Praise for Robert Newcomb

The Gates of Dawn

"Fans of epic fantasy will be thrilled that Robert Newcomb continues his winning streak with *The Gates of Dawn*. . . . Newcomb brings a fully realized fantasy world to life, with compelling characters and innovative magic."
—*Romantic Times*

"Lavish descriptions and complex characterizations."
—*Library Journal*

The Fifth Sorceress

Robert Newcomb "spring[s] into fame and literary maturity in a single bound. . . . Tristan is the novel's main strength, an intriguing and all-too-human hero who becomes a dashing warrior challenging an empire."
—*Orlando Sentinel*

"Impressive . . . These personifications of light and dark are beautifully and vividly drawn. The intense emotions on both sides are expressed with astuteness and feeling."
—*SFX* magazine

"Surprisingly original . . . Firmly in the George R. R. Martin camp of realistic fantasy . . . It leaves you wanting more."
—*Publishers Weekly*

By Robert Newcomb

THE CHRONICLES OF BLOOD AND STONE
The Fifth Sorceress
The Gates of Dawn
The Scrolls of the Ancients

THE
GATES OF DAWN

VOLUME II

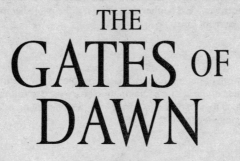

THE CHRONICLES OF BLOOD AND STONE

ROBERT NEWCOMB

BALLANTINE BOOKS • NEW YORK

A Del Rey® Book
Published by The Random House Publishing Group

Copyright © 2003 by Robert Newcomb
Excerpt from *The Scrolls of the Ancients* copyright © 2004 by Robert Newcomb

Del Rey is a registered trademark and the Del Rey colophon is a trademark of Random House, Inc.

This book contains an excerpt from the forthcoming book *The Scrolls of the Ancients* by Robert Newcomb. This excerpt has been set for this edition only and may not reflect the final content of the forthcoming edition.

www.delreydigital.com

Map illustration by Russ Charpentier

ISBN 0-345-44895-2

Manufactured in the United States of America

First Edition: July 2003
First Mass Market Edition: June 2004

OPM 10 9 8 7 6 5 4 3 2 1

For my parents, Harry and Muriel.

ACKNOWLEDGMENTS

Many thanks must go to those who helped make this, the second of my books, all it could be. To my agent, Matt Bialer, whose faith in me seemingly never wavers, and to my hugely patient editor, Shelly Shapiro, who is my trusted literary gyroscope. And to my publicist, Colleen Lindsay, and all the other folks at Del Rey who have helped make this series a success. A large helping must also go to the many booksellers—the folks in the stores who help introduce the reading public to the realms of the fantastic. And last, but surely not least, to my wife, Joyce, who started it all by daring me to succeed.

CONTENTS

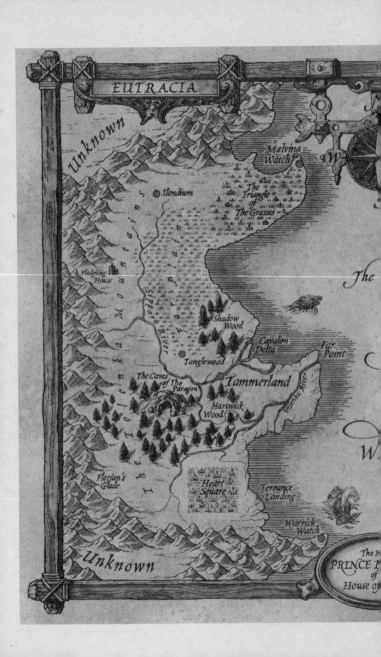

Blessed are the children of endowed blood. They are the very future of both the craft and the practice known as the Vigors. For without the merciful side of the craft, all semblances of order and compassion shall become as dust upon the wind. And it shall then be for those very same innocents—the children—that we shall forever weep . . .

—FROM THE PRIVATE JOURNALS OF WIGG, ONETIME LEAD WIZARD OF THE DIRECTORATE OF WIZARDS

PROLOGUE:
THE SERVANTS

❦

It is therefore from the following that you shall know him—the vile mutant who was chosen to lead the nation in the pursuit of the Chosen One. For his consciousness shall be as part of the gifted, yet also part of the damned. But it is within the mind of one of the heirs of the Chosen Ones that he shall find his true guidance. He shall rule the under-earth with his slave—she who is also the progeny of his greatest enemy, and who sits at the side of her keeper in his depravity. With him shall also be his assassin, aiding the vile one in his addictions . . .

—PAGE 673, CHAPTER I OF THE PROPHECIES OF THE TOME

*H*E reached up slowly to feel the thick, warm fluid at the side of his head, the fluid he both loved and hated so intensely. As he ran his fingers luxuriously through the yellow liquid, his thoughts went for the thousandth time to what he had become.

A blood stalker.

I bleed again today, he thought. He smiled to himself. *Though it is not truly blood.*

The half-human wizard, half-mutated blood stalker named Ragnar walked to the candlelit mirror on the opposite wall. He gazed carefully at the fluid running down the side of his face from the small, never-healing wound in his right temple. The wizard Wigg, onetime lead wizard of the Directorate, had given him that wound over three hundred years before, saying that the incision would help cure him—perhaps even help him gain his rightful place among the Directorate of Wizards. But it had not. And Wigg had gone on to other things, leaving Ragnar in his tortured, addicted, half-transformed state.

Looking into the mirror he saw the shiny, bald head, dangling earlobes, and long, sharp incisors of a blood stalker. The bloodshot, blue-gray eyes stared back at him from the mirror with a hunger that only vengeance could satisfy.

But he was so much more than a mindless stalker, he mused.

His other half was still human wizard. And Wigg had no idea that he still lived.

Wigg has finally returned to Eutracia, he exulted. *And with him have come both of the Chosen Ones.* He smiled briefly. *Good. The child will be pleased.*

He liked the changes the child had made in the stone fortress. The room reflected in the mirror, his private drawing room, was sumptuous. The walls were of the deepest red marble. Oil sconces and candles gave off a soft, enduring glow. Colorful, luxurious furniture, intricately patterned rugs, and various works of art adorned the room. But the harsh, acidic scent of the fluid seeping from his wound returned his mind to his current task.

It must never be wasted, he thought. He placed the first two fingers of his right hand, the hand already wet with the fluid, into his mouth. Almost immediately he felt its searing heat run through him, teasing him. The fluid was both his curse and his blessing.

Turning to the other person in the room, he asked, "Are you ready?" It was much more a command than a request.

"Yes," came the reply.

Ragnar turned to look upon Scrounge, his trusted assassin, personal servant, and spy. Tall and ravenously lean, Scrounge had a ferretlike face and dark, overly long hair. He had been an orphan his entire life, and the name that had come to him so early in his career of crime upon the streets of Tammerland fit him perfectly. He knew every inch of the ravaged city, and also a great many of the people still residing there—people who could be particularly useful, especially now that crime and violence had overwhelmed Tammerland in the absence of the Royal Guard.

In his hand Scrounge held a small glass beaker, the base of which was connected to a tube. At the end of the tube was a broad needle. In between the needle and the beaker, connected into the tube, was a crude wooden handle. Scrounge smiled, revealing several dark, decaying teeth. "All is ready," he said, in his brittle, high-pitched voice.

"Then let us begin," Ragnar replied.

Taking a seat in one of the ornate chairs, the blood stalker watched as Scrounge approached him with the beaker. Gently,

Scrounge inserted the needle directly into the wound in the side of Ragnar's head.

"You may proceed," Ragnar said, closing his eyes.

The assassin carefully began to pump the wooden handle. The yellow fluid that had been freely oozing from the wound slowly flowed into the tube and began filling the glass container. Ragnar continued to sit there quietly, almost blissful in the knowledge that he would soon have collected a sufficient quantity of the precious liquid to see him through yet another month.

When the glass beaker was full, Scrounge removed the needle from his master's wound and opened the top of the container. "As usual?" he asked. "Two-thirds for you, one-third for myself?"

"Yes," Ragnar answered. "And be judicious in its use. Wigg and the Chosen One will soon be here, and the time of our victory upon us." A smile played at the edges of his lips at the prospect of seeing the lead wizard again, and of laying his eyes upon the Chosen One for the first time.

"Both the wizard and the Chosen One will curse the day they find us," the blood stalker added softly as Scrounge picked up the beaker.

Making sure not to touch the liquid, Scrounge very carefully poured the thick, yellow fluid from the beaker into two other containers. He handed the larger of them to Ragnar, who immediately dipped the first two fingers of his right hand into it and placed them into his mouth, closing his eyes in ecstasy.

Scrounge placed his own vessel upon a nearby marble table and turned to look at Ragnar. "He asks for you," he said simply.

The blood stalker stopped what he was doing and placed his beaker on the table next to the other one. "In that case, I need to know how far you have progressed."

Scrounge retrieved a leather satchel from across the room. Opening it, he shook the contents out onto the floor.

Ragnar smiled. "How many today?"

"Over thirty, Sire," Scrounge replied, a wicked grin beginning to walk the length of his mouth. "They came even more easily this time."

"Then the child's creatures are proving ever more effective," Ragnar mused.

He looked down at the items on the floor. They were small, square, and quite obviously recently removed from their victims.

They were pieces of human skin.

Each of the small, rectangular patches of freshly incised skin carried an identical tattoo: the perfect image of a blood-red, square-cut jewel. Some of them still dripped blood.

Endowed blood. Ragnar smiled. This was quickly becoming a very good day.

"And the consuls these came from? Where are they now?" he asked.

"In the areas beneath, as usual, Sire," Scrounge replied. "And the endowed children that were available have been separated from their fathers."

"Well done," Ragnar answered. "We must have as many of the Brotherhood as possible stripped of their markings and under our control before the arrival of our very special guests."

The child would be pleased to learn that so many have been taken in a single day, he thought. "I will now go to him."

Ragnar turned away from Scrounge and left the room, his slow, heavy steps curiously quiet upon the shiny marble of the floor. Through numerous corridors he went, until at last he stopped before a heavy door of the finest black marble. From beneath the door seeped an intense glow, its radiance flooding the marble floor where he stood. It was far brighter, he noticed, than the dimmer, more ethereal glow that accompanied the actions of those less powerful in the craft. It seemed to possess a genuine physical presence that could be actually touched.

His aura is even brighter than before, the stalker mused. *His knowledge and stature grow daily. And the Chosen One is not yet trained in the craft, nor does he know the child lives.*

Ragnar continued to stand there for a moment, remembering the day not so long ago when the child, little more than an infant at the time, had literally materialized before him and begun speaking. Ordering Ragnar to do his bidding, the child had partially explained from where he had come, and why. And after hearing the wonder of it all, the blood stalker had gladly obeyed him.

Gathering up his nerve, Ragnar slowly opened the great door, and stepped inside.

In the stillness of the room, a young boy hovered above the marble floor, unmoving, silent. He was surrounded by an incredibly intense azure glow. The last time Ragnar had seen him, he had appeared to be no more than eight Seasons of New Life. Already his power had been immense. Now the boy seemed to be around the age of ten.

All his attention was focused on the table before him—and what sat on that table.

The Tome, the great treatise of the Paragon.

The boy's face was observant and peaceful as he continued to regard the pages of the Tome. His eyes were of the darkest blue and slanted upward at the corners slightly like those of his mother, giving him an exotic, attractive appearance. He had high cheekbones, the beginnings of a strong jawline, and a firm, sensual mouth. Black, straight, shiny hair that could have been made of strands of silk reached almost to his broad shoulders. His simple, unadorned robe was of the purest white, untouched by the glow that surrounded him and radiated ever outward, constantly waving to and fro in its strength.

Ragnar went down on both knees. "You summoned me, Lord?" he asked, head bowed in supplication.

It was like kneeling before a god.

As the boy narrowed his dark eyes, the gilt-edged pages of the great book turned themselves over. He read them in the blink of an eye—far more quickly than Ragnar would have ever dreamed possible. Successive pages flashed by hauntingly one after the next in the ghostly silence of the room. The child didn't even require the Paragon to read the Tome; he had told Ragnar that his "parents above" had gifted him with the power of doing so. After what Ragnar could only guess to be several hundred more pages had flown by in mere moments, the child finally lifted his face to the stalker, his eyes going to the wound at the side of Ragnar's head.

"The fluid has come?" he asked quietly. His voice was young, but neither pliant nor soft.

"Yes, my lord," Ragnar answered. "There was a sufficient quantity for my needs, and for the requirements of Scrounge, as well."

"And the single, dead consul that I requested?" the child said. At Ragnar's nod, he went on. "You will now have him taken to the palace, his tattoo intact. As for the others, I am inducing the spell of accelerated healing upon them as we speak."

Without emotion, the boy returned his attention to the great book. The pages again began to hurry by at unbelievable speed.

His abilities grow every day, Ragnar thought.

"And the hatchlings?" he asked the child. "They continue to perform their deeds well?"

"Yes," the boy answered without looking up. "The maturation of the first generation is complete." He paused for a moment.

"The two Chosen Ones and the lead wizard have returned to Eutracia," he went on at last. "And the crippled wizard of Shadowood is with them. I can feel the twisted, flaccid return of the Vigors, and the pestilence it has caused within the endowed blood of the two wizards."

"As can I, my lord," Ragnar responded. "It was wise of you to order the moving of the Tome to this place." He paused for a moment, wondering if he had overstepped his bounds. "Your reading goes well?"

The youth raised his face again. A short, menacing smile flashed briefly. "The Tome amuses me, nothing more," he said. "I find this supposedly magnificent work to be both boring and sophomoric. But it is interesting from a historical standpoint, written as it was by the Ones Who Came Before. In truth, I do not need it to practice the craft. Nor shall I eventually require the Paragon, that bauble they all seem to prize so highly."

The child looked down to the great, gilt-edged book. The pages resumed flying by at a dizzying speed. "The ones we seek will soon be here," he said suddenly, "and all must be ready. It is now time to spread the word of the Chosen One's return, and also the news of the bounty that is to be offered for his life in punishment for his murder of the king. The wizards will never allow him to be caught, but there are other, more compelling reasons for what I now do. Reasons far beyond your ken." The child lifted his exotic eyes to the stalker.

"They have without question taken refuge in the Redoubt of the Directorate," he said. "But there is no need for us to go to them, for they shall come to us. And my father of this, the lower, lesser world, shall know of my existence soon enough."

"Yes, my lord," Ragnar said reverently.

Without being told, the blood stalker knew it was time for him to leave. He rose and walked softly from the room. And though he closed the door behind him, the child's radiance again spread across the floor, spilling out into the darkness of the serpentine hallways.

PART I

❧

The Hunted

CHAPTER ONE

It shall therefore come to pass that the Chosen Ones shall suffer individual agonies regarding the use of their gifts. He in his blood, and she in her mind. For it is only through such terrors that the true art of the craft shall be revealed to them.

—PAGE 1,016, CHAPTER I OF THE VIGORS

*T*RISTAN of the House of Galland smiled slightly to himself as he looked down at his twin sister Shailiha. He was watching her sleep, just as he had for so many days now.

They were in the Redoubt of the Directorate, the secret haven where the many consuls of the Redoubt, the lesser wizards of Eutracia, had been trained. It was also the place where he had first reluctantly admitted to both his now-dead father and the murdered Directorate of Wizards the secrets he knew regarding the Caves of the Paragon. He had found that day so painful and difficult, but now he wished with all his heart that he could have it back.

The happy times, he thought. *Before all the madness began.*

Sometimes during his quieter moments, his weary mind still tried to convince his heart that everything that had so recently occurred had been long ago. As if year after year of his life had already passed. In reality it had only been several months. But because so much had changed, it still sometimes felt as if it were all a dream.

No, he told himself as he continued to look down into Shailiha's beautiful face. *Not a dream—a nightmare. One from which Shailiha is finally waking up.*

Running a hand through his dark hair, he uncoiled his long legs and walked the short distance to where Morganna, Shailiha's baby daughter, lay sleeping in her crib. The baby girl had been born both healthy and alert, despite the horrific circumstances of her arrival into the world. Her birth had come on the same day that both the Coven of Sorceresses and Kluge, their taskmaster, had been killed by Tristan. She had been born in Parthalon, before Wigg, Geldon, Shailiha, Morganna, and Tristan had finally returned to Eutracia.

A tear came to one eye as he thought of the one he'd had to leave behind.

The droplet gathered slowly in size until it finally overcame the lower lid and rolled down his cheek. *My son, my firstborn, did not survive to come back with us. For that I shall be forever sorry. Nicholas, forgive me.*

Taking a quick breath he looked up at the ceiling, remembering what the palace above had been like before the horrible onslaught of the Coven and their Minions of Day and Night. The palace had once been his home, and full of gaiety, life, and love.

He shook his head, staggered by the madness of it all and the confounding fact that he was now the new lord of the Minions. They were the winged army of over three hundred thousand that had butchered his family, the wizards of the Directorate, and much of the populace of Eutracia. The incredibly potent force still resided in Parthalon, awaiting his orders.

So much has changed, he mused. *And I must change with it.*

Looking up from the crib and into a mirror that hung upon the wall, he saw a man who had matured, who had killed and would kill again, if need be, to protect his family. He also saw a man who had discovered many secrets about himself, but also knew that there were so many more to learn.

He took in the longish dark hair, deep blue eyes, hollow cheeks, and what some would call the rather cruel mouth. Along with black breeches, he wore the same knee boots and worn leather vest that laced across his bare chest in the front that he had worn daily for the last several months. The dreggan, the Minion sword he had been forced to use to kill his father, lay in its black, tooled scabbard across the back of his right shoulder, beside his throwing knives.

The familiar yet at the same time unknown figure in the mirror stared back at him with a calmness that was born of a certain, hard-won knowledge: that he was the male of the Chosen Ones, and the only person in the world who possessed azure blood. Very soon Wigg and Faegan would want to begin training him in the craft of magic. For Eutracia—because his nation desperately needed him.

Their travels from Shadowood back to Tammerland had been arduous, since both Shailiha and the wizard Faegan had been difficult to transport. Shailiha was difficult to move because she was still suffering the lingering effects of her mental torture at the hands of the Coven. Faegan's journey had been even more problematic because of the crippled legs that kept him bound to his chair on wheels. And traveling with the princess' newborn further complicated matters. But with the combined efforts of both the wizards and more than a modicum of the use of the craft, they had finally succeeded in reaching Tammerland. And now the Redoubt, the secret place below the palace, had become their home.

They had been accompanied by Geldon, the onetime slave of the Coven, and two of Faegan's irascible gnomes and their wives. Despite his worries, Tristan managed another little smile. The gnomes had been helpful, if difficult to control. Both the bombastic Michael the Meager, the gnome elder, and the egotistical, ale-loving Shannon the Small had come. They were accompanied by their wives, Mary the Minor and Shawna the Short.

"Tristan," Shailiha called out sleepily. "Is that you?"

He turned quickly and went to her bed, looking down into her face. Thanks to the constant ministrations of Faegan and Wigg, the Shailiha he had known and loved was continuing to return a little more each day. The blond hair, hazel eyes, and firm jawline that he knew so well remained as lovely as ever.

"Yes, Shai, it's me," he answered softly. On the trip back from Shadowood he had begun calling her by this pet name. Somehow it had stuck, despite the expected, vociferous protests from Wigg that one of the royal house should not be called by such abbreviations. But just as they had done in their youth, the two of them had simply smiled at him in his huff. Deep down, Tristan knew Shailiha really liked the name. But sometimes, to tease him, she would wrinkle up her nose when he said it. Just as she was doing now. Then a different concern seized her, and she quickly sat up in bed.

"Is Morganna all right?" she asked anxiously.

"Yes, Shai," Tristan answered quietly. "She's fine. Just like her mother is going to be." He gently pushed her back down into the luxurious bedsheets.

She wrinkled up her nose again, something he loved to see, though he would never tell her so. "I'm hungry," she said suddenly. "No, actually I'm starved! I have to get something to eat!"

"Then it's a good thing I came prepared," Tristan answered happily. From a nearby table he produced a silver tray of breakfast pastries and a pot of tea that he hoped was still hot. "Fresh from the gnome wives," he told her. "Actually, they're quite good." Shailiha grabbed up one of the pastries. He watched as she quickly went on to devour two of them.

Shailiha's recuperation had been slow but steady, thanks largely to the attention of the wizards. They had worked with her constantly, using the craft to help her both forget her torture by the Coven and regain her other memories and identity. The most difficult part for all of them had been watching her as she learned for the second time that her husband, Frederick, and her parents had been murdered.

It had been especially difficult for her to learn that her father, the king, had died by Tristan's own hand. The prince's heart ached for her, and he had vowed to take the best care of her that he could.

Looking up into his deep blue eyes, she put her teacup down.

"Tristan," she began uncertainly, "Wigg has mentioned to me that we are somehow special. That our blood is the most highly endowed in the world—yours slightly more so than mine. Because of that we are something called the Chosen Ones." She paused, taking the measure of her words. "I am still unsure of what all of this means. But please tell me something. Did our parents and Frederick go to your coronation knowing that they might die that day? Die in the hope that you and I would survive?"

Lowering his head slightly, Tristan closed his eyes against the pain. *My tragic coronation day,* he thought. *The day everything changed.*

"Yes, Shai, they did," he answered. "Even the Directorate of Wizards knew of the potential danger. Their plans were designed for Wigg and the two of us to survive if anything happened. Those plans were not completely successful, and you and the Paragon were taken." He managed a small smile through the pain. "But Wigg and I came to Parthalon to get you, and we brought you home. And now, thank the Afterlife, not only are you home, but both you and your baby are well. Frederick died that day, but lives on in your child. And our parents live on in our hearts, because you and I are still together."

She bit her lower lip, and a small tear came to one eye. "Wigg also tells me that your child, Nicholas, did not live to see his birth. And that you buried him there in Parthalon . . ." She trailed off, clearly not knowing how to proceed.

"Yes," Tristan answered. "I hope to go back one day soon to visit the grave. I would like to return the body to Eutracia, and bury it with the rest of our family." A short silence followed.

"I forgive you, Tristan," she said finally, softly.

"You forgive me?" he asked, confused.

Swallowing hard, Shailiha looked down. The next words were going to be difficult for both of them. But she wanted her brother to be absolutely sure of how she felt. "I forgive you," she said. "I forgive you for killing our father. In fact, there truly is nothing to be forgiven. For I know from Wigg that you were forced to do it. That father even ordered you to do it. I forgive you, and I shall love you always."

There were simply no words. He just continued to sit there in the moment with his sister—the twin he had come so close to losing forever. His heart was so glad that she and her baby were still alive.

Finally she gave him the impish smile she was so famous for, at the same time reaching out to grasp the gold medallion around his neck—the one that had been a gift from their parents, just before his coronation. It carried the lion and the broadsword, the heraldry of the House of Galland.

"So you still wear this," she said happily. "I'm glad. And it seems that I have acquired one of my own." She reached down to touch the exact duplicate of his medallion that lay around her neck. "Although I haven't the faintest clue of how I acquired it," she added.

"Nor do Wigg, Faegan, or I," Tristan answered. "But the wizards feel that it may somehow be the physical remnants of the incantation the Coven used upon you. By some unknown means it remained with you, even after the sorceresses' deaths. The wizards have examined it closely, and say that it is all right for you to continue to wear it. But what is most important about the medallion is that wherever the two of us may go or whatever we may do, all we have to do is to look down to that bit of gold to know that there is still someone in our family who continues to love us."

Tristan paused for a moment, thinking back to the many times his own medallion had helped keep him going through the hardships of finding his sister and defeating the Coven. "My medallion is what finally saved you, you know," he said thoughtfully.

"What do you mean?"

"It twinkled in the light, and you saw it. It apparently sparked something in your subconscious just before I was about to be forced to . . . just before I . . ."

Again no words would come. How could he explain to her what Wigg had told him on that fateful day? That he must steel his resolve and kill his own sister. That her mind and soul were still infected with the Coven's spell, making it impossible for her to come back to Eutracia with them. But just as he was about to bring his dreggan down upon her neck she had recognized the medallion, and blinked.

"Tristan," she asked, "will you do something for me?"

He narrowed his eyes, pursing his lips in mock ferociousness. "Haven't I done enough already?"

She smiled, but he saw the underlying sadness in her gaze. "I'm serious," she said. "I truly do need you to perform a special task for me. Something important."

"Anything, you know that."

"Wigg and Faegan tell me that our parents and Frederick are buried a short distance from here. They also say I am still too weak to travel. I would ask you to visit their graves for me, until I can go there myself. Please let the spirits of Mother, Father, and Frederick know that I live, and that I love them." She looked with tearful eyes to the child in the crib, and then added, "Let them also know that there is now another of their blood in the world." She burst into tears.

He took her in his arms. "Of course I'll go," he said quietly. "I'll leave first thing tomorrow."

Collecting herself, she pulled away a little, tentatively smiling up through her tears. "Wigg and Faegan probably won't like the idea, you know." She sniffed. "Whenever they're together they fuss at each other like a pair of old scullery maids."

Tristan just couldn't help it. He laughed long and hard, for the first time in what felt like forever. "That's the best description of those two I have ever heard!" he exclaimed.

Before he could say more, they heard a soft knock, and the door slowly opened a crack. "Begging your pardon, Tristan, but the two wizards are calling for you," a voice said, the door opening farther. "They say you are to come at once."

Shannon the Small stood rather sheepishly in the open doorway. The little gnome was bouncing from one foot to the other, as was his habit when nervous.

Shannon had red hair and a matching beard, and dark, intelligent eyes. He was dressed as usual in a red shirt, blue bibs, black cap, and upturned boots. A corncob pipe stuck out jarringly from between his teeth. The gnome seemed quite anxious to deliver Tristan to the wizards and be done with the entire affair. "They say it is quite urgent," he added tentatively.

"It's always urgent with those two." Tristan winked at Shailiha. He turned to the gnome. "Very well," he said with a sigh. "I will come." He turned to his sister to say good-bye.

"You promise, Tristan?" she asked him again. "To do what we talked about?"

He gave her a kiss on the forehead and then stood up, stretching the sleepy muscles in his legs. "Yes, Shai," he said. "Tomorrow, I promise."

When he approached the doorway he gave the gnome a serious look. "Once we have reached Wigg and Faegan, please ask your wife to come and sit with the princess," he said. "I want to make sure the baby is watched over, in case Shailiha falls asleep again."

"Yes, Prince Tristan," Shannon answered respectfully.

The prince turned to blow a kiss to his twin sister. After gently closing the door he began to follow the anxious, waddling gnome down the labyrinthine hallways of the Redoubt.

CHAPTER TWO

$\mathcal{T}$RISTAN never ceased to be amazed at the sheer size of the Redoubt of the Directorate—the vast, hidden, interconnecting series of hallways and rooms below what had once been his home, the royal palace. It was only several months ago that he had even learned of the Redoubt's existence. The only other persons sharing the secret had been the Directorate of Wizards, the lesser wizards called the consuls, who studied here, and his now-deceased parents. How such a huge place could exist, and the comings and goings of such a large order as the consuls be kept such a closely guarded secret, was truly one of the great accomplishments of the wizards.

That accomplishment had proven invaluable for Tristan and his companions. Not only did the Redoubt house most of the nation's resources for the use of the craft, but it also provided a much-needed hiding place until the situation in Tammerland could be more thoroughly assessed.

Geldon, the Parthalonian hunchbacked ex-slave who had returned to Eutracia with them, had become their eyes and ears out in the world, using his talent at coming and going virtually unnoticed. From what he had learned so far, Tammerland was still a very dangerous place. Lawlessness was commonplace, especially at night.

The prince wanted desperately to leave the Redoubt and see the city for himself. He knew this was something the wizards would vehemently object to. But his twin sister's request of him to visit the graves in her stead provided him with a perfect excuse. He would go—with or without the approval of Faegan or Wigg. As he anticipated their joined outbursts of protest, one corner of his mouth turned upward into a wry smile.

As he followed Shannon, Tristan took the opportunity to look around, amazed as always at the triumph of subterranean architecture that was the Redoubt of the Directorate. It was built in the form of a wagon wheel, with a large central hub that had once served as a meeting place for the thousands of consuls who had visited and studied here. Outward from the center hub ran the many seemingly endless hallways, connecting at their far ends to the outer edge of the wheel. Smaller hallways connected the larger ones every hundred paces or so, allowing the traveler to reach his destination without the burdensome task of always going to the end of any given spoke, and numerous circular stairways linked the various levels. The subterranean chambers could be dizzying in their vastness.

Each hallway or room was more beautiful than the last. The walls, ceilings, and floors were of the finest, highly polished marble. Wall sconces and chandeliers gave off a delicate, ethereal hue, offsetting the massiveness that might otherwise seem overbearing. Each of the rooms was elaborately decorated; the doors were hand-carved of solid mahogany. The prince sighed inwardly. He doubted he would ever come close to seeing the interiors of even the slightest fraction of these rooms.

Before actually living here, Tristan had never known that there were so many different colors of marble. Each of the hallways had its own distinct color; the entire spectrum was represented. Just now Tristan and Shannon were walking up a hallway of the most delicate violet, shot through with streaks of indigo.

As the heels of his black knee boots rang out against the marble floors, the prince's mind went back to the day he had first been brought here by Wigg, the day he had been dressed down by his father and the entire Directorate. Hundreds upon hundreds of talented consuls had been in the Redoubt then, scurrying to and fro, each wearing a dark blue robe. Now the emptiness that filled these halls brought more than a hint of sadness.

So much had changed since that day. Even Tristan himself had been changed irrevocably. After he had unexpectedly used his untrained endowed powers to help defeat the Coven,

his very blood had altered in color from red to azure. Azure—
the color of the various manifestations of the craft. The amazing change to his blood had first been discovered after his
battle to the death with Kluge, the commander of the Minions
of Day and Night.

*"We are unsure of what other changes might occur within
you, should you continue to try to make further use of your
still untrained gift, or continue to wear the stone,"* the wizards had said as they removed the Paragon, the bloodred
jewel that empowered endowed blood, from around his neck.

He had been forced reluctantly to agree. But he still had a
great many questions to ask the old wizards, especially now
that his sister was well. And he intended to get his answers
very soon.

He already knew something of the Vigors, the beneficent
side of the craft to which the wizards had devoted their lives.
And he had seen firsthand the evil of the Vagaries, the darker,
more damning side. He had learned and come to accept that
he was the male of the Chosen Ones, supposedly meant to
lead his nation forth to a new age. He knew that he was the
only person destined to read all three volumes of the Tome—
the Vigors, the Vagaries, and the Prophecies. His mind whirled
with the complexities of it all. His supremely endowed blood
constantly called out to him to begin his education in the
craft. But still the wizards put off his training.

At last Shannon stopped before one of the massive mahogany doors that lined the violet hallway. Moving from one
foot to the other, he looked up at the prince.

"They await you inside," he said anxiously. "I will now make
sure that someone goes to watch over Princess Shailiha and
the baby." He seemed eager to be gone.

Watching the gnome waddle back down the corridor, Tristan realized that he was standing in an area of the Redoubt with
which he was entirely unfamiliar. One corner of his mouth
came up. Not knowing exactly where he was hardly seemed
unusual, considering the size of this place. What did perplex
him was why the wizards would require his presence so suddenly. He opened the great door.

The room he entered was large, and elaborately decorated.
The walls, ceiling, and floor were of a very rare and elegant
Ephyran marble, dark blue swirled with the lightest of gray.

Numerous oil lamps and chandeliers added to the soft glow of the fire burning in the light blue marble fireplace in the right-hand wall.

Wigg, seated at a long table, looked up calmly from the volume he had been reading. The wizard's gray hair fell from a widow's peak at his forehead only down to the nape of his neck. The customary braided wizard's tail had been cut off during his imprisonment by the Coven less than one month ago. Tristan smiled inside, knowing that Wigg would let it grow back out of respect for his dead friends, the deceased wizards of the Directorate. The bright, aquamarine eyes in the craggy face had lost nothing of their intensity, and the gray robe of his once-lofty office draped loosely over a body that remained muscular, protected from old age and disease by time enchantments.

As always, Faegan was seated in his rough-hewn chair on wheels. His legs, useless as a result of torture by the Coven, dangled down over the edge of the seat. His worn, black robe seemed too large for him, and the wild salt-and-pepper hair that was parted down the middle of his head fell almost to his shoulders. His eyes were an unusually intense, green-flecked gray. His impossibly dark blue cat, Nicodemus, sat patiently in his lap.

Then Tristan noticed the fourth person in the room. He automatically backed away, drawing his dreggan from its scabbard. The deadly song of the dreggan's blade resounded reassuringly through the room, bouncing briefly off the marble walls before finally, reluctantly fading away.

"You can put that away," Wigg said wryly. His right eyebrow arched up into its familiar expression of admonishment. "He is in no condition to harm any of us. He is, in fact, a consul."

Embarrassed, Tristan replaced the dreggan into its scabbard. He then slowly walked to where the inert figure reclined on an overstuffed sofa that sat along one wall. The prince looked down into the face of the battered consul who lay before him.

The man on the couch was a little older than the prince—perhaps thirty-five New Seasons of Life. He seemed to be in a very bad way. His dark blue robe was ripped and dirty, and only partially hid the fact that the poor fellow was apparently half starved. His blond hair was in knots; his face was bruised and bloodied; his cheeks were hollowed from malnutrition. Despite his condition, he was still a good-looking man.

Tristan bent over to grasp the man's right arm. Lifting it up, he slid the sleeve up to view the right shoulder. He saw what he was looking for. The tattoo of the Paragon, in bright red, identified the man as a consul of the Redoubt. Satisfied, the prince slid the sleeve back down and gently placed the arm back alongside the body. Then he turned back to Wigg.

"As I mentioned, he is a consul," Wigg said rather quietly.

"Do you know him?" Tristan asked.

"As a matter of fact, I do," Wigg answered. "His name is Joshua, and despite his relative youth he is one of the more gifted and powerful of the Brotherhood. He was one of those in charge of the squads I sent out to hunt down the stalkers and harpies, just before the arrival of the Coven. As far as I know, he is the only one to have ever returned." Wigg closed the book that lay in front of him. Placing his hands into the opposite sleeves of his gray robe, he suddenly seemed lost in his own thoughts.

"And you, Faegan," Tristan asked the wizard in the chair. "Do you know him, too?"

"No, Tristan, nor do I know any of the others of that brotherhood," Faegan replied in his gravelly voice. A look of mild envy crossed his face. "The Redoubt is an entirely new concept to me, since it was formed after the Sorceresses' War and I was already living in Shadowood by then. But I am truly interested in what this man will have to say when we revive him." The elder of the wizards sat quietly, thinking to himself, and Tristan was reminded that unlike Wigg, who was used to being in the Redoubt, Faegan was still overwhelmed by the place and what it represented. Being envious of another wizard's knowledge was something Faegan was not used to, and sometimes it showed.

Layers of thought and deed, Tristan thought, as the often-repeated phrase jumped into his mind. It was said that the thoughts and actions of wizards were piled one atop another, like the layers of an onion. One layer was removed, only to reveal another beneath it. He thought for a moment about what his sister had said to him, about how these two wizards could forever argue with each other like a pair of old scullery maids.

They were probably trying to outthink each other right now, he realized. But it was also apparent that whatever bitterness might have remained as a result of the war some three centuries ago had been forgiven.

"How did this consul get here?" Tristan asked. "Do you know what happened to him?"

"Geldon found him as he started out through one of the tunnels, to go to buy food in the city," Faegan mused, half to himself. "When he found Joshua unconscious and bleeding, he immediately brought him here. We examined him and found him to be basically sound, despite the malnutrition and a dislocated right shoulder. Wigg used the craft to reset the joint, and I invoked an incantation of accelerated healing over it. I then induced a deep sleep within him. We were only waiting for you to come before we woke him up, so that you too might hear whatever he has to say."

"Then I suggest you revive him," the prince said simply.

Wigg looked to Faegan, and the elder wizard nodded. Narrowing his eyes, Wigg stared intently at the consul, and an azure glow began to surround the stricken man. It was the glow that always accompanied any significant use of the craft, and it was proof that the wizard was working his magic on the consul.

As the clear blue glow intensified, the consul began to stir. Tristan walked over to the couch and looked down.

The glow faded away. The consul opened his eyes and slowly looked around the room. When he saw Wigg, tears filled his eyes. "Wigg," he whispered breathlessly, "is it really you?"

Wigg quickly stood, picking up his chair to go sit at the side of the couch. "Yes," he said compassionately, "it's me. You're safe now, and in the Redoubt. You're all right, but you had a dislocated shoulder, and you're starving. You need food and rest. But first we must know what happened to you."

As if Wigg's question had suddenly triggered a flood of horrific memories, the consul cried out, trying to get up off the couch. Wigg gave him a narrow-eyed stare, and Joshua settled down. But it was plain to see that he was still in shock.

"It was horrible!" he said, his hazel eyes wide with the terror of his memories. "The things, they came from the eggs . . .

the eggs in the trees . . . endowed . . . dripping azure . . . unbelievable . . . Then the awful birds came out of them . . ." His forehead bathed in sweat, Joshua collapsed farther down onto the couch and began to sob again.

Faegan wheeled his chair closer and looked down at the consul. It was clear that both he and Wigg were very concerned.

"Try to calm yourself," Wigg said softly, "and tell us what happened. Start at the beginning."

"I lost my entire squad to a harpy, and I was traveling alone," Joshua began. "I did not find another squad for a long time—much longer than I thought it would have normally taken. My food was running out . . ." He paused, trying to control his emotions. "I finally found another squad of four and joined them. They were led by Argus."

A hint of recognition came into Wigg's aquamarine eyes. "Argus," he said. "He was one of the best of the consuls."

"Yes," Joshua said. "With us were three others: Jonathan, Galeb, and Odom. Did you know them?"

"I knew all of the ones that I sent out," Wigg replied.

"We had only been together for three days when we started to feel it."

"When you started to feel what?" Wigg asked.

"The sensation of being near such unusual, highly powered, endowed blood," Joshua continued. "I had never felt anything like it, nor had any of the others. We were only one day away from the Redoubt when they struck us . . . Only one day . . ."

His voice began to trail off, and the tears came again. "We had decided to stop looking for stalkers and harpies and come straight here, to see if there was still anyone of endowed blood to report this to," he added weakly. "Both Argus and I thought it that important."

"And then?"

Joshua swallowed hard, as if still fearful that whatever had attacked the squad was somehow now here, in this very chamber. "The trees above us began to glow, and very large eggs started to take shape in the branches," he said softly. "After a little bit we could see that they were actually transparent, with birds of prey curled up inside each of them, waiting to hatch. And then they broke free of their eggs, and came for us."

Joshua began to cough, and Tristan reached to the table for some water. He held out the glass to the stricken consul. Seeing him, Joshua's eyes went wide. "Your Majesty!" he exclaimed. "Forgive me; I did not recognize you."

"That is unimportant," Tristan said kindly. "Please continue as best you can."

But now Joshua, curious about his audience, was looking around again. His eyes fell on the strange man in the chair with the blue cat in his lap. "And you, sir, do I know you?" he asked.

"No, you do not," Faegan replied. "I am Faegan, and I am a wizard. But please continue."

After another swallow of water, Joshua began again. "The first of them that broke free of its egg made an awful noise, and Argus and Galeb sent bolts against it. But the thing just shook them off, as though their gifts did not exist." He glanced at Wigg. "It was unbelievable. And then it flew in a direct line toward Argus, knocking him to the ground. The other creatures went after the rest of us in the same way. I was somehow sent flying down over an embankment, where I hurt my arm. I crawled back up as best I could to take a look, and what I saw . . ." He shook his head.

"And that was?" Wigg prompted.

"The birds' eyes . . . ," Joshua said, seemingly lost in the moment. "It's their eyes, Lead Wizard. I shall never forget them."

"What about their eyes?"

"They were bright red, and glowed with an intensity that was almost blinding." He closed his own eyes for a moment. "It was hideous. They did this for some time, apparently surveying the campsite. Then they carried off the consuls in their claws. The entire squad, except myself . . . My friends . . . now all gone . . ."

Faegan wheeled his chair even closer and looked hard at the consul with his intense, gray-green eyes.

"About the eyes," he said. "Tell me, did they glow constantly?"

Wigg frowned, not pleased that Faegan was pushing the consul so hard.

"Yes," Joshua answered, "but sometimes more than others."

Faegan let loose a small cackle and sat back in his chair. Tristan shot a quick glance at Wigg. *Faegan has some knowledge of this,* Tristan speculated. He made a mental note to speak to Faegan of it later. But right now he had some questions of his own.

"And our nation?" Tristan asked anxiously. "How fares Eutracia? None of us except one has been outside of these walls for weeks, and even on our way here it seemed that Eutracia was in the grip of something we did not fully understand. Can you tell us more?"

"It is indeed as bad as you fear," Joshua said, his heart obviously heavy. "The entire nation is in chaos. There is simply no authority to enforce the laws and restore order. Crime, murder, and looting are everywhere, and food is growing scarce. More people are moving into the cities every day, mistakenly believing places like Tammerland to be their best chance for survival. Many of these cities, *especially* Tammerland, are now straining with the flood of refugees. I fear that very soon famine may take hold in the cities, since few farmers dare to bring their crops or livestock to the market, for fear of being assaulted and robbed on the way." He paused for a moment.

"It is said that the citizens are killing each other for the mere basics of life," he went on. "Many men—husbands, fathers, and sons—were lost in the recent hostilities. The poorest of the women have been reduced to selling their bodies in the streets, even in the light of day."

Tristan couldn't bear any more. He walked slowly to the fireplace at the other side of the room. Leaning his hands against the mantel, he looked down into the glowing embers. With his nation in tatters, how could he remain in this marble tomb and do nothing? He *had* to get out and at least see for himself. *I will leave tonight instead of tomorrow,* he resolved. *And I will not tell the wizards.*

"But what about the consuls?" Wigg asked urgently. His hands were balled up into fists, his knuckles white with anger. "It is their very mission in life to do good deeds among the populace, and hopefully at least some of them survived the attack by the Coven and the Minions of Day and Night. Are they not helping?"

Joshua looked down at his hands. "I fear, Lead Wizard, that there are perhaps too few of us left to do any real good," he answered. "And if the things in the trees that carried off the others of my squad are still active, perhaps we now know why. Especially if there are more of them than I saw. I had to travel for weeks to find Argus and his group. We both know that such a thing could not have happened under normal circumstances. With all of the consuls away from the Redoubt and in the countryside, we should have been bumping into one another."

Joshua paused for a moment, to let his words sink in. "But now, I fear, even the consuls of the Redoubt may be few. This could add immeasurably to our troubles," he said weakly.

The strain was clearly starting to show again in the consul's face, and both Wigg and Faegan could see he was near the point of total exhaustion.

"It is time for you to rest," Faegan said gently. "I am going to put you into a deep, induced sleep. When you wake we will feed you, wash you, and give you a new robe. But right now, your most important mission is to rest. Do you understand?"

Joshua nodded weakly and closed his eyes. The elder wizard closed his eyes also, and immediately the consul was surrounded by the azure glow of the craft. In a moment, he was deeply asleep, and the glow was gone.

Faegan turned to look at Wigg, and Tristan finally returned from his stance in front of the fireplace to rejoin the wizards. A seemingly interminable period of silence reigned in the room.

Finally it was Faegan who broke the silence. He closed his eyes as he began to speak.

" 'And there shall be a great struggle in the skies, but it shall be as only one part of the larger, more perilous carnage below,' " he began. " 'In this the ones of the scarlet beacons shall struggle with the others who also have dominion in the firmament. And the blood of each, endowed and unendowed alike, shall flow down upon the ones below as rain, and caress the white, soft ground of the nation before it is completed. And the child himself shall be forever watching.' "

Faegan opened his eyes and smiled slightly, waiting for the inevitable questions.

"Another quote from the Tome?" Wigg asked. Faegan was the only living person to have read the entire volumes of both the Vigors and the Vagaries. Gifted with the very rare power of Consummate Recollection, the older wizard could recall anything he had ever seen, heard, or read throughout his entire lifetime. Wigg leaned forward intently, his curiosity at equal measure with the sadness he felt at hearing the consul's disturbing words.

"Yes, quite," Faegan whispered almost to himself, obviously lost in his own thoughts. "It is a quote that has long intrigued me." He looked up and smiled again. "For over three hundred years, in fact. I have never been certain of its meaning, but I believe we may be at least one step closer to learning its secrets. The 'ones of the scarlet beacons' I believe to be Joshua's birds with the bright red, glowing eyes. There has been no other creature in my personal experience with such unique attributes. Still, I have absolutely no idea about what is meant by 'the white, soft ground of the nation.' And I certainly do not know what it means when it says that 'the child himself shall be forever watching.' The only child I can think of that might in any way be relevant would be Morganna, Shailiha's baby. But for the life of me I can't understand how or why." He sat back in his wooden chair and stroked his cat.

Tristan turned to Wigg to see that the lead wizard was also lost in the maze of questions that lay before them. "Do you believe the consuls to be dead?" he asked bluntly.

Pursing his lips, Wigg placed a thumb and forefinger to either temple. "That is impossible to say at this time," he answered. "It would certainly explain why none of them have returned to the Redoubt."

"One thing is sure," Faegan ruminated. "These things— these birds of prey—are definitely not a product of the Vigors. They are without compassion, and their ends are served only through violence. Azure radiates about them, meaning that they are a product of the craft. But they also do not sound as if they are of great intelligence, and therefore may be controlled by another, higher power somewhere."

He paused for a moment, then turned his gray-green eyes to Wigg and Tristan. "This means, my friends, that someone in Eutracia is again practicing the Vagaries," he said angrily. He looked down at his useless legs and, as if in shame, pulled the hem of his robe down a bit, covering them more completely. "There is nothing in the world that angers me as much as the misuse of the craft," he added softly. The meaning of his words was not lost upon the prince and Wigg. It had been the Vagaries that had destroyed his legs.

Tristan would never forget that day upon the mountain when Wigg had called forth the physical manifestations of both the Vigors and the Vagaries. The Vigors had appeared as a giant orb of dazzling, golden light. The Vagaries had been an orb of the same size, but black, ominous-looking, and literally dripping with the energy of destruction. The two opposite orbs of the craft were constantly attracting each other but never able to touch, immediately repelling each other when coming too close.

Wigg had explained to him then that the improper combination of their energies would result in the total destruction of everything they knew. Supposedly Tristan, the Chosen One, was to be the first to successfully join these opposite powers for the good of the land. Just now it seemed such a day was far off, indeed.

"Joshua remains our only key to the answers about the flying creatures," Wigg added. "But we must wait until he awakens. Then we shall tend to his health. He has been through a great deal."

A dense, almost palpable silence reigned, the only sound the occasional snapping of the wood burning in the fireplace. Tristan looked down into the face of the sleeping consul as a sad, ironic notion suddenly came to him.

Even this injured consul has more freedom than I do now. I have been a virtual prisoner in this cavern of marble. Perhaps even a criminal in my own country—for crimes I was forced to commit. But tonight, at least, I will see the graves of my family—wizards or no wizards.

Feeling the need to check on his still-fragile sister, the prince walked slowly to the door. Wearily, he faced the others. "I will meet with you both again in the morning," he said. "Now I go to see Shailiha."

He turned and walked through the door, leaving the two wizards lost in their contemplations.

CHAPTER THREE

❖

THE afternoon was darkening as Geldon carefully guided his bay mare through the ragged streets of Tammerland. A rainy night was coming, and he made a mental note to be sure to leave the city early enough to avoid it. The strengthening wind occasionally picked up litter from the unkempt streets, blowing it around into little maelstroms of filth and debris. It only added to the general drabness and oppression that now characterized this place.

Such a pity, the hunchbacked dwarf thought. *This city must have been magnificent before the coming of the Coven and the Minions of Day and Night. Perhaps the wizards and the Chosen One can somehow make it so again.*

Out of habit he reached up to his throat, the place where he had once worn the collar of the second mistress of the Coven. He would never forget the jeweled band of slavery he had worn for over three hundred years, until Wigg had removed it after the fall of the sorceresses. But all of that sometimes seemed a thousand lifetimes ago. The members of the Coven were all dead, and their soldiers, the Minions, were stationed far away in Parthalon, the nation across the Sea of Whispers. Tristan had ordered the Minions to stand down from their violence. They were to rebuild Parthalon, helping the citizens there to regain free and useful lives.

Geldon could see evidence of the Minions' depraved butchery as he went down the various streets. As was their custom, they had used the blood of their victims to paint obscenities and symbols of their victory on the walls and buildings, just as they had done in Parthalon. Geldon knew that the psychological stain of what they had done would remain long after their horrific, telltale artwork had vanished.

He patted his horse to take his mind from the butchery, then smiled to himself at how clever the two wizards living in the Redoubt were. Fearing that the horses would be stolen from the palace stables above ground, Wigg and Faegan had converted a small part of the Redoubt to underground stables, and the horses were now boarded there full time, along with the tack and feed. It had become a part of Geldon's duties to care for them, and he loved his job.

He had ridden his bay mare out one of the many secret tunnels leading out of the Redoubt. Each of the winding tunnels exited in a different area of the palace or its surrounding landscaping. Their entrances were cleverly disguised, and he had to be very careful never to be seen entering or exiting. From the palace it was only a short ride into the heart of the city. But each time he visited this place it depressed him.

He was headed for the section that had once been the center of Eutracian culture and commerce. Most of the storefronts and shops had been long since looted, but there were still a handful of them open, their owners apparently well heeled enough to pay hired thugs to protect them. This was also the place where most of the idle citizens now seemed to congregate, as if being together would somehow add to their own safety.

The area known as Bargainer's Square was now a hotbed of whores, thieves, con artists, mercenaries for hire, and beggars. But it was the place where he was most likely to pick up the latest gossip. He knew the danger factor there was high, especially for a hunchbacked dwarf whose size might well make his self-defense more problematic.

As he approached the huge, cobblestone square he could see that it was unusually busy today. In fact, the place was literally teeming with life. He kept his pace slow and his head down, purposely trying not to invite attention. No one need tell him that simply being a hunchbacked dwarf might be enough to invite harassment from rowdies looking for fun.

Street whores with come-hither glances brazenly plied their trade in the open. From many of the alleyways could be heard the homely, visceral sounds of crude, urgent intercourse. Oftentimes the men could be seen standing in line, waiting their turn. Beggars approached him at every corner. Some of them seemed truly needy, while others were simply looking for a coin or a piece of bread to get them through another day without having to work. He bit his lip as he went along, almost crying at what he saw. Some of the unfortunates here were mere children. Orphans, he assumed. Lost and alone in a giant world not of their making, many were filthy and starving.

He would sometimes come across the menacing eyes of those he knew to be the most dangerous—the killers for hire. Professional assassination had become a healthy business since the loss of the Royal Guard. There were many citizens who were more than happy to spend the necessary kisa to eliminate a wealthy relative, adulterous spouse, or more successful business rival. Kisa, the gold coin of the realm, was the only thing that guaranteed survival. And what these mercenaries were willing to do to get it was without limits. With enough money, virtually anyone here could be killed, with no trace remaining of the assassin.

And then there was the final group of unfortunates. The hobbling, crippled souls who were wounded, and nearly dead. Those who had somehow survived the clash with the Minions, but had lost an arm, a leg, or an eye. These men and women were the ones who seemed truly lost, walking the streets as if in a daze. Their eyes were constantly searching, but they seemed to recognize little. Every such encounter with the Minions, Geldon knew, bred such poor souls like flies. And it was plain to see that many of them here were soon to lose it all to the ravages of their quickly advancing gangrene. They had apparently never found anyone of the craft capable of properly tending their wounds.

Thank the Afterlife Tristan has not seen this, Geldon thought. *There would be no end to the rage and sorrow he would feel.* As if mere cloth could somehow protect him from the horrific scene, he slowly pulled the hood of his robe up over his head and traveled on.

Geldon had made six other such visits to the city. He had purposely not been trying to find out too much, for fear of seeming overly inquisitive. The last thing he needed was undue scrutiny. But he had struck up several potentially valuable acquaintances—people he thought he could now trust enough to tell him at least some semblance of the truth. It was to the first of these he steered his mare.

Familiarity first, the wizards had warned him. *Then and only then should come the questions.*

He stopped his horse in front of one of the more rowdy, notorious taverns and looked down at the partial amputee seated on the walk. The fellow's legs were gone just below the hips, no doubt a result of the Minions' carnage. What was left of his squat body was strapped to a rather poorly made wooden box. Around both of his hands were wrapped dirty bandages, and in each fist he gripped a handle. Each handle was connected to a separate block of wood. In this way he could move along much faster than one would have ever imagined. He would repeatedly extend the blocks of wood before him, then lift his body-box upward and forward, placing it down into the space between them. He was known only as Stubbs, and his dark, dirty hair and black eye patch were always the same. He seemed to be quite sure, as he looked up at Geldon, that at least a few kisa were about to come his way. He smiled, several of his front teeth missing.

"And how are you this fine day?" Stubbs asked the dwarf, his greedy smile far from retreating. "Have you come for yet more supplies?"

Geldon took a quick look around the unusually crowded square before responding, making sure there was no one else within earshot. "Yes," he said simply, continuing to gaze down at the cripple.

"For the life of me, I don't know why you don't get a wagon," Stubbs added, rubbing a hand over his grizzled, salt-and-pepper chin. "It would make life a lot simpler, and you wouldn't have to come into town so often." Reaching out, he placed the blocks one step in front of his truncated body. Hoisting himself into the space between them, he moved a little closer to the hooves of Geldon's horse. He used his good eye to look up at the dwarf. "Nobody honest ever comes to this part of town 'less they have to. That is, unless they're in need of a good time from one of the ladies." He winked knowingly. "I could do with a bit of that myself, if you know what I mean."

Geldon opened the leather cinch bag that was tied around his waist and took several low-denomination kisa from it, holding them casually in his hand. He jingled them lightly together. "Perhaps I could help you with that," he said softly.

Stubbs took another of his small leaps forward, his eyes shining with greed. "What do you need, m'lord?" he asked quickly. "I can get you anything you want: liquor . . . women . . . or perhaps there's someone you'd like to see out of the way?"

"Just some information," Geldon answered shortly. He looked around again, pausing to let a group of loud, drunken men go by. "Why is Bargainer's Square so busy today?" he asked. "I've never seen it like this."

Stubbs tilted his head and smiled again, holding out his hand. Geldon flipped one coin down. Before he knew it, the cripple had bitten hard into it, testing its worth. Stubbs smiled with approval. "News is there's goin' to be some kind of big announcement today, and very soon now," he said conspiratorially.

"What kind of announcement?"

Stubbs just smiled. Geldon tossed down another coin.

"They say it's goin' to be big doin's, and has to do with somebody important." Again he stopped. Yet another coin came down.

"Who?" Geldon asked.

Stubbs smiled nastily. "The prince," he said softly.

Geldon froze. *That's impossible,* he thought. *No one knows Tristan is here.*

He tried to keep his composure. "What about the prince?" He pursed his lips as if the information he had just paid for had been a bad bargain. "I don't know very much about him, much less care, and I've half a mind to come down there and get my money back." He glared angrily at the cripple. "There must be more to it than that."

"Only that there is to be some kind of announcement in the Hog's Hoof Tavern, in about one hour," Stubbs said. "I swear to the Afterlife, m'lord, that's all I know."

Finally believing him, Geldon tossed down one more coin. "Consider that to be a down payment on my next visit," he said sternly. "As for now, do the smart thing and erase me from your memory until you see me again. We never talked."

"Yes, m'lord," Stubbs said gleefully. He headed off, leaping and bounding awkwardly across the cobblestones of the square, aiming straight for the first of the street whores he could find, happily holding out his kisa like a schoolboy entering a candy shop.

But the amusement Geldon felt at watching Stubbs quickly vanished as he turned his horse toward the Hog's Hoof. His thoughts were darkening with every moment. No one, as far as they knew, was aware that the prince and Wigg had returned to Eutracia. The thought of some kind of announcement about Tristan unnerved him. And the only way to learn more would be to go to the tavern—a prospect he was not particularly fond of.

The Hog's Hoof had the worst reputation in all of Tammerland, and had long been known as a gambling house, a haven for criminals, and a brothel of the most perverted standards. Geldon had been there only one other time, during one of his first trips into the city. He had quickly left in fear of his life. Still, he had no choice but to brave the place again. He owed Tristan his freedom and his life—a debt he would never stop trying to repay.

Dismounting in front of the great, overbearing edifice of the tavern, he tossed the leering brutes on the sidewalk several coins to watch his horse, then stepped inside the belly of the raucous, human carnival that was the Hogs's Hoof.

It was exactly as he had remembered it. The noise, smells, and laughter coming from the various areas of the great front room seemed to have a unique, dangerous texture all their own. A very long, hand-hewn bar of highly polished hibernium wood stretched from one end of the rear wall to the other. The rest of the entire room seemed to be a mass of tables, chairs, and men in various stages of drunkenness. Women worked the room constantly, either serving liquor or plying their other trade, trying to entice the men into going upstairs. There were many takers.

But everyone was not always happy in this place, and he knew a fight could break out at any moment. Anxious, oftentimes angry men leaned over the gaming tables, seemingly trying to throw their money away as fast as possible. From the far corner of the room he could see more of them standing in a small crowd, yelling down at the floor and throwing their kisa into the circle before them. There was obviously a cockfight going on. And the vast majority of the men in the room were armed, wearing both sword and dagger.

The square, open room was two stories high; on the second

floor, the chambers of the whores opened onto a railed balcony that overlooked the main tavern below. Scores of oil lamps hanging from the elaborately carved ceiling gave off a harsh, glaring glow, and the various hues of red, the predominant color, gave the tavern a cheap, glaring, dangerous cast. The entire place smelled of liquor, sweat, and greed.

Carefully walking through the crowd to reach the bar, Geldon realized that it would be the man standing behind it who would most probably be the best source of information. The dwarf laboriously hoisted himself up onto one of the relatively high chairs.

"Ale," he said simply.

The man behind the bar gave Geldon a curious look. Then, with a slight smile, he poured the dwarf a tankard of the tavern ale. Geldon took a draught of the strong, bitter swill, smiled his approval to the bartender, and jangled several kisa down on the bar top.

The server was an older man, with a liquor-induced, ruddy complexion. He had a shiny, bald head, save two tufts of unruly, white hair on either side. He wore a white, stained apron that did little to cover his protruding stomach. But underneath it all Geldon could see that this man was heavily muscled, and no doubt exceptionally strong. *He probably needs to be,* the dwarf realized.

But the server's demeanor seemed kind, so the dwarf decided to chance a conversation.

"Bargainer's Square is very busy today," he began casually, "and so is the Hog's Hoof. I've never seen so many people here."

"Business is good," the man said. He began wiping glasses with a cloth that was less than clean. "Rumor has it that something is going to happen here, and very soon. I don't know what it is, but if I were you I'd keep my ears open, say little, and be prepared to leave in a hurry if need be. In my opinion, we were all given two ears and only one mouth for a reason. And that is because we should listen twice as much as we talk. One never knows what's going to happen next in this place, and drawing attention to yourself is never a good idea."

Excellent advice indeed, Geldon thought. He was beginning to like the fat, red-faced man behind the bar, and he decided to press a little. "My name is Geldon," he tried.

The man nodded. "Rock," he said.

"Rock?"

"Yes, Rock." He smiled. "Can't you imagine why?"

Geldon smiled back as he looked at Rock's bulging arms and large, gnarled hands. "Yes," he said. "Indeed I can."

Rock leaned forward a little, motioning for Geldon to do the same. "Like I said, something is about to happen," the barman whispered. "And I think it has to do with—"

Suddenly Rock's voice trailed off as he looked up to the door at the other side of the room. He swallowed hard, then straightened back up, saying nothing. His face had lost some of its color, and he stood stock-still, as if waiting for something. The entire room had also gone amazingly silent. Geldon turned around, trying to see what it was that would stop such a powerful man dead in his tracks.

Someone had entered the tavern. Standing in the doorway, the stranger was backlit by the streetlight outside, and Geldon could not make out his features. As he walked farther into the large room it became clear that he was very well known. Tables and chairs screeched and scratched out of his way as he moved forward. No one spoke. As the man finally came into view, Geldon knew that he was looking into the face of a cold, professional killer.

It was true that a great many such men had sprung up since the assault by the Minions, but somehow this man was different. Geldon could immediately tell that he would not only be one of the fastest, most efficient of assassins, but would also have absolutely no remorse regarding his chosen craft. This one was a true professional.

He was tall, just a bit taller than Tristan, yet also quite thin—almost emaciated. His face was long, narrow, and angular, his leanness showing up in the gray hollowness of his cheeks and the sallow, almost sunken eyes. His aquiline nose ended just above a fairly small mouth, and his eyes were dark and piercing, their gaze missing nothing. Long, dark hair reached almost to his sharp jawline. His broad shoulders and narrow hips moved quickly and gracefully, almost like a dancer.

Looking closer, Geldon could see that the man was holding something under his left arm. A roll of papers, perhaps. His clothes were mostly of dark brown leather, and his high, black boots had silver riding spurs attached to the heels. A long dagger in a black sheath was fastened low on his belt at the man's left hip, a tie-down strap holding it to his thigh. But what caught Geldon's nervous attention was the man's right arm.

The right sleeve of the man's leather shirt was rolled up to the biceps. Strapped to the top of his right forearm was a miniature crossbow, the likes of which Geldon had never seen. Its general shape and construction at first seemed fairly basic. But on closer examination it could be seen that instead of carrying a single arrow, this one carried five. They were arranged on a circular wheel, attached between the bow and the string. The bow was cocked, with an arrow notched in it and ready to fly. The width of the cocked bow was not more than that of the man's forearm. Beneath and behind the bow ran a series of several tiny, interlocking gears. Geldon was at first stymied to understand why, until he deduced that after one arrow was shot, the gears could apparently automatically cock the bow, notching another one. It seemed quite possible that the man could literally loose one arrow after another until all five were gone. The entire affair took up so little space that if the man had been wearing his sleeves down, one would hardly notice the difference. And then the dwarf noticed something else strange.

The tips of each of the five miniature arrows were stained with yellow. Geldon turned back to Rock with a questioning expression.

"Scrounge," Rock answered quietly. "The most accomplished assassin in all of Eutracia. It is said that he works for only one benefactor, but no one seems to know who that is. Nonetheless you should not cross him, for he also kills for pleasure. The death of a hunchbacked dwarf would mean nothing to him."

The one called Scrounge walked up to the bar and arrogantly stood up on one of the chairs, then walked back and forth on the top of the bar itself, his spurs jangling lightly. He kicked off many of the liquor bottles and glasses in his way, including Geldon's ale tankard. Smiling, he watched them explode on the tavern floor in broken splatters of liquor and glass. He looked down at the dwarf for a moment, and Geldon's heart missed a beat.

But Scrounge simply smirked at him, then lifted his face to the waiting crowd. The room was as silent as death.

"Good," he began in a loud voice. "I can see that I have your attention. Therefore I shall be brief. My benefactor has been gracious enough to ask me to come to you today with a proposition that I believe shall interest you all. It seems he has proof that a very dangerous criminal has returned to the land. My employer has offered a substantial reward for this man's capture. Dead or alive. Actually, my benefactor would prefer him taken alive. But to my mind, dead is just as good." He smiled, revealing several yellow, decaying teeth.

"The reward for this man is to be immediately paid in kisa. Let there be no mistake. The reward is high—the highest ever seen in the history of our nation." He paused to allow the tension in the room to build. "The price for the head of this criminal is one hundred thousand gold kisa."

The silence in the room was shattered by high-pitched, almost hysterical cries of delight and some loud applause. In a moment, feet were stamping the floor, and fists pounding the tabletops. Ale tankards and wineglasses jumped with the commotion, spilling their contents. Scrounge politely waited for the din to subside before continuing.

One hundred thousand kisa, Geldon thought, stunned. He had not been in Eutracia long, but he certainly knew enough to understand that such a sum amounted to more than most of these people could earn in fifty lifetimes. He turned back to watch Scrounge.

The assassin took the roll of paper from beneath his left arm and began to unfurl it, smiling. "And now for the identity of this man," he said. He unrolled the first of the posters and held it before the crowd. Geldon's blood froze. The crowd fell silent.

The likeness on the poster was that of Tristan of the House of Galland, prince of Eutracia, and there were words in large, dark print beneath it.

PRINCE TRISTAN OF THE HOUSE OF GALLAND,
Wanted Dead or Alive
for the Murder of the King, Nicholas the First!
One Hundred Thousand Kisa Reward, Paid in Gold!

Geldon simply sat there, staring at the awful thing. The prince, the one so instrumental in not only saving his nation but also the entire world as they knew it, was now a common criminal.

No, he suddenly thought. *Not common at all. This is a king's ransom. And no one in the nation knows he is innocent except for the few of us living in the Redoubt.*

Scrounge walked back and forth along the wet bar top, making sure that everyone could get a good look at the poster.

"Harbor no illusions as to the guilt of this man, this onetime member of the royal house," he shouted. "His crime, that of taking the head of his very own father, was witnessed by hundreds of our good citizens on the very day of his coronation. It cannot be disputed. For this my patron has decided he must be brought to justice, and swiftly." He looked out over the crowd as he continued to hold up the awful warrant. "These are about to be posted in every corner of the kingdom. As citizens, it is your duty to bring the prince in. The fee will be paid promptly upon proof that the man brought to us is indeed Tristan, prince of Eutracia."

He unfurled the remaining posters in his arms, throwing them among the crowd. The frantic spectators began to push and shove, reaching for them. Some brief scuffles broke out, and upon seeing them Scrounge smiled widely.

"Good!" he shouted. "It is heartening to see your level of enthusiasm! Bring him to us, and you shall be rich beyond your wildest dreams!"

Geldon lowered his head, imagining the effect of these awful posters. At last he looked up and, pretending to be a part of the enthusiastic crowd, took a poster off the bar. Carefully folding it, he placed it inside his shirt.

This changes everything, he realized.

All around him, people were hungrily reading the posters and taking in the likeness of the prince. Then, from the back of the room, a man came slowly forward to stand along the wall to Scrounge's right. His beard and hair were shot through with gray, and he had a tall, mature bearing. Ex-military, Geldon thought. The newcomer stood there glaring at the assassin as if he didn't care what Scrounge thought of him. A Eutracian broadsword identical to those once used by the

Royal Guard hung low on his left hip. He folded his arms across his chest in a clear posture of challenge, and Geldon could see that the look in his eyes was one of hate.

This cannot end well, Geldon thought.

In the relative quiet of the great room, the man suddenly drew his sword from its scabbard, the blade making a defiant, unmistakable ring through the air. Scrounge immediately turned toward the source of the sound, for the first time illustrating just how quickly his reflexes could take hold. His eyes locked upon the man brandishing the sword as its blade reflected off the oil lamps.

"You're a liar, and a filthy one at that," the man said almost quietly, the words dripping like venom from his mouth.

At first Scrounge seemed intrigued. "And just why is that?" he asked almost cordially. The room had become as still as a graveyard. Table and chairs began to screech away from the man with the sword. Still he held his ground, continuing to glare up at Scrounge.

"Because I had the privilege of once being a commander in the Royal Guard, and I knew Prince Tristan personally," the man snarled. "I do not know where he is now, or why he left us. But I also know that if he killed his own father, which I seriously doubt, there must have been a good reason. A great many things happened to a great many people that fateful day—the prince included. I refuse to believe he willfully committed patricide." He paused briefly, the light still glinting off the razor-sharp blade of his sword. "I will not let you foul the land with your perverted posters. Even if I have to kill you to stop you." The words hung for a long time in the stillness of the room, as if begging to be answered. The challenge had been made.

"Ah, a relic from the past," Scrounge said mockingly. Arms akimbo, he shook his head back and forth in derision. "I knew there were still a few of you left limping about the land. From what I have seen of you fellows, you really don't constitute much of a presence. And certainly not enough to regain control of this poor, beleaguered nation. The only thing that matters these days is how many kisa a man has in his pocket, and everyone knows that. No, I'm afraid your particular brand of antiquated honor just doesn't count for much anymore."

The crowd burst into laughter, hoots, and hollers. Realizing the crowd was on his side, Scrounge cleverly let the jeering run its course.

"Besides," the assassin continued almost happily, "hundreds of people saw the treacherous prince do it! They can't all be wrong! He used one of the winged monster's own swords to take his father's head upon the very altar of the Paragon. No, my friend, I think you should just go back to your rather deluded memories of the past. Leave such things to those of us who know what to do, and how to do it." The crowd jeered as the man with the sword grew red in the face.

"If you will not desist in this madness, then I shall kill you where you stand!" the Royal Guard officer exploded, taking a step closer.

This will be his mistake, Geldon thought. *He is acting with his heart, instead of his brain.*

Strangely, Scrounge lowered his head and closed his dark eyes. A faint smile played on his lips. Finally he looked up again and shook his head knowingly, snorting out a soft laugh. "I don't really think you're going to get the chance," he said softly.

In a fraction of a second he raised his right arm, and snapped his fist toward the floor twice. Immediately two of the miniature arrows from his crossbow were flying toward the officer. They pierced him through the muscles above his clavicle and impaled him to the wall. Screaming in pain, the officer tried to free himself but could not. No one moved; no one spoke. Geldon sat stock-still at the bar. He had never seen such a fast weapon, he realized—except, perhaps, for the prince's dirks.

Scrounge jumped down from the bar and walked to the man pinned against the wall. The officer's toes were several inches from the floor, and rivulets of bright red blood ran down his clothing. Scrounge bent over to pick up the broadsword that the officer had dropped in his pain.

"Thank you," the assassin said softly, wickedly. "I have long wanted one of these for my collection." He placed the point of the blade beneath the officer's chin, viciously forcing the man's face up. "No wonder you couldn't vanquish the winged ones when they came," he added nastily.

He backed away from the man, admiring the scene as if he

were a painter or a sculptor trying to decide what feature he was going to change next. He then stepped in closer, leaning conspiratorially in to the officer's ear.

"I hope you don't mind, but these are really quite expensive, and I need them back," he whispered. With that he reached up and yanked the arrows from the man's body. The officer crashed to the floor and screamed in pain. The blood from his wounds came much faster now, little rivers of it running slowly into the cracks and crevices of the dirty floor. After wiping the tips of the arrows on a nearby tablecloth, Scrounge very carefully rearranged them on the wheel of his crossbow. He acted casually, like a man who had just been target shooting rather than mutilating a fellow human being.

Bravely, the officer looked up from the floor and spat upon Scrounge's boots. "I will yet live to kill you," he whispered through his pain.

Scrounge smiled that curious smile again. "Oh, I doubt that," he said. "For you see, you ignorant bastard, you're already dead."

He then carefully put the spur of his right boot up against the officer's cheek. With a violent, forward thrust of his foot he ran the silver spur into and along the man's face, tearing a wide gash in his flesh from the bottom of his right earlobe to the hairline. The officer groaned and fainted from the pain.

Scrounge turned back to the spellbound crowd. "Is there anyone else here who would choose to disagree with what has been asked of him today?" he shouted. The silence in the room was palpable, and there was no hint of movement. "Good," he said. "The next time I see any of you, it had best be because you have the prince of Eutracia in your grasp."

Still holding the stolen broadsword, he walked purposefully from the room. Geldon, still sitting at the bar, looked down in horror at the injured officer and then back up to Rock. What had Scrounge meant about the officer already being dead?

"This is only the beginning, you know," the barman said, shaking his head slowly. "I fear our land is in great distress indeed."

Geldon felt the poster against his skin beneath his shirt and took a long, deep breath.

More than you know, Rock, he thought to himself. *More than you know.*

CHAPTER FOUR

I⊤ was good to feel Pilgrim beneath him again, Tristan thought as he made his way along the secluded trail. Even the rain on his face was a welcome relief from the confinement of the Redoubt.

The night was dark and cool. The light of the three red moons seemed to follow him as they sailed silently across the night sky. They cast a soft, almost eerie glow upon the rain-laden foliage, pointing up the silver prisms created by the raindrops still clinging to the branches and trees.

It had stopped raining only shortly before. He had actually been glad of the downpour, for it made his stallion's hooves just that much quieter each time they struck the ground. And the clean, unmistakable scent of fresh rain had helped to blot out the horror of all he had learned and seen that night.

The purloined dark-blue consul's robe he was wearing was cold and clammy, sticking uncomfortably to his skin. But he was appreciative of it, nonetheless. It covered both the dreggan and the dirks lying across his back, and its hood could be pulled up to hide his face if he came upon anyone.

He had chosen this particular trail because it was so seldom used, especially at night. Just the same, he chose to take no more chances than he had already committed himself to. If the wizards learned of his departure from the Redoubt they would be furious.

Rather than using the tunnels to exit the Redoubt, he had chosen to come up through the royal palace above. He had no desire to bump into Geldon upon the dwarf's return trip from Tammerland and be forced to explain his presence in the tunnels. Although the odds of that happening were very small, it wasn't a chance he was willing to take. Second, there was a more personal, compelling reason. He wished for the first time since the death of his family and the Directorate to visit the Great Hall, the scene of their demise.

He had walked through the palace halls quite slowly at first, overcome by a feeling of dread, as if he might be confronted by the Minions of Day and Night, or even by one of the Coven. But he was now Lord of the Minions, he reminded himself, and the members of the Coven were all dead. Here in the palace, at least, there was nothing left to fear.

He walked toward the Great Hall slowly, almost reverently. The flood of memories from that awful day, the day everything in his life changed forever, came rushing back to him in an unexpectedly powerful torrent of grief.

The royal palace, the only home he had ever known, had been ransacked and looted from one end to the other.

In truth he had expected as much, but seeing it this way for the first time was still a great shock. Virtually everything of value had been taken—presumably by the Eutracian citizens, after the Minions had left. The Minions' mission at that time had been to destroy, not to steal. The knowledge that his own countrymen had helped destroy this place only increased his pain as he walked through the broken, shattered shell that had once been his home.

The paintings, sculptures, and other works of art, including the tapestries his mother had so lovingly created, were all gone, the hallways and rooms stripped bare. Each of the passageways and chambers he now silently crept through yawned back at him sadly in their abject emptiness. Even the castle furniture was gone.

Moonlight swept through the many open and destroyed windows, casting his shadow across the walls. He approached the Great Hall with trepidation, knowing that this room would be the most difficult to bear. Finally standing at the entranceway to the room he had so longed to see, he thought at first that his heart might burst.

Like all the others, this room was empty. The windows were all smashed, their frames dangling drunkenly off the hinges. The remnants of the once-fine lace curtains were shredded and bloodied, fluttering uselessly in the night breeze. Despite the fact that this room had been looted, some responsible citizens had apparently retained the foresight to remove the hundreds of dead bodies that had once rested here. Presumably to forestall the vermin that would carry disease to the rest of the city, he reasoned. For that much at least, he found himself thankful.

But they had not cleaned the floor of its blood. The warm, crimson waves of death had simply been left to dry, virtually covering the black-and-white checkerboard floor. Upon the walls could still be seen the Pentangle, the symbol of the Coven, painted in the blood of his countrymen.

He slowly turned to find what it was he had truly come to see, to discover for himself whether they had taken that, too. He had to admit that he did not know how he would feel if it was still there. Part of him hoped that it too would be gone, so that he would not have to look upon it. But his eyes finally found it. He walked to it slowly. Gently going down on his knees, he started to weep.

He was before the altar of the Paragon—the marble edifice upon which he had been forced to take the life of his father.

He remained that way for some time, the tears coming freely as he was taken back to that awful day. Finally he stood, looking down at the top of the altar, where the Minion warriors had held his father down. Tristan forced his hand out, as though touching the marble could grant him some small measure of peace. But when his fingertips unexpectedly found the narrow groove created when his dreggan had gone through his father's neck, he pulled his hand back in horror, the tears coming again. The altar's top was still covered with the dried blood of the king. Tristan knew that even if the bloodstains faded into invisibility, for him their taint would live on in this piece of marble forever.

Forgive me, Father, he cried silently. And then he left the palace, hoping to leave behind the ghosts that plagued him so.

Guiding Pilgrim along the rather dark and muddy path, he knew in his heart that he was not visiting the graves simply as a favor to his sister. He was also going for himself. Turning his palms over, he could see the scars on each of them—the results of the blood oath he had taken upon himself the last time he had come here.

He stopped Pilgrim a short distance from the grave site and

tied him to a tree. Then slowly, silently he drew his dreggan and stepped into the moonlit clearing.

This place had been chosen for the royal cemetery both because of its secluded location, and the fact that it overlooked one of the finest views of Tammerland. One side ended just short of a very high cliff; the other three sides were surrounded by forest. The graves appeared to be undisturbed, and for that he was thankful. The forest surrounding the grave site rustled quietly in the wind, the only other sound the quiet, reassuring calls of the tree frogs. Both the dew and the remains of the recent rain covered the ground, shimmering in the light of the three red moons. Everything seemed peaceful, and deserted.

Then, as Tristan started toward the graves, he realized that he was not alone.

Someone was standing across the clearing, his dark robe blending into the edge of the woods to Tristan's left. The hood of his robe was up over his head. His face bowed down and his hands clasped in front of himself, he was apparently giving homage to the dead. Heart racing, Tristan waited to see what the stranger would do. And then it hit him.

He's a consul of the Redoubt, he realized. *He must be. Who else would wear such a robe and pay his respects to these graves? But how did he know who was buried here?*

The unknown consul began to sob. Tristan debated whether he should make his presence known. After all, the consuls were friends. Thinking back to Joshua's plight, he thought that perhaps this consul had suffered the same fate of losing his entire squad to brigards—or to those so-called birds of prey. But before the prince could make up his mind, the consul started to move. Running as fast as he could, the consul headed directly across the tops of the graves and toward the edge of the cliff.

Tristan froze. The consul was committing suicide!

The prince dropped his dreggan and tore from the edge of the forest, running across the graves at a right angle to the speeding consul. But the consul had been too fast, and Tristan had to change direction to have any hope of catching him before the man went over. With a last effort of will the prince launched himself forward, tightly gripping the consul around the knees. They both landed hard upon the wet earth, skidding to a stop just feet from the edge.

Tristan immediately got up on both knees, trying to turn the consul over to speak to him and to get a better look at his face. What he got instead was a quick, unexpected fist to the side of his chin—a very hard right that nearly knocked him unconscious. The consul then tried to push the prince away with pounding fists.

Tristan's first reaction was to raise a fist to strike back, but he stopped himself. No doubt the consul did not realize who the prince was—only that he had been suddenly attacked. If the man was truly alone, he was probably frightened to death, especially if he had lost his squad.

Lowering his fist, Tristan held the consul's arm strongly with one hand, and pulled back the hood of the man's robe with his other. What he saw there in the moonlight took his breath away. The person in the robe was a woman.

Tristan sat there, stunned. Not only was this person no consul, but she was the most intensely beautiful woman he had ever seen. When the Parthalonian Gallipolai named Narissa had died in his arms, he had felt sure no other woman would ever equal her raw, physical beauty. But now he knew he had been wrong. Still holding her arm, he simply sat there in the wet grass, staring.

She leveled her eyes upon his with a look that seemed to go straight through him. "You're hurting me," she said hesitantly. There was a great deal of fear in the dark, husky voice, and her declaration to him was more than a simple statement of fact. It was an undeniable plea to let her go.

Unsure of what to do, he kept her in his grip. "If I release you, do you promise not to try to kill yourself again?" he asked. Knowing that a battle of wills had begun, he looked hard into her eyes. The memory of her blow still recent, he smiled slightly, rubbing his chin with his free hand.

"I suppose it really is true," he said wryly. "No good deed goes unpunished. And I shouldn't like to be struck again, especially since my deed was such a truly good one." One corner of his mouth came up in hope that she would return his smile, but she did not. "Do you promise not to try for the cliff?"

"No," she said simply.

Nonetheless, he let go of her arm. As a precaution, he turned his body slightly. Sitting directly across from her would make it much harder for her to get past him. The knowing look in her eyes told him she was well aware of what he had done. Still, she did not speak.

Tristan used the moment of silence to take in her beauty. Thick, dark red hair that was parted on the side cascaded in undulating waves down past her shoulders. A small swell of those same waves curved gracefully down over part of her forehead, all the while turning slightly in the night breeze. Below the hairline were large sapphire eyes, heavily hooded but never seeming to blink. Her gaze was commanding, and direct. The whites of her eyes could be seen completely encircling the bottom portions of her irises, giving them a knowing, seductive quality. Dark, fine eyebrows arched up and over them gracefully; the slim nose rested above a mouth whose lips were almost too full. The high cheekbones and perfect, white teeth helped complete the picture, the final detail being just a hint of a cleft in the firm, proud jaw.

Although the rest of her was covered by the robe, he could tell that her form was tall, yet curvaceous. Strong, yet also sensual. He caught just a hint of myrrh from her hair as the night breeze flowed around them.

He looked at her robe. Dark blue, and obviously far too large for her, it had clearly once belonged to a consul of the Redoubt. But how had she acquired it? She might have stolen it—but how could she have managed to steal the robe of an endowed consul? Had there been another, more insidious reason for her to come to these cliffs in the middle of the night? He also sensed danger. Given the alarming information he and the wizards had just acquired from the consul Joshua, he was determined to learn more. Beautiful woman or not.

"Who are you?" he asked gently.

"No names," she responded quickly. "Nor do I wish to know who you are." Her tone told Tristan that she was doing her best not to seem afraid.

"Why are you wearing that robe?" he pressed. "Where did you get it?"

He thought he saw a touch of sadness come to her face, but she regained her composure. "It is of no matter." She frowned, running one hand back through her hair. As her locks moved heavily across her shoulders, the scent of myrrh came to him again.

"Why were you trying to kill yourself?" he asked bluntly. "There are easier ways to do it if you're really serious about it." He smiled, hoping for some hint of her mood lightening.

Her eyes closed for a moment and opened again, this time with just a glimmer of shininess. "It's easy for people like you," she said softly, looking directly at him. "Besides, you wouldn't understand."

"What do you mean?" he asked.

Her face lowered slightly. "You want to live," she whispered.

Her words went through the prince's heart like a knife. *I've captured a bird with one wing down,* Tristan realized. *And I don't even know who she is.*

He looked up to the sky, realizing that he must finish his business and leave soon if he was to return to the Redoubt before daybreak.

"At least tell me where you live," he said to her. "Perhaps I could see you again. We could talk further." He tried to take her hands in his, but she pulled them away.

"No," she said simply. She began to stand up. He stood with her, making sure she did not try to run off the cliff. Her eyes were almost on the same level with his.

"You have done me no favor by saving me from myself this night," she said sadly. "And it would be impossible to involve you in my life." She paused for a moment. "Besides, you would not like what you found there. Your heart would never survive it." The shininess had reappeared in her eyes. Blinking her tears into retreat, she again proved herself the mistress of her emotions.

"Is your situation truly so bad?" he asked her honestly. "Perhaps I could help."

"No one can help me," she told him. "It would be foolish of you to try."

"At least promise me that you will no longer try to take your life," he said seriously. "You are far too beautiful to leave this world so early. The Afterlife can wait." He reached out to touch her cheek. Almost as if it was a habit, she flinched.

"I cannot make such promises," she said. "But if for some reason you cared enough to save me from myself, then care enough to let me go without further questions. Just let me leave this place, and you may then do whatever it is you came for." The sapphire eyes did not waver as they stared into his own with strength and candor.

He had no choice, and he knew it. No matter how badly he wanted to know more about why she was here, there was no time. Another Tristan from another time would have let her go and then followed her, his curiosity overriding his common sense. But not this Tristan—and not on this night.

This Tristan would honor his promise to his sister, then return to the Redoubt. Taking this mysterious woman with him was out of the question. He felt his heart tug, knowing he would most probably never see her again. He drew a deep breath and let it out slowly.

"Very well," he said finally. "You are not my prisoner, and you are free to leave. But if you can, please find some peace for yourself in this life. You are far too rare a thing to live in such pain."

Her expression softened a bit. "Thank you," she said. With that the nameless woman walked away into the forest, the leaves and branches closing behind her.

A final, brief hint of myrrh came to his nostrils and then quickly vanished, telling him she was gone. He stood there, gazing at the place where she had reentered the forest. He wondered again who she really was. But his heart told him he would never know.

He turned to the graves. Going down on both knees before them in the fading moonlight, he bowed his head and grasped the gold medallion around his neck with both hands. He remained that way for a long time.

So much had happened to him, yet so much still seemed unresolved. He missed his parents deeply, just as he missed the wizards of the Directorate who were also buried here. This small clearing by the cliffs would always have a special place in his heart of hearts.

Finally he stood and walked to the edge of the clearing to retrieve his dreggan. Before he left the little glade he turned, almost hoping to see her there again. But of course he did not.

When he returned to Pilgrim, the horse immediately rubbed the length of his face against Tristan's shoulder, telling the prince it was good to have him back. Tristan mounted and wheeled the horse around. The morning sun was just beginning its struggle up over the jagged horizon of the mountains as he made his way sadly back to the Redoubt.

CHAPTER FIVE

F_{AEGAN} sat in his wooden chair on wheels, happily playing his magnificent, centuries-old violin, one of the few personal treasures he had allowed himself to bring from Shadowood. All around him, the fliers of the fields turned and wheeled through the air, their colorful wings tracing delicate patterns as if in response to the music. Sometimes they teased him, flying close then suddenly darting away; sometimes they actually landed upon his shoulder or knee as he played. Each one had a body as long as a grown man's forearm, with a wingspan of several feet. And each pair of diaphanous wings contained a riot of colors, in patterns that somehow were never duplicated from one flier to the next. There was nothing else like them in the world, and they were particularly special to Faegan.

He had not personally created the giant butterflies, for they had become endowed more than three centuries earlier, due to their accidental consumption of the waters of the Caves of the Paragon. But it was he who was responsible for the amazing attribute that set them apart from all the other creatures of the world, save man himself. For these butterflies were able to communicate with humans.

One of the first things Faegan had done upon arriving at the Redoubt was to construct an aviary for his winged treasures. He had spent several days conjuring it from one of the larger rooms. The chamber in which he now sat was over three stories tall, made from light blue marble, and lit by numerous glowing oil lamps. A balcony provided a wonderful view of the entire space.

Inlaid into the floor of the room were two very large, black marble circles. One contained the letters of the Eutracian alphabet, fashioned in white. The other contained the numbers one through ten, all fashioned in red. Recently Faegan had been busy trying to teach the butterflies the basics of the Eutracian numerical system. Wigg had originally been rather critical of the elder wizard spending so much of his time in this manner, but he had finally relented when Faegan had explained.

We may have great need of these friendly, beautiful creatures, the master wizard had said. *And perhaps much sooner than we would like to think.*

So far Geldon had been their only link to the outside world. They had briefly considered sending one or more of the gnomes out into the city to collect information, but they were afraid that would only invite undue attention, since none of their kind had been seen in this part of Eutracia for over three centuries. Therefore it was Faegan's plan to eventually use the butterflies, who could fly unseen—at least at night—and reach places the gnomes and Geldon could not. Using the two wheels in the floor, they could then report their findings.

He laid his violin gently down on his lap. Then he raised a hand, and a particularly beautiful flier of violet and yellow came to rest upon his forearm. It remained there calmly, slowly opening and closing its great, elegant wings. They sat there, man and butterfly, regarding each other.

Faegan knew of Wigg's impending presence long before he saw him. Wigg approached slowly, coming to stand next to the elder wizard's chair. He admired the fliers as they soared about the room.

"And how does it progress?" he asked.

"They are coming along well, but are still not yet ready," he replied. "I fear they still need more time than we may have, especially since we are unsure of the dangers that seem to be gathering against us."

Wigg leaned his long, lanky frame against the balcony rail. "Do you have any more thoughts about Joshua's flying creatures?" he asked hopefully. "I have been endlessly scouring the libraries here for a clue, but I have not yet found anything to enlighten us. Other than the fact that they are of the Vagaries, they remain a complete mystery."

Faegan scowled. He had not been able to produce more insight into the situation other than his initial, cryptic quotation from the Tome. He slammed his free hand hard on the arm of his chair in frustration. Startled, the yellow-and-violet flier flew away. "You realize, Wigg, that we are looking in the wrong places," he said. "If we truly wish to solve this riddle, there is another, far more valuable source where we must seek the answer. Perhaps when Geldon returns, he can tell us it is safe enough to venture out."

"Yes," Wigg said sadly, rubbing the back of his neck in frustration. "Perhaps."

Each knew what the other was not saying: that the truth of whatever was behind both Joshua's birds of prey and the mysterious disappearance of the consuls could most probably only be found in the Tome, somewhere within the volume of the Prophecies—the only volume Faegan had not read. But the Tome was deep inside the Caves of the Paragon. Faegan sighed. The Caves might as well have been a thousand leagues away, for all the good they could do them right now.

"And how is Joshua?" he asked.

"He is better. Now that he is eating properly, his strength continues to improve. But despite my continued questioning, he has been able to add little to his original story. It appears that everything happened so fast, much of it is still just a blur to him. Perhaps it always will be."

The two wizards remained quiet for a time, lost in their individual thoughts as they watched the fliers soar about the aviary.

At last Faegan decided to force himself free of his depression. Carefully placing the violin on the floor, he called on the craft and suddenly levitated his chair up and over the brass rail, joining the fliers. Laughing raucously, he whirled about the room, chasing the magnificent butterflies.

Wigg simply scowled. Placing his weight upon one foot, he folded his arms across his chest, shook his head, and arched his right eyebrow sarcastically. *Despite his mastery of the craft, he can be such a child!* he thought, irritated. There was a task they both needed to attend to, and now was not the time to be frolicking with butterflies.

"You really must try this!" Faegan exclaimed as the giant butterflies careened and swooped about him. "Come on, Wigg!" he shouted. "Don't be such an old curmudgeon!"

Smiling widely, the wizard in the chair soared to the brass rail directly before Wigg and hovered there. Two brightly colored fliers came to land, one upon each of Faegan's shoulders. As far as Wigg was concerned, it only made the entire situation more ridiculous: Faegan looked more like some bizarre vendor at a Eutracian province fair than the most powerful wizard in the world.

"You take life far too seriously!" Faegan exclaimed, grinning at the imperious lead wizard from the other side of the rail. He pursed his lips, thinking. Then he smiled.

"I can *make* you participate, you know," he added cryptically. "I'm more powerful than you are."

Wigg narrowed his eyes. "You wouldn't dare!"

That was all Faegan needed to hear. Narrowing his eyes, he caused Wigg to levitate. Wigg struggled to fight it, but it was no use. Faegan's gift was too strong. He took Wigg higher, over the rail, to join him and the fliers in the aviary.

Faegan promptly turned Wigg upside down, so that his robes fell over his face, blinding him, and revealing bare legs that kicked futilely at the air. Faegan snickered like a schoolboy who had just dipped an unsuspecting girl's braid into the inkwell. Or worse.

"Put me down, you fool!" Wigg shouted from within the folds of his robes, arms waving wildly.

Faegan smiled. "Say please," he shouted back.

"Never!"

"Suit yourself," Faegan answered happily. Leaving Wigg alone in his distress, he resumed soaring about the massive room in his chair.

"She awaits us!" Wigg finally shouted, his voice oddly muffled by his robes. "Or have you forgotten, *most powerful one*?" he added sarcastically.

"Yes, very well," Faegan answered, turning his chair away from the butterflies. Waving his arm, he righted Wigg, whose face was more red from anger than from his time spent upside down. They both floated back to the balcony.

"Do you have some water from the Well of the Redoubt?" Faegan asked, his mood having turned serious again.

Still angry, Wigg gave him a nod. Saying nothing more, Faegan retrieved his violin and wheeled his chair out of the chamber and into the adjoining hall, acting for all the world as if he thought Wigg had nothing better to do than follow him wherever he went.

Wigg let out an exasperated sigh. With a thought, he commanded the doors to the aviary to close silently behind him as he followed his eccentric but benevolent tormentor.

Shailiha smiled bravely as the two wizards entered her room. As always, she managed somehow to summon up the necessary courage to endure what the wizards said they needed to do to make her whole again. She drew strength from their concern for her, from Tristan's love and support, and from the fact that she had a daughter to care for. Even now, Morganna could be heard cooing happily in her crib, just a few feet away.

"Your Highness," Wigg said gently. "How are you feeling today?"

"Much better, Wigg, thank you." Shailiha stood and walked across the room to the wizards, the silk of her pink, floor-length gown rustling with her steps. "I want to thank you both for your constant care," she said then, her words almost a whisper. "Without you and Tristan, Morganna and I would surely have been lost forever."

Wigg cleared his throat. "Are you ready?" he asked.

"Yes," she said simply. She walked back to her chair and sat down, waiting for the wizards to begin.

Wigg drew up another chair, while Faegan wheeled his into place in front of the princess. She closed her eyes, just as she had done so many times before.

She has been through so much, Wigg thought. *But it is almost over.*

It had taken a great deal of insight, coupled with Faegan's knowledge of the Vagaries, to finally unravel the secret to the incantation the Coven had used upon her. Shailiha's torment at the hands of the sorceresses had proven more of a riddle than they had first thought. The spell had been treacherously seductive. Not only had it infused itself into her mind, but it had also taken command of her endowed, but still-untrained blood.

The wizards had found an answer in the water of the Caves.

Untrained, endowed blood could be empowered—temporarily—by proximity to water from the Caves of the Paragon. The effect could either be painful or pleasurable. When Tristan had accidentally discovered the Caves, he had found the water irresistible. In Shailiha's case, the closeness of the thick, red liquid had proven to be difficult to bear. However, the process was proving successful. The princess' trials had been painful both in body and mind, but the wizards believed that she was near the end of her torment.

Wigg reached beneath his robe to retrieve a small pewter vial full of water from the Well of the Redoubt, where water from the Caves was always kept. He watched as Faegan closed his eyes and began to call forth the spell that they hoped would banish yet more of the chaos from the princess' mind. Shailiha sat completely still in her chair. The room was wrapped in total silence. Nothing stirred, not even the baby in her crib.

Slowly Faegan nodded his head. At this signal, Wigg removed the stopper from the top of the vial. Again Faegan nodded, and Wigg automatically responded by pouring a single drop of the fluid upon the open palm of the princess. The effect upon her was immediate, and far more startling than it had ever been before.

Shailiha screamed. Sweat began to soak through her gown in dark, ominous splotches. At the sound of her mother's voice the baby immediately began crying. Shailiha's entire body began to shake uncontrollably, her hazel eyes rolling grotesquely up into her head, leaving only the whites exposed. She tried to stand, but Wigg forced her back down, holding her in place. This time her strength was such that he was forced to use the craft to augment his own brawn, just to keep her in place. She tossed her head violently, sending long blond hair flying back and forth, and foam began bubbling from the corners of her mouth. It snaked wetly down her chin and onto her already soaked gown.

"Hold her!" Faegan shouted, his eyes still closed. "This is what we have been waiting for!"

With a last, earsplitting scream, the princess slumped forward in her chair, unconscious. Wigg barely caught her before she fell to the marble floor. Faegan opened his eyes, ending his spell. He examined Shailiha intently, looking for the sign he and Wigg hoped would prove the final banishment of the first mistress' awful work.

From all about Shailiha now came the beginnings of a soft blue glow. It built in intensity until it had become one of the brightest ever seen by the two wizards. Then it began to coalesce, spinning into a maelstrom of swirling light that flew from her body and spun crazily around the chamber. Oil lamps crashed to the floor; the silk sheets from Shailiha's great four-poster bed flew violently into the air. Furniture crashed and tumbled, noisily splintering against marble walls. Wigg quickly handed the inert princess to Faegan and ran to the baby's crib, covering its open top protectively with his body.

And then, with a last, insane howl, the azure maelstrom rose to the top of the room, flattening out against the ceiling, where it dissipated into nothingness. The objects it had picked up in its whirling madness immediately fell, crashing and smashing down upon the marble floor. Bits of glass, cloth, and furniture were scattered everywhere. The shrieking of the wind ceased, and all that remained was the ordinary sound of a baby crying.

Shailiha, lying in Faegan's arms, groaned softly and sleepily opened her eyes.

After calming the infant, Wigg returned to Faegan's side. He gazed intently at the princess, and then a smile broke out across his long, creased face. "You're finally well," he said softly, a tear beginning to gather in the corner of one eye. "Free."

She stood slowly, shakily. Reaching out, she hugged Wigg close, then bent over to embrace Faegan. But even this low level of exertion proved too much for her, and she started to fall. Wigg swept her up in his arms.

"The best thing for you now is sleep," he said, smiling into her eyes. "The next time you wake up, you will be a new woman." He turned her to face the crib, where Morganna lay. "A new woman with a new baby," he added happily.

Then he laid her down upon the bed and covered her with blankets that had been caught up in the maelstrom. Faegan wheeled his chair over to look at her. Already, Shailiha was asleep, and for the first time the wizards could see in her face the true, rejuvenating sleep of the peaceful and the just.

Faegan reached one of his hands out and placed it upon the sleeping princess' head, closing his eyes. He remained like that for several moments, then opened his eyes and smiled. "She is truly well," he murmured gratefully. "We have done it, Wigg. I am proud to have been of service to her. I only wish I could have been here to help guide her and her brother all these years—and to witness their remarkable birth."

Wigg was about to open his mouth to speak, but suddenly he felt something inside of him slip, and his body jolted a bit.

He turned to Faegan, wide-eyed, and saw that the elder wizard had obviously felt it, too. His face white, Faegan gripped the arms of his chair in an autonomic response to his panic. Neither one spoke, as if putting words to their suspicions would somehow, unbelievably, make them true.

Lifting the Paragon from his robe, Wigg held it to the light—to see what for three centuries had always been their greatest fear.

CHAPTER SIX

$\mathcal{A}$s he always did when being summoned by the child, Ragnar walked through the many labyrinthine halls quickly. Scrounge followed dutifully behind him. The blood stalker had indeed expected to see the youth this day, but earlier, rather than at such a late hour. His mind, busy with the possible reasons for his delayed but still-required attendance, contemplated many answers—none of which readily fit.

He always liked going to the lower places, the farthest down and darkest of the many rooms here. He had been honored to watch the child use his already-immense powers to carve the great chambers out of living rock, creating the magnificent areas through which he now walked. But even the blood stalker Ragnar did not understand the full impact of what he was about to witness upon entering these, the deepest of all the chambers.

Finally standing with Scrounge before a door of black marble, Ragnar narrowed his eyes, calling upon the craft. Immediately the door turned itself silently upon its hinges, exposing the immense room that lay below. The many winding, marble steps went down several stories and took some time to navigate.

Ragnar had been here before, but this time something was different, and standing at the entrance to the room at last, the stalker stopped short, amazed at what he saw before him. From all around the room came the glow of the craft. A vein of glowing azure rippled through the living rock walls as if it were part of the very chamber itself. Many feet wide in most places, it completely encircled the chamber like a glowing, undulating snake. It was like looking at the purest vein of Eutracian gold as it lay there, waiting to be mined. But this vein glowed, and he knew instinctively that it was infinitely more valuable than gold.

This vein is endowed, Ragnar thought as he stood speechless before its beauty. He shook his head, fully understanding that this was undoubtedly the work of the young master, and astounded at the breadth of the power the child now apparently possessed.

"Beautiful, is it not?" came the young, controlled voice from somewhere behind him.

Ragnar and Scrounge turned around to see the boy hovering before them, the amazing glow about him as always. Immediately they went to their knees.

"Yes, my lord," Ragnar said. "I have never seen anything like it."

"And once it is gone, you will never see its equal again," the youth responded quietly as he watched the undulating vein throb within the living rock. He stretched out his arm to pass one hand lovingly over the glowing ribbon.

"Please, my lord, will you tell us how it has so suddenly come?" Ragnar asked, then wondered if he had overstepped his bounds. "And, if it also pleases you, for what purpose is it intended?" He raised his face to look up at the boy, taking in the dark, upturned eyes; the long, black, silky hair; the bright white robe.

"You have many questions," the boy said quietly, sending a shiver up the spines of both the stalker and the assassin. "The vein is a subject best left for another time. Besides, you are here for different reasons."

The young adept began to glide toward the door at the far side of the chamber. "Follow me," he said simply. Then, only a short distance away, he stopped. Suddenly turning, he smiled briefly, showing perfect, white teeth. "For your purposes, you may call me Nicholas," he said calmly, turning around as he made for the door.

Nicholas, Ragnar thought, looking knowingly at Scrounge. *How appropriate.*

Nicholas led them into another room, so large that it literally dwarfed the one from which they had just come.

Hewn out of living rock, it was over twenty stories and measured several hundred meters across in both directions. The flickering, orange flames of dozens of wall torches, enchanted by Nicholas to continue burning forever, cast sinuous shadows across the walls and floor, creating an imposing sense of dread. A door led out of the room at the far side. And carved into all four walls were row upon row of open, azure-glowing crypts. There were several thousand of them, and over half were occupied by male bodies, lying head outward, into the room.

Nicholas looked up, carefully examining the crypts.

Very soon now, my father, the child thought. *Very soon you, your twin sister, and the pestilence that is the two wizards who practice the Vigors shall all know of my coming.*

He glanced down to Ragnar. Softly, he said, "Come with me." With that he began to ascend toward the highest of the rows of occupied crypts, his white robe billowing gently as he went.

Leaving Scrounge standing on the floor, Ragnar levitated himself to Nicholas' side. From here the blood stalker could see the true size of this massive place. He estimated that with a little more than half of the crypts filled, there were at least two thousand bodies already here.

But the child would not be content with those numbers, Ragnar realized. Nicholas would not rest until he had them all . . .

Ragnar hovered closer to one of the crypts for a better look. The glow seemed brighter to him from this proximity. And although the face of the man inside was unknown to him, he recognized what the man was: a consul of the Redoubt.

Lying as if asleep, the consul was still wearing his dark blue robe. The blood stalker did not have to examine him further to know that the tattoo, the representation of the Paragon, had already been removed from the man's right shoulder. This particular consul had a great, gray beard, and was rather mature. He had probably been a consul for some time, Ragnar reflected, perhaps even holding a station of some prominence within the secret organization of the endowed. He may even have known Wigg personally.

Ragnar reached up to feel the never-healing wound in the side of his head. He was to be awarded the honor of punishing the lead wizard—the child had promised him that. He smiled, relishing his eagerness for revenge. And it would be his assassin who would destroy the Chosen One. But he had no idea what Nicholas was doing with all these consuls.

The youth glided closer to the stalker, his head tilted back, his long, dark hair hanging toward the ground below, his upturned eyes mere slits. He seemed to be lost in the rapture of some private thought. Finally he looked into Ragnar's gray, bloodshot eyes with a newfound intensity.

"I bring you here to show you how many consuls we now have," he added. "It is my understanding that there are now fewer consuls left in the countryside than there are interred here. I wish them all to be delivered to the catacombs quickly, before any of them can return to the Redoubt. Do you understand?"

"Yes, my lord," Ragnar answered obediently.

"And the lone consul?" Nicholas asked. "Has he been delivered to the Redoubt as I ordered?"

"Yes, with a message from Scrounge. I approved it myself. It is sure to acquire the attention of the prince."

"Good," Nicholas said. "My father, he of the azure blood, is soon to know the sting of your particular alchemy—that which was inadvertently created by Wigg himself. It has a certain poetic quality, don't you agree?"

For the first time ever, Ragnar smiled in the presence of the amazing child. "Yes, my lord," he responded.

"Just so," Nicholas said. With a gesture beckoning the blood stalker to return to the ground to collect Scrounge, he led his servants toward the large, ornate portal at the far side of the room.

Each chamber seemed to be more immense than the last. This one was not carved of rock, but constructed of light green marble, shot through with streaks and swirls of black. It shone beneath the light of hundreds of enchanted sconces and chandeliers lining the seemingly never-ending walls. But despite the great size of the room, the air was stifling and oppressive. The temperature was warm, bordering on hot, and smelled somehow of both old and new life.

The glowing vein Ragnar had seen in the first room ran completely around the walls, undulating and coursing mightily, as if it were trying to break free of the stone in which it was imprisoned. But even more impressive were the contents of the room: The floor was covered with thousands of azure, glowing, slime-ridden eggs.

Nicholas' hatchlings, Ragnar realized, awed. *But why does he need so many?*

"The answer is simple," Nicholas said, as if reading the stalker's thoughts. "Despite the fact that he is now hunted by his own countrymen, the allies of the Chosen One will be many in the coming struggle. We shall therefore have need of all you see before you. In addition, there are others maturing outside of the Caves, in the trees of the countryside— something that will make the capturing of the consuls go just that much quicker."

The glowing, translucent eggs were arranged in rows upon the floor, their lines stretching out of sight to the farthest corners of the chamber. Each of the eggs dripped a thin, runny, azure fluid down the outside of its shell. The stinking fluid from the many eggs eventually joined, pooling upon the floor, adding to the earthy, fetid odor in the room. Inside each of the translucent eggs could be seen a hatchling—grotesque, curled up, growing.

Nicholas must have far more in mind than the mere taking of the consuls, Ragnar mused.

Nicholas turned to Scrounge. "You may leave us now," he said.

"Yes, my lord," the assassin answered without hesitation.

When he was gone, Nicholas turned his dark, upturned eyes on the stalker. "You trust him completely?"

"Without reservation," Ragnar replied. "He has been with me virtually his entire life. I discovered him as a young orphan. Although he is not blessed by the time enchantments as you and I are, his talents for killing and gleaning information are unsurpassed."

"Good," Nicholas said. "For just as you are my link to the Chosen Ones, Scrounge is our link to the outside world." He paused for a moment, smiling. "In truth, our relative situations are not that different. The Chosen Ones and the wizards are imprisoned within the Redoubt. And we, for other reasons, are imprisoned here. But they will soon come to us, rest assured."

Ragnar again touched the unhealed wound in his head, realizing he was in sudden need of ingesting more of the odorous, yellow fluid. It had been Wigg who had chained him to the ecstasy of his own stalker brain fluid—and it was that very liquid by which both Wigg and the Chosen One would suffer. Poetic justice indeed. He smiled.

Nicholas smiled back. "I have plans for the wizards. I also have very specific intentions for the Chosen One—my father of this world. None of them are to be killed, nor is my presence to be revealed to them until I tell you differently."

"Yes, my lord."

"Now leave me," Nicholas said calmly. "I still have much to do."

With that the stalker left the boy, making his way back to his personal quarters, where he wasted no time in grabbing up the vial containing the yellow fluid. He drank deeply, feeling its ecstasy ripple through him as it went down.

Revitalized, he replaced the vial and headed out again, this time to one of the several bedrooms he kept occupied. Without announcement he abruptly entered the room.

The woman seated before the mirror was his favorite of

those he kept here. She looked up tentatively at him. Seeing in his eyes the power of the fluid, she braced herself for what she knew would follow.

He fell upon her, taking her roughly, as though she were a mere possession.

CHAPTER SEVEN

I T cannot be true," Faegan breathed as he looked at the Paragon. It was lying on Wigg's palm, and the lead wizard's hand was shaking.

"Nonetheless, there it is," Wigg answered softly. A quick glance at Shailiha's bed reassured him that the princess continued to sleep peacefully. He looked back at the Paragon in his hand.

The square-cut, bloodred stone that sustained the power of the craft of magic would have seemed, to the untrained eye, to be quite normal. But to Faegan and Wigg its subtle, yet discernible alteration was readily apparent. Especially when coupled with the subsequently small, almost minuscule loss of power they had both felt in their blood during their time with the princess. Quite clearly, the Paragon was beginning to die.

The uncalled-for change in the stone was a calamity of unparalleled proportions. Such a circumstance had never occurred since the Paragon's discovery, over three hundred years ago.

"Why?" Wigg whispered in horror.

"I do not know," Faegan answered quietly but with equal emotion, moving his chair a little closer to the stone.

They both stayed that way, each of them trying to absorb the disaster that was unfolding before their eyes. What they were now witnessing had always been believed to be a complete impossibility. The continued, unchecked ramifications of this would mean the end of all they loved, had for so long held dear, and had so many times risked their very lives for. Faegan sat back in his chair, his normally crafty, mischievous expression replaced by one of defeat.

"How is such a thing possible?" Wigg asked. "The stone, provided it is being worn by one of the endowed blood, has kept its power for over three centuries. Why would it suddenly begin to dissipate?"

"I can only believe it is being influenced by someone or something beyond these walls," Faegan answered, already lost within his own thoughts. "That is the only possible explanation, and the philosophy from which we must start. Although we still do not know how such a thing is possible, it must be tied to the appearance of Joshua's creatures. Someone is once again practicing the Vagaries, and these two occurrences simply cannot be coincidental."

Wigg wondered if Faegan even knew his hands were balled into fists. The elder wizard's face was a study in contempt.

"How can you be so sure?" Wigg asked, his constantly skeptical attitude launching one eyebrow up.

Faegan closed his eyes. He searched his mind with the power of Consummate Recollection, attempting to retrieve the obscure passage from the Tome. After several long moments, he began to speak.

" *'And the stone shall one day begin to expire. With this shall come those of the scarlet beacons,'* " he began. " *'The guardians of the stone shall therefore struggle to maintain its life in a great conflict, part of which shall be determined in the firmament. For if the stone dies, all those of the Vigors shall die with it, the child forever watching from his place of victory.'* " He opened his eyes again.

"Yet another reference to 'those of the scarlet beacons,' " Wigg ruminated. He carefully replaced the Paragon beneath his robes.

"Indeed," Faegan answered, almost to himself. "But what disturbs me most is the repeated reference to 'the child.' The only child of importance I am aware of is Morganna, and for the life of me I cannot comprehend what meaning she may have in all of this. For she is truly an innocent." Taking a deep breath, he shook his head in frustration.

"There is something else that makes no sense, assuming your theories are correct," Wigg said cautiously.

"And that is?" Faegan asked.

The lead wizard turned back to the wizard in the chair. His right index finger went up into the air, just as it had done so many times before when he had been Tristan's teacher. "Assuming that someone or something is indeed causing the stone to lose its power, you have postulated that this unknown presence is of the Vagaries. I now agree. And as the stone loses its power, so shall we. But because the stone empowers *all* of endowed blood, the force behind this shall therefore lose its powers, as well. This will eventually render us all equal, and quite powerless in the craft. Why would such an endowed person or thing want to dissipate its own power of magic, despite the fact that we lose our powers, as well? Assuming this scenario to be true, we all lose. It makes no sense."

Faegan furrowed his brow and pursed his lips in thought. "Well done, Wigg," he said. "A point that up to now had escaped me, much as I hate to admit it. Why would he or she want to do such a thing indeed?" Yet another question was now swirling its way through his mind, just as he suspected it was bothering Wigg. He finally decided to bring it out into the open. "Based upon the rate the stone is decaying," he asked quietly, "how long do you give us before our powers become of no consequence?" He already had his own estimate, but wished to see what Wigg's would be.

The lead wizard put a finger to his lips as he contemplated the answer. The loss of power he had felt had been minuscule, but real nonetheless.

"Several months, at most," he said. "Then the craft as we know it shall cease to exist."

Faegan's guess exactly. Neither of them spoke for the moment.

"You realize what it is we must do, despite the danger?" Faegan asked finally.

"Yes." Wigg had known the answer in his heart the second he had first seen the stone. He was immensely glad that Faegan, the rogue wizard who loved riddles and could prove so prank-ish, was alive and here by his side.

We shall need all of our combined talents to survive this, he thought. *And both of the Chosen Ones must be told. For their help in this will be essential.*

Saying nothing more, the two wizards left the room. Clos-ing the door quietly behind them, they entered the endless hallways of the Redoubt in search of the prince.

CHAPTER EIGHT

*A*s Tristan guided Pilgrim down the narrow, little-used path back to the palace, the sun was just coming up over the hori-zon. He knew he had to hurry if he was to return before his disappearance was discovered, but a part of him couldn't re-sist flaunting the rules of the wizards. And he wanted to see more of the country he should have been ruling over.

Eutracia was in the waning days of the Season of Harvest. The leaves on the trees had long since turned scarlet and or-ange, and many of them had already fallen to the earth. The cities would normally have been teeming with trade as farm-ers brought their crops to market and the citizens bought their provisions for the coming cold period. But this season had been particularly harsh, bad weather destroying many of the crops. Coupled with the damage wrought by the Coven and the Minions, there was now little to eat. That much they had learned from Geldon. And as the prince had made his way back to the palace this morning he had seen that many fields were indeed barren. His countrymen were starving before his eyes, and there was nothing he could do to help them. The unusually harsh Season of Harvest was a sign that the next period, the Season of Crystal, would be particularly cruel. The thought made him shudder.

Adding to the problem was the fact that Eutracia was geographically isolated on all sides, allowing her no other nation with which to trade easily. Until Tristan and Wigg had learned of the nation named Parthalon that lay across the Sea of Whispers, the entire populace had always thought their nation to be the only civilization in the world. The jagged Tolenka Mountains bordered Eutracia on the northern, western, and southern sides, making a great semicircle of solid granite. A pass through the mountains had never been found.

The Sea of Whispers, the great body of water that lay to the east, had never been successfully crossed by boat until the exile and unexpected return of the Coven. Before this feat, no one had ever sailed easterly farther than a fifteen-day journey and returned home to tell about it. Nor could the Sea of Whispers be explored past a certain point to the north or the south, due to treacherous ice floes. No one in Eutracia even knew why it was named the Sea of Whispers; it just was. The prince had long felt that this great ocean held more than its share of secrets. One day, when his nation was whole again, he would try to discover what they were.

Traax, second in command of the Minions, might know how the warriors had been able to cross the Sea of Whispers, but the Minions of Day and Night were still in Parthalon. The thought of seeing the murderers of his family again, despite the fact that he was now their leader, gave rise to many mixed emotions within his heart. Because of this, his mind usually sheered away from the subject.

Before he entered one of the secret tunnels leading to the Redoubt, he wanted to view the exterior of the palace in the daylight. He wanted to be able to hold the image of his once-happy home in his mind, especially if it became necessary to spend another long period of time in the depths of the Redoubt. But as he finally came to the moat that surrounded the castle, he was dismayed by what he saw.

The very fine, pale gray Ephyran marble of the palace was scorched and destroyed in many places; the once-magnificent stained-glass windows were all smashed. Every sign of the lion and the broadsword, the heraldry of the House of Galland, had been eradicated. The drawbridge was lowered and partially destroyed, making him wonder about its safety. All of the once-beautiful flags of his family crest were gone. In their places flew the banners of the Coven, the symbol of the five-pointed star. Seeing this token made his blood churn with hate, and he did his best to remind himself that the sorceresses were dead, killed by his own hand.

He lowered his head for a moment, trying to comprehend the meaning of the death and destruction that had occurred here. He knew his life would never be the same. And then what was perhaps the most painful memory of all came to revisit him.

Nicholas, his heart whispered. *Your firstborn, your heir, lies in a shallow grave in a foreign land. And it is your fault.*

After what seemed a long time he finally opened his eyes and raised his face, as if by doing so he would somehow see the palace reborn in all of its previous glory. But of course it was not.

He turned to go, and then stopped, as his eyes focused upon something he had missed before.

Lying near the drawbridge, curled up in shadow, was a naked body. It appeared to be male.

He jumped down from his horse, drew his dreggan, and walked forward slowly, listening and watching as he went. When he finally reached the corpse, he had to swallow back bile.

The man lying on his side was of middle age, with red hair. Tall and athletic-looking, he was clearly dead and had been for some time. The tattoo of the Paragon could be clearly seen on his upper right arm. The prince slowly lowered his sword.

He rolled the body over carefully. When he saw the man's face the air went out of his lungs. He closed his eyes for a moment, trying to regain his composure.

One of the consul's eyes had been gouged out. A rolled-up parchment, neatly tied with a red ribbon, had been inserted directly into the gaping socket.

Looking more closely, Tristan could discern a second, less-visible insult to the man's face. There was a very small but deep hole directly in the center of the consul's forehead. Dried brain matter and blood spattered its edges. The hole appeared to be a wound from an arrow, but it seemed too small.

Refocusing his attention on the bizarre parchment, Tristan reached out and removed it from the dead consul's eye. The now-empty socket glared silently back at him, almost as if in anger. Tristan stood there for a moment in silence as he held the scroll, wondering whether to read it here or take it directly to the wizards.

Glancing quickly around, the prince saw that he was still alone. He quietly replaced the dreggan into its scabbard, then untied the red ribbon and unrolled the gory parchment. The note seemed to be written in blood. The hideous nature of its words made his endowed blood cry out for vengeance:

> *I enjoyed killing this one, and taking his blue eye,*
> *Killing him was simple, yet I found it so sublime.*
> *But please, dear prince, when we finally meet,*
> *For your life do not beg and whine.*
> *Please try to be a better foe, and more truly worth my time.*
> *S.*

His hands shaking with anger, Tristan rolled the parchment back up and replaced the ribbon around it. This murder had been committed in cold blood by someone truly depraved, one who also challenged the prince to the same fate. And killing a consul of the Redoubt could not have been a simple thing.

As Tristan continued to stare down at the dead consul and the scroll, he searched his mind for anyone with the first initial "S" who might want to kill him. Or, for that matter, who would want to kill one of the consuls of the Redoubt. No answers came.

But I will find you, wherever and whoever you are, Tristan promised himself. *And you shall not find me such easy prey.*

He hoisted the dead consul on his back and walked the body to Pilgrim, then laid it just before the saddle. As he mounted, he scanned the area around him, but saw nothing else of note. Finally he prodded the stallion toward the closest of the secret tunnels leading into the Redoubt.

The long, lean figure hiding behind the trees just past the prince's gaze retreated farther into the woods.

Good, he thought gleefully. *The Chosen One has found the dead consul and the scroll. This is even more than we could have hoped for. Now he will surely come to us.*

He very quietly walked back to his horse and climbed up.

Checking the odd, yellow-tipped arrows in the crossbow on his arm, he smiled.

One of these is for you, Prince Tristan, he thought. *And your day shall shortly be upon us.*

Launching his horse forward, the assassin named Scrounge quickly disappeared into the woods.

CHAPTER NINE

*T*RISTAN was missing. His bed had not been slept in, and his quarters were empty. If for some reason he had actually left the Redoubt and not yet returned, it could only add to their troubles.

The two frantic wizards ordered Shannon to go and awaken Joshua and have him join them in the quarters of the princess. Tristan might have slept the night in her room, watching over her. But Wigg felt in his heart that the prince was not in the Redoubt.

Wigg's mood darkened even further as he followed Faegan down the hallways. They desperately needed the Chosen Ones now. The wizards knew they must win a battle against time if their world was to remain safe.

Tristan, where are you? Wigg shouted silently as they approached the princess' door. After a soft knock, they heard Shailiha bid them to enter.

The princess was fully dressed and sitting in a rocking chair, holding Morganna. Her pale blue gown flowed beautifully down around her waist and ankles. The gold medallion that carried the heraldry of her family lay around her neck, twinkling in the soft light of the room. Morganna cooed softly, and the princess smiled and wrinkled her nose at the baby as the wizards walked in.

The Shailiha that Wigg and Faegan saw before them was

the woman they had hoped she would be—the woman she had for so long deserved to be again. Her hazel eyes and firm mouth showed both her intelligence and strong sense of purpose, where for so long there had been only lost, sorrowful gazes. A happy, compassionate personality radiated outward from her, just as it always had before the coming of the sorceresses.

Shailiha was indeed an image of her mother, the late queen—except that the princess had more strength, and an even greater sense of purpose. Like her twin brother, she also had a commanding sense of both physical and moral courage. Unlike many other women of her day, she had never been afraid to speak her mind in the company of men.

"You are well, Your Highness?" Faegan asked first. He wheeled his chair closer to the princess, looking deeply into her hazel eyes. "No ill effects from yesterday?"

She smiled at him. "I feel wonderful, thanks to the two of you."

"And the prince—have you see him today?" Wigg asked quietly. "Did he stay here with you last night?"

Shailiha rose to walk to the crib. She put down the baby and then turned back to the wizards. "I'm afraid I have a confession to make." She pursed her lips into a slight, mischievous smile.

This is the Shailiha I used to know, Wigg thought. "And what confession would that be?" he asked sternly, placing his hands into the opposite sleeves of his robes.

"I asked him to visit the graves for me," she answered. "If he is not here in the Redoubt, then that is no doubt where you will find him."

"The graves?" Faegan asked, looking up at Wigg. His jaw hardened a bit. It was clear by the look on his face that he had just realized that there were yet more secrets he didn't know—and Faegan was the type who liked to tease others with mysteries, rather than the reverse. So much had happened in Eutracia without him, during his self-imposed exile in Shadowood—so much tragedy that he'd been unable to prevent, or even deal with. Since he had returned to Tammerland, it seemed as if he'd resolved to make up for lost time. "Whose graves?" he demanded sharply.

"Those of the wizards of the Directorate and the royal family," Wigg answered softly. He rubbed his chin with one hand, remembering the night when the prince had sat on his heels before the fresh graves. Tristan had remained there a long time, motionless in both the darkness and the rain, and had finally used one of his dirks to cut an incision into each of his palms. Squeezing the blood down and out over the fresh, soft mounds of earth, he had sworn an oath to find and return his sister.

"We can only hope that he comes back soon," Wigg said, worry showing on his craggy face. Looking back into the eyes of the princess, he said, "The truth is that we need you both very badly right now. Every moment he is away worsens the situation."

Shailiha had always been able to discern when Wigg was worried. A short pang of guilt went through her—a result of having asked Tristan to do something that was apparently dangerous, coupled with the fact that there was obviously something the two wizards had not told her. "What happened?" she asked softly.

Faegan started to speak, but another knock came upon the door. Shannon appeared in the doorway, the consul Joshua standing obediently behind him. "I have brought the consul, as you requested," the gnome said, blowing a whiff of smoke out the bowl of his corncob pipe.

"Thank you, Shannon," Faegan answered. "You may go. Joshua, please come and join us."

As Shannon retreated into the hallway, Joshua walked into the room. Upon seeing the princess, he was clearly taken aback. "Your Highness!" he exclaimed, bowing slightly.

"Princess Shailiha, may I present Joshua, of the House of Linton," Wigg said. "He was one of the consuls I sent out to destroy the screaming harpies and blood stalkers, just before the attack by the Coven. He has returned to us by the skin of his teeth, and with an amazing tale to tell."

Shailiha took in the tall, sandy-haired man in the dark blue robe, noticing his strong jaw and hazel eyes. He was a bit on the thin side, and his right arm was wrapped in a sling.

Joshua walked to her and bowed again, took one of her hands and kissed the back of it lightly. "Your Highness," he repeated softly. "The pleasure is mine." He straightened up, calmly looking into her eyes.

"And what is this story that so intrigues the wizards?" she asked him with real interest.

At a nod from Faegan, Joshua began to tell the princess of the loss of his squad, and of finding the other group of consuls. He explained being attacked by the giant birds of prey, and how the others had been taken away. Shailiha listened intently, her face darkening as the story progressed.

Despite the incredible tale, though, she surmised that this was not what the wizards had come to discuss with her. Shailiha sensed that whatever they wanted to tell her would be for her ears only. She decided not to be inquisitive in the presence of the consul unless Wigg or Faegan offered to speak of it first.

"I hope I have not frightened you with all of this," Joshua said earnestly. "But the wizards and I believe the threat from these creatures to be very real, and I only hope that a way can be found to deal with them."

Indeed, Shailiha thought. She could remember her father, the king, as he sat in his great chair in the Chamber of Supplication, where he met with citizens who had special concerns or favors to ask. Sometimes he had taken her with him to those meetings, allowing her to sit quietly by his side with the wizards as he dealt with the problems that were brought to him.

"Someday this responsibility, along with many others, shall belong to your brother," he had said. *"And there may be times when he will seek out your advice."* But the princess had not understood him then. Now her thoughts went to Tristan, and she bit her lower lip in concern.

"We have assigned Joshua to the Redoubt libraries, to research anything that might be useful in discovering more about these flying creatures," Wigg told her. "But nothing has turned up yet. These beings remain a mystery, as do so many other things.

"There is much to tell you, Your Highness," he continued rather sadly. "We not only have a great many challenges to face, but we also find that there is now a distinctly limited amount of time with which to deal with them. But to better explain our concerns to you, we would prefer to retire to another room. Due to your inexperience in the craft, this problem must be actually seen with your own two eyes for you to truly understand it."

. Seeing the concern in both of their faces, she immediately agreed. "Of course," she said. Reaching to a nearby table, Shailiha picked up the sling that the gnome wives had made for her and donned it. Then she lifted Morganna from her crib, and gently placed her into the sling. The baby cooed softly.

Wigg went to the door. Morganna cradled closely before her, the princess followed the two wizards and the consul down the great hallways of the Redoubt.

CHAPTER TEN

NICHOLAS hovered several feet above the stone floor of the chamber, surrounded by the powerful glow radiating outward from his body. The simple, white robe he usually wore was gone, his muscular, perfect form naked and glistening in the light. Since he had last come here his smooth, black hair had grown slightly longer, his demeanor more mature. He was now the equivalent of approximately fourteen New Seasons of Life.

It was time for him to glean yet more power from the vein. Rising higher into the air, he closed his eyes fully. Lost in the ecstasy of the craft, he began to revolve slowly in the azure light. He shuddered slightly as he stretched his arms out in supplication, welcoming the dynamism he so badly needed. His parents of the Afterlife had called upon him to perform this act today, and he would not fail them.

His body began to shudder more violently with the power, his mouth turning up into a strange, constricted smile of both pleasure and pain. The vein in the walls pulsated more vigorously now with a deep, undulating presence. Very gradually, the glow reached blinding proportions. As its vibrancy increased, Nicholas turned faster and faster in the air, the light from the vein screaming all about the chamber.

And then the vein running through the walls began to bleed out onto the floor of the cave into pools of azure, glowing liquid.

The shimmering puddles undulated with the immense power of the craft. Then slowly, hauntingly, they slithered toward one another, gathering into a larger pool that seethed and writhed with a life of its own. Finally revolving into a whirlpool, it rose slowly into the air just below the boy.

The whirling maelstrom finally stopped turning. With a great cracking sound, it converted itself into bolts of pure energy, shooting upward toward the boy's body, striking his naked skin over and over again.

Nicholas twirled frantically in midair, screaming aloud, as his body absorbed the ecstasy of the craft—both the Vigors and the Vagaries alike. On and on the azure bolts came, as if they would never end. And then, almost as suddenly as they had begun, they stopped, and the glow of the craft receded.

Immediately he fell to the floor, crashing hard. He stood slowly upon trembling legs, head lowered like an animal. His breathing was ragged and labored, his body bathed in sweat. Finally lifting his head up, he smiled and raised each of his hands, turning up his palms and curling his fingers. Waves of dynamism began coursing back and forth between his palms, and he laughed aloud, reveling in the increase of the pure, unadulterated power he now possessed and the fact that there was still so much more to come. Eventually he lowered his hands and began to speak aloud, even though there was no one in the chamber to hear him. His naked body continued to glisten in the glow of the light.

"Chosen One," he whispered softly, "my father of this world, you of the azure blood, it will soon be time. Time for you to learn the true reasons for my coming. That day you shall be at my feet, begging for both your own life and the life of your nation." He paused for a moment, gliding slowly across the short distance to where the vein, seemingly undiminished, ran through solid rock. Lovingly, he ran his hands across its surface, watching it undulate within the hewn stone that imprisoned it.

"You should not have freed me that day, my father," he continued softly. "For you allowed me to escape both the womb of my sorceress mother and also eventually be released from the common, inferior trappings of this lower, lesser world. It was you, Chosen One, who allowed me to rise to the heights of the Afterlife, and discover my other parents in their omnipotence. Your tears will be great when you learn that the downfall of all you cherish and protect was your doing, and yours alone. Your nation is about to hear a cry such as it has never known, even with the coming of the sorceresses."

He lay his feverish brow against the cool, pulsing vein. "Your consuls are quickly becoming mine, as is your craft of magic, Father. Soon they shall both join me in my struggle, as shall my hatchlings and yet others of my invention. Only near the end of your life, Chosen One, shall I grant you the true, undeniable knowledge of my existence—I, who embody the unexpected survival of your seed."

Nicholas turned away from the pulsing vein and floated out of the chamber. The glow of the craft followed him, eventually vanishing from the room.

CHAPTER ELEVEN

TRISTAN approached the hidden entrance to the tunnel slowly and carefully. The dead consul lay across his horse's back; the bloody parchment and the poem it contained were tucked snugly beneath the prince's black leather vest.

Finding the special boulder, he reached out and touched the spot on it that the wizards had specially infused with the craft. The giant piece of granite slowly rolled away, revealing the darkness of the tunnel beyond. He walked Pilgrim into the tunnel, then touched yet another spot on the inside wall and watched the massive stone roll back into place before touching one of the pale green stones lining the length of the tunnel roof. A soft, ephemeral sage glow immediately illuminated the entire way back to the Redoubt.

He dismounted and pulled the body off of Pilgrim. He removed the dark blue robe he was wearing, then dressed the dead consul in it to give the deceased man a modicum of decency. Both the neat, small hole and the ghastly, empty eye socket stared abjectly up at him.

With a great heave, he lifted the body back onto Pilgrim.

When he finally reached the tunnel's end, he pulled the body down and left it by the door into the Redoubt. He wished to place the consul in what had once been his father's private chamber, the room the king had reserved for meetings requiring the greatest secrecy. The odds of it being used at this hour of the day seemed slim. After taking Pilgrim to the underground stables and securing him there, Tristan went back to the body, hoisted it over his back, and walked to the room he had chosen.

Wigg, Faegan, Joshua, and Shailiha, Morganna in her arms, were sitting at his father's long meeting table in midconversation when he walked in unannounced, the dead consul over his back. Upon seeing the dead man Shailiha immediately wrapped her arms tighter around her baby. The wizards were obviously surprised, but remained calm. They turned to look at each other's reaction as the prince laid the body down on the couch along the wall.

Knowing he had a great deal of explaining to do, Tristan then turned back to the wizards. He started to speak, but Wigg quickly raised one of his hands, stopping him before he could start.

"We already know you were gone last night, and we also know the reason why," he said in that casual, yet somehow all-knowing way of his. Shailiha set her jaw slightly in defiance. "But what we don't know is why you have an obviously dead man in a consul's robe with you." Wigg stood and approached the body.

Faegan wheeled his chair closer, while Shailiha rose to join her brother. "Are you all right?" she whispered.

Tristan's first reaction was to realize that his sister was finally free of her torment by the Coven. A new strength and sense of personality radiated from her. It was a look he had not seen since that awful day on the dais, when their whole world had collapsed. Tears started to form in his eyes, and he put his arms around her. Between them, Morganna wriggled slightly.

"They've finally done it, haven't they, Shai?" he asked joyfully. Still holding her by the shoulders, he gently pushed her away from him so that he might look into her face. "You're finally free?"

"Yes." She smiled back. "The wizards have cured me."

He kissed her cheek, bent to kiss Morganna's downy head, and then turned back to where Faegan and Wigg were intently examining the wounds in the dead man's head.

"Is this the way you found him?" Faegan asked him bluntly.

"Yes," Tristan answered, walking over to the two wizards. "He was already dead. The wound in his forehead looks like one from an arrow, but it seems too small for that. As for the missing eye, there is a little more to the story."

"Such as?" Wigg asked.

Tristan beckoned for everyone to sit down at the table. Then he removed the bloody parchment from his vest, unrolled it, and laid it out so that the others could read it at once. After they had finished, Shailiha looked a little green, and the two wizards became lost within their own respective thoughts. Joshua said nothing. For several moments the only sounds in the room were the crackling of the fireplace and the purring of Faegan's ever-present cat. Finally, Wigg broke the silence.

"Joshua," he asked the consul as he pointed to the body on the other side of the room, "did you know this man?"

"No," Joshua answered sadly. "But he certainly seems to have come to a terrible end."

Faegan studied the poem closely. "This is more than mere boasting," he said softly. "This is also a challenge to Tristan to come and find whoever did this. It is clear that someone wants to confront him, and they have begun that process by killing the consuls. Or at least this particular one. This entire act was designed to taunt the prince."

Tristan removed his dreggan and its baldric from over his right shoulder and hung them on the back of his chair. "And they succeeded," he said angrily. His face had gone dark. "I do not plan to let this challenge go unheeded. Whoever has done this must pay."

Shailiha stared at her brother intently, almost as if she were looking at him for the first time. She had never seen him so clearly determined. She had very little memory of her time with the Coven, and before that the brother she had known had been much more carefree and irresponsible. But the Tristan who sat before her now had become a much more focused, mature warrior, and the difference in him impressed her.

He truly is the Chosen One, she realized. *But he is still impulsive. And with that, at least, I can be of help.* She gently placed one of her hands upon his and said, "Before you do anything, Brother, you need to hear what it is the wizards have to say. Much has happened of which you are still unaware, and it may change your perception of things."

Seeing the calming effect she had over Tristan, Wigg smiled to himself. He cleared his throat. "Before that," he said, "I still have some questions. First of all, on a personal note, were the graves undisturbed?"

"Yes," Tristan answered. He smiled sadly at Shailiha.

"And do you think," Wigg asked, "that the death of this consul and the appearance of Joshua's flying creatures are related?"

Tristan reached out to the large, silver pot of morning tea on the table, poured himself a cup, and took a deep draught. He narrowed his eyes in thought for a moment.

"That is impossible to say at this time," he said at last. "Clearly neither of these acts was random, and both had to do with the consuls. But that does not necessarily mean that they are related."

"Where did you find him?" Faegan asked.

"At the entrance to the palace," Tristan answered. "Just in front of the drawbridge."

Faegan looked at Wigg, the two of them apparently coming to the same conclusion. "Given the existence of the poem, does that tell you anything?" Faegan asked the prince.

Tristan knew they were testing him. "The answer to that is simple," he said. "First, whoever wrote the poem knows I am back in Eutracia. That was a secret we tried very hard to keep, but it still seems to have leaked out somehow. And second, it is obvious that they believe we are hiding somewhere in the palace, for that is where they placed the dead consul."

"Precisely," said Wigg, his right index finger in the air.

"Is there anything else about your little trip to the outside world we should know?" Faegan asked, spearing the prince with his gray-green gaze.

Looking over to Shailiha, Tristan thought for a moment. He briefly considered telling the wizards of the woman he had rescued from suicide, but for reasons even he did not fully understand, he decided not to speak of it. "No," he said simply. "Nothing of importance." Shailiha wrinkled up her nose at him, tacitly telling him that she knew better.

She could always tell, he thought happily. *She truly is back.*

"Very well," Wigg said, his eyebrow high in the air. He didn't completely believe Tristan, but he was willing to let it go for the moment.

"There truly is something important you must know," Faegan began seriously, "and I'm afraid it—"

Just as the wizard managed to garner the prince's complete attention, a soft knock came upon the door. Tristan reached over his back to draw one of his dirks, then stood and went to the door. He opened it sharply, his knife at the ready.

A very surprised Geldon stood there. With an apologetic smile, Tristan replaced the knife into its quiver, as Wigg beckoned Geldon into one of the vacant chairs.

"Thank you for not killing me, Your Highness," Geldon said, a touch of sarcasm in his voice. "Begging your pardon, but you need to hear what it is I have to tell you, and you need to hear it now."

Tristan's dark eyes took in the expression on the hunchback's face, and saw clearly that whatever he was about to hear would not please him.

Without speaking, Geldon removed from his shirt the wanted poster for the prince, then unceremoniously flattened it out on the table. As the others read it, Geldon studied the bizarre poem written in the blood of the consul. The color drained from his face. He then saw the dead consul lying on the couch and noticed the neat hole in the man's forehead and the gaping, empty eye socket. But it was the forehead wound that most interested him.

Standing from his chair and walking closer, he saw the dried, yellow fluid that lay crazily around the edges of the small, perfect wound. He thought of the mysterious letter "S" at the end of the poem. *Scrounge! It has to be!* He very quietly walked back to his chair and sat down.

Tristan was speechless. Faegan had warned him of this day back in Shadowood. And Kluge, the winged monster he had killed with his own hands, had boasted the same thing as he died in the dirt at Tristan's feet. The prince closed his eyes, remembering the words Kluge had uttered with his last breath.

"Our struggle is not over, Chosen One," Kluge had said. *"Even in death it shall go on for me. There are still things you do not know, and even if you should somehow return to your homeland you will be a wanted man, hunted day and night because of me, your forever-damaged sister a mere shadow of her former self. No, Galland, your victory over me here today is far from complete. Our battle goes on, even from my grave."*

Tristan looked over to his sister. Kluge had been only partially correct. Shailiha was cured, no longer the damaged person Kluge had said she would forever be. But apparently the other side of his prediction had come true: Tristan was now a wanted man in his own nation, being hunted by the same subjects he had risked his life so many times to protect. And someone was willing to pay one hundred thousand kisa to bring him in.

"How is it that you came by this poster?" Wigg asked Geldon softly, obviously taken aback by the news.

"It was being distributed in the Hog's Hoof Tavern," Geldon answered, "and it caused quite a stir." He looked over at the prince with sad eyes. "I'm afraid they all quite believe it."

"Believe what?" Tristan whispered back, finally finding his voice.

Geldon looked down at his hands. "The fact that you killed your father . . . They believe it was intentional, and that you were in league with the Coven and the Minions."

Lowering his head with the pain, Tristan closed his eyes. *This simply cannot be happening.*

"Who was distributing these posters?" Faegan asked, calmly stroking the cat in his lap. "Did you see him?"

"Oh, yes," Geldon replied, looking again at the dead man on the other side of the room. "I believe him to be the same one who killed this consul."

Tristan's head quickly came up. "Why?" he asked sharply.

"He walked into the tavern with a roll of posters under one arm and jumped up on the bar, shouting his invective at the crowd," Geldon explained. "He condemned you as a traitor, saying that the reward would be paid in gold." He turned his attention back to the table as a whole.

"He also viciously attacked an ex-member of the Royal Guard," the dwarf continued. "The man tried to stand up for you, and the assassin hurt him badly. He used a miniature crossbow, strapped over his right forearm. It is very ingenious, and the only other weapon I have ever seen to be as fast as your dirks. I believe it caused the wound on the consul's forehead. The points of the arrows were coated with some kind of strange yellow stain."

At the mention of the yellow stains on the assassin's weapons, the two older wizards looked quickly to one another. Narrowing his eyes, Wigg placed either hand into the opposite sleeves of his robe while Faegan continued to stroke his cat, his gaze turning far away.

"What is his name?" Tristan asked, his knuckles white around the chalice he held.

"Scrounge," Geldon answered. "This killing of the consul, combined with the fact that the poem is signed 'S,' leads me to believe that he is the murderer. The bartender also told me that Scrounge is a professional killer, and one of the most accomplished assassins in all of Eutracia. Yet he is rumored to have only one employer—the same sponsor who is putting up the money for Tristan's capture."

"And the name of his employer?" Tristan countered.

"Unknown," Geldon answered softly. Again the room went uncomfortably, deafeningly quiet.

"After he wounded a soldier with his crossbow, the soldier swore that he would one day kill Scrounge. And then the assassin said something strange."

"And that was?" Wigg asked calmly from the other side of the table.

"Scrounge told the officer that he doubted it, since the soldier was already dead. But clearly he was not. What did he mean?"

Wigg glanced over to Faegan, and said, "Would you like to tell them, or should I?"

"Be my guest," the elder wizard answered rather blankly, still off somewhere in his own private world.

"The reason this Scrounge person said the officer was already dead was because he wounded the man with a weapon that was dipped in a very special fluid. A poison, actually." Wigg paused, wondering how to say the next words. "The yellow stain you saw was the dried fluid from the brain of a blood stalker."

"But you told me once that the fluid from a stalker's brain was instantaneously fatal," Shailiha said from across the table. "If that is the case, then why did Scrounge's arrow not kill the officer immediately?"

The princess could still remember the day not so long ago when she and Wigg had been in the Hartwick Woods, searching for Tristan. Wigg had killed a stalker that had been secretly tracking them. It was the first and only time she had ever seen one, and the wizard had gone on to explain the stalkers to her. Each stalker, he said, had once been a wizard, but had been captured by the sorceresses and mutated by incantation.

"Well done, Princess," Wigg said, smiling for the first time.

"So what is the answer?" Tristan asked.

"The fluid kills instantaneously only in its liquid form. Once it dries out, the resultant powder must somehow get into the victim's bloodstream in order to be deadly. And that effect is not immediate."

"So that is what Scrounge meant when he said the officer was already dead," Shailiha whispered, almost to herself. She looked up at Wigg in horror. "How long will it take him to die?"

"That depends upon the type and strength of the person's blood," Wigg answered. "If the officer is unendowed, which is most likely the case, then he will die in a matter of only days. But if the victim is one of endowed blood, the torment can last much longer."

And all because someone stood up for me against Scrounge, Tristan thought. *Yet another reason to kill him.*

"Why would someone bother to dip the ends of their weapons in this fluid and only wound them, when they could just as easily kill them outright and be done with it?" Shailiha asked.

"Because a person like that doesn't kill just for the money, Shai," Tristan said. His expression had turned dark again. "I have seen this before, in Parthalon. Such a person also kills because he enjoys it. He takes pleasure in knowing his victims continue to suffer, even after he has finished with them."

"That much is true," Geldon interjected. "And he is very good."

So am I, Tristan thought viciously.

"In truth, the yellow liquid dried around the forehead wound on the consul had not escaped Faegan and me," Wigg said thoughtfully. "But I first thought that he had been killed by a stalker. Now that we believe it was Scrounge, this puts an entirely different light on things."

"Indeed," Faegan responded simply.

"How so?" Geldon asked.

"Well, for one thing," Faegan began, "how did Scrounge get the fluid to dip his weapons into, and who taught him about all of this? Such things are not common knowledge. An obvious conclusion is that a blood stalker is actually in league with this man. But such a relationship would be highly unlikely, since stalkers have relatively little ability to communicate, and are almost always completely mad as a result of their transformation. No, this issue is far from resolved." He paused for a moment, his gray eyes shining with thought. Anger chased sadness across his face, and he looked down at Nicodemus in his lap. If only he had not stayed in Shadowood all those years! He shook his head. There was no time for regrets. There were puzzles to solve and action to plan. He had to concentrate on what he could do now. He looked up again.

"There is an even greater problem we must still discuss," he continued. "And I now believe that the two are related."

"And that is . . . ?" the prince asked, unable to fathom what else might possibly be wrong.

Faegan did not immediately answer. Instead, he looked across the table at Wigg, who nodded. Wigg stood to walk to the spot at the left of the fireplace, touching the wall gently with his fingertips. Immediately the fireplace began to pivot, causing Geldon's and Shailiha's jaws to drop. "Shall we?" Wigg asked, motioning everyone through.

The Well of the Redoubt was exactly as the prince remembered it from that day when the lead wizard had first brought him here, just after the murder of his family. The black trough of marble was as breathtaking as ever, the dark red waters from the Caves still happily, noisily splashing down and out from the spigot in the wall. He couldn't imagine what the problem might be.

They stood before the trough. "Do you see anything different about this place?" Wigg asked darkly.

Tristan was perplexed. Absolutely nothing, as far as he could tell, was unusual about the Well of the Redoubt. "No," he answered. "I do not." He was also feeling the effects of the waters on his untrained blood. His heart beat faster, and he felt flushed. He knew neither he nor his sister would be able to withstand the proximity of the waters for long.

"And those of you here with endowed blood, have you felt anything unusual in the last several days?"

"What do you mean?" Shailiha asked, now clearly dizzy and holding on to her brother for support.

"I mean, other than just now, have you sensed any unusual weakness in your physicality, or mental abilities?" Wigg answered.

"No," Tristan said, and Shailiha shook her head in agreement. Joshua, however, nodded.

"Just as we expected," Wigg said. He carefully removed the Paragon from beneath his robes and held it before them. "Look closely at the stone, and tell me what you see."

Tristan looked hard at the Paragon, the jewel that controlled the power of the craft. At first it seemed absolutely normal to him. And then he saw the anomaly. His breath caught in his lungs. *It can't be!* his mind cried out.

There was clearly something wrong with the stone. Instead of being deep red, the upper right-hand corner of the gem was pink. The Paragon was losing its color—and therefore its power, as well.

Tristan regarded the stone in horror. "Why?" the prince whispered to Wigg. "How can this be?" Now dizzy, he was finding it difficult to get the words out. He knew that Shailiha was faring no better, and Morganna had begun to cry. He hoped the wizards would let them leave the room soon, despite the drastic nature of the circumstances.

"Now that you all understand, we shall leave," Faegan said

simply. He turned his chair toward the door and started to wheel his way out. The prince and Shailiha also made for the door, Geldon, Wigg, and Joshua following them. Wigg closed the secret door, and almost immediately the prince began to feel somewhat better. He could tell that Shailiha did, too.

Nonetheless, Tristan felt as if he had just been struck down by some kind of terrible blow. The combination of the effects of the waters and the awful knowledge regarding the stone left him stunned and questioning. For a moment he simply sat there, trying to collect himself, watching his sister do the same. Finally, he spoke.

"But why?" he whispered to the wizards. "What would cause the Pargon to lose its color?"

"We do not know," Wigg replied. "Faegan and I both felt the decay in the stone before we actually saw it. It happened to each of us at the same time, just after our last session with the princess. Although at this point the loss is minute, we did sense a slip in our powers. At the current rate of decay the stone will soon become clear, and lose its power in no more than several months."

"It is truly distressing," Joshua said, concern plainly showing in his face. "I have also felt a decrease in my gift, but I thought it was malnutrition," he said simply. "Now I know differently."

"Has this ever occurred before?" Tristan asked, still overwhelmed by the implications of it all.

"The only time the stone ever loses its color is when it has been removed from a human host, or prematurely from the waters of the Caves. Otherwise, there is no reason for this phenomenon," Faegan interjected, still stroking his cat.

"I don't understand," Shailiha said, now almost fully recovered. "If the stone loses its power when removed from a human host, then how is it that it can be moved from one person of endowed blood to another?"

"An excellent question." Wigg smiled at her. "And one that took us a great deal of time in the early days of the monarchy to unravel. It was Egloff, our resident expert on the Tome, who first came up with the reason. Simply put, the stone needs a host for its continued survival, and there are only two types it will accept. A person of endowed blood, or the waters of the Caves. Nothing else will do." He paused for a moment, thinking of how best to explain.

"In order to change human hosts, such as at the coronation of a new king, the stone is first removed from around the person's neck. The Paragon, because it now has no host, will immediately begin to lose its color. If this process were allowed to continue, the stone would eventually die without either the waters or another human host of endowed blood to sustain it. But because the relationship between the wearer and the stone is so strong, it must first be prepared for another wearer, or returned to a 'virgin' state, if you will. For this reason it is immersed in a small quantity of the water. The procedure must be performed exactly right, or the stone is in great peril of being extinguished forever. As the Paragon returns to its normal color, the waters become clear. This signals that the waters have performed their task—that is, to reenergize the stone and make it ready to accept another host of endowed blood. The Paragon is then ready to be placed around the neck of its new human host."

"Then why is the stone losing its color now?" the princess asked.

"Wigg and I think that the stone is actually being drained in some way, by some other power," Faegan answered. "Perhaps even from a long distance. If that is true, then our chances of stopping its decay are much less."

"But why would someone wish to do such a thing?" Geldon asked. His understanding of the stone was no doubt less than that of anyone else in the room, but his question was important, nonetheless. "If this decay is being accomplished by someone of endowed blood and the stone loses its power, then will the person causing this to happen not also lose his mastery of the gift? It doesn't make any sense."

"Indeed," Faegan replied. "Frustrating, isn't it?" His mouth quirked up at one side in a half smile, as it always did when he was presented with a seemingly contradictory problem of the craft.

The prince was suddenly concerned with the long-term effects of all of this. "Assuming all that you say is correct," he began, "and the stone loses all of its color several months from now, what is the ultimate effect on our lives?" He felt sure he already had the answer, but he wanted to hear it from the ones who were the true experts on the Paragon.

Wigg and Faegan looked at each other as if they were about to discuss the end of the world. *Perhaps they are,* Tristan thought glumly.

"The first and most obvious effect will, of course, be that Wigg, Joshua, and I will begin to lose our powers," Faegan said quietly. "This will happen slowly, over time. The end result will be that when the stone is completely clear, we will be totally stripped of our use of the craft. It will also of course mean that we are no longer protected by the time enchantments. Therefore, if we don't find the cause for all of this and correct it quickly, as time goes inevitably forward our abilities to perform the craft and also to remain healthy and alert will be greatly diminished. This will vastly reduce our chances of success. But there remains another, even more dangerous result of all this—one that we have feared for over three centuries."

"And that is?" Tristan asked quietly.

"A world without magic," Wigg whispered. "Or, I should say, a world such as the one Faegan and I inhabited three centuries ago, before the Paragon was discovered and we accepted its powers over what were at that time our far less powerful practices of the craft. But given the fact that this calamity has no precedence, we simply can't be sure. It is possible that with the Paragon drained, there may finally exist no magic at all."

For a moment the prince was stunned, unable to imagine such a thing. But then he realized that what the wizards were saying was of course quite true. The Paragon empowered the craft. Without the stone, the craft would die. And a great many dreams and hopes carried over from the last three centuries would die with it, never to return.

"Such a situation, namely our world without the craft, would be disastrous. Especially now," Wigg said. "As time went on and our knowledge of the stone grew, the Directorate, through its compassionate use of the Vigors, was always able to keep control of the nation. We accomplished this via a monarchy that carefully ruled in the interests of the populace as a whole. Chaos is the natural order of the universe, and without the use of the craft to combat it and keep it in check, it will no doubt return. True anarchy will reign, just as it did during the Sorceresses' War of three hundred years ago. And this time there will be no Paragon to save us."

Tristan turned to his sister and saw in her eyes the pain that matched his own. She placed a hand over his, telling him that whatever they must endure, this time they would at least go through it together.

"Do you have any idea who might be responsible for this?" he asked the wizards.

"No," Faegan said. "That is the maddening part. And now that the country is in chaos and there is a price on your head, going out from the Redoubt in search of the answers is doubly dangerous."

"Nonetheless, that is exactly what you and I must do," Wigg said, looking at the prince.

Tristan knew that the wizards must already have something in mind, and he was eager to hear whatever it might be.

"It is imperative that you and I leave at once for the Caves," Wigg said. "Faegan and Shailiha will remain here, with Joshua and the gnomes. Shannon will accompany us there, to watch our horses, while we are inside. While we are gone, Geldon will continue his travels to the outside, providing those living here with provisions and gleaning whatever information he can. Joshua will also remain here as he continues to recuperate."

The Caves of the Paragon, Tristan thought to himself. *I am finally going back to the Caves.*

He could still remember that warm, bright afternoon as if it were yesterday. The day he accidentally discovered the Caves—the day so many questions about his life suddenly came brimming to the surface. He had followed Pilgrim there in the horse's mad chase of the fliers of the fields. He had accidentally fallen into the Caves, only to awaken in an unknown world of magic and secrecy. To him it was a sacred place, and his heart had ached to return ever since he had first found it, but until this moment, the Caves had been forbidden to him. Now, the thrill of going back made his endowed blood rise in his veins.

"Can you imagine why this is our strategy?" Faegan asked him, distracting Tristan from his memories of the Caves.

Tristan was stymied by Faegan's question. "I understand the Caves is a place of magic, and our many problems clearly have to do with the craft. But other than that I do not see your reasoning," he replied honestly.

"Understandable." Faegan smiled impishly. "Tell me, what have you learned about the blood of the endowed?"

Tristan's mind went back to another unforgettable day not that long ago. He and Wigg had been in this very room, and Wigg had told him—at last—why he was special. Wigg had also explained that the blood of the endowed was actually a living entity of its own. But until a person was trained in the craft the blood remained dormant, sensitive to the waters of the Caves but unaffected by the Paragon.

Again the prince was without a sufficient answer. "Endowed blood must first be trained to become active. But my blood and Shailiha's is untrained, and therefore technically dormant," he replied, "despite my blood being azure instead of red, as a result of my experiences in Parthalon."

"Correct," Faegan said. "Now follow that concept, and tell me where it takes you."

Layers of thought and deed, the prince reflected in frustration. He had no immediate answer, but tried to delve deeper into the mystery of the wizard's question. And then, after some thought, a kernel of realization came to him. "My sister and I are different," he finally said, almost to himself.

"Ah," Faegan said, nodding. "And in what way would that be?"

"We will not be affected by the decay of the stone."

Faegan smiled. "And why will you not be affected by the decay of the Paragon?" he asked.

"Because we have not been trained in the craft, our blood is still dormant. As such, we have little or no powers. Therefore, unlike you, Joshua, and Wigg, as the stone decays further, Shailiha and I will not sense it." Pleased with himself, Tristan sat back in his chair. But the wizards were not done with him.

"And?" Wigg asked from across the table, the infamous brow arched up over his right eye.

"And what?" Tristan asked, perplexed.

"And what truth logically follows this fact that you have just told us?"

Tristan cast his mind back through all he had learned

recently—and then he came right up against something he was sure he did not want to see.

"You and Faegan are the only two here protected by time enchantments," he began. "The Paragon is decaying. Therefore, so shall the enchantments. This will gradually leave the two of you subject to both aging and the ravages of disease for the first time in over three hundred years." He paused, closing his eyes briefly in pain. "But as for the rest of us, other than Joshua's loss of the craft, we shall feel no change in our lives. For us, things will remain the way they have always been."

"I thought time enchantments were forever," Shailiha said quickly. "That's what they do, isn't it? Keep the subject free of sickness and aging for all time?"

"An understandable assumption," Faegan replied, "but incorrect. Consider the following: The time enchantments, like everything else of the craft, rely on the continuous power of the Paragon. As we said before, ours may soon become a world completely without magic. And such a world certainly would not be able to sustain time enchantments."

Tristan hated seeing the stunned expression on his twin sister's face. Neither of them had ever seen one of the wizards of the Directorate growing old or becoming ill. It was awful enough that most of the Directorate was now gone, murdered. The thought of watching Wigg and Faegan age and die was almost more than he could bear.

And then he realized what else Wigg had been saying.

"We're going to retrieve the Tome," he whispered, barely able to get the words out. The Tome of the Paragon. The giant book that was rumored not only to explain the craft's many secrets, but to reveal much of Tristan's future, and the future of his nation. The first volume of the Tome was the Vigors, and was dedicated to explaining the compassionate side of the craft. The second went into the Vagaries, the darker, far more self-serving aspects of magic. The third and last was the Prophecies, or the foretelling—the volume that only he, the Chosen One, was destined to read. "And you are about to begin my training in the craft." He could feel his blood sing with the prospect.

"Yes," Wigg said, finally smiling. "It is now time for you.

But perhaps beyond time for our nation. Eutracia desperately needs the powers that you will eventually possess. Powers that are fabled to be beyond anything even Faegan or I could ever summon. But time is not on our side. Eutracia needs your training now more than at any other time in her history. Perhaps even more than during the recent return of the Coven. Whatever training we can give you, however slight, may be of great help in augmenting our own power. It is something that we simply cannot afford to delay." He paused for a moment, the smile on his face disappearing before he continued.

"In our estimation even the Coven, as powerful as they were, could not have accomplished this apparent draining of the stone," Wigg added. "And if we are truly up against a power of the craft that can perform such a terrible thing, then we are immersed in the depths of something even more deadly than our experiences with the sorceresses."

"But there is yet another problem," Faegan added. "And that problem has to do with what may be our most important foe: time. Do you remember what Wigg taught you about needing the stone to decipher the Tome?"

"Yes," Tristan said, now beginning to understand Faegan's ominous point. "The Tome is written in a different language. Wigg has sometimes referred to it as Old Eutracian. It is believed to be the language of the Ones Who Came Before—the civilization of ancients who preceded us here in this land. They were the ones who wrote the Tome, leaving it behind for ongoing generations of the endowed to find, and employ. Since I have not studied Old Eutracian, the only way I can comprehend the language of the great book is to wear the stone. It immediately allows a wearer of endowed blood to read the text."

"Excellent," Faegan said, giving an approving glance toward Wigg.

"But there is still something I do not understand," Tristan said. "If Faegan has the power of Consummate Recollection, then why can't he simply recite the entire Tome to us, here in the Redoubt? Can we not find the answers we need without making this journey?"

"Although I have read the first two sections of the Tome, I have not read the Prophecies," Faegan said sadly. "To do so is forbidden by anyone but the Chosen One. Wigg and I fear that much of what we may need, not only to help stop whoever is doing this but also to train you, may well reside within that last volume. And if the Tome is not brought back to us soon, it is quite possible that whatever we learn from the Prophecies we might not be able to employ. Because by then our powers may be too weak."

Tristan looked around the table at all of the people who were now so heavily relying on him. Shailiha, Morganna, Wigg, Faegan, Geldon, and Joshua. And then he turned to look at the dead consul on the other side of the room, knowing that the lives and dreams of whatever consuls were still left in the countryside also rested squarely upon his shoulders.

"As much as I wish to retrieve the Tome," he said, thinking out loud, "there is great danger, is there not, in simply bringing it back to the Redoubt with us? We will be out in the open. If we are accosted and they manage to take it from us, we might never see it again. This sounds far too risky to me! Is there no other way?"

"I must agree with the prince," Joshua interjected. "Master Faegan, the lead wizard has told me of the portal that you summoned to transport them to Parthalon and back. Could that not be used for this purpose, making it safer to transport the Tome?"

"There simply is not enough time," Faegan said. "The portal is summoned to a specific location through a series of complex calculations. And in truth, I have only ever directed its use between Parthalon and Shadowood. It takes weeks to complete the computations for a new destination, and that is a luxury that we just can't afford."

Tristan tried to take in the ramifications of everything he had heard that day. So much bad news had arrived in such a short period of time that it was difficult to comprehend it all. The vanishing consuls, the decaying Paragon, and an assassin named Scrounge who killed for pleasure and was bent upon not only distributing wanted posters of him, but sending him taunting notes written in blood. Not to mention Joshua's strange flying creatures and the fact that there might be at least one blood stalker still on the loose who might somehow be in league with the one named Scrounge. He wondered if all of this was somehow intertwined, or whether these events were random acts, a result of the madness sweeping the land. He thought of the nation of Eutracia, lost in the chaos that had been brought by the Coven.

It pained him to know that his leaving the Redoubt with Wigg would be hard on Shailiha. But he tried to take heart in the fact that here in the Redoubt with Faegan, Geldon, and Joshua was the safest place for her. Even he could not protect her as well as the master wizard in the chair, and he knew it. But there remained yet another concern, one that had been haunting him since his departure from Parthalon. He was still unaware of the status of the Minions of Day and Night.

The Minions—the savage Parthalonian fighting force of over three hundred thousand who were responsible for the sacking of his nation and the deaths of his family. Incredibly, he now found himself to be their undisputed leader. Traax, the Minion second in command the prince had left behind to carry out his orders, had seemed completely committed to doing whatever Tristan ordered. But that did not mean things in Parthalon hadn't changed.

The prince had given several commands to Traax that day. He had demanded the elimination of the brothels and the freeing of the Gallipolai—the enslaved offshoots of the Minions who had white wings, instead of the customary black. He had also ordered the task of reconstructing the terrible place called the Ghetto of the Shunned, the holding area the Coven had employed to contain the "undesirables" of the nation.

I am not only responsible for the welfare of Eutracia, he thought, *but now for Parthalon, as well. For the nation across the sea is not advanced, nor does it have any history of the craft other than the Coven. If they chose to, the Minions could cut the Parthalonian citizenry down like locusts through a wheat field.*

"If Wigg and I are to go to the Caves, there is something that I insist be accomplished while I am gone," Tristan said adamantly. "I wish for Geldon to be sent through the portal to Parthalon. I want him to review the actions of the Minions, and to be sure that the nation is still at peace. And I want to know the warriors are continuing to carry out the orders I issued. Far too much time has gone by without such an inspection, and in my temporary absence I wish Geldon to do it. He has the most experience of any of us in this regard. He is, after all, Parthalonian himself."

Tristan turned to look at the hunchbacked dwarf, the small man of such great stature and heart who had come to their aid time and time again. "Will you do this thing for me?" the prince asked. "Will you go as my emissary and bring me back a report?"

Geldon was stunned, and his face showed it. He owed Tristan his life, and would do anything he asked—but what if the situation in Parthalon was not as it was expected to be? He looked around the table for a solution to his dilemma, and then quickly realized what it was.

"I will gladly do as you ask, Tristan, but I have one request," Geldon said. "We do not know what this journey might hold. None of us has been back since we left. I would therefore ask that Joshua accompany me on this trip. I may need someone to help protect me. And clearly you, Wigg, and Faegan must stay here. Joshua is trained in the craft. He is not as highly trained as the wizards, I know. Nonetheless, his gifts would be of great help, should we find it necessary to use his skill to either impress the Minions or to actually try to fend them off."

Well said, Tristan thought.

The prince automatically turned his gaze to Faegan and Wigg. They seemed far from pleased. But Tristan meant to have his way in this. The responsibilities he had left behind in Parthalon had come to weigh heavily upon his mind in recent days, and he needed to know. Without giving either of the wizards a chance to object, he spoke directly to the consul.

"Will you do it?" he asked Joshua bluntly. "Will you accompany Geldon to Parthalon for me?"

"My authority has always come from the lead wizard," Joshua said without hesitation. "But you do need my services, and you are the Chosen One. Meaning no disrespect to Wigg, I will do as you ask."

"Thank you," Tristan said. The wizards remained silent, but Wigg's arched eyebrow was as high up into the furrows of his forehead as the prince had ever seen it.

"Then all is agreed," Tristan said with finality. "Wigg and I shall go the Caves to retrieve the Tome, and Geldon and Joshua shall carry out my orders in Parthalon."

From the other side of the table the prince heard Faegan take a deep breath and let it out slowly. It was as if the entire weight of the world had suddenly fallen upon the crippled wizard's shoulders. The intense, gray eyes looked into the prince's with a sadness Tristan had seldom seen.

" '*And the search for the volumes shall draw them into dark, unknown places. Their minds shall be turned and deceived, their endowed blood strained to the utmost. For it is only in this way that they may truly attain their prize. But the ultimate victory that they seek shall remain elusive and ephemeral, the child forever watching,*' " Faegan said.

"Another quote from the Tome?" Tristan asked.

"Yes," Faegan answered softly. "But as usual, its meaning escapes me." He looked around at Tristan, Wigg, Joshua, and Geldon.

"May the Afterlife see you all safely home," he whispered.

CHAPTER TWELVE

❧

*A*s Tristan made the long walk to his sister's chambers, he couldn't help but reflect upon how lonely this place was. Lonely, yet at the same time so incredibly beautiful. The Redoubt was gigantic in size, originally meant for the training of the several thousand consuls who had once inhabited it. The relatively few people who lived here now seemed lost within the expanses yawning before them.

He knew that Shailiha greatly missed both her husband and their parents. Despite the fact that Faegan, Geldon, and the gnomes would still be here with her, it would be even lonelier for her with him gone.

But he had mixed feelings about leaving, he realized, as he listened to the heels of his knee boots ringing out against the marble floor. Although part of him wanted to stay here with his sister and see personally to the safety of both her and her baby, he also longed to be outdoors. He selfishly wanted to feel his stallion beneath him again, and to take in the pine-laden scent of the Hartwick Woods. Tristan was a man of action, and always had been. When there was no task before him his spirit always died a little, these last weeks in the Redoubt having been no exception.

As he finally approached Shailiha's door he knocked softly once, then twice more. At the sound of her voice, he walked in.

Standing in the doorway and looking into her room, his first reaction was one of shock. But then his mind slowly uncoiled, realizing that what he saw before him was only the re-creation of a pleasant memory, nothing more. Shailiha was sitting with her back to him, before a great loom. As she sat there calmly working the threads, her long, blond hair trailing down over her shoulders, the prince had immediately mistaken her for their late mother. Morganna had sat tirelessly at her looms, eventually passing the art on to her daughter. Just as the queen's mother had taught her, so long ago.

Shailiha is so much like her, he thought. *And I am so fortunate to have her back in my life.*

His sister turned to smile at him, but he could tell her expression was a bit forced. Clearly, his impending departure weighed heavily on her mind.

"Where did the loom come from?" Tristan asked her. "I thought everything in the palace was destroyed or looted."

"Wigg was kind enough to conjure it for me," she answered. "It helps to pass the time, and somehow seems to help keep me closer to the memory of our mother." She paused for a moment, then looked up into her brother's eyes.

"You're leaving sooner than expected, aren't you?" she asked, already knowing the answer.

Tristan nodded. "Wigg and I thought it best we leave in the dark."

"I see," she said softly. "Then I shall have to see to it that Morganna and I give you a proper good-bye."

Standing, she looked at him and was struck again by how

much he had changed. She glanced at the weapons he constantly carried, one of which—the dreggan, the curved sword of the Minions—was still rather unfamiliar to her.

"You look like you're going into battle," she said darkly. As she so often did when distressed, she bit her lip.

He grinned. "Don't worry. Wigg will be with me. Should anyone try to interfere with us, he probably won't even need his magic. In truth, I doubt there's anything his sarcasm can't overcome. He will probably just insult them to death." He laughed, trying to lighten her mood.

He walked across the room to the crib and looked down into the face of his niece, Morganna. She always seemed to be such a happy baby. What hair she had was wispy, blond fluff; her large, expressive eyes were blue, like his own. He knew it was too soon to determine what her coloring would eventually be, but something told him she would remain blond, like her mother and her grandmother.

Looking down at her, his own sad memories of leaving his son in the little grave in Parthalon came back to revisit him. He no longer struggled to push away the pain of these thoughts, as he had tried to do immediately following the tragedy. There was clearly no longer any use in trying. His memories of burying the child had been returning to him in very graphic dreams lately. Several times he had almost talked to Wigg about it, to see if there was anything in the craft that could be employed to help make the nightmares stop. But in the end he had decided to hang on to his memories, the nightmares included, and let them come whenever they may. For it was all of Nicholas he had left.

Nicholas should be here, in the family cemetery. One day I will bring him back, and bury him where he rightfully belongs. He heard Morganna coo up at him then, and he returned his attention to the living, breathing child who lay before him.

Shailiha walked next to him, linking her arm in his, her smile apparently genuine as she too looked down into the crib. "So tell me something, little brother," she teased, wrinkling her nose up at him in that special way of hers. "Just what is it that you did not wish to tell the wizards this afternoon in our meeting with them? I got the distinct impression you were hiding something. What exactly happened out there last night that you aren't telling us?"

Turning back to her, Tristan snorted a short laugh of surrender. He might as well give in. She would be relentless in this, just as she always was whenever his welfare was concerned.

"I met a woman," he said simply.

"Ah. Well, that's nothing new, now is it?" she teased. "And just who is this woman?" Her face became humorously conspiratorial. "Is she beautiful?"

"Oh, yes, very," he answered, pursing his lips and narrowing his eyes slightly at the memory. Thinking back, he could almost smell the scent of myrrh that had come from her hair. His face grew a bit more serious. "She is perhaps the loveliest I have ever seen."

"Really!" Shailiha answered, one of her eyebrows raised. "That's quite an accomplishment, given some of the ones you have been with. Tell me, what is her name? Perhaps I know her."

"I seriously doubt that you know this one." He smiled.

"The *name*," Shailiha demanded, lowering her voice in mock ferociousness.

"I don't know, Shai," he answered quietly.

"You don't know?" she exclaimed, far too incredulously. Shailiha shook her head back and forth in comic ridicule, while she waggled an index finger in his face. "You're slipping, little brother! The Tristan I knew would have gotten her name and much, much more."

She took in the almost serious look on his face and decided to press a little more. Reaching out to grasp his chin with one hand, she turned his head to level her hazel eyes on his. "Why, if I didn't know you better, I'd think you were smitten!" She laughed.

"Don't be ridiculous," he answered tersely, determined to change the subject and regain control of the conversation. "I don't even know who she is."

"No matter. Your secret's safe with me," she teased. But just as in the old days, she had something to hang over his head, and she loved it. They smiled at each other, happy to know that their relationship was back to normal.

Then she remembered that he was about to leave her, and

her face darkened. "Tristan," she said, more softly this time, "what would our world truly be like without the craft of magic?"

He didn't really know how to answer her. "I'm not sure," he said. "But what concerns me most is the fact that if the Paragon is depleted, neither Faegan nor Wigg will be protected by the time enchantments. Their powers will wane, and then they will most assuredly die. And time is short, making things even worse."

Her expression became more introspective, and she reached to touch the medallion around his neck. "I want to help," she said, "but there seems so little I can do. Tell me honestly—do you think there ever might come a day when the wizards would let me learn the craft?"

He could see the hunger in her eyes, and understood it well. After all, her blood was nearly the equal of his, so her desire for the learning of the craft must be nearly as strong. But ever since the Sorceresses' War, the Directorate had banned the teaching of magic to women—a custom that he now found to be cruel.

"I hope you may one day be trained," he said. "Just as I am to be. But for now, the emphasis must be placed upon retrieving the Tome and stopping the decay of the stone. Until then, all of our other wishes must be put aside."

He put his hands on her shoulders, pulling her a little closer. "I must go now," he said softly. "Wigg will be waiting."

"Before you leave, would you please tell me about the graves?" she asked. It was almost as if she was afraid she would never see him again. "Were they truly undisturbed, as you told the wizards? Did you tell Mother, Father, and Frederick the things I asked you to?"

He closed his eyes, trying to fight back the rising grief. "Of course I did, Shai," he answered. "I got down on my knees and told them everything. And they heard me, I know."

Closing her eyes in gratitude, she gave him a long embrace. "Come home safe," she whispered.

"I promise," he assured her. With that he turned and walked out the door, purposely not looking back at her. Looking back would have been much too hard—for both of them.

Shailiha reached down into the crib and picked up her baby. She held Morganna tightly in her arms, as if by keeping the child close she could somehow also keep her brother safe. Then she looked over at the door her brother had just gone through.

Suddenly, from deep inside her, a cold, gnawing voice told her something she did not want to hear.

Neither Tristan nor Wigg will come home to you the same men as when they left.

PART II

The Stricken

CHAPTER THIRTEEN

It is not how much one hates that is important, but rather how that hate is manifested. Nor is it how much one plans for revenge, as much as how that revenge is carried out. And it is not even so much the form of the revenge itself that matters, but how long one can make it last. It is therefore not in the doing of the thing that one derives the greatest pleasure—for the act itself shall surely be fleeting. No, it is much more than this. It is the sublime knowledge that the pain administered shall be never-ending.

—FROM THE PRIVATE DIARIES OF RAGNAR, BLOOD STALKER

GELDON and Joshua stood in the cool morning sunshine of the country called Parthalon, looking down at the city that for over three centuries had imprisoned all of those deemed undesirable by the Coven.

The Ghetto of the Shunned.

The Ghetto's walls had been repaired, the dwarf noticed, and the drawbridge over the filthy, dank moat had been reconstructed. The drawbridge was raised and locked, seeming to haughtily reject all visitors to this once-desperate place. The flags of the Coven had all been removed, and from their perch high up on the hill, Joshua and Geldon could see movement upon the catwalks that lined the top of the wall. But the area surrounding the Ghetto was strangely abandoned, an eerie sense of quiet pervading it.

The figures standing guard atop the walls of the Ghetto were easily discernible to the dwarf. They were some of the winged warriors and former taskmasters of the Coven—the Minions of Day and Night.

Joshua and Geldon had not been able to come to Parthalon immediately, as Tristan had wished. After discussing their journey with Faegan, the three of them had decided it would be best for the consul and the dwarf to be delivered outside of the city walls, rather than inside. This would hopefully allow them to take stock of the situation before trying to enter. And since the wizard's only calculations for the portal would exit them at Geldon's destroyed aviary in the heart of the city,

Faegan was forced to restructure the spell slightly. Despite the proximity to the original destination, it took him three days of working day and night to produce the desired effect.

The trip through Faegan's azure portal was dizzying, but worse for Joshua since it was his first experience. Faegan had instructed them that when they wished to return home they should go to the exact spot of their arrival at high noon, just as Geldon and the others had done the previous time, that day not so long ago when Tristan had become the new lord of the Minions. The wizard would re-create the portal and hold it open for an hour each successive day, until such time as they returned.

The dwarf and consul had then walked into the swirling maelstrom . . . and landed in the grass at the top of the hill. It had taken them both several moments to regain their bearings and for the dizziness to stop. But they were now themselves again as they looked at the city below, trying to decide what to do.

"It is amazing!" the consul exclaimed softly. "Just as you said it would be. Did the Coven truly banish anyone here who was not to their liking?"

"Oh, indeed," Geldon answered, his eyes still locked upon the drawbridge as he wondered what to do.

"Why did the Coven send *you* here, if I may ask?"

Geldon closed his eyes for a moment. "I stole a loaf of bread," he answered sadly. "A simple loaf of bread. My family was starving, and I was sent here to languish. I never learned what became of them, or whether I have any descendants still living. I suppose I shall never know. It was shortly after my internment that Succiu, second mistress of the Coven, found me here and made me her personal slave."

His hand automatically went to his neck, where he had worn the jeweled collar for three centuries, until its removal by Wigg. "She made me wear a collar. At night she would chain me to the floor of the Recluse, the Coven's palace."

"I'm sorry, Geldon," Joshua said.

"We have other things to worry about," the dwarf said quickly. "As much as I hate to say it, our only option seems to be to walk right up to the drawbridge and demand that the Minions lower it for us." He gave the consul a hard look. "You have no experience with these beings, so let me do all the talking. I can only hope that there are some of those still present who will recognize me as a friend of the prince. Under no circumstances are you are to display your powers unless I order it. Do you understand?"

"Yes."

"Very well, then," the dwarf said with finality. "Let's go." With that the two of them began to approach the drawbridge.

As they neared the moat, about one hundred paces from the city walls, Geldon looked up to see two silver whirling disks flying toward them: returning wheels, the throwing weapon of the Minions.

He immediately grabbed the unsuspecting consul by the robes, stopping him short. The wheels, purposely underthrown, landed in the dirt at their feet. Geldon looked up to see the silhouettes of several dark, winged figures standing on the city walls, and he raised his hands high in a gesture of surrender.

The Minions would wish to speak first, to establish their control over the situation. Geldon gave the consul a tacit glance that spoke volumes. Joshua nodded.

"Come no closer!" a strong, masculine voice cried out from atop the walls. "We have express orders to allow no one near. If you persist in advancing, you will be killed! You have been warned."

"I am Geldon, the emissary of the Chosen One, your new lord," the dwarf shouted back. "I have come from across the Sea of Whispers to confer with you. This man next to me is Prince Tristan's representative of the craft of magic. Are you going to lower the drawbridge, or must I return to Eutracia and tell your lord that you will not let the servants of the Chosen One enter?"

A long silence followed. Then, from atop the wall, came the next words.

"If you are who you say you are, you may enter. But first you must prove that what you say is true."

Momentarily stymied, Geldon thought for a moment.

"Joshua, can you damage the drawbridge?" he asked the consul quietly. "For many of these warriors, violence is all they respect."

"Yes," Joshua answered. "I do not have enough power to destroy it completely, as Wigg or Faegan could. But I can surely cause it damage."

"Good. When I tell you to, do so," Geldon answered. He turned back to the figures on the wall. "Remove your troops from the area of the drawbridge," he shouted. "For it is now *you* who have been warned!"

Complete silence followed for several moments as Geldon and Joshua waited. Then the dwarf nodded to the consul.

Joshua raised his hands. Slowly the familiar glow began building around them, and finally a small, azure bolt of energy flew from his hands toward the center of the drawbridge, making a great crashing noise as it hit. Splinters of wood careened and whirled into the air, some falling into the water of the moat.

As the smoke cleared, a neat hole could be seen directly through the drawbridge. The figures once atop the walls were gone. The drawbridge began to come slowly rattling down.

"You may enter," a voice called out.

Geldon turned to look at Joshua. There was no going back now. Awkwardly they made their way across the sound sections of the shattered drawbridge. The scene that greeted them inside the city wall stunned Geldon.

Hundreds of Minion warriors were down on bended knee, just as they had been that day when they recognized Tristan as their new lord. And then, in a single, earthshaking chorus came the familiar oath.

"We live to serve!"

Hundreds of Minion warriors, kneeling before me—the onetime slave of the second mistress! Geldon thought in disbelief. But calmly, he said, "You may rise."

Standing, the Minions were even more impressive. They were all large and muscular, most over six feet tall, some approaching seven. They were uniformly armed with both the dreggan and the returning wheel. They all seemed to have dark hair worn long; some of them had braided it down the center of their backs. Their uniforms varied slightly, but for the most part consisted of black leather body armor, with long leather boots and gloves. And over the top of each of their shoulders could be seen the tips of dark, leathery wings.

One of the larger ones stood before all of the rest, and Geldon took him to be the leader. He was tall, with brown hair down the back of his neck and a matching, dark brown beard.

"Are you in command here?" Geldon asked bravely.

"Yes," the warrior answered. "I am Rufus. There are approximately fifty thousand of us here." The warrior stood before the dwarf with a defiant gaze.

Geldon realized he must be supremely careful in how he handled this. A revolt by the Minions was not something they needed to deal with just now. "Is there somewhere in the shade we could talk in private?" he asked.

"Of course," Rufus replied. After dismissing his warriors to their duties, he directed Joshua and Geldon to a nearby building, where they sat together on the porch.

"We come under the protection of the Chosen One's wizards," Geldon said calmly. He indicated the consul seated next to him. "This is my friend Joshua. He is the Chosen One's representative of the craft while I visit here."

Rufus looked with curiosity at the young consul. "You say little," he said, narrowing his eyes. "Do you have no tongue?"

Joshua looked to Geldon, and the dwarf nodded. "Uh, er, yes, of course," the consul answered politely.

Rufus snorted a short, almost insulting laugh, then turned back to Geldon. "At least it is good to know that you received our messages, asking for your help. That is why you are here, is it not?"

Geldon paused for a moment, his heart pounding. He took a deep breath. "Your messages?" he asked politely.

"Yes," Rufus answered quizzically, furrowing his brow. "We considered sailing to Eutracia to express our concerns directly, as the armada we used to invade your land still rests intact at anchor just off Eyrie Point, waiting to be used. But it would have proven too problematic."

Their armada is still intact, Geldon thought. *But of course it would be! That could prove very useful.*

"Many times we sent you requests for help by way of the enchanted pigeons." He stopped for a moment, obviously perplexed. "Did the birds not arrive in Shadowood, as they should have? We stopped sending them out when the first ones did not return, since we began to fear for their safety and they are known to be very rare."

Geldon's heart sang. He had thought his beloved pigeons lost. How he had mourned them!

He had repeatedly risked his life to release them with messages to Faegan. When Kluge and his Minions had ransacked the Ghetto looking for any of the prince's conspirators, the Minion commander had destroyed the aviary. To now discover that some of the birds had survived was news that the dwarf had never expected. The ones that had been sent to Shadowood must still be there, as the gnomes would not have known what to do with them or how to contact Faegan in the Redoubt. He could only hope they were being well cared for.

"The ones that remained here—where are they now?" he asked, trying to contain his glee.

"In the aviary, of course," Rufus responded, still confused. "It was one of the first buildings we reconstructed upon the orders of our new lord."

But before the dwarf could express his desire to see the new aviary, a cloud seemed to gather above, blotting out the sun. Geldon and Joshua heard a great rustling of wings and looked up to see several hundred Minion warriors flying overhead in pairs, each pair carrying between them some kind of litter. Geldon turned to the consul with questioning eyes, and then looked back up to the hundreds of flying Minions.

"What do they carry?" Joshua asked.

"These warriors are bringing us provisions," Rufus answered. "Traax, the acting Minion commander, has regular shipments sent in from his base at the Recluse, just north of here."

The consul and the dwarf watched in awe as the Minions wheeled and careened above them, then finally soared down. Flying very low to the ground they dropped their precious cargoes, then climbed back to the sky. When they were done, a giant mound of food and other supplies lay in the middle of the square.

The aviary would have to wait. It was Traax they most needed to see, and Geldon thought he had just found the fastest way to get there.

"Rufus," he said, turning to the Minion officer, "can you command them to take us to our next destination?"

The Minion smiled. "Of course." He immediately walked into the square beneath the circling warriors and motioned them down. Selecting two pairs of them and ordering them to stay, he sent the others back into the sky to wait.

"I wish them to take us to the Recluse," Geldon said. He

turned to the consul, seeing distinct horror on the younger man's face. It was obvious that Joshua did not like this idea at all.

"Uh, er, isn't there any other way to do this?" the consul stammered. "Can't we just ride horses to the Recluse?"

"Look around you," Geldon said impatiently, "and tell me how many horses you see here. Given the fact that they can fly, the Minions have very little use for them. Besides, it is a hard two-hour ride with horses. The other choice is a long four-day walk. So which do you prefer, eh? The walk of several days, or a free ride of only several moments?" Confident that his logic was inescapable, he stood defiantly before the apprehensive consul.

"There is another reason one should not travel across this land on foot," Rufus said, a serious look darkening his face.

"And that would be?" Geldon asked.

"I think it better that you ask Commander Traax that question," Rufus answered cryptically.

Geldon wondered what the Minion officer wasn't telling him, but decided not to make an issue of it. Climbing aboard one of the empty litters, he beckoned the fearful consul to enter the other.

"Is there anything you would like me to tell Traax?" Geldon asked as he grasped the sides of the litter.

He heard Rufus let out a great belly laugh. Turning, Geldon saw that Joshua was only holding on to the litter with one hand, desperately covering both his eyes with the other.

"Just that it has been a most interesting morning," Rufus shouted back.

That is something I can certainly agree with, Geldon thought as the litters began to ascend.

In mere moments, they were aloft.

CHAPTER FOURTEEN

❧

THE rose-colored light from the three Eutracian moons shone down brightly on the riders as they made their way along the narrow, familiar trail. They were heading up into the hills of the Hartwick Woods. The night was cold. The dew upon the fallen leaves and grasses of the forest floor had crystallized; the horses' hooves crunched quietly down into the twinkling, silver prisms of water and light. The pine-scent somehow cleansed everything in that strange, yet familiar way only it could. These woods seemed to be the catalyst for so much that had happened in his life, Tristan mused. There was magic here. He could always feel its presence in this place as he could in no other—except, perhaps, the Caves. He drew a breath, reminding himself that the peaceful scene before him clearly belied the sad state of his beleaguered nation.

The prince, Shannon, and the wizard had taken consuls' robes with them to fend off the cold and to disguise themselves should they encounter anyone upon the same path. But the likelihood of such a thing was not great. Tristan had therefore, to the intense but blessedly silent scowling of Wigg, removed his robe and tied it to the back of his saddle. He had no intention of not being able to reach for either his dreggan or his dirks—especially in light of the terrible news he had received regarding his status as a wanted man.

The three of them had spoken little since their departure from the Redoubt. Except for Shannon, of course, who seemed even more talkative than usual. Tristan knew that this was because the little man was frightened, and he really couldn't blame him. But he would have preferred that the gnome be quieter. Shannon occasionally drank from his ever-present ale jug, raising objections from Wigg, who had never approved of the gnomes.

Perhaps Wigg could be distracted. Tristan spurred Pilgrim a little to come up alongside the wizard's mare, just out of earshot of the gnome.

Turning to look at the lead wizard's craggy profile, Tristan asked, "Wigg, may I ask you a personal question?"

Wigg did not look at him, instead keeping his attention directed into the darkness that lay before them. Tristan knew that the wizard would be trying to stay alert for the presence of endowed blood, such as that of a stalker.

"Given your impulsive nature, the asking is guaranteed," Wigg replied calmly. "The answering, however, is not. *Especially* when the question is of a personal nature."

Tristan thought to himself for a moment.

"How was it that you first met Failee?" he asked courteously, half holding his breath as he wondered whether the old one would answer him. He had been shocked to his very core to learn that Failee, first mistress of the Coven, had at one time been Wigg's wife. There had never been any inkling of this fact until finally reaching Parthalon and bringing back Shailiha and the Paragon. And Wigg had never spoken of it since.

Wigg took a very long stream of evening air in through his nostrils, finally letting it out slowly. Tristan could virtually feel the wizard's consciousness flowing back through three hundred years of time as the old one sorted through the kaleidoscope of his memories.

"That was a long time ago," Wigg began, "and things were much different then. Eutracia was not as she is now—or should I say, the way she was before the reappearance of the Coven. Magic was still in its infancy, for we had not yet found the Caves, the Paragon, or the Tome. Women were allowed to learn the craft. For the most part an equal, if not always harmonious relationship between the genders had been struck regarding the use of magic. Unfortunately, however, it did not last. The balance of power went briefly to the women, just as Failee started her revolution."

"What do you mean?" Tristan asked.

"What I mean is there was no monarchy, no Royal Guard,

and very few formal laws. Birth records were not kept. Marriages were often prearranged. As you can imagine, this often added to the resentment some of the people felt—especially the young endowed. I can't say I blame them. Arranged marriages are a barbaric custom, one that was outlawed after the war." He paused for a moment, shifting slightly in his saddle and gathering his thoughts.

"Anyway," he continued, "as I said, the Paragon had yet to be discovered. Still, what magic there was ruled the land, not law. It was vitally important that no faction of endowed blood gain a stranglehold over any other. That is why the monarchy was created, and why the wizards eventually imposed the death enchantments upon themselves, to keep them from practicing the Vagaries. In this manner the sovereign would not need to concern himself that the hunger for total power would again erupt among the endowed. We could no longer take that chance after the sorceresses' failed civil war." Wigg pursed his lips in thought for a moment.

"However," he added, "the newly formed Directorate, no matter how brilliant its members eventually proved to be, was not without its mistakes. I now believe that our prohibition against women being trained in the craft was an unnecessary, gender-driven overreaction to the agonies of the war. But, for right or wrong, the custom was ultimately accepted."

Tristan thought for a moment. "That's how you and Failee met, isn't it?" he asked quietly. "Your marriage was arranged."

"Yes." The wizard sighed, smiling slightly. "Failee's blood was very highly endowed, as is mine, of course. She was beautiful and brilliant. But then her madness set in, and she began to turn. She left me and founded the group of sorceresses who ultimately chose the Vagaries as their weapon, and would later lay such waste to the land."

Tristan vividly remembered Failee. She truly had been a beauty, just as Wigg said, with an hourglass figure and deeply lustrous, hazel eyes. He could easily understand the attraction the young wizard of the time would have felt for her, arranged marriage or not.

"And there were no children," Tristan said softly.

"No, there were not," Wigg replied rather sadly. "We were not together very long. After the war, I often wondered if she had been purposely keeping herself barren. Perhaps it was the madness, or perhaps she had come to hate me so much that she couldn't bear the thought of ever having my child. I suppose I will never truly know. Like so many things of those days, the dust now lies so deep upon my memories that it is difficult to see things for what they really were."

Saying no more, Wigg altered their path a bit, and the prince realized that the wizard intended to make a detour to the grave sites. Tristan was pleased. Wigg had never visited the place since that fateful day he and Tristan had first buried the bodies, and the prince hoped that by going there, the wizard's heart would be comforted as his had been. Perhaps it had been this talk of the past that had prompted his decision. Or perhaps Wigg had wanted to go there since the determination had been made to visit the Caves. But as far as the prince was concerned, Wigg's personal reasons were just that.

Tristan turned around to check on the gnome and found him falling behind. Shannon's robe was several sizes too large and his face peeked out from its depths as though he were hiding in a cave. The gnome was clearly quite tipsy. He slid around drunkenly in his saddle, which was far too big for his little bottom, trying to maintain his balance. He waved one hand at the prince, then almost fell off, grabbing the pommel and righting himself at the last moment. He hadn't spilled a drop of the precious ale. Beaming proudly, he raised the jug in triumph.

"That's enough!" Tristan hissed. "I can't have you unable to find your way back! I want you to put the jug down now!"

Glowering at the prince from the depths of the hood, the irascible little man did as Tristan asked. He rather defiantly corked the jug, then awkwardly tied it to the back of his saddle. Wigg turned to smirk at the prince in obvious agreement. Then they approached the clearing that marked the area of the graves.

Wigg's expression took on a sad darkness as he stopped his mare and dismounted. He took a deep breath, looking out into the clearing. Finally he walked slowly to stand by the graves, the rose-colored moonlight casting his larger-than-life shadow across the deep grass.

Tristan brought Pilgrim to a quiet stop at the clearing's edge. *I have already had my own quiet reflections in this place,* he thought. He touched the medallion that lay round his neck. *It is now time to let the wizard have his.*

Shannon finally caught up and saw the robed figure of Wigg in the clearing. The wizard's head was bent down, and his silent presence was surrounded by the silver prisms of frost that lay upon the forest floor like scattered, rose-colored diamonds. Shannon for once remained blessedly silent.

As Wigg stood there in the moonlight, Tristan could not help but again be reminded of the woman he had met here. The memory of the myrrh in her hair came back to him.

He knew in his heart that he would never see the mysterious stranger again. She would no doubt find some other way to take her life before that could ever happen. Perhaps she was dead already. She had seemed so determined to end it all, her demeanor suggesting she had experienced a great deal of pain in her life. He shook his head a bit, thinking of what a waste her death would be.

Finally walking out of the clearing, Wigg remounted his mare. Without saying anything to each other the three of them again set upon their path for the Caves.

They had not gone much farther when the lead wizard suddenly stopped his mount and held up his arm, indicating that the others should stop and remain silent. Tristan watched him bow his head and close his eyes. After a brief moment, Wigg looked seriously at the prince.

"There is endowed blood ahead," he said quietly. "It is a type I have never before encountered. We could go around it, but I feel we should investigate. It may have a great deal to do with our problems."

"Can you tell who it is?" Tristan whispered.

"No," said the wizard. "But the presence is strong. Follow me closely, and do not speak." They started to move.

They had gone perhaps another half league when Wigg stopped again and dismounted, silently motioning for the other two to do the same.

At the top of a small rise, Wigg beckoned them to lie down on their stomachs. Crawling forward on the forest floor, they slowly approached the crest. The depression in the ground that lay below them was rather large, and what they saw within its borders staggered them all. The clearing was full of Joshua's birds of prey.

Tristan's jaw dropped at the sight. He had never before seen anything quite like this, and doubted he ever would again.

He quickly counted the birds, finding fifteen. Each was at least the size of a man, and their bodies and long wings were covered with leathery, reptilian skin instead of feathers. They had exceptionally long, dark claws. They stood upright upon what appeared to be very strong legs.

What fascinated him the most were their eyes. Each of the birds' bright red orbs was located far to the side of its head and could rotate in virtually any direction, even opposite directions at once, probably giving them incredible eyesight. The overall effect was horrifying. Their movements both birdlike and incredibly fast, the things often tilted their heads quickly this way and that to enhance their view. Then Tristan took in the entire scene, and his breath caught in his lungs.

The birds were standing guard over about a dozen captive consuls of the Redoubt.

The men, each still in his blue robe, were in varying states of injury. Most of them simply lay upon the ground, terrorized by the great birds glowering over them. Occasionally one of the things would find a consul trying to edge his way out of the clearing, and with a great shriek would rush to him and strike him hard with the bony protuberance that ran down the center of its long, angular head, herding the hapless consul back to the center.

The chilling scene made Tristan's blood churn, summoning him to kill them all. He silently drew his dreggan, laying it in the grass by his side. He then looked over to Shannon, to see the gnome shaking uncontrollably with fear.

Wigg looked into Tristan's darkened expression. "Under no circumstances do we interfere in this!" he hissed, as if reading the prince's mind.

Tristan couldn't believe his ears. "Are you mad?" he whispered back angrily. "In case you haven't noticed, those are consuls down there! Do you really expect us to simply watch and do nothing?"

"That's exactly what I expect us to do!" Wigg growled softly. He clearly meant to have the upper hand. "Don't you think I would like to try to save them from whatever fate these creatures have in store? Of course I would! But there are fifteen of those beasts down there, and we don't know their power. In addition, our mission to the Caves must take precedence! _Nothing_ can jeopardize that! The very fate of both our nation and the craft hang upon us successfully retrieving the Tome. If we stop to interfere in this, all might be lost for the sake of a precious few. Besides, I believe if these creatures truly wanted our people dead, they already would be." He paused for a moment, the pain of his difficult decision clearly registering on his craggy face. "No," he whispered finally, his tone a bit softer. "We wait, and we watch."

"And just what will that accomplish?" Tristan asked angrily.

"We will learn all we can, for I have no doubt we will encounter these things again. All that we can glean here will eventually prove useful, I assure you." Wigg glanced down to Tristan's dreggan as it glittered sharply in the light of the moons. "You will yet have your chance," he added softly. "But not today."

Tristan's jaw tightened, and his knuckles turned white as he gripped the hilt of his sword in frustration.

It was just then that Shannon, still shaking with fear, accidentally brought his hand down upon a dry branch. As it broke beneath his weight, the snapping sound it made reached out through the night air and into the clearing. The awful birds suddenly came to attention, their grotesque heads turning this way and that.

Tristan froze, holding his breath.

Several of the awful things stretched their long wings and half flew, half jumped into the trees at the farthest edge of the clearing. Their speed was astounding. Perching almost gracefully upon the bending branches, they closed their wings, becoming quite still. The silence surrounding this place was suddenly overwhelming, for now even the captive consuls did not move. And then the creatures' eyes began to glow even more brightly.

The red within their orbs became brighter and brighter, un-

til it was actually painful to look at. The beams of red light
shot from them, tearing across the clearing and into the night.
The intensely focused tunnels of scarlet illumination were so
vivid that Tristan and the two others were forced to turn their
heads.

They're looking for us, the prince realized.

The three of them slid back down behind the crest of the
knoll just as the scarlet beacons shot out in their direction.
Once behind the lip, the prince looked up to see the red lights
shooting crazily to and fro, crisscrossing almost constantly as
they searched out any sign of movement. It seemed to go on
for an eternity, imprisoning the three of them there. Finally
the crimson beacons vanished. At an approving nod from
Wigg the three of them slowly made their way back up to the
crest and peered over it cautiously. The hideous birds were all
back on the ground, again tending to their containment of the
consuls.

Suddenly, many of the birds turned their heads to one side
of the clearing. Looking toward the edge of the glade, Tristan
squinted into the darkness, trying to see whatever it was the
creatures were looking at. A figure upon a horse appeared
from out of the woods and rode slowly into the midst of the
stricken consuls.

The birds were not alarmed, Tristan realized. They knew
the rider.

The fellow jumped down from his horse, the spurs at the
heels of his boots jangling lightly. Walking in between the
various consuls, he began examining them closely. He was
tall and lean, and looked to be dressed in brown leather. A
dagger hung low at his left side, tied down to his thigh. He
carried no sword. The cruel face that showed up in the rose-
colored moonlight was sharp and angular, revealing sallow
eyes and gaunt, sunken cheeks. His unkempt hair was long
and dark. Then he turned just right in the moonlight, allowing
the prince to see the miniature crossbow that was laced along
the top of his right forearm. Tristan's endowed blood immediately began to swirl hotly in his veins.

Scrounge.

Wigg turned to the prince, his raised eyebrow telling Tristan without the need for words that he was not to move, no

matter what happened. His lips in a snarl, the prince could hardly contain his anger. Nonetheless, he nodded a curt agreement back to the old wizard and turned to lock his dark eyes upon the assassin in the glade—the man who had become the object of his unyielding hatred.

Scrounge stood before one of the larger birds. "They are in good condition this time?" he asked. "None of them are damaged severely?" The bird he was addressing tilted its grotesque head and made a harsh call into the night. It was clear that not only could the birds understand, but that they could answer back, as well.

Scrounge smiled at the awful thing. "Very well, then. Let's begin."

The bird began extending and retracting its deadly-looking claws, as if in apparent anticipation of what was to come, and then jumped upon one of the consuls lying on the ground. Straddling him, it pinned his arms to the earth with its long, dark claws. Another of them did the same to the consul's feet as the remaining birds began to contain other men. One bird kept watch over those consuls who were not yet restrained.

Scrounge smirked. He removed a dagger from inside his shirt, rather than reaching for the one at his side. In the bright moonlight the prince strained his eyes to look at the blade. It did not appear to be stained yellow. And then, with the methodical, painstaking precision of an expert butcher, the assassin began his grisly work.

Bending down, Scrounge reached for a pinioned consul's right arm and pulled back the sleeve of his robe, exposing the tattoo of the Paragon. The consul tried frantically to get away, but he proved to be no match against the strength of the two horrific birds. With four quick, surgical strokes Scrounge excised the tattoo completely as the consul's screams reverberated through forest. Then Scrounge lifted the tattoo, impaled on the end of his dagger, into the moonlight. He smiled as if it were some bloody, sick prize he had long coveted, then walked back to his horse and retrieved a leather satchel from the back of his saddle. He deposited the tattoo into the satchel and brought it back to the center of the clearing with him.

The consul he had just cut fainted. Scrounge and the birds

ignored him as if he did not exist. Instead, Scrounge selected another of the captives and began the same process, the screams commencing anew into the cold night air.

And so it went, one victim after the other, the great, obscene birds holding down the consuls while the sadist employed his dagger. The screams and the begging ripped into the hearts of the wizard, the prince, and the gnome as they watched silently, helplessly, from the knoll.

Wigg lowered his head in the midst of all the madness, tears coming from his eyes. He looked over at Shannon and the prince and again shook his head, silently telling them both that they must also do nothing, despite how much it hurt. Tristan's eyes were not full of tears. Instead they held the same kind of darkness Wigg had seen in them whenever the Chosen One had thought of Kluge, the previous commander of the Minions of Day and Night.

Despite how much Wigg wanted to reach out a hand to try to stop what was happening, he was still unsure of the birds' powers. He looked over again into Tristan's face, knowing how hard it was for him to remain still.

And then, blessedly, the assassin's work was finished.

Scrounge picked up all of the tattoos from the ground, carefully placing them into his satchel. Turning to the birds, he said, "Take these consuls to the master. And be careful with them. They are no longer to be harmed. Should any of you drop one, you will pay for your mistake with your life. Go now."

With that, each of the great, awful things grasped one of the consuls firmly in its claws. Tristan noticed that the birds now seemed to be concerned for the men, rather than simply trying to contain them in the glade. They took the greatest of care when gripping them with their long, black talons. Then they flew up and away. For a moment their silhouettes, bizarre-looking with the consuls' bodies dangling below their wings, flashed across the rose-tinted light of the moons. As a group they wheeled into the dark sky and were gone.

Scrounge remained alone on the bloodstained grass in the middle of the clearing. For a moment he simply stood there, looking at the moons, a wicked smile creeping across his angular face.

Placing one of his hands into the satchel, the assassin ran his fingers luxuriously through the twelve bloody pieces of human flesh he had obtained. He then walked back to his horse, tied the satchel to the back of his saddle, and galloped away. The sound of his mount's hooves eventually retreated into nothingness.

Someday, Tristan swore to himself as he gripped the hilt of his dreggan.

With another nod from the wizard, the three of them carefully walked down into the clearing. Blood could be seen everywhere—far more than they had noticed from their hiding place. The redness lay like a specter of defeat, adding to the sadness each of them sensed as they stood in the spot where the consuls had suffered.

"Why?" Tristan asked the wizard angrily. "Why would anyone do such a thing? And where did these awful birds come from? I can now completely understand Joshua's fear."

"Indeed," Wigg said simply. He squatted down, taking some of the consuls' blood between his fingertips. He examined it closely in the moonlight.

"But the other question is, 'how?' " he continued. "How was it that the consuls did not try to use their gifts and fight back? Did you notice how powerless they seemed to be in the face of those things?"

The wizard stood up, turning his bloody fingertips to the light of the moons. A sudden flash of recognition came over his face. "Tristan," he called softly. "Come here." The prince walked around Shannon to where the wizard was standing.

"Tell me," Wigg said, holding his bloody fingertips before the prince's eyes. "What do you see?"

"All I see is the blood of the consuls upon your hand," he answered. "What more would there be to see?"

"Perhaps nothing more to see, but much more to be known from the seeing," Wigg answered cryptically. "Look at the blood again. *Think.*"

Another test, Tristan thought to himself.

He stood there, perplexed. Then something tugged at the back of his mind, and he realized he had the answer.

"The blood is not moving," he breathed, unashamedly fascinated at his own discovery.

"Exactly." Wigg nodded. "And why is this significant?"

Tristan's mind went back to that day in the Redoubt, when Wigg had told him so much about himself, his blood, and his destiny.

"If the blood of the endowed does not move, it can only be for three reasons," he said slowly. "First, its owner could be dead. Second, the endowed was never trained, as is the case with Shailiha and me. Or third, he has for some reason lost his powers—the blood returning to an inert state. Since we know the first two reasons are not possible, it must therefore be the third." The importance of his statement hit him all at once. "The consuls have somehow been stripped of their powers," he whispered, not even believing it himself.

"Well done," Wigg replied. "But the question remains, 'how?' How could someone or something strip all of the consuls of their power? And if the cause is a blanket incantation, covering all of them at once, then why has Joshua not lost his powers, as well?" he asked. The wizard paused, rubbing his chin with his clean hand.

"I believe Joshua has not lost his gift because he has been in seclusion with us at the Redoubt," he continued. "At first, when I saw that the consuls were not using their gifts to try to fight off the birds, I concluded that it was due to the weakening of the Paragon. Because their blood is less endowed than ours, any variance in the quality of the stone would affect the consuls' powers much more quickly—far more drastically than it would mine or Faegan's. Compared to us, the rate at which the consuls would lose their powers would be virtually exponential. But now I'm not so sure that the decay of the Paragon is the only reason." Wigg paused, lost in his thoughts.

"In addition," he added, "Joshua told us that the squad he was with tried to use the craft to fight off the birds. That means that whatever took their powers did so *after* that incident. This must be yet another reason why Joshua retains his gift. For that we should feel thankful, for we shall need all of the endowed blood on our side that we can muster."

"And all of this means?" Tristan asked.

Wigg's face darkened. "What all of this means is that whatever we are up against is growing in its power," he said softly. "And probably continues to do so with each passing moment."

Tristan looked around at Shannon, finding that the gnome was still speechless. Curious about something Wigg had said, he turned back to the wizard. "What is a blanket incantation?" he asked.

Pursing his lips, Wigg took a long breath in through his nose. "A blanket incantation is one designed to influence more than one person at a time, in exactly the same manner. If, for example, I wished to have everyone at a dinner party believe that the common gruel being served to them was Eutracian pheasant under glass, the incantation used would affect all of them at once, in the exact same way. A 'blanket' incantation, if you will, 'covering' them all. Such spells can be very useful, as I'm sure you can imagine."

"You also used your powers to mask our blood from them, didn't you?" Tristan asked.

"Yes, as a matter of fact, I did," Wigg answered. "At first I could not be sure whether the birds had the power to detect endowed blood. I masked our blood anyway, just to be on the safe side, but I now believe that they do have this ability. How else would they be able to find and hunt down the consuls? In any event, I'm glad they did not find us with those very interesting eyes of theirs. Yet another curious topic . . ."

"But why take the consuls at all?" Tristan asked. Suddenly realizing he had been wielding his dreggan all of this time, he quietly replaced it into its scabbard. "And what would Scrounge want with all of the tattoos? Are they simply some form of sick, twisted proof of his conquests?"

Wigg looked up at the moons. "I don't know why the consuls are being taken," he answered simply. "I only wish that I did. But as for the tattoos, perhaps that is not really what they seek. Perhaps it is the consuls, *without* their tattoos, who are for some reason the true prize."

Above, the inky black of night was beginning its daily retreat into the softer, more fluid shades of pink and orange that would soon accompany a beautiful sunrise. Tristan knew that the wizard would want to get under way again before they lost their cover of darkness.

Remembering Scrounge's final words to the flying creatures, though, he found he had one more question.

"Wigg," he asked, as the wizard began to wipe the blood from his hands, "who is the 'master'?"

His face darkening again, the wizard stopped what he was doing and looked the prince in the eyes. "There have been many masters, Tristan," he said softly. "Faegan and I are but two of them. Some of them I have known, and many of them I have not. Only time will tell. But what I can tell you is that we are up against someone or something of inordinate power—the likes of which I have never seen. And our odds of surviving this entire situation do not appear to be particularly good."

With that the wizard began to walk out of the clearing to retrieve their horses. The prince and gnome followed, their footsteps sadly trailing the blood of the consuls as they went.

CHAPTER FIFTEEN

As Faegan wheeled his chair down the labyrinthine halls on his way to the princess' quarters, his mind turned over endlessly. So many problems had so quickly presented themselves to the small group of people living here in the Redoubt. The price on the Chosen One's head, the disappearance of the consuls, and the sudden emergence of Joshua's birds of prey all weighed heavily on his mind. But no problem concerned him as much as the decay of the Paragon.

He and Wigg had properly prepared the stone so that it might take a new host, and Faegan had put it on, hiding it beneath his robes. He had dutifully checked the Paragon several times since Wigg and Tristan had left for the Caves. Any subsequent change in the color of the jewel was still undetectable to the untrained eye. Nonetheless, he could sense the minute decay of the stone. The several months he and Wigg had estimated would rid the stone of its color would pass quickly, indeed, unless the process of decay could somehow be reversed. His sense of dread increased with every moment of every day.

He turned his gray-green eyes to look at Shawna the Short, Shannon's wife, who was patiently walking alongside his chair. He had asked her to accompany him to the princess' room so that she might stay with the baby while he and Shailiha went about their business. Business that the wizard felt was long overdue.

Shawna the Short was an incredibly hard worker. Her hair was gray and tied at the back of her head in a bun, so that it would never interfere with her tasks. The simple dress she wore was covered in the front by a white apron that she washed out every night. Her no-nonsense shoes were flat and sturdy. Her blue eyes and strong chin showed a fierce independence, and Faegan had learned to rely on her very much over the last three hundred years. He had also come to love her as he would a daughter.

At last they arrived at the princess' door, and the wizard knocked softly. At the sound of Shailiha's voice he narrowed his eyes, opening the door with the craft, and wheeled himself in.

Shailiha was at her loom, and both the wizard and the gnome wife could begin to recognize the pattern that had begun to take shape in the woven lengths of thread. It was clearly a representation of a king and queen—her parents, he assumed. They were standing side by side in one of the great rooms of the once-sumptuous palace above.

Faegan suddenly realized that this was Shailiha's way of dealing with her grief in this massive, lonely place. The young woman had been so used to light, gaiety, and love in her previous existence. It was apparent to him that her work at the loom was, at least in some small way, an attempt to relive those days. Smiling at his sudden insight, he found himself wholeheartedly agreeing with her methods.

She deals with her pain through the process of creation, Faegan thought. *And Tristan dealt with his personal tragedies through the process of destruction—the killing of the sorceresses and the commander of the Minions of Day and Night.* He paused in his thoughts for a moment, still regarding the lovely young woman at the loom. *The Chosen Ones. So alike, so different.*

Shailiha turned from her work and smiled at the two visitors. "Good morning," she said cheerfully, rising and walking to them. She wore an off-white gown, with ivory satin shoes. A matching string of pearls lay around her neck, accompanied by the gold medallion she always wore.

She gave the elderly wizard a quick kiss on the cheek, then did the same for Shawna. "I am glad you have come," she said. "I was just about to take the baby for a walk. Would you like to join me?" Faegan smiled, hoping that the blush on his cheeks wasn't noticeable.

Shawna pulled a chair up before the princess and stood upon it. Without asking for permission, she rather grumpily began rearranging the way Shailiha's dress lay upon the princess' shoulders. Muttering under her breath, she tugged at the material until it was more to her liking—as if the princess were somehow her own personal charge. Getting down off the chair, she then looked into the crib to check on the child. Apparently satisfied, she started on the room itself, carefully fussing with things that were already in perfect order, like an old, contrary mother hen in need of something useful to do for her brood of chicks.

Shailiha shook her head and laughed. "You really needn't do all of that," she exclaimed. "The room is just fine as it is. So is Morganna. How you fuss over us!"

Shawna turned around to face the young woman. "You know how much I care about you," she snapped. A short, knowing smile came to her lips, quickly vanishing behind the deceit of her supposed sternness. "Besides, you wouldn't take these duties away from a poor, broken-down, three-hundred-year-old gnome, would you?"

Shailiha winked at Faegan. "There's nothing broken down or old about you," she replied. "You can do the work of a hundred. I've seen you." With that she let the little woman alone, smiling as Shawna happily went about her loving but quite unnecessary labors.

Faegan cleared his throat. "Actually, I *was* hoping you would take a walk with me," he said simply. "There is something I would like to show you. But I think it best you leave Morganna here. That is why I brought Shawna with me. So that she could look after the baby while we are gone."

"I would be honored," Shailiha answered. "But what is it you wish to show me? Will I be impressed?" She lowered her voice and raised one eyebrow high into the air in an obviously satiric imitation of Wigg. Faegan couldn't help but laugh out loud.

"Yes," he said. "You will be impressed!"

"Very well, then, go along now," Shawna said from a corner of the room as she began furiously dusting a shelf near the loom. "Go and do whatever it is you have to do. Just leave me and the baby in peace."

Smiling at each other, the princess and the wizard left the room to negotiate the endless halls of the Redoubt. They talked of Morganna and of Joshua as they went, and of the trials that Wigg and Tristan had gone through to bring both the Paragon and the princess back to Eutracia. Her face darkening slightly, Shailiha also mentioned the loss of her husband and her parents. But she quickly regained her composure as they finally arrived at the door Faegan wanted.

He smiled at the princess. "Brace yourself. What you are about to see will, I'm sure, bring a smile to your face." And with that he again narrowed his eyes, commanding the doors to open. As the wizard wheeled his chair through, the princess followed him into the massive atrium containing the fliers of the fields.

Faegan wheeled his chair into its usual place on the balcony. The princess came to stand next to him, on the side nearest the brass rail that was attached to the wall. Her smile expanded as she watched the giant, multicolored butterflies swoop and dart, careening endlessly but somehow never colliding. She stood transfixed, radiating a sense of happiness that the wizard had never before felt from her except in her moments with Tristan and Morganna. Grinning at her expression, Faegan cackled and slapped the arm of his chair.

Shailiha looked all about in amazement. The atrium was several stories high and constructed of the palest light blue, Ephyran marble. Plants, trees, and flowers of every color and description lined the floor. The light from the oil sconces helped to make the room seem full of magic and the promise of discovery.

Looking down, she saw the two curious wheels of marble upon the floor. One contained the letters of the Eutracian alphabet, the other the numbers, both in sequential order. But it was the butterflies that entranced her the most. She just gazed at them, wide-eyed, as they flashed by in the pale light of the great room.

Faegan was reminded of the fact that this was the first time the princess had truly seen the giant butterflies. Shailiha had not been aware of their existence before her abduction by the Coven, and during her trip home from Shadowood she had still been under the influence of the Coven's incantation, and thus had no memories of the butterflies that had accompanied them here.

As he watched her, she slowly, silently extended her right arm out over the railing of the balcony. Almost immediately one of the larger fliers, a violet-and-yellow one, came fluttering up to land on her arm. The flier rested there patiently, its only movement the slow opening and closing of its large, diaphanous wings.

There were few things left in the world that amazed the wizard Faegan. But now his jaw literally dropped. *How can this be happening?* he wondered. *A bond between a flier and one of untrained blood!*

Shailiha seemed mesmerized. It was as if she had entered another world, oblivious to everything around her except for the flier perched on her arm. Even the butterfly was unusually calm. It did not dance about, as was so often the case whenever Faegan called one to himself. Shailiha with the flier was one of the most beautiful, unexpected scenes the wizard had ever witnessed. For a long moment he simply watched. Finally his wizardly curiosity overcame the moment.

"Shailiha," he said carefully, "will you please turn and look at me?"

Mechanically, slowly, the princess turned toward the wizard. As she did so the flier remained perched upon her arm. Shailiha had a faraway expression in her eyes that seemed to look straight through Faegan, rather than at him. She did not blink. Her only movement was her deep breathing, matched by the equally exaggerated rising and falling of her chest.

Faegan was now worried for her, since she had been so recently cured of the Coven's spell.

"Please release the flier," he told her calmly. "Just lift your hand into the air a little, and the butterfly will leave your arm."

But Shailiha did not seem to hear him.

"Release the flier, Shailiha," he said again, a bit more sternly.

"No," she finally said in a monotone voice. "The flier does not yet wish to leave me."

"And how do you know this?" Faegan asked, wheeling his chair a bit closer.

"It told me," she said.

Faegan felt something inside of him slip. The blood drained from his face.

Beads of sweat had begun to break out across the princess' brow. Her breathing had become quite irregular. The strain of whatever was happening to her was clearly beginning to show, and the wizard knew that he must somehow end this.

Reaching up, he gently grasped her arm. She made no attempt to shake him off. Faegan shook her arm slightly, and the butterfly flew off to rejoin the others.

Almost immediately the princess' eyes began to regain their focus, and her breathing returned to normal. The wizard gratefully noticed that not only did the princess seem to be quite well, she had actually been refreshed by the experience. Her eyes were brighter; her demeanor was more serene.

"Your Highness," he asked gently, "are you all right?"

For a moment Shailiha stood without speaking. She looked out at the fliers as they playfully soared and careened in the pale light of the atrium. Finally turning to Faegan, she said, "Yes, I believe I am fine." She took a deep breath and stretched a bit, smiling as she did so. "In fact, in some ways I am not sure I have ever felt better. But what just occurred was an experience far beyond anything else in my life."

"Tell me about it," Faegan said, wheeling his chair closer to her, as if that might bring him deeper into the riddle he was trying to solve.

She pursed her lips as she thought for a moment, trying to

find a way to put her feelings into words. "For some reason, when I saw the butterflies I was compelled to raise my arm. To this moment I do not know why. Something just told me to. And when one of the fliers came to me, something happened. I felt something change within me—in a way I have never before experienced."

"And that was?"

"I began to hear voices," she said softly, as though she did not believe it herself. "Many of them at once. Then the cacophony of voices died down, and there remained only one. Strong and clear." She shook her head a little. "Somehow I knew that the single voice remaining was coming to me from the flier on my arm."

"It spoke to you?" he asked.

"No, not exactly. Rather, it revealed itself to my mind."

"What did it say to you?" Faegan asked, his intense curiosity growing by the moment.

"It told me that I was the one for whom they had been waiting so long," Shailiha answered. "What does it mean? Am I going mad? Am I truly not healed of the Coven's spell?"

Faegan took her hand in his. He did not completely understand what had just happened, but he felt that this phenomenon was a gift, rather than something to be feared.

"I believe you may have just discovered the beginnings of your personal destiny," he said to her. "This is something to be treasured and refined, rather than an evil to be avoided. We must explore this further. But before we do I need time to consider it all. I also need to consult with Wigg. Promise me you will not come here without at least one of us in attendance."

"I promise," she said earnestly. "But I will find that promise difficult to keep. I now feel drawn here—as surely as I am drawn to both my brother and my child. I won't rest until I have the answers to what has happened to me." She turned from him again to watch the butterflies.

So much like her brother, Faegan thought at the sight of the determination in her hazel eyes. *Had their parents lived to see these days, they would have been proud.*

He suddenly felt the tug of Consummate Recollection upon his mind, telling him that there was something in the Tome that spoke of what she had just witnessed. Slowly, as was his custom, he closed his eyes and relaxed his intellect, letting the passage come to him rather than sending his consciousness to chase after it. And then the quote appeared to him, as though he could see it written upon the page of the great book.

" 'And each of the Chosen Ones shall be allowed certain gifts before their training in the craft,' " he said aloud. " 'These gifts shall be different, yet in some ways the same, and shall remain forever with them, even unto death.' " He opened his eyes and looked at her.

"What was that?" she asked innocently.

"I am able to recall with accuracy anything I have heard, seen, or read since the very day of my birth. The quote you just heard is from the Tome of the Paragon. I am the only living person, as far as we know, to have read the entire first two volumes."

"Is it really true?" she asked, wide-eyed. "Can you really remember all of your experiences if you choose to?"

"Oh, yes," Faegan said, smiling. "And I can assure you that it is as much a curse as it is a blessing."

"And the section you just quoted—what does it mean?" she asked.

"Ah," the wizard said, shaking his head. "That is always the difficult part. The speaking of a quote from the Tome is always far less difficult than the deciphering of it. The Ones Who Came Before certainly did not make it easy for us. Presumably they had some motive for being so cryptic. But I suppose we shall never be sure." He paused for a moment, looking out at the butterflies. Their whirling, colorful wings continued to dart through the scented air of the atrium.

"As for the quote, it probably means just what it says—that you and the prince each have as-yet-unrealized gifts," he resumed. "Some powers of which neither he nor you have ever been aware."

"How is it that Tristan and I could have such powers without being trained?" she asked. "I thought our blood was still dormant. And what is Tristan's gift?"

"How things are possible, I cannot say at this time," he answered. "I am sure, however, that it must have something to do with the fact that your blood, and the blood of the prince, are both of such unsurpassed quality. And as for Tristan's gift, we may have already witnessed it."

"What do you mean?"

"When he destroyed the Coven, he did so by causing the Paragon to move. He did this strictly through the use of his mind. Such a feat had never before been accomplished by an untrained person of endowed blood. Even with the proper guidance, such a breakthrough usually takes years. This may be Tristan's gift. That is, the ability to move objects. But then again, it could be something else entirely, something that has yet to reveal itself."

Faegan could see that the princess was tired. "It is time for us to go," he said, turning his chair away from the fliers and wheeling back through the door. "We will return tomorrow, and every day thereafter, if it pleases you. We must explore the mysteries of your bond with the fliers." He paused, looking up at her beautiful face. "And what we find should be very interesting, indeed."

Taking a final look at the butterflies, Shailiha reluctantly followed the wizard out of the room. Faegan closed the great doors of the atrium behind them.

And then, from seemingly nowhere, a mesmerizing idea overtook Faegan's mind.

It was possible that Shailiha's bond with the butterflies was *not* one of her natural gifts! He was filled with a strange mix of excitement and foreboding as he pondered his new idea. Impossibly, it seemed, the bond might be a sign of something else, something always thought to be mere myth: an Incantation of Forestallment. Not wishing to alarm the princess with either his actions or his words, he wheeled his chair forward.

If what he had just witnessed was truly a sign of a Forestallment, then there was a great deal more going on than he had ever imagined.

His mind whirling, he continued to roll down the magnificent hall. The unsuspecting princess followed obediently behind.

CHAPTER SIXTEEN

❧

THE cold wind tearing through the lengths of his dark hair, Geldon held on tightly to either side of the litter that was carrying him through the sky. He found the feeling of flying totally exhilarating. Looking down, he delighted in seeing familiar landmarks of the Parthalonian countryside passing by as he soared along, the Minions upon each side expertly holding his litter between them.

At first the sensation of being carried up and away by the winged warriors had been frightening. Not only was this something he had never done before, but the Minions, his onetime enemies, very much had his life in their hands. But after the first few moments he had settled down, coming to trust the fact that if the warriors had wanted to drop him they probably already would have. He then embraced the flying with a kind of glee he had not felt since he was a child.

Joshua, however, was having an altogether different experience. The consul's litter was close enough that Geldon could see the blatant terror on his face. Joshua's eyes were clamped shut, and he was holding on to his litter with both hands. Even as Geldon soared bouncingly along, he could see that the younger man's knuckles were white.

Occasionally they would swoop straight through a bank of clouds. The dwarf had at first tightened his grip, holding on for dear life as if they were about to smash headlong into a solid object. From his inexperienced perspective, that was exactly how it seemed. But he had quickly learned to love tearing into the clouds and feeling the cool, fine mist striking his face before bursting out the opposite side over a changed panorama.

Geldon looked in awe at the Minion warriors flying all around him. Their powerful, leathery wings reached through the air in great, broad strokes, propelling them through the sky. Flying seemed as natural for them as walking across the ground. He soon found himself admiring—even envying—this marvelous advantage.

But Geldon had not come to trust the Minions yet, despite the fact that they were helping him. As they continued to soar through the air he focused his mind on the upcoming meeting. Traax, the Minion second in command, was no fool. Geldon needed to be as prepared as possible when he finally landed. He would have to put into his own words whatever the Chosen One would say if he were here, to impress upon the Minion leader the importance of what must be done.

For over three hundred years Geldon had been the butt of the Minions' cruel jokes. But now things were different. Now he was the emissary of the Chosen One himself. His job was to see to it that Tristan's wishes were being carried out, and see to it he would. Assuming, of course, that Traax recognized his authority. But deep down he was starting to worry that such a thing might be a very large assumption, indeed.

It was then that he first noticed the anomalies in the Parthalonian landscape, as its familiar beauty flashed by below him.

Something was different—he was sure of it. They had already flown over several landmarks he knew quite well, so he was sure they were on the correct course to the Minion fortification closest to the Recluse, north of where Faegan's portal had exited them. He had seen both the Black River and the Vale of Torment, the valley where Tristan and Wigg had first learned of the Gallipolai. He looked down steadily now, his mind awash with curiosity. And then he realized what had changed.

The ground below him was covered with lakes and ponds. Some had huge waterfalls spilling into them. Others emptied more serenely into babbling brooks that stretched into the distance. Still others were calm, their placid surfaces reflecting the sky and clouds back to him as if some great force had placed a series of huge mirrors upon the earth. In all of them, the water was a strikingly beautiful blue.

But these waters were not here when I left Parthalon! he thought, confused.

Just then, a group of Minion warriors detached themselves from the flying mass and dived down toward one of the largest lakes. They winged their way around the edge of the lakeshore and then soared back upward, seeking out their leader.

Almost immediately the entire flight of warriors plunged down toward the lake at an alarming speed—faster than Geldon had known the Minions could fly. The warriors seemed to have absolutely no regard for their own personal safety; the way they were falling through the sky bordered on suicidal. So rapid and violent was their descent that at one point Geldon feared his litter might come apart.

The Minions landed close to the lake and roughly dropped the hundreds of litters they were carrying—Geldon's and Joshua's included. And then the warriors did something very strange.

From pouches located in each of the litters they began producing what appeared to be fishing nets of unusually strong, thick rope. Each of the warriors seemed to have one. The warriors quickly tied the nets together, ending up with one of very great size. Completely ignoring the consul and the dwarf, they all flew above the lake—the huge, circular net before them— and hovered only meters above the calm waters.

After regaining their composure, Geldon and Joshua ran closer to the lake, straining to see what invited such urgency. When they reached the shore, Geldon felt sure he was going to be ill.

Human skeletons—small and large, child and adult—lay scattered all around. The skeleton's bizarre postures were completely random, as if some powerful force had dumped them there from a great height, yet not a one was broken.

Surrounding everything was an acrid, almost toxic stench, unlike anything he had ever smelled. As his eyes began to water, he placed his hand over his mouth. And then he realized the source of the sickening, overpowering odor.

An oozing, slimy substance covered some of the bones. In places, it actually seemed to hiss, a small amount of steam coming off hauntingly to waft back and forth upon the breeze.

Gray-green and quite thick in places, it was eating into and actually melting whatever flesh was left clinging to the bones.

He looked quickly to Joshua, but the consul seemed to be as confused as he. The Minions seemed to know, though. They hovered over the dark blue waters, holding the massive net, their eyes trained upon the surface of the lake, as if waiting for something.

An insidious sense of dread began to coil up inside Geldon like an angry, frightened snake.

Suddenly, one of the Minion warriors swooped down toward the surface of the lake, coming to hover barely a single meter from the surface. Slowly, silently, he drew his dreggan. All the warriors not holding the net drew their dreggans at once and extended the hidden tips of their swords with a great clanging sound that bounced off the surface of the dark blue water and back into the air. Then everything went silent again.

The water beneath the lone Minion warrior began to rile and swirl. Geldon and Joshua stood transfixed, holding their breath in anticipation.

With an unimaginable burst of energy, something huge and black vaulted from the depths. It leapt straight upward, its speed amazing. Teeth flashed as it tried to reach the lone warrior hovering above it.

The warrior reacted, trying to gain altitude. But the thing was too fast for him. It took the Minion's foot off at the ankle and plunged back into the lake. The warrior flew to the lakeshore as fast as he could, his face a picture of agony, his blood pouring from his torn stump.

Geldon and Joshua ran to the spot where the wounded Minion came to land.

"Can you help him with the craft?" Geldon asked Joshua breathlessly.

The consul closed his eyes, and the familiar, azure aura of the craft began to surround the mangled end of the warrior's leg. Blessedly, the Minion fainted. Joshua took a deep, sad breath and let it out slowly.

Geldon studied the warrior. Even for a Minion he was large, and he had long, dark hair and a black beard.

"I have sanitized the wound and accelerated the healing process," Joshua said. "In addition I have used an incantation that will render him unconscious. He will live, but he will never be the same again."

And then the dwarf realized at least part of what was happening. *This lone warrior had been bait!* his mind exclaimed. *Living bait, intended to lure out whatever was down there in the lake!* Geldon turned his eyes back to the Minions, expecting to find them still hovering over the surface of the lake with their swords and their nets. But they were gone.

The dwarf raised his eyes to the sky. At first he saw nothing. But then, very high up, he saw what at first appeared to be a giant flock of geese hovering so high that they were no more than specks in the sky. He had never before seen the Minions fly so high.

Then the pinpricks in the sky began to grow larger, at an alarming rate. On and on they came, approaching the lake. Within only moments Geldon and Joshua could see that the Minions were soaring downward in a giant circle, wings closed behind their backs, their formation perfect, clearly in free fall. The huge, circular net was stretched in front of them. A few held their dreggans pointed before them.

Geldon's mouth fell open with wonder.

With a great noise and a massive, explosive splash, the perfect circle of several hundred hurtling Minion warriors plunged headfirst into the body of water. A giant gush of water leapt upward in the form of a perfect sphere from the lake, like several hundred connected geysers bursting into the air at once. Then the Minions were gone into the depths, and the water fell back noisily. The surface of the lake became still again, as if nothing had happened.

The moments came and went agonizingly. Geldon wondered how long the warriors could hold their breath under water. He was holding his own breath, as if that would somehow help those below. Both the dwarf and the consul began to wonder whether all of the warriors had by now met their end.

At last the water near the center of the lake began to churn and swirl, this time more violently. Several Minions broke the surface, gasping for breath. Finally the entire circle of warriors that had plunged into the water was again visible, and the net was rising in their midst, a great, dark, humped shape trapped within it.

The hump began to writhe and scream.

Shouting to their fellows in unison, the Minion warriors began to fight the thing in the net. Their screams combined hauntingly with the urgent, insane shrieking and struggling of the creature they had captured as it desperately tried to free itself and return to the depths. But slowly and surely the Minions managed to bring it closer to shore, finally dragging the convulsing, snarling beast to the water's edge.

The thing was covered with smooth, black, velvety hair, much like a Eutracian otter, and stood on four legs. Its back was at least as high as any of the Minion warriors were tall. Its body was easily five meters long, and quite large around. Its four feet were scaly and reptilian, quite unlike the torso, and each ended in five sharp, webbed claws that looked especially suited for tearing.

It seemed to be a strange and grotesque amalgam of creatures. The head ended in a pointed nose, much like a rat. Its large but still somehow beady black eyes looked out from within the net with intense, almost intelligent hatred. An unusually wide, thin mouth sat just below the nose, and large, ratlike ears sat on either side of its head. Its tail—reptilian, like the feet—was barbed all along its length and ended in a point much like the head of an arrow. It switched back and forth violently, occasionally slicing through the net. The creature's amazing strength was more than obvious.

Then Geldon took a quick breath of surprise as he noticed the beast's most unusual characteristic: It had both gills and lungs. The double, vertical, pink-colored slits in the skin and hair behind its jaw were clearly gills, but they were not moving, as would those of a fish out of water. Yet the creature's chest heaved with its labors. Geldon was amazed. Possessing both lungs and gills, the beast could live both beneath the water and upon the land.

The beast was truly remarkable. But where had it come from?

In defiance of its captors, the awful thing opened its mouth farther. Geldon took a step backward, as its jaw hinged open as far as a Parthalonian serpent's. Two great incisors stood out in each corner of the upper row of teeth, glistening wickedly in the afternoon sun. It hissed in anger at the warriors as they struggled to contain it, snapping its jaw shut with a force that could easily bite a man in half.

The Minion leader was a man of rather short stature for his kind, and looked familiar to Geldon. The dwarf thought for a moment and dredged up the Minion's name: Baktar. From what Geldon had seen he was particularly capable.

Baktar walked up to the dwarf and the consul. "Ugly bastard, is it not?" He laughed, obviously proud of its capture.

"What in the name of the Afterlife is that thing?" Geldon whispered incredulously.

"It is called a swamp shrew," Baktar answered. "At least that is the name we have given it. Appropriate, don't you think?"

Baktar motioned for several of his troops to come to his side. They drew their dreggans and stabbed the swamp shrew, their swords plunging deep into its chest. When its struggles and burbling screams ceased, they slashed through the net. Quickly lifting it from the dead body, they beheaded the creature and scrambled to begin another, even more grisly task.

Lining up alongside the slick, black, beheaded body, with a great heave they turned the shrew over on its back. One of the Minions quickly jumped up on its underbelly, and with his dagger began to open its abdomen from head to tail. Placing his hand within the shrew's abdominal cavity, he reached in up to his elbow and pulled out several bloody organs. He quickly and expertly cut their connecting tissue away from the creature's body, letting them slide sloppily over the side and to the ground. Another of the warriors descended on one of the organs—a grayish sack of some size. He sliced it open quickly and cleanly, then pulled out the contents.

The dwarf and consul stared in unbelieving horror. Geldon covered his mouth.

Lying before them was the foot just taken from the Minion warrior. And next to the foot lay the clothed, partially digested body of a human being.

Baktar sighed sadly, then wiped his dreggan in the grass at his feet and slid it back into its scabbard. "We were too late."

The body that lay before them appeared to be male. But the only way such a determination could be made was from the style of dress. In all other respects the identity was impossible to discern. The face and extremities had been eroded; the skin was sallow and gray; the facial features were virtually gone. A large quantity of the same gray-green, slimy fluid that had covered the bones lining the lake had spilled out along with the foot and the semidigested body. Its stench was overpowering.

"Shrews feed both during the night and the day," Baktar continued. "And only upon either humans or Minions. In the short time since they appeared, they have taken thousands of victims—civilians and Minions alike. We estimate their numbers to be in the hundreds, perhaps even the thousands. They always return to the water after they hunt, remaining out of sight to rest. They can run as fast across the land as they can swim in the water."

Joshua, whose eyes had remained on the foot, went over to it and picked it up. He closed his eyes, and the glow of the craft engulfed the severed appendage, remaining there. He gently placed the foot down next to the wounded warrior.

Baktar bent to examine the strangely glowing, severed foot, then turned back to the consul. "Can you use the craft to reattach this?" he asked earnestly. "Tempting the shrew to come to the surface requires indomitable courage, and volunteering for this task has become a great honor among us. The warrior who was brave enough to tempt this shrew is a particularly excellent fighter, and I would not like to lose his services."

"Unfortunately, I cannot reattach the foot," Joshua answered. "Such an incantation is beyond my ability in the craft. I have seen to it that the wound will heal quickly, with no infection and with less pain than normal. But there are some others who might be able to do as you ask. That is why I have enchanted the foot—to preserve it. Tell me, what is the wounded man's name?"

Baktar smiled slightly. "Ox," he replied. "What he lacks in wit he more than makes up for in courage." He paused for a moment, looking down at the stricken warrior.

"Why is it that you were so eager to cut open the shrew's stomach?" Joshua asked.

"It is a matter of Minion honor that we cremate our dead," Baktar replied. "When we take a shrew, the stomach is opened to see what it contains. If it is a warrior, we burn the dead body in honor. If it is a civilian, a selected group from the participating squad of shrew slayers buries the corpse."

"Shrew slayers?" Joshua asked.

"Yes," Baktar explained. "Commander Traax formed the slayers soon after the shrews first made their appearance, since our last orders from the Chosen One were to protect the populace. Hunting the shrews has partially kept us from doing all else that the Chosen One ordered. Still, we felt this work was important. There are now many groups of shrew slayers who do nothing else, day and night. They are all volunteers. In my opinion they are to be commended."

"That's why all of the bones are here, isn't it?" Joshua asked. "The shrew swallows its prey whole. It then slowly digests the organs and flesh, regurgitating the bones and clothing back up on the shore."

"Yes," Baktar answered. "Sadly, one of the best ways to find a shrew, just as we found this one, is to look for the bone trail of its victims. But there is yet another reason for opening the stomach of a captured shrew as quickly as possible."

"And that is?" the consul asked.

"Their stomachs have sometimes been known to contain victims that were still alive," the Minion warrior said simply.

Geldon felt his stomach turn over. "You must be joking!" he exclaimed.

"Oh, it is quite true," Baktar said, then snorted as if he did not quite believe it himself. "There is in fact one warrior here among us today who has survived that very ordeal."

"Who is he?" Geldon whispered in awe.

"He is Ox, the one who lies at your feet."

Now Geldon understood why the warrior would volunteer for such a thing. This had become personal for him.

But there was something else that puzzled Geldon. "Where did all of these bodies of water come from?" he asked Baktar. "They were not here when I left Parthalon, and I have only been gone a matter of weeks."

"We were hoping you, the Chosen One, or his wizards could tell us that," Baktar answered discouragingly.

"What do you mean?"

"Several days after the death of the sorceresses, certain areas across our land began to take on the glow of the craft, both day and night. This lasted for several days. We were not at first concerned, assuming it to be the work of the Chosen

One and his wizards. But when the glow finally faded, in every place where it had come and gone there was a body of water, each one somehow more beautiful than the last. This is when the shrews first appeared."

Geldon turned questioningly to the consul. Joshua merely shook his head.

"Only Wigg and Faegan would possess the knowledge to unravel such a thing," the consul said quietly.

Geldon let out a long breath, but before he could say anything else, a young Minion officer stepped forward from the ranks. He clicked his heels together. "Forgive me, sir, but our work here is done. Is it your order that we continue north, as previously planned? Or are we to camp here for the night?"

Baktar looked to Geldon. "What are your wishes?" he asked.

"My business with Traax is important," Geldon said. "Provided your troops are not too tired, I would like to carry on."

Baktar smiled. "Minion troops are never too tired," he said.

Baktar gave the order to regroup and watched his forces as they picked up the hundreds of litters. As only one of the craft could, Joshua reached through the azure glow that surrounded the severed foot and placed the appendage carefully within his robes.

Geldon and Joshua returned to their litters. The wounded, still-unconscious warrior named Ox was carefully placed into another. Geldon looked over to see that Joshua again had one hand firmly clamped over his eyes.

Without further fanfare they rose into the sky, their great numbers briefly darkening the land below them as they went. As the sun set gracefully into the retreating horizon of the lake, Geldon pondered that there was much more to learn about what had happened here.

But first he would have to deal with Traax.

CHAPTER SEVENTEEN

CLOSING his eyes, Ragnar placed his thick index finger into the gaping wound along his right temple. He found no fluid there today. But he soon would. The three rose-colored moons of the Eutracian night sky would again soon be full, and his gash would produce anew the yellow fluid. Just as it had been doing for the last three hundred years.

He dipped his finger into the vial of brain fluid that Scrounge had drawn from him not so long ago, then inserted it into his mouth. Immediately he felt searing heat run through his tortured body.

He stood from the ornate, velvet-upholstered chair and paced slowly around the room like a caged animal. Ever since the child had told him of the impending arrival of his enemies, his memories had come to haunt him even more than usual. His eagerness to face Wigg grew with each passing day.

His personal chambers were both his prison and his home. The furniture and draperies were of the highest quality. Magenta streaks darted across the black marble walls like shooting stars in the sky. The candlelight flickered softly, barely piercing the darkness that he preferred for his personal reveries.

He reached to the marble table that stood nearby and took up a sheathed dagger that lay there. He fondled it gently, almost lovingly, then placed the coolness of its scabbard along the length of his brow. This dagger had once belonged to Wigg. It would serve in the plans Ragnar had for the lead wizard. The child had already granted him permission.

Slowly he pulled the dagger from its highly patterned, gold

scabbard to read the flourished, centuries-old engraving on the blade. The words lay just above the patterned blood groove: *In Brotherhood We Serve the Vigors*. The symbol of the Paragon, the square-cut jewel of the craft of magic, was also fashioned in solid gold, and adorned the top of the hilt.

Such daggers had at one time been carried by all of the more powerful wizards, prized as the weapon of choice before they eschewed such crude devices in favor of their quickly increasing knowledge of the craft. Over the last three centuries, this particular dagger had been the focus of Ragnar's intense, compelling hatred. For this was the very tool with which Wigg had not only given him his wound, but had caused his addiction to his own brain fluid, making Ragnar unique in all the world. The stalker smiled.

He closed his eyes, and memories came flooding back as if they had happened only yesterday. His knuckles turned white upon the dagger's golden handle.

It had been during the Sorceresses' War, when the fighting had still been somewhat crude and had as much to do with physical confrontation on the battlefield as it did with the manipulation of the craft. The sorceresses, led by Failee, Wigg's onetime wife, had employed blood stalkers and screaming harpies to overcome much of the civilian population. They had conquered vast amounts of land with their largely conscripted army and were closing on the fortress city of Tammerland. The end had seemed very near for the wizards who continued to resist them.

And then the tide of the conflict had started to turn in favor of the wizards, for they had unraveled the secrets of the Caves, the Tome, and the Paragon. They used their increasing knowledge of the craft to push the sorceresses' forces westward, into retreat. And Ragnar, once one of the most powerful of the wizards, had been there to witness it all.

Looking back on it now, the very thought of having served against the sorceresses, swearing to pursue only the weak, altruistic Vigors, made him angry almost to the point of self-destruction. Wigg, Tretiak, Killius, Maaddar, Egloff, and Slike. How easily he remembered their faces and their names, and what hatred these same names always conjured within him! These were the so-called "brilliant" wizards who would not only win the war, but also drive the sorceresses into exile. They would then go on to selfishly grant themselves time enchantments, form the Directorate itself, and oversee the rule of Eutracia for the next three hundred years.

But not Ragnar. Instead, he was to be given the great privilege of knowing the combined joys and power of being simultaneously a blood stalker and a wizard. Failee herself had carefully converted him to the superior creature he was now, at the same time showing him the ecstasy of the fundamental practices of the Vagaries.

He had been on patrol under Wigg's orders, in charge of one of the companies of civilian troops loyal to the wizards. They were chasing what they had believed to be the Coven itself. Night had fallen, and they had been forced to make camp. It was then, deep in the night while they slept, that the Coven had quietly fallen upon them, massacring all of his troops. Failee had then told the lone, terrified wizard that he had been saved for a specific reason, which would only be revealed to him later, when she knew the time was right.

And then Failee had relentlessly worked her magic upon him, employing the incantation that would convert him to a blood stalker. Surprisingly, she stopped before the process was complete, leaving him half human and half stalker, the only such mutant ever created. She spent the next several days teaching him some of the arts of the Vagaries, and revealing to him that the exclusive practice of the Vigors was a waste of time and knowledge for one with his immensely high quality of blood.

Finally, the first mistress opened his mind, showing him that the cause of the Coven was both just and true, forcing his sensibilities away from the greedy pestilence that were the wizards. And then she left him to explore his newfound talents on his own.

It was during this time that Wigg and Tretiak came upon him. Wigg was much younger then, not more than thirty-five Seasons of New Life. The Directorate was not yet formed, so he wore no wizard's tail of braided hair down the center of his back, nor had he yet donned the gray robes of office. But he was among the strongest wizards of his day, and the appointed commander in chief of all of the forces warring against the sorceresses. The golden dagger, the chosen weapon of the wizards, lay in its sheath at his side.

As they rode up over the rise to find the horrible, ghastly scene that lay before them, the wizards could not know that Ragnar was now a mutated stalker. Ragnar watched cautiously as Wigg pulled his stallion up short.

The battlefield Ragnar lay upon was staggering. At least one hundred civilian troops were dead, their bodies strewn carelessly across the lush, contrasting grass of the field, like so many fallen leaves. Smoke from the recent struggle rose faintly up into the sky. Carrion birds had already begun to circle, so that they might start to pick apart their next easily stolen meal. The stench of death was all around him, and nothing moved, nor was there any sound.

Ragnar watched hatefully as the wizards rode down into the midst of the carnage. Wigg stopped his horse and jumped down, as did Tretiak. Ragnar's body and extremities twitched back and forth as if he were in the midst of some form of horrible seizure.

Then Ragnar did something no stalker should have been able to do. He spoke to them. "Pestilence of the craft!" he growled, turning his horrible features up to his onetime allies. "I shall kill you both! You will become my first two trophies in my war against the wizards!"

With that he raised his hands, sending twin bolts of energy toward Wigg. They struck the wizard in the center of his chest, lifting him into the air and throwing him violently to the ground more than a dozen feet away, nearly rendering him unconscious.

Tretiak responded immediately, and the glowing, azure bars of a wizard's warp rapidly surrounded Ragnar. Ragnar struck out at the sides of the barrier like a cornered animal, snarling with hate as he continued to glare at the two wizards who had once been his friends. Tretiak ran to Wigg and helped him stand.

"Forgive me, but how is it that you are not dead?" Tretiak asked Wigg. His eyes were the size of saucers. "When I saw his twin bolts go to you, I was sure it would be the end of first you, and then of me, as well!"

Despite his weakened condition, Ragnar could easily hear what Tretiak had said.

Before responding, Wigg looked quickly at the gleaming cube. He smiled briefly as he collected himself, brushing the dirt from his clothes.

"A little gift from Faegan," he said. "There is an incantation, something that Faegan has just come across in the Tome, that creates a sort of shield around one of the endowed. He taught it to me before we left, thinking that it might be useful." Wigg rubbed his chin for a moment.

"And thank the Afterlife for your quick use of the wizard's warp," he added. "It was exactly the right thing to do. Now we may be able to find out exactly what it was that happened here, and help him if we can. But be very careful as we come closer to him. The warp you created should keep him from harming us further, but the fact that he is a stalker, yet is still able to speak and use the craft, is something we have not seen before, and is more than a little disturbing." Wigg paused for a moment, lost in thought. "This is no doubt something new that Failee has developed," he added sadly.

The two wizards approached the gleaming cage slowly and stopped before it.

"It seems my former wife has finally learned how to perform her stalker incantation without bringing it to its logical conclusion, leaving Ragnar both a stalker and a wizard at the same time," Wigg mused sadly. "What you see before you has been one of the greatest fears: a still-effective wizard who has also become a stalker, complete with the unyielding desire to kill males of trained, endowed blood. I need not tell you what this would mean, should the number of halflings grow. If we now have two separate sects of the endowed to struggle against, it could mean the end of us."

Ragnar remained silent as he listened to the two wizards, waiting for an opportunity to strike.

"There is something else that I find interesting," Wigg went on, his eyebrow launching upward. "Ragnar is still convulsing. That makes me think that even though Failee's part of it is done, and the incantation is advancing rapidly, the transformation is still incomplete. If that is true," he added slowly, "we may be able to reverse it, and save him."

Tretiak's jaw dropped. "In the name of the Afterlife, how?"

"We already know that the stalker's brain fluid is what makes each one unique, and perpetuates the horror he has become. If we can drain the fluid from his head while the process is still taking place, thereby taking away what it is that makes him so, we may be able to reverse its otherwise inexorable progress. The odds are slim, but I feel we at least owe it to him to try."

"And just how do we accomplish such a thing?"

"I want you to control his limbs," Wigg answered, "but keep him conscious. Then remove the cage. I will make an incision in his skull and try to use the craft to drain off the fluid. But we must act quickly. Are you with me?"

"Of course."

"Then we are wasting time," Wigg said with finality. "Begin the incantation."

Come and try, pestilence of the craft, Ragnar seethed. *I will fight you with everything I have.*

Tretiak closed his eyes. Almost immediately Ragnar began to strain against the onset of Tretiak's incantation. The two fought each other's minds for what seemed to be an eternity. Sweat broke out upon Tretiak's brow as he struggled against the mutated powers of the stalker. Finally Ragnar slipped to his knees and fell to the grass. He was still alert, but unable to move. The azure bars of the wizard's warp began to fade away, finally retreating into nothingness.

"Can you hold him in that state?" Wigg asked nervously.

"I am not sure," Tretiak responded, strain in his voice. "His ability with the gift is strong, perhaps even more so now that he is a stalker. We must hurry."

Wigg ran to seat himself the grass next to Ragnar and carefully lifted the stalker's head into his lap. Removing his wizard's dagger from its scabbard, he gave Tretiak a meaningful look.

"Above all, we cannot come into contact with the fluid," he said sternly. "To do so would mean a horrible and instantaneous death. I will make an incision in his temple, and when the fluid begins to drain I will accelerate the process with the aid of the craft, causing it to pour out upon the ground. When I am done I want you to reactivate the cage at once. Are you ready?"

Tretiak nodded.

"Very well," Wigg said. "May the Afterlife grant us strength."

No sooner had Wigg made the incision than the stalker started to move again, the combination of Ragnar's innate desire to kill the wizards and the sharp, sudden pain from Wigg's knife apparently overcoming Tretiak's incantation. Tretiak tried to keep him under, but Ragnar finally broke partially free of Wigg's grasp. The quickly flowing, stinking brain fluid splattered in all directions, narrowly missing the two wizards. A few drops landed on Wigg's boots, causing them to sizzle and smoke.

Wigg still had hold of his dagger, its blade covered with the yellow fluid. He desperately tried to control the stalker and activate his incantation at the same time. "Hold him with the craft!" he screamed at Tretiak.

Ragnar continued to struggle. With a surge of unexpected strength, Ragnar broke farther free, then turned his face up toward Wigg, screaming in triumph. Still trying desperately to perform his incantation, Wigg had inadvertently turned his dagger-point down toward Ragnar's face, and some of the awful substance dripped down the blade.

The fluid fell directly into Ragnar's open mouth. The mutant would hold that pain in his memories forever.

His eyes bulging, screams of torment tearing from his lungs, Ragnar yanked himself away from Wigg and sent a bolt into Tretiak's chest, knocking the wizard to the ground. He then instinctively reached for what he perceived to be the instrument of his torture—Wigg's dagger. He first tore the dagger from Wigg's grasp, and then the scabbard from the wizard's side. Running from his former friends and jumping on Wigg's stallion, he was gone in an instant. Perhaps knowing that they could never catch Ragnar with the two of them atop the only remaining horse, the wizards had not given chase. As soon as he dared, he had stopped to bandage the wound in his temple, but it was too late for the horse. Continuing on foot, he reflected that he had gotten away, but he would never be the same again.

His mind finally returning from his reveries, Ragnar opened his eyes.

Failee's mistake was not realizing you were near, Wigg, he thought. *Your mistake was not killing me the moment you saw me lying there on the bloody grass of that field. And the Chosen One's mistake was to leave his seed behind in Parthalon. So many mistakes are about to intersect upon the tightly woven tapestry of time.*

He smiled into the gloom.

It was you who caused my addiction, Wigg. And it is now you who shall pay. Both you and the Chosen One shall very soon know your fates, by my hand and the hand of the child. Each of us is now your enemy—the living, breathing results of your mistakes.

The blood stalker gently replaced the dagger into its golden scabbard. With a brief glance he extinguished the candles in the room, then sat alone with his hatred, his madness, and his thoughts.

CHAPTER EIGHTEEN

T RISTAN, Shannon, and Wigg stood at the top of the small rise in the depths of the Hartwick Woods. The sun was at its zenith, and the promise of a beautiful day had been fulfilled. Shannon held the reins to all three of their horses as they watched the giant butterflies soaring colorfully in the afternoon sun.

Tristan was reminded of the day he had first encountered the fliers of the fields and the Caves of the Paragon. That single afternoon had seemed to set so much in motion, almost as if he had never been truly alive before that point in time.

Soon we shall have the Tome, and my training can begin. He could feel his endowed blood sing with the promise of it.

But his heart held no joy. His mind was filled with unanswered questions about Scrounge's abuse of the consuls, and he found himself worrying about Geldon and Joshua. He had no real assurances that the Minions would obey his orders, much less be respectful to the two rather odd emissaries he had sent to do his bidding.

Looking down into the glade, Wigg said, "We may not be alone here. There remains a lingering presence of endowed blood. Someone was here . . ." He took a deep breath and let it out slowly. "And they may still be present."

To their surprise the wall of gray fieldstone in the center of the grassy bank across the clearing was missing several of its pieces. The hole that had been created did not seem sufficient for a person to pass through, but it was sizable enough to allow for the entrance and exit of the fliers. Tristan watched as they occasionally alit near the opening, then folded their wings and went through, just as he had seen them do the first time he was here.

"I thought you reactivated the warp that guarded this wall," Tristan whispered to Wigg.

"I did," Wigg replied. "Apparently someone powerful enough in the craft dismantled it again." One eyebrow came up. "How convenient for us."

He turned to Shannon. "This is as far as you go," he ordered quietly. "And I insist that you pour out the rest of your ale here. Considering everything we have witnessed on this little journey, you'll need your wits about you."

Blowing a puff of smoke from his corncob pipe, Shannon glared back at the wizard with a look that spoke volumes. But he finally relented, pouring his precious swill out over the grass.

"What a waste!" Shannon moaned, as if he had just lost his best friend. "That was one of my finest concoctions yet."

Tristan couldn't help but break into a grin.

"Now I want you to tie the horses," Wigg ordered, "and find a good place to hide—one where you can not only watch our mounts but that also affords you a clear view of the entrance to the Caves. Stay long enough to make sure no one follows us in—if no one has appeared by dusk, then return to the Redoubt. If someone does appear to be following us, be sure to get a good look at them, then leave for the Redoubt immediately, to report to Faegan. Leave our horses when you go. If no one has come after us by then, they should be all right on their own."

"Why would you want me to leave if someone does follow you into the Caves?" Shannon asked. "You might need my help."

Wigg smiled slightly. "Your offer is brave, but you would be serving us better to be able to give Faegan a description of whoever may be after us, in case we don't survive this. At the very least, it will give him a place to start looking."

Grumbling, Shannon tied up the three horses and headed toward a stand of thick brush that looked to be a likely hiding place. But at the last moment he turned back toward Wigg and Tristan, and they could see that his expression had softened a bit. "Good luck," he said. "And may the Afterlife watch over you."

"And you," Tristan said. Shannon ducked into the brush and was gone from view.

Wigg turned to look at the prince. "Are you ready?" he asked.

Staring at the breach in the wall, Tristan reached behind his right shoulder and tugged on the hilt of his dreggan and then the first of his throwing knives, making sure neither would stick should he need to call upon them. One corner of his mouth turned up in anticipation.

"I have been ready to return ever since I first came here," he said.

"Very well, then," Wigg answered. "Let's go."

They walked cautiously across the glade, the giant butterflies scattering as they went. Wigg stood before the wall, carefully examining the breach. Then, using his hands, he began to remove more stones, widening the gap so that they would be able to enter.

"Wouldn't it be easier to use the craft?" Tristan asked, helping the old one loosen the stones.

"Of course," Wigg said in that all-knowing way of his. "But it might also help alert someone of endowed blood to our presence—something I do not feel would be wise just now. In addition, I have begun to cloak our blood from anyone who might be able to sense the fact that we are endowed—just as I did back in Parthalon, to screen our presence from the Coven. That will make it difficult for me to use the craft for anything else."

When the hole was large enough, Wigg led the way through.

"Mind your feet this time," he said snidely, reminding Tristan of how he had fallen down the rough-hewn steps the last time he had been here. "We will secure some illumination at the bottom."

They descended slowly, the rushing sound of the water from the falls in their ears. The prince began to experience the now-familiar, exhilarating feeling of being close to the waters of the Caves. The farther down he went, the more his blood rose in his veins, making him slightly dizzy. Soon they were at the bottom, standing next to each other in the gloom. Wigg took a few careful paces to the side and reached up to take one of the torches from its holder on the nearby wall.

"Take out your flint and strike this torch alight," Wigg ordered. "I dare not use the craft to do so."

Tristan did as he was asked, and the torch came alight quickly. As the prince looked around, Wigg lifted the flame higher.

They were standing on the floor of a spectacular subterranean cavern, the high, cascading falls tumbling ever downward into a stone pool to their right. The sound was almost overpowering in its majesty, and the water was calling Tristan to again dive into its depths, to immerse himself just as he had so obsessively done on his first visit here. Giant, multicolored stalactites and stalagmites reached to join floor and ceiling. Some of them had already found their mates, creating majestic columns of slick, gorgeous stone.

From the rent in the wall above several of the fliers reentered, their wings adding to the riot of color and movement that surrounded the wizard and the prince. Some of them perched next to the pool.

From all around him Tristan could sense the serene, yet overpowering presence of the craft infiltrating his mind and his heart. Growing increasingly dizzy and short of breath, he found himself forced to go down on one knee. He looked up weakly at the wizard.

"Wigg," he breathed, "you must get me away from the water! It is calling to me again!" He gasped for breath as he turned his head toward the enticing pool.

"I know," the old one said. He helped Tristan up, putting one of the prince's arms over his shoulder for support. "Come with me."

Wigg hurried the prince across the stone chamber, to the entrance to the square-cut tunnel in the wall at the opposite side. But as they approached the tunnel, the breath left his lungs in a rush.

Sensing Wigg's apprehension, Tristan looked tentatively to the tunnel entrance.

"What's wrong?" he asked weakly. "Why aren't we going inside?"

"The warp guarding the entrance to the tunnel is gone," Wigg said hesitantly.

"How can you tell?" the prince asked. "It looks the same to me."

"That's because it was invisible. You would not have been able to see it during your first trip here. Nor could you see it now, because you are still untrained. The Directorate designed it so that it could not be seen by anyone except us. We had hoped that this would make it less subject to tampering by unknown forces. That strategy has apparently failed. But what I do not understand is how it could have been dismantled without my sensing it."

"Wigg," Tristan whispered, "you must either take us down the tunnel, or carry me back outside. I will not be able to last much longer, this close to the falls . . . I have begun to hear my own heartbeat in my ears, despite how loud the falls are, and I . . ." His voice trailed off as he collapsed into unconsciousness. His face was bright red, reflecting the exertion being placed upon his heart by being so close to the waters. Wigg picked him up and carried him quickly, desperately through the entrance to the tunnel.

Holding both the torch and the prince, he ran down the length of the passageway, continuing until he estimated Tristan would be a safe distance from the falls. He put the prince down against the tunnel wall and checked his condition.

The redness in the prince's face was starting to dissipate, and his breathing was coming back to normal. Wigg looked up at the torch in his hand, not happy with what he saw. The flame was fading.

Tristan finally opened his eyes to see the wizard looking concernedly down at him. Beyond the circle of the sputtering torch, the silent, impenetrable darkness of the tunnel completely surrounded them.

"How do you feel?" Wigg asked cautiously.

"Better," Tristan answered slowly. "But I have never been so intensely affected by the waters of the Caves." He shook his head back and forth, trying to regain his focus. "Will I be all right?"

"Yes," Wigg answered, smiling for the first time since they came underground. "But right now we have a bigger worry."

"And that is?" Tristan asked, rubbing the back of his neck.

"The torch," Wigg said simply.

Tristan looked up to see that the ancient, oil-soaked torch was beginning to fade. Soon they would be engulfed in total darkness, a prospect that was less than reassuring.

"We planned poorly," he said.

"I had no idea that the warp would be dismantled," Wigg replied. "The ceiling of this tunnel is lined with radiance stones, which were to have been our means of illumination. But now, with this failing torch, we have only two alternatives."

"To either go back the way we came and leave the Caves, or throw caution to the wind and permit you to use the craft," Tristan said glumly.

"Precisely. The radiance stones that light the tunnels in and out of the Redoubt have been enchanted so that even the unendowed can activate them with a touch. But these stones have not. Only one of endowed blood may employ them, and to do so I must first stop cloaking our blood."

"I understand," Tristan said. "But you must activate the stones." He stood up, testing his legs. "We have come this far, and we must have the Tome. You said so yourself. If there are problems ahead, we shall simply have to deal with them."

"Very well," the wizard said reluctantly.

Tristan watched the old one's face relax, indicating that he had stopped cloaking the quality of their blood. Wigg held the torch high, examining the ceiling of the tunnel, where the dormant radiance stones lay. Closing his eyes, Wigg activated the stones. The familiar pale green glow appeared, brightly illuminating the tunnel for as far as the prince could see. Almost immediately the slightly pinched, strained look returned to the wizard's face, telling the prince that their blood was again being cloaked.

The wizard sighed. "There. At least we now have light." He extinguished the torch and dropped it on the tunnel floor. "I think it best that we make our way to—"

He never finished his sentence, for that was when the sound started.

It was a strange, grating sound in the hollowness of the tunnel. Almost immediately Tristan recognized it for what it was—stone against stone. He watched in horror as black marble walls shot down from the ceiling to the floor on either side of them. They descended with great thuds, creating a stone cubicle of no more than two meters in any direction, trapping the wizard and the prince inside.

Tristan glanced at Wigg, hoping against hope that this had for some reason been an action of the wizard's. But the expression on Wigg's face told him that was not the case. They looked around desperately.

"What happened?" Tristan exclaimed. "Is this another safeguard? Some type of device to trap intruders?"

"It is definitely the use of the craft, but I had no hand in it," Wigg answered. "Someone or something obviously does not want us to move from this spot."

Tristan was finding it difficult to breathe. "Do the radiance stones have any bearing?"

"Very possible," Wigg said. "Illuminating the stones may have been the trigger that brought down these walls. But there is yet another problem." He paused for a moment, thinking. "We shall run out of breathable air in short order. Device of entrapment, indeed . . ."

"Can you destroy the wall, or raise it back up with the craft?" Tristan asked hopefully.

Wigg raised his arms, sending a bolt against the farthest of the walls. The glow of the craft slowly snaked over the entire surface of the slick marble wall, remaining there. Wigg then lifted his arms in an attempt to raise the wall. Nothing happened. He sent another bolt at the wall, much faster this time, the magic crashing against it with great intensity. Noise and smoke followed, the calamitous sound and acrid smell made even worse by the small confines of the chamber. But when the harsh, bitter smoke partially cleared, the deadly wall was still intact.

"Whoever is responsible for this is of great power," Wigg said sadly. "I fear that there is little I can do."

The smoke in the room had dissipated slightly, but it was making the air more difficult to breathe. They both began to cough.

Then they noticed the glow.

The familiar radiance of the craft in the shape of a circle had begun to appear on one of the walls. As it grew in size and intensity, its illumination flooded the chamber with an azure light that combined with the sage glow from the stones in the ceiling. Then the circle began to change shape, parts of it fading away to reveal an emerging pattern. The pattern that the glow had taken on was the lion and the broadsword, the heraldry of the House of Galland.

Tristan stood there weakly, his breath coming with increasing difficulty. The glowing pattern was beautiful. He looked down at his gold medallion and took it into his hands. Then he looked back up again. The pattern in the stone wall was an exact duplicate of the jewelry he held. The brilliant, azure veins that made up the image of his heraldry pulsated and undulated as if they were trying to free themselves from the rock wall.

Before Wigg could protest Tristan extended his hand, touching the glowing heraldry. Immediately the glow intensified, becoming almost blinding. Wigg moved to take the prince's hand away from the wall, but he was too late. At that moment, another sound came to their ears: a hauntingly beautiful voice.

"Tristan," the voice said softly from both nowhere and everywhere. "If you wish to live, you must do as I tell you."

Tristan staggered backward, almost falling to his knees in shock.

The voice that had just spoken to them belonged to his deceased mother: Morganna, the last queen of Eutracia.

Speechless, Tristan turned to Wigg to see shock on the wizard's face, as well. Nonplussed but also knowing they were quickly running out of air, the wizard nodded, indicating to the prince that he should answer.

It took Tristan several long moments to gather himself, finally finding the breath with which to whisper an answer. The pain in his chest was unbearable; it was becoming more difficult to breathe by the moment.

"Mother," he whispered tentatively. "Is that you?"

"Yes, my son," came the lovely, familiar voice again, filling their stone prison. Its timbre was both caring and reassuring, just as he had always remembered it to be. It was in stark contrast to his own weak, rasping whispers. "You must do as I now tell you, or you and the wizard will perish here. There is little time left."

Gasping, Tristan asked, "What must we do, Mother?"

"When the wall rises, you must go quickly through the exit it creates. Always take the path that is marked by the lion and the broadsword. To do other will only lead you on an endless quest, going nowhere, resulting in your death." Morganna's voice paused for a moment as if it were finally retreating with the vanishing, breathable air. But then it came again.

"Much has changed here since Wigg last trod these paths," she continued softly. "There will be many obstacles in your way, some of them deadly. But you must persevere. The object you seek, the treatise of the craft, shall be elusive. But follow your heritage, my son, and you will reach your prize."

Tristan finally went down on one knee, his breath rattling a final, deadly song in his starving lungs. Wigg, too, was losing the fight.

"Follow the entrance," Morganna said. "Go forth and live."

"But how is it that you can speak to me?" the prince gasped from the floor. He still saw nothing but the four dark walls of the suffocating prison and the glowing heraldry of the House of Galland. "Do you live?" he whispered. He would have died to know how it was that he could hear the voice of his mother—the beautiful, compassionate woman who had been so horribly raped and murdered at the hands of the Minions.

"There is no time, my son," Morganna said, her voice fading away.

Teetering on the cusp of unconsciousness, Tristan was unable to form his next words. His eyes closing in defeat, his head finally sank to surrender upon the almost welcoming coolness of the stone floor.

"Behold," the voice of Morganna said.

With that the slick, marble wall barring their entrance to the tunnel began to rise, disappearing into the ceiling from which it had come.

The prince suddenly felt two arms beneath his own, dragging him from the room. Wigg managed to pull Tristan a short way down the tunnel before collapsing to the floor next to the prostrate prince.

It was Tristan who finally opened his eyes first, coughing and hacking. He propped himself up weakly against the wall of the tunnel, helping the wizard do the same. "Wigg," he asked, half coughing, half speaking, "was I dreaming, or did I hear my mother's voice?"

Wigg took a deep breath, gratefully refilling his starved lungs with the sweet, humid air of the tunnel. "I heard it, too," he said slowly, trying to marshal his thoughts. "But I still do not know what it means."

"Is she still alive?" Tristan asked. He dared not believe it, but he felt compelled to ask the question, nonetheless. "Or perhaps somehow able to communicate with me from the Afterlife?"

"I simply do not know," Wigg answered honestly, rising slowly on trembling legs. "But I also believe that there is no time for such a discussion right now. We must keep going."

"Did you hear what she said about always taking the path marked with the heraldry?" Tristan asked, standing up. He checked his weapons, and was relieved to find they were still intact.

"Yes," Wigg answered.

"And is that what we should do?"

"I can only answer that when we come to such a place," Wigg said cautiously. "*If* we come to such a place. There were no such intersections here before—at least as far as we had previously explored. Forgive me, Tristan, but I find it hard to believe such an unlikely possibility now exists, simply because a voice from the past says so. But I suggest we get moving. Too much has already happened that I am uncomfortable with, to say the least. And there is no telling what may lie before us."

Tristan looked down the tunnel to see that the radiance stones were continuing to illuminate its depths. "How far must we go?" he asked as they began walking down its length.

"That depends," Wigg answered, "on whether what the voice said is true."

They walked in silence for a long time. Apparently lost in his thoughts, the wizard took the lead. Following behind, Tristan was still consumed by the memory of the voice he had heard.

After what seemed to have been at least half a league, Wigg stopped short. From his position in the rear the prince could not easily see what was up ahead. He walked around to get a better look.

Directly in front of them, literally daring them to enter its tempting puzzle, lay a gigantic intersection. At least a dozen tunnels split off from it, each leading in a different direction, each lit with radiance stones, beckoning them to enter.

But the glowing, azure sign of the heraldry of the House of Galland was embedded into the rock of only one of them. Tristan could see that the marked tunnel led to a flight of stone steps going downward, curving around and out of sight.

"This intersection never existed before," Wigg breathed.

"Nonetheless, here it is," Tristan countered. "I say we take the tunnel that is marked. The voice told us to."

"That does not necessarily mean it is a good idea," Wigg responded.

"Her voice saved us, did it not, by raising the wall?" Tristan asked adamantly. "If the voice of my mother had wanted us dead, we would be already. To me, there seems no other choice but to follow her instructions."

"Very well," Wigg said slowly. "But keep your wits about you, and do as I say. Be ready to act on a moment's notice. We cannot be sure of what awaits us, especially if the voice is correct."

With that, the wizard and the prince tentatively entered the tunnel marked with the heraldry and cautiously began navigating the cold stone steps leading downward into the earth.

CHAPTER NINETEEN

❧

$\mathcal{F}$AEGAN sat in his wooden chair on wheels, finding the silence of the room almost oppressive. His gray-green eyes bore down intensely into the ancient book that lay on the table before him, its pages so dry and fragile that he had decided to turn them using the craft, instead of his fingers. Nicodemus lay in Faegan's lap, purring softly.

Faegan sighed, sitting back in his chair. After two days of searching through volume after volume, he still had not found what he was looking for. But he knew he would.

The master wizard looked up from his work to gaze around the room. He was in the Archives of the Redoubt, the greatest collection of books and scrolls ever assembled in one place, second only to the Tome in its importance to the craft.

The Archives occupied a vast room of Ephyran marble, one of the most beautiful of the entire Redoubt. His mouth turned up in a knowing smile. It was only fitting that the late wizards of the Directorate would have made this sanctuary one of the most sumptuous and secure of all the chambers in this amazing complex.

The square room measured at least two hundred meters on each of its four sides, and was seven stories high. Each story had a railing that overlooked the central area. Each level was lined with books from top to bottom, and a magnificent set of curved, mahogany stairs with a brass railing ran up and around to each of the floors, giving access to the thousands of works.

The floor and ceiling of the Archives were of the most delicate, dark green marble, shot through with swirling traces of gray and magenta. Several hundred finely carved desks, reading tables, and beautifully upholstered chairs were tastefully arranged on the bottom floor, and the delicate, golden light was supplied by a combination of oil chandeliers, sconces, and desklamps, all enchanted to burn eternally. The entire chamber smelled pleasantly of must, knowledge, and the thrill of discovery.

"I'm afraid this one won't do either, Nicodemus," Faegan said affectionately, rubbing the cat beneath the nape of his neck. "But we will keep trying, won't we? The stakes are too high to give up."

He narrowed his eyes at the book, and it rose into the air and floated to the fifth floor, to glide gently back into place between two equally imposing volumes.

Ever since he had witnessed the amazing connection between Shailiha and the fliers of the fields, Faegan had known that there would be only two ways to explore the incredible, unexplained phenomenon. One would be to continue to go to the aviary with the princess and see what happened through a process of trial and error with the fliers. The other was to come here, to the Archives, to discover all he could about such connections—especially with those untrained in the craft. It had consumed his mind even to the point of having stopped trying to research Joshua's birds of prey. Something in his heart told him that the fantastic bond between Shailiha and the fliers was going to become even more important.

"Time to go searching again." He sighed softly and wheeled his chair over to the rather odd-looking desk in the center of the floor. Wigg had shown him how to use it before leaving for the Caves with Tristan, and Faegan had found it to be a marvel of the craft. It was called the Index of the Ages, and it was the key to negotiating the complexity of the Archives. Once activated, it provided the location and document number of any book or scroll, depending on the subject matter or author.

Faegan closed his eyes, relaxing his mind. "Open," he commanded softly.

As the familiar glow built around the desk, its marble surface slowly separated from top to bottom into equal halves, which slid to opposite sides. He opened his eyes and looked down into the seemingly limitless, azure depths that had been left behind.

"Forestallments," he said. "Both event- and time-activated.

Of and relating to endowed blood only, and the possibility of bonds that may be created with nonhuman creatures." He waited.

From the depths rose the glow of the craft. Swirling as it came, it finally stopped spinning at the level of his eyes and coalesced into gleaming, azure letters of the Eutracian alphabet. They hung there silently, like long-forgotten, dead ghosts of language. It was a list.

He slowly ran down the titles of the hundreds of related documents, seeing that he had already examined many of them. Most had not been helpful. And then, at the bottom of the shimmering list, was an entry that had not appeared with his previous queries:

A Treatise on Forestallments and Their Possible Uses
Author: Egloff, of the Directorate of Wizards
The Vault of the Scrolls
Sixth Floor
Section 1999156
Document 2037
Date of completion:
Seventy-third Day of the Season of New Life, 327 S.T.

Faegan closed his eyes and recalled all he could of Egloff. The highly precise wizard had always worn spectacles. He had been slight in stature but great in intellect, with a rather diminutive head and an incongruously long nose. He had also been highly respected among the wizards as a master of the Tome.

Faegan opened his eyes again and reread the words that hung there, motionless in the silence of the room. And then it hit him.

The blood stalkers and screaming harpies, the horrific tools of the Coven that had been revisited upon Eutracia just before the sorceresses returned, might have been brought forth from their hibernation by Forestallment, the same aspect of the craft Faegan suspected the princess' bond with the fliers to be!

The wizard's blood raced as the possibilities whirled through his mind like pinwheels. He placed his cat on the floor, turned his chair toward the only section of wall that was not lined with books, and raised his hands. "Open," he ordered.

The marble wall separated down the center, becoming twin doors opening to either side. Wasting no time, the master wizard wheeled his chair through—into the Vault of the Scrolls.

The Vault of the Scrolls was constructed of black marble, and held countless racks of ancient, dusty rolled-up parchment.

Searching his mind, he retrieved the section number: 1999156. The level upon which the scroll was to be found was represented by the last number of the series. He therefore needed to be on the sixth floor. Since the winding staircase was useless to him, he levitated his wheelchair up to the appropriate floor and over the railing, coming to a gentle landing in the appropriate alleyway between racks.

The first three digits of the section number indicated the number of the alley: 199. The fourth, fifth, and sixth digits were indicative of the particular section of racks in which the document could be found: rack 915.

Finally stopping in front of the correct section, he reached into his memory and retrieved the number of the individual scroll he wished: document 2037.

Once he spotted its resting place, above his reach, Faegan used the craft to call the scroll to him. Slowly, one of the parchment tubes began to slide itself out from among its brothers and gently floated down into the wizard's lap.

Faegan looked at it for some time, feeling overcome by emotion. Having been isolated in Shadowood for so long, he had not read a true scroll of the craft for over three hundred years. And this particular scroll had been written by Egloff, one of his old friends who was now buried in a nameless grave.

The golden tag that traditionally hung from the leather strap surrounding the scroll was still there. Glistening as if new, it was engraved with Egloff's signature. *He always did prefer scrolls to books.* As he unrolled it, he felt old, dusty memories tugging at his heart. His friend had had a beautiful script, and preferred to write in red ink. The treatise was very long and detailed—just as he would have expected it to be.

It is truly a window to Egloff's intellect, Faegan told himself. Then his heart skipped a beat. What he had been searching for was the method by which one could empirically prove the existence of a Forestallment in another. And he had just found it.

The existence of a Forestallment residing in another can be proven by the subject's blood signature! His gray-green eyes continued down the parchment, searching for more clues. Finally, near the end of Egloff's treatise, came the answer. *That's it!* he realized.

At the bottom he saw Egloff's signature, the accompanying signature of one of the many consuls of the Redoubt needed to authenticate it, and the document's date of completion. The air went out of his lungs in a rush as he reread the date, the importance of which had eluded him until now.

The Seventy-third day of the Season of New Life, 327 S.T.

The treatise had been written the same day as the attack by the Coven. The very day Egloff and all of the other wizards of the Directorate, except Wigg, had been murdered.

That would explain why the other wizards of the Directorate had never learned of Egloff's findings, Faegan realized. There would have been no time to tell them. They would all have been preparing for that evening's coronation of the prince, and Egloff no doubt had planned to tell them afterward. Faegan sadly looked away from the parchment, trying not to think of all Wigg had told him of that fateful day. *But Egloff never got the chance,* he thought.

It was forbidden to remove any document from the Archives or the Vault of the Scrolls, so he decided to make a copy in the event that Wigg would want to study the scroll, as well.

Opening the drawer of a desk he found sheets of extra parchment. Carefully he laid a clean sheet directly over the original, then closed his eyes.

Almost immediately the glow of the craft appeared and the words from the original began to bleed upward into the developing copy, creating an exact duplicate. When the process was complete, he rolled the fresh copy up and placed it in his robes. The original rolled itself up and, with a thought from Faegan, floated gently upward to replace itself in the spot from which it had come.

Faegan levitated his chair over the railing and wheeled himself out of the Vault of Scrolls and into the Archives proper, where he retrieved Nicodemus. He gave the cat an affectionate scratch under the chin, and Nicodemus stretched to ask for more.

"We have found it, my friend," Faegan whispered. "This could change everything."

In his excitement he allowed himself to use the craft again to levitate his chair. Cackling with glee, he went sailing down the halls of the Redoubt in search of the princess.

CHAPTER TWENTY

*T*RISTAN carefully followed Wigg down the narrow, curving steps and into the bowels of the Caves. The radiance stones glowed more softly here, and the deeper they went, the colder it became. Moisture seeped visibly from the walls, and the air grew increasingly musty. There was no sound save that of their boots on the unforgiving rock. Tristan thought the journey would never end, his sense of apprehension growing with each pace downward.

After what seemed leagues Wigg stopped short and held up his hand. He turned around in the stairwell to look at Tristan with a silent expression of complete disbelief, then beckoned the prince to follow him into the room at the bottom of the stairs.

Embedded in the walls of the large stone chamber was a continuously circling vein of azure. Glowing brightly, it pulsated and throbbed as if it had a life of its own—as if wishing to free itself from this place in which it was imprisoned. At the opposite end of the room was another door.

The vein's amazing glow bathed the entire room; it was perhaps the most beautiful thing Tristan had ever seen. But the look on Wigg's face told him that it was also something terrible.

In horror, he watched the wizard fall to his knees before the vein, a tear rolling down one of his cheeks. "So this is where it is being taken to!" he exclaimed. "And as the vein grows, our world above collapses around us!" His hands were balled up into fists, his knuckles white with tension.

"What are you talking about?" Tristan asked gently. He walked to the wizard and placed a hand on the old one's quivering shoulder.

"It has to do with the stone," Wigg whispered. Tristan was not sure when he had ever seen Wigg so distraught.

"The vein you see here, this abomination of the craft, is in some bastardized way the true physical embodiment of the power locked within the Paragon," Wigg said sadly. "I'm sure of it! The power of the stone is somehow being drained off, attracted to the Caves, and captured within these walls. And as the vein grows, the stone weakens." He shook his head in disbelief.

"Do you see how the vein undulates, its power clearly evident?" he asked the prince. "When the process is complete and the stone is colorless, this vein will imprison all of the power that the Paragon once held. The power gleaned from the stone will then be at the disposal of the one who drew it here, and completely unavailable to us."

"I still don't understand," Tristan answered. "How do you know all this?"

"There's no way you could understand," Wigg responded, slowly coming to his feet. He wiped the tears from his cheeks. "Faegan and I barely understand it ourselves. There is a passage in the Tome that mentions a method of drawing the power from the stone without removing it from its human host. It says that someone will eventually come who will be capable of such a feat. That person, however, would have to be of such immense power that we had always thought it could only be you, or your sister, Shailiha. Therefore our concern regarding this issue was not great. But we were obviously very wrong." He paused, lost in his thoughts.

"There is now one who walks the earth who has far more power than any of us," the wizard continued slowly, half to himself. "The superiority of this being is without precedent, and his or her strength grows every day, just as the stone weakens. I need not tell you how dangerous this—"

He was interrupted by the eerie, grating scratchiness of stone on stone. As the prince spun around to see where the sound came from, another marble wall came shooting down, blocking the entrance to the stairway from which they had just come. Tristan instinctively turned to the door at the opposite side of the room. It remained unblocked, and on it glowed the sign of the lion and the broadsword.

Then the voice of Morganna filled the stone room. "Tristan, you must hurry. There may already be too little time."

The prince looked to the wizard, who was also listening intently.

"Why must we hurry, Mother?" Tristan asked. "What is it we are to do?"

"There is not time to tell you *why,* my son," the voice said, already starting to fade. "But take the wizard and go quickly through the other door, before it is too late."

Wigg nodded, and they began to run.

As they approached the portal Tristan heard scratching, scrabbling sounds. He drew his dreggan with a swift pull, the ring of its blade bouncing off the stone walls. Tossing the heavy sword into his left hand, he reached back to his knives, loosening the first of them. Then he threw the dreggan back into his right palm again and looked down to where the sounds seemed to be coming from.

A pair of dark gray hands were beginning to dig their way out of the ground. First only the fingertips were visible. Then came the fingers themselves, and finally the entire hands and upper arms. They agonizingly twisted and turned their way up and out, loosened particles of dirt sprinkling eerily back down as they came. Their skin was gray and bleak, the folds of the knuckle joints black, the nails broken and torn. And then from the dirt came another pair, and then another and another.

Wigg came to stand cautiously next to Tristan as the things continued their inexorable climb from the earth. The wizard and the prince watched in horror as the ground before each of the pairs of hands seemed to obligingly open even wider, the rents created in the earth becoming deep, dark crevices.

Then bodies rose from the earth, heads and shoulders first, until they were standing directly before the wizard and the prince. Tristan stood aghast, not wanting to breathe, as if that simple act would somehow bring the awful things closer. They were consuls of the Redoubt.

It had taken the prince several moments to recognize them for what they were. It was only their dark blue robes, torn and covered with dirt, that gave a clue to their identity.

Their faces and hands appeared to be quite bloodless. Loose, sallow skin hung down from their bones in horrible, sagging folds. Their eye sockets were sunken and dark; the whites of their eyes were a sickly, bloodshot yellow, and the irises were inky spheres that seemed to be vacant, looking at nothing. Their gaping mouths were red and drooling, their teeth black, their expressions utterly empty.

Now other pairs of hands were beginning to claw their way to the surface. It was painfully clear to the prince that they would soon be surrounded. Then one of them spoke.

"You are to come with us," it said. The lifeless consul's voice seemed to crack with the strain of simply trying to speak. "Our master wishes it," he rasped, his blank, doll-like eyes still looking at nothing.

Tristan turned to look at the wizard, and then back to the consuls. "I don't think so," he hissed. He raised his dreggan slightly.

"Who is your master?" Wigg asked, taking a step forward. "Why does your master wish to see us? Does he wish us harm?"

"You will not be killed," the consul said emotionlessly. "Of that you may rest assured. But before you will be allowed to stand before him, you must first be prepared."

"I do not understand," Wigg said cautiously. "How is it that we must be prepared?"

Tristan looked around the room to see that several dozen more of the gruesome pairs of hands had broken through the dirt floor.

"Your preparation is to be completed by others," the consul said. His arms outstretched, he began to walk slowly toward Tristan and Wigg. "You must come. It has been ordered."

The lifeless thing opened its grotesque hands, attempting to grasp the wizard. Tristan had now withstood all that he was able.

Raising his dreggan, he slashed straight across the center of the thing's body, cutting it in half. With a great scream it tumbled to the floor in two separate parts, gray matter spurting from the cleaved portions of its torso. Suddenly, the rest of the consuls were upon them.

Sensing several behind him, Tristan turned on his heel and swung the heavy sword in a great arc. The razor-sharp blade sang shoulder-high through the air, slicing cleanly through the necks of two of the horrible things at the same time. Their heads rolled off their shoulders and onto the floor, and putrid gray matter shot into the air from their headless bodies, its stench coming to his nostrils for the first time. Some of it landed sickeningly upon his whirling arms as he completed the cut. For a brief moment the headless torsos staggered aimlessly about the chamber, walking crazily into the rock walls before finally falling to the earth.

Tristan turned frantically to Wigg to see that the wizard was finally employing the craft. Bolts of energy shot from his hands to strike many of the advancing consuls in the chest, burning them in agony, but another was approaching Wigg from the rear. Tristan tossed his sword over into his left hand and gripped one of his dirks with his right. The silver-bladed knife wheeled through the air almost before he was aware of throwing it, burying itself in the eye of one of the consuls and killing him instantly. More gray matter leapt from the gaping, destroyed eye socket. But there were too many of them, and Tristan knew it.

As he swung the great sword endlessly, striking down one after the next, it seemed that for every one he and the wizard cut down several more rose to take their place. The door at the other side of the room with the glowing, beckoning heraldry of his family seemed a hundred leagues away.

Sweat ran maddeningly into his eyes, and the stench of the dead consuls smothered him. He had lost track of Wigg. He began to sense the desperation in his tired arms, the heavy dreggan almost becoming too much to lift.

It was then that the blow came to the back of his head. Blindingly white light shot through his brain, and then his entire world went suddenly, completely black.

* * *

*T*he softly crashing sounds came quietly to him at first, as if from a dream. He found them very reassuring. Gently caressing his ears and his mind, the harmonious ebb and flow of their timbre made him feel welcome and safe.

What beautiful sounds. His eyes still closed, he had only partially risen to the surface of awareness. *It sounds like the sea. The roar of the ocean, like waves crashing. But that would be impossible . . .*

And then came another, more familiar sound.

Women's voices, laughing . . . speaking my name . . .

His mind suddenly rebelled, his body twisting in futility and fear. His frightened subconscious recalled the time he had been in the depths of the Coven's Recluse—when he had heard the voices of the four mistresses while teetering on the cusp of death.

For a moment he thought he heard Wigg call out to him in pain, and he felt discomfort in his arms and shoulders. Then all went silent again. He lost his fight to rejoin the world around him, falling back down into a long, dark tunnel of sleep.

When he finally opened his eyes, Tristan took an astonished breath and immediately closed them again. He must be hallucinating. He shook his head, trying to understand. He hoped that when he opened his eyes, the scene would be different.

But pain barreled through him, forcing him to face reality. A great ocean lay before him, its blue waves stretching away from the rocky shore.

He was still in the depths of the Caves. A ceiling of rock lay above him where the blue of the sky should have been. The radiance stones ensconced within it lit this place brightly, stretching as far as his eyes could see. Even the ocean itself, wide and foam-crested, seemed endless.

The smell of the cool, almost comforting breeze blowing in off the water reminded him of the coast of Eutracia. Unbelievably, the froth-tipped waves were the exact hue produced by the craft. They tumbled toward him over and over again, crashing noisily upon the sandy shore only meters away from his feet.

The scene mesmerized him so much that it took him several moments to fully realize his plight.

His hands were in iron manacles, his back against a very high stone wall. He was hanging by his wrists, and his shoulders suddenly reminded him of how much pain he was in. Looking down, he saw that his boots were dangling at least a meter off the ground. He still had his weapons, but there was no way to reach them. His shoulders and wrists on fire, he looked to his left and finally saw Wigg. The wizard's condition was even worse.

Also hanging from manacled wrists, Wigg was clearly unconscious. His eyes were closed, and his head was slumped forward on his chest. His right foot was clearly injured. An incision had been made along the inside of his boot, running halfway from the toe to the heel. Dried, endowed blood was caked all around the leather of the opening and had created an odd-looking red trail that ran crazily up and over the top of his foot.

Straining his neck, Tristan tilted his head to look down at the sand below the wizard's feet. It was red. Wigg had been purposely drained of his blood.

For a moment the prince was perplexed. Then he understood.

The consuls we fought with said that we must first be prepared, he realized. *They have drained blood from Wigg, so as to render him powerless in his use of the craft.*

Tristan's memories took him back to the fateful day when Succiu, second mistress of the Coven, had taken her own life and the life of their unborn child. Before doing so she told the prince that when an endowed loses a significant amount of blood, his powers of the craft are drastically reduced. He knew that this was what had been done to Wigg. *But by whom?* he wondered.

He looked around at the sandy beach, trying to find a clue. But now the puzzle grew even more complex. There were no footprints. Just the undisturbed beauty of the sand as the ocean continued to rush up against it.

"Wigg!" he called out loudly. "Wigg! Wake up! Talk to me!"

But it was to no avail. In a sudden panic Tristan narrowed his eyes to peer at the wizard's chest. With great relief he saw that it continued to rise and fall with the old one's labored breathing. At least Wigg was still alive.

The prince looked sadly at the impossible ocean that lay so beautifully, so incongruously before him. His shoulders and wrists seemed about to dislocate. The only sound coming to his ears was the crashing of the waves. He suddenly felt very alone.

Then he saw the glow of the craft forming in the air before him. Wondering if he was seeing things, he closed his eyes once more. When he opened them again, a door frame had formed. Slowly, hauntingly, it began to move closer.

"Wigg, you must wake up!" Tristan shouted. "I need you!" But the wizard did not move.

The portal now floated directly before him. For a brief moment Tristan thought he saw some movement within it. Then the azure fog began to dissipate, and three beautiful women flew directly out of the mist on large, diaphanous wings. Rather small, they would not have quite reached to his shoulders had they all been standing on equal ground. Their entire presence glowed with the craft as they whirled about his face and body as if examining him. At first Tristan recoiled. But then, after a time, he relaxed as he realized that they did not seem to be harming him.

They were all exquisitely beautiful. They wore elaborate, low-cut gowns of the palest white. They all had very long, curly hair, and their eyes were the deepest blue he had ever seen.

At last one of them spoke. "We are here to prepare you." Her voice was earthy, welcoming, and smooth.

"Who are you?" Tristan whispered back in awe.

"We are the master's wraiths," she answered, looking deeply into his eyes. She shook her head gracefully, as if wondering how it was that the prince did not already know that. Her long azure hair flowed out behind her on the breeze from her wings.

"And who is your master?" Tristan asked. He instinctively recoiled a bit as the two other wraiths moved to either side of him.

The first one smiled. "He is the one who has waited so long to see both of you. But we had no idea that the Chosen One would prove to be so compelling."

Before Tristan could ask what she meant, the two wraiths

hovering on either side of him began to caress his body. Their hands softly teased his groin; their tongues and lips circled his own. The sweat of his nervousness ran down into his eyes, and he twisted as best he could to avoid them. But he could only hang there, receiving whatever it was they chose to do.

"Please let them pleasure you," the one before him said softly. "It will help you deal with what I must do."

Tristan looked directly into her face, and in horror watched her beautiful eyes begin to change. Her deep blue irises slowly narrowed, running vertically, and turned yellow. The deep, black pupils were now mere slits. Snakelike eyes looked calmly at him, and she opened her mouth. A forked tongue appeared.

"You do not like me this way?" she asked coyly. The long, pink tongue slithered in and out between her full lips, flicking back and forth as it tested the air.

"No!" Tristan snarled angrily. Trying hard to keep his concentration while the other two wraiths continued to caress him, he glared into her yellow, reptilian eyes. "Whatever it is you intend to do, get it over with!"

She smiled. "Very well." Whipping her pink tongue back and forth, she wetly ran the flat of it up and down his right cheek. Moving lower, she slithered her tongue in and out between the laces of his leather vest, toying with the hair on his chest, then finally ran it down the length of his torso.

Not knowing what would happen next, Tristan closed his eyes and tried to steel himself.

The serpentlike wraith shot her tongue out, cleanly slicing through the leather of his left boot. She then probed it into the cut in the boot to carefully slice a wound in his foot. Tristan cried out, trying to shake her off. But he was too late. Blood was already running out of his boot and into the sand. As the blood came more quickly, a silver bowl appeared on the ground below him.

Once his azure blood began to drip into the bowl, the two wraiths on either side of him stopped their molestations and hovered quietly before him.

"Why?" he snarled. "I know why you would want to bleed the wizard, but why me? I am untrained, and represent no threat to you while still in these chains!"

"We have bled you and the wizard for the same reason," the first wraith said, smiling. Her eyes and tongue had returned to normal; her incredible beauty was restored. "We wish you to become weak, and therefore controllable. An appropriate amount of blood loss will accomplish that in the Chosen One, just as it would in any human. Trained or untrained. But in your case there is yet another reason. The Chosen One's blood has uses all of its own."

Looking into Tristan's puzzled face, she smiled again. "Ah, I see you do not understand," she purred. "So much that you still do not know, Chosen One. But the days of your ignorance are finally coming to an end."

Tristan did not know what she meant by that, and part of him was past caring. He struggled against the manacles as his foot throbbed. His shoulders and wrists felt as if they were being burned away from his body, and additional rivulets of azure blood began to run crazily down the length of his arms from where he had been struggling against the iron. He looked back up into the eyes of the wraith with hatred.

"So what happens now?" he spat at her.

"We wait," she answered pleasantly.

"For what?"

"For enough of your blood to have been collected. We have no need for the wizard's blood, only yours. Then the master's other servants will come."

Tristan wanted to ask them what other servants were meant, but they flitted away along the beach. He sought desperately for a means of escape as he listened to the dribble and plop of his life's fluid hitting first the metal and then later its own pool, but no answer presented itself.

Just as the blood in the bowl began to splatter over the edge with the continuing flow from his foot, the wraiths reappeared.

The one who had cut him looked down into the bowl and smiled. "There now," she cooed. "That wasn't so bad, was it? Now we can heal you and the wizard."

Tristan had been greatly weakened from the loss of blood, and he knew it. He hung limply in his chains, doubting that he would have the strength to raise his dreggan even if he were free.

He immediately began to feel the itching in his foot that

signified the incantation of accelerated healing. Turning, he saw that Wigg's wound was closing, as well. The wraiths were hovering over Tristan's bowl. The one who was their apparent leader picked it up, then smiled at him.

"Good-bye, my sweet prince," she whispered. "We may never meet again. But if we do, by then there will be far more for us to discuss." She looked him up and down, then gazed reverently into the bowl containing his blood. "So many questions, aren't there?" she teased. "And so few remaining of the craft who can answer them for you."

The chains holding the wizard and the prince snapped open, dropping them to the sand. Tristan tried to stand and somehow slowly came to his feet. But when he attempted to reach for his dreggan he fell back down, unable to rise again.

Noticing the wraiths had directed their attention to the ocean, his tired eyes searched the sea, trying to find what it was they were waiting for. Finally, he saw three small black dots against the sage horizon. As they drew closer, he could tell what they were. The horrific birds of prey.

Tristan crawled across the sand as best he could, coming nearer to Wigg. Shaking the wizard did no good, nor did several sharp slaps across the face.

The birds of prey came nearer. Stretching their pointed wings to buffet the air, they landed softly on the beach. Tristan narrowed his eyes in disbelief. These were not the same kind he and Wigg had observed in the Hartwick Woods. These birds were more advanced. As he looked closer, the grotesque, obvious differences in them made his breath come quickly to his lungs. These birds had human-looking arms and hands in addition to their wings.

Their arms extended from just beneath the top of the middle wing joint, and ended in hands of five perfectly formed fingers each. The arms were sculpted and muscular. Black leather gauntlets adorned their wrists. Around the chest of each bird was a black leather baldric holding a long, sheathed sword. In addition, their mannerisms told the prince that they were far more intelligent than the ones he had seen the previous night. The birds before him did not possess the jerking, uncertain movements of the others. Rather, they seemed calm and in control.

Everything else about them seemed to be the same as the

others, however. The long, pointed heads, the leathery wings, and the great black claws at the ends of the feet were identical. Their scarlet, grotesque eyes rotated constantly, taking in the wizard, the prince, and the wraiths all at once. And then, unbelievably, one of them spoke.

"They have been bled?" it asked, turning its awful head toward the wraiths. Its voice was high and eloquent.

"Yes," the wraith who had cut Tristan said. "We now have a sufficient quantity of the blood of the Chosen One. I am pleased to present the bowl to my master's hatchlings." Hovering nearer, she placed the bowl of azure blood into the waiting arms of one of the other birds.

Without speaking further, the hatchling who seemed to be their leader walked closer to the prince, drawing his sword. Tristan's breath came harder. He wished with all of his being that he could find the strength to take his dreggan into his hands.

The hatchling placed the tip of his sword beneath the prince's jaw, raising Tristan's face painfully upward. After regarding him for a time, the great bird lowered his sword.

Another time, I promise you, the prince swore silently.

The hatchling turned to address the wraiths. "You are free to go."

Without further discussion, the wraiths flew through the waiting door frame, disappearing, leaving the wizard and prince alone with the three awful birds.

"What do you want?" Tristan shouted weakly, trying to stand and take his sword into his hand. But standing was impossible, as was pulling the heavy dreggan from its scabbard.

Somehow, impossibly, the thing with the long, pointed beak full of teeth smiled. "We want you," it said softly.

With that, the other hatchling that was not holding the bowl walked over to take the inert body of the wizard into its claws. Using one of its powerful feet, the leader roughly pushed the prince down into the sand and curled its long, black claws around Tristan's body. Struggling against the bird's unyielding talons, Tristan used up the remainder of his strength.

Stretching their leathery wings, the hatchlings flew toward the horizon of the magnificent, azure sea.

As they did so, Tristan finally lost his battle to stay conscious.

CHAPTER TWENTY-ONE

$\mathcal{G}$ELDON looked down from his litter to see the lush Parthalonian countryside flying by. Joshua, in the litter next to him, still had his eyes closed. It made the dwarf wonder whether the younger man would ever get used to this form of travel.

Peering out into the distance, Geldon could pick out the island upon which the Recluse had stood before its destruction by the aftershocks accompanying the sorceresses' deaths.

Tristan had given the Minions many orders that day, not the least of which had been for them to rebuild that terrible, imposing fortress. They had also been ordered to strip away any reminders of the Coven, such as the five-pointed star.

Not an easy task, Geldon thought. He squinted, trying to see the remains of the once-great structure. *It will be interesting to see what they have done.*

As they approached the Recluse, Geldon could not help but be reminded of his life of servitude there. He also thought of the coming of Tristan and Wigg to find Shailiha, who had been kidnapped and subverted by the Coven. Tristan had regained his sister, but he had lost his son. Geldon looked down at the moat surrounding the island and took a deep breath, making a decision.

Geldon waved to Baktar. The leader of the Minions nodded back, coming to fly alongside the dwarf's litter.

"Drop us at the outside of the Recluse, near the moat!" Geldon shouted to him. "And then go on ahead without us! Please tell Traax that we will join him shortly!"

Baktar nodded. "As you wish!" he shouted back. With that he indicated to the warriors flying the litters of the consul and the dwarf that they should descend.

After a gentle landing, the dwarf and consul climbed out of their litters and, on rather shaky legs, watched the four warriors fly back up to join their brothers. The entire group wheeled around to fly over the broken walls and down into the midst of the Recluse.

"Why are we here, outside of the palace walls?" Joshua asked as he rearranged his robes. "I thought you wanted to meet with Traax."

"I do. That's what we ultimately came here for. But there is something I feel should be done first." Geldon's dark eyes searched the ground around the moat. "Walk with me," he said to the consul.

The walk around the perimeter of the island took some time. Finally the dwarf saw what he was looking for. He began walking toward it, the flood of memories from that day coming back to him in a strangely reassuring torrent of both grief and joy.

The little grave lay undisturbed. The many stones still lay peacefully atop it, and a crudely carved marker of wood overlooked the spot. It was the grave of Nicholas, the unborn son of Tristan and Succiu.

Geldon looked down to the rough-hewn wooden marker, reading the words Tristan had carved there.

NICHOLAS II OF THE HOUSE OF GALLAND
You will not be forgotten

Not far from here, according to Tristan, Succiu had jumped from the castle walls, killing herself and the unborn child she carried. Tristan had excised the corpse from her womb to bury it, and Wigg had burned the second mistress' body, to ash. Nothing whatsoever of her was left now, and the thought did not sadden him in the least. Finally, he turned to the consul.

"I have a thought," he said tentatively. "It might be rather extreme, but—"

"To unearth the child and return his body with us to Eutracia for a proper burial with the royals and the Directorate," Joshua said softly, finishing his sentence for him. "That is what you were thinking, is it not?"

"Yes," Geldon answered, returning his gaze sadly back to the little grave. "How did you know?"

"Because it has been in my mind also, ever since the Chosen One asked us to come here," Joshua answered. "Wigg told me the story, and he also believes it to be Tristan's wish to eventually bury his son in Eutracia." He paused for a moment, thinking. "But I have my misgivings," he finally added.

"And they are?" Geldon asked.

"This child was Tristan's, not yours or mine. The decision to do such a thing, and also the timing of it, should therefore be his and his alone." Joshua looked into the dwarf's eyes with a candor and simplicity of purpose that Geldon found hard to contradict.

"I suppose you're right," the dwarf finally said. He took a deep, resigned breath. "We should be getting to the Recluse. Traax will be waiting."

Joshua peered around, as if looking for something. "Just a moment," he said cryptically. He spied some orange and yellow flowers on a nearby bank and pointed his right hand at them. The stems obediently pulled their roots from the ground. Narrowing his eyes, Joshua caused the roots to be cut away. The colorful blossoms floated over to the grave, hovered there for a moment, and finally dropped gently down on the cairn.

"Thank you," Geldon said, finding it difficult to speak.

Placing his hands into the opposite sleeves of his robe, Joshua nodded. "Tristan is now my friend, too," he said quietly.

Turning away from the grave, the dwarf and the consul began walking toward the massive wood and iron drawbridge that would carry them over the moat and onto the island, into the scarred, broken castle known as the Recluse.

They have done well here, Geldon thought. They had traversed the great drawbridge, passed through the first portcullis, and were approaching the second. The partial rebuild of the castle could be seen rising within the center of the spacious courtyard.

Every sign of the Pentangle, the five-pointed star of the Coven, had been dutifully eradicated. The Minions had completely cleared away much of the original structure, though light blue marble had again been chosen as the Recluse's color. The first floor was almost completed, and the circular towers at each of the corners were starting to take shape. The arched windows that would eventually hold heavy, leaded glass could be seen here and there in the walls.

Walking up the marble steps and into the open, still roofless expanses of the first floor, Geldon and Joshua were amazed at the level of activity here. The Minions were swarming over the place like a giant gathering of committed worker bees.

Seemingly thousands of them came and went, many of them shouting orders. The officers, Geldon presumed. Some of them gathered to huddle over drawings laid on crude wooden tables. Others carefully cut and fashioned marble, the dust from their labors flying into the air and occasionally choking off their breath. Still others had the tedious job of using pulleys and ropes to lift and place the magnificent stones into position. Light blue marble dust, noise, sweat, and the groans of physical labor filled the evening air. Some of the workers were lighting torches, to allow the work to continue throughout the night.

The warriors took little notice of Geldon and Joshua. The dwarf was unbothered by this. He realized that of the hundreds of thousands of their total population, many of them here would not know him. Then, he finally saw the Minion women.

He was greatly surprised to see Minion women among the workers. He had never seen one before. Until Tristan had commanded that the brothels be opened, and the women be allowed to take an equal place in Minion society, the females had been strictly relegated to the services of the males. Now they worked alongside the men, seeming quite sure of themselves in their new tasks. Only their awkward gaits—due to the deformities caused by foot binding—remained as a legacy of their previous cruel treatment. Geldon was pleased to see that, according to the prince's orders, none of their feet were bound.

Continuing up another flight of steps to what would eventually become the great foyer, the dwarf and the consul finally saw Baktar and Traax in huddled conversation, bent over a series of drawings.

Baktar saw them first and immediately went down on one knee. "I live to serve," he said solemnly. Quickly turning, Traax looked hard at the dwarf and the consul, wariness in his expression. For a torturous moment the dwarf felt an acidic sense of panic rise in his chest, as he wondered whether the younger, more aggressive second in command would honor the representatives of the Chosen One. Finally Traax also went to his knee. "I live to serve," his deep voice said with authority.

Trying to regain his composure, Geldon silently let out a long breath. *So far so good,* he thought. "You may rise," he commanded. As Traax stood, Geldon examined him. After Tristan had beheaded the previous commander of the Minions, Traax had been first to fly to the prince and lay down his sword, thereby retaining his position as second in command.

Unlike most of the warriors here, Traax was clean-shaven. He was approximately thirty Seasons of New Life—the same age as Tristan—and was tall and strong, even for a Minion warrior, with serious green eyes and an intensely commanding presence. Geldon knew him to be of very high intelligence. The dwarf would only get one chance to do this right; he must choose his words carefully.

"The Chosen One has sent me and this other emissary to secure your report." He indicated the consul. "This is Joshua, Prince Tristan's representative of the craft. Is there somewhere we might sit?"

"Of course," Traax answered perfunctorily. He led them to a tent with chairs and a table beneath it. "Would you like food and drink?" he asked, removing his dreggan from his side and laying it on the table. Baktar, Geldon, and Joshua all sat down.

"Yes," Geldon answered, the mention of food making him realize his hunger.

Traax waved one of his hands, and a Minion woman came over to the table and stood, waiting for Traax to speak. Neither her posture nor her attitude seemed subservient.

"Bring us food and wine," Traax said abruptly. He glanced at Geldon and then turned his face up more courteously to the woman. "Please," he added quietly. Despite the importance of this meeting, Geldon found it difficult to contain a smile.

The changes must be so hard for them, he realized. A Minion warrior would never have been required to say please to anyone other than the Coven, and now the sorceresses were all dead. The Minions' entire world had been turned upside down, and he would do well to remember that.

He had a job to do, though. "Your report?" he asked Traax.

"As you can see, the rebuilding of the Recluse goes well," Traax began. "I estimate that the entire structure should be finished in approximately one year's time. In addition the brothels have been closed and the Minion women freed. As the Chosen One gave us permission to marry, there have already been many unions. Birth records are now being kept. The Gallipolai have also been freed. Neither the Minion females nor the Gallipolai will ever have their wings clipped again. Foot binding also no longer occurs." He stopped for a moment, smiling. "It will be interesting trying to teach them to fly when their wings recover from the clipping," he added drily. Then his face became more serious. "There are, however, other concerns in the land that do not fare as well."

"And those are?" Geldon asked, placing a critical expression upon his face, as if suddenly disappointed.

"Since the death of the Coven, strange things have happened," Traax answered. "We have been plagued by the sudden, unexplained appearance of the swamp shrews. They raid the land constantly, taking refuge in the depths of the many lakes and ponds that have so mysteriously appeared. I have formed groups of shrew slayers to try to kill as many of them as we can."

Geldon looked up to see that the food had come. Two Minions, a man and a woman, began to put it on the table. It looked to be wild Parthalonian boar served on a great rotating spit, with fresh vegetables and dark brown bread from the Minion hearths. He inhaled the aromas with anticipation.

The Minion woman, a particularly beautiful and statuesque being, smiled at Joshua. As she placed some of the food on the table, her long, dark hair brushed the young consul's face. Geldon was sure that it had been no accident. Joshua turned beet red, shifting uncomfortably in his chair. Both Baktar and Traax broke out into raucous laughter.

"Beware!" Traax said. "The fact that they now have their freedom has emboldened them. It has become their custom to—how should I put this?—make sure a man is 'capable,' before considering him as a husband. And by the look of you, I'm not sure that you could stand the strain—craft or no craft!" The two Minion warriors guffawed again as the woman walked away. Baktar actually went so far as to heartily slap the hapless consul upon the back, making him cough. Geldon considered rebuking Traax for his comments but finally decided not to push his luck.

Besides, Geldon thought, watching the stately, commanding woman walk away, *he's probably right.*

In a moment she was gone. Joshua turned his wide eyes to the dwarf, sighed, and then began to eat. After several bites of the excellent food, Geldon returned his attention to the Minion second in command.

"Tell me about the state of the civilian population," Geldon said, taking a sip of deep, rich wine. "I have seen few of the locals since I arrived. I assume it is because of the shrews."

Traax's face darkened again, and Geldon could see that the news would not be good. "The people are terrified of the shrews, and are afraid to venture far from home. But also, the population has yet to trust us," he said, "despite the death of the Coven. And I cannot say that I blame them. We have done all we can to try to earn both their trust and respect. But with the task of rebuilding the Recluse and hunting the shrews taking so much of our time, it has been difficult."

As if reading the dwarf's mind, Traax asked, "Is there anything our new lord can do to help? I feel that the presence of the Chosen One and his wizards, no matter how brief, would go far. Especially where the civilians are concerned. The Minions are strong and brave. But we are not accustomed to practicing politics, or solving national concerns. In these matters we need help."

Geldon found himself actually beginning to like Traax. "We will convey your needs to the prince," he said compassionately. "But you must understand that there is a great deal in his own nation that needs attention just now. Your legions did much to destroy Eutracia, and his first concern must lie there."

He decided to change the subject. "I have been told by Rufus, your commander at the Ghetto, that the armada you used to invade Eutracia still lies intact at Eyrie Point. Is this true?"

"Yes," Baktar replied in between bites of the delicious pig. "The fleet is sound, and its captains have been given other duties. Does the Chosen One have need of it?"

"I do not know," Geldon replied. "Nor is it for me to say. But I believe both he and the wizards will be glad to hear it."

"There is an issue of which I would now like to speak," Joshua said suddenly. Traax and Baktar turned quizzical eyes on him, waiting. "You are familiar with the Minion warrior named Ox?" the consul asked.

Traax smiled. "Yes. Although not quick of wit, he is one of the most loyal of us."

"I would like to take him back to Eutracia with us," Joshua said. The sudden, unexpected words hung over the table like a cloud, and everything went silent.

Geldon tried not to show surprise. *I hope he knows what he's doing,* he thought nervously.

Traax scowled. "May we be made aware of your reasons for this request?" he asked darkly.

"He was wounded during the capture of the shrew," Joshua answered.

"That is your reason?" Traax asked with a snort. "Because of a simple wound? The Minions have seen many wounds, and we have always dealt with them ourselves. Fighting, dying, and being wounded are the very reasons for our existence!" Then he glanced over at Geldon, wondering if he had misspoken. "Or at least that used to be our mission," he added.

"But his is not a simple wound," Joshua answered. "The entire foot is severed. I enchanted both the foot and the end of the leg immediately after the attack to preserve them. If we return Ox to Eutracia, the Chosen One's wizards may be able to reattach the foot."

Traax's mouth opened slightly in awe. "You can do such a thing?" he asked softly.

"No," Joshua answered simply. "My powers do not extend to such realms. But there are others of the craft across the sea who may be able to accomplish it."

Traax waved a hand in the air. A Minion officer promptly appeared, clicking the heels of his boots together. "Send for the one called Ox," Traax ordered.

"I live to serve," came the quick reply. The warrior ran off.

Ox appeared several minutes later, limping along on a crudely made crutch. The strange, azure glow of the craft continued to surround the base of his footless leg.

"I live to serve," he said, trying to go down on the knee of his good leg and causing himself obvious pain.

Geldon winced as he watched the warrior try to assume the traditional Minion position of servitude, and he temporarily considered commanding him to desist. But Traax stepped in at that point.

"That will not be necessary," he said. Ox straightened to a standing position, leaning heavily on his crutch, and Geldon realized the devoted Minion would have stood there that way all night if ordered to.

"These emissaries of our new lord wish to take you with them back to Eutracia. It is possible they may be able to heal your foot. Would you like to do that?" Traax asked.

Geldon could see Ox struggling with the concept of healing a severed limb, but the Minion finally responded. "If you send, I go," he said crudely, his deep, resonant voice matching the power so evident in his body.

"Very well." Traax nodded, turning his attention to the consul. "But I have a request."

Joshua put down his goblet as if annoyed, then looked Traax squarely in the eyes. "That depends," he said. "The Chosen One is not used to demands."

Geldon froze, watching the unexpected test of wills. *The consul is perhaps far more brave than I gave him credit for,* he realized. *He learns quickly, just as Wigg said.*

Joshua rather rudely took his eyes from Traax and returned to eating. "What is it?" he asked, fork poised before his mouth.

"That should Ox die in your land he be given the right of any Minion warrior. That his body be burned, his ashes scattered."

Joshua looked up for a moment, considering the request. "Done," he said.

"Very well, then," Geldon interjected, wanting to regain

control of the conversation. "It is decided. We will stay here for several more days. I wish to watch the reconstruction of the Recluse unfold further." Smiling, he turned to look at the young consul. "And perhaps Joshua would like to become better acquainted with the young woman who just served us," he added coyly. While everyone else at the table laughed, Joshua only scowled, and turned bright red.

Geldon looked at Ox and wondered what the wizards would say when out of the portal came not only a consul and hunchbacked dwarf, but also a wounded Minion warrior. He smiled slightly to himself.

May the Afterlife have a sense of humor, he thought.

CHAPTER TWENTY-TWO

RAGNAR turned over luxuriously in his bed to gaze into the eyes of the woman he had just brutally taken—the one who had for so long been his favorite. He had brought a great many females here over the centuries and continued to do so, usually letting them go after he had taken his pleasure from them. Sometimes he held them for days, sometimes for years, depending upon how much they pleased him. But none of them had been the quality of the one he now regarded.

This one he had selfishly kept, her time enchantments allowing them to lie together in perpetuity, here in this place that was both his prison and his sanctuary.

In truth it had not been his idea to grant the time enchantments to the magnificent creature lying beside him, he knew. He had been ordered to.

Ragnar gloated over how differently things had evolved from the way they had been planned all those years ago. If the one who had ordered the time enchantments placed upon the woman were here now, Ragnar would surely be dead, rather than praised or thanked.

Smiling to himself, he thought of how lucky he had been. How the synchronicity of events had woven itself into an amazing, colorful tapestry of revenge that was finally coming to fruition. The finished product would soon be taken from the loom, as it were, and put to his use.

"You shall leave me now, my sweet," he said to her, almost gently. "For there are things to which I must attend." She slowly rose from the bed, not looking at him as she put on her silk robe.

Reaching to the bedside table, Ragnar placed a finger into the vial of yellow brain fluid and licked it hungrily, feeling the familiar, comforting heat go through him. Slowly he turned back to the curvaceous beauty.

"Did I make you happy this time?" he asked, knowing what her answer would be.

She was still standing with her back to him, shivering.

"No," she said. "You disgust me, and you always shall." She paused for a moment, lowering her head in shame.

"Even if you take me for yet another three centuries, my answer will remain the same," she said wearily. "My only blessing is that your madness and addiction have made it impossible for you to leave me with child." She finally turned to him, her eyes brimming with hate, her hands clenched into tight fists. "I would rather die than carry the abomination of your seed within my womb."

Had Ragnar been near enough, he would have reached out to strike her. But as it was he simply lay back upon the sheets, lazily tasting another drop of the precious fluid. He leered at her.

"Rest assured, my dear," he told her, "that we have centuries of this bliss still lying before us."

"May I take my leave now?" she half begged, half demanded.

"The Chosen One and Wigg will be here within hours. I wish for you to be present when they face us," Ragnar said unexpectedly, enjoying the sudden look of surprise upon her face. He smiled wickedly. "It is important to me that they both see you."

"Why?" she asked. "I do not know who they are or why they have come. How could my attendance make any possible difference?" She had never been a part of his plans before, and his suddenly wanting her there now perplexed and frightened her.

Ragnar rose from the bed, walking naked to where she stood. She cringed. Reaching out, he grasped her face with one hand and then quickly backhanded her with the other, forcing her to her knees. She reeled drunkenly for a moment near the floor. She slowly stood again, hate flashing in her eyes.

"My poor sweet," the blood stalker said softly. "There is still so much you do not know. So much that you most probably will never know. But be there you shall, or I shall give you to Scrounge for his amusement. I don't wish to share you, and I never have, but if that is what it takes to make you obedient, then so be it."

Tears running down her cheeks, she lowered her head. She had long seen the way Scrounge looked at her, and she cowered at the thought of being made his plaything, as well.

"Very well," she whispered. "I will do as you say."

"Of course you will." Ragnar smiled, his bloodshot eyes and long teeth twinkling in the soft light of the room. "And you always shall. Go to your chambers and put on your finest dress—the green one, I think. You will be called for."

Without speaking further she walked to the door, then opened it and went through. Smiling, the blood stalker returned to the vial, tasting the fluid. At last he dressed, also donning the golden wizard's dagger that been owned by Wigg so long ago.

Soon now, Wigg, Ragnar thought to himself. *Soon.*

"They are close," Nicholas said softly, his dark blue, up-tilted eyes registering a smile. "Both the lead wizard and the Chosen One. I can already feel the pestilence of their blood. I have seen to it that each of them is unconscious, and that fits our needs perfectly."

Nicholas was wearing his simple white robe, sitting in one of three highly polished marble thrones of the deepest blue. The azure glow radiating from him flooded the stone chamber, overpowering any light from the large oil chandelier hanging from the center of the ceiling. The room was sumptuous, the floor and ceiling of palest green marble.

Ragnar gazed at the young man. Nicholas had grown again since Ragnar had last seen him. He now appeared to be at least fifteen Seasons of New Life. His dark, shiny black hair fell to his shoulders, and his high cheekbones, exotic eyes, and firm jaw were becoming more reminiscent of his parents with each passing day.

Beside him, on a white marble altar, sat the Tome, its pages open.

Why would he bring the book here? Ragnar wondered. *Surely he cannot want the wizard and the Chosen One to have it.*

"Oh, but I do," Nicholas said softly. "I wish the wizard and the Chosen One to take the Tome with them. It is, after all, what they came for. It seems the least we can do." He smiled.

"And for reasons beyond your simple understanding, the Tome is now of more use to us in their hands than in ours," the young man continued. "Besides, I have already read it. I told you not long ago that I would eventually have need for neither the Tome nor the Paragon, that ridiculous bauble of jewelry they all prize so highly. I already no longer need the book. And soon the stone will have no significance for me, either."

Ragnar and Scrounge were stunned. They looked at each other and then back at the young man on the throne.

"I do not understand," Ragnar said. "Will the Tome not help them?"

"Nothing can help them now," Nicholas answered. "The wheels have been set into motion, and there is no return—for any of us."

Ragnar turned to look at the great book. Covered with shiny, finely tooled white leather, its pages gilt-edged, the Tome of the Paragon was so enormous that it would have taken at least two strong men to carry it. The weakened wizard and prince would never be able to do it—Ragnar was sure of it. More puzzled than ever, he turned his attention back to Nicholas.

"Do not worry about how they are to carry the Tome back

with them," Nicholas said from his throne. "I will employ a secret method of transportation for the book. Do not be alarmed when this happens. Wigg will surely recognize the incantation for what it is, and believe that it was you who accomplished it. They will be skeptical, of course, that you wish them to have it. But in the end they will take the book—of that you can be sure. I will be in hiding, but within earshot. For I do not yet wish to reveal myself to the Chosen One." Nicholas' eyes narrowed; his lips turned up in a sneer. "That will come later, at a more opportune time. But I do wish to hear the voice of the one who dares call himself my father."

Ragnar stood silently, wondering what the young man had planned.

"Both the wizard and the Chosen One have been bled by my wraiths," Nicholas added. "Although their strength will eventually return, they will be of no immediate danger to you. In addition, a chalice of the prince's blood is being brought here with them. It is to be taken to your quarters for safekeeping until such time as I shall call for it." He lowered his head slightly, leaning forward to look into the stalker's mutated face. "The azure blood of the Chosen One is of the utmost importance. You are to guard it with your life. Should one drop be spilled, your existence is forfeit. Slowly and painfully."

"Yes, my lord," Ragnar said nervously.

Nicholas sat back in his throne. "In addition, there are other things you must know before the arrival of the wizard and the prince," he went on. "First of all, the hatchlings that bring them here are not like the ones you are accustomed to. These are representative of the second generation of my work, and are capable of both thought and speech. In addition, these hatchlings carry weapons. These are but three of the developing birds you witnessed that day in the catacombs, all of which are now fully mature. They number in the tens of thousands and gather in camps to the north, awaiting my command. Do not be alarmed at the appearance of these three hatchlings, for they are both your allies and your servants." Ragnar and Scrounge shook their heads in wonder.

"I need the hatchlings because there is to be a great conflict," Nicholas whispered. "In the firmament, as well as upon the land. The Tome ordains it, but makes no mention of its outcome. It is this, coupled with my plans for the Chosen One, that give us the opportunity to reshape the Prophecies to our liking." He paused for a moment, thinking, his eyes glistening with the power of the craft. "But the reasons for my capture of the consuls are mine, to be revealed to you only at the proper time."

"My lord, may I ask a question?" Ragnar asked.

Nicholas nodded silently. "You are about to ask me of the azure vein that runs so brightly through the walls of this place, are you not?"

"Yes, my lord," Ragnar answered.

"To this I will deign to respond, for the wizard Wigg will have already witnessed it, and will no doubt have discerned the answer for himself. The power you see within the vein is coming from the Paragon itself. Its entire dynamism is being transferred to this place, to be stored. It is slowly being imparted into me a little at a time—for even I cannot absorb all of its majesty at once. Think of it, if your feeble mind will allow. The stone, which empowers *all* of those trained in the craft, is now instilling its power into just *one* being. Myself. As I once told you, I shall eventually have no need for the Paragon. For the Paragon, as it were, will be inside me. Within my blood, and mine alone." Nicholas paused for a moment, letting the import of his words sink in.

"This draining of the stone is the reason for my rapidly advancing growth and wisdom," he continued softly. "My reading of the Tome has enhanced this process, and was one of the reasons I took refuge here, below ground. I will eventually have unquestionable authority over the craft, both the Vigors and the Vagaries, at the same time leaving all the other endowed of Eutracia quite powerless. As this occurs, the stone slowly dies. Wigg will believe Ragnar to be the cause. He will have many questions, some of which it will be to our advantage to answer.

"Taking the power of the stone for myself is not the ultimate goal, just one more step in the total endeavor," Nicholas went on. "There is still so much you do not know. But you eventually shall."

"Will I therefore not also begin to lose my powers as the stone fades?" Ragnar asked nervously. "For my abilities of the craft are tied to the stone, as well. I have already felt a minuscule loss in my powers, but could not imagine the cause."

"Have no fear in that regard," Nicholas answered. "For reasons you do not yet understand, I have chosen you as my servant. And as my servant, you shall retain your powers."

Smiling, Nicholas closed his eyes for a moment. "Your woman," he asked Ragnar. "She will of course attend?"

"Yes, my lord."

"And she is still completely unaware of my existence?"

"Again, yes."

"Good," Nicholas said, his eyes still closed. "I have approved of the revenge you have planned for the wizard. I find it uniquely fitting. And Scrounge knows of my personal instructions regarding the prince. But it is ironic, don't you agree, that your woman should be included here today? I can think of no better revenge than that which you are already taking. And still they will have no concept of its importance. Nor will they after they have left us, and you continue to take her. A true treat for the body as well as the mind, is it not?"

"Indeed, my lord." Ragnar smiled wickedly. He again touched the never-healing wound at the side of his head. *Soon, Wigg,* he thought. *Soon you will stand before me. And I will have my revenge.*

Turning his head, Nicholas smiled. "I can sense they are near," he said quietly. "Make ready."

CHAPTER TWENTY-THREE

*T*HEY'RE back!" Shailiha exclaimed happily to Faegan. "They have reached the last portal!"

They were together on the balcony, watching as a veritable cloud of giant butterflies circled the large, black marble door at the bottom of the atrium.

"Well done, my dear," the wizard said, and he meant it. Closing his eyes, he commanded the massive black door to open, and the twelve handpicked fliers shot into the great room in a stream of rainbow colors. Quickly he caused the door to close again, sealing the atrium from the tunnel that led to the outside world.

"Bring them up," he said quietly to the princess.

Shailiha looked down to the fliers. Almost immediately the squadron of special butterflies soared to the brass rail at her left and perched there quietly, the twenty-four beautiful, diaphanous wings opening and closing silently.

She has done it! Faegan thought, amazed. *She has successfully sent her first group of fliers out of the Redoubt. And they have returned at her command, finding their way back through the tunnels perfectly.*

He had not yet explained to Shailiha his suspicions that her power was the result of an Incantation of Forestallment. He needed more time to absorb all the information contained in the long, detailed scroll that had been left by Egloff: Consummate recollection, unfortunately, did not automatically grant consummate understanding. He was quite aware of the fact that Forestallments had heretofore only been the stuff of myth and legend, and to put such a concept before Wigg and the others required that he be absolutely sure.

But he was becoming more convinced by the moment that this was the result of an event-activated Forestallment, rather than a time-activated one. And the more he saw her with them, the more convinced of it he became. He postulated that it had been the princess' first physical contact with the butterflies that had initiated it. Even she did not know how it was that she had suddenly been able to do such a thing. To the wizard, this provided even more evidence for his theory. And he now also had a very good idea who had created the forestallment.

The second reason that he had not yet discussed his theories with the princess was because he preferred to explain his discovery to everyone at once. He would therefore wait until the prince and wizard returned to the Redoubt with the Tome of the Paragon. *If indeed they ever return,* he thought worriedly.

Tristan and Wigg had already been gone too long. It should not have taken them so much time to retrieve the Tome and come back to the Redoubt unless they were in trouble, and the likelihood of just such an occurrence increased with every moment. Given the immense power of whoever was draining the Paragon, he shuddered to think of the forces they might be up against.

With a scowl, he reached down and gathered his robe more closely about his feet, as if by doing so he might also be able to cover up his shame at not succeeding in healing his own legs of the damage done to them by the Coven. If he'd had the use of his legs, he'd have gone with Wigg and Tristan, and perhaps they all would have been there and back again by now.

Still, he was determined to move ahead where he could. He had spent the last two days hurriedly trying to explore the inner workings of Shailiha's amazing talents with the fliers, yet explaining relatively little to her. Much to his delight, her progress had been dramatic. She no longer trembled or perspired when bonding with the butterflies, and her ability to communicate with them seemed to improve with every moment.

To his mind this had become vital, for there was no one else left in the Redoubt to do his reconnoitering for him. Joshua and Geldon had not yet returned from their trip to

Parthalon. And although he had not expressed his concerns to the princess, to his mind Tristan and Wigg should now be presumed missing.

Shannon had returned with the horses, and had also told him of their seeing Scrounge, the captured consuls, and the hatchlings. But despite Shannon's loyalty, the wizard still dared not use the gnome as his other pair of eyes. The appearance of a gnome among the already frightened population could cause more potential harm than good.

The fliers were now the only choice the wizard had to discover what was happening in the world above, and he felt it imperative he teach both the butterflies and the princess how to exit and enter the Redoubt on their own.

As if reading his mind, Shailiha asked, "How is it that the butterflies are able to move the boulder that guards the end of the tunnel, and release themselves into the outside world?" As her talents with the fliers had progressed, so had her thirst for knowledge.

Faegan smiled. "Wigg and I had to change the spells on the boulders and the radiance stones so that they can now be empowered without the aid of endowed blood. We are not altogether happy about it, but it had to be in case one of the unendowed now living here needed quick entrance or exit." He looked down at the butterflies as they chased happily around the great room. "The fliers need only to touch the roof of the tunnel to enact the radiance stones, and again touch the boulder that hides the entrance to the other end to open the exit. Just as Geldon does when he goes into town. It is only the large black door at the bottom of the aviary that they fliers cannot move by their own powers. I insisted on that for reasons of security when I constructed the aviary. I was in the process of teaching them how to enter and exit the end of the tunnel by themselves when we first became acquainted with your particular abilities.

"Now then," the wizard said, "let's try again."

Shailiha turned to the twelve fliers on the brass rail next to her. *Tell me,* she thought, concentrating. *Outside of this place, is it night or is it day?*

And then came the familiar voice to her mind—what she now knew to be the combination of all twelve voices at once.

It is night, Mistress, she heard.

Tell the wizard, also, she silently ordered. *For he cannot hear you in his mind as I can.*

Immediately five of the fliers fluttered down to the black alphabet wheel, landing gently, one by one upon the letters. N-I-G-H-T.

"And what was your question?" Faegan asked her.

"Whether it was night or day outside."

"Very good." Faegan smiled. "Time for a different kind of test." He crooked the index finger of his right hand, indicating that the princess lower her face to his. Whispering into her ear, he said, "Do not forget that they understand what is communicated to them verbally, at least by you and me; I doubt they would understand anyone of unendowed blood. I will whisper my question to you, so that they may not hear it. Ask them to spell their answer, rather than communicate it to your mind."

Faegan thought for a moment, then whispered, "Ask them where they came from, before being brought to the Redoubt. It should prove interesting, and their answer might tell us much." Shailiha turned her intelligent, hazel eyes once more to the fliers and concentrated.

Tell me the name of the place where you lived, before coming here, to the Redoubt, she thought.

For a moment the butterflies upon the wheel hesitated. Their great wings stopped opening and closing, a sight seldom seen. Uncharacteristically, it was as if they were having trouble deciding on the correct answer. Finally they leapt into the air; several others joined them, and they landed again on some of the letters. S-H-A-D-O-W-O-O-D.

Shailiha turned to the wizard and was about to speak when Faegan placed his index finger across his lips, indicating silence. Smiling and bouncing his eyebrows up and down in delight, he pointed back down to the butterflies. They had taken to the air, and they now alit on another group of letters. A-N-D E-U-T-R-A-C-I-A.

"Ah-ha!" Faegan chuckled, obviously pleased. "Well done!"

"They did it!" Shailiha exclaimed. But the look in Faegan's amazing, prankish eyes told her that she had not yet grasped the entirety of what had just happened.

"There were two reasons for my particular question," he said slyly. "Can you tell me what they were?"

Shailiha thought for a moment. "You wanted to know whether they could hear you if you whispered," she said triumphantly. "They apparently could not, for they did not respond until I asked them with my mind."

"Yes," Faegan agreed. "What was my other reason?"

Shailiha thought hard. Finally, and without the wizard's permission, she looked down to the fliers still perched upon the letters and silently commanded one to come to her. The large yellow-and-violet flier, the one that had become her favorite, launched itself from the alphabet wheel and landed on her outstretched arm. The princess stood there, lost within the moment, and then smiled. "They remember," she said.

She has truly become their master, Faegan realized. *Even more so than I.*

"Please explain," he said calmly.

"Not only did they tell us where they lived until being brought here, but they also named Eutracia, their original home of three centuries ago. This means that they not only relate to the present, but also to the past, as well." She turned back to the butterfly, obviously communicating with it. Then she looked at Faegan. "They can recall as far back as the day that they ingested the waters of the Caves, when they first became endowed." She turned her hazel eyes to him, confident in her newfound knowledge. "This is significant," she said with understated authority.

Indeed, Faegan thought. *"And the Chosen One shall come, but will be preceded by another,"* he remembered. The ages-old quote from the Tome rang out just as clearly in his mind now as it had the first time he had read it. *The female—the twin to the male. Had the Coven succeeded in keeping her as their fifth sorceress, she would have been unstoppable.*

"Faegan," the princess asked, "I know these creatures belong to you, but would you mind it terribly if I named this one?" The yellow-and-violet flier continued to perch quietly upon her arm, its wings opening and closing gracefully as it kept its balance.

"The fliers belong to no one," Faegan answered compassionately. "I am only their guardian."

"Do you know which of them are the males and which are the females?" she asked, pursing her lips coyly. The wizard got the distinct impression that she was toying with him, as if she knew something that he did not.

"I never really thought about it," he admitted. "For all of these years I have not had a need to know."

Shailiha turned back to the flier on her arm. "This one is female," she said. "She just told me."

The wizard shook his head. "Of course," he answered. "And your name for her?"

"Caprice," Shailiha answered softly.

Faegan smiled. "Very well. Caprice it is." Then he grew serious.

"There is a matter of which we must now speak," he said. "Would you please release Caprice, so that I may discuss it with you?"

The princess shook her arm slightly, and the giant butterfly took flight. After twice circling the princess' head, it flew down to the lower area of the atrium, rejoining the others.

Shailiha turned back to Faegan.

"I am very worried about Tristan and Wigg," he said as compassionately as he knew how. "They should have been back by now." He paused for a moment, the sudden worry on Shailiha's face stabbing him in the heart. "I fear they may be in danger."

She bit her lower lip, and then a stronger, more determined look surfaced on her delicate features. Drawing a deep, resolute breath, she asked, "Do you have any idea what kind of trouble this may be?"

"No," Faegan responded. "I only know that in my heart I believe they should have been back before now. And I also believe we need to take whatever action on their behalf we can."

The princess did not speak as she weighed her very limited options. Finally she turned back to the wizard. "You want me to send the fliers out looking for them, don't you?" she asked. "And you also want me to use my newfound gift to stay in touch with them as they go."

"Yes," Faegan answered. "Just a few of them. It is now night, and they should be safe, provided they fly high enough and return before dawn. I do not want them out and about in the Eutracian countryside during the light of day. The simple, unendowed citizens would love nothing better than to capture one of these amazing creatures of myth." Another thought came to him. "It will also give us valuable information regarding your bond with the fliers," he said.

"How so?"

"Since this will be the first time they have traveled any appreciable distance outside the Redoubt, we will be able to discern the range of your abilities. It should prove interesting."

"Yes," Shailiha said softly. "Unless they are captured, or die in the attempt . . ."

Knowing she was quite right, he let the statement stand. He could tell how much it hurt her to release the precious butterflies from the safety of the Redoubt, but he also knew that her love for her brother and Wigg surpassed that fear.

"Very well," she said. "Tell me what to do."

"Thank you," Faegan said. "And don't forget: I love them, too. Call Caprice back up."

Shailiha raised her arm, silently calling the giant butterfly to her. Almost immediately Caprice left the ground, flying happily back to the arm of her mistress.

Faegan remained amazed at her abilities with the fliers. Though still untrained, she possessed a power that even he did not have.

"I am going to give her spoken commands," Faegan said. "This way we shall both know what is expected of them." He turned to look at the delicate creature on Shailiha's arm. "Pick five others of your kind, and exit the Redoubt," he said gently. "Fly to the west, high in the sky, and try to get as close to the Caves as you can. But do not enter. Be careful to avoid all other forms of life, especially human. I wish you to communicate as best you can with your mistress, informing her at regular intervals if you see what it is I am sending you in search of. However, under no circumstances are you to fly so far that you are unable to return to the tunnels by dawn. This is paramount. You are searching for the prince and the wizard Wigg. If you see them you are to inform your mistress at once, and immediately return to the Redoubt. Open and close your wings twice if you understand."

Caprice's diaphanous wings gently folded together once, then twice.

"She understands," the princess said. Raising her arm, Shailiha released the flier into the air. "Good-bye, Caprice," she said softly. The giant butterfly circled Shailiha's head, then fluttered down to the others. Five of them separated from the group and then followed Caprice toward the door of black marble, waiting for the wizard to release them into the tunnels.

As Faegan closed his eyes the great door of black marble swung open, and the fliers soared into the passageway. Just as quickly the wizard caused the door to close again, securing the room.

After a moment Shailiha turned to him, the concern plainly showing upon her face. "Will Tristan and Wigg be all right?" she asked hesitantly.

Faegan smiled, trying to raise her spirits. "Do not underestimate them. They are two particularly capable individuals, especially together. They went through much to find you and bring you back—more than you will probably ever know. If they did that, they can certainly negotiate their way home." He reached up to give both her hands a comforting squeeze, and she finally let go a little smile. Turning back to the atrium, the wizard looked down to the remaining butterflies as they careened about the room.

Unless they are both already dead, he thought.

CHAPTER TWENTY-FOUR

THERE was something cold and hard against Tristan's right cheek. He was lying on one side, and he squirmed a bit, trying to become more comfortable. All he wanted to do was sleep.

Then his tired, blood-deprived brain slowly began to work again, bringing him around, and he gingerly opened his eyes. His vision was crazily skewed, the vertical having traded places with the horizontal. As a result, nothing in the room was where it should have been.

And then he remembered the ghoulish consuls. With that also returned the memories of the wraiths and hatchlings. Then he and Wigg had been carried out over the azure, impossible sea.

Slowly, warily, he sat up, looking around. The room he was in was very large, with three dark blue marble thrones against one wall, the center one higher than the others. Perched on the right-hand arm of the center throne was a glass vial that contained some kind of yellow fluid. Chairs, tables, patterned rugs, and artwork tastefully adorned the room. The pale green marble of the walls, floor, and ceiling was of the finest quality. A huge oil chandelier hung from the center of the ceiling, giving off a soft, subdued light. Then, what he saw to the left of the thrones caused his jaw to drop in admiration. *The Tome of the Paragon!* his hazy mind told him. *It has to be!*

It lay on a white marble altar, its pages open. A white light shone down upon it from above.

The Tome was huge—far greater in size than Tristan had ever imagined it to be. At least a meter long and an equal distance in width, it was also at least half a meter thick. From his vantage point the prince could not see the tops of the pages, or the writing upon them. But he somehow knew that the words contained there would be tightly packed, with no wasted space. It was absolutely magnificent.

But how did Wigg expect them to remove it from the Caves and carry it all the way back to the Redoubt? he wondered. It looked as if it would take at least two strong men just to lift it.

Testing the weight across his right shoulder, he could tell that he still had all of his weapons. He tried to stand, but clumsily fell back to the marble floor, ending up half kneeling, half sitting. The cut was still there in his left boot, he noticed, and his foot still itched from the incantation of accelerated healing the wraith had placed upon him. He felt a cold sweat break out along the length of his brow.

It wasn't a dream.

He looked around for Wigg. The wizard lay curled up on the floor a little way from him. He appeared to be unconscious. Tristan crawled to the old one and tried to shake him awake. It did no good. Finally the prince began slapping the wizard across the face. Eventually Wigg slowly opened his eyes, and his breathing quickened. Tristan helped him to sit up.

"Where are we?" Wigg asked weakly. His aquamarine eyes were dim, his speech slurred.

"I don't know," Tristan answered. "Do you remember being bled by the wraiths?"

"Yes," Wigg said thickly.

"Are you in possession of your powers?" the prince asked anxiously.

Wigg closed his eyes for a moment, his face becoming dark. "They are minimal, at best," he answered sadly. "The loss of blood has been too great."

With some difficulty Tristan reached behind his right shoulder, taking one of his dirks into his hand. Knowing full well that he would never be able to handle the heavy dreggan, it was the only thing he could think of. He slid the throwing knife into the pocket of his trousers.

"They bled me also," he said. "They kept a portion of my blood, handing it to three hatchlings for safekeeping. I don't know why. Nothing makes sense here. And the hatchlings were not the same as the ones we saw before. They had arms and hands, and wore weapons. At least one of them could even speak. They picked us up and flew us across the sea."

"Can you stand?" Wigg asked.

"Not on my own. But perhaps we can help each other," Tristan answered.

The two of them struggled to their knees, each using the other for support. They finally stood upright on trembling legs in the center of the strange room.

"Welcome, Wigg and Chosen One," a deep, male voice suddenly said. "I have been waiting for you a very long time. Three hundred years, in fact."

Tristan and Wigg looked up to see someone standing on the other side of the room who had not been there before. His back was turned to them, and he wore a shiny, black, hooded robe. It was gathered at the waist by a golden belt, from which hung some kind of weapon. Looking closer, the prince could see that the back of the man's head was misshapen and bald; the grotesque, dangling earlobes were exceptionally long. The shiny skin of his head glistened eerily beneath the light of the chandelier.

From this angle he almost looks like a blood stalker, Tristan thought. *But blood stalkers cannot speak.* Reaching slowly into the pocket of his trousers, he ran his thumb along the blade of the dirk.

For the first time Tristan noticed the doorway in the right-hand wall near the thrones. And from that there came a glow—the most magnificent evidence of the craft he had ever seen. A chill ran up his spine.

Like a dense fog, the azure glow crept out of the hallway and across the floor of the chamber. Its power and density were such that he felt certain he could hold it in his hands.

"Wigg, lead wizard of the former Directorate," the strange-looking man suddenly said. "King maker, and protector of the Paragon. Onetime husband of Failee, the dear, departed first mistress of the Coven of sorceresses. And Prince Tristan, the male of the Chosen Ones. For whom the Directorate waited so long. Brash, impulsive, and said to possess the highest quality of endowed blood the world has ever known. Or ever will. However, despite his magnificent blood he is yet to be trained in the ways of the craft. How frustrating that must be. Nonetheless, welcome to you both. It is indeed an honor to be in the presence of such important guests." The man had still not turned around.

"Who are you?" Wigg shouted. "I demand to know why we are here!" He took a weak step forward.

Slowly, the man in the black robe turned around. Seeing the thing's face, Tristan thought he might be ill. He heard the breath leave Wigg's lungs in a rush, and he whirled to see the blood draining from his friend's face.

"Ragnar," Wigg finally breathed. "You're alive! This cannot be . . ."

The wizard clearly had no more words and just stood there, speechless before the monster in the black robe.

Tristan looked more closely at Ragnar. The shiny, bald head was elongated; the eyes were gray and bloodshot. Two long fangs ran down from the top row of teeth, overlapping the lower lip. An angry, oozing, unhealed wound could be seen in the right temple of his head, and his eyes glistened back at them with a madness that was sickeningly evident. A beautiful golden dagger hung from the belt at his left hip, contrasting sharply with the shiny black robe. He was an odd combination of both human and blood stalker, and the effect was chilling.

Walking away from them, the one called Ragnar turned and sat in the center throne.

"So many questions, aren't there, Wigg?" he asked sarcastically, settling himself into the great marble chair. "But before we begin, there are two others here I should like you to meet. First of all, my servant. Someone I believe the prince will be especially eager to see."

Tristan felt his blood rise as Scrounge sauntered into the room, the silver spurs on his boots ringing out loudly upon the marble floor. Once seated on the throne at Ragnar's left, he smirked nastily at Tristan. Remembering what Geldon had told them, the prince looked carefully at the tips of the arrows in the crossbow strapped to the man's right forearm. They were stained in yellow.

Tristan remembered the dead consul he had found outside the palace, and the parchment scroll so violently placed into the empty eye socket, containing the taunting, sick note the assassin had written in the victim's own blood. Tristan continued to stroke the blade of his hidden knife with his thumb.

"And now," Ragnar suddenly said, "for the finest prize of all. Please come in, my sweet, and meet our guests."

A woman walked into the room wearing an emerald green, floor-length gown.

"I present to you my . . . companion," Ragnar said slyly. "This is Celeste." He nodded, and slowly, gracefully, the woman turned.

Tristan froze, his heart racing wildly. The woman standing before him was the mysterious beauty he had rescued from suicide that night on the cliffs.

Her clothing was different, but it was the same woman. Of that there was no doubt. He took in the long, red hair that swooped down over the forehead, the brilliant, sapphire eyes almost hidden beneath it, and the hint of the cleft in her strong chin. His mind raced, searching for answers.

After looking first to the wizard, Celeste finally turned her eyes toward the prince. The color drained from her face, and her lovely red mouth opened partially in disbelief. Recomposing herself, though, she narrowed her eyes and very minutely shook her head once, indicating that she did not want him to speak of their previous meeting. Tristan gave a small nod of agreement. He looked away as Celeste seated herself on Ragnar's right.

A centuries-old hate evident in his eyes, Ragnar looked at Wigg. "So tell me, *Lead* Wizard," he asked sarcastically, "how does it feel to see me, your old friend, after all these years? I observe that you no longer have your wizard's tail. No matter. The Directorate is no more, anyway. It is my understanding that Failee herself took your tail from you. How appropriately disgraceful."

Wigg at last collected his thoughts.

"How is it that you live?" he demanded weakly of the blood stalker. "You were never granted time enchantments, because your transformation by the Coven happened before the enchantments were ever developed! You should be dead!"

"Oh, but I was granted the enchantments." Ragnar smiled. "And by someone you knew well. I have been waiting all of that time, here within these caves. Be that as it may, I am anxious to complete my business with you."

"And what would that business be?" Wigg asked.

"Several things, actually," Ragnar responded. "Not the least of which is to give you what you came for."

Wigg again seemed stunned, but recovered quickly. "And that is?" he asked skeptically.

"Why, the Tome, of course," Ragnar said. He dipped his right index finger into the vial of yellow fluid. Placing the fingertip into his mouth he closed his eyes for a moment, smiling again before reopening them. Tristan's sensibilities recoiled at the brazen vulgarity of it.

The three individuals in their thrones stared down on the prince and the wizard as the amazing radiance continued to flood the marble floor of the room. Tristan looked with hate into the ratlike eyes of Scrounge, and the assassin shot back an unafraid glare that each of them understood well. After a time, Wigg spoke again.

"You're addicted, aren't you?" he asked. "Tretiak and I believed that might happen. Especially if you survived long enough."

"Of course I am addicted, you conceited bastard!" Ragnar hissed back. "You had to realize that I would be! And still you did nothing! Not a single search party sent out to come and look for me!" He finally collected himself, settling back into his chair. "But all of that will be paid for in full today," he said more softly.

"We were unaware at the time you would become addicted. We had no way to know," Wigg said sadly, taking a step forward. With the wizard's unexpected movement, Scrounge raised the miniature crossbow slightly. Tristan curled his fingers around the knife in his pocket.

"It was only later, as our knowledge of the craft grew, that we realized what we had done," Wigg continued. "You must also know that the ingestion of your own brain fluid was an accident! Tretiak and I were only trying to help you!"

His eyes turned to the golden dagger on Ragnar's belt. "That's mine, isn't it?" he asked solemnly.

"Yes," the blood stalker sneered, slowly sliding the blade from the scabbard. He held it to the light of the chandelier. " 'In Brotherhood We Serve the Vigors,' " he quoted sarcastically. "A truly ridiculous concept. Had you ever been properly exposed to the Vagaries, you would know that the drivel of the Vigors is not only less powerful, but quite insipid, as well."

Tristan had suddenly endured quite enough of listening and doing nothing. "Why do you want my blood?" he shouted at the stalker. "And who are the wraiths?"

Ragnar smiled. "The wraiths are only several of an entire host of servants. Why I have need for the blood of the Chosen One will be revealed to you at a later time. For now, suffice it to say that you will find it very interesting."

"The ghoul-like consuls and the hatchlings," Tristan hissed. "I suppose they are simply more of your followers?"

"Not followers, exactly." Ragnar smiled, pursing his lips in thought. "More like servants. The consuls you fought with and killed are simply those that were 'left over,' so to speak. They are the ones who initially resisted me, so I turned them into what you saw there in the Caves. They are now relatively mindless, but still have their uses. You also might be interested to know that the second generation of hatchlings, those which carry weapons and can speak, now number in the tens of thousands and are already camped here in your beloved Eutracia. To the north, in the fields of Farplain. They will also prove to be extremely useful."

Tristan looked to Wigg in horror. The wizard seemed as shocked as he. But the blood stalker had not finished taunting them.

"Please forgive me," he said politely. "For I digress. Living underground for three centuries has a certain effect upon one, if you will. I believe you were asking about 'followers,' were you not? Oh, I will indeed have followers, but they are not ready just yet. Only when the time is right shall they be brought forth." He paused, leering wickedly at the prince. "Tell me, Chosen One, can you guess who they are?"

Tristan shuddered inside. He did not dare utter his suspicion for fear that saying it might make it come true.

"Ah," the stalker said. "I can tell that you already know. Yes, Chosen One, it is indeed so. My followers will be your very own consuls of the Redoubt." Again he paused, savoring his statement. "And Wigg! Frankly, you surprise me!" he continued. "It was quite foolish of you and the dearly departed Directorate to send them forth from the Redoubt, searching for stalkers and harpies during such a fragile time in the history of your pompous monarchy! And then you and the Chosen One ran off to Parthalon, leaving them all here to fend for themselves in this shattered, chaotic shell of a nation! What *were* you thinking? But I thank you, nonetheless." He grinned at the wizard, relishing every word. "By the way, there is no longer any point in searching for them," he whispered vehemently. "I have them all."

Tristan looked up at the woman called Celeste. He thought there was a hint of shininess in her sapphire eyes, as if she was fighting back tears. But then it was gone; he had probably been mistaken. Regaining his focus, he looked over to Wigg.

The wizard was psychologically beaten—both from the loss of his powers and the devastating revelations he had been forced to listen to. He raised his eyes to Ragnar.

"You're draining the stone, aren't you?" he asked weakly. "Its powers are somehow being transferred to the vein that runs through the walls of this place. Don't lie to me. I know it to be true."

"Quite right, *Lead* Wizard," Ragnar said, taking another fingerful of the yellow fluid and placing it into his mouth. "I knew you would recognize the meaning of it immediately. Just think! In less than three months' time, all that you have ever worked for, including the impending training of the Chosen One, will be of no consequence. A beautiful thing, is it not?"

Ignoring Ragnar for the moment, Tristan turned his attention to Scrounge, who was sipping from a cup of wine that had appeared in his hand.

"Why the reward for me?" Tristan shouted at him. "Don't you have anything better to do than walk atop tavern bars, handing out illicit posters? If it's me you want, I will gladly come to you right now!" He fingered the knife in his pocket. "I won't need another note of invitation," he whispered viciously.

"As far as your reward goes, you will learn later why it has been offered," Scrounge replied. "Interestingly enough, despite the hugely handsome sum, we don't want you to be taken. Curious, isn't it? And as to your offer of a duel, please know that I would like nothing better than to take you on right now." He smiled, happily taking another sip of the wine as if none of this mattered.

"Rumor has it that you're very good," he continued. "And that you somehow even managed to slay the commander of the Minions. Even so, I doubt you're good enough to take me. Besides, it wouldn't be fair. Right now you couldn't even raise your sword. And what a shameful act it is, you carrying around the same disgusting, foreign-made weapon you used to willingly murder your own father. The same blade those ignorant, winged freaks from Parthalon employ. No, Chosen One, we will not fight, at least not now. But another time, I promise you." Scrounge mockingly raised his cup in a gesture of false courtesy.

Tristan could contain himself no longer. Despite his relative weakness, he sent his hidden dirk unerringly across the room, straight for Scrounge's forehead.

Lazily, almost effortlessly it seemed, the assassin lifted his miniature crossbow, and a yellow-tipped arrow seared across the expanse of the room, striking Tristan's knife in midair. Both fell noisily to the marble floor, disappearing into the ankle-deep glow still rolling in from the hallway.

"You see?" Scrounge said, clucking his tongue in condemnation. "Just as I said. Too slow."

Tristan stood there weakly, seething at the arrogant assassin, not knowing what to do. His eyes full of hate and frustration, he looked to Wigg for guidance.

"Pick up my arrow, Chosen One," Scrounge's voice ordered from the other side of the room.

"What?" Tristan asked, momentarily nonplussed.

"Are you deaf as well as difficult?" Scrounge asked cattily. "Pick up my arrow and bring it to me on bended knee. *Now.* They're expensive, and I wish it back. And don't touch that crudely made piece of iron you call a throwing knife that is lying beside it." He smiled at the prince. "I don't have the patience to shoot one of your toys out of the air again."

Tristan's endowed blood began to rise in even greater anger from the insulting demand.

"I will never kneel to you," he growled. Lowering his eyes in hate, he took an aggressive step toward the assassin. "If you want your weapon so badly, come and get it yourself.

There are several ways in which I would enjoy giving it to you."

Scrounge laughed. He stood, placing his hands on his hips. "The Chosen One's reputation indeed proves true! Impetuous to a fault! No matter, though." He turned to Ragnar. "I believe now is as good a time as any, don't you agree?"

"Indeed," Ragnar answered.

Almost immediately Tristan felt his arms being clamped to the sides of his body, his feet no longer able to step forward. Ragnar had enveloped him within a wizard's warp. The prince could see that Wigg had been similarly affected.

"This is not necessary!" Wigg shouted at the stalker. "Why are you doing this?"

"We simply wish you both to remain quite still for a moment, while Scrounge and I take care of some long overdue business," Ragnar said almost happily. "It is especially important for the prince to be held, for he has a famous habit of becoming unpleasantly athletic. Scrounge, you may go first."

The assassin jumped down from the throne, looking into the azure haze that curiously covered the floor. Finally recovering his arrow, he held it in his right hand as he approached the prince.

Sweat ran into Tristan's eyes, and his breathing came faster. He struggled desperately against the invisible bonds holding him, but it was clearly no use. If there was one thing in the world that he could not abide it was being contained or restricted. He desperately wanted the chance to circle Scrounge and actively engage him on his own terms, his dreggan slashing as he went. But locked within this unforgiving warp he had no choice but to stand frozen to the floor and let the assassin do whatever he chose. Then his eyes fixed on the yellow-tipped arrow, and his heart skipped a beat with the sudden, horrific understanding of what was about to happen. The sickening arrow was now only inches from his face.

"Ragnar!" Wigg screamed. "I beg you, do not do this! He is the one for whom we have waited so long! Kill me if you want, but let him live!"

"He will leave here alive, Wigg, of that you can be sure," Ragnar said softly. "And, given the purported quality of his blood, he may not even feel the effects of the poison coursing within his system for as long as several days. But to let him live indefinitely is not something that we are prepared to do. The Tome states that he will lead the world forward to a new age. But we have other plans. We wish to do that job ourselves."

Tears began to run from the wizard's eyes as he continued to plead for the life of the prince, his words the only weapons he had left. "How could you do such a thing?" he whispered incredulously. "You used to be one of us!"

"But I am one of you no more!" Ragnar snarled back. "You helped see to that yourself."

Tristan struggled to muster his courage as the assassin brought the arrow close to his face. A slow and horrifying death. That was what Faegan and Wigg had told him happened when someone was scratched by a weapon coated in the brain fluid of a stalker.

"If you want me dead, why don't you just get it over with!" he shouted.

"Because we do not wish for you to die quickly," Scrounge answered. "There are many more interesting things we wish you to witness before you finally leave this earth."

"Before all of this is done, I shall kill you," Tristan whispered, his voice barely audible. He spat all the saliva he could muster directly into the assassin's face.

Scrounge smiled and wiped off the spittle. "Still giving orders, even in the face of death!" He laughed. "I commend you! And as for your invitation to a duel, as you already know, I heartily accept." Scrounge looked to Ragnar for permission to commence.

Smiling, Ragnar nodded. "You may place the blade anywhere within the warp you wish," he said.

Scrounge walked slowly around the prince, his spurs ringing out coldly against the marble floor. He savored each moment like a cat toying with mouse—a mouse that was trapped in a corner, and could not move.

Tristan strained uselessly against the confines of the warp as Scrounge wandered behind him, out of his sight. Then the assassin came full circle to face him.

Slowly, carefully, Scrounge pushed the tip of the arrow

through the warp, touching Tristan's right shoulder. With a quick, unforgiving stroke he incised a straight line into the prince's skin. Tristan's azure blood began to well up and trickle down his arm, dripping through the haze, splattering softly onto the floor.

Then Tristan felt the familiar itch of accelerated healing. He craned his neck to look at his shoulder, and his eyes went wide. He could literally see the wound closing. Before several more moments had gone by it was completely gone, as if Scrounge's weapon had never touched him.

"Yes," Ragnar said to the prince as if reading his mind. "I healed you. We couldn't have your famous azure blood dripping all over the floors, now could we? It would have created such a mess. But I healed your skin only. Your blood is still polluted by my brain fluid." The stalker smiled, stabbing another finger into the vial of fluid and placing it into his mouth.

"Now both of you and the Paragon you love so much will die at approximately the same time," he said softly. "Separate phenomena, to be sure, but with the same timing and ultimate effect. Interesting, don't you think?"

A thousand emotions swirled through Tristan's mind. He looked at the woman named Celeste. Again he thought he could see a hint of shininess in her eyes, but perhaps it was simply the light. Turning his dark eyes to Wigg, he saw that the lead wizard was crying softly. Then Wigg raised his face and glared at the mutated blood stalker.

"Ragnar," Wigg breathed through his pain and hate. "He is the Chosen One. You have no idea what you have just done."

"Oh, but I do," Ragnar purred back. "Things have now been set in motion, the likes of which your feeble mind could only dream of."

"I assume you have some type of similar fate in store for me." Wigg now sounded resigned.

"Similar, but not exactly the same," Ragnar answered. "Your fate is to be special, and it is to happen now. I have had the luxury of three centuries to perfect it, and you will be impressed."

"Before you do whatever you intend, I have some questions," Wigg said. "At least satisfy my curiosity."

"By all means ask them," Ragnar answered politely.

"First: the great sea, here within the Caves. Where did it come from? How is its existence possible?"

"I cannot take full credit for the phenomenon," Ragnar answered. "It was a by-product of the excavation needed to house the hatchlings as they matured. It seems there is an underground river that runs through this area, not unlike the falling, red waters of the first chamber that for so long supported the life of the stone. The first time an attempt was made to acquire room for the second generation of hatchlings, the unusual spring was laid bare, and it flooded the entire space, creating the sea. But rather than being red, the waters of the sea are azure, like the manifestations of the craft. I have not fully researched whether there is any connection between the two, but I shall. After all, the waters must be azure for some reason, mustn't they? I feel there is much, much more to learn about the Caves than any of us ever expected. In fact, it is now my belief that there are worlds here, below ground, that we never knew existed."

"And the voice of Morganna that came to us in the Caves?" Wigg asked.

Ragnar laughed. "The good Queen Morganna is as dead as dead can be. I imitated her voice to draw the two of you here, knowing that the prince would be compelled to follow it. The sliding walls blocking your retreat were also of my doing, as were the glowing signs of the heraldry the prince prizes so much."

"But why go to all that trouble?" Wigg asked.

"For exactly the reasons that the false voice of the queen told you," the blood stalker responded. "The protection of your well-being. We wished to herd you here to this precise spot, without delay or unnecessary risk. Had we not done so you would have become lost within the Caves' newfound complexities, most probably starving to death. Besides, without my 'help,' how would you have ever crossed the sea?" Ragnar grinned over his long incisors while taking a bit more of the yellow fluid. "It could be said that I saved both of your lives."

"But why do you want Tristan's blood?" Wigg asked. "If I am to die, then there is no reason to keep the answer from me."

Smiling, Ragnar waggled a finger at the wizard. "Some things are better left unsaid. Besides, my good fellow, who said anything about you dying? What I have planned for you is much more refined. But first we must discuss the Tome."

Wigg glanced toward the great book resting peacefully on the white altar. "What of it?" he asked skeptically.

"Since your powers are temporarily gone, I will perform the spell of compression and pagination for you now. It will be given to you after you've departed. When you are finally back in the Redoubt, I suggest you restore the book to its natural form as soon as possible."

Wigg's expression registered surprise. "Why are you giving us the Tome? You must know that we will only use it against you!"

"I have already read it," Ragnar answered quietly. "I have no further need for it."

"That's impossible!" Wigg exploded. "Even if you could somehow have read it without the Paragon, you couldn't possibly recite the entire treatise! It's tens of thousands of pages long! Only Faegan can do that, for he is the only known living being with the Power of Consummate Recollection! And it is difficult, even for him!"

Ragnar smirked at Wigg. "Is that so?" he asked quietly. Tristan saw the color drain from the wizard's face.

"Enough of this chatter," Ragnar said suddenly. "Time to get down to business."

The blood stalker pointed one of his extremely long fingernails in the direction of the Tome. The entire book began to glow. Then it became smaller and smaller, until it was the size of an extraordinarily thick personal journal. Finally Ragnar dropped his arm. "There," he said almost casually. "That should make things much easier for you on your journey home."

He rose from his throne and walked to the altar, where he picked up the once-gigantic book. Then he sauntered over to Wigg and reached through the warp surrounding the lead wizard to deposit the Tome within Wigg's robe. "There is, however, one more piece of unfinished business," he whispered nastily.

Ragnar snapped his fingers. Scrounge jumped down from

his throne, coming like an obedient dog to his master's side. From a pocket in his dark brown leather trousers he produced a small silver tube, which he handed to Ragnar.

"Tell me, Wigg, how much do you know about stalker brain fluid?" Ragnar asked. "It's a fascinating subject all of its own, quite full of riddles and complexities. Did you know, for example, that if enough of it is collected at once, it can be condensed and dried into a powder? And that the older the powder is, the less power it contains?" He slowly opened the top of the silver tube.

Removing the golden dagger from its scabbard at his side, he sprinkled some of the fine, light yellow powder along the length of the blade, holding it to the light of the chandelier.

"This powder is almost three hundred years old," Ragnar continued. "I have been saving it all this time for you, and you alone. It has taken all of those centuries for it to lose just the right amount of its power. You should feel complimented. Unlike the brain fluid that was placed into the bloodstream of the prince, this powder will not kill you. I do not wish you to die. I do, however, wish for you to suffer, just as I have suffered for centuries."

He held the shiny blade of the dagger before Wigg's face. "Fitting, is it not, that the instrument of this act should be the very same blade that you once used to harm me?" And with that, the stalker blew the powder from the blade directly into Wigg's eyes.

Wigg screamed and snapped his head back and forth as torrents of pain cascaded through his eyes and into his brain. Long minutes passed, until Wigg let out a final, great scream of torture and his head lolled down onto his chest. Tears of pain and sadness ran down upon his robe, creating dark blotches as they went. Then he groaned softly and fainted.

"You bastards!" Tristan screamed, fighting the warp that held him. "What have you done to him?"

"Why don't we let him tell you?" Ragnar answered pleasantly. He reached through the warp and began slapping Wigg viciously across the face.

Wigg finally opened his eyes, and Tristan stared in horror. The wizard's eyes were totally white and lifeless.

"Wigg!" Tristan screamed. "Can you hear me?"

"Yes," Wigg responded thickly. "But I am quite blind."

Now it was Tristan's turn to cry. Trembling with hate, he whispered to both the stalker and the assassin at once, "I swear to the Afterlife, I shall kill you both. By all that I am, I will see you die at my feet."

Ragnar smiled. "Given your condition, that is quite doubtful. You have unknowingly hit upon one fact, however." He leaned in conspiratorially. "The Afterlife is more responsible for all of this than you know.

"And now it is time for the two of you to leave us, for my work is done," he said. "When you wake, you will find yourselves back on the trail leading to the Redoubt. You will find your horses there. During your return you will not be harassed by any of our forces. The Tome will still be in the wizard's robe."

Tristan felt the wizard's warp fall away—and then everything went black.

Ragnar turned to Celeste. "You are dismissed, my dear," he said. Without a glance at him she left the room, closing the heavy door behind her.

As soon as she was gone, Nicholas emerged from the hallway, coming to hover quietly over the inert body of the prince. He bent to run his smooth, white palm across the face of the Chosen One.

"So this is he who dares to call himself my father," Nicholas said softly. "The Chosen One, his azure blood now polluted with the brain fluid of a stalker. How fitting. And next to him lies his sightless, quite useless wizard." He closed his eyes, lifting his head toward the ceiling. "The Chosen One shall soon see who the true parents are."

He turned to Ragnar. "Call for two of the hatchlings to return them to the trail, as promised. Make sure the Tome goes with them."

"My lord," Ragnar whispered back.

With that, Nicholas glided from the room, followed by the blue glow that receded down the hallway and out of sight, like a shimmering wave.

Ragnar and Scrounge bent over to pick up the bodies.

CHAPTER TWENTY-FIVE

❦

TRISTAN! Wake up! Drink!"

The urgent words came to the prince's ears as a distant, hazy sound, growing ever clearer as he regained consciousness. The voice was familiar. A flask of water met his lips, and some of it was poured carefully down his parched throat. He swallowed automatically, greedily. Lying in Wigg's lap in the dark of night, he finally opened his eyes. What he saw was not comforting.

The wizard's eyes were still that milky white.

"We are safe, at least for the time being," Wigg said weakly. "The basket of food and drink and even the fire were already here when I came to. It appears Ragnar kept at least part of his promise."

Finding that some of his lost strength had returned, Tristan tentatively stood. For several moments he carefully surveyed the scene. Their horses stood nearby, tied to a tree. He checked his weapons; they were intact.

They were on the trail to the Redoubt; he recognized the bend just ahead, and the fallen tree lying partly across it. A campfire burned brightly before them, its comforting, wood-laden scent reaching for the sky. Alongside the wizard was a basket of food, with two flasks inside. A soft breeze rustled through the night, and the stars in the dark sky competed for attention with the three magenta moons.

Once convinced that they were alone, Tristan sat down next to the blind wizard. He raised one hand, slowly passing it before Wigg's face. But there was no reaction; the wizard's dead, white eyes registered absolutely nothing. And then Wigg spoke.

"Yes, it's true," he said. "I am blind." He paused for a moment, as if trying to find the words. "And I may be so forever."

Tristan put his hand on the old one's shoulder. "I'm so sorry," he whispered. "Other than your vision, are you all right? Have your powers returned? I hope so. But Wigg, I understand nothing of this. Who is Ragnar? And why does he hate you so much?"

"Ragnar . . ." Wigg sighed. "What happened between us was over three hundred years ago, during the height of the Sorceresses' War, long before you were born, and long before we learned of the eventual arrival of you and your sister." He paused for a moment. "When I first awakened I discovered the flasks, and smelled wine in one of them," he said. "Would you give me some? I fear that just now I could use it."

Tristan placed the wine flask into the wizard's hands. Wigg took a long pull from the opening. "First things first," he said finally, the wine seeming to fortify him. "How do you feel?"

"I'm better," Tristan answered, moving a little nearer to the warmth of the fire. He looked to his shoulder; there was absolutely no evidence of what Scrounge had done to him. As was sometimes his habit, he pulled his knees up to his chin, holding them there. "It is as if nothing ever happened to me."

"Other than my vision, I am also well," the wizard told him. "My powers have not completely returned. But they will certainly have done so by the time we return home—or at least to some semblance of what they once were, considering the continual draining of the stone." He turned his lifeless, once-beautiful eyes in the direction of the prince. "But right now we should both eat."

"I can't," Tristan said angrily.

"But you must," Wigg answered. "It has been a long time since we had any nourishment. Especially you. You must keep your strength up for as long as you can . . ."

The prince knew the answers to his many questions about Ragnar would eventually come, but only in the wizard's good time. He took a piece of cheese and a hunk of bread for both himself and Wigg, placing the wizard's portions into the old one's hands. He did it for no other reason than to get Wigg talking. It worked.

In between bites of cheese and bread, Wigg related the story of Ragnar. Of how he and Tretiak had tried to heal him, only to have their well-meant compassion end in tragic results. Tristan listened in silence.

"How did he become so needful of his own brain fluid?" he asked when Wigg was done. "If it is of his own body, then how can it be addictive?"

"If you better understood the craft, you would have a keener grasp of that," Wigg answered. "Simply put, since Tretiak and I interrupted the process begun by the Coven, it was never completed. This means that, unlike other, fully developed stalkers, his process of transformation goes on unabated, even to this day, the incantation still trying to turn him. Some incantations, such as those used upon the stalkers by the Coven, had an infinite timeline until purposely discontinued by their creator. But that is another subject, for yet another day." He paused again, taking another drink of the wine as he continued to collect his thoughts.

"Anyway," he continued, "what all of this means is that his system continues to produce fluid, driven relentlessly forward by the ongoing incantation. But the wound in the side of his head releases it again, partially negating the process. Ingesting it is one way to get it back into his body, thereby simultaneously slowing down the need to create more, and causing a pleasurable sensation of release upon his nervous system. This process has apparently gone on for centuries, and will continue to do so unless he is killed. He is, in effect, his own prisoner of time. And also a prisoner of the craft. One must always be careful in the application of the craft, Tristan. For each way in which an incantation can proceed successfully, there are a hundred ways for it to go awry."

"And he blames you for his addiction," Tristan concluded.

"Yes. That is why he blinded me. He wanted to satisfy his desire for revenge by using the same weapon I tried to help him with. In those days we all carried the golden daggers as a symbol of our brotherhood. As difficult to believe as it may now seem, Ragnar was once a part of that. But never forget that as a stalker, even a partial one, he is quite mad." He shook his head. "There remain, however, many things I do not understand."

"Such as the amazing azure glow that crept out from the doorway," Tristan said. "I felt very drawn to it for some reason, as if it were somehow a part of me, a part of my very own blood."

"Yes," Wigg agreed. "I could see the effect it was having on you. That glow was the most awe-inspiring manifestation of the craft I have ever witnessed. But Ragnar never had that kind of power, and I very much doubt that he does now. No, someone else was there also, listening to every word. I believe it to have been the same being who is responsible for the draining of the stone. I am convinced that much of what Ragnar told us is lies, designed to throw us off. And much of it, conversely, I also believe to be the truth. A great portion of this riddle remains unexplained, purposely shrouded in a dense fog much like that glow we saw there in the chamber."

"Such as placing a bounty on my life, when they have no desire of my ever being caught?" Tristan wondered aloud. "That makes no sense. And what is their need for the consuls, especially with all of their tattoos removed? What possible difference could that make? Not to mention the purported thousands of hatchlings camped at Farplain."

His face darkened, especially at the thought of so many of Ragnar's second-generation hatchlings loose upon the land. Wigg turned blindly toward the prince. Tristan winced at the memory of the wizard's once-commanding aquamarine eyes.

"And then there is the greatest threat of all to our safety," Wigg said solemnly. "The Chosen One has been polluted with the brain fluid of a stalker. I know you feel well at this moment. But soon, very soon, you will begin to feel its effects. We *must* get back to the Redoubt and inform Faegan. With the aid of the Tome, perhaps there is something we can do."

"And about your blindness, as well?" Tristan asked.

"Perhaps. But it is you who are most important." Then a look of concern crossed Wigg's face. "The Tome! It is here, as Ragnar promised, is it not?" He stretched out an arm and began to pat the ground beside him, searching.

Suddenly anxious, Tristan looked around. At last he saw the thick, white leather book sitting in the grass a few feet away. "Yes! It's here!" he exclaimed. For the first time that night, he saw Wigg smile.

Slowly, reverently, Tristan took the Tome into his hands. He could not believe that the once-gigantic treatise he had seen in the Caves could in fact be the same book. Very carefully he opened it—the collection of volumes that were to explain the very meaning of his life and the life of his sister. It was a moment he had waited impatiently for.

But what he saw within the Tome made his breath come out in a rush. Quickly, almost in a panic, he thumbed through the rest of the pages in utter disbelief.

Every single page of the Tome was solid black. No words, no letters, no symbols.

He looked at Wigg in horror. "I don't understand!" he exclaimed. "The pages are all black. The Tome is ruined! This must be some trick of Ragnar's!"

Despite his affliction, Wigg smiled. "The Tome is not ruined," he said compassionately. "The great book has been made smaller for the purposes of transporting it from one place to the next."

"What good is the Tome if it cannot be read?" Tristan asked in frustration.

"There is, in fact, great value in not being able to read the Tome," Wigg answered. "Think for a moment. Right now the Tome is out in the open, where anyone could conceivably take it from us. When the spell is enacted, the Tome's cover and pages shrink, but the *writing* upon its pages does not. As the pages compress, the words written upon them are therefore literally forced into and over the top of one another. So much so that all of the white space is covered over, creating a completely black page. In this way not only can the great book be easily hidden or moved, but if it falls into hands that have also captured the Paragon, it still cannot be read." Wigg took another sip of the wine.

"As the book shrinks, the pages also become rearranged, or 'repaginated,' if you will, in a completely random order. Pages from one volume may even appear within another. So even if a thief were somehow able to restore it to its original size, it would remain impossible to use. Clever, don't you think?"

Tristan shook his head. "But why would Ragnar let us have the Tome?" he asked. "Is possessing both the Paragon and the Tome not an incredible advantage?"

Wigg's face darkened. "I do not know," he said slowly, the wheels turning in his mind. "Unless you take him at his word and believe that he has read the entire treatise, and requires it no longer. But for him to voluntarily relinquish his grasp of the Tome would also mean that he has somehow acquired the gift of Consummate Recollection, and to my knowledge Faegan is the only living wizard who is so gifted. Why Ragnar gave us the Tome remains a puzzle as truly confounding as why he let us live and put us back here, on the trail to safety. But then again, do not forget that he is at least somewhat mad. His words and deeds may have no meaning whatsoever, sending us uselessly chasing our tails. His apparent study of the Vagaries may also have harmed his mind, just as it drove Failee to the edge." At the mention of his wife of so long ago, Wigg's face fell slightly.

Tristan thought for a moment, finding something about all of this that was confusing him. "But it was my understanding that I was the only one who was to read the Prophecies, the final volume of the Tome. How then is it that Ragnar may have also read it? And how did he decipher it without the stone?"

"It is true that the Ones Who Came Before decreed in the Tome that only you should read the Prophecies," Wigg said, "and we all respected that. Even Faegan has not read them. But there is, in fact, nothing keeping someone else of endowed blood who is wearing the stone from doing so. That is one of the prime reasons we placed the Tome back into the Caves. So that the book and the stone would be separated, keeping someone from doing that very thing. At this point in our history, we have translated and now even teach Old Eutracian—the language of the Tome—to select wizards." He paused. "Also, the Prophecies are not inviolate." He took another sip of wine.

"But aren't the Prophecies the true story of what is to happen—of what *must* happen?" Tristan asked.

"Yes and no. The Prophecies can only come true if you and your sister live to fulfill them. You and Shailiha are the keys to the Prophecies, not the other way around as the Directorate first believed in the early days. Should you or your sister die, they will be altered. That is why Ragnar ordered Scrounge to cut you. They want you dead so that they can reshape the future. He even said so himself. It is this possible reshaping of the future by others that makes your survival and the survival of Shailiha so important. We also believe that this is the reason the two of you came to us as twins. A double safeguard, if you will, in case one of you should die. One day, not so long ago, your father told you that the lives of you and Shailiha were the very future of Eutracia. Now, after all you have been through, you finally know what he meant."

Tristan was about to ask yet another question when Wigg stiffened. The wizard's brow drew down, and he tilted his head, as if testing the air.

"What is it?" Tristan whispered. He silently drew his dreggan from its scabbard.

Wigg raised one palm. Finally, he turned to the prince.

"There is someone near," he whispered urgently. "Someone of *very* highly endowed blood. I can sense that there is only one, but his blood is of amazing quality. Other than you and your sister, I have never sensed such excellence. Find this person and bring him to us, if you can. I hate to send you alone, but under the circumstances this is how it must be. It is imperative that we know what this is about! But be careful."

"Which direction?" Tristan whispered back anxiously.

Wigg pointed a long finger toward the area directly behind them. "There," he answered softly. "Only about ten meters back. But make some excuse about leaving me before you go."

After loudly telling the wizard he was going to search for more firewood, Tristan entered the brush and began a slow circle in an attempt to come up behind whoever it was. The damp evening grass beneath his feet, he crept forward, his dreggan before him.

The intruder was hunched down behind some brush and facing away from Tristan, watching the wizard's every movement. But there was little else Tristan could tell about him, since the brush between them was thick, and the stranger's dark, hooded cloak covered most of him.

For a moment Tristan paused, wondering what to do. The intruder continued to crouch there, watching the wizard before the fire. Wigg went calmly about eating and drinking more of the wine, carefully sustaining his pretext of ignorance.

Finally deciding, Tristan slowly, silently, replaced the dreggan into its scabbard and drew instead one of his dirks. The brush here was too thick to use the sword properly, and a shorter weapon was called for. He crept forward again.

He put his boot down, taking the first step and closing the distance.

He reached down with his left arm and took the intruder under the neck, wrenching him upward to a standing position as he whipped his dirk to the man's throat.

"Do not attempt to move or speak!" Tristan snarled, his lips at the man's ear. He was in no mood for argument. "If you do otherwise I will kill you instantly. Now walk!"

When they reached the campfire, Tristan used all of his strength to throw the intruder down into the dirt next to Wigg. The man finally lifted his face to them, the light of the campfire dancing upon his features.

No! Tristan's mind called out to him. He continued to stand there, unable to grasp the meaning of what he saw. For the man on the ground before him was not a man at all.

It was Celeste, Ragnar's woman.

Even though her features were still partially covered by the cloak, there could be no mistake. The beautiful wave of red hair curved down across her forehead, and the amazing sapphire eyes looked up at him with the wariness of a cornered animal.

She looked around, then back up to the prince as he continued to glower over her, holding his knife. Despite Tristan's aggressive stance, she seemed to remain defiant.

"Tristan?" Wigg called out urgently.

"It's all right," the prince said, keeping his eyes on Celeste. "But first things first. Do you still detect any endowed blood other than what is here by the fire?"

Wigg again tilted his head for a moment. "No," he said with finality. "But who is here with us?"

"It is Celeste, Ragnar's companion," Tristan answered. He addressed the woman. "Why are you here?" he demanded.

"Spying for your lover, I suppose? Well, you did a particularly poor job of it. After what was done to us back there in the Caves, I should kill you on the spot! And take off that cloak! Now!" Tristan had no particular interest in the woman's body, only in discovering whether she was armed.

She removed the cloak to reveal the same emerald dress she had been wearing in the chamber. She appeared to be carrying no weapons.

Tristan replaced the dirk into its quiver. "You haven't answered my question," he said angrily. "Why are you here?"

"I need help," she said without hesitation. "That night I first met you on the cliffs, you helped me. You were kind. So I took a chance, hoping that you might be kind enough to do the same for me now. That is why I indicated for you not to speak to me, when we first saw each other in Ragnar's chambers. Had he known, there is no telling what might have happened. I had no part in what was done to you and the wizard—you must believe that. My only desire is to escape the stalker and Scrounge. I don't know where you are going, and to me it doesn't matter. I only ask that you take me with you." She lowered her head slightly, her red hair falling a bit farther down over her forehead. "Please take me away with you," she repeated. "I will do anything . . ."

"Tristan," Wigg said, his curiosity showing in his voice. "What in the name of the Afterlife is she talking about? Do you mean to say that you know this woman?"

" 'Know' is too strong a word," Tristan answered, his eyes still locked on Celeste. "We are, however, acquaintances. But that story is best left for later. Right now I want some answers." His heart had allowed other beautiful women to trick him before—such as Lillith, the member of the Coven who had almost killed him. Trying not to be swayed by her beauty and supposed vulnerability, he glared down at her.

"Who are you?" he asked sternly. "Other than a woman who always seems to need my help."

"I don't know who I am," she answered rather defiantly.

"What do you mean, you don't know? You know your name, don't you?"

"I was raised by Ragnar—but he is not my father," she answered. "Ragnar told me little about myself, other than the fact that a long time ago, I was brought to him for safekeeping. By the end of the Sorceresses' War, as he calls it, I was fully grown. At that point he began to abuse me." Slowly, her sapphire eyes became harder. "It has been that way ever since. I *hate* him. All I want is my freedom."

Tristan's thoughts careened through his mind. *If what she said is true, then she is over three hundred years old! And if she is, then she must be the subject of time enchantment!*

Tristan looked over to Wigg and saw that the old one's eyebrow was arched over his lifeless right eye.

"Tell me something," Wigg asked skeptically. "Assuming for the moment that you are telling us the truth, is there anything else about you that Ragnar might have told you?"

"Only that my entire existence had been originally intended for some great purpose," she answered uncertainly. "One that apparently never came to pass. But he never told me what that was."

"Anything else?" Tristan asked, almost casually.

"Only the name of my mother," Celeste said. "She was someone called Failee."

Tristan froze and looked immediately to Wigg. The wizard's eyes had gone wide, his mouth hanging open in disbelief. Wigg's lips began to move, but he said nothing. It was as if he was in shock, and Tristan knew why.

Wigg never knew the reason Failee left him, he remembered, *except for her apparent madness. But if Celeste is truly Failee's daughter, then it is possible that . . .*

Tristan looked back at the woman sitting across from him. And then he saw it: the thing that had been plaguing him ever since he had first discovered her on the edge of the cliffs. It was her eyes.

For all of his life Tristan had never seen a pair of eyes as beautiful as Wigg's had once been—until he had come upon Celeste. The lead wizard's spellbinding eyes had always been his most imposing feature. And it was this way with Celeste's eyes, also. He also remembered what Wigg had said of this one's blood just before sending Tristan out to find her.

"Other than you and your sister, I have never sensed such excellence."

A union of Wigg and the first mistress of the Coven presumably could have produced such blood. Tristan looked again to the beauty before him, feeling the harshness of his attitude starting to slip away. Still, he wasn't even close to trusting her.

Concerned, Tristan looked at Wigg. It seemed that the wizard had partially regained his composure.

"There is something I do not understand," Wigg asked Celeste. "If you are clearly able to leave the Caves on your own and join us, as you profess to have just done, then how is it that you were never able to escape?"

"I tried many times," Celeste replied angrily, balling her hands into fists. "There are numerous ways in and out of the Caves, and I used many of them. But Ragnar always found me and brought me back. Then I would be punished in ways you couldn't imagine. Eventually he laughed about my departures, seeming not to care whether I tried or not. He told me that because my blood was so special he could easily find me wherever I fled to, and it was always true. I don't know how he did it. I don't understand the workings of magic, and I never want to. Magic has never given me anything but pain. That night on the cliffs I had finally decided to take the most drastic measure of all."

Something else tugged at the prince's memory—something Celeste had said just after he captured her. *She was intended for some great purpose that never came to pass...*

Could it be true? he wondered. *Am I looking at the woman who was originally meant by her mother to become the fifth sorceress? But if that is so, then why did they take Shailiha instead of Celeste?* His mind a whirling maze of questions, he looked at the wizard.

It was clear that Wigg had come to the same crossroads, his face a mask of concentration as he struggled with his decision. "Celeste, you may be coming with us after all," he said softly.

"Wigg, are you sure?" Tristan asked quietly. "Where we are going and what you carry are both of the utmost importance. I'm concerned that we don't know enough about her to trust what she says."

"In theory I quite agree," Wigg announced, carefully standing up. "But there are several things we need to determine regarding her, and they cannot all be confirmed or disproved here in these woods. However, one of them can." He turned his face toward Celeste. "Tell me," he asked, "have you been trained in the craft?"

"No," she answered forthrightly. "Ragnar would never allow it. I've had little education of any kind."

"Tristan, take her hand and hold it," Wigg ordered.

Realizing what Wigg intended to do, Tristan carefully grasped Celeste's right hand. She quickly started to pull it away.

"Don't touch me!" she exclaimed.

"This will not hurt, I promise you," Wigg said compassionately.

Reaching out, the blind wizard felt along her arm until his fingers were touching the ends of hers. A very small incision appeared in Celeste's index finger.

"Tristan," Wigg ordered, "catch a single drop of her blood in the palm of your hand, and tell me what you see. If she is truly untrained, she can do us little harm."

Tristan collected a warm drop of blood as it fell from her finger. It sat completely still in his hand.

"It is dormant," he said. "She has not been trained."

"Very well." Wigg let out a sigh of relief. "Celeste, you are indeed coming with us. I believe there is a great deal that each of us is about to learn from the other."

"Where are we going?" she asked, wrapping herself in the cloak.

"To another place of magic." Wigg smiled. "But this time it shall be a place you will like. You will be safe there, and we have much to discuss. But it is imperative that we leave now, for if Ragnar has learned of your disappearance he may well already be after you. The farther away we are from the Caves, the better."

Celeste tentatively took one of the wizard's gnarled hands into her own. At her touch, Wigg's eyes became shiny.

Tristan went to the horses and untied them. Walking them back, he helped the wizard mount, then took the Tome and tied it to the back of Pilgrim's saddle, checking twice to see that it was secure. Satisfied that it would not fall, he helped Celeste onto Pilgrim and took the reins of both horses in his hands, preparing to lead them down the trail.

But before they took their first step, something came out

of the sky, swooping dangerously close to Tristan's head. He ducked as it went by; he could feel the air from its wings on his face.

It was a yellow-and-violet flier of the fields. Five others were just behind it.

"What is it?" Wigg asked nervously, sensing Tristan's sudden movement.

Tristan smiled into Celeste's surprised eyes. "We have a reception committee," he announced. "Faegan's butterflies."

With that, Tristan began to guide them down the trail, the multicolored butterflies leading the way as they careened in and out of the rose-colored moonlight.

PART III

The Children

CHAPTER TWENTY-SIX

It is this pollution of the blood of the Chosen One that shall plunge him into one of his greatest personal trials, should no answer be found as to the conundrum of his disease. For without the solution there shall occur a great shift in all things—the future and the very Prophecies themselves will be forced to change, just as shall the azure blood flowing through his veins.

—PAGE 2,337 OF THE PROPHECIES OF THE TOME

$\mathcal{M}$ARTHA, a rotund, compassionate matron, smiled proudly in the glow of the sun. The normally harsh Season of Harvest had surrendered an unusually warm day, and she had therefore allowed the children to take their midday recess outdoors, rather than inside. Smiling proudly, she watched them play in the orange and red leaves scattered upon the ground. Their incessant laughter combined happily with the crunching of the dry foliage beneath their feet, the crimson and magenta bits and pieces flying colorfully away in the Harvest wind. The air had a cool, crisp scent, the tattered leaves adding an aroma of spice to the mix of noise, color, and playfulness.

Martha had been here since she was a young woman, her hair now gray for more days than she could remember, her girlish figure long since gone. She had seen so many of the girls come and go, their faces still locked within her memories as if it had been only yesterday for each of them. Some of those she had raised here had returned to her as women, bringing their daughters to her.

But the recent troubles in Eutracia had created a great many hardships for her, and her tenuous hold upon both this place and the special children who lived here was becoming more fragile by the day. It was now the sixty-seventh day of the Season of Harvest. *May the Afterlife help us,* she thought.

Duncan, the blue-robed consul who had for so long been in charge here, walked up beside her. He gently placed one arm around her generous waist. He had been sent here by Wigg and the Directorate, as had she. But without having been granted time enchantments he had aged naturally with Martha, and for this she was ever thankful. They had become lovers many years past, and the bond between them in their subsequent marriage was as strong today as it had been when she had first taken him to her bed. The fact that there had never been any offspring from their time together only made them care all the more for the happy brood before them.

Martha looked up into Duncan's gentle face, watching his long, gray hair move softly in the wind. Seeing the disappointment in his dark brown eyes, she already knew the answer to her coming question. "There is still no one?" she asked hesitantly.

"No," Duncan replied. "I have had no contact with any of my brotherhood for weeks now. It is as if they have all somehow vanished. There should have been many of them who would have wished to come here—needed to come here. And yet not a single consul has visited for weeks. I fear that many of the girls' growing questions will be even more difficult to put off as the unexplained absences of their fathers become ever more mysterious." He paused for a moment, then continued as if finally coming to some internal decision.

"I did not wish to disturb you with this, my dear," he said, "but it may become necessary for me to return to the Redoubt. I simply must try to discover what is going on. These are virtually unprecedented times. I fear that most of the Directorate is dead—slaughtered by the hideous creatures with wings from across the sea. But it is rumored that Wigg still somehow lives. If that is the case, he will know what to do."

He watched two of the girls as they tossed leaves at each other, laughing in the sun. Several of the older ones stood by, talking in hushed, private tones as they watched their friends engaged in what they perceived to be the very height of childishness. "I simply cannot believe that the lead wizard, provided he lives, has forgotten us," Duncan added. "Or why this place exists."

"The food grows short, Duncan," Martha said back to him softly. "By now the Directorate and the consuls would have normally filled our larder for the coming Season of Crystal. But this year no one has come. Perhaps it would be better if we took all of the children back to Tammerland. We could leave a scroll behind for any of their fathers who might arrive, to inform them of what we have done." She turned her head to look at the Sippora River, watching it lazily flow by a short distance away. "If the river freezes early this year, as I fear it shall, it will make the use of supply boats impossible. Then any food would have to come to us overland from the Redoubt. Don't forget the several years when the snow drifts on Farplain have been too deep for even horses to make it through."

"I have considered this," Duncan answered seriously. "But the impracticality of taking the girls away from here is overwhelming. The children would have to march at least as far as the city of Tanglewood before we found any relief—and given the trouble in the realm, we don't know what we may or may not find there. Besides, with over fifty children here, we could never carry enough food for the journey. If we tried north, Ilendium is no closer, and even farther away from the Redoubt. And the stalkers and harpies are still rumored to exist. Our ultimate charge is the protection of the children, and the risk to them in such an undertaking would simply be too great."

He turned around to look up at the dark, jagged, impossibly high peaks of the Tolenka Mountains only two leagues away. They had always seemed yet another constant reminder of their seclusion.

"This sanctuary was placed here between the Tolenkas and the Sippora River for a reason, my love," he said gently. "You know that. What we have accomplished here over the last three decades has helped to secure the survival of the craft. Even more so now, in these times of trouble. We have every right to be proud. But in return for this honor we have paid the price of secrecy. Now that the entire Directorate may be dead and none of the few consuls who know of us have visited for weeks, we may be forced to fend for ourselves. Just as so many of our fellow citizens are now doing."

Duncan turned to look at the small stone castle in which he, Martha, and so many different children had lived. It stood peacefully just to the north, in the shade of the trees. "The Directorate built this place so that the craft might live," he said quietly. "But we are only overseers, charged with trying to do our duty. Therefore, I must do what I feel to be in the best interests of the children. If I leave now, by boat, I can be in Tammerland in perhaps five or six days. Far more quickly than if I go by horse. I do not wish to leave you alone, my love, but I now see it to be the only way." He paused for a moment, thinking. "There is another reason for me not to take the horse," he said softly.

"And that is?" she asked.

He turned to her with sad eyes. "If you run out of food, you must kill him and eat him. But try to do so without telling the children."

Still refusing to believe that such a necessity could befall them, Martha turned to look at the rowboat that was always tied to the tree near the banks of the rushing Sippora. Since he loved to fish, Duncan had used the boat often. He had always preferred to do it the normal way, with pole and line, rather than being aided by the craft. She smiled to herself, remembering the day not so long ago when, to amuse her, he had employed his gift to make a dozen or more multicolored Eutracian trout literally jump into the boat. He had then quickly released them, saying that the process had not been fair and that it went against the teachings of the Vigors. Just one more of the many things she so loved about him.

But he had never made so long a trip in his boat as attempting to reach Tammerland, and that worried her. They had always known in their hearts that such a day might come. But as happens with things that threaten to invade one's life and mind, her consciousness had always sheered away from such a possibility, preferring to dwell upon her love for him and the children they protected.

"There is yet another reason why I must go," Duncan said concernedly, breaking into her thoughts.

Detecting the worried tone in his voice, she turned to him. "And that is?" she asked.

"I am slowly losing my ability to perform the craft," he said.

She looked at him aghast. They had endured much together, but an impossibility such as Duncan losing his gifts had never occurred to her.

"How can that be?" she whispered back to him, making sure the children could not hear.

"I have no idea," he replied. "But if I am losing my gifts,

then perhaps so are others of trained, endowed blood. We could be left in a world without magic. The very idea is almost inconceivable. It is therefore not only for you and the children that I must go, but also for the sake of the craft itself. I need to reach the Redoubt before I become useless in my gifts, and they can no longer aid me in my journey."

"You will go tomorrow, won't you?" she asked, already knowing the answer to her question.

"Yes," he replied, letting out a long sigh. "But before then I will provide as many fish and as much fresh game for you and the children as I can, and I will enchant it to stay edible for you, for at least as long as my powers hold out." Despite the situation, he managed a smile for her. "It should be interesting to see how many trout I can make jump into the boat this time, don't you think?" he asked. "I can tell you remember that day, don't you, my love?"

"Of course," she answered.

But suddenly she felt him stiffen next to her, as darkness filled the sky.

Quickly turning, Duncan gazed upward. Then he whirled back around to Martha with terror in his face and a life-or-death urgency in his voice. "Get the girls into the castle! Now!" he shouted, grabbing her by the shoulders. "Hurry!"

Gathering up her skirts, she immediately ran to the children. Many of the girls were already huddled together, looking into the sky and starting to scream. Seeing this, she too stopped for the briefest of moments, looking above herself.

There were hundreds of them, and she had never before seen their like. As they came closer and the hideousness of their forms came into sharper view, she immediately scooped up two of the smaller girls, screaming orders to the others to run with her back to the castle. Finally overcoming their initial shock, the children did as they were told, running as fast as they could back to the dark gray building that was their home. But they were too slow.

Martha was knocked to the ground by one of the awful things. As she landed, the air left her lungs in a rush. The two girls she had been carrying went flying, landing some distance away in the grass. Amid the screams and crying of the panic-stricken children, all she could do was look up, trying to breathe again, and watch it all happen.

The great birds with the awful, leathery wings were descending by the hundreds. Duncan was already surrounded.

The aging consul started to raise his arm, but it was already too late. One of the birds cut Duncan's head away from his shoulders with a single, powerful stroke of a sword. The consul's body collapsed to the ground as if it had been made of paper, his precious, endowed blood spraying out, landing everywhere.

Martha tried frantically to get up, slipping back down to the bloody grass twice before finally finding her feet. Tears running down her face in torrents, she tried to run to her husband. But then she found herself caught up from behind in the iron grip of yet another of the hideous things with wings. It was then that she saw what the birds were doing to her girls.

As the frantic, screaming children ran in every direction, the great birds were landing upon them, grasping them in their long, black claws. The children struggled mightily, screaming hysterically in what was now a single, uncontrolled chorus of terror. But it was no use. As each of them was gathered up, the bird holding her called immediately out to the others in victory and then flew south, eventually disappearing into the afternoon sky. Oddly, she noticed, the birds seemed to be taking great care not to harm them.

In no time, all of the children had vanished. Perhaps one hundred or so of the awful attackers remained standing in the grassy field before the castle. All around her, the wind buffeted about the remnants of the once-happy, laughing children: Some of their small, orphaned shoes and the occasional torn, lonely article of lost clothing tumbled across the grass or flapped helplessly in the gathering wind.

The girls. Her girls. Carried away.

A strange kind of quiet crouched over the scene, the horrible birds standing very still as if waiting for something else to happen. Their terrible, scarlet eyes stared at her menacingly. And then, through her tears, Martha saw something else that would remain in her memories forever.

Another pinprick in the afternoon sky began to form. Low and near the horizon, it grew larger by the moment. As it came into view, she could see that it was yet another of the strange birds. But this one was carrying a rider.

The bird approached slowly, spreading its wings to land

expertly upon its powerful lower legs. Like the others, it had arms, wore black gauntlets upon its wrists, and carried a sword at its hip. But this one also wore a wide, black leather collar around its neck. The back of the collar had loops for its rider to hold on to. Having finally settled, the great bird bent down, the figure atop it rather unceremoniously slinging one leg over the thing's back and gracefully sliding to the ground.

Through her terror and grief, Martha saw the tall, lean figure approach. She took in the angular face, aquiline nose, and long dark hair that ran down to his jawline. His clothes were of brown leather, and a highly unusual, miniature crossbow adorned the top of his right forearm. As he stepped closer she could hear the jangling, disconcerting sound of spurs. His careful eyes took her in. Finally he stopped before her, examining her in the fading light of the afternoon as though she were some unusual creature he had just paid to see at one of the province fairs.

The man smiled. "Martha, is it not?" he asked almost politely. "Headmistress of this, the place known only to the privileged few as Fledgling House. Wife of the consul Duncan, of the House of Janaar, acting headmaster." The man looked about, finally focusing on the small castle nearby.

"A novel idea, this place, I must say," he went on nastily. "But quite obviously its time has come and gone. And the girls, Martha! Those oh-so-bright girls! The charges you and your husband failed so miserably to protect, now proving to be exactly what we needed. We thank you. And you have been here so long, haven't you, my dear? But all of that is about to change."

Martha's lower lip quivered so badly that she could hardly speak. Her legs were weak from fear and exhaustion. She looked to the headless corpse of her husband as it lay in its own blood. The only man in the world she had ever loved—butchered at her feet, gone forever.

"Why?" she finally whispered, her voice cracking with the strain. "Why is my husband dead, and where have you taken the children? When the Directorate hears of this abomination—"

"Oh, but there is no Directorate, my dear," the man said. "Or haven't you heard? Wigg is the only survivor of that ill-fated group. He's in hiding in the belly of the Redoubt with another wizard, named Faegan, who is little more than a helpless cripple. They're there with the prince, who is a wanted man for the ruthless murder of his father, the late king. They are a very unsavory group, to be sure. But you will be seeing them all soon enough, I promise you."

The man then removed a parchment from his vest and unrolled it. Producing a quill, he walked to Duncan's body. Reaching down, he filled the quill with blood and began to write. Martha thought she would vomit.

Noticing her weakness, the man said, "Oh, please forgive me, my dear, but I find that endowed blood makes for the finest of writing fluids. It flows so evenly, you see. But first one must wait a bit for the blood to die. Otherwise it keeps trying to form its own patterns." And with that he finished his ghastly handiwork.

He rolled the parchment into a scroll, tied it with a red ribbon, and handed it to her. She wanted to refuse, but the look in his eyes finally made her take it into her trembling hands.

"You are to be taken to the Redoubt," he said, "where the wizards and the traitorous prince hide. One of my hatchlings will fly you there. Upon arriving you will be deposited at a great boulder, near the royal palace. Simply touch the stone at its top and it will roll away, allowing you entrance to the tunnels. You are to give this scroll to the prince, with my compliments." The man in leather smiled once more, wickedly. "He and I are old friends."

Martha simply stared at both the man and the creatures he controlled as if they had all just arrived from another world. The man then turned to another of his birds. This one had a broad leather saddle strapped to its back.

"Do you understand your orders?" the man asked the hatchling sternly. "If she falls off and dies, or if the scroll is lost, you pay for your mistake with your life."

"I understand, my lord," it answered obediently.

Martha was then roughly picked up by several of the winged things and deposited on the hatchling's back. Not knowing what else to do, she gripped the scroll and the saddle pommel for all she was worth as her tears streamed down her face. After climbing on the back of his own hatchling, the man with the spurs and the crossbow wheeled his bird around to look at her for the final time.

"Follow my instructions to the letter, Martha," he said quietly, his dark eyes boring directly into hers. "Or the girls shall be forfeit for your failings." With that he spurred his great bird into the sky. The many others followed him, their wings again blotting out the sun.

The hatchling Martha was astride then gently lifted itself up and away. Desperately trying to hang on, she felt the bird beneath her turn south, to Tammerland.

CHAPTER TWENTY-SEVEN

*A*s Wigg, Tristan, and Celeste neared the Redoubt, Shailiha ran to Faegan, joyously telling him that Caprice and her squadron had found them. But after another message from the flier, the princess' joy quickly faded. Apparently things were not as secure as they had at first seemed.

Wigg was injured, and there were now *three* people returning, not just two. The third person was female, but unknown to Caprice.

Faegan made sure the fliers would return well ahead of Tristan, Wigg, and the stranger they were apparently traveling with. The unknown woman had him worried. He considered barring all three from entrance into the Redoubt until he knew more. But if Wigg had been injured, he might well need immediate help.

Finally Faegan decided he had no choice but to allow all three of them entrance. When he and Shailiha first saw Wigg's eyes and then the beautiful stranger known as Celeste, they were horrified and surprised at the same time.

After examining Wigg, Faegan took him away to a separate room. After an agonizingly long period the wizards emerged, stating that the five of them, including Celeste, were going to another location in the Redoubt. They gave no explanation why, but quickly led everyone away. Tristan and Wigg then spent the next several hours discussing their experiences with Faegan and Shailiha.

So much had happened in so short a time span that Tristan, his sister, and even the wizards seemed at a loss. They did not know how to control, even in the most minute sense, the horrific events they had all been caught up in.

Tristan looked around, taking in the grandeur of the magnificent chamber in which they now sat. The room was huge—perhaps larger than any of the others he had seen in the Redoubt. The floor and ceiling were of black Ephyran marble. Completely encompassing each of the four walls were row after row of very wide mahogany pull drawers, each with its own elaborate, solid-gold handle. The drawers were labeled with gold plaques, but the prince was too far away to read what was engraved on them.

The table at which the five of them sat on elegantly upholstered, high-backed chairs was huge, of highly polished, inlaid mahogany—one of many such tables here. Soft light was supplied by large, solid-gold oil lamps. A certain indefinable mustiness hung in the air. It was as if the ancient odor somehow knew that there were people in the room, and was trying to share its secrets with them.

Sitting in this chamber made Tristan feel the need to speak in hushed, respectful tones—as if the heart of the world had somehow been secreted here.

"Wigg," Faegan said at last, "please hand me the Tome."

Removing the book from his robes, Wigg placed it on the table. "You will restore it now?" he asked.

"Yes," Faegan said.

Tristan and Shailiha watched Faegan close his eyes. An azure haze began to surround the small, leather-bound book, and the Tome began to grow until it was once again full-size. The process was spellbinding.

Faegan then narrowed his eyes, and the great treatise rose, floated over to another of the nearby tables, and landed gently. "It is a great thing you have done—bringing the Tome back to the Redoubt," he said solemnly to Tristan and Wigg. "And you have, each in your own individual way, paid a terrible price to do so. The craft of magic is seriously in your debt." He sighed, carefully taking the measure of his next words. "The most important issues to discuss, of course, are the blinding of Wigg and the wounding of Tristan," he continued. "But Wigg has made a personal request of me to resolve certain other concerns first, and I have agreed."

Wigg took up the conversation. "This magnificent room is called the Hall of Blood Records," he said. "It is the resting place of one of the most fascinating of all the aspects of the craft. Here within these many drawers can be found the identification of almost all persons of endowed blood who have lived within the time since the discovery of the Tome and the Paragon. It is one of the most sacred and revered of all of the chambers in the Redoubt."

Faegan nodded. "Wigg has explained to both of you how trained endowed blood is alive and can move on its own, has he not?" he asked Tristan and Shailiha.

They nodded.

"What you do not yet know, though," Faegan went on to say, "is that when the blood of a trained endowed is exposed, it always moves about in its own *particular* way. The same way every time, forming a pattern. When the pattern is completed it begins again, retracing its journey over its original track, until the blood finally dries up and dies. Every such pattern is completely unique. There are no two alike, except in the case of twins—and even that is not a hard and fast rule. These patterns are called blood signatures. Please allow me to demonstrate."

The wizard caused one of the many mysterious drawers to open, and a large sheet of blank parchment rose from it, coming to land gently in the center of the table. "Wigg, if you will allow me," Faegan said.

Using the craft, Faegan created a tiny incision in Wigg's index finger. A single drop of blood came from it, landing with a soft plop on the parchment.

Almost immediately Wigg's blood began to move, creating a distinct, red pattern. Fascinated, Tristan watched as the blood drop completed its gyrating pattern, then began anew over the exact same track it had just laid. Gradually drying, it finally stopped.

Tristan was amazed. "Do you mean to say that it is exactly the same every time?" he whispered incredulously.

Faegan smiled. "Indeed. Observe." With that the chair-bound wizard turned his attention to the many drawers and ordered, "Wigg, lead wizard of the Directorate."

Almost immediately one of the highest of the drawers began to slowly open, another sheet of parchment fluttering down to land on the table. But this parchment was not bare. Looking down, Tristan and Shailiha read:

Wigg, Lead Wizard of the Directorate
Trained Blood Signature
Date: Forty-fifth Day of the Season of Harvest, 002 S.T.

The blood signature just below the words, although faded with age, was identical to the one just created from the fresh drop of Wigg's blood. Tristan turned to Shailiha and Celeste to see that they were as mesmerized as he.

"What does the '002 S.T.' mean?" Celeste asked. "I have never seen such a phrase used."

Faegan stroked his ever-present cat. "This is the manner in which all documents kept here in the Redoubt are dated," he responded. "All dates are located on the same timeline, with the discovery of the Tome and the Paragon being the focal point from which all things are measured—either before or after that event. That precise day in time therefore happened in the year zero. 'S.T.' means Subsequent to the Tome. Any years previous to the zero demarcation point are labeled 'P.T.,' or Prior to the Tome. My birthday, for example, would be written as the Seventy-third Day of the Season of Crystal, 032 P.T., or thirty-two years prior to the discoveries."

Shailiha spoke up. "Tristan and I, because we are untrained, do not yet possess blood signatures," she reasoned. "They will only appear after we become educated in the use of the craft."

"A logical assumption, but quite untrue," Faegan responded, eyes twinkling at her obvious confusion. He leaned closer to the princess and bounced his eyebrows up and down slightly.

"Training in the craft does not *produce* the signatures; it only activates them, allowing them to be seen and thereby recorded," he went on. "Every endowed we know of, trained or not, has his or her blood signature on record in this hall.

Finding newborn endowed and recording their blood signatures was one of the main tasks of the consuls." Faegan smiled.

"But if my blood does not move, how then can my signature be recorded?" she asked. "Or for that matter, anyone else's who has not yet been trained? And do you mean to say that mine has already been done somehow?"

"*Especially* yours," Faegan answered. "Yours and Tristan's. Which, by the way, are very similar to each other, since you are twins."

"But how?" she asked.

"Why don't you tell us yourself?" Faegan answered. Wigg smiled in agreement.

"I still don't understand," Shailiha answered in frustration.

"Then I shall give you a clue." Faegan winked. "Think of how it was that Wigg and I finally cured you of the last remnants of the Coven's spell."

Shailiha smiled. "The water from the Caves."

"Now tell me how this applies to our current problem," Faegan continued. Shailiha gazed down at Morganna, asleep in her sling, and pursed her lips in thought. At last she looked back up at the wizards. "We know that the waters agitate untrained, endowed blood within a person's system. It might therefore also stand to reason that the water, when placed near the blood when *outside* of the body, would have the same effect." She paused to collect her thoughts.

"But in the second case," she finally continued, "because the blood is away from the body and therefore has much more freedom of movement, the waters may have an even greater effect upon it, convulsing it into revealing its signature prematurely." She raised her eyebrows tentatively, wondering whether she had gotten it right. "Or something like that . . ."

"Exactly," Faegan said softly. "I am impressed." And he meant it. He looked to Wigg to see him smiling, as well.

"Can Tristan and I be permitted to see our signatures?" she asked hesitantly.

Faegan smiled. "Of course. I thought you would never ask. Your hand, please."

Shailiha tentatively held out one hand, and Faegan created a small incision in her first finger. A single drop of her blood fell gently onto the parchment alongside Wigg's signature.

"And now, Wigg, a drop of the water if you please." Faegan smiled.

Wigg reached beneath his robe and produced a small pewter vial. He held it out, waiting for Faegan to take it.

Faegan very carefully poured a single drop of the precious fluid directly onto the waiting blood of the princess.

The joined liquids began to writhe, and the same process commenced as had occurred with Wigg's blood: The fluid moved hauntingly across the parchment until Shailiha's blood signature was complete.

Faegan stared down at it. He could have come here to the Hall of Blood Records and pulled a copy of it beforehand, but that would have done nothing to prove his theory. He knew that only seeing the princess' fresh signature created before his eyes would produce the answer. He continued to examine the trail left by her endowed blood, finally seeing the anomaly he was looking for—the anomaly that Egloff's scroll said would prove his theory.

It's true! he thought exultantly. *The Forestallments exist! This will change so much!*

Faegan turned his eyes toward Wigg. "Old friend," he said compassionately, "I know there is something very personal that you long for me to do, but I must ask your indulgence one more time. Please wait just a bit longer, for there is something that we must first discuss."

Wigg's face fell a little, but he nodded back with curiosity. "If you insist," he replied. "But what is this about?"

"It is both my great pleasure and my great worry to inform you that I have just categorically proven the existence of Incantations of Forestallment," Faegan whispered.

Tristan immediately looked to Wigg to see that the lead wizard's mouth was open in astonishment, his white, milky eyes wide.

"Impossible!" Wigg exclaimed. "Forestallments are only myth! Everyone of the craft knows that the calculations required for such a thing are far beyond us, and always have been! This time your imagination has gone too far!"

"What are you two talking about?" Tristan asked warily. "I've never heard of a Forestallment."

"Simply put, the principle behind a Forestallment is the relativity of time," Faegan responded. He gave Nicodemus another affectionate stroke. "I believe there are a great many such ties binding the craft to the fabric of time—ties that we have yet to explore. The Forestallments are merely one such example. But to answer your question, a Forestallment is a gift, placed within the blood of one endowed person by another. This can presumably be accomplished either with or without the subject's knowledge. But this incantation is different, in that the spell does not take immediate effect. In fact, it may not become evident for years, decades, or even centuries. It lies in wait, as it were, in the recipient's blood until activated. It is thus forestalled, or delayed, until the preselected time of its activation."

"Or so goes the theory," Wigg said skeptically from the other side of the table. "But what is your proof?"

Faegan smiled. "I will tell you shortly. But first I will finish the prince's question. Incantations of Forestallment may be either time-activated or event-activated. In other words, the Forestallment within the blood may become active only after a prescribed amount of time has passed, or it may become active only after the occurrence of a specific event. In addition, it can either be open-ended, or can be set to terminate after the passage of a prescribed period of time or after the occurrence of yet another specific action. You can well imagine how useful or destructive such a spell could be."

Tristan's head was spinning. "But what does all of this have to do with us?" he asked.

"Indeed!" Wigg said. "What you have just described has long been the theory. But it is now time for you to tell me something I *don't* know."

"Very well, then," Faegan said. He took a deep breath. "What you *don't* know is that Princess Shailiha, without a scintilla of training in the craft, can mentally communicate with the fliers of the fields. She has been accomplishing this for days, and each time she does so her ability increases. It is clearly an innate, rather than a trained talent. And it is a feat that even I, after three centuries in the craft, have been unable to perform. The most likely explanation for this is that she has been unknowingly placed under a Forestallment. An event-activated Forestallment, initiated when she first came into contact with the butterflies."

Tristan looked at Shailiha as if she had somehow just

descended from the heavens. "Is this true?" he whispered incredulously.

Shailiha raised her eyes to his, a slight blush of embarrassment on her face. She began to rock Morganna gently. "Yes," she said. "It is. The fliers reveal themselves to my mind, and I can answer them back without speaking. I have absolutely no idea how I do it. It was Faegan and I who sent the fliers to find you and Wigg. Caprice called back to me, saying that Wigg was injured, and that there was an unknown female traveling with you. We therefore knew these facts even before you arrived at the Redoubt."

Tristan shook his head in disbelief. *"Caprice?"* he asked.

Only slightly less chagrined, Shailiha smiled. "Caprice is the name I have given to the violet-and-yellow flier who usually speaks to me for the rest of them," she said, raising her eyebrows as if expecting neither the prince nor the wizard to believe her. "It is she who led the group to find you." Her smile turned mischievous. "She is the one who flew so close to your head, trying to get your attention. I must admit that she did so under my orders."

Tristan turned his awestruck face to Faegan. "This is all true?" he asked, still not entirely willing to believe.

"Oh, yes." Faegan chuckled. "True as the day is long. I have seen it with my own eyes."

"But the proof!" Wigg countered. "Where is your proof?"

Smiling, Faegan withdrew a scroll from his robes. "I hold in my hand a copy of a scroll I found by Egloff," he said quietly. "Its existence was apparently unknown to the rest of the Directorate. It seems that just before his death he was deep into research regarding the possible existence of Forestallments. It was the sudden reappearance of the stalkers and harpies that finally placed him on the right path."

Wigg's face began to register a hint of understanding. "Do you mean . . ."

"Yes, Wigg," Faegan answered rather sadly. "It is now my belief that the blood stalkers and screaming harpies, the tools of the Coven that we had all prayed were dead, were actually infected with Forestallments, waiting to be activated. After you sent the consuls into the field to try to wipe them out, Egloff finally had the one thing he had lacked to prove his hypothesis. Their blood. The three-hundred-year-old, endowed blood of the beasts that before then had not been available for examination. It is all here, written in his scroll." He paused for a moment, letting the import of his words sink in. He gently placed his copy of the scroll onto the table.

"I still don't understand," Tristan said, rubbing his forehead in frustration. "What does the endowed blood of the stalkers and harpies have to do with Shailiha's bond with the fliers?"

"It seems that when a Forestallment is inserted into the blood of an endowed, be it human or creature, the blood signature is altered," Faegan replied. "But only slightly. Look down at Wigg's blood signature, and then at the princess'. Tell Wigg the difference you see between the two."

The prince and his sister looked down intently at the two signatures lying side by side on the parchment. Shailiha spoke first. "The shapes are very different."

"True," Faegan responded. "But I have already told you that they always are. To understand the Forestallments you must do better than that. Look again."

After a brief time, Tristan thought he saw what the wizard was referring to. "Shailiha's signature has branches leading off from it," he said softly, half to himself. It was a series of branches—like tributaries of a river—that led off from the main body of the signature. There seemed to be dozens of them.

"Exactly!" Faegan exclaimed.

Looking over to Wigg, Tristan could see that the expression on the lead wizard's face had become one of great surprise. "What do you mean, her blood signature has *branches*?" Wigg asked. "There was no such an anomaly in her signature at her birth. Why should there be one now?"

Placing each hand into the opposite sleeve of his robe, Faegan leaned forward in his chair, his expression quite serious. It was as if he knew that his next words would hurt Wigg, and he didn't know how to say them. "Because she has been with the Coven," he answered quietly. "I believe Failee perfected the Forestallments, and placed a number of them into the princess' bloodstream. I also believe this act was an enhancement to their plan of making Shailiha their fifth sorceress."

"But why would Failee bother to do such a thing?" Wigg countered, obviously still unconvinced.

"Because the more Failee could immediately influence the princess' blood, the easier her overall task would be. I ask you to consider the following possibility: Once Shailiha had truly become their fifth, it was likely that Failee would turn control of the Coven over to her, because of the vastly higher quality of Shailiha's blood. And if the princess' blood contained Forestallments, it would empower a gift immediately, without the tedious, time-consuming teachings of the craft. I believe Shailiha's sudden, unexplained bond with the butterflies to be just such a Forestallment, accidentally activated when I took her to the atrium."

"But why would she want to give Shailiha dominion over the fliers?" Wigg interjected. "There are no known fliers in Parthalon. It seems a particularly wasteful use of a Forestallment."

"I agree with you," Faegan answered. "I therefore do not believe that this particular Forestallment was originally meant for the fliers. I feel that is simply a by-product, so to speak, of the original incantation."

"What do you mean?" Tristan asked.

Faegan looked soberly to the group as a whole before answering. "She was to be their fifth sorceress and eventual leader. I believe this Forestallment was meant to give her a bond to the Minions of Day and Night."

For a very long moment the room went silent, each person trying to grasp the stunning importance of the wizard's statement.

"Then why does it succeed with the fliers also?" Shailiha finally asked.

"We may never be sure, but perhaps it is because both the Minions and the fliers are winged creatures of the craft. In fact, you may eventually be able to perform this gift with *any* winged creature that has been either created or otherwise affected by magic. And only time can tell us that," Faegan answered. He gave Nicodemus a short stroke under the cat's neck.

"Your argument is very enticing," Wigg said skeptically from the other side of the table. "But again I must ask you, where is your proof?"

"In Egloff's scroll," Faegan answered. "You see, unknown to the rest of the Directorate, he was already deep into studying the blood of the screaming harpies and the blood stalkers. It was the sudden reemergence of these creatures after three hundred years that initially piqued his interest. He knew there had to be a logical reason. He used the waters of the Caves just as we have done here today, and his field experiments revealed the undeniable existence of an anomaly in their blood signatures, compared to the samples you and I took from stalkers and harpies during an earlier part of the Sorceresses' War. Do you remember now? The early signatures had no Forestallments. But the later ones, the ones that surfaced just before Tristan's coronation, did. It is my belief that near the end of the war even Failee could see that her cause was hopeless, and she planted the Forestallments within the remaining of her creatures, causing them to lie dormant until her eventual return. We never knew how it was that the stalkers and harpies suddenly seemed to vanish at the end of the war, then returned just when the Coven needed them. Now we do. This also proves the approximate time of her mastery of these incantations—very near the end of the war, yet after you and I took the initial blood samples from her creatures." Lost in his thoughts, he closed his eyes for a moment.

"When coupled with the unexplained, similar anomaly in Shailiha's blood, and her sudden ability with the fliers, it is the only answer that fits," he added finally.

"But what activated the Forestallments within the stalkers and harpies, and at just the proper time?" Wigg asked, apparently becoming more convinced. "The Coven had been exiled from Eutracia for over three hundred years, and could not possibly know when or even if they would ever return. How did they know when the creatures would be needed, if ever?"

Faegan's eyes became shiny with the unmistakable advent of tears. Using the sleeve of his robe, he wiped them away. "Telling you this is perhaps the most difficult of my duties this day," he said sadly. "You are forgetting Emily, my only child, the first reader of the Tome. Also known as Natasha, the duchess of Ephyra. The unknown sorceress Failee so cleverly left behind. I believe it was she who activated the Forestallments in the stalkers and the harpies. This was designed to scare both the citizens and the wizards, just before the invasion of the Coven and the Minions."

"I'm sorry, Faegan," Wigg said compassionately. "I know how much all of this must hurt. But there is still one thing that doesn't make sense. If Egloff knew all of this, why didn't he tell us?"

Finally regaining his composure, Faegan looked at the prince. "Tristan," he said softly, "would you please read aloud the date at the bottom of the scroll?"

The prince obediently unrolled Egloff's scroll. "Seventy-third day of the Season of New Life, 327 s.t.," he read aloud. The import of the date did not register with him.

Clearly, however, it was not lost on Wigg, whose mouth opened slightly in sudden realization. "So now we know why . . . ," he said gently.

"What do you mean?" Tristan asked.

"The Seventy-third day of the Season of New Life, 327 s.t.," Wigg answered, "was the day of your ill-fated coronation."

Tristan closed his eyes for a moment.

"This is why Egloff didn't tell us of his findings, isn't it?" Wigg asked Faegan. "He probably planned to do so right after the coronation. But as it turned out he never had the chance."

"Correct," Faegan answered. "The scroll confirms the fact that he had not formulated his final theories until late that day."

Shailiha had suddenly had enough of talking about magic. She was deeply concerned for the well-being of both her brother and Wigg, and was determined to broach the difficult subject. "I wish to speak of what Tristan and Wigg suffered at the hands of Ragnar and Scrounge," she said emphatically. The look in her eyes said that she would not be dissuaded. "There must be something we can do for them."

Faegan took a deep breath, letting it out slowly. "I truly hope you are right, my dear," he said wearily. "But only a detailed study of the Tome will tell us whether we can help either of them. The problem, of course, is that such a thing takes time. And time is the one commodity that we are in short supply of . . ." His voice trailed off for a moment as he retreated into his thoughts. "Adding to the confusion is the fact that there are now other complications making the researching of the Tome particularly difficult."

"Such as?" Shailiha pressed.

"First and foremost is the decay of the Paragon," Wigg said. "Soon it may not be powerful enough to allow Tristan to decipher the Tome."

Smiling bravely, Shailiha reached her free hand out and placed it atop one of her brother's. If there was any way to cure him, she would find it or die trying. He had risked his life time after time to bring her back from Parthalon, and she would do no less for him. Realizing she was hugging the baby too tightly, she relaxed her arm and looked over at Faegan. "Please tell me what Tristan can expect, given his condition."

Faegan lowered his eyes slightly. "Given the fact that he is the Chosen One and his blood is the most pure in the world, it is difficult to say," he began. "I can only describe to you what has always happened to others of endowed blood. It will consist of a series of convulsions that are sometimes preceded by fever and sweating. The area of the original wound will grow weak and painful. In between these attacks the victim often feels fine, as though there is nothing wrong with him. But as the infestation progresses, taking over more and more of the victim's blood, the attacks begin to come closer together. In the end one dies either during a convulsion, or due to his or her weakened state." He looked down at his hands for a moment, then back up at the prince. "No cure has ever been found. In every single case, the victim died."

After a long period of silence, Shailiha spoke again. "And what of Wigg?" she asked, her voice cracking a bit.

"Wigg was more lucky, should one choose to characterize it as luck," Faegan answered. "I don't believe that the powder used on him can kill him, though I don't know if we can restore his sight." He raised his eyebrows slightly. "There is one ray of hope in all of this, however."

"What is that?" Shailiha asked eagerly.

"The fact that both Wigg and Tristan were infected with the same thing—the brain fluid of a stalker, and the same stalker. Had their afflictions been due to separate causes, our task would be twice as onerous. And given the limited amount of time before us, the future would be much more bleak."

Wigg cleared his throat. "We also now believe we know the reason for the bounty on the prince," he said.

Tristan snapped his head around, staring intently at the wizard. "What is it?"

"Faegan and I discussed it at length," Wigg answered. "The most obvious conclusion is that they want to keep you from doing what you are supposed to do—commune with your citizens in their time of need. Branding you a criminal will turn many against you, and the price on your head will embolden some to try to capture you. In this way you are also kept from garnering support and raising a civilian army to fight off their hatchlings, assuming such a thing is even possible. All in return for one hundred thousand kisa in gold that Ragnar can very easily conjure up, ultimately costing him nothing. Clever, when you think about it."

"The hatchlings must be stopped," Tristan said adamantly. "With the Royal Guard gone the nation has virtually no means of protection against whatever it is they plan to do."

"True," Faegan said, "but that would be difficult, indeed."

"You forget that I am still lord of a different army," Tristan answered, his face darkening. "An army of the fiercest fighters I have ever seen. We must make use of the Minions. It is the only way."

Again the table went silent. Tristan recalled the death and destruction caused by the winged warriors during their relentless onslaught against his homeland.

"Wigg and I have considered that, but it presents a great many problems," Faegan responded.

"How so?" Shailiha asked.

"For one thing, how would we accomplish it?" Wigg asked. "Even Faegan can only hold his portal open for one hour each day—hardly enough time to bring a sizable force through very quickly. The first time the Minions arrived here they came by armada. We still don't know how they managed to cross the Sea of Whispers, or how long it took them. We cannot even be sure whether the Minions continue to accept Tristan's rule over them, for we have yet to hear from Geldon and Joshua. In fact, we have no way of even knowing whether our emissaries are still alive. Until we do, we can assume nothing. If the Minions of Day and Night do not recognize Tristan as their true lord, once they are here they might decide to take the nation for themselves, or even join in with the hatchlings. For all we know right now, this could be yet another of the things that Ragnar wants us to do. We must consider all the possibilities before acting." The lead wizard's eyebrow arched characteristically over his right eye.

"Additionally," he continued, "there is also the prospect of Tristan's personal involvement. Even if the Minions accept his leadership, it is only he they will follow. And if he does lead the Minions in a war against the hatchlings, he will only solidify in the minds of the populace exactly what Ragnar and Scrounge have been saying all along: that the prince is not only in league with but also commands the ones who butchered their nation." He let out a great sigh. "Ragnar and Scrounge have planned exceedingly well," he added softly.

Closing his eyes and rubbing the back of his neck with one hand, Tristan turned away. He felt very frustrated—an emotion he didn't always deal with well. And it seemed that no matter what was proposed the wizards always had a thousand good reasons why it couldn't be done. He understood Wigg's points about the Minions, but he still felt in his heart that it was the only way.

"And in addition to everything else, we still do not know why Ragnar abducted the consuls," Tristan muttered discouragingly. "Or what caused the incredible azure glow that Wigg and I saw in his chambers."

"That's true," Faegan said. "Or why Ragnar needs some of your blood." Then a hint of a smile appeared on his face. "But I believe that there is now another within these walls who might be able to help us." He looked over to Wigg. "Old friend," he said compassionately, "it is now time to learn the truth."

Wigg took a breath, nodding slowly. "Thank you," he replied softly.

"Can you discern whether she is truly Wigg's daughter?" Tristan asked.

There was an audible gasp, and he turned in dismay to see the shock on Celeste's face. Her full lips worked silently for several seconds before she uttered a word. "D-daughter?" she stammered at last.

Wigg turned in the direction of her voice. "It is possible, my dear, though I would have preferred to bring up the subject more gently."

Tristan tightened his lips and shook his head in annoyance at himself. He *had* to learn not to be so precipitious, he told himself harshly.

"But before we discuss it, we should ascertain whether it is true, I think," the lead wizard continued kindly.

"You will activate her untrained blood with the waters of the Caves?" Tristan asked.

"Correct," Faegan replied.

"But what will that tell us?" Tristan countered, a puzzled look on his face. "Her blood signature, like everyone else's, will be unique, will it not? How does that in any way indicate who her parents were?"

Smiling into the prince's face, Faegan said, "Failee, one-time wife to Wigg, lead wizard of the Directorate. Blood signature, please."

With that, yet another of the many drawers obediently opened, and a single sheet of parchment floated into place atop the table, next to the others. The prince looked down at the blood signature.

"I still don't understand," Tristan said. "How does this help?"

"Look at each of the blood signatures in turn," Faegan replied. "First Wigg's, then Shailiha's, and finally Failee's. What is it they all have in common?" He smiled craftily. "I will even give you a hint. In a way, it is actually their differences that make them the same."

Truly puzzled, Tristan looked down at the signatures for some time. To his eye, each of them seemed unique. "I still do not see it," he answered.

"That is because you are looking *past* it, not *at* it," Faegan said.

"I see it!" Shailiha suddenly said from the other side of the table.

"And that is?" Faegan asked.

"The tops are all made the same way, as are the bottoms," she answered.

Faegan smiled. "Please explain."

"In each of the signatures, there is a basically horizontal dividing line. All this time I had been regarding the signatures as a single design. I can now see a duality present in them that I had missed before."

"Please go on."

She furrowed her brow for a moment. "The lower portions are made up of straight lines, connected by sharp angles. But the top halves are softer, more fluid, and more roundly shaped."

"And this helps us with our problem because . . ." Faegan said.

"I still do not know," she answered.

"Go back to the word you yourself used to describe them," the crippled wizard said gently. "That word was 'duality.' "

She tilted her head for a moment. "Duality," she said softly. "That means two sides. We are looking for two things, the mother and the father." Her face lit up. "One of the halves represents the signature of the father, the other that of the mother!" she exclaimed.

"Excellent!" Faegan said. He looked over to see that Wigg was also smiling. "Now tell me, which is which?"

"The lower halves, the ones of the sharper angles and straight lines, are probably of the fathers," she said. "And the top halves, the more fluid and softer of the two, would be from the mothers."

Faegan sat back in his chair to give Nicodemus another scratch. "Well done, Your Highness," he said softly.

"Indeed," Wigg replied.

"I then take it that Celeste's signature, if she is truly the product of Wigg and Failee, will be made up of Wigg's male signature, and Failee's female signature," Tristan interjected. "This is why each signature of the endowed is the same in some ways, yet completely different in others."

"Exactly," Faegan answered. "Allow me to demonstrate."

Narrowing his eyes, he enchanted two incisions into the parchment containing Wigg's signature, neatly separating the upper from the lower. The bottom part then floated over the table to neatly cover the lower half of Failee's signature, creating a new one.

Faegan sat back again in his chair, obviously pleased with the results of his labors. "If Celeste is truly the daughter of Wigg and Failee, then this is what her signature shall look like," he said simply. "The top half indicating the father, the bottom half the mother. The result will be inviolate. She either will be their child, or she won't."

Tristan looked over to Wigg. He could tell that the old one's anticipation was mounting by the second.

"This doesn't make sense," Tristan said.

"How so?" Faegan answered.

"You said that only twins, such as Shailiha and myself, have identical signatures. But if the blood signature of a child is always constructed in this way, then how is it that all of the children born of the same set of parents do not have identical signatures?"

"It's really quite simple," Faegan answered. "You see, each blood signature is really made up of three parts—not just two, as one might first suspect. One distinct pattern comes from the father, one from the mother, and a third part forms during conception that is a unique combination of them both. This third part varies from sibling to sibling. When that child has a child of his or her own, a third, newly unique part is of course again created, in combination with the spouse. The differences between the blood signatures of siblings are difficult to discern—even more difficult in the case of twins. Only an endowed person, trained in the art of reading them, can tell the signatures of two siblings apart. This became one of the tasks of the consuls, and was the secret method by which paternity disputes were settled in the kingdom. Provided, of course, the issue was brought before your father for an official ruling by the crown."

Tristan snorted in disbelief. He remembered the day not so long ago when Wigg told him how the study of the craft was infinite. *Little did I know,* he thought.

Wigg turned his white eyes to Celeste. "My dear," he said softly, "give me your hand."

She slowly placed her hand into his.

Wigg felt along the length of it, stopping at the tips of her fingers. "Do you remember what I did to you in the forest?" he asked gently.

"Yes."

"And did it hurt?" he asked.

"No."

"I am going to do the same thing to you now, nothing more."

Almost immediately, a small incision began to appear. "Faegan, if you please," Wigg said.

Reaching out, Faegan turned her hand over, and the single drop of bright red blood landed softly on the parchment that held the combined blood signatures of Failee and Wigg. He then poured a single drop of water from the Caves onto it.

Tristan watched, transfixed, as the fluid moved and the design began to take shape. After a few moments he could clearly see the result.

The two blood signatures looked identical.

Faegan reached past Celeste and gripped his old friend's shoulder.

"Wigg," he said gently, "it's true. The two signatures are a perfect match." Then, after a silent moment he added, "There are also Forestallments in her blood, much like those of the princess."

Faegan tried to smile, but his eyes filled with moisture. Memories of his own daughter flooded him—the girl who had been taken by the Coven, turned into one of them, and later used to destroy Eutracia. And all the while he had thought she was dead. He would never forgive himself for not somehow *knowing,* and for not being able to prevent all the evil that was done to and by his daughter. Blinking back tears, he looked down at his useless legs and turned his chair away from the table.

Wigg was already crying. No one else knew what to say as he pulled himself together and wiped his blind eyes with the sleeve of his robe.

He finally shook his head sadly, and held his palms out toward Celeste. She placed her hands in his.

"What we have just proven, beyond a shadow of a doubt," Wigg said to her, "is that you are a product of my time with Failee. She became enamored with the darker aspects of the craft, leaving me to study them on her own. She never told me she was with child. You, Celeste, are the daughter I never knew I had. And I will protect you with my life."

"Welcome, Celeste," Shailiha said softly. "Welcome to our home, the Redoubt of the Directorate. The time of your coming is long overdue."

"Indeed," Faegan said, and Tristan nodded his approval at the same time.

Celeste's beautiful face darkened. "If you and Failee are

truly my parents, then why would you abandon me, leaving me with someone like Ragnar?"

"I have had three hundred years to consider the tangled history of those days," Wigg said. "And now that I have discovered your existence, I believe I can answer much of what you ask. I will make it as simple as I know how. It is a story that I have only recently pieced together from both fact and long since dusty memories, so please bear with me as an old man tells his tale." Every pair of eyes and ears in the room was intently focused on what Wigg had to say.

"It is now clear that Failee left me immediately after discovering she was pregnant, and gave birth to you during the war," he began. "As the war worsened for them, it became obvious to her that she would need a place to hide you—to both remove you from harm's way and to keep your existence a deep secret. Failee was fully aware that if I ever learned I had a daughter, I would move earth and sky to find her. This she could not afford, for it would have ruined her plans for the future." He paused for a moment, hoping he was not being too blunt for her, but then continued.

"She no doubt hoped to either return and retrieve you should they be victorious, or find an equally safe, permanent place of safety for you should they not," Wigg continued. "After they lost the war, the sorceresses were banished to Parthalon, the nation across the sea. She could not take you with her, for fear of revealing your existence. She also knew that I would surely intervene, demanding that you stay here with me. Despite the fact that she was your mother, she was nothing if not pragmatic, her cause more important to her than anything else. I do not wish to hurt you when I tell you this, but bringing you into this world had more to do with her plans of conquest than it ever had to do with any maternal instincts she might have possessed. It was only after three centuries had passed that one of her mistresses and her army finally returned."

"But why give Celeste to someone as hideous as Ragnar?" Tristan asked. "That doesn't make any sense."

"In retrospect, Ragnar was the perfect choice," Wigg answered. "Consider the following facts. First of all he was a powerful wizard, and could use the craft to protect her, if need be. Second, as a blood stalker, he would devoutly obey Failee.

This would also have been the time when Failee laid the Incantation of Forestallments in Celeste's blood. Tell me, Celeste, do you have any special powers? Powers that you have not been trained to use, but that have instead simply occurred naturally?"

"No," she said flatly. "I have no such gifts. At least none that I am aware of."

Wigg rubbed his brow, thinking. "It is apparent to me now that Failee first intended you, her own daughter, to become her fifth sorceress. Then, much later, she chose Shailiha instead."

Faegan then looked up from his cat. "And Failee gave Ragnar orders that once Celeste reached a certain age, he was to endow her with time enchantments—thereby further protecting her from disease and old age," he mused aloud, still stroking Nicodemus.

"But why didn't she do that herself and make sure of it?" Shailiha asked. "Why would she entrust that task to Ragnar?"

"She had to, because Celeste was still far too young," Wigg replied. "The time enchantments work amazingly well. They literally 'freeze' the subject at the chronological age during which they are applied. Faegan and I, for example, received the time enchantments during our later years. Failee obviously wished Celeste to come to adulthood and be in full command of her faculties when this was performed, so that she could be more useful to her purpose."

There was still something about all of this that Tristan did not understand. At first he was hesitant to bring it up, knowing that it would cause both Celeste and Wigg a great deal of pain. Taking a deep breath, he finally decided.

"Wigg, there is something that makes no sense," he said. "Assuming Ragnar was obliged to obey Failee, then why would he have ever abused Celeste?" He regretted having to conjure up hateful memories for her, but it had to be. "Didn't he know that once Failee discovered it, he would have incurred her wrath forever?"

"There are several possible reasons," Wigg said, his right eyebrow arching up over the white eye beneath it. "First and foremost, never forget that he is at least partially mad. Clearly not as insane as a full stalker, but mad nonetheless. Second, he would have known that the Coven had been banished from Eutracia, to the Sea of Whispers. He, like the Directorate, never imagined their possible return. No doubt he believed he was safe to do with Celeste as he pleased." Pausing, he took a deep breath, as if his next words were to be the most difficult.

"And then there is the final, and perhaps most convincing reason of all," he said. "I am positive he was aware that Celeste was my daughter. What better way to simultaneously take pleasure for himself and revenge against me?"

For the first time Celeste lowered her head in shame. She wished all this talk of her time with Ragnar would end. But she was slowly coming to learn that the people here were vastly different than the few she was used to. She turned her eyes to Wigg with what seemed to be a newfound respect. Then her expression hardened again, as yet another thought came to her.

"I will kill him one day," she said softly, almost inaudibly, her sapphire eyes shining with hate.

"What?" Wigg asked her.

"I will kill him one day, for the things he has done to so many of us in this room."

"No," Wigg said forcefully. He turned his white eyes in the general direction of the prince. "Nor will you, Tristan. When the time comes, Ragnar is to be mine. Mine alone. I shall be the one to destroy the monster I helped create."

Tristan had never heard Wigg speak this way. Frankly, it surprised him. The usually calm, discerning wizard had always been slow to anger, always presenting a demeanor of contemplated reason. But the Wigg who now sat before them was different somehow, the hate clearly radiating from his face despite the lifeless nature of his eyes. This time it was personal, and it showed. Still, there was something tugging at the back of the prince's mind.

"But there remains yet another puzzle," he said thoughtfully. "We know that Failee purposely left Emily, Faegan's daughter, behind. At that point Emily was an adult, and a sorceress in her own right. Why then didn't Failee leave Celeste in her keeping? To me it would seem a much safer thing to do than leaving her with a partially mutated blood stalker."

"I can certainly understand your thinking," Wigg responded. "But the fact of the matter is that you never knew Failee as I did. As I have said, she was pragmatic. Her cause was everything to her, and her personal needs meant nothing. Taking care of Celeste was never to be Emily's task. Failee needed Emily to be free to roam the nation in search of both information and the company of powerful men, in order to eventually be received at your father's court, so she could keep Failee abreast of any news regarding you and your sister."

He squeezed Celeste's hands. "What we now know is that Failee did not leave just one person behind, as we first thought. She left two."

"You also said that it was Failee's original intent to make Celeste her fifth sorceress," Shailiha said, thinking out loud. "Then why didn't she do it? Why didn't she have Succiu search for her daughter when the second mistress was here, with the entire army of the Minions to help? And then, above all, why would she choose me over her own daughter? It all seems pretty coldhearted."

"Coldhearted," Wigg murmured softly. "I am sorry to have to tell you this, Celeste, but that is a very good description of the woman who was your mother. The truth is that Shailiha had by now been born, her supremely endowed blood making the princess a better candidate for Failee's plans. And do not forget that Failee could not send the Minions to Eutracia until they had evolved to her liking, and were present in sufficient numbers to overwhelm us. I do think it was originally Failee's desire to make Celeste her fifth sorceress. But when she learned that the Chosen Ones had been born and that one of them was female, her blood of a purity never before seen, Failee's path was clear. If she could turn Shailiha, one of the Chosen Ones, to their side, Shailiha would eventually make an even better leader than either she or her daughter. She would therefore take Shailiha first, and after her success had been assured she would return for Celeste."

Celeste's face fell slightly. "Where is she now?" Celeste asked.

"She is dead," Wigg answered sadly. "Never to return. Tristan killed her, and the others of the Coven. Except for Succiu, the second mistress, who committed suicide, taking Tristan's unborn child with her."

Tristan looked down at his hands.

From the other end of the table Faegan's voice came strong

and clear. "There are two very important things you have overlooked, Wigg," he said, "and they should both be dealt with as soon as possible."

"And they are?" Wigg asked.

"Of the greatest urgency is the matter of Celeste's time enchantments. If the blood stalker comes to the conclusion that she is now in hiding with us rather than having simply gone missing again, he may, in a fit of rage, issue an Incantation of Discontinuance. Upon discovering your daughter after all of these years, I'm sure you do not wish to lose her again." Raising his eyebrows, he scratched his cat once more. "Especially because of him."

Wigg let a sudden rush of air out of his lungs. "Of course," he said, shaking his head. "Thank you, Faegan."

"What we must do, therefore, is to issue her another enchantment, one that envelops the first," Faegan added. "Then if Ragnar's is suddenly taken away, ours will instantaneously take effect. After we do she will feel a slight shudder if she loses the blood stalker's protection, but she will suffer no ill effects." He looked to the beautiful woman in the green dress. "If you feel anything abnormal after we enchant you, my child, you must tell us at once." Celeste nodded her agreement.

"You said there were two things that must be done," Tristan said to Faegan. "What is the other one?"

"Two additional things, actually, now that I think about it," Faegan answered, smiling. "And they are related. Can you guess either of them?"

Tristan was suddenly out of patience with talk of magic. "I do not wish to guess," he said bluntly. "I am tired, and would like to have a simple answer for once."

Wigg's infamous eyebrow rose up in surprise, and Faegan sighed, pursing his lips in contemplation.

It will begin soon, Faegan thought sadly. *I must find a cure for him as quickly as possible, if indeed one exists at all.*

"First of all, Egloff's scroll makes reference to the fact that he believed Forestallments could be passed from one generation to another, provided the Forestallment had not already manifested itself in the parent," Faegan said. "If such is the case, then we must immediately check Morganna's blood signature. Her mother gave birth after her time with Failee and before the manifestation of her bond with the fliers, fitting exactly within Egloff's requirements. A positive reading would prove Egloff's theory of inheritance, since Morganna has been only in our care since her birth, and none of us have tampered with her blood." He paused for a moment, narrowing his eyes in thought. Then he took a deep breath. "The proven inheritance of Forestallments could bring forth convolutions in the craft the likes of which we have never dared dream," he said quietly. After a time, his thoughts returned to his next concern.

"In addition," he continued, "the prince's blood must also be checked. There is no telling what the ramifications of a Forestallment in the male of the Chosen Ones could bring."

Faegan wheeled his chair a little closer to the table, placing both palms down on it. His face was grave, making it abundantly clear that he had something else very important to say.

"I now believe that Failee was far more brilliant than any of us first thought," he said slowly. "Her calculations resulting in the art of Forestallments bring with them an entirely unknown world of possibilities, both good and bad. In many ways I hope that her knowledge of these things died with her. And yet, in other ways there is a part of me, the ever-curious wizard, that desperately wishes to learn how she accomplished it. I fear that the appearance of the Forestallments may have much more to do with our current difficulties than we first thought."

He was interrupted by a sudden, urgent pounding on the massive door. Without waiting for permission, Shannon entered, his ever-present ale jug in one hand. He wobbled drunkenly back and forth, using either side of the door frame to keep from falling down. Tristan often found the gnome's inebriation comic, but this time things were different. This time Shannon was scared to death.

"What is it?" Faegan asked urgently.

"Forgive me, Master, but someone not of our group has somehow entered the Redoubt!" Shannon slurred through his drunkenness, the seriousness of his words nonetheless coming through. "And she demands to see Master Wigg. There is news. And none of it is good."

CHAPTER TWENTY-EIGHT

RAGNAR was full of fury and concern as he stomped his way through the labyrinthine passageways to his young master. When Nicholas summoned him, the stalker had no choice but to stop what he was doing and obey. But the anger that flowed through his veins at having been interrupted in his quest was now far more consuming than whatever the boy could conceivably want of him. It had been only hours since he first sensed Celeste had left the Caves. She had left before. But this time it was different. This time he feared it was forever. He had even wasted precious moments before setting out to find her, luxuriating in the thoughts of the slow, delicious retribution he would administer to her body after he recaptured her.

But upon exiting the Caves and using the craft to search for her highly endowed blood, he had been stunned. Because of its great purity, he had always been able to detect it, no matter how far she had gone. But this time he had been able to sense absolutely no trace of her. Someone of the craft was cloaking her blood, and he had his suspicions about who it was. Her father. The man he hated most in the world.

As always, the glow of the craft seeped out beneath Nicholas' door. Trying to remain calm, the stalker took a controlled breath, squaring his shoulders. As he opened the door he saw that Nicholas had not only enlarged the size of this particular chamber, but had also changed its appearance. The young master sat cross-legged in his simple white robe, elevated at least a meter above the highly polished floor. His body revolved slowly in midair, and his eyes were closed in meditation.

The stalker could see that the undulating ribbon of energy

now encircled this room, as well. Deeply embedded within the marble walls, it seemed to be a living, breathing entity. Wherever one found Nicholas, one also found the vein.

There were hundreds of endowed children here, happily at play in the great chamber. Nicholas had transformed the walls of this chamber into oddly playful checkerboard squares of the faintest blue and pink, creating a calming, cheerful environment for them.

Throughout the room, boys and girls of different ages practiced simple aspects of the craft. They played and talked among each other, their laughter bouncing happily off the walls, contrasting starkly with the controlled serenity of the master.

Ragnar was stymied. He knew that Nicholas had sent Scrounge and the hatchlings off on a mission, but he had never expected this.

"Sit down," the young adept said in his soft, commanding voice. He had stopped revolving but continued to hover in midair. A short throne of marble appeared behind Ragnar, and the stalker obediently took a seat. Nicholas opened his dark, almond-shaped eyes, leveling them upon the stalker with a seriousness Ragnar had seldom seen.

"Your mind tells me you are disturbed," the young man said quietly. "Do not be. Celeste is of no consequence. True, after only myself and the Chosen Ones, her blood is of the highest quality ever seen. But that fact has no bearing on my plans." His eyebrows rose slightly in mock appreciation of what he sensed to be Ragnar's concern. "But it was not the quality of her blood that attracted you to her, was it? It was her great beauty, your twisted, centuries-old subjugation of her, and the fact that she is the daughter of Wigg that enticed you so. Do not be concerned for her absence. Soon you shall be able to take all of the women of Eutracia, should you wish to."

"Do you know where she is, my lord?" Ragnar asked anxiously.

"She is surely in the Redoubt of the Directorate, with her father and the others," Nicholas answered. "In truth, you brought this upon yourself. Your insistence upon displaying your trophy to Wigg and the Chosen One only resulted in her final, desperate departure. Indeed, even I did not know this would happen. However, I could sense that she was somehow familiar with the prince. I do not believe she knew who he was or was aware of his importance, but for some reason she felt she could trust him. I sensed she was leaving the Caves, and that she had found the prince and the wizard on the trail where we left them. In the end I let her go to them."

Ragnar was stunned. "You let her go, my lord?" he asked incredulously. Had Nicholas been anyone else, Ragnar would have killed him on the spot. "But why?" he asked breathlessly. "Why would you let her go?"

"She meant nothing to me." Nicholas smiled. "She was your toy, never mine. And should I ever require her, she is easily found. In fact, she is in far safer hands with the wizards then she ever was with you," he said, enjoying the insulting reference to the stalker's perverse inclinations. "And the fact that she is no longer here to distract you only means you shall be more attentive to your duties, does it not?"

"Be that as it may," he continued, "Wigg and Faegan will not immediately try to remedy the fact that she is untrained. For we have seen to it that they have far too many other pressing concerns to deal with." Nicholas was no longer smiling. Seeing this, Ragnar forced down an anxious swallow.

"I'm sure it was a very tearful reunion," the young man went on. Glancing down at some scampering children, he smiled briefly. "Celeste has finally reunited with her long-lost father. The synergy of it is fascinating. And Wigg is of course shielding her blood. But even he cannot cloak it from *me*."

"That traitorous bitch," Ragnar fumed. "With your permission, I would like to issue a discontinuance of her time enchantments. Let Wigg watch his beautiful daughter, the child he never knew he had, turn to a pile of dust before he even comes to know her." He relished the thought, even if it meant Celeste's death. If Nicholas would no longer let him possess her, then he would keep Wigg from having her also.

Nicholas shook his head as if he were addressing an uneducated child. "At this point it would assuredly accomplish nothing," he replied.

"Again, my lord, I do not understand," Ragnar said shortly.

"Wigg and Faegan's first reaction to Celeste's presence will be to suspect that she is in league with us, even though she is not," Nicholas replied. "They will also examine her blood to see whether it is dormant or trained. In fact, I have no doubt that this has already occurred. Then they will examine her blood signature, revealing that she is truly the product of Wigg and Failee. Once so assured, they will cast an overlapping time enchantment upon her—and have almost certainly already done so. Your discontinuance would be for naught."

As he looked at the young man, Ragnar took in the fact that Nicholas' appearance had again changed. He now appeared to be approximately twenty Seasons of New Life. His face and body had reached full maturity, coming to more closely resemble his father. Never again would the blood stalker be able to think of Nicholas as the "child." He wondered how long it would be before Nicholas commanded all of the power of the Paragon. But his thoughts were interrupted by the young adept's voice rising above the happy din of the children.

"You are fortunate that Failee does not still live," Nicholas said almost coyly. "Not only would she be merciless because of your abuse of her daughter, but you also failed to fulfill the one responsibility she charged you with," Nicholas went on. "Namely, keeping Celeste from her father. As it now stands, you have only the wrath of a blind wizard and a crippled one to concern you." Nicholas smiled, as if the combined powers of Wigg and Faegan were a fly that he could simply brush away with one hand. "But do not bother yourself unnecessarily. When all is said and done, Celeste will again be yours."

Ragnar looked to the hundreds of laughing children. "If I may be so bold, my lord, how is it that all of these children are here?" he asked. "And am I correct in assuming that they are all of endowed blood?"

"Oh, yes," Nicholas answered. "They are indeed of endowed blood. They have been brought here only recently by my hatchlings. Some are the children captured with the consuls, and others of them are the girls from Fledgling House."

Ragnar narrowed his gray, bloodshot eyes in curiosity. "Fledgling House?" he asked quizzically. "I have never heard of such a place."

"It remains one of the greatest secrets of the dearly departed Directorate of Wizards," Nicholas replied. "I doubt Wigg has told even Faegan of its existence. That means only you, myself, Scrounge, Wigg, and a particularly frightened woman named Martha know of its existence." He paused to look at the youngsters. "Aside from the girls who were taken from there, and their parents, of course," he added casually. "All of these children before you are the especially gifted sons and daughters of the consuls. Those very same men of trained, endowed blood now ensconced in the catacombs. But at this time it does not serve my purposes to speak further of Fledgling House," he added.

"And may I also ask, why are the children here?"

"The answer to that is simple." Nicholas smiled. For a moment he paused as if deciding whether to answer the question, his deafening silence settling over the blood stalker's mind like a shroud. Finally, the young adept spoke. "I will have need of their blood," he whispered.

Ragnar went suddenly cold inside. Even to his mad, seasoned mind, the prospect of such a thing was hideous. *First he collected the blood of the Chosen One,* the stalker thought. *And now he has need of the blood of these relatively untrained children, as well. Whatever for?*

"My reasons will be revealed soon enough," Nicholas said, answering the stalker's silent, unasked question.

Ragnar felt the unmistakable need to return to his chambers. He desperately wanted to ingest more of the odorous yellow fluid waiting for him there. But his mind was a swirl of curiosity, sparked by Nicholas' statements. "And how is it that the children are so happy?" he asked. "Have they not all been suddenly ripped from their homes?"

"Oh, indeed," Nicholas answered. "But they now believe this place is where they belong." Again he paused, clearly relishing his next words. "They now all believe me to be their father. It has to do with something called Forestallments."

Despite what he already knew Nicholas to be capable of, Ragnar was stunned. He had seen many ministrations of the craft over the last three centuries, but none so powerful as this. To enter the consciousness of another was truly an immense power. But to enter the minds of so many, at the same time controlling their thoughts while also erasing memories of the past, would require an ascendancy that was truly inconceivable. The stalker sat unmoving, in complete awe of the young man floating before him.

Ragnar was burning with the one inquiry he had for so long wished to put to Nicholas, but had been afraid to broach. Now he found his lips forming the words. "My lord," he whispered, lowering his grotesque head in supplication, "forgive me, but I have never seen such power. From where is it you have come?"

Enjoying the children as they began to congregate at his feet, Nicholas smiled. Some turned their faces up to look at the one they believed to be their father, each of them now also certain in the false knowledge that they were all brother and sister to one another.

"I come from a place of light and darkness," Nicholas answered softy. "A place of pure, unadulterated power and knowledge. It is a concept your feeble mind could only begin to dream of. I come from the same place where my mother, the departed second mistress of the Coven, now exists. The same place I intend to send any of those not worthy of the new order."

Nicholas reached down to the face of a particularly pretty young girl, raising her bright, shining eyes up to his own.

"I come from death itself," he whispered.

CHAPTER TWENTY-NINE

*A*s the very drunken Shannon stood in the doorway, it was immediately clear that something had affected him deeply. His knees were trembling, making it even more difficult for him to remain upright.

Wigg and Faegan, however, remained calm. "What's wrong?" the lead wizard demanded of the terrified gnome. "Who is it that has asked to see me?"

A heavyset woman of some years burst past Shannon to fall at Wigg's feet. Wrapping her arms around his legs and burying her head in his lap, she sobbed, her entire body trembling with fear. Tristan looked to Faegan for an answer, but a quick shake of the elder wizard's head told the prince that even he did not know.

"Who are you?" Wigg demanded. Her tears were beginning to create dark blotches on his robe.

She finally lifted her face, and her gaze went wide at the sight of his eyes. She searched his ancient face for the meaning behind his obvious impairment. "It is I, Martha," she said tremulously. "But tell me, old friend, what has happened to you?"

At the mention of her name Wigg immediately placed his hands upon her face. "Martha," he finally whispered, "is it really you?" Then his face darkened. "Why have you come here? You know it is forbidden, so I'm sure your reason must be grave."

She lowered her head in pain, the tears coming anew. "They are all gone, Wigg," she whispered. "All of the girls—every one. Taken by a man in brown leather, who rode through the sky on a hideous bird such as I have never seen. Hundreds of the awful things came, and there was nothing we could do . . ."

Fearing the worst, Tristan turned to Shannon. "Is this woman the only being to have breached the entrance to the Redoubt?" he demanded.

"Yes, Tristan," Shannon answered thickly. "She apparently came alone. The various safeguards protecting the tunnels are all still in place. After telling me her story I brought her here."

"Shannon, please come in," Wigg said, "and shut the door behind you." Shannon joined the others at the great table.

Wigg asked Martha to sit and turned his face to hers. It was clear to everyone that he had been greatly struck by what Martha had said, for tears were gathering in his eyes. As best he could, he quickly made Martha aware of the identities of the others in the room.

"As for my sight," Wigg said to her, "I have been afflicted by the same ones who came to you. Now then, tell me everything," he prodded gently. "Leave nothing out. But first, what of Duncan?"

A look of intense grief passed over her face as she closed her eyes. "Duncan is dead," she whispered, her voice cracking. "My husband of fifty years, gone in a matter of moments. One of the great birds beheaded him when he tried to resist them. As we speak, his endowed blood lies spilled on the grassy fields of Fledgling House."

At the mention of Fledgling House, Tristan turned to Faegan. It was clear the elder wizard was fascinated by this sudden turn of events. His eyes twinkling, he leaned forward eagerly. But it was also clear that he had absolutely no knowledge of what was being discussed.

Lowering his head, Wigg winced at the pain of hearing Martha's words. "I am so sorry," he whispered to her. "Duncan was one of my dearest friends and closest allies." The lead wizard paused for a moment, taking the measure of his next words. "He was one of the best of them. That was why I picked him for the very special task that the two of you performed so well. I shall miss him with all my heart."

"As shall I, Lead Wizard," Martha whispered back. "As shall I."

Tristan could contain his curiosity no longer. "Forgive me, Wigg, but what are you talking about?" he asked. "Who is this woman? And what is Fledgling House?"

Despite Wigg's blank eyes, his expression made it clear that there was yet another secret hidden within him—and that the telling of it would be difficult. With a great sigh, he began his explanation.

"Fledgling House was one of the greatest secrets of the Directorate," he began. "The late king and queen also knew of it."

Tristan cast a surprised look to his sister. "Our mother and father knew of this place?" Shailiha asked softly.

"Indeed," Wigg answered. "It was, in fact, Queen Morganna's idea. She felt it necessary that we dispense with some of the old ways, putting the two genders of the endowed back on equal terms. In the end the Directorate finally agreed."

Tristan narrowed his eyes in thought. "I still do not understand," he said to the wizard. "What 'old ways' are you referring to?"

Wigg took a deep breath, gathering himself up. Finally he said, "The 'old ways' to which I refer is the ban on the teaching of the craft to females."

The prince sat back in his chair, stunned. Looking to Faegan and Shailiha, he could see that they were equally surprised. Faegan leaned forward, his gray-green eyes flashing with curiosity.

"Wigg," the elder wizard began in a whisper, "do you mean to say that—"

"Yes," Wigg said, cutting him off. "It was the desire of the king, queen, and Directorate to resume allowing females to practice the craft." For several long moments the room was silent.

"And it was Mother's idea to do this thing?" Tristan asked.

"Yes," Wigg answered. "She labored long and hard, endlessly petitioning both the king and the Directorate for the right of endowed women to be trained in the craft. She wished for them to one day take their place alongside the men who commanded such power. She even foresaw the day when women would serve in the Directorate. Morganna was a wonderful woman, and far ahead of her time. In many ways she was much stronger than the king. But there eventually came another reason for her feelings on this matter. One that finally tipped the Directorate in her favor. It was a very compelling reason that no one could ignore."

"And that was?" Tristan asked.

"The twin births of you and Shailiha, and the azure light that accompanied the event as prophesized in the Tome," Wigg answered. "The event for which we had waited for over three centuries. As the male of the Chosen Ones and the somewhat stronger of the two, Tristan was to rule Eutracia first. And then Shailiha, if need be."

Intensely interested, Tristan leaned forward in his chair and looked directly into Wigg's lifeless eyes. "That's why we were born as twins, isn't it?" he asked softly. "So that if I should fail or die in the attempt to eventually join the two opposite sides of the craft, Shailiha would be trained and then succeed me in my efforts. That's what you mean by 'if need be.' "

"Yes," Wigg answered. "But there is far more to it than that." *Indeed*, he thought. "But more of this topic another day," the wizard ordered. He turned back to Martha. "Please tell me what happened."

"Hundreds of the awful things flew to the ground, just as the children were at their noon recess," Martha began, the pain of her words showing clearly on her face. "Duncan tried to fight them, but he was killed immediately." Remembering what had happened next, with a trembling hand she removed the scroll Scrounge had given her, placing it before Wigg.

"The one in brown leather wrote this in Duncan's blood, telling me to deliver it to the prince," she continued. "The other birds took the children in their claws, and flew away. Then they forced me atop one of the birds, and it carried me here. But there is something else of importance, Lead Wizard. They obviously know where you are hiding. And worse, they know how to breach the tunnels of the Redoubt. It was the one in the brown leather who told me how to cause the boulder to roll away. After I entered, the gnome found me. I told him my story, and he led me here."

Tristan looked to Shannon. The gnome had regained some of his composure, but not much. "Is this what unnerved you so?" the prince asked. "Martha's story?"

"Yes," Shannon admitted. "In my three hundred some years I have been witness to some of the most horrible things imaginable. But to take children . . ." As if unable to continue, his voice faded away.

Tristan nodded gently in Shannon's direction, then he picked up the scroll, unrolled it, and read it aloud. The muscles in his hands tightened even harder with each new word.

We took your cherished children today,
It was such an easy task.
The feeble consul Duncan has surely breathed his last.
And when the moment comes, my friend,
When we again shall meet,
You will grovel like an obedient dog
In the dirt before my feet.

S.

His endowed, poisoned blood rising hotly in his veins, Tristan slammed the scroll down on the top of the table and shot to his feet. He violently pushed his heavy chair back a good meter and began pacing back and forth in an attempt to release his surging, pent-up anger. The heels of his black knee boots rang out loudly on the marble floor as his lips curled into a sneer of hatred for the ones called Scrounge and Ragnar, and for the vile acts they were committing.

Holding Morganna closer, Shailiha looked aghast at her brother. This was not the mature, controlled warrior she had been so impressed with just after she had been cured. This was a different Tristan. He was clearly in the grip of something, uncontrollably raging against all of the injustices being inflicted on his beloved Eutracia. Hoping for reassurance, she turned to Faegan. Giving the princess a quick shake of the head, the chair-bound wizard indicated that Tristan should be left alone.

Faegan knew what was happening to him. The poison was already causing the occasional agitation of Tristan's blood, and therefore of his mind. He also knew that the first of Tristan's convulsions could not be far behind. If the prince was not quickly cured of the poison, the unbelievably high quality of his blood might soon make him uncontrollable, even for the two wizards.

No one in the room moved; no one spoke as they waited for the prince to calm himself. Finally, the attack passed. The tension in his face subsided, and he again took his place at the table. Shailiha placed an affectionate hand over his, giving him a small smile.

Uncharacteristically, Tristan did not smile back. Instead, he focused his dark blue eyes on Wigg. "I believe you have some explaining to do," he said bluntly. "What is Fledgling House, and who are the children Martha refers to?"

"Indeed," Faegan added from the other side of the table.

Wigg took a deep sigh. "Tristan," he began, "do you remember the first day I brought you to the Redoubt and you saw the nursery—the place where the sons of the consuls were being looked after?"

"Of course," Tristan answered angrily. That day, among many others, was one the prince would never forget. He had been overwhelmed at the amazing acts of the craft the many young boys were performing. The wizard had sworn him to secrecy on the spot.

"Well," Wigg said, "those boys were only the tip of the iceberg, so to speak."

"What are you talking about?" Tristan asked.

"I'm talking about Fledgling House," Wigg answered simply. "When your mother convinced us of the need to begin training the girls in the craft, we decided to do so in secret, somewhere away from the boys and the majority of the consuls. You see, despite how long ago the Sorceresses' War ended, there is even today great sentiment against the teaching of the craft to women. It was our hope that we could eventually introduce the trained females into the population gradually, thereby reducing confrontation, bigotry, and misunderstanding." He sighed.

"The neophytes of Fledgling House are neither sorceresses of the Coven, nor practitioners of the Vagaries," he added. "They are only young girls, trying to do their best."

"In any event," Wigg continued, "the boys of the Consuls' Nursery and the girls at Fledgling House were very special. Only those of the most highly endowed blood were allowed to enter these schools, and neither group of students knew of the other. Duncan, the headmaster of Fledgling House, was one of the very best of our teachers. I named him to the post myself. Martha, who is not of endowed blood, oversaw the other needs of the girls. Having one's child accepted for training at Fledgling House or the Nursery of the Redoubt was truly deemed an honor." Suddenly Wigg's face became grave. "But now those very same children have been taken by Ragnar and Scrounge. And we still do not know why."

After many long moments, it was Faegan who spoke. "There is still something I do not understand," he said. "You mentioned to Martha that it was forbidden for her to come here. Why would that be?"

Wigg managed a half smile. "For the simple reason that she is female, of course. This secret place of learning is still available only to men, and Martha would be known only to those consuls whose daughters attended Fledgling House."

"Yet another safeguard?" Faegan asked.

"Yes."

"And Fledgling House itself," Faegan asked. "Where is it located?"

"A small castle was secretly constructed for our needs, in the highlands between Ilendium and Tanglewood," Wigg answered. "It lies just west of the Sippora, close to the base of the Tolenka Mountains."

"It sounds like a special place, Father," Celeste interjected, calling Wigg by that name for the first time.

"Oh, it is," Wigg answered his daughter. "It is a very special place indeed."

"And how long has Fledgling House been in existence?" Faegan asked.

Already knowing where this inquisition was heading, Wigg smiled. "The training began five years after the birth of the Chosen Ones. It took us that long to see the reason in Morganna's plans, determine the site, build the castle and the nursery, and select the first groups of students."

Tristan looked quickly to Shailiha. The equally shocked expression on her face told him that she had also figured it out. "That was twenty-five years ago!" the prince exclaimed. "That means—"

"Yes," Wigg said, purposely interrupting him. "There is already one mature generation of females, at least partially trained in the craft, living in Eutracia. Presuming, of course, that they still live."

"But there is more to this, isn't there?" Faegan asked. His eyes shone with certainty that he had unraveled a riddle. "These women, the first of their kind in centuries, were to eventually form their own group, weren't they? Queen Morganna was apparently both wise *and* persistent."

"What do you mean?" Shailiha asked.

"Unless I'm wrong"—Faegan smiled—"there was to have been an adjunct to the Brotherhood of Consuls. A secret sisterhood, if you will, made up of these women who had studied the craft. In this way two things could be accomplished."

Again Wigg smiled. "Go on," he said.

"First of all, if and when Shailiha was to be trained, the citizens would accept the princess more readily, if there were already other endowed women of training acknowledged in the kingdom." Faegan smiled. "Cleverly done, Wigg."

"Thank you," Wigg answered. "But you mentioned two reasons. What do you believe the other to be?"

"The formation of this other secret society," he mused, "would have finally given the queen something she wanted so much for Eutracia. Namely, equality for females of endowed blood." Looking first at Tristan, then Shailiha, Faegan cackled in glee and slapped one knee. "I knew it!" he exclaimed. "I never had the privilege of knowing your parents, but all that I have heard about them leads me to only one conclusion—they were two of the finest persons in the realm." He rubbed his chin with one hand. "And do these women now practice the craft?" he asked.

"Yes," Wigg answered. "But only in secret, doing anonymous good deeds about the countryside, like the consuls of the Redoubt. And just like the consuls, should any of these women attempt to practice the Vagaries, death enchantments would immediately be enacted."

"What are they called?" Shailiha asked.

"What do you mean?"

"Such men are called consuls," Shailiha said. "What name was given to the women?"

"We call them the acolytes of Fledgling House," Wigg answered. "Just as the consuls all wear dark blue robes, the acolytes wear robes of the deepest red. And they bear a tattoo of the Paragon on one shoulder, as do the consuls."

"I see," Faegan mused. "Considering everything that transpired, you took a great risk in doing this."

"The Coven had been gone for over three hundred years," Wigg countered. "And the queen was adamant." Smiling, he turned his face in the direction of Tristan and Shailiha. "She could be quite persuasive, as well."

"All things change, don't they?" Faegan asked. Then his face became more serious, his voice lowering. "And where are these women now?"

Sighing, obviously not wanting to answer, Wigg placed his tongue against the inside of one of his hollow cheeks. "I don't know," he replied softly.

Faegan leaned forward on his arms, more than a hint of disapproval showing on his face. "You don't *know*?" he asked incredulously.

"After they leave Fledgling House, they, like the consuls, are free to scatter throughout the realm," the lead wizard answered. "They are waiting for the official announcement of the existence of their society by the Directorate—the Directorate that no longer exists. But as for keeping track of the specific location of each of these women, well, that was the task of Tretiak. But of course, Tretiak is now dead."

"And did Tretiak keep any written records of these women?" Faegan asked.

"Yes," Wigg answered rather sadly, "but I do not know where. They could be anywhere in the vastness of the Redoubt."

"Do the consuls know of the acolytes?" Tristan asked.

"Only those who are their fathers," Wigg answered. "And they were of course sworn to secrecy. Just after what was to have been your coronation, the Directorate was planning to bring them all together at once—the consuls and the acolytes—and reveal the existence of one to the other. It was to have been a wonderful day—one your mother was especially looking forward to. But then the stalkers and the harpies began to reappear, followed by the invasion of the Coven. Your mother's dream of a sisterhood of the craft still survives, but she never lived to see it come to complete fruition."

"And how do we know that whoever is doing this has not gone after the acolytes the same way they have the consuls?" Faegan asked.

"We don't know," Wigg said. "But I don't believe they have."

"Why not?"

"The training of the consuls has been going on far, far longer than that of the acolytes," Wigg explained. "The oldest of the acolytes would be only about thirty New Seasons of Life, making them far less experienced—and thus less powerful—than most of the consuls. Also, there are far fewer of them. However, we cannot assume that the acolytes are safe. Our enemy may well be going after them—or have plans for them later. Only time will tell."

Scowling, Wigg laced his fingers and placed his hands on the table. Recognizing Wigg's mood, Faegan finally became silent.

Tristan sat back in his chair, stunned at the revelations that had just been unearthed.

"But still more important questions remain, old friend," Faegan said darkly.

"Such as, why did Ragnar and Scrounge abduct the children," Wigg replied, "not to mention the source of the power behind the strange, immense glow Tristan and I saw in the Caves."

The situation descended on the people seated at the table like it was the weight of the world. But to the minds of the wizards, things other than worry over Fledgling House had to take priority.

"The attack at Fledgling House was indeed a travesty, as was the death of my friend Duncan," Wigg said quietly. "Nonetheless, these recent events must not dissuade us from the most important of our goals. We must concentrate our efforts on the cure for the prince, and on solving the riddle of the draining of the Paragon. For if these two things are not correctly and quickly addressed, all is lost."

Wigg turned to his left, searching for Martha's hands. Finding them, he took them into his own. "My dear friend," he whispered, "despite your recent loss, there are still things of importance I would ask you to do for both the realm, and for myself. That is, if you will consent to remain in my service."

Her tears came again, and the kindly matron bowed her head slightly. "Anything, Lead Wizard," she whispered back.

"First, I would like you to help my daughter," Wigg said. "As I will explain to you later, she is not really of our world, and knows nothing of either the history or customs of Eutracia. I would like you to teach her these things for me. Please instruct her as quickly as you can, so that she may become an equal, participating member of our group. Other than the prince and princess, her blood is of a quality never before seen. And I can think of no one more ideally suited to help her than you."

Martha looked over at the tall, red-haired beauty. "It would be my honor," she said. "And the other request?" she asked.

"That you would also care for yet another young lady, if need be." Wigg smiled. "Unknown to you, there is a new royal in the world. Shailiha has given birth to her first child. A daughter, named after the queen. We have just learned secrets regarding new, unexpected talents that Shailiha now possesses, related to a spell lying within her blood. If these things are indeed true, her services may prove invaluable. Therefore, please care for the daughter of the princess if Shailiha is required elsewhere."

"Of course," Martha answered.

Although pleased to hear these requests, Tristan's mind had already been taken to a different place. Parthalon.

He closed his eyes against the pain of his memories, wondering if he could summon up the courage to again confront the brutal, winged killers of his family.

"Wigg," Faegan said from the other side of the table, "we have talked long enough. Now is the time for action. One of us should immediately recite the incantation for Celeste's time enchantments, before any discontinuance is used by Ragnar." He smiled again. "But I think, given the circumstances, the honor should be yours."

"Thank you," Wigg said.

"Shannon," Faegan said, turning to the gnome, "would you please familiarize Martha with the Redoubt?"

"Yes, Master," Shannon answered. He and Martha started toward the door. The little man raised the ale jug to his lips again on the way out.

"Now then," Faegan said, looking to Wigg.

"Celeste, please kneel before me," Wigg said.

Celeste obediently rose from her chair, going down on her knees before her father. Wigg reached out his hands, turning up his palms.

"Place your hands in mine, close your eyes, and bow your head," he said quietly. She did so. Then Wigg began the incantation:

"Your form and substance shall remain forever new,
The progress of time around you, rather than through.
Of neither disease nor time shall you further fear,
Nor the sands of the hourglass seem so dear.
For from this time on you shall be forever the same,
Frozen in the moment from which you just came."

The people at the table remained still as death as the familiar azure glow of the craft appeared all around Celeste. It filled the Hall of Blood Records with its majesty, increasing in intensity until Tristan thought he might have to cover his eyes. Then it finally faded away, leaving the room as quietly and quickly as it had come.

"Arise my daughter," Wigg said, quietly brushing away a tear that had formed in one of his milky eyes. "You are henceforth protected by my time enchantments. Now, even if Ragnar decides to discontinue his enchantments, mine shall protect you. But please always bear in mind that should you feel any unexpected shudder in your blood, you must tell us immediately. For that will mean he has discontinued his ministrations, and that is something we should know."

"Yes, Father," she answered, her voice cracking slightly. "Thank you." Celeste returned to her seat.

"Princess," Faegan said, "if you would, please place your child down on the table." Shailiha did so, the baby remaining still and content.

Faegan silently commanded one of the many drawers in the walls to open. Another blank sheet of parchment arose from it, coming to rest on the table next to the child. Then Morganna gently rose into the air, landing quietly back down on the paper. A tiny incision painlessly appeared in the first finger of Morganna's hand, and a single, perfect drop of her blood fell to the paper. Morganna immediately began to cry, so Shailiha reached out and took the baby back into her arms, kissing the cut finger. Slowly, the baby calmed.

Faegan poured a single drop of water from the Caves onto the child's blood. The fluids then began to wend their way hauntingly across the thirsty paper, revealing the infant's signature.

At seeing Morganna's blood signature, Shailiha's first reaction was to take a sudden breath and cover her mouth with one hand, fearing that there was something wrong with her baby. Tristan was also perplexed. The signature looked somewhat like the others he had seen this day, but was also radically different. Looking at it more closely, he finally realized why. The father's portion of the signature was missing.

"Is something wrong with my baby?" Shailiha asked urgently, pulling Morganna close to her breast. "Why does her blood signature look like that?"

"There is nothing wrong with Morganna, Princess," Faegan answered reassuringly. "In fact, had her signature been any different, you would have had some rather difficult explaining to do." In that way in which only Faegan could, he smiled cattily at the inference. "Your husband, the father of this child, was of common blood, was he not?"

"Yes," she answered, her eyes still glued to the parchment.

"As such, Frederick had no blood signature. Nor would he ever have. Therefore nothing of his blood can be shown in this way. Only your portion and the child's own form Morganna's signature. A 'partial' endowment, if you will, and entirely normal when one of endowed blood reproduces with one of common blood."

"Of course," Shailiha answered softly. "Now I understand."

"But look more closely," Faegan said. "For the reason I wished to reveal your daughter's blood was not to teach you this, but to look for something else." The princess looked down at the child's blood signature again, and this time she saw it. There were branches leading off from it; they looked identical to the ones in her signature.

She drew a quick breath, immediately understanding. "Morganna has my Forestallments," she whispered. "It's true. Forestallments can be passed from the parent to the child."

Faegan smiled. "Well done. This is exactly what I thought we would see. But we needed to confirm it with our own eyes."

"Is it really true?" Wigg asked from the other side of the great table. "Forestallments can be handed down?"

"Apparently so," Faegan said absently, thinking to himself. "But now the question becomes, will Morganna's talents be the same as her mother's or something quite different? Only time will tell."

"And now there remains but one more thing to do, before you and I turn our attention toward other, more pressing matters," Wigg said to Faegan. "We must examine the blood of the Chosen One himself."

Faegan nodded. "Tristan, if you please," he said.

Tristan obligingly held one hand out. An incision appeared, and a single, azure blood drop fell with a soft plop onto the parchment next to the signature of the child. Faegan carefully placed a single drop of water from the Caves onto it.

This time, however, due to the very high quality of Tristan's blood, the signature was revealed far more quickly than any of the others. None of the people at the table, though, not even the master wizard Faegan, were prepared for what they saw in it.

Tristan's signature was identical to Shailiha's in form. That was to be expected. But branching off from his signature were far more Forestallments. Some were long, some short, and some thicker than others, crazily leading away from the body of the signature itself. More than half of them showed their own additional offshoots, like branches from a tree limb.

After a period of silence, it was again Faegan who spoke first. He described the unusual configuration to Wigg and then asked, "Tristan, do you have any idea why this would be so?"

"No," the prince said solemnly. "Unless it has to do with the poisoning of my blood."

"That is not the reason," Wigg interjected. "Faegan and I have seen stalker blood poisoning before, and it has never manifested itself this way in a signature. Unless I miss my guess, these are truly Forestallments, though of a complex nature we had yet to see. But as to how or why there are so many of them, I am at a complete loss to say."

"Then we shall start with what we do know," Faegan said. "We originally postulated that the Forestallments placed in Shailiha's blood were a ministration of Failee. Of that I feel we can be relatively certain. While the princess was with the Coven, there was ample time for the first mistress to accomplish such a thing. But, as the prince and Wigg have previously told me, their time with the Coven was much shorter. Nonetheless, the presence of so many Forestallments in Tristan's blood must still be a result of his time with them." He paused for a few moments, collecting his thoughts.

"Tell me, Tristan," he began, "exactly in what ways any of the mistresses physically touched you while you were with them."

Faegan's blunt request brought back Tristan's dark memories of his time with the four mistresses in the belly of the Recluse. Wigg and Geldon had been with him and were tortured, as he had been. But his abuse had come in a very different fashion. As he searched his mind, he could only remember one single time that any of them had actually touched him.

When Failee had sent Succiu, the second mistress, to rape him. He swallowed hard.

"The only time I was ever touched was during Succiu's forced union upon me," he said slowly. "She gloated about it, telling me that it would be the most intense physical pleasure I would ever receive. But instead there was great, unexpected pain. It shot through my entire system, and I almost blacked out. Afterward the glow of the craft formed around her. She said that she had already conceived, and would give birth in only three days. But because of the quality of my blood, she actually went into labor much sooner."

"Did you tell me once that Failee said it was her intention to continually use your seed to breed what she called a race of superbeings, all female, who would use the Vagaries to rule forever?"

"Yes. But what are you getting at?"

Faegan sat back in his chair, stroking his cat. "I believe that is when so many unique, branched Forestallments were placed into your blood," he ruminated, half to himself. "During Succiu's rape of you. Ever since I read Egloff's scroll, something has been troubling me. Namely, how is it that a Forestallment could be implanted within the blood of another without his or her knowledge? Such a strong, ongoing spell would surely have some form of immediate, physical reaction. In your case, I think it was the pain you described, though that may not be the case for everyone so affected. This also confirms another theory of mine: that the installation of the Forestallments within the blood of another can only be accomplished when actually touching the receiving party." He paused for a moment, looking around the table. "It appears there was much more going on during your time in the Recluse than we first thought."

Lowering his head and closing his eyes, Tristan let out a sad, lonely sigh. He remembered, too, some of Succiu's last words to him, just before she committed suicide. *"There is still so much you and the wizards do not know,"* she had said.

"But *why?*" he asked, his eyes still closed. "They already had me to do with as they chose. Why this, as well?"

"You were given Forestallments for the very reason your sister and Celeste have them," Faegan answered gently. "But your case was different. The greater the number of Forestallments in your blood, the less Failee would eventually have to teach her superbeings when they matured. And because of the nature of your blood, your Forestallments would be even stronger than those inherited from Celeste or Shailiha. For this reason also, you apparently received many more than they did. But do not be alarmed. Because you escaped, in many ways this may truly be a blessing."

Angry and restless again, Tristan raised his head and opened his eyes. He looked at Faegan as if the wizard had suddenly gone mad. "How could such an abomination be a blessing?" he hissed.

"Because you now have talents, dormant in your blood, that do not require training to come alive," the wizard answered. "Just like Shailiha's amazing bond with the fliers. And if your Forestallments are event-activated, as hers were, you may discover them at any time. They may be truly wondrous."

"Or something horrible," Tristan said through gritted teeth.

"That possibility also exists," Faegan answered softly. "Only time will tell."

Tristan was suddenly very anxious. Though the room was huge, he felt like the walls were closing in on him.

He began to shake. At first slightly, but then with greater intensity until his entire body was firmly in the grip of uncontrollable spasms. His eyes rolled back into his head, and drool formed in the corners of his mouth.

Shailiha's scream sounded far away to his ears.

The last thing he remembered before the awful blackness closed in was the horrific, painful convulsions throwing him from his chair onto the hard, cool, marble floor of the room.

CHAPTER THIRTY

❦

THE wind in his hair and his weapons at the ready, Scrounge gripped the specially made leather band strapped around the body of his personal hatchling as the awful bird carried him higher into the golden glow of the evening sky. He had been longing for this night ever since Ragnar had outlined this newest plan to him. It had been almost two days since Scrounge and his birds had raided Fledgling House, taking the girls. But the dramatic, difficult task that now lay before him thrilled him even more. The night sky was clear and calm.

The bird that carried him was also heavily armed. A long sword dangled from the baldric around the creature's strong shoulders. At the hatchling's hip lay a dagger, and the black leather gauntlets it wore were studded with long silver points for ripping and tearing into its victims at close quarters.

Scrounge looked down at the land of Eutracia as it passed dizzyingly below. He was still amazed at how fast the master's new generation of creatures could travel through the air without ever seeming to tire. And then he looked behind him, and smiled. Traveling with him were thousands more of the great birds.

They flew due west in a giant formation shaped like a highly compacted arrowhead, with Scrounge and his bird at the forefront. None of the other creatures carried a rider, but each of them was armed in the same fashion as his mount. Ragnar's assassin narrowed his eyes, trying to make out the unfortunate city that would soon bear the horror of their orders. Ilendium—one of the true jewels of Eutracia.

He didn't yet see their target, so Scrounge allowed his

mind the luxury of traveling back in time a few hours, to his visit to the amazing camp the hatchlings had established at Farplain, in the Triangle of the Grasses.

At Nicholas' orders, thousands of black tents had been erected everywhere, the campfires before them sending smoke high into the sky. Hordes of hatchlings milled about on their strong rear legs, those in positions of command shouting orders. Some were performing tasks such as sharpening weapons. Others were flying patrols, guarding the perimeter.

The largest and most ornate of the tents, set on a small rise overlooking the entire scene, held Ragnar. After completing his mission at Fledgling House, Scrounge had reported there for further orders.

The tent was furnished with items that had been brought here from the stalker's underground chambers. Included among them was the ever-present vial of yellow fluid. Most of the furniture was upholstered in deep red. Decorative tapestries hung on the insides of the tent walls, and highly patterned rugs covered the grassy floor. Oil sconces adorned the tent poles. A golden table sat in the center of the room, a silver platter atop it containing fruit, olives of several colors, cheese, and wine—all of which looked untouched.

Long and languorous, a brunette woman with deep blue eyes lay propped up on one arm along the length of a curved, bloodred sofa. She smiled when Scrounge came in. Only a single, diaphanous piece of fine Eutracian silk covered her; it left little to the imagination. Her face was badly bruised, no doubt from some form of punishment administered by the stalker. But by her coy look the assassin decided she hadn't minded, and had perhaps even enjoyed it.

Ragnar was seated in a high-backed, red velvet chair at the end of the room, a vial of brain fluid in his hand. His robe was of the deepest purple, and Wigg's three-hundred-year-old golden dagger was at his hip. He placed two fingers into the vial and then into his mouth before beckoning the assassin forward. Scrounge took several steps into the room, the silver spurs of his knee boots jangling lightly.

"The raid at Fledgling House went well?" the stalker asked, already knowing the answer.

"Yes, my lord," Scrounge answered.

"And are you ready for the next of your assignments?"

"Indeed," Scrounge answered, his eyes flashing. "This latest mission promises to be the most satisfying yet."

"Good," Ragnar answered. "You fully understand Nicholas' instructions? That nothing is to be taken except life. Also destroy as much of the city as possible. Make the evidence of your actions lasting, and particularly explicit. How you accomplish this part of it I leave to your rather considerable talents. But remember, Nicholas wishes to make a clear example of this first attack. It is not the city itself he wants; it is the people living in it. And after you have made the necessary preparations for the master's other servants, be sure to avoid their impending arrival."

Ragnar stood from his chair, going to the table. Selecting a grape, he walked to the brunette on the couch. He held it for her as she opened her mouth, seductively taking it in. Ragnar smiled.

"While it is true she is not Celeste, she is nonetheless very talented," he said. "Would you like to partake of her charms before you leave?"

Scrounge looked down to the beauty before him, and then back up to his master. "Not now, my lord. Frankly, the prospect of the mission lying before me is far more exciting. But perhaps, when I return . . ."

"Of course," Ragnar answered. "Go and carry out your orders. And do not disappoint us."

With that, Scrounge had turned on his heel and walked out.

Straining his eyes against the wind, the assassin could now make out the lights of the city of Ilendium, about one league away.

He looked behind him to make sure that the birds he had selected were still grasping torches.

"You know your orders! Fly in low and drop the torches first. Then proceed as planned. Be sure to leave several hundred survivors, and herd them into the square in the center of the city." With quick nods of their grotesque heads, the hatchlings began a long, descending glide toward the unsuspecting city, and the thousands of other birds of prey immediately followed suit.

Descending low over Ilendium, they dropped the billowing flares onto the quiet, sleeping city.

The roofs made of straw went ablaze first. They caught quickly, the sudden, intense flames snapping and popping as they went roaring up into the darkness of the night. The buildings with stone or marble roofs, those housing the wealthier citizens, were treated differently. In those cases the hatchlings landed in the streets, smashing out windows with the hilts of their swords and tossing the torches inside. On and on it went, building after building, street after street. The entire city was soon a raging inferno.

The assassin flew over the expanses of the desperate city, intently watching the master's hatchlings go about their work. He smiled viciously, enjoying the moment, and then spurred his bird lower, and soared recklessly through the city streets. His sword at the ready, he watched for survivors as the flame-ridden buildings flashed by on either side. His first victim was a little boy, lost and alone in the mayhem, screaming wildly as he tried to find his parents.

Many more such defenseless victims followed. So many, in fact, that near the end he was barely able to raise his sword.

As they ran madly from the burning buildings, the citizens were cut down by the sword-wielding hatchlings. Sometimes a particular group of hatchlings chose to use their long, black talons to trap their living victims on the ground, and would then use their daggers or the points of their gauntlets to tear through the clothing and abdomens of those beneath them. Then they employed their long beaks and sharp teeth to peck and pull the organs from their victims. Often, at the end of such brutality, the birds would lift their faces to the flame-ridden skies, calling out shrieks of victory to the others, their mouths and teeth dripping with blood. The streets and gutters eventually ran red, and the screaming of the citizens evolved into agonizingly helpless crying and moaning.

Some of the fires had begun to subside, while others still raged furiously. The orange-and-red flames threw their light up into the night and across what was left of the burning buildings, spotlighting the grisly specters of the hatchlings going about their work. Acrid, soot-laden smoke billowed everywhere as Scrounge finally sheathed his bloody sword. He then turned his bird toward the center of the city, toward the gathering place known as Ilendium Square.

His hatchling landed softly and bent down, and Scrounge swung one leg over to slide to the ground. The cobblestone square was already full of the living. Some were wounded; some were not. The birds kept prodding and poking their captives, forcing them to remain in the center of the square. Other hatchlings flew the corpses of the disemboweled to the square, dropping them on their backs. At last, Scrounge issued his orders.

"Begin the search for stragglers!" he called out. "Leave no stone unturned. And place all the disemboweled here, in the center. The master's other servants shall arrive at any time. We must be in the air by then, or suffer the same fate as our conquests."

Scrounge watched as some of the hatchlings before him rotated their endowed, scarlet eyes partially out of the sockets in preparation for the search. Beacons soon shot from their orbs into the blackness of the night, criss-crossing crazily through the sky and across the ground. Then the birds flew off, searching for survivors. As they went, the red shafts coming from them shot down the streets and through the flickering orange of the flames, adding to the macabre nature of the scene. Amid the blood, the carnage, the corpses, and the wailing, Scrounge waited.

The hatchlings eventually returned with hundreds more survivors, and unceremoniously dropped their captives to the stones of the square amid the dead and the living alike. Scrounge smiled. He walked back to his personal hatchling and remounted, then wheeled the bird around to face the thousands of other hatchlings on the ground and in the air.

"Those of mine still standing in the square," he shouted, "come join your brothers in the sky!" With a great flapping of wings, scores of hatchlings took to the air, joining the others. "Hover above the square and wait. Eventually you will see what it is that your master has created," he shouted, his face twisting into a grin. "And be glad you are not one of those below!"

Patiently hovering over the barbaric scene, the hatchlings bided their time. Occasionally a survivor would try to run, only to have one of the great birds swoop low to snatch him up in its talons and return him or her to the center of the carnage. An incongruous silence gradually crept over the scene—almost a peacefulness of sorts—as the thousands of birds kept watch over the captives below.

At first, all that could be heard was a soft scrabbling sound. Faint and distant, it grew nearer by the moment. It was almost like thousands of bits of metal scratching against themselves to create a sinister, uniform din. On and on it came, growing louder until it was a roaring, living wall of noise descending on the square from every direction. It was then that Scrounge, safe atop his hatchling, saw the first of this new breed of Nicholas' servants: carrion scarabs.

Scrounge watched, transfixed, as hundreds of thousands of black beetles deluged the square. Each one was about the size of the palm of his hand, with an indentation down the center of its hard, shiny shell. A pair of black fangs, curved and sharp, protruded noticeably from the front of each of the heads. Their many legs scrambling, their antennae stretched forward and hungrily scenting the carrion before them, they filled every entryway leading into Ilendium Square. They came relentlessly, so many that they finally poured out of the shattered doorways and windows of the weakened buildings, knocking down the charred window frames and doors that had been loosened by the fires. It was a virtual sea of blackness, undulating and flowing as if a single entity—a seemingly never-ending torrent of fluid motion.

They tore into the people in the square, both the living and the dead, like a rolling sea of death.

Scrounge smiled at the incredible scene below him. Some of the carrion scarabs scrambled quickly over the dead, and then seemed to slow down, busying themselves atop the eviscerated bodies. The others clambered up the feet and legs of the living, their victims' bodies and faces quickly becoming black with their numbers. The curved, black fangs tore relentlessly into the screaming victims, who fell to the bloody square, dying slowly and horribly as the scarabs consumed their living flesh.

When all of the humans were dead, many of the beetles began congregating around the bodies that had been disemboweled. And then it became almost quiet, and the carrion scarabs started going about the second of their tasks.

As Scrounge watched in fascination, the female scarabs began to lay thousands of white, slippery, glistening eggs directly into the warm body cavities of the dead.

Each of the eggs, about the size of a child's marble, came slowly from the females' bodies, falling gently into the soft, warm abdomens of the dead men, women, and children. When a cavity became completely filled, the females would go on to the next, and then the next. When the grisly task had finally been completed, about half of the carrion scarabs marched away. The other half formed a protective ring around the dead, presumably waiting for their eggs to hatch.

Satisfied, Scrounge looked down at the ruined city a final time, then wheeled his bird around to face the others hovering nearby. Once they gathered into proper formation, he gave them a nod of his head, and the entire flight of hatchlings soared away, melting into the blackness of the sky.

A shadow moved within the recesses of the top of the bell tower, one of the few buildings not completely consumed by flame. And then the shadow moved again.

Caprice, Shailiha's graceful violet-and-yellow flier of the fields, her wings folded, finally revealed herself, walking tentatively along the ledge that lay just below the great bell. She looked down upon the carnage of the square, and then to the still-blazing remnants of the once-great city of Ilendium.

For a moment she bowed her head, as if an overpowering sadness had come to her. And then, sensing that the danger for her had passed, she launched herself into the air. Her diaphanous wings began carrying her to the west, carefully following the hatchlings.

CHAPTER THIRTY-ONE

NICHOLAS, his eyes closed and his body naked, hovered high above the floor in the darkness of the antechamber. The azure glow of the vein surrounded him, running brightly through the walls. He extended his arms at his sides, and the light from the ribbon of energy glistened brightly against the pale skin of his perfect body. His mind turned commandingly, proudly to the awesome power and knowledge that he had already attained. Of the Vigors and the Vagaries alike.

He tilted his head back, and his dark hair fell toward the floor as he revolved in the brilliant atmosphere of the subterranean room. He had come here after having been instructed to do so earlier this day. After his parents above had again revealed themselves to his mind.

This time their voices had been much stronger, much clearer than the time before. So too was his grasp of the craft. And this day he would come another step closer to that which would eventually become their means to conquer. He would continue to absorb the power of the Paragon, and imbue it into a single being. Himself.

Before commencing he smiled, allowing himself the luxury of returning to the earlier moment this day, when the ones from above had again called out to his mind.

Nicholas, he had heard. *Nicholas, it is we. We who exist on the other side. Those who remain in perpetual struggle with the Ones Who Came Before. Your parents above, the true masters of the Vagaries. Hear us now when we tell you that you have done well, but that there is still much more to be accomplished before we may return to the land of the living. And it is only you, our messenger on earth, who can make this possible.*

Continuing to revolve in the light, he thought back to the time when his consciousness had first materialized. The moment when he had found himself unearthed from a shallow grave, reborn in azure hands that had arrived so mysteriously from above. And then had come the flight skyward, ever skyward, cradled in those same delicate hands. He had emerged from the fog and gloom of his quasi-life to arrive before the serene masters—the ones who were the ultimate bringers of light and knowledge. Trapped in the firmament and in constant struggle with those who cherished only the Vigors, his parents could not accomplish all they desired by themselves. And so they had sent him.

And as his time with them passed, they imbued his exquisite blood with the necessary Forestallments. But in order to employ their magnificent gifts, he would first have to harness the dynamism of the stone, for they required unheard-of power.

The vein in the walls began to undulate more strongly, pulsing with energy. As its glow increased, Nicholas revolved faster, his body turning gracefully in the light. And then, his eyes still closed, he commanded gashes to open along the inside of each of his wrists. As he turned, small amounts of his blood began to run from the incisions, soaring outward and casting strangely concentric patterns on the walls and floor of the room. Finally opening his eyes, he looked down to regard the blood that was so prized: the glowing, unequaled, azure blood he had inherited from the male of the Chosen Ones.

From this time forward you shall absorb the power differently, the voices from above had said. *This time you will take the power directly into your blood. You are strong enough now. But you must take the vitality little by little as it leaves the stone, giving your blood time to adjust. For to do so all at once, even for you, would mean certain death. And even though you absorb both sides of the craft, it is forbidden for you to try to use them in concert with one another. Only we hold that key.*

As he called upon the energy of the vein, its magnificence slowly poured out onto the floor of the antechamber in its other form—the liquid, unadulterated power of the Paragon. Small pools of it developed as it slithered forth. Twisting and turning with a life of its own, it seemed to desperately want to join with his exposed blood. It writhed into a whirlpool, rising slowly into the air beneath the young adept. Nicholas held his wrists out to it, begging it to come closer.

A great cracking noise exploded, the vein converting itself to bolts of azure energy. The bolts struck the incisions in his wrists with blinding speed, and the young man screamed and screamed again.

And then the glow softened, the bolts dying away as Nicholas revolved more slowly in the silence of the room. Unconscious, he crashed the distance to the floor of the chamber.

As he slowly regained his senses, he came to all fours. He was unhurt, but his chest was heaving, his blood more alive than ever with the power of the craft. He knew he had been successful. Although aware that he had as yet absorbed only a portion of the dynamic of the stone, he felt more arrant than ever. He raised his hands, and laughed aloud as he caused the incisions to vanish, the azure waves of strength cascading to and from between his palms in an awesome display of his newfound power.

You are to become the vessel into which both sides shall be poured, his parents above had told him. *Hold them for us until our return. For just as the Chosen One was to have been the emissary of the Ones Who Came Before, you are to be ours. It was the Chosen One himself who gave you to us, when he took you from the dead womb of the sorceress. And soon enough he will see the gravity of his error.*

The young man smiled again, thinking how true all of their revelations had been, and how anxious he was for them to display their remaining magnificence to him.

But you are not to venture forth into the light until you are the same age as the other of azure blood, they had said. *To walk among your enemies now would provide too great a temptation, even for you. You would be drawn to attempt joining the two sides of the craft, without doubt destroying all that we have sought to attain. Even you would not be able to resist this call, just as the first mistress of the Coven, in all her experience, could not. But it shall soon be time for you to take your place in the world above. And own it all.*

Smiling, Nicholas turned, and glided from the room.

CHAPTER THIRTY-TWO

$\mathcal{H}$OLDING her baby close, Shailiha stood with Faegan and Wigg on the balcony of Queen Morganna's once-sumptuous bedroom above the Redoubt, waiting for the coming dawn. The queen's familiar but now-ransacked chambers in the royal palace had at first conjured up a great many memories for the princess. Especially of the time that she, Tristan, and her mother had been here, not so long ago, taking tea—the day Morganna had given the prince the gold medallion he still wore around his neck, an exact copy of the one Shailiha wore.

At first, the memories had made Shailiha cry. But she had forced the tears away, determined to do all she could to help her brother.

She was terribly worried about Tristan. His violent convulsion in the Hall of Blood Records had been a revelation, showing her for the first time how ill he really was. Once the attack had subsided, Wigg and Faegan had taken the prince, still unconscious, to his quarters, and put him to bed. Martha and Celeste were keeping watch over him, for the wizards had said that once the episode was finished, there was little more they could do. They believed that he would eventually awaken on his own, and they had instructed Martha to immediately alert them when that happened.

Shailiha had remained by his bed the entire night, crying, afraid the twin brother she loved so much would never come back to her. Finally, with the advent of dawn, she had decided to accompany the wizards in their task.

She turned her attention from the horizon, looking back to the smashed, violated room. One of the great looms that her mother had loved to sit before was still there, but the half-finished tapestry that was to have been her gift to the king had long since been stolen, as had virtually everything else of value. Dust and debris lay everywhere. As if they somehow knew themselves to be the new masters of the castle, an occasional rat or spider could be seen brazenly going about the business of hunting food. She shuddered.

She was standing between Wigg on her left, and Faegan on her right. The sun was just starting to come up over the hills beyond, bringing the promise of a cold but beautiful day. The birds had begun to sing, and the ground shimmered with frost, foreshadowing the coming of snow. Indeed everything from the balcony outward, in direct contrast to the room behind her, looked almost idyllic.

Just as the sun began to peek over the horizon, casting its sharp, golden spears toward the balcony, Faegan spoke. "It is now the beginning of high noon in Parthalon," he said, "and it is time for me to begin."

Closing his eyes, he commenced the spell that would produce the portal. Slowly Shailiha could begin to see the swirling glow appear, heralding the portal's coming. On and on it came, until the entire balcony was covered by a brilliantly glowing vortex. The burden of holding it open showed on Faegan's face.

"Will he be all right?" the concerned princess whispered to Wigg. "It looks to be a terrible strain."

"It is," Wigg answered softly. "Do not attempt to speak to him or otherwise distract him during this use of the craft." Understanding, Shailiha nodded back.

The moments passed slowly, the sun continuing its climb in the east.

At last, Shailiha thought she saw a flutter in the vortex. Geldon slowly appeared from the mist, and immediately fell to his knees. Following behind him came Joshua, also obviously dizzy and disoriented. Shailiha placed her hand over her mouth in horror, not wanting to believe what she saw. The consul was holding a glowing, severed foot.

Lastly from the azure whirlpool came something that Shailiha had seen but did not remember—something Faegan had never seen. A huge, armed, bizarre-looking man with

wings fell to his knees upon the floor of the balcony. His
wings flapped weakly as if trying to help him regain his balance. He was holding a crutch, which he placed beneath his
armpit to assist him in standing on his good foot. Shailiha
could only stare, frozen in the moment.

As Faegan opened his eyes, he sent a bolt of the craft toward
the new arrival, surrounding him within a brilliant wizard's
cage.

"That will not be necessary," Joshua said quickly, taking
his first real step forward. "This warrior is an ally."

"He is right," Geldon finally said. He walked around
everyone and into the room. "He is a friend."

"What is going on?" Wigg shouted out in frustration.
"Who is there?"

"Geldon, Joshua, and, of all things, what I assume to be a
Minion warrior," the wizard in the chair answered drily. "Assuming, of course, that your previous descriptions of them
have been accurate." It was clear he had no intention of eliminating his wizard's cage any time soon.

Shailiha took in the huge size of the warrior, and his long,
dark hair and unkempt beard. Her eyes then went to the dreggan lying peacefully at the warrior's hip. A shiny wheel—a
weapon, from what she could tell—hung at his other side. His
right foot had been severed cleanly at the ankle. Despite his
fearsome appearance, she could not help but feel a small
measure of pity for his plight. Accepting his fate, he stared
silently out between the shiny bars of his cage.

"Are you sure?" Faegan asked condescendingly of the consul. He knew that he had little to fear from the single warrior
contained within the cube, but wanted answers first. "A one-
footed Minion warrior is not something that we are accustomed to seeing. It appears that you and Geldon have some
explaining to do."

Joshua was about to speak, but then he saw the lead wizard's
eyes. "What happened?" he asked urgently, walking closer to
Wigg. He looked carefully into the wizard's face, then frantically back to Faegan. "Is he—"

"Yes," Faegan interrupted angrily. "He is blind. It is a long
story, and one that we shall eventually share with you. But
first, what is the meaning of bringing this warrior back to

Eutracia? Have you gone mad?" Faegan's gray-green eyes burned with an angry intensity that Shailiha had not yet seen.

"He was injured beyond their abilities to heal him," Joshua began apologetically. "And the courageous service he provided in the slaying of the swamp shrew was highly commendable. It seemed only fitting that we try to—"

"A swamp shrew?" Faegan shouted, his eyes wide. "Do you mean to tell me that there are shrews in Parthalon?"

"Uh, er, yes," Geldon answered, both surprised at the wizard's words and hoping to deflect some of his wrath away from the hapless consul. "They appeared in conjunction with a number of lakes and ponds. The Minions are trying their best to hunt the shrews down and kill them, but it is exceedingly difficult."

Shailiha looked at Wigg. His lips were pursed in contemplation, rather than surprise. Then she turned back to Faegan.

"What is a 'swamp shrew,' " she asked, "and how is it that you are familiar with them? You have never been to Parthalon."

"The shrews once roamed Eutracia," he told her. "Yet another of the Coven's tools. Obviously the sorceresses employed them in Parthalon, as well. Possibly they prepared an incantation to make the swamp shrews reappear in the event of their own absence."

"So the incantation would have been activated by the sorceresses' deaths," Shailiha guessed.

"Exactly," Faegan said, smiling at her quick grasp of the situation, as well as her growing ability to accept the seemingly impossible.

Shailiha glanced at the Minion warrior just in time to see him look over her shoulder and suddenly go down on one knee, bowing his head. And then, from somewhere behind her, she heard the unforgiving, dangerous ring of sharpened steel.

"I live to serve," the Minion said reverently, his head still bowed in supplication. Whirling around, the princess gasped as she saw who was there. It was Tristan.

Standing in the doorway of the room, his dreggan drawn, Tristan glowered dangerously at the warrior in the cage. His chest rose and fell quickly beneath his black leather vest. No one spoke; no one moved.

Shailiha's eyes became shiny with sadness as she looked closer. This was not quite the Tristan she knew. He was a bit paler, the look in his dark blue eyes more intense and angry. And then her eyes went wide, and she involuntarily placed one hand over her mouth.

A bizarre pattern of what looked like dark, spiderweblike veins covered the upper part of his right arm.

Tristan took several quick steps toward the wizard's cage, pointing his dreggan at the warrior who was still on one knee, trapped inside. "What is he doing here?" he demanded angrily.

"As I was telling the wizards, his foot is severed," Joshua said carefully. "It was beyond my powers to help him, other than preserving both the foot and the leg in their current state. We brought him here for healing. Under the circumstances, we thought it fitting."

Tristan continued to stare at the winged one in the cage. He thought of the Minions' violation of his country, the butchering of the Directorate, and the rape and murder of his mother. Of how they had forced him to take his father's life on the altar of the Paragon with the very sword he now held. Of the Vale of Torment, where they had slowly tortured the gentle Gallipolai upon the monstrous, turning wheels of death. And lastly to the battle he had fought with Kluge, finally acquiring his long-sought-after revenge.

He took another quiet, smooth step toward the cage, then turned to Faegan.

"Drop your warp," he ordered. He stood defiantly, expecting to be obeyed.

From his chair, Faegan looked up into the eyes of the Chosen One. He too had noticed the black veins on Tristan's shoulder, and knew what they meant. For one of only a handful of times in his entire life, the master wizard was uncertain.

"What is it you are planning to do?" he asked Tristan calmly. In truth, Faegan's mind was racing. He certainly had no love of the Minions. But a highly respected consul, who had not yet been fully given the chance to explain his reasons, had purposely brought this one back. And he also expected that there was much more that the warrior might tell them, things that might be immensely invaluable, that even Joshua and Geldon might not know. With so much at stake, allowing the prince to kill the Minion was not an option.

"Drop your warp," the prince ordered for the second time. "I may have never officially taken the office of king, but nonetheless I am the only sovereign head of state that Eutracia has. And as a wizard it is your duty to obey." He continued to look at Faegan with fierce determination. "Drop your warp. Now."

Faegan closed his eyes, and the warp began to disappear. The warrior remained on one knee, unmoving, his head bowed. Slowly, Tristan crossed the remaining distance to where the winged one knelt. He pointed the razor-sharp dreggan directly at the top of the warrior's head, his thumb feeling for the button in the sword's hilt that would release its blade the extra foot.

"Look at me," Tristan said quietly.

The Minion warrior obediently raised his face. The point of the dreggan was now directly between his eyes.

"To whom do you owe your allegiance?" Tristan asked.

"To the Chosen One, of azure blood, lord of all Minions," the warrior answered crudely.

"And to whom else, after me?"

"Traax. Second in command."

"And do you swear, upon your honor as a Minion warrior, that you will do no harm to the peoples of Eutracia or Parthalon, unless so ordered by me?"

The warrior bowed his head. "Yes, my lord," he answered.

Tristan paused, inching the dreggan closer yet, until it actually touched the warrior. Its point punctured the skin of the warrior's forehead, and blood began to run down its blade.

"And lastly," Tristan snarled, "were you one of those who had a personal hand in the killing of the Directorate or the husband of the princess, or the murder and rape of my mother?" Silence again fell over the room, every person suddenly anxious to know the answer to the prince's unexpected question. And what he would do if it was affirmative.

"No, my lord," the warrior answered. "I elite assassin. I outside palace only."

Tristan, his breathing slowing, apparently made up his mind. Moving his thumb away from the button on the hilt, he slowly replaced the dreggan into its scabbard across his back. "You may rise," he ordered.

The Minion warrior stood, and for the first time their eyes truly met. Despite his reliance on the crutch, the warrior towered over the prince by nearly a foot.

"What is your name?" Tristan asked.

"I be Ox," the warrior said. "I brought here by consul and dwarf."

Tristan finally turned back to Faegan, the agitation in his face somewhat lessened. "I'm sorry," he said, uncoiling his muscles. "When I saw the warrior my instinct just took hold. He was the last thing in the world I expected to see. I also had to know if he remembered me, and to whom his allegiance is sworn. It will be imperative to know this when I return to Parthalon."

Holding Morganna, the princess walked to Tristan, looking at his arm where the deadly-appearing veins lay. "Are you all right?" she asked urgently.

"I'm fine, Shai." He smiled to her. "But I do not know what these marks are, or why they are here." He turned to Faegan. "I'm sure the wizards will tell us."

"Indeed," Faegan answered. "There is a great deal to discuss. But not in this open place. We are too exposed here. Follow me back to the Redoubt, all of you." At that Joshua took Wigg's hand, and everyone in the room, including the Minion, began to follow Faegan toward the door. Except for Shailiha.

She stood, wide-eyed, staring out at nothing, tears starting to cascade freely down her cheeks. Tristan was at her side in an instant.

"What is it?" he asked anxiously.

"Caprice," the princess said in a soft, faraway voice. "My flier. She calls to me. She is coming home. Ilendium . . . there has been a great tragedy."

CHAPTER THIRTY-THREE

RAGNAR smiled as he watched the thousands of consuls employing the craft for the benefit of the young adept. He had demanded his red-upholstered chair be brought from his tent so that he could be comfortable as he watched the amazing process unfold. At his feet sat the woman he had brought from the Caves, as well as a large assortment of food and wine.

He had been here since dawn, knowing that the work would continue night and day until they had secured all of the raw material they needed. It was the day following the destruction of Ilendium, and dawn had burst forth into beauty, providing an unusually warm day for this time of the year. But he knew snow would soon follow with the rapidly advancing Season of Crystal. Especially here, this far north.

He dusted off his robe, just as he had been forced to do so frequently this afternoon. He didn't mind. The black grime came off easily, some of it falling to the ground, the rest catching on the wind, flying away into nothingness. Pausing for a moment he reverently, luxuriously, rubbed what remained of it between the first few fingers of his right hand. He could almost feel its power.

The forbidden material of the ancients, he thought. *Finally to be unleashed after centuries of waiting. Only two others in the entire world besides the adept could ever accomplish such a feat. The Chosen Ones. But they remain untrained, and impotent. And very soon now, they will be dead.*

He reached out and grasped the vial containing the yellow fluid. As he took a taste, he felt familiar heat rush through his system. Then he cast his eyes back to the vast marble quarries just outside the city of Ilendium, in the province of Ephyra.

At least half a league wide in any given direction and several hundred meters deep, the quarry pits had for over three centuries produced the most prized marble the nation of Eutracia had ever seen. The stone had made the province of Ephyra, despite her relatively small geographical size, one of the richest in the nation. That had been the way of things until the coming of the Coven and the subsequent collapse of both the government and the economy. Since then, the quarries had remained still. Until today. He rose from his chair to walk toward the edge of the pit, taking stock of the seemingly ceaseless activity.

Over three thousand consuls of the Redoubt struggled tirelessly, mining the marble. It was a strange scene, especially considering the fact that for three centuries this particular section of the quarry had been forbidden from harvest by unanimous vote of the wizards of the Directorate. The consuls' dark blue robes were already filthy and torn with the effort of their labors. Their dirty faces emotionless masks of servitude and their movements autonomic, they toiled unceasingly at the harvesting of the beautiful stone.

Ragnar's elongated ears perked up when he heard yet another series of blasts come from the bolts of energy that were being so unceasingly summoned by the consuls. The craft was being used to harvest the marble in a manner that had not been seen for hundreds, perhaps thousands of years. As the select group of the Brotherhood sent yet more bolts to split free the marble encased in the giant limestone walls of the pit, others of them walked through the dust and debris to gather the great, jagged stones.

On and on it went, the dark, rather ominous-looking soot continually rising into the air, the consuls going about their labors automatically, unflinchingly, without words or emotion. Ragnar smiled. The marble they were harvesting was very special indeed. Of the deepest black, with brilliant azure veins running throughout, it had not been seen in Eutracia for centuries. And it was this mystical, banned substance that the young master needed most to accomplish his goals.

Turning his eyes to the sky, the stalker saw thousands of

hatchlings wheeling overhead as they monitored the endeavors taking place below in the pits. Scrounge could occasionally be seen on his personal bird, calling out orders to the others.

Deep within the quarries, Nicholas watched every move the consuls made. Suddenly he turned, rising quickly through the air to the top of the pit. His white robes billowing around him, he landed effortlessly next to the blood stalker.

Ragnar turned to look into the dark eyes of the being before him. "The mining progresses well, Master?" he asked carefully.

"It does," Nicholas answered. "The attack upon Ilendium went satisfactorily, also. You and Scrounge are to be congratulated." He paused, looking down at the gathering of the dusty, black, history-laden stone.

Ragnar considered for a moment both the hatchlings and the carrion scarabs, suddenly realizing how the two horrific types of creatures actually complemented one another. *One for swarming across the sky,* he thought. *And the other for marching across the ground.*

"The citizens of Ilendium would have been in the way," Nicholas said casually, as if he were speaking of brushing away a fly rather than annihilating an entire city. His dark eyes remained locked on the activity below. "Now we can work in peace. Besides, it would have been time-consuming to transport the marble any great distance, and I wish to employ it near a city. Ilendium was, of course, the logical choice. Summon Scrounge."

Raising his arm, Ragnar sent a bolt skyward. It traced high through an open space between the swarming squadrons of hatchlings. Seeing the signal, a lone bird carrying a rider immediately began to descend, and landed softly before Nicholas and the stalker.

Ragnar's assassin deftly threw one leg over the bird's back and slid to the ground. "You require me, my lord?" he asked Nicholas.

"Bring me one of the consuls," Nicholas said. "Any of them will do."

"Yes, my lord," Scrounge answered. In a flash he was back atop his bird, soaring into the sky to single out another of the hatchlings. The chosen bird swooped down to pick up a consul and carried him to the edge of the pit, where it unceremoniously dropped him at Nicholas' feet. Scrounge's bird landed softly, and the assassin quickly dismounted. The consul slowly rose to his feet, his expressionless eyes looking at nothing.

Nicholas cast his eyes to Ragnar's assassin. "Kill him," he said simply.

"Yes, my lord." Scrounged smiled, then walked around to face the defenseless consul. In a flash his arm with the crossbow was raised, his fist snapping once toward the ground. The miniature, yellow-tipped arrow tore across the expanse between the two men and with a sickening thud buried itself into the forehead of the consul. The man fell onto his back and shuddered as he died. Scrounge walked over to remove the arrow.

"No," Nicholas ordered. Scrounge stopped in his tracks. "Leave the arrow. It will prove useful."

"Very well," Scrounge said obediently.

Nicholas turned his palms upward, and a long, very narrow parchment appeared, hovering before him. He turned back to Scrounge. "Behead the consul," he ordered.

Scrounge drew his sword and with a single, clean strike, removed the consul's head from his body. Grasping the hair, he held the bloody, dripping thing before Nicholas. Death had come so quickly from the assassin's arrow that the consul's eyes were still open. The breeze tried to move the head back and forth hauntingly in the assassin's grip as if it still somehow possessed sentience.

Narrowing his eyes, Nicholas called the dripping blood of the consul to him. The drops hovered just above the parchment, then began to rain down lightly on the page. They arranged themselves into letters, then the letters into words, and finally the words into sentences.

At last the narrow parchment rolled itself up, moved toward the arrow, and slid its open center down the length of the shaft. Freshly conjoined ribbon then knotted itself around the parchment, securing the message to the shaft.

"This is to be delivered to one of the secret entrances of the Redoubt," Nicholas ordered. "Make sure it is placed where it will not be missed."

"I understand," Scrounge said. He tied the consul's head to the leather band around his hatchling's neck and mounted the bird, wheeling it around to face Nicholas and Ragnar. "It shall be as you order," he said. With that he prodded the hatchling into the air, turning southeast to Tammerland. Ragnar continued to watch until Scrounge and his mount became a mere pinprick in the late-afternoon sky.

"Another message to the Chosen One?" the stalker asked.

"Indeed," Nicholas replied, turning his attention back to the mining of the marble. "And my father of this world cannot afford to ignore me. There is now a choice he must make." Then he looked at Ragnar, and the stalker felt as if the dark gaze were burrowing directly into his brain. "It has to do with his blood."

CHAPTER THIRTY-FOUR

Ox stood gingerly upon both feet, testing his weight. He was stunned at what the wizards had been able to accomplish in so short a time. Faegan and Wigg had worked diligently for hours to reattach the severed foot, and had at last been successful. But it would take several weeks, they told the warrior, before he was himself again. The glow that had once surrounded both the lower leg and the newly reattached ankle had faded, and would soon disappear altogether.

"Ox still no believe," the dumbfounded warrior stammered. "Ox give gratitude."

"You're welcome," Wigg said, echoing Faegan's thoughts.

Upon hearing of the attack on Ilendium from the princess, the wizards had become quiet, and quite visibly disturbed. They had also listened intently to Geldon and Joshua's report. Then they had immediately excused themselves, going off to be alone. They had come out to reattach the Minion's foot, and then had beckoned everyone to join them in the Archives.

Despite the victory regarding the warrior's foot, the mood was both tense and morose. Tristan, Shailiha and her baby, Celeste, Joshua, Ox, Geldon, and the two wizards were present. The prince could see that Faegan wished to move on to more important, more private matters, as did he.

Wigg turned his white eyes in the general direction of Joshua. "The Minion is your charge," he said flatly. "Despite the fact that it is Tristan who is his true lord, you are the one who brought him here. And neither Faegan nor I have the time or the inclination to monitor him. You are of the craft, and should it become necessary to use it regarding the Minion, we expect you to do so. If such becomes the case, you are to report your actions to us at once."

He then turned toward Ox. "Please understand we mean you no ill will, provided nothing untoward happens as a result of your presence. Given the circumstances in Eutracia we must be careful at all times, and your appearance here was quite unexpected."

"Ox understand," the warrior said simply. He turned to Tristan. "I live to serve," he said, bowing his head.

Tristan took a deep breath, then let it out slowly. *This will take* some *getting used to,* he thought.

At Faegan's nod, Joshua escorted Ox from the room.

Anxious for answers, it was Tristan who changed the subject. "I want to know why the veins in my arm are turning black," he said bluntly. "I've had no pain anywhere, except during the convulsion. Then it was all-encompassing. What is happening to me?"

"As time progresses, the convulsions will grow in both intensity and frequency," Faegan said. "As to the veins, there is only one answer." The wizard in the chair looked glumly to Tristan's shoulder. "Put simply, your blood is dying."

An uncomfortable silence engulfed the room for several moments. "Is there nothing that can be done?" Shailiha asked in a small, tentative voice.

"Faegan and I have done little else, night or day, other than search for a cure," Wigg answered. "We have uncovered several references in the scrolls of the Archives as to the possibility of an antidote."

At the sudden glimmer of hope in Tristan's and Shailiha's eyes, Faegan quickly held up a hand.

"But the formula remains elusive," Wigg continued. "Even if we were to deduce the calculations to produce the antidote, there might not be enough time or power to do so, given the decay of the Paragon and the resultant lessening of our gifts."

"And what of the stone?" Shailiha asked suddenly. "Does its condition continue to worsen?"

"Not only is the stone's condition worsening," Faegan replied, "but it is doing so at a progressively faster rate. We calculate that it will now be approximately one month before the Paragon is completely void of color, and the world is without the craft of magic. Save for that one, still-unknown being whom we believe is garnering it for himself. You should also know that both Wigg and I have experienced a further, dramatic loss of our powers," he said sadly, "reducing our effectiveness at finding a way out of all of this. As our powers lessen, we also surmise that the strength of the being responsible for this grows in direct proportion." He paused. "And whoever that being is, he or she will be very difficult to stop," he said softly.

"But what of the Tome in all of this?" Tristan asked urgently. He glanced over to see that the white, leather-bound book was still resting securely on the table nearby. "Wigg and I risked our lives so that it might be brought here, and so I could read the Prophecies of the Tome for you. Is that not still the best course of action?"

Silence reclaimed the room as the prince and princess waited for one of the wizards to speak. It was finally Wigg who broached the reply. "No, Tristan," he said, knowing how difficult this would be for the prince to hear. "We cannot let you. At least not now."

"But why not?" the prince exclaimed, a clear mix of frustration and anger showing on his face. "Is it not true that the Tome may hold the key to our problems?"

"Yes," Faegan said. "But it is now also quite true that your blood is, to a large extent, the *cause* of all of our problems, as well. As I said, your blood is dying. Given the current condition of your blood we cannot know what putting the stone around your neck might do to you. It is for this same reason that your training cannot now begin. And all of this has become yet more complicated, given the attack on Ilendium."

Tristan looked to Shailiha to see that she was as confused by Faegan's words as he was.

"Why do you think they destroyed Ilendium?" he asked the wizards. "It has no real strategic value."

For the first time that day, a small smile began to creep along Faegan's lips. He gave the twins a playful wink. "Tell me," he asked, "what comes to mind when you think of Ilendium?"

"Marble," Shailiha said decisively. "That's where the best marble comes from."

Wigg leaned forward, placing his arms carefully down on the highly polished mahogany tabletop. "Yes," he said. "And we now believe that may be the reason behind all of our troubles."

Tristan was still stymied. "I don't understand," he said.

"Tell me," Faegan asked him, "have you ever, in your entire life, seen black marble with variegated veins of azure running through it?"

Tristan tried to think. "No," he finally said. "As a matter of fact, I have not."

"Nor will you ever," Wigg countered. "Unless you go to the quarries at Ilendium, the only place it can be found. The use of that particular marble was outlawed by the Directorate over three centuries ago. Any buildings containing it were ordered knocked down, and the marble was returned to the quarries to be buried. It has never been used since. Just like the wizard's warp that guards the entrance to the Caves of the Paragon, another guards that particular section of the quarry in which this marble can be found."

"But why?" Shailiha asked from the other side of the table. "What is so special about it?"

"It is dangerous," Faegan said softly, "and said to be of the craft. It has to do with the Ones Who Came Before."

Wigg had said that the Ones Who Came Before were the first true rulers of Eutracia, and had been responsible for first harnessing the craft and employing the orbs of the Vigors and the Vagaries.

They had written the Tome as a guide to the practice of magic. They had also left behind the Paragon, the jeweled conduit of magic, without which the practice of the craft would be impossible. It had been their hope that mankind would learn from their teachings, following only the Vigors and using the craft strictly for the practice of good.

Wigg had also made reference to a great struggle of centuries ago, in which the Ones Who Came Before had become embroiled with some dangerous adversaries. They had hidden the Tome and the Paragon to be found, hopefully, by the next generation of the endowed.

"I still do not understand," Tristan protested. "What does all of this have to do with us?"

"Tristan," Wigg said rather apologetically, "I'm afraid we have not been entirely forthcoming with you all of these years. In truth, we know more of the Ones Who Came Before than we ever let on. Your parents knew also, as did each king and queen before them. This secret, this history of the Ones, if you will, has been closely guarded ever since the discovery of the Tome, the Paragon, and the subsequent knowledge that one day you and your twin sister would walk among us."

"Why weren't Shailiha and I informed?" the prince responded angrily. "After all, as you have told us, we are the Chosen Ones. Is it not both our duty and our responsibility to know?"

"It is for that very reason you were *not* told," Faegan said coyly. "As the Chosen Ones, you were to be protected at all costs. This meant keeping a great deal of knowledge from you for your own good, training you in these things little by little when the time was right. Your parents agreed."

"How is it that you know all of this?" Shailiha asked. "And just when were we eventually to be told?"

"Tristan was to be told first," Wigg said, his white eyes gazing unseeing out across the table. "It was to have been an essential part of his training—the training that we now cannot risk giving to him. And then, should he die or otherwise fail in his attempts to join the two sides of the craft, the duty was to fall to his twin, who would then be trained, taking up the challenge. As for how we know these things, well, in truth they came to us from the Tome." Wigg pursed his lips, thinking of how to formulate his next words. "There is a small section of the great work that you still know nothing about," he said softly. His words landed on the ears of the Chosen Ones like a thunderclap.

"Do you mean to say that there is a fourth volume of the Tome?" Tristan asked, his voice nearly a whisper.

"Not exactly," Wigg answered. "It is in the form of a preface to the Tome—a history of the Ones, also written by themselves. However, it is incomplete. We believe they died before being able to finish it. The Directorate presumed this was because the great cataclysm the Ones predicted finally overtook them. The Ones wrote that should this feared disaster occur, it could wipe out the vast majority of human life. We believe that this is exactly what happened, leaving only a few humans, both endowed and unendowed alike, left to roam the wreckage of the land. We also contend that it is these survivors who eventually gave rebirth to the population that now inhabits Eutracia."

"What was the nature of this supposed struggle?" Tristan asked.

"A great war ensued," Wigg said. "They were near the end of it while writing the Tome and the Preface. Apparently a group of malcontents, bent on using the craft for their own purposes, had splintered off from these original, compassionate practitioners of the craft. They were vying for power in much the same way the sorceresses did against the wizards three centuries ago. A great, final battle ensued, and their combined use of the craft amounted to almost the total destruction of the land and the people inhabiting it. A doomsday, if you will. Their cities apparently decimated, the surviving people must have been scattered, becoming nomadic tribes or cave dwellers. We think that all forms of education and culture were virtually extinguished, including the ability to command the craft. What truly saved magic was, of course, the natural passing of endowed blood through the coming generations. But there was little possibility of practicing it or passing the knowledge down, since virtually all of the adepts had perished in the war. It was only after thousands of years had passed that nature replenished the earth and the sky. The remaining humans finally emerged from their ignorance to start again. We are the eventual result. Although over the passing centuries various of the endowed began to understand and use certain simplistic examples of their gifts, it was only upon finding the Tome and the stone that the craft was truly reborn."

"But how could the craft result in the nearly complete annihilation of everyone and everything around them?" Shailiha asked.

"We feel that both the Ones and their enemies were immensely more powerful than we are," Faegan answered. "Remember, unlike the wizards and the Coven, these mystics of old were exquisitely trained, in ways we may only be able to dream of. For all we know, they may have been studying and employing the craft for thousands of years."

Tristan felt something tugging at the back of his mind. "If the history of the Ones is incomplete because of their demise in the cataclysm, then what about the Tome?" he asked, at first even he not completely understanding the importance of his words.

"What do you mean?" Wigg asked politely.

"You say that this preface, this so-called history of the Ones, was not completed because of their demise. If that is true, then how do we know the Tome itself is not incomplete for the very same reasons?"

Faegan crackled. "Well done!" A grin and a wink followed.

Tristan's eyes went wide at the overwhelming implications of such a premise. "Do you mean to say—"

"Yes," Faegan interrupted. "Even the Tome itself may be incomplete. What we know to be the art of magic may only be a sliver of what can actually be attained."

"What were they called?" Shailiha suddenly asked.

"Who?" Wigg asked back.

"The enemies of the Ones. What did they call themselves?"

"They were called the Guild of the Heretics," he answered softly.

"But what does the black-and-azure marble of Ilendium have to do with this?" Shailiha asked. "I don't see how any of it pieces together."

At the princess' question, Wigg's face became very dark.

Faegan slumped down a bit into his chair. " *'And just as the*

Ones left behind certain instruments of the craft, the Heretics shall also leave behind marks of their mastery. One of these shall flow as azure through the darkness, and lay in wait for the coming of he who can release its power upon the land,' " he quoted.

"From the Tome, I assume," Tristan mused, turning to look at his sister.

"Yes," Faegan answered. "But this time it comes from the Preface, not one of the three volumes proper."

"What does it mean?" Shailiha asked.

Faegan looked into the eyes of the Chosen Ones with an intensity he rarely showed. Drawing a long breath, he answered, "Someone is attempting to construct the Gates of Dawn."

"The Gates of Dawn," Tristan said. "And these gates have something to do with the black marble from Ilendium?"

"They have everything to do with it," Faegan answered. "The potential construction of the Gates is the reason that the mining and use of this particular marble was banned so many years ago. The black-and-azure marble is the material from which the Gates will be constructed. No other will do."

"Why?" Shailiha asked.

"Because the azure that runs through the marble is not stone," Wigg answered solemnly. "It is the preserved, endowed blood of the Guild of the Heretics."

Tristan shook his head in disbelief. "How can that be?" he asked. "Stone is not blood, nor blood stone."

" 'And before they perish, the Heretics will perfect the Art of Transposition, thereby converting their life force to stone . . . The resultant perfection shall be embedded into the living rock, and used to facilitate their return,' " Faegan said. "From the Vigors. A warning from the Ones to whomever would eventually find the Tome and the stone. And, as you know, that person was Wigg." He looked carefully into Tristan's eyes, waiting for the prince's understandable, inevitable disbelief. It didn't take long.

"Their *return*?" Tristan whispered incredulously. "You must be joking! Do you mean to say that—"

"Yes," Wigg interrupted. "It has long been our belief that both the Ones and the Heretics were eventually able to use their powers of the craft to delve into the study of what we now call the Afterlife. The ultimate pursuit of learning, wouldn't you agree? They may have turned to this because they felt they had pushed the boundaries of magic to its limits. We feel they are still alive. In spirit only, but that these spirits reside in the heavens. Because of having lost their material presences, they are unable to take true action here on earth, despite their great power." He paused for a moment. "Unless, of course, they are able to somehow return," he added drily.

Faegan took up the explanation. "The Tome makes several references to 'those who shall reside in the sky,'" he said slowly. "As a part of their seemingly never-ending struggle, we think the Heretics now plan to unleash the power of the Gates. We also believe they could not do so until they had the use of one or more beings of immense, heretofore-unseen power residing here, with us. Otherwise they would have attempted to construct and employ the Gates centuries ago. These powerful beings now somehow here with us, these Heretics' servants, if you will, would presumably be dynamic enough to ensure the building and the subsequent empowerment of the Gates. And because of this, something formidable has happened to magic. That much is abundantly clear. It could only be something of a great, craft-altering magnitude for this opportunity to have finally presented itself after all these centuries. We must find out what it is. And we must stop the construction of the Gates."

"And just what would happen if they in fact did return?" Tristan asked.

"Due to the fact that the Heretics worship and practice only the Vagaries, they would probably see us as inconsequential, killing us all," Wigg answered. "And there would be absolutely nothing we could do to stop them. The craft would no longer exist as we know it, for they would never employ the Vigors. In fact, they would probably do all they could to stamp out forever the compassionate side of the craft. As for the unendowed population as a whole, I can only assume the Heretics would consider them to be the lowest forms of life. As such, they might do away with them altogether."

Tristan sat back in his chair, stunned. He looked to Shailiha to see that she was equally astonished. "And you actually mean to say that the Heretics may be able to return from the After-life?" he whispered.

"Yes," Wigg answered. "And that the construction and empowerment of the Gates will allow this to happen."

"But how?" Shailiha asked.

"For this to become possible, the Tome states that several things must first be accomplished," Wigg replied. "Things that the Directorate never believed could be arranged. First, the mines at Ilendium must be opened, and the black marble taken from them. Second, at least one being of truly immense power—one who could oversee both the building and the empowering of the Gates—needs to walk the earth and be under the Heretics' control. No such power of that magnitude has ever before been known to exist. And third, there needs to be a catalyst, an empowering substance, if you will, that would be used to energize the Gates. Faegan and I now believe that substance to be endowed blood."

"What would happen then?" Tristan asked.

"First the Gates must be built," Wigg answered. "And then, at dawn, they are empowered with the blood of the endowed, combined with the inherent energy of the being responsible for the process. The Tome states that once energized, the azure of the marble returns to its previous state—that is, the blood of the Heretics. The details of all of this are still very unclear to us, but apparently the Heretics will be drawn to this empowerment of their blood, and then somehow be able to descend from the heavens. Their spirits would then pass through the Gates, regaining their bodies, rejoining the world of the living in the same powerful, fully human forms they enjoyed before perishing in their struggle with the Ones. But this time they would be alone on the earth, without the Ones to oppose them." He paused for a moment, taking a deep breath. "The Guild of the Heretics are the true masters of the Vagaries, Tristan," the wizard said, lowering his voice. "This rebellious offshoot of the original harnessers and employers of the craft would make the comparatively limited abilities of the Coven seem as mere child's play."

"One other fact has become abundantly clear," Faegan said. "Ragnar is obviously not the being who has been chosen to oversee this great venture. He is a pawn in the game, rather than the king he would like us to think he is. His powers do not in any fashion possess the dynamism required to perform such a thing. There is someone else, at least one such person, who will be responsible for performing all of the more infinitely difficult aspects of the process."

"The same being creating the amazing glow Wigg and I witnessed in the Caves," Tristan said softly. "The power to which I felt so curiously drawn. Now I understand."

"Yes," Wigg said. "It was the plan of the Heretics to leave behind their blood, hoping for a practitioner to eventually come who was strong enough to aid them in their return. Just as it was the hope of the Ones to leave behind the stone and the Tome, so that the compassionate side of the craft might flourish. Faegan and I now believe we may also have the answers to some of the other things that have been troubling us so," he added.

"Such as?" Tristan asked.

"For one, if it is indeed true that someone is attempting to construct the Gates, the killing of the citizens of Ilendium seems a logical if brutal first step. They would have been in the way. And this being may have a specific use for the city. It might better serve his purposes if it were abandoned, perhaps even destroyed. In addition, the wanted posters of you that have been scattered around the countryside, blaming you for the 'murder' of your father, now seem to fit, also."

"Why?" Shailiha asked. Morganna whimpered. Smiling down at her, Shailiha stroked the baby's soft cheek and then adjusted the sling a bit. Morganna began to quiet.

"We had first postulated that the posters were a result of our enemies wanting to keep Tristan in hiding so that he could not rally the citizens against them," Wigg went on. "This was only partially correct. No citizen army in the universe could combat what we are facing. Scrounge put the posters up and offered the reward for a different purpose. To keep Tristan safe."

Shailiha furrowed her brow in frustration. "But they are our enemies, are they not?" she asked. "Why would they want to keep him safe? And how does making the entire nation want to capture him accomplish that?"

It was then that Tristan suddenly understood. "They wanted me safe so that nothing would befall me before they were able to take my blood," he replied softly. "Keeping me here, among the wizards, was the best way to accomplish that. The posters and reward were intended to drive me underground. And they worked." He looked up to Faegan, the muscles in his jaw tense. "That is why they wanted my blood, isn't it?" he asked slowly. "It is my azure blood that they plan to use to empower the Gates of Dawn."

Faegan nodded. "Yes," he answered. "Right now that makes the most sense. As I said, the Tome states that they will not only require the talents of a great adept, but also an 'energizing' agent. Wigg and I now believe that agent is to be your blood—the finest ever known. In fact, it is most probably the only substance in the world that could accomplish such a thing. We have long known that if your blood is employed correctly, not even the waters of the Caves would be as potent." The room went silent for a moment. Shailiha placed her hand over her brother's.

"But then why blind Wigg and poison my blood?" Tristan asked. "Why bother, if they already had what they wanted?"

"As far as blinding me is concerned," Wigg answered, "you must remember that Ragnar hates me with a passion that is virtually unequaled. Blinding me was a simple act of revenge. But as for why your blood was poisoned, we really have no answer. Only time will tell."

"And time is quickly running out," Tristan said darkly.

"The taking of the consuls," Shailiha said. "What of that?"

"The consuls must be helping them to mine the stone, for they shall need a great deal of it," Wigg answered. "And using the craft to get at it would be the most efficient way. It is the only answer that makes any sense. The black-and-azure marble is the hardest in the world, and is virtually impervious to ordinary, unendowed mining techniques. But of greater interest is how this being is able to control so many of the consuls at once. His or her power must be virtually without limits."

"And where did this creature come from?" Tristan asked.

"In that, as with so many other questions, we have no answers," Faegan said, his usually mischievous voice full of frustration.

"This is also why the Paragon is being drained," Wigg said. "The combination of all of the power of the stone poured into a single being, coupled with Tristan's raw, untrained blood will make for an event of unparalleled proportions."

"We also have no rationale for their raid on Fledgling House," Faegan added. "No doubt by now they have collected all of the children of the consuls—both the boys and the girls. But to what ends this was accomplished we do not know."

"And they let us have the Tome," Tristan said, looking over his shoulder to the book. "Yet another mystery."

"You mentioned the Art of Transposition," Shailiha suddenly said. "Is it this spell that allows the Heretics to return?"

"In a manner of speaking, yes," Faegan said. "But it is far more complicated than that. The Art of Transposition is the method by which one substance is converted to another, such as attempting to turn dirt into gold. After centuries of trying, even the combined efforts of the Directorate failed to unravel the calculations required."

"But I have often seen you conjure things out of the air," Tristan countered. "Isn't that the same thing?"

"Indeed it is not," Wigg replied. "At first glance one would suppose that creating something out of nothing would be far more difficult than the mere changing of one thing into another. But in fact, the exact opposite is true. Without going into detail, suffice it to say that it has to do with overcoming the strength of an object's present existence, rather than overcoming the relative weakness of nothingness. Do you see? When the Art of Transposition causes the veins of the marble to revert back to the blood of the Heretics, this shall be an example of the craft that will have no previous equal in its complexity. It shall be something never before seen upon the earth." The wizard thought to himself for a moment. "Or, should I say, at least since the discovery of the stone and the Tome, and the enlightenment of the wizards. It is yet more proof of the hugely advanced abilities of those who were here before us."

"Why can't the Ones do the same thing?" Shailiha asked.

"I beg your pardon?" asked Faegan.

"Why can't they do the same thing? Why can't the Ones also return?"

"We do not know that they can't, but to our knowledge they never have," he answered. "We have long theorized that the act of returning from the Afterlife would require a connection to at least one part of the departed ones' bodies—something of them that had been left behind upon the earth, with which to once again bond. The Heretics, of course, were somehow wise enough to leave behind a portion of their blood, encasing it for safety within the marble at Ilendium. Logic dictates that they must have accomplished this before the great cataclysm of their times. But as for the Ones, they must have left nothing of their bodies behind."

"Nothing that we *know* of," Wigg countered.

Faegan raised his eyebrows. "Quite right," he added. "Nothing that we know of. In addition, this method of return from the Afterlife is presumably an act of the Vagaries, and therefore something that the Ones would not allow themselves to do. At least not in this exact way."

Tristan suddenly remembered something. "In your first quote you recited the words 'among the other instruments of the craft,' " he said eagerly. "Is it possible that there are other things still to be found? More artifacts that may also have the power and importance of the stone and the Tome?"

"There may indeed by such things still within the earth, carrying secrets and power we could only dream of," Wigg answered. "But no such additional treasures have ever been discovered. Still, the prospect continues to exist. Tantalizing, wouldn't you agree? To that end, many parties of wizards and consuls have searched Eutracia over the years, looking for the remains of the One's civilization. It was felt that if we could discover the ruins of their cities, much would be revealed. But nothing ever came of it, and the prospect was abandoned. It was as if the Ones and the Heretics vanished into thin air."

Tristan slumped down in his chair, fatigued and stunned by all he had heard. He shook his head back and forth slowly.

"What we do not know is *who*," Tristan whispered to himself, so softly that the others at the table could scarcely hear him.

"What did you say?" Shailiha asked. Morganna had begun to fuss again, and Shailiha adjusted her clothing to nurse the baby. Her brother smiled at the two of them, and then his face turned serious again.

"What we do not know is the identity of the being Wigg and Faegan describe," he said. "Until that is uncovered, I fear we may never solve the rest of the riddle lying before us." He paused for a moment, looking around the table. "It is now more clear than ever that I must go to Parthalon. If the Paragon continues to decay and the wizards lose their powers before we find a way out of all this, the warriors may be the only means we have to help control the situation."

Faegan sighed resignedly, placing either hand into the opposite sleeve of his robe. "At first Wigg and I were skeptical about that," he said slowly. "We would have preferred to keep you here, so that you could at least begin your training and also read the Prophecies to us. But now things have changed markedly, and we are forced to agree with you. Frankly, we see little other hope for us. Whoever is controlling these events has planned exceedingly well, and we have been bested at every turn. But if the Minions come here, quickly enough and in numbers sufficient enough to matter, we may have a chance against Scrounge, his hatchlings, and those insects that were used in Ilendium. That would be a start. But as for stopping the return of the Heretics . . . Well, that is a different problem, for it is of the craft. Wigg and I must work ceaselessly on it." He turned his gray-green eyes to the prince, giving him a hard look. "But before you go," he said sternly, "there is something we must ask of you. Actually, it is more of a demand."

"I'm listening," Tristan said, folding his arms across the worn leather of his vest. He had long ago made up his mind to go, and he didn't like demands, especially when they came from the wizards. Even as a child, he had always hated constraints of any type placed upon his movements. The look in his dark blue eyes told Faegan that whatever it was they wanted him to swallow, it would not go down easily.

"We're assigning you a bodyguard," Faegan said simply. "At least until such time as you may be healed from the poison that runs through your veins."

"A bodyguard!" Tristan exclaimed. "Absolutely not! I am entirely capable of taking care of myself!"

"Under normal conditions, perhaps," Faegan said sternly. "But current conditions are far from normal. First of all you are ill. Another convulsion is certain to befall you, and probably soon. When that occurs, you will need help. In addition, suppose when you reach Parthalon things have changed?

True, Traax agreed to accept Geldon's orders. But for all we know he could have been only giving us lip service, waiting for your unsuspecting return to take your head, laying claim to your position."

"Even if that were true," Tristan countered, "there would be little two of us could do against such numbers." Fully realizing that the wily wizards had already chosen someone to be his bodyguard he paused for a moment, thinking. "And just who is it that you two brilliant mystics would send with me to defend my honor, eh?" he asked sarcastically.

"Ox," Wigg answered calmly from across the table.

"*Ox!*" Tristan exclaimed. "Can't you send Joshua with me? At least he is of the craft. Compared to a consul of the Redoubt, what possible good can a Minion warrior do me?"

"Hear us out," Wigg said calmly. "We have our reasons. I am blind, and of little use to you. Faegan remains trapped in his chair. We considered sending Joshua, but the sad truth is we now need him here, to help with our research. He is the only other person trained in the craft, as far as we know, who is free to help us. Besides, we think that with Ox at your side the Minions will come to feel that you respect them. They will surely know that as the Chosen One you could have traveled with anyone you like, but instead chose to be with one of their own." Wigg pursed his lips ironically. "Even though that really isn't true," he added drily.

Out of the corner of his eye Tristan thought he caught a quick smile on Shailiha's lips. "And if I refuse?" he asked.

"You're forgetting something, my young friend," Faegan said with a wink.

"And that is?"

"You want to go to Parthalon, and I am the only one capable of opening and closing the portal." He grinned impishly. "That is, of course, unless you would like to do it without my services, and brave the Sea of Whispers alone."

Tristan laughed—a resigned sort of snort. They had him, and he knew it.

"If not for the wizards, then do it for me," Shailiha said seriously. She reached out with her free hand and gently touched the gold medallion around his neck. "You and Morganna are all I have left of my family."

"Very well," he said grudgingly. "I accept."

"When you arrive, you must be exceedingly careful in how you handle things," Wigg said. "First and foremost, you must convince the Minions to come to Eutracia under your leadership, and go to war with the hatchlings. Second, should you feel a convulsion coming on, it is vitally important that you do not let any of the Minions see it. You are their lord, having risen to that position by virtue of a fight to the death with Kluge. They expect strength and decisiveness from you, not weakness."

"Very well," Tristan answered. "I will do my best."

At that there came a knock on the door. It opened to reveal Geldon holding a shopworn straw basket that was soaked with blood.

"What is it, Geldon?" Tristan asked urgently. "What do you have there?"

The hunchbacked dwarf walked into the room, carefully holding the basket away from his short, bent-over body as if it were filled with venomous snakes. "I found this when returning to the Redoubt. It had been placed at the foot of one of the revolving boulders." He paused for a moment, tentatively looking around the table. "I took the chance to look inside, and now I wish I hadn't," he said distastefully. "It isn't pretty."

"Please place it on the table," Faegan ordered. Geldon did so. The stench of the blood clotted between the strands of straw caused Wigg to gasp. Shailiha looked as though she might be ill.

"What's in there?" Tristan asked anxiously.

Geldon looked around, not wanting to upset those gathered any more than he had to. But there was no other way to say it. "It contains a human head," he said softly. "And there is another parchment scroll. I believe it is meant for the prince."

Tristan looked quickly to Faegan. At the wizard's nod he carefully opened the basket, withdrawing the head by the hair and placing it on the tabletop.

The victim had been fairly elderly, with gray hair and a rather long beard. The face was smudged and very dirty, covered with a strange kind of black soot. The head had been severed cleanly. Blank, emotionless eyes stared hauntingly out at nothing. Faegan raised one hand in the direction of the head, and the eyes gently closed for the final time.

Tristan immediately recognized Scrounge's miniature arrow embedded in the forehead, and saw the scroll. He carefully removed the scroll from the length of the shaft, untying the ribbon and unrolling the parchment. His eyes tore down the page, eager to read the message. But he couldn't.

It was written in blood, just as the others had been, but neither the handwriting nor the language was recognizable. This was not Eutracian as Tristan knew it. It was written in a very flowing, beautiful style, the odd-looking symbols completely unintelligible to him. Then he realized he had seen this form of writing before. It had been in the Caves of the Paragon. He had also seen it in various places within the Redoubt of the Directorate, primarily over doorways that were almost always closed. Puzzled, he laid the parchment flat upon the table. Faegan pointed to the scroll and caused it to flatten out, keeping it in place.

"What is it?" Wigg asked.

"Another scroll," Faegan answered. "But this one is different. This one is written in Old Eutracian."

"In case the two of you are bewildered," Faegan said to the prince and princess, "Old Eutracian is the ancient language of our nation. It is the dialect spoken and written by the Ones, and therefore presumably by the Heretics, as well."

"Is it written in blood?" Wigg asked.

"Yes," Faegan answered. "In that way it is like the others." He rubbed his hand across the dirty face of the head and then held his fingertips high, examining the black dust he had collected upon them. He blew on his hand, and the soot flew into the air. As it drifted harmlessly to the floor it caught the light, and to Tristan's eyes it appeared to have a bluish cast intermixed with the black. Faegan cast a knowing glance to the table at large. "This man was most probably a consul," he added.

"How do you know that?" Shailiha asked.

Faegan held his dirty palm up to the table. "This is marble dust from the quarries of Ilendium. I would bet my life upon it. It also contains traces of azure, meaning that they are indeed mining the forbidden black marble—and almost certainly using the consuls to do it. Just as we surmised."

"Aren't you going to ask me about the language?" Wigg

said in the direction of the prince. Despite both his infirmity and the darkness of their situation, the lead wizard had a short smile on his face.

"Ask what about it?" Tristan said blankly.

"How did you learn Old Eutracian?" Shailiha asked.

"Well done, Princess." Wigg smiled. "Please continue."

"If all of the Ones and the Heretics are dead, then who taught you to understand their language?" she asked.

"Think about it for a moment," Wigg said. "The answer to your question is before you, in this very room."

Tristan looked around at the vast, rather dark room, carefully observing the seemingly endless floors with their stacks of books, and the entryway to the Vault of Scrolls that lay within the far wall. He also saw the white, leather-bound Tome. And then something began to pull at his mind. Rubbing his brow with his fingertips, he thought for a moment.

"The Tome is written in Old Eutracian," he said softly, almost to himself. He thought again for a moment. "In the early days of its discovery it was unreadable, written in a language that was completely foreign to you. But after Faegan's daughter, Emily, the first to wear the stone and read the Tome, led the way with her first translation, you worked to unravel the Old Eutracian symbols."

"Very good!" Faegan pointed a long, bony finger at the prince and barked a cackle. "Emily was also able to read the language aloud in its original form—allowing us to learn how to speak it as well as read it. All the consuls and wizards have learned it, and we speak it among ourselves when the topic is particularly secret."

Tristan looked back down at the scroll, his mind alive with questions. "Would you please read it?" he asked Faegan.

"Of course," the crippled wizard answered. "I will first read it aloud in Old Eutracian, so you may hear what it sounds like. I shall then translate it for you."

Faegan looked down at the scroll, measuring the import of the words he saw there. It had been almost three centuries since he had read any ancient text, but the words came back to him as surely as if it had been yesterday. As he began to read aloud, Tristan found the language mellifluous and soothing. But as Faegan continued to read the scroll, Tristan was disturbed to see that the wizard's face darkened further with every word.

Faegan sat back in his chair, seemingly stunned. Wigg also seemed overtaken. "Please," Tristan urged anxiously. "Translate it for me."

"Very well," Faegan replied.

"I am the power behind the glow, and I am the one you seek. I am also he who has caused the wailing and torment of your nation. Have you not felt yourself drawn to me? Have you not already seen my face? There is much for us to discuss, Chosen One. I am in the Caves. Come to me tonight. Come and much shall be revealed. Leave your wizards behind in their useless pursuit of the answers. For their inferior, unenlightened gifts are useless to beings such as we. Come alone."

After a period of intense silence, Wigg finally spoke. "This is obviously not the work of Scrounge," he said quietly. "I am not even sure whether Ragnar, in his madness, could have written this."

"I agree," Faegan replied. "But now we must decide whether Tristan is to do this thing, especially without protection."

"I have seen him," Tristan said suddenly. His face was a blank, his eyes staring out at nothing.

"What?" Faegan exclaimed. "Why didn't you tell us?"

"I have seen him," Tristan repeated. He finally turned his eyes to the wizards. "At the beginning of my first convulsion, I saw a face that I was inexplicably drawn to. It was a dark-haired male. And he was quite young, little more than a boy. Just before I blacked out I remembered thinking that he reminded me of someone, but I couldn't place who. I dismissed it, thinking it was a hallucination. But now I know better." He paused, his breathing starting to visibly quicken. "Now that I have seen the scroll and remember the vision, I can literally feel his presence in my blood. It is almost as if his heart beats in time with mine . . . the same feeling that overcame me when I saw the glow sweeping across the floor in Ragnar's chambers." He paused for a moment. "But how could a mere boy be responsible for all of these wondrous, terrible acts of the craft?" he asked.

"Have you seen this face since?" Faegan asked urgently.

"No," Tristan answered, shaking his head.

Despite the lifeless nature of his eyes, Wigg's face said much. Faegan, too, appeared as if something monumental had just occurred.

"I think you should go," Wigg said flatly from the other side of the table. "And you should go tonight, alone, just as the note asks."

"I agree," Faegan replied.

"Are you both mad?" Shailiha exclaimed. She grasped her brother's hand, as if doing so could somehow keep him by her side forever.

Morganna seemed to sense her mother's agitation, and her little eyes went wide. The princess was angry, and it showed.

"Have you forgotten what happened the last time?" Shailiha continued. "He is mortally ill because of that visit! How do you know something worse won't happen this time? How could you possibly let him do such a thing?"

Wigg and Faegan remained quiet for a time, letting the princess' emotions calm. Finally Wigg said, "If those in the Caves had wanted us dead, we would be already, Shailiha. And I believe that if Tristan can use this opportunity to discover anything about this being, anything at all, he must do so. Not only for our sake, but also for the craft and the nation."

"I agree," Tristan said, giving his sister's hand an affectionate, reassuring squeeze. "I must go now, before my trip to Parthalon. Surely you can see that. If I can bring back anything that might be of help to the wizards, they can be researching it while I am meeting with the Minions." He smiled, trying to help her mood. "And in case you haven't noticed," he added, "we're losing this battle."

"But what about Ox?" she asked, knowing she was losing the argument. "The wizards said you should have a bodyguard. Shouldn't he go, too?"

"Not this time," Tristan answered. He looked to the wizards to see that they were both nodding in silent agreement. "The being responsible for the scroll said to come alone. And that is what I shall do."

Shailiha lowered her head in frustration. "Why must you always be so eager?" she whispered to her brother.

Tristan placed a finger under her chin, raising her face,

then smiled at her. "I take after you, Shai. You were born eight minutes before me, remember?"

She said nothing for several moments, searching his face as if trying to make sure she could keep it locked in her memories. "When will you leave?" she asked quietly.

Tristan looked to Faegan and said, "Within the hour."

Faegan closed his eyes, nodding approval.

Shailiha had seen her brother leave for the Caves once before. But that time he had been with Wigg, and despite her misgivings she had felt relatively sure they would return. But this time was different.

This time her heart told her she would never see her brother again.

CHAPTER THIRTY-FIVE

$\mathcal{A}$s Ragnar approached the marble steps to Fledgling House, the bitter, unrelenting wind swirled around him, teasing the hem of his robe. The coldness seeping into his bones told him, as had so many other things of nature lately, that the Season of Crystal was near. Looking up to the jagged Tolenka Mountains, he could see that some of the snow that always resided only at the very top of the peaks had begun creeping its way downward. Its whiteness would soon also come from the sky, laying a frozen blanket over the land. The air smelled of dead leaves, the once-magnificent colors of their foliage having slowly expired to orange, then brown, and in most cases dust. Nearby, the cold, blue waters of the Sippora River babbled happily onward, going about their business.

How idyllic, he mused. Pausing for a moment, he looked up at the edifice that had, until only recently, held within its walls one of the greatest secrets of the Directorate of Wizards: the training of females in the craft of magic.

The castle had been built some twenty-five years earlier, and little had been spared in its expense. Although small compared to the royal palace at Tammerland, this lesser manor was nonetheless comprised of four stories, containing more than four hundred rooms. The rose-colored marble was gracefully shot through with streaks of magenta; the columns and steps were of the faintest pink. *How appropriate for little girls,* he thought. Two massive oaken doors, their planks bonded together with strong-looking ironwork, stood side by side, seeming to bar entrance to anyone not associated with the craft. On either side of the doors was a hatchling, fully armed and standing at attention. Others flew high in the sky above, carefully watching over the scene. Still more were camped nearby.

The stalker paused at the top step, relishing the many victories that the master had already afforded them. Curious to see more, he pointed to the doors, watched them open, and stepped inside. The hatchlings obediently bowed as he passed, shutting the great doors behind him with finality.

The large foyer was also of marble, the floor a complicated pattern of dark and light inlaid mahogany. Twin staircases, their steps of marble and their railings of patterned wrought iron, curved upward from opposite sides of the floor, ascending to the higher levels. Originally the girls' quarters, he presumed. A huge stained-glass window lay in the opposite wall from the entryway doors, a representation of the Paragon inlaid into the curving, gentle grace of its design. Oil chandeliers gave off a delicate, subdued essence, and the air smelled delicately of potpourri.

From a hallway leading off to the right came the familiar, magnificent glow. The aura that existed only in the presence of the master poured forth from the doorway of the corridor, partially covering the foyer floor. Ragnar turned toward it and began walking down the hallway, his feet strangely covered in the glow of the craft.

Just before leaving the quarries, Nicholas had told him to come here later in the day. There was something he wished the stalker to see. Several hatchlings had carried the stalker in his ornate, personal litter, landing him at the doors of Fledgling House. Still intrigued by what the master wished him to witness, he finally came to the room at the end of the hall.

The huge marble room had been completely stripped of its furnishings, its emptiness a distinct contrast to the sumptuous foyer the stalker had just left behind. Nicholas hovered several feet above the floor in the center of the room, his back to the stalker, the folds of his white silk robe falling gracefully over his muscular form. He was surrounded on all sides by open-faced, coffinlike boxes. Rows upon rows of them were stacked in tiers on the walls. In each one lay a child, his or her eyes closed peacefully in sleep.

A transparent sphere sat on the floor of the room. From it, a mass of clear, flexible tubes snaked outward, one to each child. Both the sphere resting on the floor and the tubes were pulsing with red liquid.

"Enter," Nicholas said without turning around. Ragnar stepped tentatively into the room, as if his very footsteps might upset the delicate balance of what was unfolding. The master had told him not long ago that he would be needing the blood of the endowed children, but the stalker was still at a complete loss as to why. Ragnar was transfixed at the scene before him, his mind alive with questions. Even to him, what Nicholas was doing to the children had a ghastly, macabre quality.

"Interesting, isn't it?" Nicholas asked, rotating at last to look at the confused stalker. "Each day I take a little more from them. As much as their young bodies will safely allow, without placing them in shock. But even with so many children here at my disposal it will be two more weeks until I have enough. So much beautiful, endowed blood! But still the potential collected in this bowl is infinitesimal compared to the sanguine fluid of myself and the Chosen One, my father of this world.

"You are wondering why I need it, are you not?" he asked as the hundreds of tubes continued their grisly task. "All in good time, my friend, all in good time. For now let it suffice to say that their blood shall become the mortar, if you will, that shall bind the pieces of marble together, to create the Gates."

"But the blood of these children is of very low training," Ragnar countered politely. "How is it that it could be used for such a grand purpose?"

Nicholas smiled. "It is precisely because of the relatively

meager training of their blood that I require it," he answered. "The blood of the children, because they have not received a great deal of training, is more 'malleable,' so to speak. Using the blood of their fathers for this purpose would have presented a far greater challenge." He smiled again, his exotic eyes flashing. "But one I am sure I could have surmounted, nonetheless."

"Are they in pain?" Ragnar asked, looking up at the rows of children on the walls. He asked not out of compassion, only curiosity.

"Oh, no," Nicholas replied. "Not at all. And afterward they remember nothing of the experience. Aside from some initial weakness they are quite well, and ready to be used in the same manner again the following day."

He changed the subject. "The mining continues to go as ordered?"

"The consuls work endlessly in shifts, day and night," the stalker answered. "I am amazed as to how fast they are able to gather the marble. It is being cut and polished exactly to your specifications."

"When not working they are billeted in the city of Ilendium, as I asked?" Nicholas asked.

"Yes, Master," Ragnar answered. "As are the hatchlings you have ordered to remain there. In addition, the carrion scarabs' eggs that were laid in the corpses of the dead at Ilendium have begun to hatch."

"Excellent," Nicholas said. "All is going according to plan. And now I must stop the blood collection for today, for I have other matters to attend to."

The stalker watched as Nicholas narrowed his eyes. Almost immediately the hundreds of needles in the children's feet came out, and the bleeding stopped, the small pinpricks vanishing in mere seconds. Then the tubes connected to the sphere hauntingly retracted, melding into the sides of the vessel itself.

Nicholas lowered the children gently to the floor, and they began to awaken. Within a matter of only moments, the unsuspecting youths started to laugh and play happily among themselves.

"You see?" Nicholas said, placing an affectionate hand on

the head of one of the young girls. "No harm done. Now I must leave. After I am gone, order a squadron of hatchlings here to watch over the children and feed them. Walk with me."

Ragnar walked silently alongside his master as Nicholas glided above the floor. Entering the foyer, they went to the door and opened it. The hatchlings on either side bowed obediently.

"If I may ask, where is it that you now go, Master?" Ragnar asked.

"The Caves," Nicholas answered. "I am about to receive a very important guest." With that the adept spread his arms and flew away, higher and higher, until he was a mere pinprick in the sky. Ragnar stared after him, stunned. How could anyone, even one of such highly endowed blood, fly without wings?

Ragnar's eyes finally lost the adept as the whiteness of the young man's robes became one with the nighttime stars.

After ordering a squadron of hatchlings into the castle to care for and protect the children, he called for his personal litter. Four of the great birds landed with it, one of them at each corner. As the stalker climbed inside and gave orders for his return to the quarries, his mind went to other, more pleasurable pursuits.

He had been several hours without his fluid, and he needed it badly. Taking the ever-present vial down from a specially built shelf on the inside wall, he luxuriously scooped some onto a finger and licked it off. Lying back on the overstuffed pillows, he let down the velvet side curtains, so as to be alone with his thoughts.

Once he had checked on the consuls' progress with the mining, he would turn his entire attention to the beautiful woman he had brought to the quarries with him. True, she was not Celeste, but she would do for now . . . until the daughter of Wigg was again his to do with as he wished.

CHAPTER THIRTY-SIX

$\mathcal{A}$s Tristan neared the Caves of the Paragon, a flood of thoughts and memories came to his mind. Some of them were pleasant, but most were far from reassuring. Although always drawn by his blood to these remote, underground caverns, he nonetheless had a deep dread of coming here alone now.

It was cold, the clear sky above scattered with thousands of twinkling stars. Pilgrim's breath came out of his nostrils in short, streaming puffs of vapor, the dead leaves crunching pleasantly beneath the gray-and-white-dappled stallion as he carried the prince ever deeper into the woods.

The last time Tristan had come here by himself was that fateful day when he had accidentally discovered the Caves' existence. He had fallen in while trying to learn how the fliers of the fields had seemingly disappeared, as if melting into the wall that barred the Caves' entrance. He had nearly died that day, and his father and the Directorate of Wizards had been furious with him. Now, of course, he knew why. Sighing, he shook his head. So much had transpired since then. Closing his eyes, he tried to fight back the feeling that all would soon be lost.

Before donning a fur coat and setting out, he had looked at his shoulder. The dark, ominous-looking spider veins that covered the skin of the joint were slowly lengthening into his biceps. Strangely, he felt no pain from them. Nor did he feel ill or weak when not in the grip of a convulsion. The wizards had told him that that might change, though.

But he also knew it would only be a matter of time before another of the attacks came, and he closed his eyes briefly at the thought. The pain and disorientation had been so intense he wasn't sure he could survive another convulsion, and he only hoped that one of his allies would be near him when it happened.

He raised his eyes to the heavens, thinking of the incredible tale the wizards had told him and his sister about the Ones and the Heretics.

But perhaps the thing that concerned him the most was the continuing erosion of the wizards' powers. Although he had not yet seen either of them fail in attempting to use their gifts, he knew it would only be a matter of time until it happened. It was as if there was little either of them could do to stem the tide of all that was happening. Their resignation was unusual, and only added to the prince's personal sense of defeat.

And then there was Celeste. When he had first seen her that night by the graves he had been deeply drawn not only to her beauty but to her solitary, mysterious strength. *So much like her father,* he thought. Incredibly, she was one of them now— the long-lost daughter of Wigg. Whenever he and Celeste were in the same room together he was still intensely aware of her presence, but there was little time for such things. Besides, she was Wigg's only child. Becoming involved with her at this time would not only be irresponsible, but could perhaps even intrude on the delicate relationship between father and daughter that had only so recently begun to take root.

As he approached the little rise where he would tie his horse, Tristan's mind finally turned to the strange, obviously very powerful presence in the Caves—the still-unknown being Wigg and Faegan had described as able to return the Heretics to the earth. He remembered the amazing glow that had flooded the floor with its majesty the day he had been cut by Scrounge, and Wigg had been blinded by Ragnar. He had been strangely drawn to it, almost as if it was a part of him. And then, after reading the scroll and remembering the face that had appeared before him just as his first convulsion occurred, he had known without a doubt that he had to come here, that the wizards had been right. He must face whatever this thing was, discovering all he could. And somehow get back alive.

He stopped Pilgrim and dismounted, then tied the stallion to a tree and crept slowly up to the top of the little rise. Sliding his dreggan from its scabbard, he looked down to the wall of fieldstone that marked the entrance to the Caves.

There was something different about it this time. The hole that he and Wigg had made in the wall had been enlarged. Light shone from it, flashing hauntingly, an odd combination of flickering orange-red that was intermittently combined with the glow of the craft.

The being is here, Tristan realized. He wiped the sweat from his palms, contemplating his descent into the Caves. He cautiously started down the rise.

Suddenly, he stopped. Looking at the dreggan in the moonlight he took a deep breath, recalling something the wizards had said. If Wigg and Faegan were right, had the thing in the Caves desired it he would probably be dead already. He slowly replaced the sword into its scabbard and climbed through the hole.

Standing at the top of the stone landing he could see that the vein into which the power of the Paragon was being drained now ran through the walls of this room, as well. As always, the majestic falls continued to noisily spill the waters of the Caves into the stone pool at the bottom. The wall torches had been lit, and combined with the azure of the vein they gave the chamber an eerie, macabre look.

The deep glow he had seen before in Ragnar's chambers was seeping silently outward from another hallway to the left. Tristan could not remember ever seeing that corridor before. He could only assume that the being had somehow recently created it. Just as it had perhaps also created the newly discovered chambers he and Wigg had been forced to navigate. Carefully, his senses alert, he continued down the stone steps.

Once upon the floor of the chamber, the overpowering effect of the waters on his blood made him dizzy. He was forced to go down on one knee, his breath coming quicker, more hungrily to his lungs.

"Come to me, Chosen One." The voice was strong, yet somehow also soft and reassuring. It resonated deeply through the chamber and the hallway from which it came, leaving no room for misunderstanding.

Tristan stood up on shaky legs and started down the hallway to the left, following the glow.

The corridor twisted and turned. With every step he took the dynamism of the being called more powerfully to his blood. And conversely, the effect of the waters of the Caves lessened, finally vanishing. The corridor ended at a solid-black marble door. The azure glow seeped from beneath it, spilling out over his boots. Tristan slowly reached out and pushed the door open.

Before him was a man of about his own age and size, seated cross-legged in the air. His hands in the opposite sleeves of his fine, white robe, he stared peacefully at the prince. He was apparently unarmed. Long, dark, shiny hair fell down to his shoulders, framing high cheekbones and a sensuous mouth. But there was something else about him. Something that immediately unnerved the prince as he stood there, taking him in. It was his eyes.

Dark and sparkling, the eyes slanted upward slightly at the corners, giving the man an exotic, almost feminine appearance. They seemed strangely familiar to Tristan.

Looking around, he saw that the vein ran through the walls of this room also. To the right stood a black marble pedestal, on top of which was a small glass beaker.

"Who are you?" Tristan asked the man.

"You truly do not know?"

"Only that you are the being who is about to build the Gates of Dawn, unleashing the Heretics on the world," Tristan said. "It is my duty to stop you."

"Is it really?" the man asked, pursing his lips. "Are you quite sure of that? As the male of the Chosen Ones, he of the azure blood, your wizards have yet to completely tell you of your duties. But you still do not know that, do you? So much to learn, so little time left. In fact, both you and your sister have more in common with those in the heavens than you could possibly know."

Understanding the reference to time but little else, Tristan pressed. "Why did you poison my blood?" he asked angrily. "If you wish me dead, why not just kill me and get it over with?"

"First things first," the man said. He hovered closer, looking deeply into the prince's face. "You truly do not know who I am?" he asked again.

"No," Tristan answered simply.

Again the man smiled. But then the smile suddenly vanished as quickly as it had come. "Look at me," he ordered. "Do you not recognize these eyes?"

Tristan hesitated, unsure of what to say. The exotic eyes were beginning to unnerve him. It was as if something in his subconscious was trying to convince him of an impossibility—that he had seen them before.

"They are somehow familiar to me, but you are not," he answered. Suddenly he had endured enough. "No more games," he said sternly, taking a slightly more aggressive stance. "Tell me who you are. Now."

The dark-haired man before him took a short breath, then let it out slowly. "I am your son, Chosen One," he said softly. "The boy-child you so casually left behind in the shallow grave in Parthalon. Do you not remember me? I am also the son of Succiu, second mistress of the Coven. One of the four women you and your wizard killed." He paused for a moment. "I am Nicholas," he finished softly. "And I have returned."

Despite the similarity of the man's eyes to those of Succiu, at first Tristan wanted to dismiss him as mad. But then a creeping dread began to overcome him. The longer he stood there, the more he could see Succiu's eyes staring back at him. It sent a shiver down his spine. In fact, he could now see much more than that. It was as if this man somehow possessed the finest aesthetic qualities of both himself and the sorceress who had raped him.

"It is not possible," Tristan whispered. "You lie. My son died. Succiu took him to his death, when she committed suicide by leaping from the roof of the Recluse. I excised the body and buried it myself, weeping over the grave. And aside from the impossibility of him being alive, you are far too old. No—this is some kind of trick. A cruel, sick prank. And I will have none of it." He warily took a step back, wondering what to expect next. It was difficult to keep himself from reaching for his sword. But he knew in his heart that such a crude weapon would be completely useless against the creature before him.

"Are you so sure?" Nicholas asked, closing the distance between them. His dark, sparkling gaze was relentless. "If the Heretics, my parents of the Afterlife, can come back with my help, then what makes you so certain they could not save me from the grave, and return me to the earth?"

Tears began to gather in Tristan's eyes. Not because he was ready to believe, but because of the horrific memories that came with having to speak of it with a stranger. "But you are too old . . . It . . . it would be impossible," he stammered.

"Very little is impossible with the practice of the Vagaries, Father," Nicholas said. Hearing himself called "Father," Tristan felt something inside of him slip. "It is true that I first returned to your world as an infant," Nicholas continued. "But I also came with certain preordained knowledge, granted to me by my parents above. There are certain advantages to being dead, you see. At least in the unenlightened way you understand it. As I said, so much to learn, so little time. But I digress. The most important of these abilities was the taking of the power of the stone. Think of it, Chosen One. All the power of the Paragon—imbued into a single being. When I began to harvest the dynamism of the stone, my knowledge, power, and physical stature grew exponentially, resulting in the man you see before you." He paused for a moment. "I am truly your son of this earth," he said softly. "Why do you think you were so drawn to me?"

Tristan shook his head back and forth, trying desperately not to believe. But inside his heart of hearts, he was starting to have doubts. He lowered his head. "No," he whispered softly, his voice cracking. "It simply cannot be . . ."

"You are indeed as stubborn as your reputation claims," Nicholas said. "Therefore I shall provide proof. Behold." With that, the adept narrowed his eyes, and an incision opened in his right wrist. His blood began to run slowly from it. He placed two fingers against the wound and collected some, then held it up to Tristan's face. The prince's breath came out in a rush. The blood was azure.

"The wizards told me that I was the only being in the world with such blood," Tristan whispered, barely able to get the words out. "How can this be?"

"The answer is really quite simple," Nicholas answered. "If you were at one time the only such being in the world to possess it, and you fathered a child, then . . ."

Nicholas left the sentence hanging, watching amazement and pain blend in Tristan's expression.

Shock nearly caused the prince to faint. He lost his balance, collapsing slightly, going down to one knee. He finally regained his legs, standing before Nicholas with some difficulty. Tears ran down his face.

"There, there—steady, Father," Nicholas said almost compassionately. "You mustn't take it all so hard. In fact, there is a great deal of very important work still remaining we can now do together. That is if you will simply choose to cooperate."

Nicholas reached out his hand, caressing one side of Tristan's face. "You see, I am no monster. I am simply a messenger. A constructor of worlds, if you will. I do not need your help in these things I must do, but the Heretics and I would prefer it. You will find our methods not to be so crude and clumsy as those of the Coven." He smiled wickedly. "My late, extremely perverted, but very beautiful mother being no exception. I'm sure it must have been very interesting when she coupled with you."

Nicholas produced a small piece of parchment from a pocket in his robe and allowed a drop of his blood to fall on it. The blood immediately began to convolute into its own distinct signature. When it was dry, he tucked the parchment inside one of Tristan's boots. "When you return to the Redoubt, show this to your wizards. After that, you shall have no doubt. And when you are finally sure of my identity, there shall then be decisions you must make. When you have done so, you need only to come back here to find me."

"What are you talking about?" Tristan asked.

"I can see that the stalker's dried brain fluid is already taking effect in your bloodstream. Your veins are turning black, just as I am sure the wizards told you they would. Soon the pain in your shoulder will begin. By now you have most certainly lived through your first convulsion. An interesting experience, no doubt. Tell me, Father, do you know why I poisoned your blood?" Nicholas asked, backing away slightly.

"For the only reason there could be," Tristan snarled. "You want me dead."

Again came the twisted smile. "I knew your wizards would not grasp it," Nicholas said. "Their view of the world is so limited. Indeed, Father, the reason I poisoned your blood was because I wanted you to stay *alive*."

"I don't understand. What you are saying makes no sense." Tristan's heart was telling him to leave, if indeed Nicholas would let him. He desperately wanted to be gone from this place—gone from the being who called himself his son. But his mind told him not to leave yet. He must try to remain calm, keeping the adept talking for as long as he could. He had promised the wizards he would bring them back as much information as possible.

Nicholas glided to the black pedestal, holding out his hand. The glass beaker left the table, slowly levitating into his grasp. "I poisoned your blood as an incentive, Father," he began quietly. "As you know, the dried stalker fluid works very slowly. Even more slowly than usual, due to the great strength of your magnificent blood. This gave us both time. Time for me to construct the Gates, and time for you to become increasingly ill . . . and to make up your mind."

"Make up my mind about what?" the prince countered.

"About joining our cause, Chosen One," the adept said. He glided closer, continuing to look straight into Tristan's eyes. "Join us, Father. It is the ultimate goal of the Heretics above to rule the world. With you to lead us. Just as it should have been eons ago, before the Ones with their ridiculous love of the Vigors started the War of Attrition. Both you and your twin sister are of their blood, Father. Just as I am of yours."

Stunned, Tristan took a step backward. "Why would you want me?" he asked carefully. "My blood is not yet trained, and therefore of little use to you. You and the Heretics are already vastly more knowledgeable than the wizards of Eutracia, so there is nothing you could learn from me. How does my joining with you help your cause?"

"You forget something, Father," Nicholas answered. "Despite the fact that you are not trained in the ways of the craft, you are still the Chosen One. You and your sister are the only two such beings in the world. You possess the finest blood in the universe. Even I, your direct progeny, do not possess blood the equal of yours, because mine is diluted with that of the sorceress Succiu. Have the wizards ever told you what the word 'Chosen' really means? Or who it was who truly placed that title upon you? Or why the same blood and moniker were also given to Shailiha, your twin sister and my aunt? Ah, I can

The Gates of Dawn

see by the look upon your face that they have not. Your wizards know far more than they are telling you, Father. Unless, of course, they mentioned your eventual joining of the two sides of magic. That was the ultimate goal of the Ones. But never the goal of the Heretics. In fact, it was this schism that started the war. The act of joining the two sides was to be just the first of many such deeds only you—or my aunt, if need be—would eventually be able to perform. But the Heretics do not want them joined, you see. They do not wish their pure, perfect art to be adulterated by the weaker, compassionate side of the craft. And it is the Heretics, because of their ability to return before the Ones, who will come to employ you first."

Tristan's mind was suddenly awash in new worlds, new horrors, and vast new dangers. "And just what is it you would have me do, assuming of course that I agreed to join you?"

Nicholas smiled. "Lead us," he said simply. "After the return of the Heretics, we shall eliminate all the others of this earth. Our world shall become one barren of all human life other than that which is sufficiently gifted. A true paradise of the craft. Following that we will return the power from my consciousness to the Paragon. You will then be trained by the Heretics in the ways of the Vagaries."

"Why would you do such a thing willingly?" Tristan asked. "Once you have it all, why would you choose to return the power to the stone?"

"Because the Heretics, unlike you, cared for me. I am bound to their wishes in ways you could never imagine."

"And after I am supposedly trained?"

"Together we shall destroy the Vigors and their orb forever, leaving only the true, sublime teachings of the Vagaries that we have so come to love. The Heretics and I could eventually accomplish this ourselves, but it would take eons. That is why we need you, and your perfect blood. The Coven only attempted to use your sister to complete their self-indulgent ritual, and to employ you to propagate your seed." Again came the knowing, twisted smile. "An understandable desire, but shortsighted. We intend to put you to a much higher use. We shall train you to become one of us. You will come to know the more perfect, exquisite side of the craft, leading us for eternity."

"And if I refuse?" Tristan asked.

"Then you and all your loved ones will perish," Nicholas answered. "If you do not join us in this, the female of the Chosen Ones, my aunt, must also die. Despite the fact that she is one of the Chosen, she is not of azure blood, and is of no use to us. As I said before, we would prefer to have you with us, since your azure blood makes our task so much simpler. But should you choose not to do so, your end will be quite gruesome, I can assure you."

Nicholas held out the small vessel that he had taken from the pedestal. It contained a white, milky substance. "Do you know what this is?" he asked.

"How could I?" Tristan answered caustically.

"It is the antidote to your illness, Father. Swallow this, and in a mere two days your disease disappears forever. Agree to stay here with me, submit to my mind so that I know your intentions are true, and it shall be yours. Perhaps the wizards have told you of the technique used to test the quality of one's heart? A simple use of the craft, but also quite effective. That is to be my proof that you mean what you say. Come to us, and bring your sister and her girl-child. They too are welcome, but as with you, the quality of their hearts must be tested first."

Tristan was familiar with the technique Nicholas had just mentioned, for he had watched Wigg and Faegan perform it on Geldon to be certain the dwarf did not side with the Coven. His face became dark with defeat. "And if I refuse?" he asked.

"Then you condemn yourself, your sister, her daughter, your wizards, and the rest of the endowed of your world to certain death," Nicholas answered casually. "The existence of all of the unendowed has become quite academic, since they are to die whether you join us or not. So the choice is simple, don't you see? It is only a matter of taking your rightful place in the world, thereby allowing your loved ones to live."

Tristan's mind reeled. "The wizards will find the cure," he said tentatively.

"Wrong, Father," Nicholas gloated. "The wizards are quite incapable of finding the cure. First, the calculations required are very probably beyond their gifts. Secondly, the antidote, as are so many antidotes of this world, is partially made of the very thing that poisons you—the brain fluid of a stalker. Wigg and Faegan have no access to this most important of ingredients. With everything else that is going on I cannot envision them, one blind and the other crippled, combing the woods to find and kill another stalker, can you? No. Therefore, do not rely on those two relics of the past to cure you, for they cannot."

He paused for a moment, his exotic eyes boring directly into Tristan's. "You will soon see that I cannot be defeated," he said menacingly. "Things have been put into motion that even I cannot stop. The only choice you have is to relinquish yourself to us."

Tristan lowered his eyes. "If you are truly my son, how is it that you could do these horrible things to us?" he asked softly. "We are of the same blood. Does that not count for anything with you?"

Nicholas' face became commanding. "Consider my next words well, Father, whatever your eventual choice in this matter is to be. My mother of this world, the sorceress Succiu, took my life with her own. And you, my father of this world, chose to leave my body behind in that awful land, rather than return it to your own. But my fathers above took me in, trained me, and returned me here, to the world of the living. Given that, do you really believe I would ever choose you over their power and majesty? All you really did was to vomit your seed into the depths of a woman. She, in turn, chose to see me dead. After that, you ceased to care."

Tristan hung his head. In a bizarre, twisted way he could almost agree. Forcing his mind back to his many questions, he decided to keep Nicholas talking for as long as he could. "The hatchlings and the carrion scarabs," he asked. "Where did they come from?"

Nicholas smiled. "They represent but two types of the servants employed by the Heretics during the War of Attrition. I brought the Forestallments for their conjuring with me from above. After that, letting them multiply on their own was simple enough. One creature for the sky, another for the earth, just as it was so long ago. They're unusually effective, don't you think?"

Tristan thought for a moment, wondering how long Nicholas would allow his questions. "If the Heretics can send you back from the Afterlife, then why can't they simply do the same thing for themselves?" he asked. "Why do they need you? And you said that both Shailiha and I have much in common with those in the heavens. To whom are you referring—the Heretics, or the Ones?"

"Ah," Nicholas said. "Finally the Chosen One comes to the very heart of the matter. The center of the riddle surrounding his existence, and that of his twin sister. The truth is that the Heretics could not return until they had an emissary of your blood given to them. And you yourself provided it in me. The Heretics are spirit only, as are the Ones. As we speak the two forces are still in constant struggle with each other, even in the Afterlife. They have been since the War of Attrition. But my parents above desire to live again. To feel, touch, smell, and taste again. And to again know the pleasures of being a man or a woman. I will not delve into such questions further unless you choose to join us, for the answers would prove far too revealing. Similarly, I shall not reveal the truth about the link between you and your sister and those of the heavens. I am fully aware that you are trying to enhance your knowledge for your wizards."

"Why did you take the consuls' children?" Tristan asked. "And why did you raid Fledgling House? Of what possible use could the young endowed be to your far greater powers?"

"As with so many things of this world, it has to do with blood," Nicholas answered. "But I will say nothing more of that." Still holding the vessel of antidote, he looked calmly into the face of his father. "You have been given sufficient information in order to make your choice. It is now time for you to do so."

Tristan looked into the dark, slanted eyes.

"No," he said flatly. "I will never join you."

"Are you quite sure, Father?" Nicholas asked coyly. He held the bottle of antidote before Tristan, swinging it back and forth temptingly. "A little sip of this and you would be made well again. Not to mention the fact that you have not only just condemned yourself to death, but your sister, niece, and wizards, as well."

"I have given you my answer," the prince said softly. He was trembling with anger. "Now let me take my leave of this place."

"As you wish," Nicholas said, gesturing courteously to the doorway. "It was never my intention to harm you further, or to keep you captive. But hear this, Chosen One: Pain will grow within in your body as the dark veins continue to encroach. The sword arm you so prize and the weapon over your shoulder that you used to kill my grandfather will both eventually be worthless. During the onslaught of your fourth convulsion, you will die. And nothing except what I hold in my hand can stop it. I tell you this so that you will have a frame of reference as to how much longer you shall live.

"Should you change your mind, simply come to the Gates of Dawn, Father," the adept continued. "By then they shall be constructed." Again came the rather twisted smile. "As you will see, they shall be very difficult to miss."

Tristan turned to the door, taking his first few steps toward it. Stopping, he turned around. "I will kill you," he said softly. "Whether you are truly my son or not. Somehow, despite your powers, I will find a way. I will make sure before I die that what I have sired will do no further harm to this world." With that he left the room.

As he approached the chamber of the falls he could again feel the powerful effect of the waters on his blood, but he ignored it and ran up the stone steps out into the light. His chest heaving, he paused to look at the early-morning rays that had just begun to creep up over the horizon beyond. Tears of anger and sadness welled in his eyes.

How many more such dawns? he asked himself. *How many dawns before they come back, and all that we know perishes forever? And it is all because of me, and what I did not finish in Parthalon.*

"What have I done?" he cried aloud, his voice shaking desperately.

He covered his face with his hands and went to his knees in the cold, frosty grass.

Tristan stayed that way for some time. He finally sat upright in the cold, damp grass, watching the sunrise. His head was a whirl of stunning new facts and seemingly endless, frightening implications. He knew he needed to return to the Redoubt quickly, and tell the wizards everything he had just learned.

It was then that he heard it. Steel on steel—the unmistakable sound of swordplay.

Immediately jumping to his feet he drew his dreggan, the blade ringing in the air. Turning, he searched every foot of the little clearing, but could see no threat. Nonetheless the clang of swords could be plainly heard, sounding to his experienced ears like two single combatants. The action seemed intense, their swords clashing together almost constantly. Finally realizing the sounds were coming from higher up, he raised his eyes to the sky.

Above him, one of Nicholas' hatchlings was locked in mortal combat with some other winged creature. At first Tristan couldn't make it out. Then the two flew lower as they struggled, and the prince was shocked to see who it was. Ox.

The huge Minion warrior was fighting mightily with the hatchling, and it was plain to see that the great bird was at least an equal match. As they swooped and darted through the air, frustratingly out of reach, Tristan could only stand there, mesmerized by the battle taking place above him.

He immediately recognized that such fighting required skills he had never experienced. It was amazingly different from fighting on the ground, where a fighter relied upon his feet and legs for both quickness and balance. In the fight above him the entire sky was at the combatants' disposal, and they each made the most of it, covering distances with the use of their wings that an earthbound swordsman's feet and legs could not begin to address. A full three dimensions of turns and maneuvers were possible in the air.

Where the hatchling might be quicker, Ox seemed a little stronger. Whenever the bird threatened with his broadsword, Ox seemed able to counter the blows effectively with his dreggan.

But why is Ox here? Tristan wondered desperately, his frustration causing him to tighten his grip around his sword. But all he could do was watch and wait.

Stretching his wings further, Ox flew up and over the hatchling, positioning his body directly above the great bird.

With a sudden series of relentless, powerful slashes he began to force the hatchling downward, ever nearer to the ground. The hatchling fought back mightily, but Ox now held the advantage, for Tristan could see that it was much easier for the Minion to slash downward than for the bird to thrust upward.

The clanging of their sword blades became louder as Ox pressed his opponent ever lower. Tristan would soon be able to reach the hatchling's legs with his dreggan. He touched the button at the hilt of the sword to launch the extra foot of blade; then he raised the dreggan high in both hands. But he came to a sudden realization.

Tristan dropped his sword in the grass, and searched frantically through the glade. Finally he found a heavy, dried tree limb that looked sturdy enough.

Tristan's first swing barely missed, and the hatchling cried out in its desperation. Ox made a great, final effort, driving the bird even lower. This time the prince's aim was true.

The limb connected mightily with the side of the hatchling's head, and it fell unconscious to the ground, the light going out of its hideous, red eyes. Exhausted, Ox landed next to the bird, looking at Tristan as if the prince had just lost his mind.

"I sent to protect," Ox breathed, sliding his dreggan into the scabbard at his hip. "Why Chosen One no kill bird?"

Tristan did not immediately respond. He roughly kicked the hatchling's side, testing whether the bird was indeed knocked out. It remained motionless. Tristan reached down, relieving it of its sword. Finally he picked up his dreggan, retracting its blade and placing it into its scabbard.

Tristan looked at the exhausted Minion warrior, realizing that it was finally time to make up his mind about the huge Minion.

"What happened?" he asked. "Why are you here?"

"Wizards send Ox," the warrior said proudly. "To look after Chosen One. It Ox's new task in life. But they say no go into Caves after you. Only follow, and wait in sky. Ox glad Chosen One still alive." His chest was fairly puffing out with pride.

"And when I came back out?" Tristan answered. "What happened then?"

"I wait in sky. Then bad bird come. When I see bird, I fight. Then you hit with branch." His face screwed up quizzically again behind the black beard. "Why you no kill bird?" he repeated.

Tristan glanced back down at the inert hatchling. "Because I wanted it alive," he said flatly. "If I had killed it without Wigg and Faegan having a chance to study it while it was still breathing, they would have never forgiven me. Especially if this is one of those that can speak."

Looking back at Ox, Tristan thought quietly for moment. "Cut down a pile of strong limbs," he ordered. "And gather up some vines. Make sure they're all sturdy. We're going to make a cage, place the hatchling into it, and then fasten it to a litter. Pilgrim can drag it back to the Redoubt."

Although the prince knew these birds were of the craft, he seriously doubted that they were capable of using magic on their own. But the cage would either hold it, or it wouldn't. If he succeeded in returning with the hatchling, then the wizards could decide how best to control it.

"No need to make cage, Chosen One," Ox answered. "I strong. I carry."

"Oh, no," Tristan said gently, raising his eyebrows. "If the bird awakens, I don't want to take the chance of losing it."

Ox placed an index finger upon his lower lip. Tristan could sense the wheels in the Minion's head, while apparently not exactly spinning, at least grinding away with difficulty. Finally Ox said, "Chosen One right. Chosen One smart. I make cage and litter."

"Good," Tristan answered.

They completed the job together, then placed the still-unconscious hatchling inside the cage and bound the remaining logs together to enclose it. While Ox used vines to lash the cage to the litter, Tristan retrieved Pilgrim. They then secured the litter to the back of Tristan's saddle.

Tristan walked to Pilgrim's head and grasped the bridle. Giving the stallion a short, clacking sound out of the corner of his mouth, he urged the horse forward. Ox proudly brought up the rear on foot, dreggan drawn, acting as if they were about to be attacked at any moment.

Tristan shook his head slightly. Despite all he had been through, he snorted a quick, unbelieving laugh down his nose.

From somewhere an old quotation came to his mind—one that described the situation perfectly.

"Before the Afterlife makes one mad," he remembered, *"it first gives one the strangest of traveling companions."*

CHAPTER THIRTY-SEVEN

TRISTAN sat back in his upholstered chair in the Hall of Blood Records. His mind was a confusing whirl of questions and concerns. Across from him sat Wigg and Faegan, their faces dark. To his right was Shailiha with Morganna, and next to Wigg sat Celeste. Tristan stared for a moment into Celeste's lovely, sapphire eyes. She looked back at him with concern.

After successfully delivering the unconscious hatchling to the Redoubt, where Faegan had immediately secured it in a wizard's warp, Tristan had glumly told them of the many things he had learned in the Caves. The one thing he did not speak of was his shame—the realization that he should have allowed Wigg to burn Nicholas' dead body back in Parthalon. Tristan had wanted his unborn son to have a real burial, and he had seen to it that it had been done before Wigg had the chance to intervene. Now, because of his selfishness, he felt responsible for unknowingly leading them all to this most grievous of calamities. As if reading Tristan's mind, the lead wizard spoke.

"It's not your fault, Tristan," Wigg said gently from the other side of the table. "There was no way you could have known. You only did what you thought was right, and it took great courage. Even I had no inkling of what was to follow."

Tristan looked down at the parchment with Nicholas' azure blood signature. He had pulled it from his boot and laid it on the table for all to see.

Faegan cleared his throat. "We must be sure, Tristan," the master wizard said compassionately. "We must check the signature to know whether what this person told you is the truth."

Tristan nodded. But in his heart of hearts he already knew the answer.

"Prince Tristan of the House of Galland," Faegan called out to the enchanted room. "Son of Nicholas and Morganna, one-time king and queen of Eutracia." One of the mahogany drawers began to slide open, and a sheet of parchment rose into the air and floated across the room to come to rest in front of the prince. Tristan looked down at his blood signature. It was azure this time. This was the one that had been produced most recently, showing the many Forestallments and their respective branches.

"Succiu, second mistress of the Coven," Faegan said simply. Another of the drawers opened, and the parchment holding Succiu's blood signature floated to the table.

Using the craft, Faegan coaxed the sheet holding Tristan's signature to separate widthwise, dividing the top from the bottom. Then the lower half of Tristan's signature glided to Succiu's signature, covering its original lower half, creating a new one. Finally Faegan caused the blood signature of the one calling himself Nicholas to move next to it. Everyone in the room held his or her breath.

They were identical, except that Nicholas' signature held even more Forestallments than did Tristan's.

Letting out a sigh, Faegan sat back in his chair. "It's true," he whispered to the table at large. "He is without doubt Nicholas, Tristan's son." As if not knowing what else to say, he looked down, unconsciously drawing his robe closer about his legs. Finally he turned his deep, gray-green eyes toward the prince.

"The first child of the male of the Chosen Ones now walks the earth, and he does so with the blessings of the Heretics," the wizard continued. "His blood, although slightly diluted by that of his mother, is the closest in the world to his father's perfect, azure blood. And to make matters even worse his blood will soon have gathered all of the power of the Paragon. It wasn't supposed to happen this way!" Tristan had never seen the master wizard so beside himself with frustration and sadness.

"The centuries-old balance and power of the craft is about to shift," Faegan added. "Completely and irrevocably. Such a being, who commands both azure blood and the complete power of the craft held only within himself, will be the likes of which the world has never before seen. There can simply be no stopping him now."

Faegan slumped forward. For the first time since Tristan had known him, he seemed completely defeated. No one spoke for what seemed a very long time.

"But how could such a thing have happened?" Tristan asked at last. "Nicholas died! I left him in the grave in Parthalon! How could he have anything to do with the Heretics?"

Faegan closed his eyes, preparing his mind. He then relaxed a bit, letting the appropriate quote from the Tome come to him.

" 'And it shall come to pass that the Heretics, in their mastery of the Vagaries, shall attain power over those of the lower world possessing azure blood,' " Faegan said. " 'But first the mortal, azure blood of the lower world must die. It is also ordained that the Ones shall have powers in the world of the living, should what they left behind be discovered.' " Faegan opened his eyes.

"Another quote from the Tome?" Wigg asked.

"Indeed," Faegan answered, already lost in thought. "From it we can make two relevant, although incomplete assumptions. First, it would seem that the Heretics have mastered the Vagaries to the point they can take action upon those in our world who possess azure blood—provided the blood is dead, as theirs is. This of course meant that the one possessing azure blood must first have expired, as did Nicholas. I believe they were somehow able to take his body to the heavens. They then prepared him, returning him to do their bidding."

The room went silent again as everyone tried to comprehend the immense ramifications of their problems.

"You mentioned two assumptions," Wigg finally said. "What is the other?"

"That the Ones also have potential powers over our world," Faegan replied. "Provided whatever it is they left behind is eventually discovered. And we have absolutely no idea what that might be, or where to go looking for it."

"What about Nicholas' hatchlings and scarabs?" Shailiha asked. "Have you determined where they came from?"

"The horrific creatures of the Vagaries always owe their existence to four aspects of the craft," Wigg answered. "The first and by far most difficult of these methods is called 'conjuring,' or invoking their entire presence. Those are beings created from scratch, if you will, via extremely convoluted calculations of the craft. The second method is to mutate an already normal, existing being into another, such as when the Coven mutated wizards into blood stalkers. The third way is to combine a human with an animal, giving it inordinate powers. This is illustrated by the screaming harpy—a giant bird with the head and face of a woman. And the fourth way is to combine any of the aforementioned practices, in as many ways as one chooses. The combinations are virtually limitless. But to answer your questions, Princess, Faegan and I believe the hatchlings and the scarabs to be purely products of Nicholas' conjuring. The spells and calculations required for their development were most likely placed into his blood by the Heretics, via Forestallment."

"But surely there is *something* we can do on our own to stop Nicholas," Shailiha said adamantly. She had become quite tired of hearing all that they couldn't do, and she desperately wanted to take some kind of action. "I thought you and Wigg postulated that if the stone still had at least some color, we might have a chance. And I can tell the Paragon is not yet completely drained, because both of you still possess at least some of your powers."

"That's true," Tristan insisted. "There must be something we can still do!"

"Neither of you completely understand," Wigg said seriously. "What we told you was before we knew the true identity of Nicholas. His being born of Tristan's blood changes everything—for the worse. Had Nicholas proven to be someone else, anyone else, we might have had a chance. But not now. You see, only one power is strong enough to defeat his blood: the male or female blood of the Chosen Ones. Only your blood is superior. But to defeat him, your blood would first have to be trained. And we cannot accomplish that in time."

"Why not?" Tristan asked rather angrily.

Wigg sighed. "First is the fact that in order to train either of you, it is ordained that Tristan must first read the Prophecies. Only after he has done so may Shailiha then read them. Tristan cannot do that without the Paragon around his neck. And if we do that, the poison in his blood could kill him. Second, even if we were somehow able to surmount the first obstacle, it would literally take decades, perhaps even a lifetime, to bring Tristan to Nicholas' level of understanding. Sending Tristan to confront his son without the proper training would be like sending a lamb to slaughter." Wigg sat back in his chair, running an ancient hand down the length of his face. "So there it is," he said wearily. "Faegan and I don't like it any better than you, but facts are facts. It is only now that we fully come to understand the true ramifications of the Heretics' vision for the future. Their plan is brilliant."

Tristan was beside himself with frustration. He had never seen the wizards so downhearted, even during the worst of those times when they had faced the Coven. But then again, he reminded himself, they knew far more about the craft than he apparently ever would.

He looked into Faegan's eyes. "I'm going to die, aren't I?" he asked bluntly. His question did not come from concern for himself as much as the fact that he needed an answer to be able to finalize his plan.

"Yes," the ancient wizard replied softly, looking down at his legs. "In truth, unless your son can be stopped, we all are. But you will most probably be the first, due to your condition. What Nicholas told you is true: The brain fluid of a stalker is required to make the antidote. And acquiring any seems quite impossible."

"Then it is imperative that I go to Parthalon and order the Minions to come back to Eutracia," Tristan said flatly. "They are our only hope of buying time. Their numbers may be able to slow down the hatchlings and the carrion scarabs. Perhaps even tie up some of Nicholas' attention, as well, thereby slowing down the construction of the Gates. It is the least we can now do. And as their lord, I am the only one who can lead them to war. You said so yourself. I must go immediately." He paused for a moment, weighing his next words. "Because it must be done before I die," he added softly.

Shailiha turned around in her chair, facing the wall so that the others could not see her tears. Celeste placed an affectionate hand on her shoulder. The princess of Eutracia gripped it without turning back around.

"I'm sorry, Shai," Tristan said to his sister. "But we must face facts, and time is of the essence." He looked at Faegan. "For how long each day can you hold your portal open?" he asked seriously.

Faegan narrowed his eyes, rubbing his chin. "I have never been able to do so for more than one hour per day," he answered glumly. "But I could try to attempt it every twelve hours, after I have rested. That would make two hours per day. Order the warriors to assemble near the portal's entrance, ready to run through it as fast as they can when they see it appear. That will also speed up the process. But there will eventually come another problem," he added, frowning.

"And what is that?" Wigg asked.

"You all must keep in mind the Paragon is constantly diminishing in power," Faegan answered. "My abilities to form and sustain the portal will therefore be affected proportionately. If any of the warriors are in the process of coming through while my powers are weakening, forcing me to end the spell before the hour is up, those caught in between will die horribly. Even by Minion standards. And there will be nothing I will be able to do to save them. Tristan, you must tell them that if they see the color or intensity of the portal begin to waver, they are immediately to stop going through until they see its strength return, no matter how long that takes. Even as it is, I am sure we will see many of them die. It will not be a pretty thing to watch."

"There will truly be nothing you can do?" Celeste asked. She placed her other hand on top of her father's.

"No," Faegan said flatly, the frustration clearly showing on his face. "Nothing at all."

Tristan cast his dark blue eyes at Wigg and Faegan in turn. "And what will the two of you be doing while I am gone?"

"What we have been doing all along," Wigg answered. "The only things that make sense. Namely, trying to discover the answers to our defeat of Nicholas, and to unravel the cures for both you and myself. But there is something else you, Shailiha, and Celeste must know. In all fairness, it needs to be said."

Tristan looked calmly into Wigg's unseeing eyes, knowing that whatever he was about to hear would not be good. Shailiha turned back to face the table, her eyes wet and red.

"Nicholas told you that Faegan and I were keeping information from you, did he not?" Wigg asked.

"Yes," Tristan answered. "What did he mean?"

"The information we have kept from you is that we truly fear this shall be the end of us," Wigg said, rubbing his brow as if to ease an aching head. "We have no real answers to these many dilemmas. In fact, we are really no more ahead of where we started. The powers arrayed against us are just far too strong. But before you travel to Parthalon, we need you to know what is in our hearts, and not suffer from delusions or unjustified hopes as to our relatively meager abilities to solve this crisis." He sat back in his chair. It was plain to see that the old man's heart was breaking.

Tristan felt even more of his energy slip away. Looking at Shailiha and Celeste, he could see that they too had been equally affected. In truth, he had hoped that the two ancient, wily wizards had something—any glimmer of optimism whatsoever—that they had not shared with him. He had never before known them not to have at least one playing card up the sleeves of their robes. But he could tell by the look on Wigg's face that the wizard was telling the truth. And the continuing decay of the stone would only make things worse. He tried to smile.

"We all know you two are trying your best," Tristan said gently. "You and I have been through a great deal together, old one. But what you have just told me only reinforced the fact that I must leave immediately, does it not?" he asked. Wigg nodded, his white eyes shiny.

"You will take Ox with you?" the wizard asked.

Tristan thought for a moment. "Yes," he said finally.

"Good," Wigg answered. "You will need someone, in case you . . ."

The wizard never finished the sentence, immediately regretting having started it.

Tristan resolutely stood from the table. There was a little more to be said, and he and Ox needed to be going. "Faegan," he said, "if you would be so good as to meet me and Ox in one half hour?" Faegan nodded. Celeste and Shailiha also stood.

The two wizards ruminated sadly, as the younger people walked from the room.

$\mathcal{W}$igg and Faegan continued to sit in silence for a time after the three others had departed, each lost in his own thoughts. Finally, Faegan spoke.

"I am glad you informed them of our true lack of success," he said softly. He paused for a moment, as tears welled in his gray eyes. "There is something else I feel I need to say," he went on at last, his voice barely more than a whisper. In a rare gesture, he reached out and took Wigg's hand. After a moment of surprise, Wigg returned his grip.

"What is it?" Wigg asked.

"I'm sorry," Faegan said. Wigg could barely hear him. A tear finally freed itself from one of the crippled wizard's lower eyelids and began its journey down his cheek. "Despite how much I tease you, I love you like a brother. Had I been here, where I belonged, all those long years, we might not be in such dire straits today. There is so much I regret. Please forgive me."

Wigg sighed. "There is nothing to forgive, my friend," he answered. "You did what you thought was right—just as we of the Directorate did. But you are here with us now, and that is what truly matters." One corner of his mouth came up. "And in case you haven't noticed, the Directorate didn't do such a wonderful job of controlling things, either."

Silence reigned.

"I told Tristan and Shailiha the things I did because I did not want them to have any hopes that were unjustified," Wigg finally said. "That would be cruel, since Tristan and Shailiha have always relied on me for so much. Especially since the death of their parents. And now I find I have a beautiful daughter who is endowed with the gift. She is all any father could ever ask for. Yet it appears I have found her only to lose her again. Just as you did, my friend." An uncomfortable silence descended between them.

"The Chosen One will most probably die in his war with Nicholas' creatures," Faegan said after a time. "You know that, do you not?"

"Yes," Wigg said sadly. "But I agree with him that it has to be done. Going to war is one of our few options left. And he is the only one the Minions will obey. But I doubt he can win. There simply will not be enough time to bring sufficient numbers of Minion troops across the sea. By the time the battle is joined, I estimate Nicholas' hatchlings will still enjoy a great superiority of numbers. And even if we did somehow win the war, there would still remain the larger, far more dangerous problem." He paused for a moment. "Fighting the war may do little, if anything, to keep Nicholas from activating the Gates of Dawn."

"I also reluctantly agree that Tristan must do this," Faegan answered. "But we still must make the necessary contingency plans in the event of his death."

Faegan closed his eyes, again calling on his powers of Consummate Recollection. " *'And should the male of the Chosen Ones perish, those of the craft who remain shall leave no stone unturned in their care, protection, and training of the female. For it shall then be her blood, and hers alone, that shall persevere in the survival of the compassionate side of the craft,'* " he quoted. He opened his eyes.

"I am aware of the passage," Wigg said quietly.

"If Tristan dies, whatever the cause, we must immediately take Shailiha away from this place," Faegan said sternly. "For it shall then be only her blood that can effectively continue the struggle for the preservation of the Vigors. Do you agree?"

"Yes," Wigg said reluctantly. "I do."

"Very well. And now, if you will excuse me, Wigg, I have two people to send to Parthalon."

"Before you do, Faegan, would you be so kind as to hand me the parchment containing Nicholas' signature?" Wigg asked as he heard the wheels on Faegan's chair begin to roll.

"Certainly, old friend." Faegan retrieved the parchment and placed it in front of Wigg. "Good luck in your studies." With that, he wheeled himself from the room, the massive door closing behind him.

Sitting there in the quiet of the Hall of Blood Records, alone with his thoughts, a tear came to Wigg's eye. *How in the name of the Afterlife did everything come to this?* he asked himself. *But then again, the Afterlife is exactly the problem, isn't it?*

Wigg reached out to the sheet of parchment in front of him and invoked the craft to sensitize his fingers even further to the design upon it. He wished to commit its shape to memory, just as he had done with so many others of this place over the centuries. Slowly, his endowed fingers traced over the complicated design of the blood signature. And then, suddenly, he stopped.

Again he felt it, thinking it had been not quite real.

Wigg sat back in his chair, his heart and mind racing. He would wait for Faegan, and they would talk until dawn.

PART IV

The Warriors

CHAPTER THIRTY-EIGHT

The male of the Chosen Ones shall therefore be forced to return to the foreign land of his travails. And upon this journey he shall order the onetime destroyers of his nation to return with him, and to join in his struggle.

—PAGE 1,016, CHAPTER I OF THE VIGORS OF THE TOME

*W*HEN Tristan came to his senses, he was lying on his back on the cold, frozen ground. A beautiful blue sky lay above him, cumulus clouds patterned throughout. Birds sang loudly, announcing the advent of morning. His mind was cloudy, but he knew the sleepiness and dizziness would soon depart. He sat up, his head slightly spinning, and turned to look at Ox.

The huge Minion had not fared so well. His slumber was so deep and his breathing so shallow that anyone passing by might have thought him dead. Then, without moving, the warrior began to snore. Loudly. Tristan smiled, thinking of the day before, when he and Ox had captured the hatchling and dragged it back to the Redoubt.

Tristan pulled closer the gray jacket of Eutracian fox that Shailiha had insisted he wear to ward off the cold. He decided to let the Minion sleep for a few more moments.

He looked around, reacquainting himself with the area. Light, fluffy snow blanketed the ground. Faegan's portal had deposited them in the immediate area of the shattered Recluse, and he could see the foundation of the partially reconstructed building rising nearby, on a mound of land surrounded by water.

He felt a sudden jab of pain in his right shoulder and reached under the fur with his opposite hand to rub it. Just as Nicholas had predicted, he was beginning to have pain and weakness in his arm: the arm he relied on the most. He knew without looking that the dark, ominous-looking spider veins had extended farther down the length of it.

He stood slowly, anxious to be on his way, then walked to the snoring warrior and gave the bottom of the Minion's right boot a gentle kick. "Ox," he said strongly. "Wake up. It's time to go."

Ox slowly stirred, finally sitting up. "Portal make Ox sleepy," he said thickly. He stood and stretched his arms and then his leathery wings to either side. "We go Recluse now, Chosen One?" he asked.

"Yes," Tristan said, tugging first at the hilt of his sword and then the handles of a few of his throwing knives, making sure the cold weather would not cause them to stick. "But first I wish to go to another place. It is important to me."

"I live to serve," Ox said. Together they walked around to the left of the island that held the smashed Recluse.

After about half an hour of walking, Tristan finally saw what he had been searching for. As his eyes fell upon it, his expression darkened. The little mound of earth and its wooden marker seemed to have remained undisturbed. With every step he took, the sight of it stirred within him stronger and stronger emotions. Love mixed with hate, knowledge permeated by confusion, anger swirling with compassion—they all welled up inside of him, swelling almost to the bursting point.

But he had to know, and there was only one way to be sure.

He stood with the Minion before his son's grave, his knees shaking slightly, and read the wooden marker that he had so lovingly carved that fateful day:

NICHOLAS II OF THE HOUSE OF GALLAND
You will not be forgotten

Ox's eyes widened as Tristan shoved away the stones piled atop the grave, then ripped the marker from the ground, and used one end of it to shovel away the dirt. After many moments the prince stood up, his chest heaving, to see the awful truth. The grave was empty.

Suddenly all the mixed emotions melted away, leaving a single, unrelenting sentiment coursing through his endowed veins. Hate. Gripping the marker, he threw it as far as he could into the neighboring woods, as if by doing so he could also cast off not only the terrible memories of this place but also the monstrous nightmare plaguing his nation.

Looking to the Recluse, his mind drifted back to the day

when Succiu had so brutally raped him. He returned his gaze to the empty grave. *You were conceived in violence and pain, Nicholas. And your life has been devoted to nothing else. But I shall end it for you.*

As he made this new oath to himself, he looked down, staring defiantly at the wounds he had carved into his palms not so long ago. When he had sworn a similar pledge, also upon his knees, at yet a different burial place of those he had also once loved. These scars had only recently healed—far more quickly than the ones that remained upon his heart. Or the new one that he now realized he must create. And then his mind and vision began to swim.

Perhaps it had been the sudden, unrelenting rage passing through his blood. Or the fact that he was so near to yet another place of Nicholas. But for whatever the reason, Tristan immediately knew he was in the grip of his second convulsion, and it was far worse than had been his first.

He fell the rest of the way to the ground, foam surging from the corners of his mouth. The pain wracking his body was excruciating, and he screamed out blindly into the clear Parthalonian morning. On and on the torment went, without reprieve. The last thing he remembered was Ox trying to force something into his mouth, and being dragged toward the nearby forest.

Then everything went black as night.

CHAPTER THIRTY-NINE

FAEGAN sat comfortably in his chair on wheels, his violin beneath his chin, in the spacious but stark chamber he had specially selected. He had chosen this particular room because there was only one massive, very secure marble door, and no chimney. The music he was creating was both thoughtful and soft, exactly befitting the master wizard's current mood. His eyes were closed, and he let his hands perform their art without the use of the craft, preferring this day to produce the enchanting melody from his heart, rather than from his gifts. He had been playing for hours, as was his custom when there was an unusually difficult decision to make. And the problem he now wrestled with was one of the most trying of his very long life in the service of the craft.

Finally placing the violin in his lap, he turned his attention for the hundredth time to the glowing bars, within which resided the captured hatchling. Now conscious, the dangerous-looking bird had so far said nothing, simply glaring with hatred at him. Initially it had attempted to free itself by smashing its body against the bars of Faegan's wizard's cage, of course to no avail. This much, the wizard knew, was to be expected.

Even after his painstaking examination of the bird while it had remained unconscious, he still had serious doubts as to his plan. So had Wigg. After hearing of Faegan's idea, he had instantly blustered and argued, finally saying he could not give his blessing to such a thing. He had instead gone off to meditate, trying to envision how he could somehow come to a compromise with Faegan. But in his heart Wigg knew it would probably be all or nothing. Half measures certainly would not work, and might prove to be even more dangerous.

Faegan could easily understand Wigg's concern, for such a thing had never been attempted. Their knowledge of this particular branch of the craft was still very much in its infancy. But these were extraordinary times, he had told Wigg, and they needed to make use of any advantage they could think of. Even one this tenuous. And they needed to do it quickly.

Faegan again put the violin beneath his chin and started to play, going over in his mind the few facts that he had become relatively sure of regarding the bird. The hatchling had not spoken, but the wizard believed it was able to. When Faegan had first produced the instrument and begun playing it, the bird's red eyes had widened, and it shuffled back and forth as if in surprise. It had started to form a word but had then closed its beak. It was no doubt under orders to remain silent if captured, Faegan realized.

He was quite sure that the hatchlings were a product of the Vagaries, since they were not only used for destruction but also seemed to relish their work. He knew that the spell needed to conjure such beasts was very intricate indeed, and had most assuredly been given to Nicholas by the Heretics via Forestallment. This last point, he reasoned, was the worst of the problems.

As he played, the unfazed hatchling continued to stare hatefully at him from between the glowing bars of its cage.

Faegan heard the massive door open and knew without turning that it must be Wigg. He put aside his violin to lead his old friend to a chair.

After a very long sigh of resignation, Wigg spoke. "Are you sure there is no other way to accomplish your idea?" he asked. "This is so risky I don't even know how to begin to broach my many concerns! Such a thing has never been tried before, and we still know so little about Forestallments! And it is her very *life* we are talking about, not just her mind. Are you sure there is no other way?"

"We have been over and over this," Faegan answered gently. "If you have a better plan, I am ready to listen. But as we sit and do nothing, every moment that passes Nicholas grows stronger, and we weaker. I checked the Paragon again today, and more than half of its color is now gone. I'm sure that you, like me, have sensed the acute reduction in your powers. Not a very pleasant experience, is it? It is time, Wigg. Like it or not I feel we have to proceed, before we both become powerless. And as the stone weakens, so does my warp that holds the hatchling at bay, and it's far too valuable to kill." He smiled coyly, though he knew Wigg couldn't see the expression. "Do you really want it running loose through the palace, Lead Wizard?"

Scowling, Wigg ignored Faegan's sarcasm. "But do you really believe the strength of her blood will prevail?" he asked. Uncharacteristically, he wrung his hands. "I know the theory proves itself on paper, but there is still so much about Nicholas and his spells that we do not know, not to mention the Heretics . . ."

"I too have grave doubts," Faegan said. "It is true that again exposing her mind to the Vagaries, especially after her vicious treatment by the Coven, may be the end of her. But I believe her Forestallment, coupled with the nearly unparalleled quality of her blood, will overcome. Provided she agrees, I feel we must push forward. Did she accompany you here?" he asked hopefully.

"Yes," Wigg answered. "She waits in the hall. Given the nature of the situation, I requested that she leave the baby with Martha. I have explained nothing of this to her. But if we are to do this, there is something I must insist upon. She must know everything involved—especially the reasons for this and the accompanying risks. Only then can I consent. May the Afterlife grant us success."

"The Afterlife is precisely the problem, is it not, old friend?" Faegan asked, unknowingly echoing Wigg's thoughts of the previous day. "Besides, in case you haven't noticed, I love her, too."

Wigg nodded resignedly, tacitly giving his consent.

Faegan rolled himself to the door and opened it, then ushered Shailiha in.

This was her first time to see the hatchling, and on noticing it she took a step back, looking nervously from one wizard to the other.

"It cannot harm you," Faegan said gently, motioning her to a chair.

"Is this the creature that Tristan brought to the Redoubt?" she asked, coiling up a little as she sat in a nearby chair.

"Yes," Wigg said.

Shailiha stared at it a moment longer, then turned to the wizards. "Why did you bring me here?" she asked. "What is it that you desire of me?"

In careful tones, Faegan and Wigg began to explain their plan to her. At first she did not respond. But as they finally described the most important part of it, she shrank back farther into the chair. They told her that what she was about to do must be of her own free will, but that it was not just for the sake of her brother that she would be making the attempt, but also for the survival of her entire nation. And then they told her why it must be done. Upon hearing this, her eyes went wide. They went on to say what she must do should the process be successful.

"There is another fact you need to know," Wigg said softly. "It is entirely possible that you could die in this attempt. We believe the spell used to conjure the hatchling will be very powerful indeed, having come directly from the Heretics themselves. Given your relative weakness from the Chimeran Agonies, we cannot be sure your blood will be able to stand the strain. But we feel its virtually unsurpassed quality will win out."

Shailiha nodded her understanding.

"And one last thing," Faegan added. "Perhaps the most difficult of all, in fact, given how much you love the prince. Should you be successful, no one outside of this room is to know what happened here. No one. No matter the circumstances. Especially Tristan. And for the good of us all, we will eventually be forced to tell him a lie. A lie that he must believe totally, and without hesitation. It will become imperative that you join with us in this. Do you understand?"

"I understand," she said quietly, staring at the awful thing in the cage.

"Come to me, Princess," Wigg said.

Shailiha walked to him. He felt for her hands and took them in his own. "What say you?" he asked. "Will you do this thing?"

She turned to look at the beast in the cage. The hatchling stared hatefully back at her with its grotesque, red eyes.

"Yes," she said softly. "I owe you, Faegan, and Tristan my very existence. And I love you all more than my life. I also know that you mean only well in all of this. Therefore, I will try."

"Very well," Wigg replied, his voice cracking with emotion. He turned toward the other wizard. "Faegan, if you please," he said.

"Of course." Narrowing his eyes, Faegan encapsulated the bird's body in an additional manifestation of the craft. At first the beast tried to struggle, but in the end it settled down, unable to move in any way.

Shailiha walked slowly toward the glowing cage. Stopping before it, she looked back to Faegan for a sign of support. Smiling slightly, he nodded to her.

Shailiha took a deep breath and tentatively slid one of her hands into the cage.

The hatchling was held immobile by Faegan's warp, but as Shailiha's trembling hand continued its dangerous journey toward the great bird, the hatchling's eyes began to glow an even deeper, fiercer red.

Carefully, very carefully, the princess wrapped her fingers around the leathery, pointed top of the bird's head. Almost immediately a change overtook her.

She began to perspire, and her entire body started to shake. She lowered her head like an animal, moving it back and forth as if in some kind of trance. When she finally lifted her face again, her eyes had rolled up high beneath her lids. Her teeth were bared in a kind of silent, almost vicious snarl, and her breathing was heavily labored, her chest heaving mightily. Faegan feared she might die. He watched in helpless frustration, desperately wondering whether they had done the right thing.

But then her sense of self and her breathing slowly returned to normal, and she finally removed her hand from the creature's head. Still standing before it, she adopted a stance with her legs spread slightly, her arms folded across her chest, and glared directly into the thing's bloodred eyes.

Neither bird nor woman flinched. It was as if the two of them had suddenly become locked within a place and time that somehow only they could inhabit. Everything about Shailiha now suggested an attitude of complete power and domination. Sensing the moment was right, Faegan terminated the warp holding the bird. Seeing the azure glow fade away, Shailiha spoke.

"Who is it that you serve?" she asked rather harshly.

"Only you, Mistress," the hatchling answered dutifully, breaking its self-imposed silence for the first time since being captured.

The hatchling called her Mistress! Faegan's mind shouted out to him. *But of course it would! The Forestallments in Shailiha's blood are of Failee's doing, and she would have wanted all of her endowed creatures to address the princess in that way! It makes perfect sense!*

"And who are Nicholas, Ragnar, and Scrounge?" she

asked, employing the second of the questions the wizards had instructed her to put to the bird.

"I know of no such beings," the bird answered obediently. "My entire world is only of you, my mistress."

We have succeeded beyond our wildest dreams! Faegan realized. *Not only has her touching an endowed, winged creature of the craft enacted the Forestallment, just as it did with the fliers of the fields, but the superior quality of her blood has actually pushed out all of the hatchling's memories of its original master. This bird will truly do our bidding.*

"I shall ask you a question," Shailiha continued, "and you shall endeavor to respond without the use of the spoken word, using only your thoughts to reveal the answer to my mind. Tell me, hatchling, what is my name and title?" The princess closed her eyes, waiting for a response.

And then suddenly there it was, resonating within her mind as clear as if the bird had spoken it with its tongue. *Shailiha, fifth mistress of the Coven.*

She turned, repeating the answer verbatim to the wizards.

And then she collapsed to the floor.

Faegan rushed to her and used the craft to lift her body into a chair.

"What is it?" Wigg shouted urgently. "What's going on?"

"She collapsed," Faegan answered.

The princess looked pale and drawn. Faegan lifted one of her eyelids, peering in. Seemingly satisfied, he closed it again. "I think she is going to be all right."

Shailiha stirred, then opened her eyes and sat up a little straighter, getting her bearings. "Did we succeed?" she asked thickly. Her hair was matted against one side of her face from perspiration, and she weakly hooked some of it behind her ear. "Did I really do it?" she asked again. "I cannot completely remember . . ."

"Oh, yes," Faegan answered her. "And to our wildest expectations. But there is still one thing I do not know. Are you able to communicate with the minds of all of the other hatchlings, or only this one before us?"

"Only this one," she answered, looking back at the bird in the glowing cage. "Why is that, when I can communicate with all of the fliers if I choose to?"

Faegan paused for a moment, lost in the question. "Presumably because the magic sustaining the hatchlings is stronger," he answered at last. "As such, your Forestallment, especially with your blood not having yet been trained, could only penetrate so far. Remember, we assume that this spell for Nicholas' creatures came directly from the Heretics themselves. Given that premise, it is a true testament to your blood that you were able to accomplish as much as you did."

Shailiha slowly stood, testing her legs, then walked gingerly to the cage. "I no longer fear it," she said rather absently. "It is mine now, heart and soul." Wigg stood, and Shailiha went to take him by the hand.

"Thank you, my child," he said with shiny eyes, "for all that you have done here. But I think we should leave now. I want you to get some rest."

The three of them walked to the door. Before going through, Shailiha suddenly stopped, turning back to the hatchling for the last time. She commandingly trained her eyes upon the beast.

"In my absence you are to obey these two men, and these two men only, just as you would obey me. Do you understand?"

"Yes, Mistress," the bird answered, lowering its head slightly in submission. Even the glowing sense of hatred that had once possessed its eyes was now gone.

Narrowing his eyes in thought, Faegan leaned toward Shailiha's ear and whispered something to her.

The princess nodded and again addressed the bird. "There is one other order I have for you, and it is to be obeyed to the letter, as are all of my demands. Do you remember the Chosen One, the man without wings who brought you here?" The bird nodded. "Good," Shailiha said. "Under no circumstances is he to become aware of your powers of speech. You are never to speak in his presence, nor to answer him should he ever ask you anything by which he might test you in this regard. And test you he will, mark my words. In addition, only the three people you see here before you are to know that you can speak. Should any others be present, anyone at all, you are to remain silent. Do you understand?"

"Yes, Mistress," the bird answered. "It shall be as you order."

"Well done." Wigg smiled.

"Indeed," Faegan added, winking. No longer having a reason to contain his delight, he levitated his chair and, cackling, whirled twice in a circle in the air before lowering himself back to solid ground. Wigg scowled. Shailiha smiled weakly.

And then the three of them, one wizard on each side of the exhausted princess, left the room, starting down the halls.

CHAPTER FORTY

*W*hen Tristan finally regained consciousness, pain wracked his entire body, and he was weak and trembling. His breathing was labored, and he was covered with perspiration. Lying on his back in the snow, as he looked up all he could see were the leafless tops of the trees, swaying gently in the wind. And then he vaguely remembered being dragged toward the woods by Ox. He could feel as much as see the Minion warrior sitting nearby in the snow, carefully watching over him.

He tried to raise himself, but couldn't help falling back to the ground. Immediately Ox was next to him, helping him to sit up. Then the vomiting came, and seemed to last forever. Finally feeling somewhat better, he looked over to the Minion.

"Thank you," he said weakly. He smiled at the warrior.

"Ox only do what wizards say," the warrior replied, an uncharacteristically worried look gracing his usually menacing face. "Ox again glad Chosen One lives."

"You dragged me here, didn't you?" Tristan asked.

"Ox bring here, so other Minions not see Chosen One sick. That bad for new lord of Minions."

Tristan noticed a strange taste in his mouth, coming from something that seemed to be lodged between two of his teeth.

He liberated it and spat what looked to be a tiny piece of tree bark into the palm of his hand. "What's this?" he asked. "Did you do this, too?"

Ox picked up a small, wet length of tree branch. There were deep bite marks at its center. "Ox put this into Chosen One's mouth, just as wizards say," the Minion answered. "Keep from swallowing tongue, or Chosen One could die." He smiled, almost sheepishly. "Chosen One almost bite Ox finger off." He raised his eyebrows at the prince. "Ox thinking maybe wizards would have to put it back on, like foot."

Another faint smile came to Tristan's lips. "How long have I been out?" he asked, rubbing the back of his head. Ox looked up between the tree branches, finding the sun.

"It midday. You gone about five hours."

Looking down at his right arm, Tristan saw that the menacing black veins had lengthened even farther, extending into his hand. His arm felt far more stiff and sore than before. He sat there for some time saying nothing, quietly thinking to himself before trying to stand up.

With Ox's help he finally came to his feet. He checked his weapons, also taking stock of where he was. Thankfully, the warrior had dragged him approximately twenty meters into the woods. Through a clear spot at the edge he could just make out the dark soil of the grave he had unearthed, and the heel tracks left in the snow. Choosing to say no more of it, Tristan began to exit the forest, Ox in tow. After walking silently past the grave, they headed for the Recluse.

The partially constructed foundation of the blue marble rose commandingly into the air, resting squarely atop the island in the center of the magnificent lake. But as Tristan and Ox approached the first of the two drawbridges, they could see no one. Nor were there any of the normal, busy sounds of construction work, or voices ringing out through the air that would accompany an undertaking as grand as the rebuilding of a castle. Sensing something was amiss, Tristan and Ox slowly stopped. It was then that they heard the sound. Cheering.

Turning, Tristan finally noticed a mound of earth to his right. It was approximately one hundred meters away, and covered with snow. It rose upward for about thirty meters, ran for some distance, and then descended to some depth. Looking at it, Tristan came to realize that it was a great bowl of some sort. The bowl was obviously man-made, and he was sure it had not existed at the time of Shailiha's rescue.

Looking quizzically to Ox, he asked, "Do you know what this is? Why is there shouting coming from it?" The hollering and cheering seemed to come in waves, rising and then subsiding, over and over again.

"Was built after Chosen One leave first time," Ox answered. He looked Tristan in the eyes, but it was clear he did not quite know how to proceed. "Is for Kachinaar."

Tristan looked back at the mound. "What is a Kachinaar?"

"Is warrior's vigil," Ox said. "If one warrior accuses another, then Kachinaar held. If contest fails, then warrior guilty and killed, punishment already done. If contest succeeds, then innocent, warrior set free. Kluge use Kachinaar very much, sometimes in other ways. Traax use too."

Tristan's jaw went slack. "What happens during this Kachinaar?" he asked quickly.

"Kachinaar take many forms," Ox said. "Best go look."

Tristan had originally hoped to see Traax, the second in command, in a private setting. But on the other hand, confronting a great number of the Minions at once might prove more effective. Provided, of course, that they accepted his rule over them. And besides, there seemed to be no one at the construction site to speak with, anyway.

"All right," he said resignedly. "But I do not want our appearances made known until I say so, do you understand?"

Ox clicked the heels of his boots together. "I live to serve," he said quickly. Together they started up the side of the embankment. Finally reaching the top, they looked down.

Layered from top to bottom against the inner side of the earthen walls was row after row of blue marble seats filled with shouting and cheering Minion warriors. They all seemed to be enjoying themselves, and it was apparent to Tristan that many of them were quite drunk. The amphitheater was in the shape of an oval, rather than a circle, as he had first presumed. The floor in the center was made also of blue marble, presumably having been taken from the nearby construction site. Tristan ordered Ox to lie on his stomach behind the last row, then followed suit.

There were perhaps a dozen Minion warriors on the floor of the amphitheater, where they seemed to be playing some kind of violent, deranged game. Arranged into two teams, each was struggling mightily to gain and keep control of some type of ball. As one warrior would gain possession of it and try to make it to the opposite side, those from the other team would use any and all means—short of weapons, he noticed—to try and take it away. There seemed to be no other rules whatsoever. Blood lay pooled in many areas upon the slick marble floor, and the bodies of several of the warriors, apparently smashed senseless from their previous participation in the game, lay inert along the sides of the ring. Some of them, unconscious and their mouths open, were quite obviously missing teeth. Others of them were splayed out in very unnatural directions, their limbs obviously broken. It was then, during a split-second break in the action, that Tristan could finally see the "ball" clearly. It was the severed head of a fellow warrior.

Aghast, Tristan turned to Ox. "What is the meaning of this?" he whispered angrily. "I can't believe what I'm seeing!"

Ox indicated an area segregated from the others. Small and square, it held a single warrior. He was seated in a marble chair, his hands, wings, and feet bound tightly with rope. He looked extremely worried.

"He accused," Ox whispered back. "If team on right side take head across to opposite end three times first, then he guilty, and die. If team on left get head and take across other way three times first, then he innocent, and live."

Tristan shook his head back and forth in utter disbelief. "This is insane!" he snarled. "Only a proper court can make a man guilty or innocent! Besides, I outlawed this kind of behavior before I left Parthalon! Why are they disobeying me?"

Ox looked back, an obvious expression of complete misunderstanding upon his face. "Pardon, but Chosen One wrong," he said as courteously as he knew how. "Chosen One never outlaw Kachinaar. Ox know. Ox there that day in courtyard." He looked back down to the bizarre game. "Is Minion way," he added with finality, the pride in his warriorship showing through.

Tristan thought for a moment, his mind going back to that awful day when he had slain their previous leader, subsequently being anointed the new lord of the Minions. *Ox is right,* he finally realized. *I only outlawed those things that I knew of at the time.* He looked back down at the horrific game as the warriors continued to gleefully, recklessly maim each other.

"Why do they use the head of a warrior?" Tristan asked. "And where did it come from? Did they kill someone just to provide a head for this awful game?"

"If two warriors accused for same crime, and first one guilty in different Kachinaar, then head brought here for second. Is only time this place used. Kachinaar in theater special, and much enjoyed. Minions like."

Tristan looked down again at the accused, sitting alone in the marble box. "If this man is found guilty, then how will he die?" he asked, playing along for the moment.

Ox pointed to another segregated area at the side of the amphitheater floor. "There," he said. "If guilty, warrior go to that."

Tristan's eyes followed Ox's thick arm.

Lashed beneath huge rope nets, a long, black creature was being kept under tight control. Huge, sleek, and deadly looking, it had a barbed, reptilian tail and a head and face that closely resembled a rat. Pink, obscene-looking gills lay just behind its head.

In the same area in which it was confined could be seen a rather large pile of what looked to be human bones, long since polished clean and glistening in the cold afternoon sun. Bits and tatters of what was once obviously the leather body armor of Minion warriors still somehow clung to many of them.

"What in the name of the Afterlife is that thing?" he whispered urgently.

"Swamp shrew," Ox whispered back. "If warrior guilty, they push him down shrew throat."

Tristan shook his head and closed his eyes. *For as long as I know the Minions of Day and Night, they will continue to amaze me,* he thought. *Just as with the wizards.*

He turned his attention back to the raucous game below, and to the plight of the warrior in the marble box. He knew he had to make a decision quickly, but he remained unsure of what to do.

Suddenly the warriors stood and cheered. A player in the game had finally been able to take the severed head deep enough into the opposite team's territory, placing it triumphantly on the floor of the theater for what was apparently the third and final time. His teammates ran to leap happily upon him, literally burying him with their bodies and wings.

"Kachinaar over," Ox said. Tristan held his breath, at first not wanting to ask.

"Is he—"

"Warrior innocent," Ox answered, interrupting the prince. "Warrior live."

Tristan let out a thankful sigh and tried to focus again on his now-more-pressing problem. "Ox," he whispered, "are you strong enough to carry me in your arms when you fly?"

The huge Minion smiled, puffing out his chest. "Few that strong, but Ox able."

Tristan bit his lower lip, thinking. *It would definitely create a dramatic entrance,* he thought. *That is exactly what I need. And now would be the perfect time.* It was then that he saw Traax.

Traax had left his seat and was walking toward the validated warrior, apparently to free him. Tristan took in Traax's tall, muscular stature and the fact that he was one of the few Minions he had ever seen who was clean-shaven. Younger and more handsome than Kluge had been, Traax wore his long, dark hair tied in the back with a piece of black leather. The Minion commander drew his dreggan, and the familiar ring of its blade drifted through the theater. He expertly severed the Minion's bonds with a few sure strokes, then took him into a congratulatory bear hug. The entire crowd leapt to their feet at once, arms waving in the air. Minion ale and wine slopped over many of the warriors' heads and the amphitheater seats. The cheering was deafening.

"Ox," he said quickly, "pick me up and fly me around the theater twice, then land us in the center, directly before Traax."

"I live to serve," the warrior said. Picking Tristan up, Ox snapped open his strong, leathery wings. Taking a few quick steps down the other side of the embankment, he launched himself into the air.

Tristan was mesmerized by his first experience of flight. The cold wind in his face was bracing, the sensation of freedom wonderfully intoxicating. Ox soared higher, his strong wings carrying them around the perimeter of the theater. Many of the Minions began to point into the air at them, shouting among themselves. Finally completing the two turns ordered by the prince, Ox swooped to the center of the amphitheater floor and landed gently. He let the prince down directly in front of Traax.

The entire theater went silent as Tristan and Traax stared at each other in an obvious contest of wills. No one moved; no one spoke. The only sound was the cold, swirling wind as it blew in and out of the great bowl.

Tristan stared calmly into Traax's green eyes, not giving an inch.

The initial look of surprise in Traax's eyes was quickly replaced by one of skepticism, as if he did not wish to relinquish command of his legions, no matter how briefly. His jaw hardened, one brow coming up questioningly, almost sarcastically. Every pair of Minion eyes was on Traax, waiting to see what he would do.

After several silent, excruciatingly tense moments, Traax relented, slowly going down on one knee. "I live to serve," he said in a strong, clear voice.

Immediately the entire body of warriors in the theater also went to their knees. "I live to serve," they said as one, the many voices seeming to shake the very coliseum in which they stood.

Tristan showed no outward signs of emotion, but his heart was leaping. He'd done it, he thought. But now that he had control, he had to learn to keep it.

"You may rise," he shouted to the theater as a whole. Traax came to his feet. The other warriors did the same, continuing to stand at stiff attention.

"The Chosen One graces us with his presence," Traax said, bowing slightly. Tristan thought there might be a hint of sarcasm in the Minion officer's voice, but he brushed the concern away. "It is an honor," Traax added, this time a bit more humbly. He then looked at Ox, and to the foot that had once been severed from the warrior's body. "I see your foot is healed," he mentioned. "I am glad the Chosen One's wizards were successful."

Bowing shortly, Ox clicked his heels.

"I have come for your report, as I said I would that day in the courtyard," Tristan replied calmly, continuing to hold Traax's eyes in his. "There are also urgent matters to discuss pertaining to Eutracia. Is there somewhere more private that we may speak? What I have to say is for your ears only."

"Of course," Traax said. "Follow me, my lord. But first may I request permission to return these warriors back to their duties of rebuilding the Recluse?"

Tristan had almost forgotten them, focused as he had been upon Traax. "Granted," he said.

With a wave of his arm, Traax indicated the Minions were to leave. At once the several thousand warriors took to the air, flying back in the direction of the castle. "Now, if you will follow me," Traax said.

Tristan and Ox followed him out the amphitheater and around the outer edge, finally stopping before a rather elaborate entrance of marble that had been constructed into the wall of the embankment. It was guarded on either side by very large, fully armed warriors. Opening the door, Traax beckoned Tristan and Ox within.

Once inside, Tristan was surprised. He had expected something rather stark, as was his overall impression regarding most things of the Minions. Instead the chambers here were light and airy, the marble of the palest indigo, with carpets on the floor and comfortable furniture placed tastefully about. A broad marble conference table with six chairs sat in the middle of the largest of several such rooms. Oil chandeliers gave the chamber a soft, inviting glow. It was not entirely unlike being in one of the smaller rooms of the Redoubt.

They each took a seat at the table. In an obvious gesture of respect, Traax removed his dreggan and placed it on the tabletop. Tristan and Ox replied in kind.

"Food and drink?" Traax asked.

"Yes," Tristan answered, suddenly realizing how hungry and thirsty he was.

Traax slapped his hands, and almost immediately two Minion women appeared, coming to stand by the table. Tristan realized that these were the first Minion women he had ever seen.

They were quite beautiful.

They stood proudly, rather than adopting the meek, subservient postures he imagined they had been forced to maintain under Kluge's command. It would be interesting to see how Minion society emerged, provided his orders remained in place, he thought.

"Food and wine," Traax said to the women. "The grouse, I think. And be quick about it." He then looked to Tristan, pursing his lips. "Please," he finally added, in a softer, less commanding tone. As the women walked away, Tristan thought for a moment he could see slight smiles come to their lips. He had a hard time repressing one of his own, but he managed.

"They are strong, the Minion women," Traax said thoughtfully. "Many of the warriors, especially those who have recently married as a result of your permission, seem to be even happier than before. Minion warriors prefer their women to be forceful, and sexually aggressive. Given their newfound freedoms, the females have responded in kind. Many of them have even made significant suggestions as to the rebuilding and decorating of the Recluse." He spoke almost as if it were astounding that mere women could accomplish such intellectual acts. Then one corner of his mouth came up. "As I said, my lord, your changes have been interesting."

"Please give me your report," Tristan said. "I particularly wish to hear of your progress in the orders I gave you just before I left Parthalon. But be brief. There is much left for us to discuss."

Traax nodded, quickly outlining for Tristan the progress that had so far been made.

When Traax had finished, Tristan asked, "What were the crimes of those who endured the Kachinaar? And why is this theater here?"

"The first warrior, the one whose head you saw, was accused of forcibly taking another man's Gallipolai wife," Traax said. "There was truly little doubt that he was guilty. His vigil failed, reinforcing not only the fact that other men's women are no longer to be shared, but that the Gallipolai are no longer slaves." Traax spoke as casually about this brutality as though he were discussing the weather.

"If two or more Kachinaars are to be held within days of each other, should the first accused be found guilty we also take his head, using it for the theater games," he continued. "It was said the second fellow, his friend, also took the woman after the first one did. But his guilt was far less certain. In any event he survived his vigil, and is now free." He paused for a moment, smiling.

"And to answer your second question, the theater was constructed of imperfect marble pieces left over from the site of the Recluse," he went on. "There is still more work to be done upon it, such as decorative statues and the like. I ordered the stadium built so that if more than one accused was to suffer the Kachinaar at once, or if I deemed the crime to be important enough, far more of the Minions would be able to watch. It has become quite a tradition." He smiled again, leaning in conspiratorially. "As you saw, we even keep a live shrew here, for just this very purpose. It tends to add a great deal of liveliness to things. Sometimes bets are taken on which day the shrew will vomit the bones back up."

Tristan sat back in his chair, trying hard not to appear as disgusted as he felt. "Is there a name you have given to this place?" he asked.

"Of course," Traax answered. "We call it the Proscenium of Indictment. Other places also serve as venues for the Kachinaar, of course, but the Proscenium is quickly becoming the favorite."

And just what in the name of the Afterlife do I do about this now? Tristan wondered. Allowing this form of barbarism to exist here, under his aegis, was unthinkable. But he needed these warriors—every single one of them. Eliminating something so popular and that they were obviously so proud of, and doing so on his very first visit, might well cause too much ill will.

Still struggling with the decision, Tristan tried to think of what Wigg would tell him if he were here. Many had been the time, during their search for Shailiha and the Paragon, that the lead wizard had ordered him to forget the things he saw, no matter how vile, and to concentrate instead on the larger goal. Using the Minions to crush Scrounge's hatchlings and somehow prevent Nicholas from empowering the Gates of

Dawn had to take priority. He therefore decided to speak no more of the Proscenium or the Kachinaar for the time being. He would not condemn these traditions. But he would not give them his verbal approval, either. He decided to change the subject.

"And now for the true reason I have come," he said, looking into Traax's eyes. "I am ordering as many of the legions as you can possibly spare to Eutracia. Immediately. We have a host of new enemies, and it shall be the Minions' task to destroy these monsters." He folded his arms across his chest and sat back. Holding his breath, he waited for Traax's response.

"It has been too long since we have seen action, my lord," Traax said. Gripping the hilt of his dreggan, he held the shiny blade to the light of the chandeliers. "And it will be good for our swords to again taste blood, especially since we can no longer train to the death. Your enemies are ours." He refocused his green eyes back on the Chosen One. "Tell me more," he said eagerly.

At that moment the food came. Tristan became quiet, waiting for the women to depart. The Parthalonian grouse was excellent, perhaps the best bird he had ever tasted. He quickly washed down several helpings of both the seasoned grouse and the dark, rich bread of the Minions with several glasses of hearty red wine. In between bites he gave Traax his orders.

The reconstruction of the Recluse was to be put on indefinite hold, he said. Traax was to begin assembling his men—along with weapons, support staff, materiel, and foodstuffs—and placing it all near the entrance to Faegan's portal. Also, the fleet anchored at Eyrie Point was to depart as soon as possible, carrying additional troops. Should there be any serious problems in the execution of his orders, a Minion messenger was to immediately come through the portal, informing him.

Tristan described the hatchlings and the scarabs, and Traax only smiled, his sense of anticipation growing. Tristan purposely did not mention Nicholas or the building of the Gates of Dawn. He would explain those things to Traax once the entire force had arrived in Eutracia and were at his disposal. Getting them there was the chief concern now, and he did not wish to confuse the issue for his second in command, or give him a possible reason to object.

Above all, he especially did not want Traax or any of the other Minions to become aware that the wizards were losing their powers.

"There are several other points you must adhere to strictly," Tristan continued, remembering the things the wizards had insisted upon. "Mark my words well, for your life and the lives of your troops shall depend on it. Should you see any weakness or fading in the consistency of the vortex, it is paramount that no more warriors go through. Such an anomaly will mean either that the portal is about to close, or there is something wrong with its operation. If anyone goes through at that time they could die horribly, forever lost somewhere in between. They are to run through as fast as they know how and as many abreast as the portal allows, so as to add to our numbers on the other side as quickly as possible. Do you understand?"

"Yes, my lord," Traax answered.

"You are also to leave a small skeleton force here, to continue hunting the shrews. I give you five days to organize all of this. Then you are to come to Eutracia, by way of the portal. You and I still have much to discuss, not the least of which is our plan of battle."

Traax took a deep breath as he formulated his next thought. He took another sip of the wine. "The Chosen One understands, does he not, that the ocean voyage takes at least thirty days?"

"Yes," Tristan said. "But there is little we can do about that. And in the meantime Minion troops should be pouring through the portal, especially if my wizards can find a way to enlarge it, or to hold it open longer."

"And my lord understands the bargain of tenfold times four, the agreement made by the Coven to ensure a safe crossing?" Traax asked politely.

Tristan froze, not knowing what to say. *At long last here it is,* he thought frantically. He reminded himself that he must never show weakness or a lack of knowledge, especially at this stage. He needed to get the answer without revealing to the Minion that he did not know what it was. He turned to Ox. Having been part of the force that invaded Tammerland, the giant Minion must also know—yet in their great concern for their many other problems, they had not thought to ask him.

Tristan saw a hint of concern creep into the corners of Ox's large, dark eyes.

"I forced the Coven to reveal the secret of crossing before I killed them all," Tristan finally said with hardness in his voice, hoping desperately that the Minion would accept the lie. "We must make allowances for the increased degree of difficulty, of course. I know you yourself have crossed, for you were upon the dais in Tammerland that day." He paused, his jaw hardening. "The day my family and the Directorate of Wizards were all murdered."

Traax took a long, deep breath, leveling a clearly remorseless gaze at Tristan. "I follow my orders to the letter," he said sternly, quietly. "No matter who my lord may be at the time. Do you think my great numbers could not have crushed you and your wizard that day in the courtyard when you killed Kluge? But usurping one's lord in unfair battle is not the Minion way. It is something you shall be quite glad of when we finally arrive again upon your shores."

Tristan stiffened at the tone in Traax's voice, but at the same time he knew the warrior was only telling the truth. Tristan was coming to have more than a modicum of respect for the intelligent, clean-shaven Minion sitting before him.

"Tell me your version of the crossing," Tristan said, finally using his ploy. "I wish to see whether the Coven lied to me."

Traax nodded, Tristan's bluff having apparently worked for the moment. "At fifteen days into the voyage, the ships enter a 'dead zone.' By this I mean that there is suddenly no wind for the sails, and the sea becomes smooth as glass. The air is so cold that one can see his breath. Then a thick fog coalesces into the shape of two hands, gripping both the bow and stern of the ship, holding it in place. Voices come from faces in the water, demanding the forty dead bodies. We throw them over, and they are consumed. Only then do the Necrophagians, the Eaters of the Dead, allow us to pass." He paused for a moment, thinking.

"We will, of course, require forty dead bodies. And, as you know, they must be fresh," Traax added. "If my lord would allow it, I am sure we could easily arrange for a session of training to the death on board, just before entering the dead zone. This could easily result in the required number of fresh corpses." He paused again, a look of concern growing on his face. "All of this assumes, of course, that the Necrophagians will honor the bargain despite the fact that the sorceresses are not aboard, much less still living."

Tristan sat back, trying not to appear horrified by Traax's story. He had to find a way to corroborate the bizarre tale—and the one person in this land he was so far willing to trust was Ox. He turned to the huge Minion by his side. "Is this the way you remember it?" he asked.

"Yes, Chosen One," Ox said.

Tristan nodded. "Then either my wizards shall deal with the Necrophagians, or we shall not cross by sea. One way or another, we shall find a solution."

Traax gave the prince a strange look.

"Is there something else?" Tristan asked him. "Something you don't understand?"

"Forgive me, my lord, but this is something I must ask," Traax replied. "Are you ill?"

Tristan stiffened. "Why do you ask?" he answered as casually as possible.

"The veins in your arm," Traax said. "They look inflamed. Have you been injured?"

"A battle wound, nothing more," Tristan lied. "My wizards have already begun the healing process. I shall be by your side when the time comes."

He stood from the table, indicating that Ox and Traax should follow suit. Each of them replaced their dreggans into their scabbards. Tristan turned to Traax. "Do you understand your orders?"

Traax clicked the heels of his boots together. "Yes, my lord," he answered quickly. Together the three of them walked outside, reentering the coliseum.

"Is there anything else you require, my lord?" Traax asked. "Will you be staying the night?"

"No," Tristan answered. "We must go back." With a sense of finality, he looked at the stars. "I ordered my wizard to briefly open the portal each hour until my return. We shall walk to the place at which we first arrived. Our wait will not be long."

"In that case I shall go to the Recluse, and begin informing the legions of the upcoming campaign," Traax said. He smiled again. "They will be most happy to hear of it. I shall see you in Eutracia, in five days' time."

"Five days," Tristan repeated. In a final gesture of good faith, he held out his right hand. Traax extended his, as well. With a strong slap, each man firmly grasped the inner side of the other's forearm. The pact had been made. With that Traax again clicked his heels, then walked away.

Tristan and Ox left the hauntingly beautiful, moon-shadowed Proscenium. The fresh Parthalonian snow crunching beneath their feet, they returned to the spot in which they had arrived. In the near distance the partially rebuilt Recluse shone brightly from the many torches surrounding it, just as it had during the days of the Coven. Suddenly, from the area of the castle came the sound of great cheering and yelling.

His breath leaving his lungs in frosty clouds, Tristan looked to the stars, and to the three rose-colored moons that bathed the twinkling, snowy ground with their crimson hue. He gathered his coat around him and remained that way for some time, thinking of his many loved ones who had died at Minion hands. Ox stood silently by his side, as if the huge warrior had been doing so all of his life.

CHAPTER FORTY-ONE

*W*IGG sat quietly at the rather large table. He had his doubts concerning what Faegan was about to do, but he had finally agreed to it. Faegan sat nearby in his chair on wheels. In his hands he held an oddly shaped glass beaker, its liquid contents glowing brightly with the power of the craft.

Tristan and Ox had not yet returned from Parthalon, but each of the wizards knew it was still too early to be concerned. Shailiha was sleeping safely in her bedroom. The rest of those who lived here in the Redoubt were quietly going about their duties.

The two wizards sat alone in the antechamber that protected the Well of the Redoubt. Several days before, they had removed the stone from around Faegan's neck and placed it beneath the continually running waters of the Well, hoping that might help protect the stone. That act should also have caused everyone of the craft to lose their gifts, but to their amazement, that didn't happen. Not only did they all keep their gifts, but the decay of the stone went on unabated.

Wigg and Faegan had just come from checking on the stone. The Paragon was losing its color—and at a strangely accelerating rate. To an untrained eye, the loss of color in the Paragon would have appeared fairly constant. But not to someone as highly trained as Faegan. This had set the curious master wizard to thinking. As a result he had come to view the entire problem of the fading jewel in a potentially new light.

A murky light, he thought as he sat there in his chair, holding the odd beaker he had brought with him. *But not one without possibilities in the darkness of our troubles.*

Given his tenuous but hopeful new hypothesis, he had immediately gone to the Archives to do research. It had taken some time, but he eventually found the rather esoteric calculations he was looking for. Then had come several hours in one of the Redoubt laboratories, laboring to get the mixture just right.

Due to his reduced powers, it had taken him far longer to accomplish this than normal. The hard-won result was the glowing fluid he now held.

"Are you really sure that this is going to work?" Wigg asked, ever the skeptic.

"What's wrong, Wigg?" Faegan retorted impishly. "Do you no longer trust my abilities?" His experience of being back in one of the laboratories again, even though difficult, had energized him. Just as it always did. Research, followed by the successful physical application of its results, were his favorite aspects of the craft.

"Let's see," he continued, feigning an air of ignorance. "First it was the Forestallments I had to convince you of. You fought back hard on that one. And then came the bond between Shailiha and the hatchling. You were highly skeptical about that one, too. But I was correct on both counts, I believe. Will you never be able to admit that I sometimes get things right?" His gray-green eyes twinkled, and he dangled the beaker tauntingly at Wigg, even though he knew his friend could not see him doing so. "Would you like to try for two out of three?"

Unwilling to join into the game, Wigg simply sighed. "Has Shawna the Short done her part in this foolishness?" he asked.

"Oh, yes," Faegan said happily. "She informed me this very morning that she was quite finished. And she took great relish in it, I can assure you. It took her the past two evenings to finally accomplish her mission without raising suspicion. She has, of course, absolutely no idea why I would request something so bizarre. She has also been sworn to secrecy regarding her actions." Faegan smiled. "She certainly loves a good mystery. Almost childish about it, in fact."

She's not the only one, Wigg thought. "Let's get on with it," he growled.

Closing his eyes, Faegan levitated Wigg in his chair. Then he levitated himself, chair and all, in the same fashion, and carefully removed the stopper from the beaker. He slowly poured the azure fluid out into a small, glowing puddle on the floor of the room.

His expression became more serious, and he closed his eyes in concentration. Almost immediately the fluid began to spread across the floor, finally progressing from wall to wall and corner to corner. Not one scintilla was left uncovered. And then, after several moments had passed, the fluid completely disappeared.

Faegan opened his eyes, a look of satisfaction on his face. "Time to go, Wigg," he said softly. "Our work here is done."

With that, the single door at the opposite side of the room swung open by itself and the two wizards floated from the room, coming to rest on the floor of the hallway outside.

The great mahogany door closed firmly upon its strange secret as the two ancient friends made their way back down the hallways of the Redoubt.

CHAPTER FORTY-TWO

*T*RISTAN sat with Faegan, Wigg, and Shailiha behind closed doors in the Archives of the Redoubt. As usual, Morganna slept in the sling across Shailiha's chest. It had taken the prince some time to relate his experiences in Parthalon.

The wizards' expressions had become far graver when they heard the macabre tale of the Necrophagians.

"We simply cannot allow the armada to cross," Faegan said. "The Necrophagians' bargain was with the Coven, and the sorceresses are all dead. We have no way to know whether the bargain would still be honored, and we can't risk losing all those warriors for nothing." He thought for a moment. "We must send Ox back to Parthalon immediately, with written orders from Tristan to belay the sailing." He stroked his blue cat as it contentedly purred in his lap. "It seems I shall just have to speed up my efforts to find a way of both widening the portal and holding it open longer." He sighed deeply. "But it shall not be easy."

Tristan looked to Shailiha. She seemed more pale somehow, and weaker. "Are you all right?" he asked earnestly. "Did something happen to you while I was away?"

Knowing how much she cared for her brother and how difficult it was for her to lie to him, the two wizards held their breath, hoping against hope she would say the right thing. Shailiha stifled the urge to bite her lower lip, a dead giveaway whenever she was unsure of herself.

"I'm fine, little brother," she said reassuringly. She reached out, gently touching the gold medallion that hung around his neck. "No need to worry. I think I'm just tired from all of the excitement." She saw the wizards uncoil a little. Deftly changing the subject, she took up Tristan's right hand. "Was it bad?" she asked, referring to his second convulsion.

"Yes, Shai," he said quietly. "I have never experienced such pain in my life. My right arm is now somewhat weaker, and very sore. Had Ox not been with me, I might have swallowed my tongue and suffocated. I still can't get used to the fact that a Minion has become one of my friends." He turned to the wizards. "I don't suppose there is any point in my asking whether you two are any closer to finding a cure?"

Faegan shook his head slowly. "But we do have something else for you," Faegan added. "A surprise! Something that I believe will cheer you up."

Tristan raised an eyebrow. "What is it?" he asked skeptically.

"For the answer, you must follow us to the upper levels," Faegan answered cryptically. Without waiting for Tristan's response he began wheeling toward the door. "Shall we go?"

Tristan dutifully followed the two wizards and his sister out of the Redoubt and up into the broken, looted palace rooms above. He eventually found himself standing before the doors that once barred entrance to his mother's private chambers.

"And just what is it that you all think is so interesting here?" he asked. One corner of his mouth came up.

"Why don't you open the door and see for yourself?" Wigg asked him. The smile was one of the few Tristan had seen on the lead wizard's face in weeks, and it only added to the deepening mystery. The prince took a breath and then turned the doorknob, walking purposefully into the once-sumptuous room.

Considering the fact that the wizards were involved, he could have witnessed any number of bizarre things in these rooms, and he knew it. But what stood before him now was the last thing he had ever expected. Especially here, in his mother's chambers.

The hatchling he and Ox had captured stood in the center of the room on its strong rear legs. Seeing the bird was for some reason free of its wizard's cage, Tristan began to reach for his dreggan. But then he saw that the bird was calm, and was regarding him with only mild interest.

Faegan cackled. "You won't be needing your sword. I suggest you take another look."

Tristan carefully examined the beast. Something about it was clearly different. And then, recognizing why, he immediately understood what was going on.

They've broken it, or trained it somehow! he realized.

The bird made no move to escape out the open balcony doors behind it. Tristan's eyes immediately went to the odd-looking saddle and stirrup combination that had been cinched to the hatchling's back, and then to the bridle and reins. His eyes widened with sudden realization.

They actually expect me to ride it! Ride through the sky!

He turned back to the three of them, his jaw slack, to see that they were all smiling from ear to ear. "Please tell me you're joking," he said, shaking his head in disbelief.

"Not at all," Wigg replied. "But in all fairness we have some explaining to do."

"An understatement, I'm sure," Tristan muttered. He turned to his sister. "I assume you knew about this," he added.

As she rocked the baby slightly, Shailiha could not keep from biting her lip. "I knew, but I really didn't have anything to do with it," she lied convincingly. "It was all the wizards' idea."

He regarded her narrowly for a moment, finally accepting her answer. "Can this thing talk?" he asked the wizards.

"Unfortunately not," Wigg lied. "Even though it has human arms. There were apparently three generations of these birds. We believe this one to be second generation, rather than third."

"Did you ever learn how it came to be separated from the others?" Tristan asked skeptically. "Could this be a trick of some kind? How do I know it won't simply fly me back to the enemy?"

"We considered that possibility, eventually dismissing it as illogical," he replied. "You were just with Nicholas in the Caves, and he willingly set you free. Why would he send a single bird out, simply to take you back to him? If he had wished to keep you there, he could have easily done so. Besides," he added, "the bird fought with all of its strength to keep from being captured, did it not?"

"Yes," Tristan answered. He rubbed his sore arm, thinking. "But that still doesn't explain how it came to be wandering around on its own."

"Faegan and I believe that this bird was one of those that ransacked Ilendium," Wigg suggested. "In the darkness and chaos that must have ensued, it is easy enough to imagine how one or more of them might have become lost." He raised the usual eyebrow. "I suggest you start being more positive about all this, and stop looking a gift bird in the mouth, so to speak."

Tristan turned back to the creature, beginning to think that this might be a blessing in disguise after all. "Where did the strange saddle and bridle come from?" he asked.

"You have Geldon to thank for those," Wigg answered. "He took them from the palace stables, and modified them for use on the hatchling. As it turns out, among his many other talents he is quite a good leatherworker, as well."

Being careful not to make any sudden moves, Tristan walked closer to the bird. He closely examined the saddle. The pommel had been enlarged, presumably to provide a better grip. The leather bands leading down to the stirrups had been widened. Leather belts, complete with buckles, had been stitched into them, three on either side.

"What are these extra belts for?" Tristan asked quizzically.

Shailiha smiled. "To keep you from falling off, of course. They go around your legs and buckle in the front, holding you in the saddle." In truth she had been particularly worried about this, despite the fact that Tristan had always been one of the finest horsemen in the kingdom. Nonetheless, if he fell from the bird at any significant altitude, death would be certain—Chosen One or not. It had therefore been she who had insisted on the additional straps.

Tristan simply stood there, not sure of what to say. "But none of this explains how you were able to turn the hatchling to our side, or do it so quickly," he insisted.

Faegan cleared his throat. "It seems that the bird's ties to Nicholas were not so strong, after all. I reasoned that with so many hatchlings, even he surely cannot keep perfect control over them all, every second of every day. Assuming this to be true, I invoked a spell that allowed me to sense when his control was at its lowest point. That's when I broke the bond, turning it to our side." He made a nonchalant, throwaway gesture with one hand. "But all of that is wizards' business, and you needn't concern yourself with the whys or the hows of it all." Watching the prince's reaction carefully, he sensed that his lies had worked.

"And you really expect me to ride it?" Tristan asked. "What's wrong with using Pilgrim, just as I always have?"

"You are about to lead the Minions into battle," Wigg said sternly. "Have you somehow forgotten that they fly? Or that every single lord they have ever had has always been able to join them in the air? This shall be a new kind of battle for you, Tristan. One that takes place primarily in the air, just as Faegan's prophecy decreed. In addition, this creature can give you greater speed, and the ability to see what is happening on the ground over great distances. Besides, it is our belief that the hatchlings can run as fast across the ground as any horse that ever lived. So what are you going to do, eh? Ride your hatchling into the skies to command the Minions properly, or plod around on the snowy, slippery ground atop Pilgrim, wondering what in the name of the Afterlife is really going on above you?"

Tristan glared at the wizard, finally understanding that Wigg was right. In truth, the prince was thrilled at the prospect of riding a hatchling. But there were questions he wanted answered first. The wizards had been acting strangely lately, and he wanted to know why.

But it was clear by the imperious look on Wigg's face that no more questions were going to be answered at the moment. Tristan turned to his sister. She had a curiously mischievous look in her eyes.

Grasping his medallion, she pulled his face close to hers and raised her eyebrows at him mockingly. "What's the matter, little brother?" she teased. "Afraid Scrounge can do something you can't? I hear he doesn't even need a saddle."

That was all it took. Taking the medallion from her grasp, Tristan walked to the hatchling. As if the bird knew his wishes, it kneeled down, allowing Tristan easier access to the stirrup. When he climbed aboard, the saddle felt good beneath him, almost as familiar as the one he always used on Pilgrim. He carefully cinched the straps around his thighs, buckling them tight, and finally took the reins. As if he had been doing it all his life, he expertly wheeled the bird around to face the others in the room.

"We'll see about that," he said softly. Shailiha held her breath.

Tristan turned the muscular bird toward the balcony, and the hatchling launched itself into the air.

Shailiha, Wigg, and Faegan went to the railing. The princess strained her eyes for as long as she could, as the strange bird carrying her twin brother became little more than a dark speck against the sky, finally vanishing altogether.

"Do you think he believed us?" she asked tentatively.

"That is hard to say," Wigg answered, pursing his lips. "Tristan is both highly intelligent and very stubborn. But the important thing is that he is finally on the bird." He turned his unseeing eyes toward the princess. "Your comment about Scrounge was the turning point. Well done. As to whether he believes us—well, who knows? But he must ride none other than that particular monstrosity of the craft into battle if we are to have any hope of succeeding in all of this."

The three of them finally turned away from the balcony, retreating to the depths of the Redoubt.

CHAPTER FORTY-THREE

*Y*OU *have done well, Nicholas,* the young adept heard the Guild of the Heretics say. Their many voices came to him as one—both male and female, both strong and soft. It was as if a choir sang the most beautiful songs imaginable within the depths of his consciousness. His very blood was alive with their sound. And as he hovered in the depths of the Caves, taking in their words, he closed his eyes in ecstasy.

The Gates of Dawn shall soon be complete, they said. *The Chosen One continues to grow more ill, and will soon come to you on bended knee. Complete the Gates as soon as possible, our son. At that time the Vagaries, the truly sublime side, will reign continually and without contest. And the Ones, our enemies of the craft, shall be locked within the firmament forever.*

I shall, my parents, Nicholas told them. *I shall.*

Nicholas soared through the cold, clear sky and quickly approached the construction site. He hovered near the magnificent black-and-azure Gates.

The three massive structures had climbed even higher, and their graceful, more artistic aspects would soon be in evidence. Nicholas was pleased. In only two more weeks they would be finished, and he could then activate them, bringing his parents of above back to the earth.

He had just come from yet another blood-drawing session in the special room at Fledgling House. That was the slowest part of the process: He could only take a bit at a time from the children without killing them.

But he still had time. The Chosen One's Minions were not yet here, and his wizards were already drastically weakened. His father of this earth was therefore in no position to challenge his hatchlings, much less stop the construction of the Gates. Soon, very soon now, the Chosen One would see the awesome power of his son's creations for himself.

Nicholas flew higher to examine the new construction.

The blood of the children ran freshly from the seams between the great stones, dripping lazily down the sides of the stunning black-and-azure pillars and forming little endowed ponds around each of the legs.

Satisfied, Nicholas backed away, and closed his eyes.

Almost immediately the blood of the children began to turn azure. Steaming with heat and glowing brightly, it began to pull the massive stones closer together, their surfaces grating against one another as the joints slowly, agonizingly fused.

Excess blood ran down the sides of the Gates, leaving macabre, winding trails down the smooth edifices, adding crazily patterned streaks to those already shot deep throughout the stone.

Smiling, Nicholas flew down to hover near the base of one of the legs.

Ragnar stood there waiting, dressed in his fur robes, Wigg's ceremonial dagger at his side. He bowed, then pulled the robe closer, warding off the cold.

"The bond between the most recently erected stones is now complete," Nicholas said quietly. "Later this night I will harvest yet more of the children's blood. I shall return with it at midnight to repeat the incantation for the pieces the consuls shall erect between now and then. In less than a fortnight, we shall be victorious."

"Yes, my lord," Ragnar answered obediently. He placed two fingers into his ever-present vial of yellow fluid, then sucked on them. Almost immediately he felt warmer.

"Keep the consuls working," Nicholas ordered quietly. "I will brook no slackness in this."

Again Ragnar bowed, smiling.

Nicholas soared into the sky, his white robe and dark hair billowing about him, and disappeared.

CHAPTER FORTY-FOUR

THE next two days passed in relative calm for Tristan. At first learning to control the movements of the bird and trying to stay in the saddle at the same time had been a challenge.

It was much like riding Pilgrim, he soon discovered, but more unpredictable. And far more dangerous. However, as time went on, he was becoming more and more used to the experience, finding it mesmerizing.

Not only could the bird climb swiftly, but it could also, given the proper commands, hover, seemingly indefinitely, or fold its wings to dive with great speed toward the ground. Tristan dove the bird often, from increasingly greater and greater heights. He would pull up at the last second, only to do it again. He came to love soaring through the white, humid fog of the clouds, only to emerge suddenly out the other side.

He quickly came to realize what a wonderful place these clouds—or even the branches of a tree, for that matter—could be to hide from an enemy. And seeing Eutracia from this far up gave him a unique, awe-inspiring perspective on his nation that before he had only dreamed about.

He had also purposely landed the hatchling on a large, bare, snow-covered field to test the wizards' other belief regarding the creature's abilities. Sure enough, when finally made to understand, the bird ran across the snowy ground as fast and as surefooted as Pilgrim ever could have.

When he finally landed on the balcony of his late mother's rooms on the afternoon of the second day, Geldon was there waiting. Tristan walked the bird into the chamber, then dismounted and began removing the saddle and bridle. Geldon closed the balcony doors.

"You have become very good in such a short time," the hunchbacked dwarf said with a smile. "But there is now business to attend to. The wizards ask for us."

Tristan raised an eyebrow. "Did they say what it was about?"

"No," the dwarf answered. "Only that it was important. We are both to go to the antechamber that lies outside the Well of the Redoubt. Now."

Tristan took a deep breath, shaking off the cold. Then he removed his gray fox coat and slung it over one shoulder. "Very well," he said matter-of-factly. "Let's go."

Inside the chamber, Wigg, Faegan, Shailiha, and Celeste were seated at the ornate table. Behind them, a fire danced merrily in the familiar, light blue fireplace. The prince and Geldon took seats. As always, Tristan found himself acutely aware of Celeste's presence and the way the fire showed off the highlights in her long, red hair. She smiled at him. Shailiha, on the other hand, looked anxious. Morganna was not with her. But before he could ask her what was going on, the door opened again.

Joshua walked into the room, looked around briefly, and then took a seat at the far end of the table. His hazel eyes took in the group gathered there, then settled on the princess. He smiled.

Faegan cleared his throat. "Now that we are all present, there is something of importance to discuss," he said sternly. Abruptly he raised one arm, and azure flashed from the ends of his fingers. A wizard's cage immediately formed about the young consul.

Joshua looked up first in horror, then in fury. "What is the meaning of this?" he asked angrily. "Have you lost your mind?"

Faegan pursed his lips. "No, I think not," he replied softly. He leveled his gray-green eyes at the younger man. "Tell us, if you would, how it is that you were able to circumvent the death enchantments, considering the fact that you have been practicing the Vagaries?"

Faegan's question hit Tristan like a thunderbolt.

Joshua turned to look at Wigg. "What is the meaning of this, Lead Wizard? Surely you cannot be a part of this madness! Tell Faegan that you know me well, and that I have done nothing wrong!"

Wigg sighed long and hard. "You know I cannot do that, Joshua," he answered. "For you also know that it is not the truth. I may be blind, but there are still some things I am able to see clearly." He paused for a moment. "And my eyes have finally been opened regarding you."

"What is it you are accusing me of?" the consul asked frantically, refocusing his attention on Faegan. "I have the right to know!"

"Simply put, you are in league with Nicholas, and we can prove it," Faegan answered, his face dark. He was literally shaking with anger. It was as if the formidable power he controlled was about to burst forth at any moment in some incredible use of the craft.

"I am not a traitor!" the consul protested. "You have no proof!"

"Oh, but we do," Faegan countered. "You have been instrumental in helping Nicholas drain the power of the stone. I am now as sure of this as I am my own name. But still, the most interesting piece of the puzzle is how you were able to deny the death enchantments. As a consul of the Redoubt who has willingly taken them upon himself, performing such acts of the Vagaries as I accuse you of would normally result in instant death. So the question remains. Or, put another way, how is it that you continue to live?"

At this, Joshua seemed to calm somewhat. Placing his hands into the opposite sleeves of his robe, he lowered his eyes menacingly at the master wizard across from him. This was a Joshua that Tristan had never seen; it was as though something vile had just come over him.

"First show me your proof, cripple," he shot back.

"Very well," Faegan answered calmly. He turned to Shailiha. "Princess, if you please."

As if in concentration, Shailiha lowered her eyes somewhat. And then, from the bookcase behind the table and directly across from the secret door leading into the Well of the Redoubt, came Caprice, Shailiha's violet-and-yellow flier. She had apparently been hiding in the dark space that would have ordinarily been occupied by an unusually thick, tall volume. Pausing tentatively for a moment on the edge of the shelf, she launched herself into the air, coming to rest on Shailiha's arm. From there, presumably at the princess' silent order, the flier flew down to land on the center of the table, her wings opening and closing silently.

For what seemed to be an eternity, no one spoke.

Joshua looked hard at Wigg. There was venom in his eyes. "Is this your idea of a joke?" he snarled. "Do you really expect me to accept the absurd accusations of some perverted creature of the craft? Especially one without the power of speech, who can communicate only with a woman who has just been supposedly cured of the Chimeran Agonies? No, gentlemen—I'm afraid you'll have to do much better than that."

"It's over, Joshua," Wigg said softly. "The flier, or should I say the princess, told us everything. You have been helping Nicholas drain the power of the stone. In fact, you have probably been doing so since the process first started. We had long wondered why the rate of decay varied so much from one day to the next—almost as if there were more than one force at work. After you, Faegan, and I placed the stone in the Well, Faegan and I placed the flier here, to determine whether anyone would enter the Well of the Redoubt without authorization. From her hidden perch in the bookcase, Caprice saw you. When you left she informed Shailiha, who in turn informed us. Faegan then immediately came here to check. The rate of decay had been increased, and the only changed variable was your presence."

"Even if all this were somehow true, it isn't enough, and

you both know it," Joshua protested. "For all I know this is something the two of you made up—an elaborate hoax of some kind, designed to force me from the Brotherhood." He paused, his jaw tightening. "I have never, in my entire life, been to the Well of the Redoubt alone. The only time I have ever been there is with you."

This seemed to be exactly what Faegan had been waiting for. "Really?" he asked, narrowing his eyes. "We thought you might say something like that." He turned to the prince. "Tristan," he said, "please remove the consul's right boot."

Tristan stared at the old wizard in bewilderment. "What are you talking about?" he asked.

"Remove the consul's right boot, and place it on the table in front of me," Faegan answered calmly. "I have engineered the warp so that you might reach through it without harm. Except for his right foot, I will momentarily immobilize him so that he cannot resist you."

Still nonplussed, Tristan nonetheless did as he was asked.

"Thank you," Faegan said as Tristan walked back to his seat. "Now then," the wizard went on. "Everyone please observe."

At once the chandeliers in the room began to dim, until finally the only light came from the bars of the cage holding Joshua. In the eerie glow, Faegan turned his wheelchair toward the center of the room, then raised his arm. A glowing broom appeared and hovered silently in the darkness. Then it began to sweep the floor, until its sparkling, glowing bristles had covered it all. With that, Faegan caused the broom to vanish and the lights to come back up. Tristan looked down at the floor, amazed.

A set of very clear boot prints, glowing with the power of the craft, led to the secret wall panel guarding the Well of the Redoubt, and back again.

"Tristan," Wigg said. "Go to the boot prints, and look closely at the right heel. Tell us what you see."

The prince rose, and went to study one of the prints. In the center of the glowing heel mark was a dark letter "J." He bent down, just to be sure, then turned back to the table and reported what he saw.

"Now," Faegan said, "if you would also be so kind as to turn over Joshua's boot."

Tristan walked to the table and turned over the boot. In the center of the heel had been carved the letter "J." The exact duplicate of the one upon the floor, it stared back silently at him, a clear testament to what had transpired here.

Speechless, Tristan turned to Faegan. "How?" he asked. "How was this done?"

"A little-known use of the craft," Faegan replied, turning his chair around and staring directly into the eyes of the consul. "I created an elixir that when spread across the floor subsequently vanishes, but can later reveal the tracks of anyone who walks upon it. Because only his boot prints appear in that area, only Joshua has entered and exited the Well of the Redoubt since I poured the elixir onto the floor. As for the mark on the heel, well, 'J' obviously stands for 'Joshua.' It was carved there by Shawna the Short. She slipped into his chambers while he was asleep, and did the job for me." Faegan smiled knowingly into the consul's face.

"But suppose others had gone there, even for innocent reasons?" Celeste asked from the other side of the table. "Or he had used an accomplice? How would you know who they were?"

Faegan grinned impishly. "Because Shawna did *everyone's* boots and shoes."

Reaching down, Tristan quickly removed his right knee boot and carefully examined the heel. Sure enough, a small "T" had been carved into it. He shook his head. As he put the boot back on, he looked over at the fuming consul in the glowing wizard's cage.

"What made you suspect him?" Shailiha asked.

"First of all," Wigg answered, "there was the fact that he has been the only consul to ever make it back to the Redoubt alive. Think about it. Didn't that ever strike you as strange, given the fact that there were roughly three thousand of them out there? Surely if he could escape the hatchlings and make it to safety, so could at least a few of the others. It is our belief that Joshua traveled from squad to squad as Nicholas' agent, helping the hatchlings to capture the consuls. We had often wondered how the birds could find the squads so easily, and why it was that the consuls' powers were completely useless against them. It just made no sense. In both cases we believe Joshua used a superior spell given to him by Nicholas, perhaps even placed into his blood by way of Forestallment. A simple blood signature will tell us that. His emaciated condition and dislocated shoulder were a nice touch, as well. A small price to pay for authenticity and sympathy, wouldn't you say? And so he came to us, at Nicholas' orders, to tell us his sad story, infiltrate the Redoubt, and begin helping to drain the Paragon." Wigg paused, collecting his thoughts.

"And then there was the fact that Joshua would not let Geldon unearth Nicholas' grave in Parthalon, or at least talked him out of it," he continued. He looked in the general direction of the dwarf, giving him a short, compassionate smile. "Geldon wanted to bring the body here for you, Tristan, so that you might bury it in the grave site of your parents. He thought that as long as he was there, he would do you a kindness, saving you at least that part of the grief. But Joshua couldn't allow that, because there was no body to bring back, was there? And finally there was his suggestion that we use Ox as your bodyguard. An idea Faegan and I eventually embraced, ordering Tristan to accept. Fiendishly clever, I'll give the consul that much. We never told you that it had been Joshua's idea, but it was."

"I still don't understand," Tristan said. "What has Ox got to do with all of this? Is he a traitor, too?"

"No," Wigg said, shaking his head. "Ox's heart is pure, and he would gladly die for you. Nicholas wants you protected, for he still hopes that you will join him in his madness. The poison he ordered placed into your system by Scrounge, as he told you himself, provides the ultimate incentive to do so. Things are starting to make more sense, but I'm afraid there are still far more pieces to the puzzle."

Tristan stared at the consul, stunned that he could be a traitor. "But what about placing the stone in the Well, and you retaining your powers?" he asked. "How could Nicholas do that?"

"No doubt via one or more of the Forestallments placed into his blood by the Heretics," Wigg answered. "Perhaps even the same Forestallment that allows our 'friend' Joshua to help Nicholas accelerate the decay of the Paragon. As I said, a simple test of the consul's blood signature will reveal much. For if he is innocent, his signature will contain no Forestallments. Isn't that right, Joshua?"

The consul stayed silent, his lips drawn into a thin line, his eyes seething with hate.

"Assuming Joshua was our culprit, we needed to be able to prove it without a doubt," Faegan continued. "I assumed he needed to be near the stone to help with its decay. He was occasionally in my presence as I wore it, but not always. By having him help us place the stone in the Well of the Redoubt, we gave him the opportunity—and the temptation. Wigg and I replaced the Paragon around my neck this morning, after Shailiha informed us of Caprice's observations."

"But we still have questions, Joshua," Wigg said. "Questions that you shall answer—one way or another. How was it that Nicholas was able to defeat your death enchantments? And, even more importantly, is there a way by which we can return the power to the stone?"

Joshua produced an evil, twisted smile.

"Very clever, Wigg." He nodded. "Yes, I have always been his, right from the moment he first revealed his mind to me, even while he was still a child. Even then his power and knowledge of the craft dwarfed anything you and the cripple have ever seen. But why, you are no doubt wondering. Why is it that a trusted consul would do such a thing? I'll tell you why, you pompous old man. Because Nicholas promised me the one thing you and your vaunted Directorate would never share with any of us who wear the dark blue robes: power. And with that a complete understanding of the craft, especially the darker side. The adept has promised me things that you could never, in your exclusive, infantile practice of the Vigors, ever conceive of. And I wanted them. Oh, yes, *Lead Wizard,* I wanted them badly." The wicked smile again contorted his face.

"And there is something else," he hissed, so quietly his words were almost inaudible. "There are a great many more of the Brotherhood of Consuls just like me—brothers who went over to Nicholas' cause. A greater number of us than you could ever imagine. The master removed their tattoos so that they could never be identified." He paused to stare menacingly at Tristan. "But your son didn't tell you any of that, did he, Chosen One? No. For you see, there is still far more to all of this than any of you can imagine. But you shall never understand it all, for very soon now shall come the Confluence, and you shall all be quite dead."

Wigg looked as if he had seen a ghost. Darkness passed across his face like a thunderstorm across the sky, and tears welled up in each of his useless eyes. But Faegan seemed less daunted by what he had just heard. Quickly wheeling his chair closer, he faced the consul directly.

"You said 'the Confluence.' What do you mean by that?" he demanded urgently.

"It makes no difference whether you are told, for you cannot possibly stop it now, anyway," Joshua gloated. "The Confluence is the combination of four separate, but equally necessary elements. First comes the azure blood of the Chosen One, which my master already possesses. Second: a sufficient quantity of the blood of endowed children—blood that is gifted, but still malleable. He now has that, too. Third, waters from the Caves of the Paragon. And finally the power of the Paragon, transferred into the willing, *azure* blood of just one individual—an individual who is completely devoted to the teachings of the Heretics. The individual the Chosen One himself so conveniently took from the womb of the sorceress Succiu and left behind in Parthalon. As I said, it is the Confluence. Through the unique combination of these elements, the Guild of the Heretics will be allowed to return to the earth, to rule once more."

Suddenly he smiled again. It was a more knowing and somehow more decisive smile—as if his mind was suddenly made up about something.

"But I digress," he said, almost casually. "I shall not address your first questions—those of the death enchantments and the power of the stone. Those, I'm afraid, you must decipher for yourself. But there is still one thing of the highest importance that I have yet to mention. It would be quite impolite of me not to do so."

"And that is?" Faegan asked, leaning forward.

"That death itself is not the end, nor is it even the problem," Joshua answered cryptically. "That it is, truly, only the beginning. Something the master, in his infinite wisdom, will soon demonstrate to you."

With that, the consul smiled calmly. Then his eyes began to

roll up into his head. Reaching into his robes, he produced a long stiletto with a strange-looking, very tiny hook just visible at the end of the blade. Faegan's eyes widened in realization and he raised his right arm, but even for the master wizard there was not enough time.

Joshua inserted the strange blade deep into his right ear. As blood gushed out, he slammed it in even farther, then gave the blade a sudden, forceful pull. Tristan heard a moist, muffled crack.

The consul was dead before his face hit the bars of his cage.

After everyone's shock subsided and they verified that Joshua was truly dead, Tristan dragged the body outside the room to be disposed of later, then came back to the somber gathering.

"Why would the consuls revolt?" he asked. "I thought they were bound, heart and soul, to the Brotherhood and the exclusive practice of the Vigors. And how is it that they have somehow been able to circumvent the death enchantments?"

Wigg had been deeply affected by the news of the consul's betrayal, and tears ran blatantly down his cheeks. Celeste placed an affectionate hand over his, and the lead wizard closed his ancient fingers around it. He seemed unable to speak.

Faegan, however, having had no such long-term relationship with the Brotherhood, remained more pragmatic. "For the same reasons Joshua mentioned, although I believe I can name a few more," he said quietly. "First, the nation was destroyed by the Minions. The royal family, with the exception of the Chosen Ones, are dead. As is the entire Directorate, save for Wigg. So to whom do the consuls now owe their allegiance, eh? From their perspective, it is apparently up for grabs. For the first time in over three centuries, there is clearly a power vacuum in Eutracia. Second, Nicholas supposedly offers them far greater power than the Directorate would have ever dreamed of doing. This would be a very tempting proposition, especially in light of the fact that there is now no Directorate to punish them for their actions. They may even consider Wigg to be a traitor to the nation, just as the populace at large considers you, Tristan, to be the willing murderer of your father, the king. And then there is the most compelling reason of all." Faegan sat back in his chair, his face grave.

"And that is?" Celeste asked, her sapphire eyes alive with curiosity.

"The promise of the time enchantments, granting them eternal protection from both disease and old age, and the concurrent circumvention of the death enchantments, finally freeing them to do literally anything they choose," Faegan said glumly. "A very tempting package for those already partially trained, and still possessing an overriding curiosity about the craft. Wouldn't you agree?"

Again the wizard paused, measuring his words. "We must therefore assume, at least for the time being, that the Brotherhood of Consuls is now in revolt." Like the peals of a death knell, his words hung heavy and deep over the table.

"But Joshua has been exposed, and is dead," Tristan countered, trying to find a gleam of hope. "Surely that is a good thing."

"Yes," Wigg answered. "But we are not much better off than before. All we have gained is the fact that the Paragon will not decay so rapidly."

Shailiha leaned forward, placing her arms on the table. "Joshua talked about the 'Confluence.' What is that?"

"The Confluence is mentioned in the Preface to the Tome," Faegan explained, "and refers to the spell allowing the 'rebirth,' if you will, of those who have departed to the Afterlife. It is the concurrent gathering of usually disparate powers that will allow Nicholas to perform his version of the craft, thereby empowering the Gates and the blood of the Heretics locked within them."

"And what happens then?" Tristan asked.

"It is written in the Tome that the Gates shall literally split open the heavens, releasing the Guild of the Heretics from their bondage in the firmament. The spirits of the Heretics shall then appear, descending from the heavens to come flying through the Gates, passing by their reactivated blood. They will then bond with it, taking on their original, human forms."

"But if the Heretics can be released, then why are the Ones not released, as well?" Tristan asked.

"Because their blood is not in the marble of the Gates," Wigg answered. "And is therefore not a part of the Confluence."

Tristan looked around the table at the dark, defeated faces. Sighing sadly, he turned again to Faegan. "Tell me," he asked, "why are they called 'The Gates of Dawn'?"

"The Preface of the Tome states that the activation of the Gates is to take place precisely at dawn," Faegan answered. "That is the only answer that we have."

And with that, the room went silent.

CHAPTER FORTY-FIVE

*T*RISTAN stood in the middle of a snowy field some distance north of the royal palace, watching the many individual fires as they roared high into the evening sky. From their hot orange-and-red flames came a sickening odor that brought forth his memories of the destruction of Tammerland. It was the distinctive, unmistakable foulness of burning flesh.

The funeral pyres rose high into the sky, their many levels littered with the mangled and torn corpses of Minion warriors. Tristan had given permission for the pyres to be used, and as their lord he knew he needed to be present at the burnings, to pay his respects to the dead.

There had been many such nights already, and he knew there would be more. For although Faegan had been able to widen the portal, it had not functioned entirely as planned.

It had taken the ancient wizard many hours of study in the Archives to come up with a workable calculation for the enlargement of the vortex, but doing so had drained his mind terribly. Added to this was the fact that his powers were by now very much in decline.

Despite Joshua's death two weeks earlier, the Paragon was still being drained, albeit at a constant rate. The stone was now almost colorless, and Tristan could easily see that what they had so feared was surely near—a world without magic. Or rather, he reminded himself, a world in which all of the magic had been taken into only one person, intent upon using it to commit an unspeakable act.

Tristan had never seen the usually impish and powerful Faegan so drawn and exhausted, and the prince worried for him. But still the ancient one sat defiantly in his chair each day in the cold, snowy field, holding the portal open for as long as his powers would allow.

The portal had let thousands of Minion warriors through, but with Faegan's successes had also come problems.

Just as his powers now waxed and waned, so did the effectiveness of the vortex. This meant that many of the Minions trying to come through from the other side died horribly in the attempt.

Each time the vortex collapsed, some dead bodies, or what was left of them, made it through, while others did not, forever lost in the netherworld of the craft.

Blood lay everywhere upon the snowy field. The screaming and wailing that could be heard coming from inside the whirling maelstrom was terrifying—despite the fact that these warriors were Minions, and the bravest fighters Tristan had ever seen. Sadly, the prince estimated they were losing about one of every six. Their already bad odds against Nicholas' hatchlings were growing worse by the moment.

What's more, Tristan was worried about the wizards. It wasn't just the continual loss of their powers that bothered him. They had become unusually secretive and quiet. Whenever Faegan was not operating his portal, he and Wigg shut themselves off behind closed doors. Even Shailiha seemed to be more withdrawn.

Tristan gazed along either side of the banks lining the Sippora River. From his position on higher ground, he could easily see the thousands of red Minion war tents that had sprung up. Torches twinkled gracefully within the gigantic encampment, the campfires before most of the temporary dwellings causing the surrounding, melting snow to gently give up the colors of the rainbow. In the firelight Tristan could make out hundreds of pairs of wings as the warriors landed and took off, the patrols ordered by Traax continually checking for any signs to the north that the enemy was on the move. The entire scene somehow seemed peaceful and idyllic, convincingly belying the true reasons for its existence.

The warriors were eager for the battle to be joined, and yet they waited, as more of the winged fighters poured through the vortex every day. At Traax's suggestion the prince had billeted the officers in the empty palace. It had at first unnerved Tristan to see them walking briskly through the halls, setting up their quarters in the various rooms as if they owned them. These were some of the same warriors who had killed both his family and the Directorate of Wizards. And now, impossibly, they were here once more, this time occupying the palace to protect it, rather than destroy it.

Traax, Wigg, Faegan, and Ox waited with Tristan, watching the corpses burn. Traax had come to Eutracia, luckily without harm, on the fifth day, just as Tristan had ordered him. The Minion turned to his lord.

"Why do these hatchlings and scarabs not attack us now?" he asked Tristan. "Their hesitation makes no sense. Every day we grow stronger. Surely they must know that. Even more effective would have been a powerful, continuous attack upon us just as we started to exit the portal, only ten Minions at a time. Given enough opposing forces, even we could have been picked off in this way. So why do they wait?"

"There are several answers to your question," Wigg replied, raising the usual eyebrow. "First and foremost, the Gates of Dawn are clearly Nicholas' first priority, and he wishes them to remain protected by his servants until just before he activates them. Then, and only then, will he send his creatures against us. Second, he knows we shall be heavily outnumbered, and feels victory is already in his grasp. Sadly, in this he is probably also right."

Wigg paused for a moment, uncomfortable with telling the Minion second in command so much. But Tristan had told Traax everything the previous night. Considering the fact they would probably die in battle together, the prince had decided there should be no secrets between them.

"And lastly," he continued, "is the fact that as each day goes by Tristan becomes more ill. In Nicholas' twisted world, that means the longer he waits, the better the odds are of Tristan joining him in this madness. In his own way, he is still protecting the Chosen One. But that will end when the Gates are finished and he finally realizes that his father has refused him. Then he will launch his attack, for at that point he will have little to lose."

"There will probably be only one battle," Faegan interjected, the look on his face both exhausted and grave. "Given the way we are outnumbered, they will do their best to finish us off in a single, powerful stroke, and be done with it." He turned to Tristan and Traax to see that each of their faces had become hard in the flickering light of the pyres.

"You must do your best to keep them at bay," he continued. "Even though, in the end, it probably won't matter. But you must give us all the time you can. Even with Joshua's death the Paragon continues to decay, and our powers will soon be gone. You must remember that this means the time enchantments protecting Wigg, myself, and Celeste will most certainly vanish, and we will quite literally fall into piles of dust, to be blown away on the winds of the Season of Crystal. If and when that happens, your fighting force will become the only remaining chance of stopping the Guild of the Heretics from returning to the world of the living and employing the Vagaries to rule forever."

Tristan looked down to his right hip, to the new, bizarre-looking weapon he now carried there—the device with which Joshua had killed himself. Curious of all things martial, Tristan had carefully removed it from the dead consul's ear, examined it closely, and then wiped it clean, asking the wizards if he might keep it. They had quietly agreed.

The weapon was appropriately called a brain hook, and although the prince had never heard of one before, it apparently had quite a long history with the wizards, having been standard issue for them during the Sorceresses' War, when the Coven was becoming increasingly fond of taking wizards captive to turn them into blood stalkers. This small and easily hidden weapon could be deadly at close quarters, but it had originally been intended as an instrument of swift suicide.

Tristan had decided long ago that he would not suffer through the entirety of his fourth, final convulsion. He had no way of conjuring a trance to numb the pain and slow the onset of shock as Faegan had explained Joshua had done—as indicated by the rolling back of the consul's eyes into their sockets—but when the time came, he was determined to use the brain hook as best he could, ending his life cleanly. He looked down at the simple weapon tucked beneath his belt. He took his eyes away from the brain hook and again regarded the flames of the funeral pyres.

Traax took a step forward, anger and frustration clearly showing upon his face. "For a Minion warrior to die in battle is expected, even welcomed," he said through clenched teeth, his eyes locked upon the pyres. "It is the very reason for which we are born. But to die like this, defenseless . . . Such a thing simply should not be."

Many such things should not exist right now, my friend, Tristan thought.

But they do.

PART V

The Vanquished

CHAPTER FORTY-SIX

And the male seed of the Chosen One, upon empowering the Gates of Dawn, shall release a terrible burden upon the world. And those of the blue robes, once thought to be loyal, shall turn against their masters, and attempt to employ the craft for their own service. For it is also written that the powers of the craft, once tasted by the endowed but then forbidden to be savored to their utmost, shall themselves go on to cause the greatest of unsatisfied hungers ever known. And with it, one of the most frightful of all tests the Chosen Ones shall ever undergo.

—PAGE 3,007, CHAPTER II OF THE VAGARIES OF THE TOME

IT is not only for our personal safety that we ask this thing, Princess," Wigg said solemnly. His face was a mask of concern. "It is also for the safety of the Paragon and the Tome, and those who live here in the Redoubt. But most importantly, it is imperative that you, the female of the Chosen Ones, continue to survive. Should Tristan perish, your existence becomes more important than the survival and welfare of anyone else—including Faegan and myself. I realize you don't want to hear this, but it now seems virtually certain we shall lose the prince, either to the impending battle, or to the poison running through his veins."

Wigg knew his words were hurting Shailiha terribly, but if the strong-willed young woman would accept them from anyone, it would be from him.

Shailiha, rocking a fussy Morganna in her sling, had spent the last two hours in the Archives of the Redoubt, listening to what Wigg and Faegan had to say. Their words had stunned her at first, making her angry.

Above all, they went on to tell her, it was paramount that the prince not be privy to this meeting. Even Celeste, Wigg's daughter, was not to be a party to what was discussed here on this so very important of days. For the immediate future, only the three of them in this room were to know what the wizards were trying to convince the princess to do.

Abandon her brother. The brother she loved more than her life, the same man who had risked his life time and time again to return her from the grasp of the Coven.

She simply could not believe her ears.

Wigg and Faegan had reiterated to her how truly desperate their situation was, hoping that she would eventually come to her senses and agree with them. Their powers of the craft were almost gone. Even worse, the Gates of Dawn would by now probably be completed. There seemed to be no way to keep Nicholas from bringing forth the Heretics from the Afterlife.

They had to act now. While Tristan led the Minions to battle, a battle in which he would most probably die, the rest of those living in the Redoubt should leave this place. The wizards insisted on putting as much distance between them and Nicholas' hatchlings and carrion scarabs as they could. The sooner the better, they said. In fact they wished to leave tomorrow.

Again and again she protested, telling them that they were all stronger together than they were apart. That they should all make a last stand here, in their home city of Tammerland, no matter the outcome. What had come over these two mystics that would make them want to turn and run away?

And then her patience finally turned to anger. Anger at the entire world for bringing these awful events upon them, and anger at the wizards for what she saw as their cowardice. She didn't want to run—she wanted to stand next to her brother and fight back. She looked up at them both. Her hazel eyes were resolute and defiant.

"I will not go with you," she said, her jaw clenched. "Even if it means my death, and the death of my daughter. You may run away if you want, to protect your precious art of the craft. And take with you your famous magic stone and your unreadable sacred book, for all I care! For me, all that matters is the fact that Tristan is my brother, and our blood bonds us in a way that even the two of you shall never fully understand. Just as he was willing to go to the far corners of the earth for me, I will now stay with him until the end. And if that means dying by his side, then so be it." She clamped her mouth shut.

Sitting back in his chair, Wigg let out a great sigh. "I told you she would never agree," he said drily in the direction of Faegan. "She and her brother were truly cut from the same cloth." The first smile she had seen from him all afternoon finally crept into the corners of his mouth. "So much like their mother," he added softly.

"So it would seem," Faegan replied.

Reluctantly, Faegan reached into his robes, producing a parchment. He rolled it out flat on the table as Shailiha skeptically watched.

And then he began to talk to her in quiet, measured tones, trying to make her understand. It was to become perhaps the single most important conversation of the princess' life.

CHAPTER FORTY-SEVEN

❧

T RISTAN stood on the balcony of one of the great rooms of the palace, Traax and Ox on either side of him. Light, fluffy snow was falling gently through the slowly brightening sky; he hoped the weather would warm as the sun rose. Pulling his gray fur jacket closer to him, he stared down intently at the war maps that covered the marble conference table before him. He had been studying them most of the night, trying to discern the best strategic point at which to attack Nicholas' hatchlings. He knew that his first, highly concentrated assault would have to be as devastating as possible.

For as outnumbered as he and his warriors were, they would most likely be denied the opportunity of a second one.

He reached out to bite down into one of the rich, brown rolls he had requested from the gnome wives, following it with their strong tea. The comforting warmth felt good going down. One corner of his mouth came up as he remembered Shawna the Short berating him for remaining out in the cold when he could have just as easily been inside. "You'll catch your death," she had said, one of her small fingers waggling before his face. He had simply smiled, knowing that standing here on the snowy balcony was surely not what was about to kill him.

Remembering a technique from his days at the Royal War College, Tristan had remained here to try to become more accustomed to the frigid temperatures. He would need every advantage possible if he was to lead the Minions in the manner to which they were accustomed.

Taking his eyes away from the maps for a moment, he looked out over the balcony and to the amazing scene outside. In the last two weeks it seemed the entire world had come strangely alive with the winged warriors he had once so hated.

Their campsites now stretched almost as far as the eye could see. Yesterday the wizards had sadly informed him that there would be no more Minions arriving from Parthalon. Due to his vastly decreased powers, Faegan could no longer hold the portal open. The truth, Tristan realized, was that the wily wizard was trying to preserve his remaining powers to help those still living below escape. And with this the prince had no argument. Tristan rubbed his sore, severely weakened right arm. *Each of our warriors must kill two of the enemy, simply to survive the struggle,* he realized. *And to win, many of them must kill three. Long odds against our survival, indeed.*

It was his plan to attack the following day. Unless, of course, the hatchlings appeared earlier, forcing him into action. But in his heart, Tristan knew there was another, even more compelling reason that was keeping his son from unleashing his creatures against them.

Nicholas was waiting, still hoping that Tristan would join him in his struggle to return the Heretics to the earth.

For the thousandth time he attempted to fathom how things could have ever come this far. Both his family and the Directorate of Wizards were now many months dead, and he, impossibly, was the new lord of the ones responsible for their murders. The land he so loved had been made virtually barren of the craft of magic; the only remaining wizards willing to help him had become mere shadows of their former selves. And all of them here, at one time deadly enemies but now wary allies, were struggling to defeat a son he had believed to be dead.

"Chosen One all right?" Ox asked. He looked concernedly into the prince's face.

Tristan smiled slightly. "Yes, Ox," he answered. He and the two Minions had spent most of the night talking about their battle plans. Hearing footsteps in the adjoining room, Tristan turned. Wigg and Faegan were making their slow way out to the balcony, Wigg holding weakly onto Faegan's chair for guidance.

As he looked at them, Tristan felt a great measure of sadness. The once-vibrant, powerful wizards appeared much older now. Their faces were sallow, and their bodies seemed sunken, almost hidden beneath their robes.

Tristan, Traax, and Ox spent a good deal of time showing the wizards their plans. Wigg and Faegan listened intently. On more than one occasion the two wizards gave them advice resulting in a few minor changes in geography and tactics. But overall the wizards agreed with the strategies.

At last Faegan cleared his throat, something else apparently on his mind. "If you would be so good as to leave us," he said to Traax and Ox, "we have private business with the prince. It shall not take long."

The Minion warriors looked to Tristan. When he nodded, they each went to one knee. "We live to serve," their strong voices said in unison. Then they flew off the balcony and were gone.

Tristan beckoned the ancient wizards into the adjoining room and closed the cracked, stained-glass doors to the outside. After guiding Wigg to a dusty chair, he took one himself.

"We have made a decision," Wigg began softly. "One that we are hoping you can agree with. But agree or not, we still feel it must be done."

"I will make it easy for you, old friend," Tristan answered before the wizard could continue. He leaned forward in his chair, placing his arms upon his knees. "You are going to flee the palace, and take everyone, including Shailiha, with you."

"Yes," Faegan said. "How did you know?"

"Your usefulness here is now very limited," Tristan answered. "And I have long believed that you would eventually want to get the Paragon, the Tome, and my sister as far away from the danger as possible." He looked down at his hands for a moment, trying to find the words. "Given the fact that my death is certain, your first concern, and rightfully so, must be the preservation of the craft." He looked back up to the wizards. "But if there are additional reasons for your leaving," he added, a hard edge to his voice, "I would like to know what they are."

Tristan did not mean to be harsh with them, but he had long been of the opinion that they were not telling him everything. And if they were indeed holding anything back, he was determined to find out what it was, and why.

"Our reasons are exactly as you have just described, and no more," Faegan replied. He coughed—a small, ragged sound—and pulled his gray robe closer about him. "First and foremost is the preservation of magic, if such a thing is still possible. To help protect us, we request that you grant us litters, and a host of Minions to carry them."

Tristan thought for a moment. "It's a pity the portal has become so unstable. You would no doubt be safer in Parthalon." He remained silent for a moment. "You just mentioned my fate," he finally said, looking down at the ominous veins running through the back of his hand. "There will be no antidote, will there?" Already knowing the answer, he did not immediately look back up.

"No," Faegan answered sadly. "I am truly sorry." He looked away, one of the few times in his long life he was completely unsure of what to say.

Wigg lowered his head and rubbed his white eyes, then leaned his forehead on his fist in obvious despair. "And ironically, I will actually be glad to have lost my sight," he said softly. "The death of the Paragon is not something I wish to watch."

Tristan sat back in his chair and regarded his friends—the once-imposing practitioners of the craft. They had changed so much it almost seemed as if he no longer knew them. "You will go to Shadowood, will you not?" he asked quietly.

"Yes," Wigg answered. "We will flee to Tree-Town. That makes the most sense." He looked into Tristan's dark eyes, not knowing how to say farewell to the one he had loved for so long.

"We have also come to say our good-byes." Wigg continued haltingly, "for we think it prudent that we leave as soon as possible. In fact, the Tome is already transformed, and ready to go. Shailiha and Celeste have asked to see you next, so that they might say good-bye in private. We all know you will do your best to keep Nicholas and his creatures at bay for as long as you can. You are the last hope Eutracia has. Fare thee well, Chosen One. Please know, for as long as you have left, that you shall forever remain in my heart."

Wigg raised his arms, beckoning the prince to come to him.

Tristan rose from his chair, tears in his eyes. But with his very first step toward the wizard came the horrifying, sinking feeling.

He fell to the floor, tremors jangling his body like a marionette. Spittle foamed from his mouth as his tongue slipped down the back of his throat.

Then everything went black.

CHAPTER FORTY-EIGHT

NICHOLAS, his white robe billowing gracefully around him, sailed effortlessly above the Gates of Dawn, reveling in their beauty. The magnificent archways had been finished the evening before. As he gazed upon their soaring majesty, he knew he was close, so close now, to bringing home his parents of above. But still his other father, the father who had supplied the seed of his making, had not come to him.

But he would, Nicholas knew, if he desired to live.

Joyously, the voices of the Heretics had revealed themselves to his mind again, just as dawn had crept over the hills. *You have done well,* they whispered. *The Gates of Dawn are perfect. You have also collected into yourself almost all of the dynamism of the stone, thereby rendering the Chosen One's wizards nearly powerless. But you must wait two more days before our coming, for he of the azure blood may still bow to you. This he must do freely. We must either have him come willingly to our bosom or see him dead. If he does not come to worship you, it shall be time to destroy all that he holds so dear, before we descend to rule again.*

After that the morning had broken cold and clear. The fresh snow below him was pure and unadulterated, just as he knew the Gates were. Rising two hundred meters into the air and curved at their tops, they had finally taken the form of three great archways. The azure veins running through them glimmered with the promise of an ascendancy that had not been seen for eons.

Satisfied, he looked above him to see that his second-generation hatchlings were still guarding the sky over the Gates. And looking down, he was equally pleased to see that his other powerful creatures of the Vagaries—the carrion scarabs—were arriving to guard the ground around the bases of the Gates, marching across the snow in an undulating, teeming mass of life. Covering the area surrounding the Gates for hundreds of meters in every direction, their greatly magnified numbers fanned out like an encroaching stain upon the ground.

Hovering closer to the Gates, the young adept laid his brow on the coolness of the stone, then caressed it with his cheek as if in the grip of some ravenous, sexual need. The marble seemed to welcome his touch, as if the blood of the Heretics trapped within could already sense the power he possessed. With the final construction of the Gates the three majestic arches literally called to him, silently begging him to perform the spell this very morn. Groaning softly but knowing he must wait, he finally spoke.

"Parents," he whispered. "It is now to me that the most difficult part of the burden falls—the agony of waiting to enact the Confluence. I must desist for two more dawns. In your infinite wisdom you never taught me that the call would be so wondrously irresistible. But wait I shall, for you order it." Nicholas continued to hover there, lovingly pressing his face against the coolness of the marble.

"It is to you I owe my allegiance and no one else, including the untrained one of azure blood who did nothing but unwillingly create me. Obey you I shall. In two more days, the Confluence shall be yours."

He finally pulled himself away and soared off to the embankment where the blood stalker was waiting.

Standing in rows behind Ragnar stood the hundreds of consuls who had initially resisted the young adept, before his greater powers came to control their consciousnesses. Mindless, staring out at nothing in their dirty, torn robes, they waited silently for his word.

"The Gates are completed, my lord?" Ragnar asked. He pulled his fur coat closer, then sampled some of the fluid from his ever-present vial.

"Yes," Nicholas answered softly. "All that remains is for the Chosen One to come to his senses, and join me. If he has not prostrated himself before me by tomorrow's dawn, I will send my hatchlings to destroy his Minions. The following morn I shall enact the Gates."

"And the rest of the consuls?" Ragnar asked hesitantly. "Those who joined us willingly—are they safe?"

"Again, yes," Nicholas answered. "They are some distance from here, waiting for the return of the Heretics. I have also used the Forestallment necessary to test the quality of their hearts, just as my parents of above ordered me to do. They are mine, body and soul. You need neither fear them, nor fear for them."

Nicholas glided behind the stalker to face the ones in the dark blue robes.

At the adept's signal, Scrounge called a squadron of hatchlings down.

"Take them," Nicholas said simply.

Nodding, Scrounge signaled for the hatchlings to begin the slaughter.

The great birds swooped down with their swords drawn and sliced the helpless consuls from neck to groin. The endowed blood of the Brotherhood poured out everywhere upon the white, snow-laden ground. Every remaining member of the Brotherhood of Consuls who had tried to remain true to the practices of the Directorate and the preservation of the Vigors fell dead.

Scrounge smiled, wheeling his bird around to face the young adept. "As you have ordered, Master," he said.

Nicholas nodded once more.

Scrounge then ordered the hatchlings to rip away the dead consuls' robes and organs. Once done, they flew the corpses toward the newly constructed Gates of Dawn, where they dropped them directly into the midst of the carrion scarabs.

The females immediately began to crawl up and over the corpses and deposit their eggs into the still-warm body cavities. The males stood guard nearby, their antennae sensing the air, their tiny, black eyes missing nothing.

Scrounge flew his bird back to his master's side, awaiting his next orders.

"Well done," Nicholas said softly. "You are to return to Fledgling House, to rest. Do not leave there for the remainder of the day, or the coming night. Tomorrow you lead the hatchlings against the Chosen One and his Minions. I will discuss my battle plans with you this evening."

"Yes, my lord," Scrounge answered. He nodded his leave, then wheeled his bird around and took flight for Fledgling House.

Nicholas turned his dark, exotic eyes upon the stalker. "Joshua is dead," he said simply.

Ragnar stood in the cold morning sun, wide-eyed for a moment, his mind trying to digest the news. "How?" he finally asked.

"No doubt by way of the rather crude weapon you so kindly supplied him with," Nicholas answered. "My blood felt the shudder of his passing into the Afterlife the very moment it occurred."

"But how did the Chosen One's wizards discover him?" Ragnar asked, nervously tasting yet more of the thick, yellow fluid.

"Never forget that Wigg and Faegan are exceedingly clever," Nicholas answered. "I do not yet know how they discovered

Joshua's true intentions, but it is of no consequence. Nothing can stop us now. And as for you, my friend, at last your day has come."

Thinking of his next mission, of perhaps finally reclaiming Celeste, Ragnar could hardly contain himself. "Where is it in your service you are sending me this time?"

Nicholas took a deep breath and narrowed his eyes. "To the Afterlife."

Ragnar stumbled backward, almost falling. The vial of brain fluid spilled onto the ground, hissing as it burrowed into the melting snow.

"But why?" he whispered, his voice cracking with fear. "You said as a reward for my loyalty I was to serve you always, even with the coming of the Heretics!" His breathing was heavily labored; his knees had begun to shake.

Nicholas smiled slightly as a sudden gust of wind blew through his long, dark hair. "The answer is simple, stalker," he whispered. "I lied."

"But why?" Ragnar repeated even more desperately.

"Your blood is tainted by your own brain fluid, don't you see?" Nicholas answered, gliding closer. "This makes you clearly inferior, and unworthy of life in what shall soon be our fearless, uncompromising new world. The wizard Wigg has finally succeeded, however obliquely, in releasing you from your torment after all." The young adept shook his head, contemplating the unique, centuries-old maze that lay before him.

"Ragnar," he said softly. "Once a respected wizard—one who would have surely become a member of the Directorate. Partially turned to a stalker by the same woman who was once Wigg's wife, you went on to become addicted to your own fluids due solely to Wigg's actions. The onetime wife of Wigg, now controlling you, left their child with you for safekeeping. Later, believing the mother to be banished forever, you abused the sorceress' progeny for centuries in order not only to satisfy your sick desires, but also to take silent revenge on the wizard who had been the sorceress' husband. And then you finally die at the hands of the one left behind in Parthalon by the Chosen One himself—an act made possible due to the ministrations of Failee, that same sorceress."

Nicholas paused for a moment, his dark gaze boring its way into the back of the stalker's brain. "It seems that Failee, by way of the Chosen One's seed, is about to take her revenge upon you after all," he added quietly. "How fitting, wouldn't you agree? The circle is about to become complete."

As the stalker's desperate breathing ignited the cold air into puffs of vapor, a trail of urine emptied from his body, running down the inside of one of his legs to join with the odorous brain fluid already on the ground. The two vile substances of similar color snaked their way down the embankment, melting the snow before them.

"But Scrounge!" Ragnar countered. "He will surely know that you have killed me, and will perhaps even refuse to follow you!"

"How will he possibly know?" Nicholas answered, gliding closer. "I have sent him into seclusion at Fledgling House, ordering him not to depart until he leads the hatchlings against the Chosen One on the morrow's dawn. And by the time he notices your prolonged absence, he too shall be dead. Even the hatchlings and the carrion scarabs shall be disposed of after they have rid the world of everyone but myself, my parents of above, and the consuls who have chosen to serve us." Nicholas leveled his eyes at the stalker, sending another shiver of terror through him.

"So you see," the adept finished quietly. "None of my servants were ever meant to live, much less serve me for eternity."

Without further discussion Nicholas pointed a slender, white finger toward the stalker. Almost immediately Ragnar's robes, jacket, and boots began to rip apart. Wigg's ceremonial dagger fell to the ground with the tatters of clothing. Ragnar stood naked and exposed in the snow.

A thin, scarlet line appeared down the entire length of his torso, from his larynx to his exposed groin. It quickly became a ribbon of bright red blood.

With a wet ripping sound, the stalker's abdomen and breastbone split wide open, exposing the still-living organs within. As his endowed blood rushed out, his organs were pulled from his body, collecting into a hideous pile of offal in the snow just before him.

Stunned, Ragnar looked for the last time into the eyes of Nicholas. He then fell forward, dead.

With a twist of his outstretched hand, Nicholas sent the steaming organs and dead body directly into the midst of the carrion scarabs. The shiny black beetles immediately clambered over them, rendering the stalker's body virtually indistinguishable from the other corpses lying there. The females started to burrow their way into the freshly steaming body cavity to lay yet more of their eggs, while others of their kind began to feed on the bloody viscera.

Smiling, the adept took flight toward Fledgling House.

CHAPTER FORTY-NINE

THROBBING wracked Tristan's every limb and joint. He tried to raise himself up, but strong hands eased him firmly back down into the luxurious depths of a bed. He could see little, his vision blurry and off-center. Unable to fight his way out of the gloom, he allowed the blackness to overcome him again.

Pain still greeted him when he finally came around again, but his vision was better. Looking up, he saw the faces of Traax, Shailiha, and Celeste. Each of them smiled hesitantly down at him.

"You were gone a long time," Shailiha said, her voice cracking. "Almost twelve hours. We thought that we might have lost you for good this time." A tear crowded its way into her right eye, and she brushed it from her cheek.

He tried painfully to sit up, but his right arm wouldn't move.

Shailiha turned her eyes away, then forced them back to him. "The veins have blackened up the length of your neck, little brother, and they cover your arm and hand."

"I'm sorry," Tristan said quietly. "There was no need for you to see this."

Traax took a step closer to the bed, his dark green eyes looking intently down at his stricken master. "Forgive me, my lord," he asked. "But now that you are conscious, there is a question I must ask you. The wizards claim you promised them litters, and a host of warriors to do their bidding. I wished to confirm these facts with you before granting their requests."

Tristan smiled weakly. "Give them whatever they desire," he said softly. "And any other aid they may need. I shall join you later." He paused. "But first tell me, given the fact that you have now seen the effects of my illness, do you still accept me as your lord?" He held his breath for a moment, wondering if he had done the right thing. Above all, he must continue to command the loyalty and respect of the warrior standing before him.

Traax's answer was both immediate and unequivocal. "I continue to serve you, and only you," he said. "And as for your illness, it only makes me want to destroy the ones responsible for inflicting it upon you even more." His hand tightened on his dreggan. "But I must also tell you that I am very glad the entire body of warriors did not see this. In truth, I cannot be sure how they would have reacted." And then an unexpected smile spread across his face. "I shall now go to the wizards. They stand just outside the castle entrance, bickering at each other. Get well quickly, my lord, for we have some well-deserved killing to do." Clicking his heels together, he turned and walked from the room, leaving Tristan alone with the women.

Tristan couldn't remember ever having been so tired in his life. "Where is Ox?" he asked his sister.

"Just outside your door," Shailiha answered. "I know of nothing in this world that could move him from his post."

Then Celeste leaned over the bed, placing an affectionate hand on one of his cheeks. As she did so, her dark red hair fell down over one shoulder. He could smell the myrrh in it, just as he had that first night when he had saved her from diving off the cliff.

"I shall leave the two of you alone," Shailiha said quietly. "When Celeste is done saying good-bye, I will return." With that his twin sister quietly left the room, closing the door behind her.

Celeste picked up Tristan's stricken right hand, holding it gently.

"I want to thank you," she said, her voice dark and husky. She reached out with her free hand and smoothed back the usual, dark comma of hair from his forehead.

"For what?" he asked.

She smiled. "For saving my life, thereby making it possible for me to find my new one. Despite the fact that we may never see each other again, I shall never forget what you did for me."

Tristan looked into her eyes and held her gaze. "If that is true, then promise me something," he said.

"Anything."

"If you should somehow survive all of this, and you truly value your new life as you say you do, then make sure you deserve it."

"What do you mean?" she asked in surprise.

"My life was once golden, with no worries or cares," he said. "I foolishly took it all for granted, and for a very long time. I lost almost all of my family and friends before realizing how precious they were. Your father tells us that your blood is inferior only to Shailiha's, and Shailiha's only to my own. Therefore, should I die, your blood shall become the second most powerful in the world. I can see that you have your father's strength and courage. You must, to have survived all that you did. Listen to your father, and learn the craft well. Be one of the strongest of people ever to master it, for I know in my heart you will be able. But follow the teachings of Wigg and Faegan only, and do so strictly for the sake of the Vigors, keeping the ethics they deem so important alive for future generations of the endowed—generations that I shall never see."

His eyes lingered on the graceful curves of her face. "There is something else I wish to tell you."

Celeste placed her fingertips on his lips. "I know," she said. "I may be new to your world, but I still see much, including the way you look at me." She closed her eyes, choking back a sigh before opening them again. "But for now, I must leave."

With that she touched her lips gently to his and then stood. Removing a scented handkerchief from the bodice of her gown, she placed it on his lap, then walked to the door. For a moment, she paused, her head lowered. And then, without turning back, she left.

Several moments later Shailiha reentered the room. She sat on the edge of his bed and smiled bravely. "It is now my turn to say good-bye," she whispered. Her voice seemed very small. "And there is so little time. The Minions have already granted the wizards' wishes, and everyone awaits me." She looked down at Morganna in her sling. "I hope you can watch your niece grow up."

Resolutely, then, she grasped the gold medallion hanging around her neck, the exact duplicate of his, and looked directly into his eyes. "I shall always wear mine, no matter what," she said softly. "You came to the ends of the earth to find me, and if I must, I will one day do the same for you."

"I know," he whispered. There was so much more he wished to say, so much more he knew he would later greatly regret not saying. But just now, the words wouldn't come. He opened his mouth to speak, but then closed it again.

Shailiha closed her eyes, nodding gently.

And then she took a deep breath and stood up. Looking seriously into his face, she said, "Trust the process, Chosen One."

Tristan's brows drew down in confusion. "W-what?" he asked.

"Trust the process, Chosen One," she repeated. With that, she kissed him on the forehead and turned to the door. Before he could speak to her again, she too was gone.

Tristan lay back in the bed, exhausted, wondering what she had meant. But he was asleep before any answer came.

*A*s Shailiha stepped up into one of the several Minion litters, Martha smiled at her.

Wigg turned his head anxiously in the direction of the princess. "Did you tell him? Are you sure he heard you clearly?"

"Yes," Shailiha answered, holding her baby close. "He did." Tears came again, and she closed her eyes.

"Then tomorrow we shall know," Wigg answered.

Gently rising into the sky, closely accompanied by the several thousand Minion warriors sworn to protect them, the litters turned north, toward Shadowood.

CHAPTER FIFTY

WHEN Tristan finally awakened again, it was to find Ox looking down at him.

"It almost dawn," the Minion said. "Chosen One all right?"

His head still swimming, Tristan got out of bed, testing his abilities. He hurt everywhere, especially in his right arm and shoulder. He found that he could move it, though it remained stiff. He shook his head.

"I'm able to fight." His grin to Ox was stark and determined. He dressed as quickly as he could, then placed the dreggan and scabbard over his back against the gray fur jacket Shailiha had given him, and donned the leather quiver that held his dirks, adjusting it so that the handles of the weapons would not interfere with one another. He reached back to check that none of the weapons would stick, though the movement caused his shoulder to burn in agony.

And then he saw the brain hook.

He picked it up from the night table and turned it this way and that. Its pearl handle and the hook at the end of the blade gleamed quietly in the light of the chandeliers. For a moment he smiled, wondering how many secrets it held, and how many more it would yet participate in. Finally he concealed it within his right knee boot. Then, remembering another item he would like to have, he retrieved the handkerchief Celeste had given him and tucked it into a pocket.

Another table was laden with food and drink: tea, long

since cold; dark bread; and cheese. The first few bites reminded him how long it had been since he'd had nourishment, and he ate and drank greedily. Finally feeling more refreshed, he squared his shoulders and walked to the door with Ox at his side.

As they neared the field to the north Tristan slowed, amazed at the sight before them.

All of the Minion warriors, some eighty thousand strong, were standing in the cold, white snow, awaiting his orders. The sun was just coming up, and its orange and golden rays illuminated the warriors one seemingly endless row at a time. When he saw what some of those in the forward areas were holding, it took his breath away.

At Traax's sharp order, battle drums began to sound. Fifty of the warriors walked forward, each holding a long pole. At the end of each pole was a blue-and-gold battle flag carrying the heraldry of his family, the House of Galland.

The gold field of each flag had superimposed upon it a blue Eutracian broadsword and a roaring lion. The sight strengthened Tristan's heart.

For the first time since he had seen them violently crashing through the roof of the palace on his ill-fated coronation day, he felt genuinely pleased to have the savage, winged warriors in his presence.

As Tristan watched, they all went to one knee in the snow, lowering their heads in submission. With a single, unified voice, they shouted, "I live to serve!" Several moments passed as Tristan looked down at them, the snow lightly falling on their bodies and wings.

"You may rise," he said, finally finding his voice.

Traax approached him, smiling. "We didn't think you would mind, my lord," he said. "We asked the wizards where we might find these, and they gladly obliged us. We march for you, and you alone. Under your banner—the banner that is now also ours."

"Thank you, Traax," Tristan answered softly. "And I don't mind. I don't mind at all."

Just as the prince was about to address the warriors again, some of them began looking upward, pointing to the brightening sky. Tristan, Traax, and Ox raised their eyes to behold what was taking shape above them.

Writing.

Spellbound, Tristan watched as a single hatchling with a rider, high over the royal palace, somehow began tracing words into the sky. With every turn the bird made, a flowing line followed gracefully behind it, leaving azure letters. Slowly, the letters began to spell out words. As he watched the twisted, sick poem continue to form, Tristan's hands balled up into fists. The rider must be Scrounge, but he knew that the power would be coming from Nicholas. Finally the verse was complete:

> *Come up, Chosen One,*
> *In the clouds we shall meet.*
> *For when the fight is finally over,*
> *And the carnage is complete,*
> *I know I shall have found your death*
> *To be marvelously, sinfully sweet.*
>   *S.*

Traax turned to Tristan and saw the look of hate in the prince's eyes. "This one called Scrounge waits for you," he said quietly. "And it is now time for you to go to him."

Tristan took his gaze from the sky just as Scrounge and his mount began to soar away to the northeast. "Yes," he answered, his eyes dark. "There is much between him and me that needs to be put right. But first I will address the warriors."

Looking to the thousands of winged ones before him, he thought for a moment. Many, if not all of them, were about to die in his service. He wanted to make sure as best he could that his address would count for something.

"Warriors! Minions of Day and Night!" he shouted. "When you first came to my land, you came as attackers. This time you come as defenders of Eutracia. I am honored by your presence here today, for you are the most skilled warriors I have ever seen. Follow my instructions and those of your officers to the letter, and you may survive. If I should fall in battle, know that for as long as the struggle reigns, you are to take your orders from Traax. But following the conflict, no matter how it ends, you are to seek out the wizards Wigg and Faegan and submit to them as your new lords. Do you understand me?"

Again came the thunderous chorus. "I live to serve!"

Tristan reached painfully behind him and drew his dreggan. The deadly, familiar ring of the blade leaving its scabbard reverberated a long time in the cool, dry air before finally fading away.

"I also charge each of you with something else this day," Tristan shouted. "It is no secret that we are greatly outnumbered. But if each of you kills at least three of the enemy, we shall win!"

With that thousands of dreggans came out of their scabbards, their blades ringing through the cold air amid eager cheering.

Tristan looked at the warriors for a time, and then over to both Traax and Ox. They were smiling broadly. "Remember our battle plan," he said. "And may the Afterlife have mercy upon us this day."

Saying nothing more, he replaced his dreggan into its scabbard and checked his knives. His hatchling was waiting nearby, and Tristan climbed into its saddle and strapped himself in. He wheeled the bird around to face his warriors a final time. And then a thought came to him.

He reached into a pocket and produced the scented handkerchief that Celeste had given him. As the myrrh hidden there came back to him for what would almost certainly be the final time, he smiled fatalistically and tied it around his left arm. Then he launched his bird into the sky.

The thousands of warriors took flight to follow him, their huge numbers blotting out the rising sun. As one, they turned north, to what would soon become the killing fields of Farplain.

CHAPTER FIFTY-ONE

$\mathcal{A}$s they soared through the sky, Shailiha clutched Morganna with one hand. Her other hand gripped one of the rough-hewn handles fastened to the inside of the litter. She had never traveled in this fashion before, and was already quite sure she never wished to do so again. She was terrified that either she would fall out, or the warriors would eventually drop them from sheer exhaustion. Neither, to her complete amazement, had yet happened.

Wigg, Shailiha, and Martha were in one litter. Faegan, the Tome, the Paragon, and Celeste were in another, while Geldon and the gnomes rode in the third. Faegan's fliers of the fields flew alongside. Several empty litters were also being carried along.

Faegan, still in his chair on wheels, would occasionally pop his head out, shouting the necessary course corrections to the warriors as they sped along. Wigg, on the other hand, seemed very self-absorbed, his mind lost in wizardly contemplations.

To distract herself from her fear, Shailiha tried to remember what Wigg had told her of their destination, Shadowood, which was inhabited by gnomes and had served as Faegan's home since his crippling by the Coven three hundred years ago. It had been created by the Directorate, using the craft, and had been intended as a refuge for those of endowed blood, should the Coven have won the war. Now it was about to serve the same purpose should the hatchlings burst through Tristan's lines.

They were exceedingly fortunate to have the Minions and litters, Wigg had said, since the normal trip to Shadowood on foot was very difficult and time-consuming. The secret place was surrounded on all sides by a deep, invisible canyon that only the trained endowed could see. To others all that could be seen was an expansive field of grass lying before a great pine forest, and if they came too close, they would fall into the canyon and perish. If one succeeded in navigating the bridge across the canyon, a deadly forest and deadlier tunnel awaited.

There was only so much to ponder about the place, though, and curiosity finally overcame Shailiha's fears. She handed her child to Martha so that she could brave the cold and look outside as their litter soared through the sky.

The experience was both wondrous and terrifying.

The white, snowy ground flashed below them. Although she was already too far away to make out the banks of the Sippora River or the capital city of Tammerland that now lay far behind them, she was just able to distinguish the outskirts of the city of Tanglewood as their litter passed by to the northeast. Soon the southern edge of the great, flat expanses of Farplain would come into view.

Reminded of Farplain, she thought about Tristan, and the battle that he might be fighting this very moment. She felt guilty that she had teased him to get him to ride his hatchling into the sky that first time, since she found herself frightened merely to sit here in her litter, speeding along to the relative safety of Shadowood.

And then, in the distance, she saw it. Tree Town.

The Minions descended, carrying their precious cargoes with them. They landed carefully and surrounded the litters protectively, dreggans drawn. Some of them remained circling in the sky, keeping a lookout.

Shailiha took Morganna from Martha and stepped out onto the snowy ground, her knees trembling slightly. Martha emerged and helped Wigg out. Shailiha turned to look down the sloping knoll before her, and her eyes came upon one of the most curious sights she had ever seen: hundreds of tree houses, each one seeming more ornate than the last, painted a dazzling array of colors. Some several stories high, they were connected by a series of wooden walkways. Shailiha smiled. It was like something from a dream.

By now Faegan, Celeste, Geldon, and the gnomes traveling

with them were all by Shailiha's side. The fliers of the fields swooped down, congregating into a riot of color directly over their mistress.

The snow fell softly upon them as they continued to look down at the sleepy village. Strangely, there was no one to be seen.

"They are without doubt quite frightened," Faegan said wryly. "They have never seen the Minions before."

"Do they know we are here?" Shailiha asked, trying to keep the snow off of Morganna.

"Oh, indeed," Faegan answered. He pursed his lips and raised his eyebrows. "Without question the alarm has already gone out."

"Faegan, I need to get the baby inside," Shailiha said worriedly.

"Of course," he answered. "Let's go. But let me take the lead, so that they can see me. Otherwise there might be trouble, and I certainly don't want any of them harmed." He looked behind, regarding the rest of the very strange group. A smile came to his face. "We shall be quite a sight to them, I can assure you."

With that, he levitated his chair above the snow-covered ground and started down the knoll. Martha took Wigg's hand. The giant butterflies soared overhead, and the huge number of Minion warriors followed warily behind.

They had only taken a few paces when a crowd of male gnomes came running around the corners of the houses, brandishing knives, axes, and bows. Shailiha recoiled, fearing for Morganna.

But the gnomes ran to Faegan. He landed to embrace them, and then they joyously hoisted him into the air, chair and all, amid great cheering and laughter.

Faegan finally became more serious, and called for Shannon the Small and Michael the Meager.

"Escort Celeste, Martha, the baby Morganna, and your wives to my mansion," he told them. "Find for Martha anything she might need for the welfare of the child. As for the rest of us, including the Minions, there is much work to do." He then gave the compressed, repaginated Tome to a warrior and told him to go with Shannon and Michael. The Paragon remained hanging around Faegan's neck.

"And now," the old wizard said sadly, "I suggest everyone say their good-byes."

Tearfully, Shailiha kissed her baby and handed her to Martha, bidding the kindly matron farewell. Celeste walked to Wigg, holding him close. "Good-bye, Father," she whispered. "No matter what happens, I shall never forget you."

"I know, my child," Wigg answered, his voice cracking. "But you must go quickly, for time is now the only remaining ally we possess." For what seemed an eternity, he held his daughter close. Then finally, reluctantly, he let her go.

With that, her splinter of the group walked down the knoll toward the houses of Tree Town.

Faegan turned to Shailiha. "It is time," he said solemnly.

Shailiha nodded. Closing her eyes, she raised her right arm. Caprice flew down to land upon it.

Go and do as I have ordered you to, Shailiha thought. *And may you all return to me safely.*

Caprice fluttered up from the princess' arm and flew back to join the squadron of twelve fliers especially chosen for this most important of tasks.

And then, Caprice in the lead, they soared away.

Those remaining—human, gnome, Minion, and flier alike—waited there for a moment, watching the butterflies disappear into the sky. Then, at a gesture from Faegan, those who were to be carried reentered their litters, the gnomes clambering into the many extras that had been brought. Snapping open their leathery wings, the Minion bearers gently lifted the litters.

Their numbers darkening the sky, both the warriors and the cargoes they carried disappeared against the horizon.

CHAPTER FIFTY-TWO

❧

$\mathcal{W}$E are outnumbered, my lord," Traax said calmly. "But we will do all we can to prevail. You have my word on it as a Minion."

Tristan's hatchling hovered high in the sky, just below the clouds. Traax and Ox, their breath coming out in little columns of frosted vapor, hovered next to him. Thousands upon thousands of other warriors fanned out around them. The blue-and-gold banners of Tristan's heraldry, which had been carried aloft, snapped back and forth with the cold gusts.

Here, on this bizarre battlefield several thousand feet above the ground, the wind sliced into the exposed skin of Tristan's face like invisible icicles. The blustery, raw day had developed into one of very dense, gray cloud cover—just what he had been hoping for. But as he looked down to the overpowering numbers of Nicholas' hatchlings swirling below, his heart sank.

There were so many of the enemy that they literally blotted out the earth beneath them.

Tristan took a deep, cold breath, thinking. Farplain lived up to its name in every respect. It was a vast, flat, barren expanse. Even at the height of the Season of the Sun it contained little more than dry, low-lying grasses, with nowhere to hide. Tristan planned to keep the battle in the sky, where his troops could make use of all three dimensions of movement.

And then, as he watched, the hatchlings below them slowly began to form airborne columns, their lines stretching almost as far as the eye could see. Then, led by a single bird and rider, as a great, disciplined army they began to soar to higher altitudes. Their formation was so perfect it seemed they were somehow bonded together. Finally they stopped, and the entire hatchling force, armed with swords, axes, and in some cases shields, faced the Minions in the sky about one hundred meters away. The tens of thousands of red, glowing eyes were unnerving, seeming to light up the sky around them. Holding a white flag, the base of its pole lodged into one stirrup, the rider on the lone bird spurred his mount toward Tristan.

The prince's hands tightened on his reins to the point that his knuckles became the same color as the snow. He reached back as best he could, tugging on the hilt of his dreggan, and then the first of his throwing knives.

The flag-carrying rider was Scrounge.

Pulling his bird to a stop about five meters from the prince, the assassin smiled. He looked quite out of place, holding his white flag of peace as it fluttered there in the unforgiving wind.

Tristan took in the sallow face, lean torso, and sunken eyes. The assassin was still wearing the miniature crossbow on his forearm, and had a broadsword at his hip. The arrows and sword tip were both stained with yellow.

"And so the day has finally come, Chosen One," Scrounge sneered. He leaned his forearm on the pommel of his saddle as his feline eyes scanned the columns of Minion warriors.

"Your fighters are most formidable," he continued. "Although there aren't as many of them as I thought there would be. Such a pity. That fact just seems to make this all too easy. I also find it highly interesting that you somehow ride upon one of my master's hatchlings. But it is of no matter, for you shall die this day anyway. And I see you go to that certain death under the heraldry of your ruined kingdom—the same colors that fared so poorly in their last battle. Such an ironic turn of events, wouldn't you agree?

"But surely even you can see that you are hopelessly outnumbered," he continued. "Therefore, I shall grant you a compromise. Surrender now, and I will promise each of you a quick and painless death. Resist, and each of you will die horribly. Also, know that this offer does not come from me, Chosen One. For I would rather see you all perish by my hand personally, if I could. Rather, this offer comes from my lord himself, he who is your only son. The choice is yours."

"Minion warriors never surrender," Tristan answered calmly. "A fact with which you are about to become painfully familiar."

One corner of Scrounge's mouth came up as he shook his head. "My lord, your son, was quite sure that was what you would say. And so, he has another message for you."

Tristan's eyes narrowed. "And that is?" he asked.

Scrounge spurred his bird closer. So close that Tristan could almost reach out and touch him. "The Gates of Dawn are finished, Chosen One," he said quietly, almost reverently. "Tomorrow at the break of day your son shall activate them, and the Heretics will return. Your wizards are useless. And your fabled stone, the so-called Paragon, is all but without life. Even the consuls of the Redoubt have turned against you. The world as we know it will soon be forever changed. For the final time, my lord asks that you, the only other being on earth with azure blood, come and take your rightful place at his side, and at the side of those who shall soon descend from the heavens. To do so, my master tells me, is to live forever within the perfect ecstasy of the Vagaries. But refuse him, and you shall die either this day by the sword, or very soon due to the poison that runs through your body." The assassin paused, looking at the veins that lay darkly on the back of Tristan's right hand. "Tell me, Chosen One," he asked, the wicked smile returning. "How is your sword arm? Can you even lift it?"

"Well enough to see you die by it," Tristan whispered. It was all he could do to keep himself from unleashing a throwing knife right then and there. But he held himself back, knowing he must stick to the strategy he and Traax had so carefully formulated. And then there was the unsettling memory of how fast the assassin had been that day in the Caves. How his crossbow had deflected Tristan's throwing knife as if it had been mere child's play. Tristan knew himself to be an amazingly fast warrior, but Scrounge was clearly his equal.

Scrounge glanced curiously to the handkerchief tied around Tristan's left arm, and again he smiled. He took a deep breath of the cold, crisp air. "I see you carry into battle a token given you by a woman," he said. "How quaintly gallant. And the familiar scent of myrrh reveals the identity of the one who gave it to you. Don't tell me, Chosen One, that you actually have designs on Celeste?" He shook his head again, as if tutoring a particularly ignorant schoolboy. "After all of this is over and you are quite dead, Ragnar will be very pleased to have her back. And I imagine the things he will do to her in punishment for abandoning him will pale in comparison to what she has already suffered. Perhaps even I will finally be allowed some private time with her." His tongue emerged to touch his upper lip. "After all, she is quite beautiful," he added wickedly.

Tristan had endured all that he could. He urged his bird closer, bringing his hatchling little more than inches away from Scrounge's. "I grow tired of all your talk," he whispered. "It is now time for us to do this thing. And when it is over, your guts will be splashed red upon the earth below me." He drew his dreggan. The ring the curved blade made lasted a long time in the dry, cool air before finally fading away.

"Very well," Scrounge answered. He reached down to his hip, and slowly drew his own sword. Tristan could easily identify it as a broadsword of the Eutracian Royal Guard.

"But before you die, there is something else I must tell you, Chosen One," the assassin added. "It is about the children."

Tristan froze.

"That's right," Scrounge said. "The children of the consuls. Their blood is the mortar that built the Gates of Dawn. And they will be needed further—perhaps even forever."

With a final, cold look of superiority, Scrounge wheeled his bird around and flew back to his troops.

Tristan turned to look at Ox. The giant warrior smiled grimly back.

"Remember your orders," Tristan said to him. "Go now."

A combination of disappointment and worry crowded onto Ox's face as he remembered the orders Tristan had given him back at the palace.

"But my lord, Ox want—"

"No buts!" Tristan ordered sternly. "We have been all through this. I can take care of myself." His face softened a bit. "So much of what happens here today depends on you, my friend. We need you."

His chest puffing out with pride, Ox finally smiled. From a string around his neck a silver bugle hung down the center of his back between his wings, out of sight of the enemy. Upon its bell were the markings of Tristan's heraldry, indicating that it had once been a tool of the Eutracian Royal Guard. Ox slowly, stealthily hovered backward into the towering clouds that lay directly behind and above them, until only the outline of his face could still be seen.

Tristan turned to Traax. "Scrounge is mine, and mine alone," he said menacingly. "But should I die before that bastard has met his fate, you must kill him. If I go to my grave this day, I want to do so knowing that he will not survive."

Traax looked into the dark blue eyes of his leader. "It will be my honor." He grinned. "Consider it done."

"Thank you," Tristan answered. "And remember, if our plan fails, I intend to save whatever troops we have left and regroup, rather than sacrifice them all here, in this one place. Despite what the Minions may have believed up until now, there is little honor in suicide." He turned his eyes back to the overwhelming force behind them. "Wars are not won by those who die for their cause, Traax. They are won by making the enemy die for his."

Traax bowed his head. "I live to serve," he replied solemnly.

Looking up and thinking for a moment, the prince took a deep breath. For the first time in his life he truly did not fear dying, for he knew in his heart he was already dead. It was such an amazingly clear awareness that he actually smiled as he took in the beautiful sky and clouds around him. It was almost as if he were looking at them for the very first time. He could fight today with absolute abandon, caring nothing for his personal welfare, for he had already said his good-byes to the ones he loved.

Raising his left arm to his face, he took in the light scent of myrrh. Then he looked down at the gold medallion around his neck, thinking of his twin sister, and the identical one she wore.

His thoughts were interrupted by a piercing, insane noise—the shrieking calls of the hatchlings readying themselves for battle.

And then, their thousands of swords waving back and forth like wheat stalks in a summer field, the legions of hatchlings flew toward the Minions.

Tristan raised his sword.

"Now! For Eutracia!" he shouted at the top of his lungs as he spurred his mount. All at once, weapons at the ready, Tristan's Minion warriors started to move.

Gathering speed, both hatchling and Minion alike tore across the sky, covering the distance between them in mere moments. Amid relentless battle screams and the brutal sounds of smashing bodies, the two forces tore into one another.

Tristan immediately went high, pulling his bird up at the last moment, just before the armies clashed. He turned around in his saddle, waving his dreggan.

Almost at once, Ox's bugle rang out.

Tristan looked down to the battle. It was progressing exactly as he had anticipated, the bulk of the hatchling legions attempting to hack their way through the center of his forces, separating them into two parts. For now, the Minions were holding their ground, their front lines uniform. But he knew that not all the hatchlings had reached the fighting. From each side of the struggle blood, bodies, and severed limbs and heads went flying into the cold air, falling almost in slow motion, bathing the ground below in red.

Tristan heard the bugle ring out for the second time, and he turned to stare at the towering clouds behind him. *Now!* he ordered silently. *You must come now!*

On cue, twenty-five thousand Minion warriors—almost a full third of Tristan's forces—came pouring from the clouds, Ox in the lead. Their wings folded back, their bodies pointed straight down, and their weapons held out before them, the Minions dove directly at the rear, still-uninvolved lines of unsuspecting hatchlings at full speed.

Tristan held his breath.

Nearly twenty-five thousand hatchlings died on the spot. Most of them never saw their attackers as the Minions came plummeting out of the sky, the sun at their backs. Rent apart by dreggans, daggers, and axes, blood flying, the mangled bodies of the grotesque birds fell in convoluted postures of instant death.

The idea had actually been Traax's, based on one of the strategies the Minions used to capture the swamp shrews in Parthalon. Tristan and the wizards had agreed.

But the prince could also see that the Minions remained

badly outnumbered. With the scattering of the hatchlings' rear lines, the battle was quickly decaying into individual struggles, each fighter for himself. With the two foes filling up what seemed to be the entire sky, Tristan continued to hover, his anxious eyes trying to find Scrounge. And then, in the midst of the melee below, the prince finally saw him.

Scrounge was diving his bird toward the back of an unsuspecting Minion. Raising his broadsword in his left hand, the assassin took the warrior's head off with a single stroke, only to wheel his bird around and approach yet another of his enemies from the rear.

Although tempting, this deceitful approach was not for Tristan. *You shall know it was I who killed you,* he swore. He swung his bird around and dove. "Scrounge!" he screamed as he approached the assassin.

Scrounge wheeled about and raised his broadsword. As the two men met, he struck a vicious blow that Tristan just barely parried; only the thigh straps saved the prince from falling off. Tristan countered from overhead with his dreggan, but the weakness in his arm and shoulder made him too slow. Dodging, Scrounge raised his right forearm and snapped his wrist; a poisoned arrow flew straight for Tristan's breast. The prince whirled his bird at the last moment. The arrow just missed him, going on to bury itself deeply into the neck of an unsuspecting hatchling behind him, sending it crashing to the earth.

Tristan dropped the reins and tossed the heavy dreggan into his left hand. Then he reached back with his right, grabbed one of his knives, and sent it end over end toward Scrounge's heart.

Twisting in his saddle at the last moment, the assassin was able to keep the spinning blade from entering his chest, but not the shoulder of his sword arm. The dirk buried itself into his flesh up to the handle. Screaming wildly in pain, Scrounge yanked out the bloody weapon and sent it tumbling to the ground.

Tristan dug his heels into the sides of his bird, directing it to hover just above and to one side of Scrounge. Trying to ignore his pain, he raised his sword with both hands and began hacking at the assassin with everything he had.

Wounded, and his broadsword too heavy for overhead

fighting, Scrounge lifted his crossbow and let go another of the yellow-tipped arrows. It missed widely. In desperation, he wheeled his bird around, trying to dive to safety by outrunning the prince. Tristan followed him down.

The intense coldness of the wind slammed into Tristan's face and eyes, blurring his vision so that he could hardly see. They approached the lower levels of the fighting, but Scrounge descended even farther, actually soaring beneath the battle. Then he pulled his bird up at a seemingly impossible angle, in an attempt to hide among the massive numbers of warriors and hatchlings above him.

Tristan tried to follow suit, but the pain in his arm kept him from pulling back on the reins as hard as he wanted. He lost sight of the assassin almost immediately. Before he could continue in his pursuit, a hatchling was upon him, its sword held high, its red eyes gleaming. Just as it approached, Tristan reached back and threw a dirk, burying it into one of the awful thing's eyes. It died screaming, blood and vitreous matter spurting violently from its head as it tumbled to the blood-soaked ground. Two more birds died at the prince's hand before he had a safe opportunity to look around and take stock of the battle.

The Minions were losing.

For what Tristan assumed to be the first time in their history, the winged warriors were giving ground. Many of the hatchlings continued to fall, as well, but it was clear that if the situation was not reversed, the Minions would soon lose the struggle altogether.

Not yet ready to signal a retreat, Tristan swooped down, trying to find Traax and Ox. But neither of them came into view. Yet another hatchling bore down on him, and he found himself again locked into swordplay. For what seemed an eternity the advantage harrowingly seesawed back and forth, Tristan's right arm growing weaker by the moment. Finally seizing his chance, the prince leaned forward, placing the point of the dreggan against the bird's breast and simultaneously pressing the hidden button in the hilt. The tip of the dreggan launched forward, slicing directly into the bird's rib cage. Tristan retracted the bloody blade, and the hatchling helplessly pawed at its fractured chest with its strangely human arms, turning over free fall.

The screams of the dying resonated in Tristan's ears. Looking around, he still could not locate Ox or Traax. He would have to alter the course of the battle by himself.

Rising higher into the sky, he tried to rally the Minions. He wanted to get as many of them as possible to retreat, in order to regroup into a cohesive fighting unit again, at a far greater altitude. But before he could get the attention of his officers, his hatchling rebelled.

Disobeying his commands, it flew straight down into the battle, swooping and darting among the struggling fighters with unmatched speed and dexterity. Tristan tried desperately to control the bird, but nothing he did worked. It flew unerringly through the worst of the havoc, seemingly searching for something. Several harrowing near misses later, they finally came upon Traax and Ox, fighting grimly back to back.

Tristan pulled on the reins with all his might, trying frantically to get Traax's attention. But his rebellious hatchling swooped quickly by without pause, and the prince's raging words were drowned out not only by the wind of his swift passage, but by the screams and shouts coming from the carnage all around them.

The hatchling climbed with amazing speed up through another sky-blue gap in the fighting, heading high in the air over the carnage. Then it slowed to a hover in the cold, blustery air, momentarily safe from the raging battle below, and turned its head around to face Tristan as best it could, its glowing orbs staring directly into his.

"Trust the process, Chosen One," it said in a deep, controlled voice.

Stunned, Tristan thought he might be hearing things, or that the fourth of his convulsions was upon him, making him hallucinate. But no convulsion came. Raising his dreggan higher, he looked around to see if someone or something was playing a trick. But there was nothing near. The bird's head was still turned toward him; its glowing eyes continued to bore their way into his own. The hatchling could speak!

"Trust the process, Chosen One," the bird repeated. With what seemed to be a strange kind of finality, it turned its head forward once again.

The hatchling had just said the same words that Shailiha

had so cryptically whispered to him while he was recovering from his third convulsion. *But what is the "process"?* he wondered frantically. *What is it I am supposed to trust?*

"Speak to me!" he shouted at the bird. "I command you! In whom or what is it I am supposed to trust?" But the bird refused to acknowledge him, and it still would not move.

From below, Tristan heard the peal of four bugle calls. *Ox! They understood my meaning, and are sounding a retreat!*

Then, as if at the behest of the bugle but still in defiance of Tristan's direct commands, the hatchling started to move. As it circled lazily in the sky, Traax and Ox neared, followed by what remained of the Minion army. Then, just when Tristan was about to shout orders, the bird turned and flew off again.

Tristan pulled back on the reins with all of his strength. He had to speak with Traax and Ox! But whenever the two Minions gained on them, the hatchling would speed up. Then it turned east.

We are in a full-fledged retreat! Tristan realized with growing horror.

Sensing imminent victory, the entire hatchling army, with Scrounge at the lead, chased after them.

"Trust the process, Chosen One." He wondered what it meant.

Finally bowing to the inevitable, Tristan leaned forward a little in his saddle as his hatchling mysteriously continued on its way.

*S*hailiha stood with her back to the magnificent pine forest; before her, to the west, lay the barren, snow-laden fields of Farplain. Her eyes were closed, her face raised, her arms outstretched. The only sound she could hear was the soft brushing together of the pine needles in the boughs of the trees behind her as the cold wind moved them about.

And then, suddenly, she heard it—the mental call of the flier, Caprice. Dropping her arms to her sides, she opened her eyes.

"They come," she said softly. "Tristan, Ox, and Traax remain unhurt."

"It is Caprice who has told you this?" Faegan asked.

"Yes," the princess replied.

"And the hatchlings follow?" Wigg asked.

"Yes."

"How long?" Faegan demanded.

"One hour, perhaps a bit more."

"Then it is time to make ready," Wigg replied.

The wind blew the snow back and forth into little drifts of ever-changing shape; the deceivingly calm, blue skies overhead were soon to be full of the coming fury. Behind Shailiha stood the most magnificent forest she had ever seen. And just before her, though she could not see it without proper training, lay the invisible canyon guarding the borders of Shadowood.

Within that dark, enchanted forest, the Minions and the gnomes had hurriedly begun to go about the tasks the wizards had given them. The various sounds coming to her ears from their work seemed strange, and foreign-sounding.

Everything else seemed so peaceful here in this place of the craft, but in her heart of hearts she knew all of that was about to change.

Tristan held tight to both his reins and his saddle pommel as the snowy ground below him flew by at an astonishing speed. Almost an hour had passed since they departed the battle scene. By now it was abundantly clear that they were heading for the coast, or at least as far as Shadowood.

In sheer desperation he pulled once more on the reins, trying to change the bird's direction and thus veer the monsters behind them off course.

But still it was no use. Exhausted not only by the poisoned blood swirling through his veins but also by the recent battle, he carefully replaced his heavy dreggan within its scabbard and slumped forward. The bird carried him across the sky at what now seemed to be an even greater speed.

They are here," Shailiha said, opening her eyes. She looked up to the sky, where tiny dots were beginning to form. "First come Tristan, then Ox and Traax, the Minions, and finally Scrounge and his hatchlings." Her voice was cracking with the strain. "They will be over us in moments." She closed her eyes once more.

Wigg turned his own white, unseeing eyes toward where

he knew Faegan to be. Desperation showed clearly in his face. "Are they ready?" he asked.

"If they are not," Faegan answered softly, "then all that we know is truly and finally lost."

With Shailiha and Wigg standing quietly in the snow to either side of his chair, Faegan reached out and linked hands with the princess and Wigg. He turned his eyes to the sky before speaking again.

"May the Afterlife have somehow granted us the wisdom to be right."

Tristan clung to his hatchling as it tore across the sky. Looking up, he could just begin to make out the edge of the dark forest protecting the western border of Shadowood. He still didn't know precisely where his bird was taking him, but one thing was now blindingly certain: It was no use trying to get the hatchling to change direction.

But then, quite unexpectedly, it did on its own.

Pointing its head down in an incredibly steep dive, the bird plummeted headlong toward the white, cold earth. Turning around as best he could, Tristan was able to see that all of the Minions were obediently following him, with hatchlings still in relentless pursuit.

It was then that the insidious realization gripped him.

It was a trick! His hatchling had not been successfully tamed by Wigg and Faegan. It was one of the enemy still— and it intended to dive straight at the ground, killing Tristan along with itself. How could he have been so blind and trusting? And what about the Minions? Would they follow him to their deaths, as the hatchlings driving them onward pulled up at the last moment?

He tried to raise his hands to wave the Minions off, but the force of the oncoming wind was too strong.

Finally, as the white, snowy ground raced up to meet them, Tristan remembered the invisible canyon. And then it all became clear.

"Trust the process, Chosen One." Now he understood!

For a split second, as the earth approached headlong toward him, he saw three figures holding hands. *Shailiha?*

One second later, as the white, snowy ground rose up into

his face, he gripped the bird around its neck for all he was worth, wondering if he was about to die.

He didn't. But all he could see was blackness.

What seemed like an eternity passed as the hatchling continued its steep descent into the canyon. Then he felt the bird begin to level out, and his eyes started to adjust to the gloom. His hatchling made a curving turn to the left and went speeding along what seemed to be the floor of the canyon; the walls flashed by so quickly they were just a blur. Looking down, he saw bones scattered everywhere. They were no doubt the result of having gone one step too far in the pursuit of the magical place known as Shadowood.

Glancing up, he could see the sky overhead, sunlight streaking down here and there between the clouds. Then he looked behind him, and his mouth fell open.

The entire Minion army, led by Traax and Ox, was following him along the floor of the canyon. There was no way to tell whether the hatchlings were still pursuing them.

All Tristan could do was hold on as best he could while the floor of the cavern and its macabre carpet of bones flew by at an astonishing speed.

*A*re you quite sure of the timing?" Wigg asked nervously. "It must be absolutely perfect!"

Faegan pursed his lips, trying to retain his concentration. "I am well aware, Wigg," he responded curtly.

The three of them were still at the edge of the invisible canyon, and had watched both the prince and the Minions dive into its depths, followed by Scrounge and the hatchlings. With the rapid disappearance of the two forces, the skies above had gone still. But Faegan, Wigg, and Shailiha knew it was not to last.

Turning around to face the forest, hoping against hope, Shailiha held her breath.

Now also turning, his eyes closed, Faegan silently employed the craft to calculate the variables of time, speed, and distance.

Still concentrating, Faegan slowly raised his right hand. Then he opened his eyes and sent an azure bolt from his fingertips into the sky. At the signal, the trees in the forest seemed to tremble.

The Minions who had brought Wigg, Faegan, and Shailiha here flew from the woods. Many of them carried something in their hands other than weapons. And others of them carried something on their backs that seemed stranger still—the gnomes of Shadowood.

Each of the little men had one of his small arms wrapped tightly around the neck of the Minion he was riding, and in the other he gripped what appeared to be a canvas bag.

Rising quickly into the sky, the Minions fanned out over a section of what the wizards had previously shown them to be the unseen outline of the canyon's facing edges and unwrapped their cargo. Faegan again sent a bolt of magic shooting skyward. Without hesitation the Minions dived for the earth, spreading something before them.

Swamp shrew nets.

Holding the nets out before them, the Minions plunged headlong into the canyon. Shailiha watched in amazement as they disappeared, as if they had been literally swallowed up by the earth. As quickly as they had come, the Minions and the gnomes were gone. Turning to the princess, Faegan nodded.

Closing her eyes, Shailiha raised her arms.

*W*ithout warning, Tristan's hatchling lurched upward, soaring toward the top of the chasm. The prince watched, mouth agape, as the walls of the canyon flew by, vertically this time, and wondered what was to become of him.

His bird stopped about midway to the top. The Minion forces quickly caught up, coming to hover in the gloom before their leader.

"What is happening, my lord?" Traax called out. "What is this place? Why are we stopping? Are we to finally turn and fight like warriors?"

A glance downward told Tristan that Scrounge and the hatchling army would shortly be upon them.

"Everyone turn around, and get ready to fight!" he hollered at the top of his lungs. "There is no time for explanations!"

But just as Tristan's forces started to fan out, their other brothers, carrying the shrew nets before them, gnomes still clinging perilously to their backs, plummeted down above the unsuspecting hatchlings. Approaching with incredible speed, the Minions drove the heavy, whistling nets lower, finally muscling them over the top of the awful birds. Realizing what was happening, Minions from Tristan's group soared downward, helping their brothers to secure the great rope webs over the hatchlings in clumps as far down the length of the canyon as the prince's eyes could see. The Minion warriors then began forcing the trapped birds closer to the canyon floor.

Tristan watched, dumbfounded. Amidst the confusion, the gnomes leapt from the backs of the Minions and began using stakes and mallets with a vengeance, securing the outer edges of the nets to the canyon floor and trapping the screaming hatchlings securely inside.

Realizing at last that what had just happened had largely been the work of Wigg, Faegan, and Shailiha, the prince drew his sword, ready to search for Scrounge somewhere beneath the nets. But just as he did so, his bird lurched upward again, carrying him up and out of the chasm.

Tristan fully expected the hatchling to drop him off next to where he could now see Wigg, Shailiha, and Faegan waiting for him. But it didn't.

He finally realized where he was being taken. Exhausted, he had no choice but to lean forward on the neck of the bird, closing his eyes, and trust his life to the fates.

As she watched the tiny speck in the sky disappear, Shailiha wiped an errant tear from her cheek. "Will he live?" she asked Wigg.

"We have been fortunate this day, Princess," he answered softly. In his unseeing way, he placed an affectionate arm around her shoulders. "But what you ask is not in our power to grant. I must tell you from my heart that there is no way for him to survive. What we do now is simply give him additional closure to his life, nothing more. For that is all we can do. His fourth and final convulsion will soon be upon him, and there is nothing that either Faegan or I can change about that. Nor is there any action we can take to stop the Confluence. As we said before, we didn't think Nicholas would send his hatchlings after us until the construction of the Gates had been completed. My guess is that they are now finished. The Confluence thus cannot be far behind—perhaps as soon as tomorrow."

"We should be going with him," she said, her eyes still locked on the empty sky. "I simply cannot say good-bye to him like this . . ."

"We have already said our good-byes, Shailiha," Faegan replied softly. "What he does now he must do alone."

Looking up, the princess saw Caprice and the other fliers finally returning. She raised her arm, and the magnificent yellow-and-violet butterfly obediently came to rest there; the others swirled gently in graceful circles over their mistress' head.

Her tears coming fully now, she grasped the gold medallion that hung around her neck.

Good-bye, my brother. I shall always love you.

CHAPTER FIFTY-THREE

TRISTAN kept nodding off atop the hatchling, but despite his exhaustion, the pain in his right arm kept him from truly resting. He had been traveling northwest for many hours, and the sun had long since set, bathing the world in darkness. The heavy, gray clouds he had so relied upon in the recent battle had finally departed, revealing a clear, frigid sky. Amidst uncountable stars, Eutracia's three rose-colored moons hung against the inky, impenetrable night. Sunrise—when Nicholas, his only son, would begin the Confluence—could only be about two hours away.

Tristan coughed deeply and pulled his coat closer trying to keep out the cold. But the wind had become even more icy with the advent of night, and he could no longer feel his hands or his feet. Still, the hatchling beneath him soared unerringly to the place he was now sure his sister and the wizards were sending him, the only destination that made any sense: the site protecting the Gates of Dawn.

For that was where Nicholas would be.

He harbored no illusions about surviving. He was growing weaker by the moment, and he knew his fourth convulsion would come soon. His body shook, the fever that had overtaken him about an hour ago still rising.

He thought of the brain hook still hidden in his right boot, and again vowed that when his time came he would do his utmost to use it upon himself, rather than suffer the indignities of a final, mortal convulsion.

As the moonlit, rose-colored ground raced by below him, he couldn't help but recall all the horrific things that had so recently occurred in his life. He thought of the death of his father, and of the rape and slaughter of his mother at the hands of the very troops he had just led into battle. He thought of the murders of the Directorate of Wizards, and of the travails he and Wigg had suffered to return his sister and the Paragon to Eutracia. In that, at least, they had been successful.

But this time there would be no happy ending. Everyone and everything he had ever held dear would soon perish. The Vagaries, the dark side of the craft that it was to have been his destiny as the Chosen One to combine with the Vigors for the dawning of a new age of enlightenment, would rule. Not only alone, but also forever, guided by the Guild of the Heretics, who would ensure that a new age of darkness reigned.

He had few illusions as to why the wizards and Shailiha were ordering his hatchling to fly him to the Gates. It wasn't because they thought he could somehow stop the Confluence, or that by going there he would magically survive the agonies of his fourth convulsion. Nothing could stop those things now. Rather, it was because they knew he would want to confront his son for the final time.

He had already said his good-byes to those he left behind. Dying in a bed in the royal palace or in Faegan's mansion in the trees while his body was being wracked by the fourth convulsion would only heighten the pain and grief of everyone involved. He was glad they would not be there to see his death. He wanted their memories of him to be of the strong man that he had once been.

This way, he would at least behold Nicholas one final time. It would be his last chance to look into the face of the son who, unbelievably, had survived that tragic day in Parthalon. No matter what kind of monster he had become.

He closed his eyes. His mind was becoming increasingly feverish, and his pain-wracked body was covered with sweat, despite the unrelenting cold.

He had sworn an oath to destroy his only progeny, and he understood that going to Nicholas would afford him some small, strange measure of peace. And Faegan and Wigg, he realized, knew that, too. One corner of his mouth came up in irony. That was assuming, of course, that his final convulsion did not occur before he got there, leaving the hatchling flying far across Eutracia only to deliver a white, frozen corpse.

Scrounge would have no doubt been amused, he thought.

Coughing again, Tristan wrapped the reins tightly around his numb left wrist. Painfully reaching down with his right hand, he located the brain hook in his boot. With his hand still on it, he leaned all his weight onto the hatchling's neck as it raced through the clear, cold night.

Somehow, he slept.

The combination of the hatchling's great, descending turn and the first rays of the sunrise awakened him. He groaned and tried to sit up, but found he was frozen to the hatchling. Another coughing fit wracked his body, but when it finally ended he pushed hard against the bird's neck. The fur on the front of his coat tore away, leaving bare suede. He didn't care—he knew he wouldn't need it much longer.

Frost stiffened his hair, and his eyelashes were frozen together in places, making it difficult to see. He couldn't feel his face. Numbly rubbing his cheeks and eyes with what had once felt like his right hand, he looked down.

The three Gates of Dawn lay just below him, about one hundred meters apart, in a row running east and west. Rising hundreds of meters from the ground, they resembled gigantic horseshoes, curved at the tops, their ends planted firmly into the earth.

Made of the finest shiny, black, Ephyran marble, they were shot through with brilliant azure. The blood of the Heretics, he realized.

As the hatchling soared closer, he noticed what he could only assume to be Nicholas' carrion scarabs. Undulating back and forth in a black, riverlike mass, the hundreds of thousands of shiny beetles surrounded the legs of the Gates. Then his heart skipped a beat.

Within the dark ocean of seething scarabs were torn human bodies, their bloody abdomens overflowing with white, glistening eggs. The hundreds of torn, dark blue robes that lay everywhere, flapping hauntingly in the wind, told him the corpses must once have been consuls.

And then he noticed the lone figure standing atop the wide curve of the easternmost Gate.

Nicholas.

The young adept faced the rising sun, his white robes billowing in the wind, his long, dark hair flying out behind him. He seemed oblivious to the cold. Several strange-looking objects rested on the marble at his feet.

Tristan's hatchling buffeted its leathery wings as it approached the Gate. It landed softly near Nicholas, then bent down so that the prince might dismount. After several tries with his numb fingers, Tristan managed to unfasten the leather straps that had held him in his saddle for so long. Then he weakly raised one leg up and over to slide off the bird and down to the top of the windswept Gate, where he fell to all fours despite his best efforts to remain upright. He remained that way, his head down, until he gathered the strength to make one attempt at standing. He pushed himself up—staggered, and almost fell again but caught himself—and finally managed. The bitter wind swirled around him.

Nicholas had watched, doing nothing to help as Tristan tried desperately to face his son on his own terms.

Tristan looked into Nicholas' upturned, exotic eyes of hard blue. They gleamed almost as if they were made of polished stone.

Succiu's eyes, he thought. *And mine.*

From all around Nicholas' body radiated a glow such as Tristan had never seen, a power so immense that neither Succiu nor even Failee herself could ever have summoned it.

He looked briefly to the sad, tattered handkerchief on his arm as it fluttered in the harshness of the wind.

Tristan's breathing came quickly, in ragged, hard-won gasps, and it was becoming all he could do to remain standing against the gathering wind. Sweat ran from his face and body. His right arm, throbbing madly with pain, was virtually useless. He looked back into the unyielding depths of Nicholas' eyes. The first rays of the sun were just starting to show themselves in the east, illuminating the majesty of the Gates with their glow.

For many long moments Tristan and Nicholas simply stood there, silently looking at each other, the wind howling around them as the thousands of black, angry scarabs swarmed below. The world was about to change forever, and Tristan knew there was absolutely nothing he could do to prevent it. Finally, Nicholas spoke.

"And so you have returned to me, Father," he began softly, his words almost drowned out by the wind. "You have chosen to become one of us after all. I am very pleased."

From within his robes Nicholas produced a small vial. Tristan immediately recognized it as the same vessel he had seen in the Caves—the vessel containing the antidote to the poison running through his veins.

"If you will agree to join us, and allow me to confirm your intentions by testing the quality of your heart, I will administer the antidote." Nicholas smiled.

Tristan stood silently for another long moment, staring hungrily at the vial his bastard son so tantalizingly held before him. Its contents would save not only his life, but also the lives of his sister and her only child.

"No," he said thickly. "I reject your offer. To bargain for my life is not why I have come."

Nicholas narrowed his eyes, replacing the vial into his robes. "Then why *have* you come to me, Chosen One?" he asked politely. "Do not tell me that it is simply so that I may see you die? My poor, misguided father! If that is true then you misunderstand, and have therefore traveled all of this way for naught. I have no need to see your death actually occur, simply to know that it soon shall. Just as I have no need to see the sun rise tomorrow, in order to know that such a thing shall also occur." His face became a bit graver. "Your fourth convulsion is almost upon you. I can tell."

"I come one final time to ask you to stop this madness," Tristan said softly. He was swaying back and forth now, too weak to steady himself in the strengthening wind. The normally reassuring weapons he carried across his back seemed to be made of lead, threatening to topple him over at any moment.

"Please come back to Shadowood with me," Tristan whispered weakly. "Allow my wizards to try to help you . . . to bring you to the Vigors, and the light. I beseech you to release the power of the stone back to the Paragon, so that we might all work together to find a way . . ."

Life ebbed inexorably from Tristan's body, and he did not know what to say. He weakly raised his palms in supplication. "My son," he whispered. "I beg of you . . ."

Nicholas' expression suddenly turned to one of extreme anger. He pointed a long, accusatory finger straight at his father's heart. "You beg of *me*!" he thundered. "You of the azure blood, the Chosen One himself, who rejected his only son not just once, but three times? The son you ripped from the comfort of the womb with one of the very knives you still carry, leaving him to rot in a shallow grave of a foreign land? Then only to reject out of hand his compassionate offer of truly everlasting ecstasy in the craft, so graciously made to him that day in the Caves? And finally to reject his own seed yet again, at this exact moment, on the Gates of Dawn themselves? This time to insult that son's vastly superior power and knowledge of the craft, by suggesting that it could be augmented by his powerless, vastly inferior wizards! And to ask his son to willingly consent to do nothing for all of eternity except to practice the deceitful, flaccid Vigors! He dares ask *me* to come to *him*? To therefore spurn the very ones who gave me back my life, returning me to the land of the living?" His eyes grew even harder. "No, Chosen One. What you suggest for me is slavery, nothing more. You would have fared much better had you allowed the lead wizard to burn my tiny body while it still rested, dead, within that of my mother," he added softly.

Nicholas took a deadly, meaningful step toward Tristan

and extended his right arm, palm outward. "Clearly, Father," he said softly, "you haven't been listening."

With that, Nicholas pushed his white, perfect palm closer to the prince. Tristan collapsed, falling hard upon the cold, smooth marble, wracked by a scorching, twisting pain so excruciating he thought he would pass out. He felt as if he were actually being disemboweled with a searing, red-hot knife. But there was no blood. Nor was there any respite.

Wanting desperately to end his torment, he tried to reach down and grasp the brain hook in his boot. But his hands wouldn't work. All he could do was lie before his son, silently begging that the horrific pain stop.

But it didn't.

Somehow, he raised his face from the marble. "All of your hatchlings are dead," he whispered. "And so is Scrounge." A tiny, defiant smile came to his frozen lips. "At least I accomplished that much . . ."

Unperturbed, Nicholas placed his hands into the opposite sleeves of his robe, but the agony torturing Tristan did not abate. "It is of no concern," he said simply. "How you and the wizards managed to accomplish their demise is of some small interest to me, but the truth of it is that the hatchlings only served to buy me time. Time to collect the consuls and have them construct the Gates, and time to keep your Minions at bay, once you finally brought them here. Which, of course, I knew you would. You had no other choice. But in the end all you have really accomplished is to grant me a blessing, don't you see? For now I needn't waste the time or the energy killing them myself. Neither the hatchlings, nor Scrounge, nor your Minions are worthy of any place in our new world. Nor even Ragnar, for that matter. He too has gone to his reward. As have the consuls who tried to resist me."

Nicholas looked down briefly to the congested, swirling mass of carrion scarabs, black against the snow. "After the Confluence, the scarabs and their eggs shall also perish, their duties fulfilled. Like all my servants, they were never more than a simple means to an end. The spell that will destroy them is already in place. Even the wraiths who bled you are gone—easily conjured, and just as easily done away with."

Tristan could scarcely breathe. Writhing and trembling on

the cold, unforgiving marble, he curled up into a fetal position and clutched his abdomen, the searing pain slicing through him mercilessly.

"Tell me about . . . about the children," he gasped, his tortured brain finally remembering what Scrounge had said. "What . . . have you done with them? Why must they live with you . . . forever?"

"Ah, yes, the children." Nicholas finally smiled. "One of the greatest of the keys to all that has transpired, and all that is yet to." He bent down, staring directly into Tristan's eyes. "Did you know, Chosen One, that you should have gone to Fledgling House long before Scrounge, and taken the children for yourself? And do you also know that had your egocentric, blind lead wizard not been so protective of his silly secret of the training of young females in the craft, you could have easily stopped me from accomplishing all that I have? Not simply due to the fact that I needed their blood to bring forth the Confluence, because I would have taken the children back. No, Chosen One, there is far more to the story than that. It has to do with an ancient, underlying concept regarding young endowed females that even your wizards are not completely conversant with. The answer to stopping me was, as they say, right under your nose the entire time. But, as they also say, that is a topic better left for another day. Except you have no other such days left." Nicholas paused to take a deep breath, then let it out slowly, as if relishing the freedom from pain that the prince would never again enjoy.

"And . . . the rest of the consuls—" Pain caused Tristan to retch, but there was nothing in his stomach to come up. When he could speak again, he whispered, "What . . . of them?"

"Safe and sound, I assure you," Nicholas answered. "And obediently awaiting the Confluence."

Tristan took a short, deep breath in a final attempt to beat back the incredible agony, but it was unrelenting. With a supreme effort of will, he managed to lift his face from the marble again.

"I refuse to believe that my seed could have vomited forth upon the world something as evil as the being that now stands before me," he whispered, the words dripping from his tongue like venom. "Even though you were the product of rape, and forcibly taken before your time from the womb of a sorceress." It had required every scintilla of strength he had left to speak the words without passing out.

Then, completely beaten, left with nothing with which to fight, he placed his head back down on the marble, certain he had spoken the final words of his life.

Nicholas examined his father closely, as if Tristan had suddenly evolved into some kind of sick, twisted experiment. " 'Evil,' Chosen One?" he asked curiously. "History is written by the victors—don't you know that? And our history— that is, yours and mine—shall be recorded for all time as the story of a father who failed to realize the importance of not only the past, but the future, as well."

Nicholas turned his attention to the hatchling that had brought the prince to the Gates. It stood quietly to one side, waiting. "I can feel the influence of another's endowed blood within the bird," he said softly. "Fascinating. I am unsure of how this came about, but it is of no consequence."

Slowly, he raised his right hand toward the creature, and pointed his index finger. A bright azure bolt shot from his fingertip and screamed across the Gate to slam into the hatchling's breast. The bird exploded. Bits of leather and offal rained sickeningly down on Tristan as he lay there, his body twisted in excruciating pain.

Nicholas lowered his arm and smiled. "And now, if you will be so good as to excuse me, I have a great mission to complete," he said quietly. "I leave you to die alone. But you are young, and strong. You may even live long enough to have the pleasure of witnessing their coming."

Standing, the young adept turned to walk across the top of the Gate, back to where the gleaming, silver objects rested.

Through his pain, the prince looked away from the beautifully sweeping curve of the Gate, out toward the snow-covered fields of his beloved Eutracia. He then looked down, wondering if he might be able to manage killing himself without the use of the brain hook.

Even from this angle he could see the hungry, black masses of beetles. Perhaps he could roll himself off the Gate. At least the fall would kill him, rather than the scarabs. Either way, what did it matter? The pain would stop. He curled up a little tighter, the torture cascading through his nervous system in nauseating, unbearable waves. His mind teetering on the edge of madness, he looked toward his son.

Ignoring his father's plight, Nicholas stood calmly before three silver goblets that glimmered beautifully in the gathering rays of the sun. Arranged in a row, each of them rose in height to about the level of his knee. Even through his pain, Tristan knew what they held.

The fluids required for the Confluence.

One goblet would contain the endowed blood of the children, one some waters of the Caves, and the last would hold his own, perfect azure blood, taken from him that fateful day by Nicholas' wraiths. The final ingredient—the other brilliant, azure blood of the Heretics—was already held within the marble of the three Gates, silently waiting to be called upon. When combined with the power of the Paragon, these seemingly disparate elements would allow Nicholas to separate the heavens, bringing forth the Guild of the Heretics.

It was clear to the prince that his son was about to begin.

Closing his eyes, Nicholas turned his body to face the rising sun. Bowing his head, he raised his arms in supplication.

Almost immediately the first of the glimmering goblets began to rise into the air. Rotating slowly, it poured forth its contents: the dark red waters of the Caves. But instead of falling through the air and splashing down upon the Gates, the waters gathered hauntingly into a thin, flat, square sheet that hovered gracefully before the young adept.

Then, just as slowly, the second goblet began to rise. It too poured its contents—the blood of the endowed children— into the air. Another square sheet of fluid formed, moving down to hover against the first. And finally, the third goblet rose. Pouring forth the azure blood of the prince, it formed yet another sheet, which layered itself against the first two. The three goblets came back down to rest at Nicholas' feet.

Struggling to control his mind against the pain, Tristan tried to think back to Faegan's explanation of the Confluence. First . . . the necessary fluids would somehow be joined. Then Nicholas would use them to empower the Gates. And finally the heavens would literally part, allowing the Heretics to come through. Their endowed blood, locked within the marble for eons but now charged and alive, would animate them as they flew between the legs of the three structures. The returning Heretics would then reclaim their original forms, free to walk the earth once more, just as they had done ages ago. But this time their circumstances would be different. This time the Ones Who Came Before would not be here to defy them.

Tristan watched, spellbound even within his agony, as the unified sheets of fluid rose higher into the air.

Nicholas opened his eyes and gestured with his hands. First the enchanted, twinkling square turned to stand on one of its four corners. Then, like a child's top, it began to spin.

Faster and faster it went, finally twirling at such an amazing speed that the wind created by its revolving sides threatened to blow Tristan off the top of the Gate. As it spun, the different colors of the three endowed sheets of fluid coalesced in his mind's eye to create a solid cube of amazingly beautiful amethyst, glistening brightly against the almost-risen dawn. Then it began to grow to several hundred times its original dimensions. From where the prince lay, its gigantic magnificence seemed to blot out the entire sky.

And then came the noise. As the cube grew, the maelstrom of sound created by Nicholas' creation howled, screamed, and shrieked to such an extent that it nearly tore apart Tristan's eardrums, adding not only to the pain he was already being forced to suffer at the hands of his bastard son, but also to the agony of the poison swirling within his bloodstream. The rectangle was moving with such blinding speed that even its edges were only a blur of motion. Tristan tried to place one hand before his face to protect him from the blasting, relentless wind it was creating, but still could not move his arms.

Lifting his hands higher, Nicholas closed his eyes once more. The spinning dervish slowed, then finally stopped its frantic revolutions. Nicholas maneuvered it even higher into the sky.

It started to drip.

The drops came slowly, one at a time, landing softly on the very center of the apex on which Tristan lay. They came gently, quietly at first, and Tristan watched, horrified, as the fluid pooled, gathering more of its own glowing matter to itself. Then it began to slither across the smooth, black-and-azure marble in many directions at once.

The drops running from the sides of the magnificent, hovering square quickly developed into a small stream, which in turn became a rushing cascade. As it did, the amethyst fluid began to cover the entire curve of the Gate. Tristan's body was soon awash in its warm, almost comforting slickness, and he could do nothing but let it cover him.

Nicholas continued to command the fluid, watching carefully as it ran down the sides of the Gate, until the entire structure was coated with the mixture.

Apparently satisfied, Nicholas lowered his arms. Without looking at Tristan he gracefully turned around to face the other two Gates behind him. Raising his arms again, he spread the fingers of each hand. Tristan held his breath, wondering what would happen next.

A smattering of the amethyst fluid covering the first Gate leapt into the air and flew toward the second Gate. Covering the expanse between them in a heartbeat, it landed squarely on the apex of the second Gate, where it split, leaving some of itself behind before launching across to the third Gate.

The glowing square continued to supply what seemed to be an endless quantity of the mixture, bridging the Gates and at the same time dripping down to cover them. Then both it and the bridges disappeared. All three Gates carried the sheen of the liquid over their entire surfaces.

It has begun, Tristan thought.

Nicholas faced the east again, then calmly hovered up, crossed his legs in the air, and stretched his arms skyward. He closed his eyes and began to speak.

Tristan could not understand the language, but he was sure it was Old Eutracian, for it sounded very much like the words Faegan had read to him from the scroll Nicholas had sent to the Redoubt.

The Gates took on the glow of the craft—but this time the effect was different from anything Tristan had ever seen. Bolts of lightning were loosed from every area of the Gates, their branched, fingerlike tentacles flashing up into the sky. Each was followed by an earthshaking crash of thunder. It was as if the huge bolts had been ordered to swallow up the entire firmament in their menacing, relentless anger.

And then the sky began to darken. The rising sun was being blotted out by layers of black, fast-rolling clouds.

Tristan was surprised to notice that his pain lessened as the gloom increased. He could only imagine it to be due to the fact that Nicholas was focusing so much of his power on the Gates. With terrific effort, the prince sat up and looked to his son.

Nicholas seemed engulfed in a trance, his face lowered, his eyes rolled upward. His breathing was labored, as if he were struggling mightily with something. Then he slowly raised his head.

The lightning stopped, and the world became bathed in an eerie, almost calm silence. The three Gates of Dawn glowed spectacularly, silently, in the overwhelming darkness.

Nicholas still hovered over the glowing Gate, serene now, as if infinitely sure of himself. He waited for a few moments. Then, without warning, he extended his arms and spread his fingers.

A single, giant bolt of lightning flew from the apex of the Gate up toward the heavens. But this time, instead of flashing and then quickly retreating, as the others before it had, it persisted in the darkness of the sky, remaining motionless, the ends of its forked fingers lost in the gloom. And then it began to grow, spreading its lustrous branches as far as the eye could see.

It was parting the darkness of the heavens.

Tristan watched, his mouth agape, as the branches of the bolt pushed aside the clouds. Rays of soft, azure light descended through the opening. The lightning bolt fell away, and the thunder also ended. All went strangely quiet for a time, the only sight in the heavens the great gap with its descending rays, the only sound the restless swirling of the wind.

It was then that the screaming began.

A horrific chorus of human voices came down through the opening in the sky. On and on it came, the many voices shrieking, crying, wailing, and moaning all at once. Tristan managed to place his hands over his ears, but it did little to keep out the overpowering noise.

They are coming, Tristan realized. *The Guild of the Heretics, the ancient masters of the Vagaries, are about to reclaim the earth.*

Finally Nicholas turned to look down at his stricken father. Using the craft to overcome the wailing coming down from the sky, he spoke, his voice carrying a thunderous power. "Behold, Chosen One," he said calmly, the wind moving through his long, dark hair. "My parents of above finally return to the earth."

Tristan looked up to the rent in the sky, his eyes wide with wonder.

Faces had begun to develop. Huge human faces, thousands of them, men and women alike, were being illuminated from behind by a celestial source of light such as the prince had never seen. Their eyes were exquisitely sad, their mouths calling out beseechingly to Nicholas. The faces soared and turned in the heavens just behind the edges of the great opening, as if waiting for something. The wailing coming from their open mouths became even louder.

Nicholas stood upright in the air, his form still hovering over the Gate. The glow all about him was nearly blinding.

He will bring them now, he thought. *There is no force that can stop him.*

As Tristan watched, the energy and glow of the Paragon imbued into Nicholas' being increased wondrously, as if it had finally come to the bursting point.

The wailing, beseeching faces of the Heretics crowded forward to the very edges of the gigantic rent in the heavens.

And then Nicholas screamed. As if gripped by some horrific, unexplained agony, he covered his eyes with his hands.

The faces in the heavens did not descend; their wailing grew even louder and more pleading.

Removing his hands from his face, Nicholas looked down at his palms and screamed again. It was a plaintive, helpless, agonizing sound that tore through the heavens, drowning out even the wailing of the Heretics. Tristan looked at his son, aghast.

Nicholas was bleeding from every orifice of his body.

From his eyes, ears, nose, mouth, and groin poured shimmering, azure blood. It streamed down the length of his white robes and dripped onto the Gate, where it mixed with the fluid already there.

Screaming madly, his face registering nothing but abject

astonishment and pain, Nicholas fell, landing on the apex a short distance away from his father. The adept looked pleadingly into Tristan's face. And then his eyes, the eyes so reminiscent of Succiu, slowly closed, and the aura that had always surrounded his being slowly faded away into nothingness.

Stunned, Tristan looked back to the hole in the sky. The faces of the Heretics were slowly retreating, their wailing and crying subsiding. With the unexpected collapse of Nicholas had apparently come the cessation of his spell. The great rent in the skies eventually closed; the faces of the Heretics disappeared. But the rolling darkness that had preceded it all remained, and the deafening thunder began anew.

Trying to marshal whatever strength he had left, Tristan found that the pain Nicholas had been torturing him with was gone. But the poison in his veins, and the illness that went with it, were still with him. He forced himself up, knowing what his mission must be.

To reach the antidote.

He put his right foot slowly forward and nearly collapsed with the effort of that single step. As he shook his head in pain, the thunder crashed relentlessly, making it even harder to concentrate. Lightning again tore across the heavens, occasionally illuminating his path to Nicholas in ephemeral, ghostly snatches of light.

He took another agonizing step, determined to cross the distance to his son's body and remove the life-saving vial from Nicholas' robes.

Another step came somehow, and then another.

Four more paces, he told himself. *Only four more!*

But just as he began the next step, the Gates of Dawn shuddered.

Smoke, dark and acrid, rose from the apex of the Gate he was on, and a fissure opened in the surface of the fluid-ridden, marble curve, directly between the place he was standing and the inert body of his son.

With a terrible, wrenching, cracking sound, the crevice widened, its branches threatening to creep toward the sides of the curve and extend down into the legs, sending the entire structure tumbling down. The structure shuddered again, and Tristan lost his already shaky footing, falling facedown on the disintegrating Gate.

Looking up amid the smoke and noise, he could see that the crevice was far too wide for him to cross. Even if he had been healthy, he could never have made the jump required to land safely on the other side. Looking to his right, though, he saw that the jagged sides of the crevice rejoined about ten meters away. With what he was sure would be his last reserves of strength, he somehow pulled himself upright again. Weaving drunkenly, the Gate cracking beneath him, he shakily started to make his way, one agonizing step at a time.

But it was not to be.

In the midst of his second step, excruciating pain enveloped him. Foam erupted from his mouth, and he crashed woodenly to the sticky, disintegrating Gate, his body trembling.

His fourth, final convulsion was upon him.

He knew he would never reach the antidote in time. Twisting in agony, he reached down to his boot with his trembling right hand, finally coming upon the pearl handle of the brain hook he had hidden there. Just as he grasped it and pulled it out, the three Gates of Dawn began to collapse.

The tops of the second and third Gates cracked open entirely, their marble blocks crashing to the earth. With an agonizing, torturous sound, the Gate he and Nicholas were on shook again, and the cracks in its top split open from end to end.

Raising the brain hook to his right ear, he felt his tongue begin to slip down the back of his throat, choking the life from him. He looked to the tattered handkerchief tied around his left arm, and then down at the gold medallion around his neck as blocks nearby tumbled to the ground.

He placed the end of the brain hook into his ear, his final thoughts resonating through his mind.

Die, Chosen One! . . . Die, Chosen One! . . . Die! . . . Die! . . . Die! . . .

CHAPTER FIFTY-FOUR

As she so often did now, Shailiha sat quietly with Celeste, rocking Morganna softly in her arms. A fortnight had passed since they had returned to the Redoubt after learning of the destruction of the Gates and Nicholas' apparent failure to return the Heretics. But there still had been no word of either Tristan or Nicholas.

Ox and Traax had gone out to search the area of the Gates, but had not found anything. If their bodies were ever to be recovered, they would no doubt eventually be found somewhere beneath the many tons of black-and-azure marble. And the wizards were uncertain about attempting to move the rubble, concerned as they were about what other calamities might transpire if they tried.

That being the case, Wigg and Faegan had ordered that no one be allowed to return to the site until they had inspected it in person. Strangely, though, the wizards had not yet visited there, remaining cloistered in their quarters instead. No doubt they still could not bring themselves to see the place of Tristan's death, Shailiha reasoned.

After the hatchlings had all been killed and their bodies burned to ash in the depths of the canyon surrounding Shadowood, Traax had requested that the bodies of his slain Minion warriors be brought from Farplain and Shadowood to Tammerland, the home of their departed lord. The wizards had agreed. Additional litters had been constructed, and the corpses were flown back to the royal palace for the traditional burning of the dead.

Hundreds of pyres, stacked high with dead warriors, had eventually dotted the fields outside the castle grounds. Out of respect for those who had defended them, everyone living in the Redoubt had attended the lighting of the pyres. The flames and smoke had risen into the sky over Tammerland for five days and nights. Now their soot littered the whiteness of the snow for as far as one could see, turning it gray with the refuse of death.

Traax's officers had also constructed an additional pyre, upon which no bodies were placed. It was an empty, silent tribute to Tristan.

Traax had asked Shailiha to light it. With a trembling hand, amid the cries of "We live to serve!" she had tentatively placed a torch to it. The flames roared into the sky, marking the passing of he who had been the lord of the Minions. It had been more than she could bear, and she'd had to turn her face away to hide her tears.

After that, Shailiha had been inconsolable. But Celeste had come to sit with her every day, and it had been those daily visits, more than anything else, that had finally helped to bring the princess partially through her grief. They had also solidified the bond between the two women.

But having no body to bury only made it harder for Shailiha. With no Tristan to hold for the last time, it sometimes felt to her as if the grief would never end. And worse, a great sense of sadness, along with a deafening, overpowering quiet, had captured the Redoubt, as if no one living there would ever be truly happy again.

The princess looked down at her sleeping child, wishing with all her heart that Tristan could have been buried with their parents and her husband at the family grave site.

But he is buried, she had finally realized one day, looking at the gold medallion around her neck, the one that matched the medallion her brother had once worn. *He is buried with his only child, beneath the rubble of the Gates of Dawn.*

"Do you think it is possible . . ." Her words trailed off as she realized she was asking Celeste the same question she had been asking almost every day. Lately, as both time and logic forced her mind toward reality, she found herself asking it less. Or at least trying to.

Celeste placed a comforting hand on Shailiha's arm. "We must be strong," she said quietly. "That was part of your brother's last words to me. Despite the short time I knew him, I think perseverance is what Tristan would have wanted, perhaps even demanded of us. He is gone, Shailiha. And no one can change that. I do not mean to be hard, but I think we must believe what my father and Faegan have told us, and look to the future. I shall miss Tristan, and I know you shall even more. But for the sake of your country, your child, and the continuance of the craft, you must accept this." She paused for a moment, to let her words sink in.

"You have lost so much, especially for one so young," she went on. "But you are now the Chosen One."

A tear ran down Shailiha's cheek. Though she brushed it away, its moistness still clung to her eyelashes. She had long known that the mantle of Chosen One would fall to her should her brother ever perish. But she had certainly never wished for the title, nor expected it to come so soon. Sometimes she wished she had never heard of the craft.

Then a new thought struck her. "With Tristan gone," she replied quietly, "your endowed blood is second in quality only to mine." She remained quiet for a time, her mind again going over the other quite-unexpected occurrences that had transpired since the loss of her brother.

First was the fact that Wigg had slowly, miraculously, regained his sight. And the secretive wizards, although obviously very pleased by this event, had said virtually nothing about how it was accomplished.

The second and vastly more important occurrence was that power was very slowly returning to the Paragon. The jewel of the craft now hung around Wigg's neck, and the gifts of the two ancients were gradually coming back from the brink.

But as had been the case with Wigg's returning vision, the wizards had said nothing of how this wonderful thing had come about. The princess assumed that with the death of Nicholas had also come the cessation of his spells, thereby releasing the stone's power and allowing its natural return to the Paragon.

Shailiha was, of course, very pleased by these things, but in the end they did little to assuage the torment she felt over the death of her brother.

"You cared for him a great deal, didn't you?" she asked Celeste.

Celeste took a long breath, letting it out slowly. Her heavy-lidded, sapphire eyes lowered slightly, as if her mind had been taken to a different place and time.

"Yes, I cared," she answered quietly. "Or should I say, I was starting to. But I am still . . . fearful of men. Perhaps I always shall be; I do not know. I hope not. There remains a hard spot in my heart that is reluctant to let anyone in. Even Tristan— the one who saved me. But he was the first man ever to treat me with kindness. And I shall never forget that." She paused for a moment, thinking.

"Father and Faegan have told me that they have plans for me," she said tentatively.

"Plans?" Shailiha asked. "What does that mean?"

"I don't know," Celeste answered. "Only that they have to do with the craft. Something they apparently think is very important."

Celeste watched as Shailiha continued to rock her sleeping baby. More and more, she now dreamed of having a baby of her own some day, for she had finally achieved the freedom in which to foster such hopes. But when these thoughts started to creep into her mind, so too did her memories of Tristan. And then her fears would come again, forcing such pleasantries aside.

"Despite the unexplained death of Nicholas and the collapse of the Gates, there are still many problems," Shailiha said thoughtfully, interrupting Celeste's reveries. "The consuls that Nicholas said were under his control have still not been heard from. And we still do not know the whereabouts of the endowed boys and girls, or for that matter, the locations of the women our own age who have been trained in the craft."

A sad sort of quiet reigned over them for a moment. Aside from the death of Tristan, it was the unnerving disappearance of the boys and girls that had affected Shailiha and Celeste the most. And on this subject, too, the wizards had remained strangely quiet.

"And that is to say nothing of the situation in Parthalon," Shailiha finally added. "The swamp shrews continue to plague both the warriors and the civilian population alike."

"And without Tristan," Celeste said, "overcoming these problems shall be far more difficult."

Shailiha did not answer, for she did not know what to say.

* * *

𝒯rying to cross over had been difficult. There had been voices. Frightening voices. Voices that came and went, hauntingly wending their way through the fog. Unintelligible words at first, then sometimes less so. But always, finally, they retreated into nothingness. Words that came from nowhere, went to nowhere, meaning nothing.

There had also been azure, the color of the craft. Swirling everywhere. Its dense, glowing texture always surrounding and caressing, but somehow never really touching. Finally also fading away into the blackness that always came, retreated, and came again.

And there had been pain. Pain everywhere. Unrelenting, and horrible. Pain in both the azure and the darkness. Always, always, the pain.

Voices, azure, darkness, and pain. Swirling, mixing together, everywhere.

"This is the last of our chances," one of the voices said from somewhere far away.

"I know," replied the other. "There is no other choice."

"Are you ready?"

"Yes."

A long silence followed. Then more voices. More azure. More darkness, more pain.

"Let us begin," came the first voice.

"Very well," replied the other.

𝒯he knock on the door was strong, insistent, and decidedly masculine. "Come," Shailiha said.

The door opened to reveal Traax. "Forgive me, my ladies," he said almost apologetically. "But the wizards ask that both of you come with me."

Shailiha turned to Celeste, a worried look on her face. Celeste looked back quizzically. The wizards had barely spoken to either of them for a fortnight. Something was very wrong. Even the look on Traax's normally calm face said that some recent turn of events had affected him deeply. A rare thing, especially for an officer of the Minions.

Shailiha swallowed. Hard. Then she stood and squared her shoulders.

"Very well," she said calmly. Cradling Morganna in one arm, she donned the sling; then she placed the baby in it, careful not to wake her, and walked to the door, Celeste following behind.

They continued through the familiar areas of the Redoubt and eventually turned down long, cloistered hallways that were quite unknown to her. Shailiha was glad to see Traax finally slow before a rather large door.

"We are here," Traax said simply. He walked to a place of subservience behind both her and Celeste and stood quietly, waiting for them to enter. Shailiha knocked once, then twice. Upon hearing Wigg's voice, she opened the door and walked in.

Wondering what the wizards wanted of her, she glanced around the room. Then her eyes went wide, the blood rushed from her face, and she fainted away, falling like the dead into the arms of the Minion warrior behind her. A startled Morganna began to wail.

CHAPTER FIFTY-FIVE

❦

A short chuckle came from one side of the room, followed by a deep, hacking cough. "I told you she would react that way," the voice said weakly. Then another cough came. "She always has. Trust me, she will never forgive you. Either of you!"

Prince Tristan of the House of Galland sat up in his bed as well as his sore muscles would let him. He hurt everywhere, and was still so weak he doubted he could even walk across the room. Gray and gaunt, his face carried two weeks' worth of thick, dark whiskers.

Tristan had been awake since yesterday, trying to regain

some of his strength and enjoying the simple fact that he was both warm and alive. How or why, he still did not know. Since his return to consciousness Wigg and Faegan had remained tight-lipped, concentrating solely on his physical condition. But he intended to get his answers soon, wizards or no wizards.

He looked to his twin sister lying inert in Traax's strong arms. The baby had been handed to Celeste. His eyes welled briefly with tears. He then looked around the room at the others: Shannon, Michael, Ox, Geldon, and Celeste, not to mention Wigg and Faegan, of course.

"Lay Shailiha down on that sofa," Tristan ordered Traax, pointing to the large loveseat next to his bed. Traax did so. Lying there with her golden hair splayed out, Shailiha looked like an elaborate, limp, rag doll.

Celeste stood in the doorway, her arms hugging the baby, looking as if she had just seen a ghost. Her hands trembled slightly.

"Can it be true?" she asked softly, taking a tentative step into the room. "Are you really alive?"

"Yes." Tristan smiled, holding out his hands.

Immediately Celeste went to him, and gave him a kiss on the cheek. The welcome smell of the myrrh in her hair came back, reminding him of so much he once thought had been lost forever. Between them, Morganna fidgeted, gripping Tristan's hair with one tiny hand.

Faegan looked at Wigg. His friend's lips were pursed tightly, making it abundantly clear that Celeste's embrace of the prince had not been lost on him. Faegan grinned widely at Wigg's apparent discomfort.

One of the lead wizard's infamous eyebrows came up. He then purposely cleared his throat. As he did so, Celeste stood upright. Seeing that the handkerchief she had given Tristan was still tied around his left arm, she touched it and smiled.

"It helped," Tristan told her quietly. "This handkerchief, and the medallion around my neck, always kept reminding me of what I was fighting for."

"Don't you think it's time we revived your sister?" Wigg suddenly asked in that harsh but kindly manner only he seemed able to master. "By the way, now that I can see again, I no longer need ask any others in the room about what is truly going on."

Tristan actually found himself blushing. "By all means," he said. "Go ahead and revive her. But don't say I didn't warn you."

Wigg used the craft to wake the princess. Sitting up slowly, she looked around the room, her eyes finally falling upon her brother.

"Tristan . . . ," she whispered. Tears welled up. "Can it be true?"

She reached one trembling hand out to touch him, as if expecting him to vanish at any moment. But he didn't. Standing up on shaking legs, she crossed the short distance to his bed and fell on him, sobbing.

She remained that way for some time, his hand in her golden hair, until her gentle crying started to fade away. No one in the room spoke. There was no need. Finally she raised her head.

"They told us you were dead . . . I even lit your funeral pyre . . . How . . . ?" she asked, her words trailing away.

"I do not know yet," the prince answered. He looked up at Wigg, then over to Faegan. "I'd say the wizards have a great deal of explaining to do."

"The wizards . . . ," Shailiha whispered. Her mouth twisted into a frown, and she got up and stalked toward Wigg. Raising her arm, she slapped him hard across the shoulder.

Wincing, Wigg raised an eyebrow and rubbed the stinging shoulder briskly.

"If you ever do anything like that again, you'll be sorry!" she shouted. Tristan tried hard to stifle his laughter, barely succeeding. But Faegan could not, and actually cackled out loud.

Furious, Shailiha turned her narrowed, hazel eyes on the wizard in the chair. For the first time ever, Tristan saw Faegan's face actually redden with embarrassment. The old wizard's eyes widened, and he immediately closed his mouth. But, ecstatic at having fooled so many for so long, he recovered quickly. A snicker escaped his mouth, and then, giving in completely, he clapped his hands in glee. The princess scowled at him.

Celeste walked over to Shailiha and handed her the baby.

"I told you both she would react this way," Tristan smirked. "Now then, I want some answers from the two of you. I don't know how else to ask—how is it that I'm alive?"

"It's a rather long story," Faegan answered.

"You're both protected by time enchantments, aren't you?" Shailiha countered sarcastically, tapping her foot impatiently on the marble floor. "From what I understand of the craft, you have plenty of time."

Wigg cleared his throat. "Well, to begin, as to why the prince still lives—"

"Actually," Tristan interrupted, "tell me about the battle with the hatchlings. Everything makes sense to me up until that point. But then my bird took me away from the fighting. The bird that supposedly couldn't talk! I was unable to control it, and the Minions followed me, thinking I had ordered a full retreat." He turned to his sister, raising an eyebrow. "That was your doing, wasn't it?"

Shailiha's expression suddenly became more humble. "Yes," she answered. "Mine and the wizards'. That part of things I know, but little else."

"Explain," Tristan said simply.

"Do you remember the Forestallment Faegan discovered in my blood—the one that allows me to bond mentally with the fliers of the fields?" Shailiha asked.

"Yes."

"Well, as you also already know, the wizards had been of the opinion that Failee placed it there to allow me, as her intended fifth sorceress, to have a mental link with the Minions. Wigg and Faegan believe it was her original intent, among others, for me to eventually be able to probe the Minion minds, allowing me to discern whether there was ever any desire on their part to revolt. As it happens, the Forestallment she infused into my blood apparently works with other winged creatures of the craft, as well. The wizards asked me to infuse the saying 'Trust the process, Chosen One' into the hatchling's consciousness, along with when to say it, and other precise orders for it to follow during the battle. Other than that, the bird was ordered to say nothing. I repeated the phrase to you the day before the battle, so that you would make the connection and realize that what was happening was our doing. I then ordered the hatchling to fly to Shadowood, hoping that the Minions would follow and that the other hatchlings would pursue you." She smiled. "They all did."

"But how could you be aware of whether it all worked?" Tristan asked. "How did you know we were coming?"

Shailiha smiled. "Caprice, leading a specially picked group of fliers, hovered near the battle zone," she answered. "We have much to thank them for. I am glad to tell you that they all returned safely."

Bemused, Tristan looked quietly at his sister; then he turned to Faegan. "But if you wanted those things to happen, then why didn't you simply ask Shailiha to bond with Traax, instead of my hatchling?" he asked. "Or for that matter, simply inform me of your plan. You could even have used my hatchling, since it had the power of speech, to tell me more. I would gladly have followed it, leaving the scene of the battle as you wished."

"We considered that," Faegan said. "But there were too many ways for what you suggest to go wrong, and we couldn't take any more chances than were absolutely necessary. First of all, we did not know what the use of Shailiha's Forestallment upon the Minions might bring about, and we desperately needed their services to stave off the hatchling legions. Added to that is the fact that you are the Minions' lord, and this entire plan had to be done without your knowledge. We felt that if we used the Minions for this purpose, they might not have accepted the fact that their lord remained uninformed, even tricked, if you will. Therefore, the Minions might have felt duty-bound to tell you of our scheme. That could have easily ruined everything."

"You are quite right, wizard," Traax said sternly from the other side of the room. He crossed his muscular arms over his chest. "Had we been told, we would have considered it our sworn duty to inform our lord."

Tristan nodded, beginning to understand. "And so Shailiha had my hatchling leave the battle and fly to Shadowood, hoping that both the Minions and the hatchlings would follow."

"Correct," Wigg said. He raised his index finger for emphasis. "But we also knew that you must not leave the battle too early, nor too late. If done too soon, it might not have appeared as a full-fledged retreat, signaling the beginnings of the trap that it eventually turned out to be. And if done too late, there would not have been enough of your warriors left to be effective once you reached Shadowood. You were beginning to lose badly."

"But I still do not understand why you did not inform me," Tristan countered. "I could have led us there easily, without all of the subterfuge."

"True," Faegan answered. "But we did not know what plans Nicholas may have had for you. Remember, he was still hoping that you would join him in his cause. For all we knew at the time, he might even try to force you to do so. Had this been the case, and had Scrounge and his hatchlings been under orders to abduct you, all Nicholas would have had to do was test the quality of your heart to find his answer. We simply couldn't risk that."

"And so you had Shailiha order my bird to fly straight down into the canyon," Tristan mused. He ran a hand through his dark hair, thinking. "You took a great risk, did you not? The canyon is invisible except to those trained to see it. Clearly, the Minions and the hatchlings were not. How did you know they would follow?"

Wigg smiled. "We didn't. But we thought the odds were in our favor. We hoped the Minions would follow you into the canyon out of loyalty. Especially after they saw you disappear, rather than crash to your death into the earth. And as for the hatchlings, well, after they saw all the rest of you so mysteriously vanish, they no doubt believed you were escaping."

"And the gnomes, with the Minions you had brought to Shadowood, trapped them with nets," Tristan answered. "While the Minions that followed me were left free to hack them to pieces." He smiled to himself. Suddenly very tired from all of the talk, though, he laid his head down on the pillow.

"Are you all right?" Shailiha asked.

"Yes, Shai, I'll be fine," he answered. "But it's going to take a while." He looked back to Wigg. "Are the hatchlings all dead? The entire force?"

"Yes," Traax answered proudly from the other side of the room. "Every single one. The birds and their leader will trouble us no more."

Tristan uncoiled a little, glad to know that Scrounge was finally dead.

"Ox kill many bad birds," the giant Minion said, interrupting Tristan's thoughts. The great warrior stood to the side of the room with his chest puffed out proudly. "Ox enjoy that much."

Tristan smiled at the two warriors who, despite their part in the pillaging of his nation, had impossibly become not only his servants, but also his trusted friends.

"Thank you," he said softly.

"But there is still a great deal more to tell, isn't there?" Shailiha asked the wizards. As Traax had done, she crossed her arms over her chest in a gesture that clearly said she would not be denied. "And I want to hear all of it, right now." At the sight of her characteristically defiant posture, one corner of Tristan's mouth came up impishly.

"The answers as to why the prince still lives, why his son Nicholas does not, and why the Gates of Dawn seemed to self-destruct are far more complicated," Wigg began. "The best way to tell you all is to take you into yet another room." He gestured to Traax and Ox. "If you please, help the prince to follow me."

With that, Wigg narrowed his eyes. With his use of the craft, a hidden panel in the far wall began to turn on a pivot, revealing another room beyond.

Traax and Ox went to Tristan's bed and helped him stand. With his arms over the shoulders of the two warriors, he managed to stumble into the room. Celeste and Shailiha followed.

It was very spacious, constructed of shiny, rose-colored marble. Its unusually high number of oil chandeliers gave it a bright, almost sterile look. A large table with many chairs sat in the center. An even larger table sat nearby, covered with books and scrolls.

Off to one side sat something large, covered by a sheet of cloth. There was another object, similarly covered but differently shaped, on a rather long but narrow table. And still another table lay nearby with nothing on it.

"What is under the sheets?" Tristan asked as Traax and Ox helped him down into one of the comfortable chairs.

"That question shall be answered later," Wigg said once everyone was seated. "Now then, to answer your many other inquiries. First, to explain the death of Nicholas." He paused for a moment, looking around the table. His aquamarine eyes finally landed on the prince.

"You killed Nicholas, Tristan," he said softly. "You, Succiu, and Failee."

"What are you talking about?" Tristan exclaimed, taken aback. "Succiu and Failee are dead. You burned their bodies yourself, in Parthalon."

"Quite true," Faegan said from the other end of the table. "A fact we are all certainly glad of. But please listen to what Wigg has to say."

Wigg extended one hand toward the table covered with papers, and a scroll of parchment rose into the air and floated to his grasp. He unrolled it and held it up for Tristan's inspection. "Do you recognize this?" he asked the prince.

Tristan looked down at it. "Of course," he said. "It is Nicholas' blood signature."

"Correct," Wigg answered. "Now I want you to run your fingers over the signature, and tell me if you feel anything unusual."

Reaching out, Tristan drew the parchment to him. He placed the tips of his first two fingers on the azure signature and began tracing over it. He felt nothing other than the light scratchiness of the dried blood that one might expect to feel.

"I don't feel anything," he answered, withdrawing his hand.

"Precisely," Wigg answered. "Now, please give me that same hand."

Tristan did so. Wigg closed his eyes. Almost immediately their joined hands became bathed in the glow of the craft. Tristan felt a slight tingling, but it was not painful. Wigg opened his eyes, and the glow of the craft vanished. Tristan took back his hand.

"What did you just do?" he asked, puzzled.

"I have employed the craft to temporarily enhance the feeling in your fingertips." The wizard smiled. "Now then, retrace them over the signature. Stop when you feel something unusual. And by the way," he added, giving the prince a strange smile, "it might help if you close your eyes."

Tristan placed his fingertips once more on the blood, closing his eyes. He began to retrace the path he had taken earlier.

The sensation was amazing. He could now feel every little

bump, every nuance of the dried blood as his fingers traced the lines. And then, just as he approached one of the gentle curves at the top, he abruptly stopped. He backed up, tracing over the spot again.

Sure of his findings, Tristan opened his eyes and looked down. But he could see nothing unusual about the signature he had just felt.

"There is a gap in the top line of the signature," he said quietly, still not fully understanding the ramifications of his words. "Why can I feel it with my fingers, but not see it with my eyes?"

"The answer to that is very simple," Faegan answered. "The lead wizard did not enchant your eyes."

"But what does all of this mean?" Shailiha asked. "I am assuming that this 'gap' is some kind of imperfection. But how did it get there? Does this mean that Tristan's blood signature is imperfect, too? And what did you mean about Tristan, Succiu, and Failee having all killed Nicholas?"

Wigg smiled. "One question at a time, Your Highness. First of all, as to how the imperfection came about." He took a deep breath, thinking about how to best explain.

"We shall begin at the beginning," he said. "First of all, we believe that the Forestallments discovered by Faegan were created by Failee, first mistress of the Coven, and were placed into Tristan's blood during Succiu's rape of him. Succiu's immediate, endowed conception of Nicholas meant that Nicholas not only carried Tristan's blood, albeit in a slightly less powerful form because it was mingled with hers, but that he also inherited Tristan's Forestallments. As you may remember, the fact that Forestallments can be passed on from one generation to another was proven when we examined the blood of Morganna, Shailiha's daughter."

"So it was his inherited Forestallments that killed him?" Celeste asked skeptically.

Wigg smiled. "No, Daughter," he answered. "It was Nicholas' Forestallments that made him strong."

"What is all of this leading to?" Tristan asked impatiently.

"Think back," Wigg said. "Back to that fateful day in Parthalon when you chased Succiu to the roof of the Recluse. I know this is painful for you, but tell me—was Nicholas ever really born into this world?"

Tristan closed his eyes for a moment, taking himself back in time to that day in the rain—the day he lost his son. "No," he answered. "Succiu jumped from the roof just as she went into labor. She landed in the moat and died. I took her out and incised Nicholas from her womb with my knife, then buried him in the little grave."

"That's right," Wigg said softly, understanding how hard this was for the prince. "And as such, Nicholas was never really 'born.' "

"I still don't get your meaning," Shailiha said.

"The meaning is really very simple," Faegan said from his chair. "When Succiu jumped from the roof, killing herself and her unborn child, she interrupted Nicholas' gestation."

"But that can't be correct," Tristan protested. "If Succiu went into labor, doesn't that mean that Nicholas' gestation was complete? Is that not the natural order of things? Or are you telling me that his birth was premature?"

"No," Wigg answered. "His birth was not premature. But that is not to say that his blood was fully formed."

"What are you talking about?"

"After greater study of Egloff's scroll, Faegan and I now believe that the blood signature is the last thing to form in the unborn, endowed child. We think that this happens just before birth, perhaps even occurring as late as labor. But until now, we could never prove it. However, the strange, unexpected death of Nicholas atop the gates, combined with the circumstances surrounding his aborted, earthly birth, finally do just that. You see, the act of the blood signature forming is the craft's way of placing its final, unique mark upon yet another of its potential practitioners, if you will. But the blood of Nicholas was never given enough time to do so. He was killed when Succiu jumped, just as her labor began. In essence, he was never really born. His body had been prepared for his birth, but the blood signature had not finished forming completely. The virtually microscopic size of the gap is further proof of how narrowly close his signature was to completing itself, just as Succiu went into labor. Had she not jumped when she did, and instead given birth naturally, his signature would have formed completely. Trust me when I say that had this occurred, our futures would have been very different."

"Then it was this 'gap,' this imperfection, that killed him?" Tristan asked.

"Of and by itself, no," Wigg answered. "But it was the major contributing factor. It was actually his gathering of the power of the Paragon into himself, and his subsequent empowerment of the Gates of Dawn, that finally killed him. Had he never tried to accomplish such an incredibly high aspect of the craft he might have lived among us forever, the imperfection in his blood of absolutely no consequence. But he was most certainly not sent here to accomplish the mundane."

The lead wizard sat back in his chair, seeing that the faces gathered around him were still very perplexed. "When one of the trained endowed calls upon the craft, the endowed's blood in turn calls upon the Paragon," he elaborated. "It is a symbiotic relationship, and always has been. Tristan, do you remember that day on the mountain, when I told you that the most important determinant of the power of an endowed person is the inherent quality of his or her blood? That has always been true. When Nicholas took so much of the power of the stone into himself, he magnified both his powers and Forestallments hundreds of times over. Perhaps even more. This occurred for two reasons. First and foremost, in order to have the power required to perform the Confluence. And secondly, to simultaneously reduce the powers of Faegan and myself. From the very beginning this was the plan of the Heretics, the ones who sent him here. Whenever he needed to call upon his blood for any so-called 'normal' use of the craft, such as his conjuring of the hatchlings, he had no need to draw upon all of the power of the stone and his blood could stand the strain, so to speak. Simply put, the imperfection in his blood signature did not matter." Wigg paused for a moment, letting his words sink in.

"But when he needed to call upon so much more of the power of the stone to activate the Gates of Dawn as was dictated by the Confluence, bringing to life both the mixture of endowed fluids covering them and the azure blood of the Heretics that already lay within, his blood simply could not survive it."

Wigg again looked at Tristan. "In the end," Wigg said quietly, "Nicholas died of simple blood loss." He watched the mixed emotions that played across Tristan's face.

"Do you remember how your blood reacted in the Caves, when we spent too much time trying to decide whether to enter the tunnel?" Wigg continued. "Now imagine that same kind of feeling, that agitation of endowed blood if you will, magnified literally hundreds of times over."

Out of respect for the prince, the table went quiet for a long time. Finally it was Tristan who broke the silence.

"But there is still something I do not understand," he said. "Nicholas appeared to me as a grown man. That was why I could not recognize him at first. How could he return to our world in so short a time as a fully mature being?"

"An excellent question," Faegan said from the far end of the table. "And if Wigg will allow me, I will endeavor to answer it." Glancing over to the lead wizard, Faegan saw him nod.

"First of all," he began, "it is entirely possible that Nicholas was returned by the Heretics while still an infant, or at least as a very small child. But if the Heretics were aware of the many Forestallments he inherited from Tristan, as we now believe they must have been, then they may also have been able to enact many or all of them before sending him here, giving him immense wisdom and powers for one so young. These abilities would have had little or nothing to do with his chronological age. And as we now know from Shailiha's experiences with winged creatures of the craft, Forestallments can be activated even if the subject has never been trained. In fact, it is quite logical to assume that *all* of Nicholas' gifts were the result of Forestallments. And if that is true, we may then postulate that as he took the power of the stone for himself, both his physical and mental growth continued to advance at a rate never before seen."

"So he never knew of the imperfection in his signature?" Tristan asked.

"That is correct," Wigg answered. "Neither did the Heretics, or they would not have sent him here. In this we were most fortunate."

"But how on earth did you first come upon the imperfection in his blood, when neither Nicholas nor the Heretics ever did?" Tristan asked. "Frankly, such a thing seems quite impossible."

"Yet another piece of the puzzle," Faegan said, smiling. "One that we have Ragnar to thank for."

"What are you talking about?" Celeste asked. At the mention of his name her face had gone dark, her eyes hard.

"Ragnar blinded Wigg by having the dried brain fluid placed into his eyes," Faegan answered. "When we were examining Nicholas' blood signature, Wigg had to pass his fingers over it in order to 'see' it, if you will. It was then that he first noticed the anomaly." He paused for a moment, collecting his thoughts.

"Armed with that first bit of information, we began our research," he continued. "As for the Heretics, they no doubt never employed this rather bizarre method of reading a blood signature. Why would they? It is highly untypical of beings, even those as gifted as the Heretics seem to be, to go looking for things they believe cannot exist."

"And because Nicholas was unable to complete the Confluence," Tristan mused, "the process was halted, and the Gates self-destructed. Therefore the blood of the Heretics was never fully empowered, and their spirits were forced back into the heavens."

"Yes," Wigg said. "And the spell Nicholas designed to destroy the scarabs was enacted, killing the vast majority of them before the Confluence was halted. We sent the Minions to search out and destroy the rest. But Tristan remains a wanted man. And the Brotherhood of Consuls has supposedly been turned by Nicholas' use of the craft, and that body is now leaderless. Only the Afterlife knows their state of affairs. Such a group could become very dangerous indeed."

"And we still don't know where the endowed children are," Celeste added sadly. "Or the trained, fully grown women of the craft." The resulting silence lasted for a long time.

"But now I want the answer to my first question," Shailiha finally demanded. "How is it that Tristan still lives?"

"I can remember almost dying," the prince said quietly. "I had the sensation of floating. It was almost as if my blood was trying to take me someplace far away. But most of what I recollect is nothing more than azure, pain, and darkness. I heard voices come and go, but they meant nothing to me. And then I was suddenly awake, here in the Redoubt. What happened?"

"You were having your fourth and final convulsion just as

the Gates were collapsing beneath you," Wigg answered quietly. "You were unable to reach the antidote that Nicholas kept with him to tease you to his side. Then the Gates collapsed fully, and you started down with them."

"But how can you possibly know all of this?" Tristan asked incredulously. "You weren't there!"

"True," Wigg replied, pursing his lips. "But Traax and Ox were."

"What?" Tristan exclaimed. "What do you mean, they were there?"

"After we ordered your hatchling to fly you to the Gates, we ordered the two Minion warriors to follow you," Wigg answered. His mouth turned up in a smile.

Tristan looked at the two Minion warriors as they sat there, beaming with pride. "Ox save Chosen One after all," Ox said, a huge smile on his bearded face. "It his duty."

Tristan smiled, closing his eyes in understanding. "And when Nicholas died and the Gates finally collapsed, the Minions plucked me from them, just as they went down."

"Yes," Faegan said. "But not just you." He unleashed the self-satisfied grin that told the prince there were still secrets to be revealed.

"What do you mean?" Tristan asked.

Faegan leaned forward conspiratorially. "They retrieved Nicholas' dead body, as well."

Tristan nodded. "And they took the antidote from his robes, and forced it down my throat."

"That's right," Wigg said. "And there was just enough left for me, as well. That is why my sight returned."

Tristan looked over at Shailiha. With tearful eyes she placed one hand over his.

"We knew the odds were overwhelmingly against both Nicholas dying before you did, and the warriors being able to procure the antidote from him in time to help you," Faegan added. "We also knew Traax and Ox would have to wait until Nicholas was dead, if indeed he was going to die at all, before they could risk exposing themselves. Had Nicholas seen them they would have died on the spot. But what other choice did we have? We asked for a miracle, and it was granted."

"And then Traax dropped Nicholas' body into the ruins of

the collapsing Gates," Tristan assumed, nodding slowly. "It is somehow fitting."

Taking a deep breath and narrowing his eyes, Wigg smiled at Faegan. "Not exactly," he said slyly.

"What do you mean?" Tristan asked.

Wigg turned to one of the three rather mysterious tables that stood on the other side of the room. With a turn of his hand, the sheet rose from one of them.

Nicholas lay on it, still dressed in his white robes. He was apparently quite dead. Dried rivulets of azure blood could still be seen on his face and robes.

Shailiha gasped, covering her mouth; Celeste, Geldon, and the gnomes all opened their eyes wide in shock. The Minions simply grinned knowingly.

"Why?" Tristan asked, his voice barely a whisper.

"We considered ordering the Minions to cremate him at the Gates," Wigg answered. "But then we took a chance and told them to bring his body back, if at all possible, so that we might further study his blood. We felt that much might still be revealed by such an endeavor," Wigg said. "After all, we have never been able to examine endowed blood that has traveled not only to the Afterlife, but also back again. And secondly, if it could be returned without incident, we wanted it here, in the depths of the Redoubt. We certainly did not wish to leave his remains out in the open. We felt that if the body was placed here, so far below ground, the Heretics might not be able to retrieve it again. As for why they apparently did not try to take him back at the Gates, we can only surmise that they witnessed the flaw in this blood signature and realized they had no more use for him." Wigg's eyebrow came up once more. "And a good thing, too, for we wouldn't want a repetition of what happened in Parthalon, now would we? But as it happened, there turned out to be an even more important reason for the return of Nicholas' body. One that even we were unaware of."

"And that was?" Tristan asked.

"You were very near to death when Ox finally brought you here," Wigg said. He looked over at the Minion warrior. "I am forced to say that I am not sure I have ever seen such unswerving loyalty, even among what used to be our Royal Guard," he added. "Anyway, you had almost no pulse. You were suffering from dehydration, exposure, and frostbite. Worse yet, the dark veins in your arm had covered almost your entire body. The antidote had done much to help keep you from dying, but you were too far along in your fourth convulsion by the time you ingested it. You were therefore left hanging somewhere between life and death. You were crossing over into the Afterlife, and we had to hurry." Smiling again, he looked to Faegan. "So we improvised."

"You *improvised*?" Tristan exclaimed. He looked first at his sister, and then to Celeste. "I'm almost afraid to ask," he said softly.

Without speaking, Wigg again raised his hand. The other, much larger sheet covering the third table rose into the air, revealing what was beneath. Tristan's eyes went wide.

On the table sat a very large, clear ball. Its interior was separated into two equal parts by a transparent dividing wall. One half of the ball contained what appeared to be an azure substance, waving back and forth gently. The other half contained a darker, rather murky fluid that lay perfectly still.

From the outer edges of the ball ran a great many individual tubes, also made of some clear substance. At the end of each tube was a shiny, silver needle. The strange-looking contrivance seemed to crouch on the table like some kind of horrific, multicolored, crystalline spider, its legs drooping down to the floor.

"What in the name of the Afterlife is that thing?" Tristan asked. He was truly puzzled. "Where did it come from? What is in it?"

"We don't really know what it is called," Faegan replied. "Or even if it has a name. Wigg and I have been calling it the Sphere of Collection."

"And just what does it do?" Shailiha asked.

"Well, for one thing, it helped saved Tristan's life," Wigg answered.

"How?" the princess asked.

"Let me begin at the beginning," Wigg said. "Just after Traax and Ox returned with Tristan, we administered the rest of the antidote to him. But, as I said, he was still dying. While we were attending him, we also sent a force of Minions, again under Traax's command, to Fledgling House. We wanted to see if there were by chance any children remaining there.

They found no children, dead or alive. But what they did find was another small contingent of hatchlings, camped outside, protecting the castle. Apparently Nicholas had planned to return. This time, however, it was the hatchlings that were outnumbered. Surprising them from above, Traax, Ox, and their forces dealt with them swiftly, wisely burning the bodies afterward. When they finally walked inside the small castle, they were astounded at what they saw."

"And that was?" Tristan asked impatiently.

"In a great hall sat this sphere," Wigg answered. "On the walls of the room were hung small, coffinlike structures. Remains of endowed blood lay everywhere—on the walls, the floor, and all around the sphere. Supposing it to be a device of the craft, perhaps even something important, Traax and Ox brought it here. Only later did we learn just how important it was." Wigg glanced at the ominous-looking sphere. A dark look came to his face.

"After examining some of the blood signatures taken from what remained in the sphere, we quickly ascertained that it was into this device that Nicholas had collected the blood of the children. Exceedingly clever, when you stop to think about it. Faegan and I can see many other practical applications that the sphere can lend itself to—applications for good, rather than evil. But I digress." He returned his attention to the table.

"Just how did this thing save me?" Tristan asked. Clearly tired, he took a deep breath, running one hand through his dark hair.

"Endowed blood can live, albeit briefly, outside the body," Faegan said. "This phenomenon is witnessed by the blood signature."

Tristan sat back in his chair, thinking. "But what does all of this have to do with me?" he asked.

"After the failed Confluence, Nicholas' blood, because it had been infused with such an inordinately vast amount of the power of the stone, lived far longer than normal without its host—his living body," Faegan interjected. "This amazing precedent, plus the recovery of the Sphere of Collection, got Wigg and me to thinking. We formulated a plan, and then carried it out." He grinned mischievously at the prince, knowing that in a few moments he was about to shock everyone. Except for Wigg, of course.

"So what did you finally do?" Tristan asked.

Faegan looked across the table at Wigg. Taking a breath, he pushed his cheek out with his tongue and raised his eyebrows. "We used the Sphere of Collection to remove some of your poisoned blood, simultaneously replacing it with an equal amount from the corpse of your son."

Aghast, Tristan couldn't speak. He had never heard of such a bizarre thing. It seemed to him as if they had both somehow gone completely, irretrievably mad.

"You did what?" he shouted at last.

"It was your poisoned blood that was killing you, Tristan," Wigg said. "And it was the very high quality of Nicholas' blood, empowered by the stone, that was keeping his blood alive long after his body had expired. We believed that if we removed some of your tainted blood, replacing it with an equal amount of Nicholas', your blood would in turn be 'healed' from the poison. We were right. In less than two days following the procedure the dark veins covering your body began to recede, and you regained consciousness. We are sure it shall require at least several weeks for you to return to full health, but we are also equally sure that you shall. No one else—other than Traax and Ox, of course—knew that you were here, alive and under our care. We felt it best not to get everyone's spirits up, only to have them dashed again. Your funeral pyre and our descriptions of the searches conducted by Traax and Ox were merely window dressing, so that we might work uninterrupted."

"But why couldn't you tell us?" Shailiha protested. "What you did seems terribly cruel!"

"I know," Wigg answered softly. "And we apologize. But we thought it for the best. At the time, we couldn't be sure there weren't still hatchlings about, such as those Traax discovered waiting at Fledgling House. Or, for that matter, if Ragnar was dead. Should they have regrouped and come for us again, they wouldn't be able to torture from you what you didn't know. Had that happened, and they learned that the prince lived, they would have come for him, and we would have been unable to stop them. Then he would have died in truth. I am truly sorry that we had to cause so much pain with this deception."

Tristan looked over at his sister. The look on her face was one of both amazement and consternation. She wanted to be angry at the wizards for not telling her, but she couldn't be.

Wigg then looked into the dark eyes of the Chosen One with a meaningfulness he rarely showed. "In some ways Nicholas will remain a part of your being," he said. Another long period of silence descended.

"But what are the ramifications of this?" Shailiha finally asked. "Will Tristan's blood be somehow harmed, or changed?"

"No," Faegan answered. "You see, Nicholas' blood was already partly Tristan's blood, as well. Because of that, they are compatible, so to speak. Also, we did not have to employ a large quantity of Nicholas' blood. Therefore, the blood of the son shall not overcome the blood of the father. Rather, the reverse will become true. Given time, Tristan's blood shall be just as it once was. We are certain that a simple test of his blood signature, taken several weeks from now, will confirm this."

"And then there is perhaps the most important development of all," Wigg went on. "The improved condition of the Paragon. Blessedly, the stone has completely reclaimed its power."

"But there is yet another issue that must be dealt with," Faegan interjected.

"And that is?" Tristan asked.

"Why Nicholas let us have possession of the Tome," Faegan replied. "We had always considered that to be extremely odd, to say the least. Upon restoring it to its original size and examining it closely, I got my answer."

"How so?" Shailiha asked.

"Because the great treatise of the craft, the one work we rely on the most for our understanding of magic, has been altered," Faegan said bluntly. "As Nicholas read the Tome, he was at the same time changing it. Falsifying it, to suit his plans. He no doubt had the power of Consummate Recollection, as do I, and had read the entire treatise. But in his case, the gift of Consummate Recollection would have been vastly more powerful, probably enabling him to recite specific passages, perhaps even entire volumes, immediately. Therefore he no longer required the original. So he altered it, turning it into yet another weapon to employ against us. The concept was fiendishly clever, for the changes he made were not blindingly obvious. They were designed to make us stumble and try again, rather than to fall outright. Such small changes also helped ensure that it would take much longer for us to realize it had been violated. He knew that we would rely on the great book to help us better understand our many problems. What better way to make things more difficult for us than to falsify the very text we needed the most? With great effort, I should be able to use my gift of Consummate Recollection to restore it. But the amount of work and time required will be staggering."

Tristan looked around at his friends, then at the dead body of his son.

"There is something else that you must know, Tristan," Wigg said gently. "And this may be the most difficult thing of all for you to hear." The wizard glanced at the Sphere of Collection, then looked back at the prince. "It's about Nicholas' blood," he said. "All of the power of the stone is now gone from it. Therefore the last part of your son's living being is finally dying."

Tristan looked over to see that the little azure waves in the sphere were moving more slowly now. Taking a breath, he placed his hands flat on the table in preparation to stand. Immediately Traax, Ox, and Shailiha stood to help him. Tristan looked darkly at Wigg, and the wizard understood. With a quick, sure gesture from the ancient one, Traax, Ox, and Shailiha all stopped and moved away.

With great difficulty, the prince stood on his own. Walking to the sphere on shaking legs, he stared down at the strange device that had helped save his life. He gently placed one of his palms atop it.

As he watched, his son's blood slowed its movements even further, finally stopping. And then, as if someone had silently extinguished a candle, the glow emanating from the blood softened . . . and vanished forever.

Wiping away tears, Tristan shuffled over to the table that held the body of his son. The dark blue, upturned eyes were still open. Reaching down, he gently closed the lids. Then he picked the sheet up from the marble floor and carefully draped it over the body. He knew the wizards would want to cremate the remains. And this time he would not stop them.

Nicholas II of the House of Galland, he thought, remembering the words he had carved into the makeshift marker he had shoved into the soft earth over the little grave in Parthalon.

You shall not be forgotten.

Walking back to the table, the prince leaned weakly against his chair. Extremely tired, he wanted nothing more than to return to his bed and sleep forever. He said so. With the help of the Minions, he went back into the other room and fell into bed. Celeste gently pulled the covers up around his shoulders.

Tristan looked up into Wigg's face as the old one came to the bedside. He could barely keep his eyes open. "Would you do me a favor, Lead Wizard?" he asked sleepily.

"Anything."

"The next time you and Faegan make such grandiose plans, tell me about them, would you?"

Wigg looked down, his eyes shiny. He raised the infamous eyebrow, and one corner of his mouth came up knowingly.

"We'll try, Chosen One," he said softly. "We'll try."

Tristan slept.

CHAPTER FIFTY-SIX

THE freshly fallen snow twinkling beneath his horse's hooves, Tristan rode Pilgrim ever higher up the side of the mountain. It felt good to have the dappled gray-and-white stallion beneath him again, and being here was a welcome change from the relative mustiness and seclusion of the Redoubt. The air was clean, cold, fresh, and laced with the scent of pine needles. As Pilgrim brought down each hoof, taking Tristan deeper into the Hartwick Woods, the memories of this place came flooding back.

Stretching his still-sore muscles, he looked up to the sky. For the most part, the atmosphere above him was blue, with fat, puffy clouds sailing through its boundlessness.

Two weeks had passed since Tristan had regained consciousness in the Redoubt, and much of his strength had already returned. But he still had a long way to go, and he knew it. The dark veins that had once covered his body were gone, and the searing pain had been replaced with the relative relief of fatigue, soreness in his joints, and lingering weakness in his muscles. Otherwise, he felt like himself again. He smiled as Pilgrim stepped over a fallen log half buried in the mountain snow.

The first thing he had done after getting out of bed was to shave off his two-week-old beard. Shailiha had teased him mercilessly about it, telling him that between his recent illness and the full beard, he was looking more like their late father every day.

Everyone was greatly relieved that the threat from Nicholas and his creatures was gone, and their lives had regained at least a modicum of normalcy. Tristan, Shailiha and her baby, Celeste, and the others living in the Redoubt had all taken up residence in the royal palace above. Only Wigg and Faegan had refused to budge, remaining cloistered below. For Tristan and Shailiha it was indeed liberating to again be back in their old home, where the air was sweeter and the light of day could come streaming through the windows and skylights.

But the condition of the castle above was poor, making their security questionable, at best. Not only had the structure been looted, but parts of it, especially many of the windows and doorways, had been destroyed. Tristan had had the Minions transfer some furniture and decorative pieces from the Redoubt, as well as a good bit of food, wine, kitchen utensils, and linens. But the structural repairs had only just begun.

Drawing his ragged fur jacket closer around him to ward off a gust of wind, he smiled again. Shawna the Short and Mary the Minor, each of them wanting to take full control over all the ongoing domestic responsibilities, had begun shouting orders and squabbling as badly as Wigg and Faegan ever had—perhaps even worse.

Tristan had spent most of his time trying to get well. He had been practicing a great deal with both his dreggan and his throwing knives, so as to sharpen his skills and strengthen his weakened muscles. He estimated that he had only reacquired about half of his original speed. But little by little, every day he trained, he also improved. And it was good to practice again, even though he could not do so for prolonged periods.

Shailiha, Celeste, and Martha tended quietly to life at the castle and looked after Morganna. Wigg had joined Faegan in his attempts to restore the falsified Tome, but he also took time from that tedious work to get to know his daughter better.

But whenever Tristan thought of Celeste, as he so often did, he felt strangely conflicted. He was very drawn to her. Everyone living there knew it, including Wigg. But even though he sensed she cared for him, she also showed reticence in becoming closer. Further complicating things was the fact that she was the only daughter of his lifelong mentor and friend. In truth, Wigg knew her little better than Tristan did. Sometimes the prince felt he should try to shelve his feelings in order to allow the father and daughter to first come to grips with their new, blossoming relationship, and only then try to enter her heart more deeply. If indeed he ever did.

Wrenching his thoughts away from Celeste, he turned around in his saddle to check on the object he was bringing into the woods. It was his sole reason for coming up here today alone. For the first time in what seemed forever, there was no bodyguard of Minion warriors or clutch of helpful but quarrelsome gnomes to trample on his sense of peace. For what he intended to do was strictly a private affair.

He was going to scatter to the four winds the ashes of his only child, Nicholas, at the grave site of his family.

Finally approaching the little glade, he slowed his horse, then jumped down and tied Pilgrim to a nearby tree. The stallion affectionately rubbed his long face against Tristan's shoulder as the prince untied the flap of the saddlebag to carefully remove a small urn sealed with wax.

Tristan stood at the edge of the clearing for some time, the memories of the people buried there swirling in his heart and mind. So too came back to him the thoughts of that amazing night he had saved Celeste from throwing herself off the cliff, when he was convinced that he would never see her again. He shook his head slowly.

Taking a deep breath, he walked into the center of the glade, where he had dug the graves containing his family and the Directorate of Wizards.

He went to his knees in the snow and gently placed the vase down next to him. Closing his eyes, he bowed his head, the only sounds the swirling of the wind through the surrounding pines and the occasional songs of the birds.

Had he been completely well, he might have heard the steps that came so quietly through the snow behind him. Or had his eyes been open, he might have seen the lengthening shadow as it slid silently across the ground.

But he did not.

He had barely a moment to register the pain of the blow to his head. And then everything went black.

The smell of smoke awakened him. Pine needles again, this time mixed with maple. Sooty and acrid, it was coming from a fire that burned and snapped too close to his head.

As he opened his eyes, his vision swam sickeningly. Slowly, it came into better focus, revealing white clouds sailing against the background of a bright blue sky. He was lying on his back. As he tried to sit up, his head hammered like an anvil. And then a sudden, sickening realization went through him.

His weapons had been taken.

"Welcome back, Chosen One," came a voice from behind him. "So glad to see you are finally up and about."

Tristan froze. Even without looking, he knew who spoke. But his mind refused to believe what his ears were telling him. Slowly he stood, and turned around.

The angular, almost emaciated face; decaying teeth; and dirty, wispy hair were just as Tristan remembered them. A campfire burned in the snow between them, a small stack of freshly cut wood sitting next to it. Scrounge sat rather imperiously on the gathered logs, keeping himself out of the snow. A Eutracian broadsword lay at his right hip, a dagger sheathed in a golden scabbard at his left. Tristan immediately recognized the knife as Wigg's centuries-old ceremonial dagger, the same one Ragnar had used to place the poison into the helpless wizard's eyes.

Then the prince's gaze went to Scrounge's right forearm. The sleeve of his fur coat was rolled back, revealing the miniature crossbow still strapped there, containing its five arrows. The string cocked tightly, it was clearly ready to fire. Scrounge raised it slightly, more perfectly aligning it with the prince's heart. Tristan looked closely, and his nerves jangled in his skin.

The tip of each of the arrows was still stained in yellow.

Trying to calm himself, he looked beyond the assassin for a moment. Some distance away, Scrounge's horse was tied to a tree. Hung on the pommel of the saddle were Tristan's dreggan and his quiver full of dirks. To reach them, Tristan realized he would have to go straight through Scrounge, something that now seemed impossible. Lying on the ground behind the assassin's horse was a crude litter.

Tristan looked back into the face he so hated, a flood of anger coursing through his blood. "You're supposed to be dead, you bastard!" he snarled. His head was still swimming from the blow, his footing unsteady. He tried desperately to concentrate. "Which of my Minions failed me, allowing the likes of you to live? Apparently, I am going to have to finish the job myself."

Scrounge smiled. "A great many of your warriors failed, I'm afraid. When I saw you at the bottom of the canyon, I immediately knew it could be a trap. But when I saw the nets descending, I realized that my hatchlings were surely about to be destroyed. Very cleverly done, I might add. When you suddenly soared up, I turned my bird around and flew back the opposite way, down the length of the canyon. As I did, I stopped every hundred meters or so, urging the remaining hatchlings ever forward, giving them the impression I was still actively commanding them. They were all going to die anyway. So I used them to save myself. They're actually quite stupid, you know. And in truth, I much prefer a horse." A sick laugh came from him before he continued.

"Anyway, after covering what I thought to be a sufficient distance behind my troops, I headed up and out. Two of your warriors did see me, attacking me from above." Pausing, he pursed his lips sarcastically. "But things ended badly for them." He glanced down to his crossbow, and his meaning was not lost on the prince.

"The vast majority of your flying monkeys and scrubby-looking gnomes were so enthralled with what they had captured in their nets, they forgot to look for what they might *not* have captured. Even your wizards did not see me," he went on.

"Not particularly honorable of you," Tristan said quietly, "running away like that. But then again, you're not the honorable type, are you?"

"Honor?" Scrounge laughed. "And perhaps the good and *honorable* Prince Tristan of the House of Galland will kindly tell me what one can do with honor! Can you eat it, good prince? No! Can you spend it? No! Will it buy you either the comfort of a jug of wine, or a hot meal? Or purchase for you the warmth of a willing young whore, to stave off the coldness of a night of the Season of Crystal? Decidedly not! Honor, indeed!"

Scrounge spat into the fire; the saliva hissed its way down, dying in the flames. Raising one foot on the pile of logs, he lowered the forearm with the crossbow to his knee. It still pointed directly at Tristan's chest.

"But what would you know of such things, eh?" he continued. "Has the good prince ever been alone and crying, orphaned on the streets of Tammerland? Or slept in a cold alleyway, wondering if he will eat tomorrow? Or fearing what he must do to ensure that he can? Honor, he tells me! I was never in it for the honor, you fool—only for whatever Ragnar and Nicholas would give me! Crumbs from their table, to be sure, but oh, what crumbs they were! I am an assassin, the best there is, and my services go to the highest bidder. The only problem with that is that you have now managed to kill both my employers! Now that Nicholas and Ragnar are gone, and the Gates destroyed, you are the only remaining solution to my problems." He smiled strangely. "Do you not see that, my prince?"

"No," Tristan answered angrily. "Are you insane? How is it that I am supposed to solve your problems? All I want of you is to see you die."

"Ah," Scrounge answered. "We finally come to the heart of it. The one and only thing that the two us have in common. Except, perhaps, for the mutual desire to taste Celeste. And what is that one thing that binds us together, you ask? Why, our overriding desire to see the death of the other, of course. But our reasons for wanting these things are vastly different. You, you fool, do it for honor."

"And you?" Tristan asked. "Just why is it that you still want my head? You could very easily escape, without the bother of confronting me. As you yourself just said, both of your employers are quite dead." He paused for a moment, lowering his eyes menacingly. "And as you are about to discover," he added softly, "I am not so easily killed."

The crossbow continued to point straight at Tristan's heart. At this range if the assassin released one of the yellow-tipped arrows, there would be nothing the prince could do to avoid it.

"Can't you guess why I'm here?" Scrounge asked.

"No," Tristan answered calmly. "Why don't you enlighten me?"

"It's the reward, of course!" Scrounge exploded. He snorted derisively, as if he were speaking to some dullard. "The one hundred thousand gold kisa your son offered for your life! A veritable king's ransom! Or, in this case, should I say 'prince's'? The reward Nicholas never wanted collected, and believed would never be. Or have you forgotten? The prize still stands, and I plan to be the one who collects it."

Tristan's heart skipped a beat. Not because he suddenly realized that only one of them would come down off this mountain alive. He had known that from the moment he saw Scrounge. Rather, it was from the confirmation that he was still a wanted man, blamed for actions the populace did not know he had been forced to commit.

"I don't believe you," Tristan bluffed. "Ragnar and Nicholas are both dead, so there is no one left to pay you the money. And if they had conjured the kisa before their deaths, you would have simply stolen it and run, not bothering with coming after me. The pieces of your story don't fit."

Scrounge smiled. "That's because you don't have all of the pieces," he answered. "In fact, the money exists, and is still being offered—but by someone new."

Tristan narrowed his eyes skeptically. "And just who might that be?" he asked.

Scrounge tilted his head slightly, relishing the moment. "Can't you guess?" he answered quietly. "Your hunters are now the remaining consuls of the Redoubt."

Tristan couldn't believe it—the once compassionate Brotherhood of Consuls wanted to see their prince dead.

"I still don't believe you," he bluffed again. "Why would they want me killed?"

"Oh, they have their reasons, of that you may be sure," Scrounge answered. "But there is still more to this story. The story of what is about to happen to you."

Tristan could do little but stare back at Scrounge. He desperately missed the familiar, comforting weight of his weapons across his back. Without them he felt very vulnerable, and alone. But even if he had them back, he wasn't sure he would be able to kill the assassin—not in his still-weakened state. Dark edges of gloom began to press in on the corners of his mind, but he pushed them back. He cringed even more as he watched Scrounge draw the ceremonial dagger from his belt. The blade's sharp edges were still coated in yellow powder.

"If you're going to kill me, then why don't you just do it?" Tristan snarled. "Why bore me with all this talk?"

"Because I don't plan to kill you." Scrounge smiled, showing his dark, decaying teeth. "Remember, the wanted poster said dead or alive. I plan to take you back alive. Wounded, but alive. You see, there is something about the stalker's poison you do not know. Even though your health is improving, another wound, even one of dried stalker fluid such as still coats Wigg's dagger, will bond with and reenergize the traces of poison remaining in your system—resulting in not only another series of convulsions and ultimately death, but first causing almost instantaneous unconsciousness. And this time, it may be days before you reawaken. While you are unconscious, I shall return you to Tammerland. To Bargainer's Square, to be exact. The consuls will surface, paying me my reward, and they will leave you in your litter, letting you die slowly while the good citizens of Eutracia take their abuse of you. It should be most entertaining. In fact, I plan to stay and watch. But by then I shall be a much wealthier man, of course."

Tristan's breath left his lungs in a rush. The prospect of another round of convulsions, this time their outcome certain, shook him to the core. Dying, foaming at the mouth like some rabid animal in a cage, while the populace of Tammerland cheered it on. The very people he had risked his life to protect, over and over again. He tried to mask his feelings.

"But why?" he argued back gamely. "Why would the consuls do this? I've caused them no harm."

"The answers are simple, though I will not tell you all of it," Scrounge sneered. "For I value not only my head, but also the reward I am about to collect. However, this much of it I will say—if the consuls can be seen as the ones of the craft responsible for bringing in the traitorous prince, they will also appear to the populace as the new saviors of the nation. The help such a revelation would afford them in their efforts to rule would prove immeasurable." He grinned widely. "I'm sure you won't mind being poisoned again, dear prince? You seemed to enjoy it so much the first time."

Scrounge slapped his free hand against his knee with outright glee, laughing loudly. "Who knows?" he asked. "I may even become the one viewed as the hero. Perhaps even as *honorable*! An unusual turn of events, wouldn't you agree?"

"How did you get the dagger?" Tristan asked, his mind racing as he tried to buy time.

Scrounge smiled. "Convenient, is it not, that Ragnar could not take it with him where he is gone?" he said happily. "But he is quite dead, and I liberated the dagger from all that remained of him: a pile of clothing and a great pool of blood."

"How did you know where to find me?"

"Simple logic," Scrounge answered, his laughter finally fading. "I guessed that you might be saved by the wizards. And that you would insist on doing the right thing—the *honorable* thing—by your son's body, by bringing the remains to your family plot. I have been living here, in these woods, waiting for your return ever since the battle."

"If all this is true, then why didn't you just poison me while I was still unconscious?" Tristan asked. "It would have saved me the trouble of killing you."

Scrounge's face darkened. He stood, unstrapped the cross-bow from his arm, and tossed it in the snow near his horse. The broadsword followed. Looking smug, he faced Tristan holding only Wigg's dagger. Given Tristan's condition, it was apparently all he thought he would need.

"The crossbow and the broadsword are far too blunt for the work I plan," he said menacingly. "As I said, I only intend to wound you, and using those less precise weapons might cause a nasty, undesirable accident. But as to why I didn't do this before, well, the truth is that I wanted to see the look in your eyes, dear prince. The look in the eyes of one who has never gone hungry. The look in the eyes of one who needed only to snap his fingers to receive the finest of everything, or merely to beckon to the most beautiful women of the realm, only to have them so willingly fall into his bed." He paused for a moment, raising the shiny yellow-tinged blade of Wigg's ceremonial dagger higher.

"And I wanted to see the look in your eyes, you privileged royal bastard, at the precise moment you realized you were losing it all." With that, Scrounge lunged, covering the distance between them in a flash.

Scrounge slashed wickedly at Tristan's arm. His reflexes still slow, Tristan managed to pull back only at the last second, narrowly avoiding the swirling yellow blade.

If only I had a weapon! Tristan thought. Already breathing heavily, he watched as Scrounge readied himself for his next strike.

But there might be a way, he realized. *If only I can last long enough to lure him into the right position. But if it fails, there will be no second chance.*

Again and again Scrounge slashed at Tristan, the prince barely able to avoid the oncoming blade. Each time it came it seemed to reach a bit farther, the already-tiring prince reacting a fraction slower. At last the point of Scrounge's blade actually tore its way through the front of Tristan's fur jacket, narrowly missing his skin. The prince's last reserves of strength were ebbing away with each passing second; he knew he would not be able to take much more of this.

Lunging forward again, Scrounge raised the dagger high with one hand, simultaneously trying to grab the flapping tatters of Tristan's coat with the other. Concentrating on the descending blade of the knife, Tristan managed to grasp the assassin's wrist with both hands, barely keeping the yellow blade of the knife from his throat.

Sensing his chance, Scrounge yanked down on Tristan's jacket, pulling him off balance. Then the assassin placed one of his long legs directly behind one of the prince's and pushed him.

Tristan went down hard onto his back, Scrounge on top of him. Still holding the dagger, Scrounge used both hands to push it forward, slowly closing the distance between the point of the yellow blade and Tristan's throat. Tristan groaned, his entire body trembling as he tried to keep the poisoned blade from reaching his skin.

He raised his right knee and dragged his right foot back in the snow, then, concentrating all his strength into his left arm, he took his right hand away from Scrounge's wrist. The yellow blade of the knife was almost touching his skin.

Any moment now, he would be cut.

Reaching into his boot, he prayed that it would still be there. And then the smooth, pearl handle came into his hand, and he withdrew it.

The brain hook.

Tristan thrust the hooked end of the stiletto into Scrounge's ear canal. Just as the assassin screamed, the prince pointed the blade down and back, pulling forward on the handle. He felt a moist, tearing sensation through the handle of the knife, and Scrounge's eyes rolled back into his head.

Dying instantly, the assassin collapsed atop the prince just as Tristan pushed the dagger's blade away. With a last bit of strength he didn't know he had, he heaved Scrounge's dead body off him, into the snow. Scrounge's bright red blood seemed to be everywhere.

Tristan lay there for some time, gulping in the sweet mountain air, before daring to touch his fingers to his throat. Finally looking at his fingertips, he took another breath, and closed his eyes in relief.

There was no azure blood.

He stood, his chest heaving, his legs trembling beneath him. Finally looking around, he saw the black urn lying in the snow near the edge of the cliff.

He walked to it slowly and broke the wax seal, removing

the top. He stood there for another long moment, thinking of all that had happened. Then he cast the fine, gray ashes into the air. As if it had somehow known his wishes, the wind picked them up and hauntingly carried them away.

Tristan collapsed as much as sat in the snow at the edge of the cliff, looking out over the Eutracian landscape he so loved.

Nicholas II, of the House of Galland, his heart called out softly. *You will not be forgotten.*

He cast his dark eyes north in the direction of the destroyed Gates of Dawn, and his mind turned to the many problems still lingering, wondering how they would ever be overcome.

And then the same never-ending fear that had resonated through his mind ever since he had regained consciousness in the Redoubt came to him.

What will become of us now?

Standing slowly, he began the walk to collect his weapons.

EPILOGUE

The tall, lean wizard floated quietly above the shattered ruins of the Gates of Dawn. Through his use of the craft, a woman hovered silently by his side. The man's long, white hair moved casually in the swirling wind, as did the hem of his odd, two-colored robe.

Closing his eyes, he searched the rubble for the presence of other endowed blood. Sensing none, he opened his eyes and explored the scene.

Gigantic blocks of black-and-azure marble lay strewn everywhere, as if tossed there casually by giants. But nothing he saw here brought joy to his heart, because for him this was a scene of failure, rather than triumph.

Looking further, he saw both the black, broken shells of the dead carrion scarabs and the larger, partially decomposed bodies of the consuls. The remnants of their tattered, dark blue robes flapped quietly in the wind.

"Nicholas has failed," the woman said softly. "At the hand of the Chosen Ones and their wizards."

"But I shall not," the man answered. "Part of Nicholas' vision can still be completed. In fact, some of it goes forward as we speak. But to succeed completely, I must have the scrolls. And then the other."

"The other?" she asked.

"Yes," he replied. "The one of endowed blood that even the Chosen Ones and the wizard of Shadowood know nothing of. Only I and Wigg understand this one's ultimate potential. But first we must have the scrolls." He paused for a moment, watching the smoke as it continued to rise, vanishing into the nothingness of the sky. "In the end, both the lead wizard and the cripple in the chair escaped the master's grasp, but they will not elude mine," he added softly.

"And where are these scrolls?" she asked.

"Entombed within one of the legs of the Gates," he answered, his eyes still scanning the scene intently. "Yet another of the master's reasons for ordering the scarabs to surround this place. He told me that he would mark the section with an enchantment, forestalled to enact only should the Confluence fail, or he somehow perish." Unsatisfied with what he saw here, he turned to her. "We must search further," he ordered.

Finally, he saw it. Incredibly, a segment of one of the Gates still stood upright, reaching twenty meters into the air, and its azure glow was unmistakable. He headed for it as if it were some kind of beacon. But as they approached, his worst possible fears were realized.

The secret door in the side wall of the massive block had already been breached.

Pointing one of his hands at the partially open entryway, he widened the gap and maneuvered himself and the woman inside. As he reached up to touch the radiance stones his master had embedded in the ceiling, the room quickly became awash in a combination of sage and azure light. Lowering himself and his companion to the floor, he quickly took in the scene.

A huge marble table, hewn from the floor of living rock, stood in the center of the room. Something lay upon it. He immediately ran to it, hoping against hope that he would find what he had been promised, should the worst have befallen them. But to his horror, only one of the two scrolls was lying there.

"How can this be!" he railed, fists in the air. His chest heaving, he again glanced frantically about the room. But there was absolutely nothing else to see.

The woman looked carefully at the ancient, rolled-up parchment. It was about one meter long, and one quarter of a meter thick. Solid-gold knobs adorned each end of the rod running through its center. A golden band, engraved with words in Old Eutracian, secured the massive roll at its middle.

Wasting no time, the wizard picked it up. He turned to her, his eyes flashing.

"Can you locate the other scroll?" he demanded harshly.

"I—I don't know," she said, terrified of what he might do if her answer displeased him. Since she had been forced into his service, she had all too often been the victim of his sudden fits of rage. "I have never seen either of these parchments until now. Perhaps if I had either something personal of those who took it, or a piece of the missing document itself . . ."

"I don't want to hear 'perhaps'!" he snarled. Reaching out with his free hand, her took her by the throat, raised her off her feet, and slammed her against the nearest marble wall. "Besides, you ignorant cow, I cannot give you a piece of a document I do not have!" His angry, dark eyes bored into hers.

"You're an herbmistress, are you not?" he hissed. "And a blaze-gazer, as well—or so you have told me. These are the only reasons I tolerate your presence, and now you tell me you don't know!" She wheezed desperately as he tightened his grip around her throat. Her arms and legs began to twitch involuntarily. He moved his face to within inches of hers.

"Now then, can you find it, or not?" he asked, his voice no more than a whisper. Her eyes began to roll up into her head. He didn't care; if she couldn't help him, her life didn't matter. There were others like her, should he need one.

"Yes," she finally gasped. "Somehow, I will . . . find . . . a way . . . but must have . . . herbs . . . for flame . . ." What sounded like a final, rattling gasp slowly escaped her lungs.

He smiled. "That's better." He let her go, and she crashed unconscious to the floor.

Ignoring her, he walked to the open doorway and again gazed out over the smoking rubble. Thinking, he looked back to the woman lying on the floor.

He would need to find another herbmistress or herbmaster, so that he could steal the necessary ingredients. That much was certain. But where to look? Then something began to tug at the back of his mind.

Searching his memory, he tried to retrieve the details of the rumor that had long been whispered down the halls of the Redoubt: the hearsay describing the only transgression supposedly ever committed by the lead wizard.

At last he remembered, and his mouth turned up into a smile. If herbs were what his seer needed, then herbs were what she would receive. And then, after acquiring them, he would pay the lead wizard and the cripple in the chair a visit they would never forget.

He walked back to the woman and levitated her body into the air. Still holding the single scroll, he grasped her with his free arm and glided back out over the steaming, hissing rubble.

Read on for an exciting excerpt from

THE SCROLLS OF THE ANCIENTS

the next book in
THE CHRONICLES OF BLOOD AND STONE
by Robert Newcomb

*B*y the time Tristan had hidden the dead demonslavers in the alley behind the apothecary shop and the three travelers were ready to go on, the streets seemed even more deserted. The few people who did venture out glared and pointed at the prince and his sister, as if the two of them had no right to be any part of the city's population.

Faegan searched out a clothing shop and, leaving Tristan and Shailiha waiting in the shadows of a nearby alley, went in alone to purchase two hooded robes to cover the bodies and heads of the Chosen Ones. Not perfect disguises, but the best he could do without the aid of the craft. Tristan worried that the robe covered his weapons, making it nearly impossible for him to grasp them quickly, but he kept his concerns to himself. There seemed little other choice.

They then proceeded to a stable, where Faegan was forced to pay the suspicious stablemaster handsomely for three run-down horses, a dilapidated cart, and extra tack. Tristan harnessed one of the mounts to the cart and hoisted Faegan atop its seat, and at last the three of them made their way to the harbor area of Far Point.

Although the sun was beginning to set, the docks were alive with people. A large crowd had gathered here, and it was clear they were waiting with trepidation for something to happen. The air was full of the smells of salty sea air and freshly caught fish.

Tristan slid off the swaybacked roan mare, and as Shailiha dismounted her aged gelding, he went around to the back of the cart and got out Faegan's chair. Shailiha held the chair while Tristan lifted Faegan from the buckboard seat and got him settled.

Then he turned to study the inn where Faegan had directed them to stop. Many of its shutters were broken and peeling from the constant exposure to the strong, salty winds. Some of the windows were cracked, and the steps to the lobby were in disrepair. The place had clearly seen better days.

"Why are we stopping here?" Shailiha asked. She was eager to get to the oceanfront. "The carriage driver said we needed to get to the docks. Can't we just quietly wend our way through the crowd?"

"No," Faegan answered adamantly as he looked around. "This inn is perfect for what I have in mind—the kind of place where few questions will be asked. Besides, Krassus may be near, not to mention more of the demonslavers. Tristan, I want you to go around back and tell me what you find. In particular, I want to know whether there is any way up to the roof, and a secure place where we might tie the horses."

Tristan nodded. After a smile to his sister, he was gone.

The alley behind the inn was inconspicuous enough, with the usual iron rings embedded in the building's rear wall to secure bridle reins. Several mounts were already tied there, telling the prince that the shopworn inn had at least a few customers. An iron fire ladder reached from the ground all the way to the roof, with platforms at each of the inn's four levels. Backing farther into the shadows, Tristan observed the inn quietly, branding the scene into his memory. Finally satisfied, he returned to the street.

"Bridle rings *and* a ladder," he said quietly to the wizard.

"Does the ladder go all the way to the roof?" Faegan asked.

"Yes."

"And does the roof appear to be flat?"

"From what I could see, yes."

"Good," Faegan answered. Tristan and Shailiha could see mischief coming to the ancient wizard's eyes as his plan continued to form.

"I want you and Shailiha to walk the three horses around back," he said. "Leave your two saddled. Unharness the cart and put it to one side. Take the extra saddle and bridle from the cart and put them on my horse. Tie all the horses to the wall. Then return. Do it quickly."

Tristan and Shailiha carried out the wizard's orders as swiftly as they could, then returned to the front of the inn.

"Is it done?" Faegan asked. Tristan nodded.

"Very well," the wizard said. "Follow me into the inn. Whatever you do, do not lower your hoods. Stay quiet, and follow my lead. Try to act as though you do not exist." He pointed to one of the loose boards of the inn steps. "Tristan, if you would?" he asked.

Understanding, the prince reached down to tear the wide, loose board away from its few remaining nails, then inclined it against the steps of the inn. It made a serviceable ramp. After briefly testing its strength, he wheeled Faegan's chair up and through the door into the lobby, Shailiha right behind.

Inside, the inn was dingy, dark, and unappealing. The large front room held several chairs, tables, and a long bar with a mirror behind it. Sullen-looking men, some obviously fishermen, sat hunched over the tables and bar, drinking quietly. Several scantily dressed women walked among the tables, flirting with the men. For hire, no doubt, Tristan thought with a slight shake of his head.

The thin, greasy-looking man Tristan took to be the innkeeper sat at a small desk in one corner, making notes in a bound ledger. A tankard sat before him. He did not look up. Indeed, no one took any great notice of the newcomers at all, save for a few furtive, curious glances at Faegan's chair. With a smile, the wizard calmly wheeled himself toward the proprietor.

"Three rooms, please," Faegan said politely.

The man looked up from his arithmetic. His eyes were dark and distrustful.

"The only rooms I have left are on the top floor," he said rudely, "but taking you up and down the stairs isn't included in the rent."

Some of the customers laughed aloud.

Faegan graciously ignored the insult. "Thank you for your

worry, but my bodyguard will take care of that. He's quite used to it, in fact. Now then, how much?"

"How many nights?" the innkeeper asked. He took a sloppy gulp of stale-smelling ale, then set the tankard back down on the desk. Letting go a wet belch, he wiped his mouth with a stained, gartered shirtsleeve.

"Three rooms, one night each," Faegan answered.

"Twelve kisa," the man replied. "Fourth floor. The washing facilities are at the end of the hall. Take it or leave it."

Twelve kisa was a steep price for such a place, Tristan thought, but clearly Faegan thought it better not to bargain. Reaching into his robes, the wizard took out the necessary kisa and dropped them on the desk. After counting them, the innkeeper produced three keys, which he handed over to the wizard. Saying nothing more, Faegan turned his chair to the stairs, Tristan and Shailiha following behind.

At the foot of the steps, Tristan leaned in, putting his lips to the wizard's ear. "Are you joking?" he growled quietly. "Four flights of stairs?"

"No." Faegan smiled. "Actually, I'm hoping there will be five." Looking over to Shailiha, he gave her a wink. She smiled back quizzically.

"What do you mean five?" Tristan argued.

"We have no friends here, and this is no time for a debate," Faegan answered urgently. "Let's go."

Sighing, Tristan began pulling the wizard's chair backward up the steps. After what seemed an eternity, they finally reached the fourth floor. Tristan looked around cautiously. Nothing seemed amiss.

"What are our room numbers?" Shailiha asked Faegan as Tristan leaned over, breathing heavily from exhaustion.

"We won't be using the rooms." Faegan smiled and looked up at the ceiling. "That was just for show."

Before either of the Chosen Ones could ask the obvious question, the wizard found what he was looking for. In the middle of the ceiling was a wooden framework, from which hung a long rope ending in a pull handle.

Faegan wheeled himself to the rope and gave it a tug. Stairs to the roof slowly descended on a pivot, revealing the first stars of the evening twinkling through the opening. Faegan grinned at the prince.

"As I told you, there are five," he said impishly. "But again you must pull me up without my using the craft. There might still be people about."

Tristan nodded. With a determined grip he pushed the chair to the stairs, and, with some help from Shailiha below, managed to pull it up and onto the roof. Shailiha scrambled up behind them, then pulled the duplicate rope on the other side, wisely lifting the pivoting stairway back into place.

The gray slate roof was large and flat. The wind had risen, and the smell of the sea came to them again. From here the prince could see much of the city, the flickering street lamps casting dancing shadows along the sides of the buildings and down the cobblestoned thoroughfares.

"Quickly, Tristan," Faegan whispered. "Lift me from my chair and put me down by the east edge of the roof. Then both of you come and lie next to me, one on either side."

Tristan did as the wizard ordered, and Faegan lay on his stomach, peering over the edge toward the docks. Tristan and Shailiha lay down beside him.

Down on the stone piers that formed the breakwater to the sea, hundreds of people were milling anxiously about. Three large ships, their sails furled, lay tied up in docking berths, their salty waterlines riding well above the waves. Even Tristan's inexperienced eyes could guess that meant the ships were empty of cargo.

A raised wooden platform had been placed in a cleared area between the crowd and the water's edge. A short series of steps ran down from one of its sides to the ground. Alongside the platform a long, crude, rectangular table sat upon the pier. Seated behind it were at least a dozen men in dark robes. Consuls' robes, the prince thought. On the table before each man lay several objects, but Tristan could not identify them from this distance. The men behind the table sat patiently, as if waiting for something.

Before the table stood two large, black kettles with strange, curved iron handles. An orange-red glow emanated from each of their circular tops. Tristan assumed that the strange auras were being produced by glowing, red-hot coals deep within them. Black smoke rose lazily from the kettles' glowing embers, vanishing into the growing darkness of the evening sky.

Near the kettles, two pillories had been constructed. The

orange glow from the black kettles mixed with the light from the dozens of oil lamps to cast strangely flickering shadows across the hulls of the silently waiting ships and the stark, empty pillories.

Then Tristan saw the white-skinned demonslavers lining the inner edges of the clearing, keeping the burgeoning crowd from approaching the raised platform by the constant threat of their nine-tails and tridents. Then Krassus came into view. The people in the crowd began to shout invectives and wave their arms in anger. Krassus didn't seem to care.

Slowly he walked to the platform in his blue-and-gray robe. An elderly woman with frizzled gray hair and dressed in a shopworn black robe followed along behind him. As they approached, the demonslavers kept the crowd back. Without fanfare Krassus and his unknown companion walked to the side of the platform and up the steps. They remained silent.

Tristan looked over at Faegan. "Is that woman the partial-adept Krassus talked about that day in the palace?" he asked urgently. "Do you know her?"

"From here, I can't tell who she might be," Faegan whispered back, not shifting his eyes from the scene. "But it is obvious she has importance for him."

Tristan expected Krassus to speak. But he didn't. He simply stood there, the woman by his side, as if he, too, waited for something.

Suddenly Tristan heard the sound of shod hooves rattling harshly against the same cobblestoned street he, Faegan, and Shailiha had just come down. Turning, he crawled on his stomach across the slate roof to its northern side and looked carefully over.

At least a dozen carriages-of-four were approaching, their teams trotting down the street and toward the docks. But as they neared, Tristan could see that the vehicles were really not carriages at all. They were more like bizarre, wooden-slatted cages on wheels, and they were being driven by yet more of the demonslavers.

They were full of people.

Each of the rough-hewn cages contained perhaps twenty or more people, men and women alike. They sat crammed upon what looked like piles of soiled straw, and he could make out black iron manacles here and there.

The cages continued rattling up the street toward the docks. Tristan crawled back across the roof to lie beside Faegan. Below, the demonslavers on the pier barked out orders, and the crowd reluctantly parted to allow the vehicles to pass.

The cages came to a stop before the long table. A group of demonslavers promptly went to one corner of the clearing, and from a pile lying there each of them took up a device that seemed to be a long iron rod with a ring at one end. Another group of demonslavers began unlocking and opening the cage doors.

One by one the rod-wielding demonslavers approached the open cages. With a quick twist of the rod handles, the rings at their ends clanged open. The open rings were shoved into the cages and forced up against the throats of the captives. With another twist, the rings closed viciously around the prisoners' necks. One by one, the men and women were dragged out, kicking and screaming.

With the captives finally free of their cages, Tristan could see them much better. It was then that he began to get an inkling of why he and his sister had been regarded so strangely all day.

All the slaves were about the same age as he and Shailiha!

Tristan looked back to Krassus. The wizard had yet to speak, but his dark eyes missed nothing as the prisoners were hauled from their cages and forced toward the table where the robed men sat waiting.

"Can you tell what's happening?" he asked Faegan quietly. All he could make out was that the robed men were busy doing something that involved the occasional azure glow of the craft, and were making notations in some kind of large books.

"I can see part of it," the wizard responded softly. "And yes, I believe I have a good idea of what is going on. But let us not speak of it now."

There was a distinct sadness in the old man's tone. Shailiha looked to her brother and placed an index finger across her lips. Tristan nodded back.

One by one the prisoners were hauled away from the table by their necks and locked into one of the two pillories. Two demonslavers pulled the rods back from the black kettles; the ends of the rods came out glowing bright red. Branding irons.

Before each of the slavers pressed his hot iron to skin, he looked up to Krassus, waiting for a sign. And each time, before giving his blessing, the wizard in the two-colored robe would look down for an indication from the men at the tables. Then he would indicate with either his right hand or his left.

As the demonslavers pressed the heated irons into the left shoulders of the prisoners, screams resounded through the night. Many if not most of them fainted away in the stocks, and were dragged by their necks to separate areas on the pier. When one prisoner was finished, another immediately took his or her place. As the excruciating process continued, Tristan saw that one group of slaves was becoming noticeably larger than the other.

Faegan lowered his head. Shailiha closed her eyes, brushing tears from her face. Only Tristan's eyes remained locked on the gruesome scene, his hands balled up into fists and his jaw clenched with the frustration of not being able to take action. Finally he, too, could take no more, and he slowly closed his eyes against the spectacle.

Those prisoners were his people, the prince realized in shame and horror, and there was absolutely nothing he could do to help them. Was that what Krassus' taunts had meant? What in the name of the Afterlife was it all about?

At last, blessedly, the branding stopped, all of the prisoners having been marked with a rod from one kettle or the other. The moaning and crying of the victims was softer now.

Those who had fainted were revived by having cold seawater splashed in their faces. Then the two groups were marched down the piers to the waiting frigates and forced up the gangways. Full of despair, Tristan lowered his head.

Suddenly a long, silent, moonlit shadow flowed darkly across the roof between him and his sister. Then came another, and yet another. Tristan tugged silently on the sleeve of the wizard's robe, slid the dreggan from its scabbard, and smoothly rolled over onto his back. He was on his feet in a flash, his dreggan in a strong, two-handed grip.

Three demonslavers stood near the ladder at the other side of the roof, the rose-colored moonlight glinting off their alabaster skin. Each of them held a short sword. Two of them smiled.

Just then Shailiha turned to see why Tristan had risen, and

the air left her lungs in a rush. Turning over, Faegan also looked. But before anything could be done, all three slavers charged at once.

Tristan ran across the roof, his dreggan slashing as he went. The first of the slavers he met died quickly, its head cleanly severed from its body.

But the next two would not be so easy. They hacked savagely at Tristan, who fended them off as best he could, his sword almost a blur. But inexorably they came on, forcing him to keep backing up toward the wizard and the princess, as the three blades clanged coldly, harshly against one another.

Shailiha looked aghast at Faegan, silently beseeching him to intervene with the craft, even if it would alert Krassus to their presence.

The demonslavers were closing on Tristan, and it was plain to see that the prince was tiring. Faegan relaxed his mind and stopped cloaking their endowed blood.

Just then Tristan lost his footing on the slick roof and fell hard on his back. Sensing victory, the two monsters rushed in, swords held high. Faegan raised both his arms.

Twin azure bolts tore across the roof, directly over Tristan. He could feel the searing heat, see the blinding azure light, and sense the rush of the wind as the force of them ripped at his hair and clothing and almost tore the dreggan from his hands. Turning his head and gritting his teeth, he held on to the sword with all his might.

Shailiha glanced down at Krassus and saw him suddenly stiffen. With a smile, he motioned to a group of about twenty demonslavers, then pointed to the roof of the inn.

Faegan's bolts struck each of the slavers squarely in the chest. Tristan, his eyes still closed, heard their bodies being ripped apart; he felt and smelled the sickening offal, blood, and sinew splattering down on him. In a matter of seconds, it was over.

He opened his eyes and saw one of the monsters' short, shiny swords lying quietly beside him in the moonlight.

But where was the other?

Wildly turning his head to the sky, he saw the shiny, silver point of the second sword. Launched skyward by the explosions of the wizard's bolts, it was free-falling straight down at him.

He started to roll to one side, realizing even as he moved that he was too late.

Suddenly an azure hand grasped the sword only inches from his throat. Wasting no time, Tristan rolled away, coming to his hands and knees in the slick, bloody mess. As the glow of the craft disappeared, he watched the sword fall harmlessly to the roof with a clang. He picked it up with his free hand and ran to Shailiha and Faegan.

The wizard was already seated in his chair, but the look on his face was far from reassuring. Tristan shoved the demon-slaver's sword into Shailiha's hands. "Do you remember your fencing lessons?" he shouted urgently.

Understanding his meaning, she nodded.

"There is no time for talk!" Faegan growled, pointing toward the opposite side of the roof. "By now Krassus will surely know we are here! Make for the horses!"

Tristan, sword still in hand, looked briefly into his sister's eyes. Then they both sprinted across the slippery, blood-soaked roof. Faegan levitated his chair and soared ahead of them.

The wizard reached the edge first and looked down. Other than the tied horses and the abandoned cart, he saw nothing, but he knew that the relative peace of the alleyway wouldn't last much longer. He swung the chair back near the prince and his sister.

"Both of you—onto my chair, now!" he ordered.

Somewhat bewildered, the two of them did as they were told. Shailiha sat on the wizard's lap; Tristan clung to one of the chair arms. Then Faegan steered his chair over the side of the roof.

On the way down Tristan saw about twenty demonslavers working their way through the crowd and up the side street, viciously using their whips, swords, and tridents to clear a path.

Faegan hurried his chair downward as fast as he could safely manage. About one meter above the backs of the horses, he stopped and looked frantically at the prince and his sister.

"Jump!"

Tristan immediately let go, falling the remaining distance to the ground. As he ran to untie their horses, out of the corner of his eye he saw Shailiha drop directly into her saddle, the demonslaver's sword still in one hand. She masterfully whirled her horse around.

Faegan levitated himself from his chair and, with a wave of one hand, let it go. The centuries-old chair fell to the ground, smashing into pieces. Ignoring it, he lowered himself into the saddle atop the third horse. Tristan leapt into his saddle and wheeled his mount around, his back to the wall of the inn, to look down their escape route toward the end of the alley.

The rear door of the inn opened a crack. A gleam of soft, yellow light cut through the darkness of the alleyway, spilling out onto the ground.

It was the greasy innkeeper. Raising a demonslaver sword high in both hands, the point forward, he charged at the prince's back.

Shailiha noticed the sudden light and raised her sword. Spurring her horse forward, she used the momentum to shove her blade directly into the man's throat; it went through his neck and came out the back. She pulled her weapon out hard and swung it.

Tristan wheeled his horse around just in time to see his sister swing her stolen blade in a perfect arc, taking the innkeeper's head cleanly off at the neck. The headless body remained standing for a moment, as if it were still somehow in control of itself. Then what was left of the innkeeper fell forward, into the alleyway, in front of Shailiha's horse. Blood poured from the ravaged neck into the thirsty dirt.

Without pause the three of them turned their horses and charged side by side for the end of the alleyway. Tristan held his breath, wondering if they could make it to the street before the passageway filled with demonslavers. But even before their horses could break into a full gallop, the prince had his answer.

The monsters flowed down the street like a river, blocking the way to freedom. There had to be at least one hundred of them. Waving swords and tridents, they shouted and hissed as they formed what seemed to be an impenetrable wall at the entrance to the street.

Tristan turned frantically around in his saddle. He looked behind him, only to be reminded that the way back was a dead end. Charging through the slavers was the only way to freedom, but he knew in his heart that it couldn't be done.

Holding up his hand, Faegan brought his mount to a skidding stop; Tristan and Shailiha followed suit. The alleyway became strangely quiet, as the slavers stopped shouting and began walking purposefully, menacingly toward them. Tristan turned frantically to the wizard.

"Can you kill them?" he asked.

"Some," Faegan answered quickly, his eyes trained upon the monsters as they came. "But there are too many, and no doubt even more are following behind them." Then a knowing look crossed his face, and he turned to the prince and princess. "Killing them is not the answer."

"Then what is?" Shailiha asked urgently.

"Avoiding them. Follow me single file, and don't look back," he ordered. "Whatever happens, don't be surprised at what you see, and just keep on going. When we finally reach the street, whip your horses for all they're worth, and stay with me. Do you understand?" His last sentence wasn't a question. It was an order.

They both nodded.

Whipping his horse with the reins, Faegan charged down the alley, Shailiha behind him, Tristan bringing up the rear.

At first the prince thought he must be seeing things. Glowing a brilliant azure, something took solid form just as Faegan's horse reached it.

It was a bridge.

Barely wide enough to allow a single rider at a time, it arched from the dirt of the alleyway, and climbed over the heads of the slavers, touching down again on the other side. Caught off guard, the demonslavers stood in confused wonder.

Faegan's horse reached it first, his mare's hooves banging down loudly upon the embodiment of the craft as she carried him to its apex and then started down the other side. Next came Shailiha. Following close behind, Tristan's horse approached the glowing ramp.

But upon placing her first, poorly shod hoof onto the glowing bridge, Tristan's mare stumbled, and went down hard on both front knees.

Tristan was launched forward. Her front legs broken, the mare fell over onto her back, screaming wildly. Somehow Tristan managed to keep hold of his dreggan, but the slavers charged him immediately. He staggered drunkenly to one knee, then finally to his feet. Forced to use both hands, he raised his sword weakly, but could only get it as high as his waist.

From where he stood, he could see nothing but slavers coming toward him, their awful faces and the whiteness of their skin strangely highlighted by the glow from the azure bridge.

On the other side, Faegan and Shailiha wheeled their horses around to look. Shailiha screamed and would have spurred her gelding back over the bridge, but Faegan grabbed her reins, forcing her horse around.

"No!" he shouted. "We have to go! There is nothing we can do for him now! We will return for him, I promise!"

Shailiha cried out as she lost sight of her brother. The glowing bridge dissolved, leaving only the mob of angry slavers as they crowded in around the prince.

Shailiha turned her terrified eyes back to the wizard. Finally she lowered her head and nodded. It was without question the hardest single decision she had ever been forced to make.

Following Faegan's horse, Shailiha thundered down the cobblestoned street just as another wave of the sword-wielding demonslavers rushed in.

Stunned and bewildered, his hands and body covered with blood from the battles on the roof, Tristan tried his best to swing his dreggan at the first of them. But the heavy blade was too much for him, and its momentum took him to his knees.

Then a blinding white light seared through his consciousness, and he collapsed to the dirt.

Go back to where it all began . . .

THE FIFTH SORCERESS

Volume I of the Chronicles of
Blood and Stone by
ROBERT NEWCOMB

It is more than three centuries since the ravages of
a devastating war nearly tore apart the kingdom of
Eutracia. In its wake, those who masterminded the
bloodshed—a quartet of powerful, conquest-hun-
gry Sorceresses—were sentenced to exile. Now a
land of peace and plenty, Eutracia is about to
crown a new king. And as the coronation
approaches, the spirit of celebration fills every
heart. Except one.

Prince Tristan is a reluctant monarch-to-be.
Though born with the "endowed" blood that will
give him the power to master magic, and destined
by tradition to succeed his father as ruler, he is a
rebel soul. And when he discovers the ancient,
hidden caves where strange red waters flow—possessed of their own mysterious magic—it only
makes him yearn all the more to escape his future
of duty . . . and succumb to the stirrings of
enchantment within him.

Published by Del Rey
Available wherever books are sold